Decision

ALLEN DRURY

Decision

Doubleday & Company, Inc., Garden City, New York
1983

Library of Congress Cataloging in Publication Data

Drury, Allen.
Decision.

I. Title.
PS3554.R8D4   1983   813′.54
ISBN 0-385-18832-3
Library of Congress Catalog Card Number 82-22231

Dedicated to
THE SUPREME COURT OF THE UNITED STATES
without whose highly independent and
individualistic members this novel—and
a lot of other things in the United
States—could never have happened.

ACKNOWLEDGMENTS

For unfailing courtesy and helpfulness during research I am indebted to Justices who spoke confidentially but with complete freedom and candor about the ways and personalities of their peculiar institution. I am also grateful to several high-ranking members of the Court's small and efficient staff whom I could name but who I am sure, in true Court tradition, would prefer to remain anonymous. They know who they are and I thank them for their help. They are a highly competent body of men and women, deeply devoted to their unique employment and their unique employers. The Court's smooth day-to-day functioning rests in large measure on their dedicated work.

For research in the laws of South Carolina I am indebted to former Rep. John L. Napier of the Sixth District of South Carolina, and to Vinton D. Lide, at time of writing chief counsel to the Senate Judiciary Committee. Their informed help was most generously and unstintingly given. Many thanks must also go to Robert Barr of *U.S. News & World Report,* an old friend from freshman reporter days on the Hill who still covers Congress and knows more about it than almost anybody else around the place, for his characteristically generous, tenacious and indefatigable pursuit of facts for me.

To Professor Gerald Gunther of Stanford University, perhaps the nation's leading constitutional law expert, I am grateful for the list of supplemental reading transmitted via my nephew, Kenneth Killiany; to my sister, Anne E. Killiany, for many helpful editorial suggestions; and to Bill Howard Eichstadt for his usual fine job of manuscript typing and his customary sound and constructive suggestions as first reader.

I am also indebted to my editors at Doubleday, Ken McCormick and Lisa Drew, who are what editors ought to be—intelligent and thoughtful individuals who help a writer better express what he has in mind and do not, like some in publishing, attempt to twist his story out of all sensible shape to suit their own rigid ideological biases.

None of my sources, of course, is responsible for my interpretations of the information they gave me, nor for the uses I have made of it.

ALLEN DRURY

The Constitution of the United States, Article III:
"Section 1. The judicial Power of the United States, shall be vested in one supreme Court, and in such inferior Courts as the Congress may from time to time ordain and establish. The Judges, both of the supreme and inferior Courts, shall hold their Offices during good Behaviors, and shall, at stated Times, receive for their Services, a Compensation, which shall not be diminished during their Continuance in Office.

"Section 2. . . . In all Cases affecting Ambassadors, other public Ministers and Consuls, and those in which a State shall be a Party, the supreme Court shall have original Jurisdiction. In all the other Cases before mentioned, the supreme Court shall have appellate Jurisdiction, both as to Law and Fact, with such Exceptions, and under such Regulations as the Congress shall make."

"Justice Douglas, you must remember one thing. At the constitutional level where we work, ninety per cent of any decision is emotional. The rational part of us supplies the reasons for supporting our predilections."

> —The late Chief Justice Charles
> Evans Hughes as quoted by the
> late Associate Justice William
> O. Douglas in his autobiography
> *The Court Years, 1939–1975,*
> Random House, 1980

The Constitution of the United States, Article III.

"Section 1. The judicial Power of the United States, shall be vested in one supreme Court, and in such inferior Courts as the Congress may from time to time ordain and establish. The Judges, both of the supreme and inferior Courts, shall hold their Offices during good Behaviour, and shall, at stated Times, receive for their Services, a Compensation, which shall not be diminished during their Continuance in Office.

Section 2. ... In all Cases affecting Ambassadors, other public Ministers and Consuls, and those to which a State shall be Party, the supreme Court shall have original Jurisdiction. In all the other Cases before mentioned, the supreme Court shall have appellate Jurisdiction, both as to Law and Fact, with such Exceptions, and under such Regulations as the Congress shall make."

"Matter, Douglas, can more or less happen one thing. At the end of... cultural and legal level where we work, interpretation of any decision is emotional. The rational part of us supplies the reasons for our parties our productions."

—Ronald Chief Justice Clarke
Evans Hughes, as quoted by the
late Associate Justice William
O. Douglas in his autobiography
The Court Years (1939-1975)
Random House, 1980.

The Supreme Court of the United States
at the time of
*South Carolina v. Holgren; Holgren v.
South Carolina,* and *CBS et al. amicae curiae*

*Edmund Duncan Elphinstone of Kentucky, Chief Justice; "Birdie"
 Richard Waldo Flyte of Illinois, Associate Justice
*Clement Wallenberg of Michigan, Associate Justice; "Maidie"
*Raymond Ullstein of New York, Associate Justice; Hester
 Mary-Hannah McIntosh of California, Associate Justice
*Rupert John Hemmelsford of Texas, Associate Justice; "Miss Sally"
*Hughie Dubose Demsted of the District of Columbia; Katherine
*Stanley Mossiter Pomeroy of South Carolina; Sue-Ann
*Taylor Barbour of California, Associate Justice; Mary

* Indicating those whose spouses accompany them

OTHER CHARACTERS IN THE NOVEL:

In California
Helen and Frank Barbour, the Justice's parents
Carl, his brother
Anne Gonzales, his sister
Erma Tillson, his teacher

In South Carolina
Earle Holgren
His mother
Janet Martinson, his companion
John Lennon Peacechild, their son
Hon. Regard Stinnet, attorney general of South Carolina
Hon. James Perle Williams, judge
Debbie Donnelson, attorney
Boomer Johnson, witness
Sue-Ann Pomeroy, Justice Pomeroy's wife
Sarah, their daughter

In Washington
Mary Barbour, the Justice's wife

Jane, his daughter
Julia Whitby, their maid
Bubba Whitby, her son
Catherine Corning, journalist
Anna Hastings, publisher
Katharine Graham, publisher
Various other members of the media
Various officials of the Supreme Court

Decision

ONE

1

The jogger came around the bend in the mountain road shortly after nine, as he had almost every morning since work on the plant had entered its final stages.

He broke stride. Stopped, hands on hips, to survey what they were doing in the valley below. Studied it all carefully for a moment. Tossed his usual grin, wave, thumbs-up.

They returned his greeting cheerfully. Someone yelled, "Hey, man!" as someone always did.

Then he resumed stride and jogged on by as he had a hundred times before.

After he was gone the day crew—as distinct from the night crew, whose members sometimes saw him more often—retained their usual distant impression of an individual: stocky, open-faced, pleasant, amiable. No one to notice, particularly; no one to stand out in anybody's mind as worthy of any particular attention. Not the sort you would turn to look at twice.

Or even once, for that matter.

The kind of face that gets lost in a crowd.

An ordinary guy.

So passed—and would continue passing until his objective, now a handful of days away, was achieved—Earle Holgren—or Billy Ray Holgren, or Billy Ray, or Holgren Williams, or William Holgren, or Henry McAfee, or McAfee Johnson, or Everett Thompson or Everett Ray.

You could take your pick, he thought wryly, a sudden grim little smile that would have much surprised the workers at Pomeroy Station Atomic Energy Installation slashing his pleasant expression with startling savagery for a moment. He didn't much care, as long as he wasn't caught.

Not that there was anything pending right now for which he should be caught—at least not anything that *he* recognized. Actually, he supposed, he was on the run as he had been for more than a decade, but in his mind he saw it as simply exercising reasonable caution in the face of the monstrous unfairness and injustice of the system.

He had a date with that system, and in one way or another he had been keeping it ever since college. Up to now only a few of his countrymen had been aware that he had this date. Very soon, he promised himself with a happy inward convulsion of glee so intense as to be almost sexual, the whole world would know.

He jogged on through the bright May morning, the air still benign and mellow, not yet far enough into the day to be stifling, the scent of pines and firs and lush mountain growth everywhere around him. Birds sang, rabbits scurried, two deer sprang startled across the road. No one else was there, no cars, no other joggers. The only indication of man was the distant sound of jackhammers, the echoing call of distant voices, the groan of a climbing truck. Only a man spoiled this perfect place. A sudden blind anger replaced the convulsive joy. *Man!* How he ruined everything.

More specifically, how *Americans* ruined everything. A scarifying contempt for his fellow citizens replaced the anger. Americans and their arrogant uncaring, Americans and their crude disinterest in everything that made life beautiful and worth living, Americans and their greed!

The moods of Earle Holgren were as shifting as the wind but they always came back to a basic rage against his country and his countrymen.

They didn't *deserve* what they had.

They were so stupid—and so overbearing—and so wanton with the infinite bounty the Lord had given them.

Such was the basic thrust of the education his generation had received. It was no wonder some of them felt themselves appointed to correct all this. And it was no wonder, given all the weapons and clever processes an industrial society so lightly left lying around, that some of them became instruments of death.

So here he was at thirty-six, child of wealth, veteran of the Sixties and early Seventies, one who had never compromised, one who had never come in from the cold—one who had managed to carry with him into new and changing decades the unchanged convictions of an unbal-

anced period and a twisted view of life in America no longer valid if it
ever had been.

Some might consider this a terrifying mental weakness, condemning
him to repeat until it destroyed him—and many others along the way—
the pattern of a hate-sprung, unrelenting vengeance. Earle Holgren
thought of it as a strength—his strength. He had to think this or go
finally and completely insane.

Perhaps he was; he sometimes thought with a giddy feeling that he
was floating somewhere out there with only his own iron will and eternal anger to support him. But the will *was* iron and the anger *was* eternal, and although to the great majority of his countrymen it might seem
that both were far beyond the norms of rational behavior, to him they
were the permanent and unyielding conditions of his life.

Because of this he had long since put aside his family and everything
that had shaped him as a child. His parents, bewildered and shattered
like so many by what they considered the monster visited upon them
unjustly by inexplicable fate, had long since ceased their futile attempts
to contact him. For nearly a decade after he vanished from their world,
which he did immediately after graduating from Harvard and receiving
Grandfather Holgren's quarter-million-dollar trust fund at age twenty-
one, their anguished appeals were to be found among the many that
filled the "Personals" columns in major newspapers from New York to
San Francisco.

"Earle Holgren, we love you and need you. Please call.
Mother . . . Earle Holgren, please contact Father at Blue Ridge
House . . . Earle Holgren, Happy Birthday. We love you. Mother,
Father and Sis . . ." And finally the last resort: "Anyone knowing
whereabouts of Earle William Holgren, formerly Greenwich, Conn.,
please notify A. J. Holgren, 'Seaswift,' Greenwich. Ample reward."

He had seen a few of these, for he and his companions got a perverse
pleasure out of following the scraps of broken parental hearts that surfaced so often in so many publications in those years. Once in a while
there was a great surge of yearning, a sudden return to childhood sim-
plicities, that almost prompted him to answer; but each time he put it
sternly aside and felt that he became stronger. Finally there was no
responsive emotion in his heart at all. He was satisfied at last that that
part of his life was dead.

Once in a great while this brought a disturbing aftermath. Perhaps
other things were dead too? Perhaps everything was dead? Perhaps he
was a zombie with nothing left to hold on to, no center to his life, nothing inside at all.

But this too he put sternly aside on the very rare occasions when it troubled him. Although many of his old companions dropped away, seduced back by the more conventional rewards of the system, still there were some who remained; and although the riots, the protests, the robberies and bombings had also dropped away for a time to almost nothing, still there were a few, enough to bolster his feeling of still belonging to a cause beyond himself. And now in the last several years violent protest had begun to revive, washed along on the rising tide of economic unrest, inflation, the swift burgeoning of all kinds of crime, all across the country. Violence, never very far away in the land of handguns and economic uncertainty, was becoming king again. And the great cause of righting the wrongs of American society could still be pursued. The endless (if endlessly disappointed) quest to bring perfection to an imperfect country was still worthy of a heart's devotion, a lifetime's dedication.

America—the America of his parents, the steady, decent, respectable, good-hearted America that had been, and remained, the ideal of so many—was becoming terrified. The steadily rising crime rate of the Seventies had surged ever higher into the Eighties, and with it the opportunity for such as he to return to the violent forms of protest that were the most satisfying because they were both frightful and usually impersonal enough in execution to free him from any feelings of direct personal responsibility.

Thus his mind could retain the serene certainty of its own righteousness—his only, but impregnable, shield against the violent horror of his age—and against the fact that he himself had made his own substantial contributions to those horrors in these recent years.

Grandfather Holgren's trust fund was still in excellent shape—he of course had never paid income tax on it, which was one of the charges society had outstanding against him—and with the aid of a lawyer in New York friendly to him and others of his kind he had made a series of carefully hidden investments that had actually increased it substantially. Thus supporting himself was no problem. It was also no problem to support Janet, with whom he had lived for the past three years, and little John Lennon Peacechild, who had come along a year ago to intrigue and interest him in a remotely unconnected sort of way. They could live where and as they pleased—underground and modestly, of necessity, but very comfortably for all that.

He was approaching the end of the road. It terminated at an old deserted mine shaft set into the hillside. So woods-wise had he become as a youngster in these same hills, when they used to come down each summer to what his father called "Blue Ridge House," that there was no sign visible to the casual passer-by that the entrance to the shaft had been disturbed since the vein petered out sixty years ago. Not even a woodsman as experienced as he could tell without very close examination that certain logs and brush, a little too carefully distributed, hid the small cave that opened just to the left of the entrance and curved back into the hillside. Part of it had once been used for storage and that was what he was using it for now; but unless someone really suspicious had a really urgent motivation to find it, the chances were that no one ever would.

And there was no one really suspicious in his world as he had presently created it. Janet was as placid as a cow, having gone through all the expected stations of the route to salvation as a certain segment of their generation saw it. She had smoked, sniffed, snorted, main-lined, finally done the conventional and turned to alcohol. Now she lived in a gentle haze, mouthing all the old slogans dutifully when prompted, paying less and less attention to causes, more and more to John Lennon Peacechild, whom she obviously regarded as the best trip of all, the very best she had ever been on. She seemed always mildly drunk, never seemed to want to leave the cabin, always seemed content to hover around the child, which was fine for his purposes because he didn't want her hobnobbing with the neighbors anyway.

The old virtues, he sometimes told himself with an ironic inward smile, had reclaimed Janet with a vengeance. Next she would want to formalize it all with a wedding ring, which he wouldn't give her because that would also give her a legal claim on his inheritance, and that he was not about to give anybody. It was all very well to advocate sharing, but what was his was his and no washed-out hippie was going to run off with any of it. Like everything in his world, Janet was a convenience (and John Lennon Peacechild an accidental, mildly interesting dividend). As long as it suited him, they would remain. When they became a bother—or a danger—or he got sufficiently bored—he would get rid of them and that would be the end of it.

He stood for a moment listening. Now the distant agitations at Pomeroy Station were too far away to be heard at all. No human sound broke the busy mountain silence. The wind sighed gently in the trees, jays screeched, a crow spoke crossly somewhere in the high branches, four more deer sprang away startled at his approach. He looked carefully all about, held himself rigidly listening for a measured minute. With a sudden pantherlike stealth that suited the mountains, he was at the mine-shaft entrance. Logs and brush were swiftly pushed aside. He reached in, dropped something, as swiftly replaced his careful camouflage, stepped back from the entrance and stood, hands on hips again, as though he were studying it with an interested curiosity for the first time.

Charade completed, he shook his head as though in amused puzzlement, turned and came back to the circular area where the road ended. He jumped up and down several times, slapped his arms across his chest, jogged in place for a moment or two and then started off down the road again as casually as he had come.

In Washington, D.C., far from the gently rolling foothills of the South Carolina Blue Ridge, others were also considering the condition of the country and their own responsibilities toward it. They were not finding it so easy to analyze and prescribe for as Earle Holgren did. Much sooner than he expected—and they of course had no way of expecting it at all—they would find Earle Holgren in their lives. They would also find the present Secretary of Labor, Taylor Barbour. The encounters would be fateful for all concerned, and for a society greatly troubled by the constant escalations of crime and violence.

For the time being, however, the unique and highly individualistic group that worked in the stately white marble building facing the Capitol across the greensward of Capitol Plaza had a wider concern, its implications not yet narrowed down to the specific of an Earle Holgren. Their canvas was infinitely broader: and today, as they gathered for their usual Friday conference to clear up the odds and ends that remained before scheduled June adjournment, the eight Justices who for the moment comprised the Supreme Court of the United States were more deeply concerned than they had been in a long, long time.

"Not since civil-rights days," Clement Wallenberg remarked after they had exchanged suitable small talk.

"Not since ever," Rupert Hemmelsford responded glumly as they took their seats around the long table in the comfortable antique-filled Conference Room just across the hall from the formal Supreme Court Chamber.

"In fact, my sister and my brethren," the Chief Justice said, employing the quaint verbal usage with which Supreme Court Justices actually do address one another on many occasions formal and informal, wry or serious, "if things keep up the way they're going, I expect we're in for one hell of a time. There must be a dozen cases on the subject already in the courts below, waiting to come up to us."

"*If* we accept them," Waldo Flyte pointed out. "We don't have to grant them certiorari. Nobody can force us to consider anything we don't want to consider. We can always sidestep the issue." He winked cheerfully. "We've done it before."

"Not if growing criminal violence continues to provoke increasingly violent response from the citizenry," the Chief, whose name was Duncan Elphinstone, said with some severity. "We can't evade our clear duty, Wally, and you know it."

"The trend isn't going to stop unless we stop it," Mary-Hannah McIntosh agreed with equal severity, inclining her close-cropped gray head to one side and peering over her pince-nez at Justice Flyte.

"Not if things continue the way they're going in *your* state," Moss Pomeroy remarked, half teasing her as he liked to do, but pointedly. She flared, as always, in defense of California.

"South Carolina shouldn't talk! Things are getting rough down there, too."

"Rough everywhere," Raymond Ullstein observed of his own state with an unhappy air. "New York City continues to trail Los Angeles in violent crimes and violent deaths, but only just. Only just."

"It's all over the country," Hughie Demsted agreed glumly. "Three hundred and seven murders in the District of Columbia already this year. Mostly involving my own people, too, God help us."

"And the majority of them everywhere so God damned pointless," Wally Flyte observed with a frustrated anger. "Just killing for killing's sake. Ten dollars stolen here, and just for extra kicks they waste the victim. One car brushes another, quite accidentally, so they shoot each other down in the street. An old lady's purse gets snatched, with no possible response from her, so they beat her head in and leave her dead in the gutter. A perfectly innocent dinner party steps out of a restaurant and three insane no-goods gun them down. Rape, robbery, murder, destruction—*just for the hell of it*. What in the hell is the matter with this crazy damned country, anyway?"

"Lack of adequate gun laws," Justice McIntosh said promptly, seizing the chance to open one of her favorite topics.

"The pointless and inexcusable death penalty," and "The lack of a sufficiently tough death penalty," Justice Ullstein and Justice Pomeroy said together, each from his own point of view seizing upon their mutually favorite topic.

"I believe," Duncan Elphinstone said, drawing up to its full and quite

sufficient dignity his five-foot-four frame (which since childhood had inspired the nickname "The Elph," mentally spelled "Elf" by all who used
it), "that this Court must inevitably come to grips with the matter of
ravenously proliferating, wantonly murderous crime, and very soon. We
did indeed, as you so charitably put it, Wally, 'sidestep' it in the last two
terms, but very soon we've got to meet it head-on. Or the country, as
has sometimes happened in the past on some other issues on which the
Court has dragged its feet, is going to take matters in its own hands. In
fact, it's starting to already. We're right on the verge of revived Vigilante Committees, a real resurgence of the Ku Klux Klan, the paraphernalia of 'law and order' about to be taken right out of our hands by
a fed-up citizenry. Under the Constitution *we're* the supreme law and
order in this land, and I think we'd damned well better get to it."

"You sound like Mr. Dooley, Dunc," Rupert Hemmelsford remarked, but affectionately. "You want us to follow the 'iliction re-
turns.' "

"Part of our function," The Elph reminded him, "is to head off the
worst before it can happen. That function has never been more important than it is right now in the area of crime. You mentioned California,
Moss. *Look* at California!"

"And I must admit, as Mary-Hannah says," Justice Pomeroy said
ruefully, "look at South Carolina too. Are you aware there's a real, genuine move afoot in my state to revive flogging—on television? And hold
executions—on television? And punish even the smallest of crimes—even
if a guy feels he has to steal bread for his family, let's say, because the
economic situation is so bad right now—with an upgrading of penalties
that would put it in the category of major crime? And the people are
beginning to *want* this. All sorts of demagogues are trying to whip them
up. It's getting positively Islamic. Jesus! It scares the hell out of me.
Even if"—and he winked at Ray Ullstein—"I do want the death penalty.
Within reason, I want it. I'm not *medieval*."

"It scares me, too," Mary-Hannah said soberly. "What's the name of
your fellow down there?"

"Regard Stinnet," Moss said, "pronounced *Ree*-gard. He's state attorney general right now, but he wants to be governor—Senator—
President, I suppose. The sky's the limit with that boy."

"We have a pretty busy one, too, you know," she said. "I hate to
admit it, but he's on the same track. Also state attorney general, also a
demagogue, also on his way to the stars—he thinks. Ted Phillips, our
boy is."

"They aren't alone," Justice Wallenberg observed. "It's catching on all over the country right now."

"People are just God damned fed up, that's all," Moss Pomeroy said. "You can't blame 'em. The whole criminal justice system is getting out of whack—and not without some assistance from this Court in recent years, I might add. To be honest about it."

"Well," Clement Wallenberg said, "I wasn't on it then—"

"Neither was I," Moss said promptly. "Neither were most of us. But we're the inheritors. It's called 'the continuity of the Court.'"

"But not necessarily 'the consistency of the Court,'" Justice Ullstein suggested with one of his rare gleams of humor.

"That *is* another matter," Justice Hemmelsford said, making the ineffable gesture that the AP's reporter at the Court referred to as "blinking his eyebrows," and peering about at them with his customary sly twinkle.

"They used to call slavery 'the peculiar institution,'" Clem Wallenberg remarked, "but I swear if there's any more peculiar institution than ours, I don't know it."

For a moment they were silent, contemplating the strange nature of the Supreme Court which, developing gradually over two centuries under first the actual, then the historical and legendary, tutelage of Chief Justice John Marshall, had given them so much power of so strange and tenuous, yet so persistent and generally unassailable a kind, over their country's destinies.

"Well," Duncan Elphinstone said, breaking the mood. "I expect we'd better get down to business and start voting on these appeals for certiorari. There's already a case from Minnesota that's pertinent to our discussion, but maybe we'd better take things in order. First comes *Cincinnati Taxpayers v. Internal Revenue Service*. What shall we do with that one?"

So for a couple of hours they discussed *Cincinnati Taxpayers v. Internal Revenue Service* and some fifty other cases, a few of which prompted as much as ten minutes of discussion, but most of which were voted up or down with none at all. When they adjourned for lunch, which they elected to take together today in the Justices' cozy formal dining room on the second floor, the nagging topic with which they had begun came back again, complicated further by a rumor that had just come in to the press room downstairs on the first floor. As reported by the UPI, it said that the enigmatic gentleman in the White House was about to nominate, probably that very afternoon, someone to fill the current vacancy created by the retirement of Homer Dean and thus restore the Court to its full nine-member capacity.

Earle Holgren jogged slowly back down the winding road, assuring himself with a smug satisfaction that it was his ability to be casual and at ease with what he did, his characteristic of being visible but at the same time so ordinary as to be virtually unseen, that had made him so successful in the activities for which the unjust system really wanted to bring him in.

Thinking of these now as he trotted along, the sounds of Pomeroy Station at first faint then louder as he approached the plant again, he congratulated himself that he had never once failed to achieve his objective in the permanent war that he and a small handful of companions still waged against their country.

He had disappeared occasionally, without explanation to Janet or anyone. During the course of his absences four banks were robbed, seventeen people died in an airport bombing in Illinois, twenty-five more in the sinking of a ferry near Seattle, sixteen in a children's parade in California. Travel was no problem, easy targets in a still-innocent, open society, were everywhere. He had by now become a very skillful expert in demolition. Along with buildings and people, he was still hoping to demolish the society. He was part of the growing mood of fear and uncertainty that fastened increasingly upon his countrymen, and proud of it.

The only thing that annoyed him considerably, he reflected as he swung down again past Pomeroy Station, gave its workers and guards a parting wave and jogged on by, was the fact that his type of protest now was not unique: much of its calculated impact was lost in the general tide of wanton crime. Violence was satisfying to those who felt they were doing it in some great social cause whose rationale only they were privileged to understand; but when robberies, rapes, molestations and wanton casual killings in public streets and private neighborhoods were becoming so prevalent, the statement seemed to be disregarded—quite disrespectfully, he felt—in the general public fear and agitation.

Everybody was getting into the act nowadays: killing for killing's sake was becoming an American habit. He wondered wryly sometimes whether it was worth making a personal effort to bring the society down. It was being consumed quite adequately, many of his countrymen felt and he sometimes agreed, from within.

Yet there must still be room for someone to make the point he wished to make—whatever it was. His alienation from society had been so conventional in terms of the Sixties and early Seventies, so predictable in all its stages from the student protests to the breaking with his family, to his disappearance, to the underground conspiracies, to the robberies and bombings, all in the name of the greatest good for the greatest number, that he had to continue to play out the charade now and never yield to uncertainty. Otherwise his whole life's meaning would be destroyed. He could not have endured this. He just had to go on, destructive and essentially mindless for all his intelligence and cleverness, repeating the past because there was no way for him, now, to find the future.

Of course he could not admit this. He *was* the future. *He* had a purpose, *he* had a goal—*he* destroyed society in order to save it—*he* knew the secret. He felt a complete contempt for the animalistic committers of animalistic murders who now befouled the land, the primitives who roamed the streets and slaughtered on a second's sick impulse. He was infinitely better than they. He was Earle Holgren, guardian of a Cause. And after he had defended it at Pomeroy Station, there would no longer be doubt of it.

The target he had chosen this time was an obvious one, given his life-long familiarity with the area and the fact that even now, after years of agitation, security at the nation's atomic energy plants was still as lax and casual as ever.

He jogged on down the mountainside for another three miles until he came to the outskirts of the little village of Pomeroy Station, turned off the paved road onto a dirt lane, came presently to the modest cabin isolated among the pines. Janet was sitting idly in the sun, crooning some sort of rambling lullaby to John Lennon Peacechild, who was sleeping sprawled across her by now considerable lap.

"Have a good run?" she asked idly.

"Yes."

"Go by the plant?"

"Don't I always?"

"You really like that old plant," she remarked, still in the same idle way.

"What makes you think so?" he demanded, suddenly sharp; probably not a good idea, but she was too dumb to notice.

"You're always hanging around there."

"I do not 'hang around there,'" he said with a measured emphasis, "so forget it."

"O.K., O.K.," she said mildly. "Just noticing."

"Don't notice. People get hurt noticing."

"O.K.," she said, finally sounding a little alarmed by his tone. "You don't have to take my head off. What are you going to do now?"

"Study," he said as he started into the cabin.

"You're always studying," she protested with a half-scornful laugh. "Anybody'd think you were going to be a lawyer, or something."

"Maybe I will," he tossed over his shoulder. "The world could stand a few good ones who believe in doing the right thing. There aren't too many of that kind who really care for the people."

"Lucky they have you," she retorted dryly. He stopped dead, turned on his heel and came back to the doorway.

"Don't be so God damned smart," he snapped. "I tell you, people get hurt like that."

"Just commenting," she said, retreating into the kind of shrugging indifference she showed when he lost his temper: which was more often as the appointed day approached. "You're getting awfully touchy, lately. Worried about something?"

"No, I'm not 'worried about something'! What would I be worried about?"

"I don't know," she said, turning to nurse John Lennon Peacechild, who had been awakened by his father's angry tone and was beginning to cry. "And," she added spitefully, "I don't care."

"Keep it that way," he said and turned and went in, slamming the flimsy screen door behind him.

There was silence except for an occasional pleased gurgle from the baby.

Just get over the next couple of weeks, he told himself.

Don't fly off the handle.

Don't get her curious.

Just keep it cool.

Keep it cool.

It was the only way.

"It doesn't say," the Chief Justice remarked when he finished reading the wire-service copy his chief clerk had placed discreetly in his hand as they entered the dining room, "whom he has in mind as our new Associate. Or"—he smiled at Justice McIntosh—"what gender. Next thing we know, we may have to establish a ladies' gym."

"I wouldn't mind the company," she said, "but I don't remember any speculation about a female appointee in the last few days. I think you men can continue to lord it over me."

"That will be the day!" Hughie Demsted exclaimed with an amused shake of his handsome black head as they took their seats informally around the dining table. "I thought Archie Gilbert of the Ninth Circuit Court of Appeals was the front-runner, Dunc."

"Sue-Ann and I were at Henry Randall's last night for dinner," Justice Pomeroy said, naming the shrewd legal mind who was senior Senator from Virginia and chairman of the Senate Judiciary Committee, "and the guessing there seemed to center around Taylor Barbour. For what it's worth."

Rupert Hemmelsford, who had been chairman of Judiciary himself before his appointment to the Court, blinked his eyebrows and assumed the disapproving look he got when contemplating the highly intelligent, highly effective, much-publicized forty-six-year-old Secretary of Labor. "Henry's a good weathervane," he said, "but I'm not so sure I can work very well with Tay Barbour. I don't anticipate he'll have any trouble with Senate confirmation, though. I'd guess two days of hearings and confirmation by about seventy to twenty-six, wouldn't you, Wally?"

"Higher than that," Justice Flyte said with a calculation harking back to his own Senate days. "More like eighty to seventeen, I hear. Tay has some problems, but I don't think they lie with the Senate."

"Things are running down with that marriage," Justice Wallenberg observed with characteristic bluntness. "It could affect his work as a Justice. It's not unheard of, in Court history."

"He'll subordinate it to the Court," Mary-Hannah suggested. "He won't let anything disturb his work here."

"You like him," Rupert Hemmelsford said, his tone almost an accusation. She nodded briskly.

"Very much, Rupe. Shouldn't I?"

Justice Hemmelsford sniffed. "You liberals always stick together."

"And you conservatives don't?" she inquired. "Anyway, you know this institution, Rupe. Today's liberal is tomorrow's conservative is next day's liberal is next day's conservative—you know how it goes."

"That's one of the great things about us, isn't it?" Hughie Demsted agreed with a grin. "Nobody can tie us down, not even our own past records. Once we come on this bench there's not a soul on earth can control us or be absolutely sure what we're going to do. That's one of our great strengths—infinitely better to have us sitting up here a bunch of unpredictable independent mavericks than it would be if we were just a gang of puppets for some transient in the White House. Right?"

"*He* wouldn't like to be referred to like that," Rupe Hemmelsford said with a chuckle. "Like all of 'em, he's got the idea he's eternal. Whereas in reality"—he gave his sly grin—"*we* are. But you're right, of course. It keeps him wonderin' and hoppin'."

"Which is all to the good for the country," Hughie Demsted said triumphantly, settling back to take a sip of his coffee. "If not, Ray, the law."

"The law has got to be consistent if it's to mean anything," Justice Ullstein insisted with his quiet stubbornness that often achieved more than another man's flamboyant dramatics.

"We're the law," Moss Pomeroy said with his usual irreverent grin, "and we're not consistent, half the time. So how can the law be?"

"It's got to be," Ray Ullstein said doggedly. "Or at least we've got to try to make it so. We've got to subordinate our personal feelings and problems, as we were saying about Tay Barbour earlier, to the needs of this Court."

"Well," Justice McIntosh said with some dryness, "we're important, all right, but I don't know that we're *all* that keeps the country from drifting. There's a whole complex of things—tradition, old habit, respect for and devotion to the Constitution, a basic respect for law and order among the great majority of our countrymen—"

"Who are about, as Dunc says, to take the law into their own hands and raise counter-hell with everything," Wally Flyte remarked dryly.

"Listen!" Justice McIntosh said, as sternly as though she were still dean of the Stanford Law School, which she had been for five years before her appointment to the Court. "Don't lecture me on the situation in this country! I know what it is. I also know that not an hour ago we voted five to three to deny certiorari to *Evans v. Minnesota,* a very pertinent case, and it wasn't *my* vote that kept us from considering it. The Chief asked us to face up to it. Well, we just didn't. What is it going to take?" she demanded with a concluding burst of indignation. "Will one of *us,* or somebody near us, have to be slaughtered or mutilated or something, before we come to grips with it?"

"Well, now, May," Dunc Elphinstone said soothingly, figuring it was time, as Rupert Hemmelsford often put it behind his back, "to spread on a little of the old snake oil," "I don't think we need to get personal about things. It's bad enough, as we all know. I'm hopeful," he added with a slight asperity that indicated he, too, was becoming impatient, "that in the next couple of weeks we'll find a case we can all agree on, grant it certiorari and *get to it*. We can't fiddle around much longer."

"I'm ready," Justice Wallenberg said, returning his gaze with a calm and unimpressed air. "But it's got to be a good case, not one we have to stretch for. Maybe South Carolina"—he turned and bowed sarcastically to Moss Pomeroy—"will provide us with something. It's already given us the Court dude."

"Clem, God damn it," Justice Pomeroy said, "will you stop sniping at me? I'm sick of it! Sick of it! Just because I have thirty years on you —or is it a hundred?—and a beautiful wife and lots of money and smashing good looks"—he began both to exaggerate and soften his tone and his usual charming grin began to break through—"and you're just a sour, wizened, nasty old sourpuss who's a liberal-conservative or a conservative-liberal or some kind of all-purpose Push me-Pull you for the Court—anyway," he concluded cheerfully as they all, even Clem, started to laugh—"what the hell are we talking about? The whole thing is too serious to fight over in chambers. Why don't you all come down to South Carolina and be my guests and we can relax and forget it for a day?"

"What's the occasion?" Justice Wallenberg inquired in a still slightly prickly, but mollified, tone.

"They're dedicating the Pomeroy Station atomic energy plant," Moss said, "and you know why I'm involved. It's out west in the Blue Ridge on what was the original Pomeroy Grant in 1693, although we haven't owned the property for at least a hundred years, I guess. But because my name's still on it, and because I was governor when they started to build it, they want me there. I'd like to invite you all, if you'd like to come."

"Against atomic energy," Clem Wallenberg said shortly. "Wouldn't be caught dead."

"Scratch one," Justice Pomeroy said with unfrayed cheer. "I'm just as relieved as you are, Clem. Any more cop-outs?"

The Chief hunched forward and clasped his hands under his chin with a thoughtful air.

"As a matter of fact," he said, looking up and down the table, "we've already had some cases on the atomic issue, as you know, and inevitably we're going to have more. I really think it might be better if we all passed. With all thanks and respect to you, Moss. Does that make sense?"

There were unanimous nods and sounds of agreement.

"Now let me offer a counterproposition. Birdie and I would like to have everyone to dinner a week from next Friday. Just to wind up the session, as it were. And to officially greet Tay and Mary Barbour, assuming he's nominated and confirmed by then, as our two distinguished ex-Senators predict."

"That's the night of my trip to South Carolina," Moss said, "but the ceremony is at noon and Sue-Ann and I will be coming right back. The President's giving us a plane."

"Oh, I say," Justice Wallenberg remarked. "How jolly."

"Yes, isn't it," Moss agreed with a grin. "You see what you're missing, Clem."

"So, then," the Chief said, "a week from this coming Friday, eight P.M., in the dining room here, black tie—"

"God, must we?" Hughie Demsted groaned.

"You look divine, Hughie," Justice McIntosh said, "and you know it, so stop objecting. Men always look divine in black tie. Why do they always balk?"

"With spouses, of course," The Elph went on. "Or," he added, bowing to Mary-Hannah, "boyfriend, as the case may be."

She hooted.

"Darling," she said, "I am fifty-eight years old, in the sere and yellow leaf, and the last time I was unfurled was—" She stopped, blushed and started to laugh, as did they all.

"When, May?" Moss Pomeroy demanded eagerly. "Oh, do tell us about it! When? When?"

But she had collapsed in laughter and so their luncheon ended on a merry note as the Chief said with mock sternness, "And now, back to those damned certioraris. We'll be lucky if we get out of here by six P.M."

"I'm afraid so," Wally Flyte said, heading for the door. As he reached it there was a knock and it was opened from the other side so quickly that it almost hit him in the nose. A clerk thrust a piece of wire-service copy into his hand with an apologetic murmur and fled. Wally glanced at it hastily and spun around, holding it high.

"It's Tay," he confirmed. "By a landslide."

2

The landslide, while inevitable, did not happen for a week, but there was never any doubt that Taylor Barbour would have no trouble with the Senate. In the interim he was the focus of immense and immediate media interest.

"And so when did you first decide you wanted to be a Supreme Court Justice?" his bright young interviewer asked when *The Washingtonian* magazine sent her to the Labor Department late on the afternoon of his nomination to do an in-depth cover story on "Our New Man on The Court."

He smiled in his pleasant, noncommittal fashion and for a moment looked far away into some private distance.

"I don't know that I ever really *wanted* to be," he said, "or ever made it a specific goal of mine. But I suppose if one is a lawyer and by good fortune and the grace of Presidents has been permitted to reach high place in government, it is an idea that occurs."

"That's very diplomatic, Mr. Secretary," she said with a smile that he found he quite liked, "but of course you know I don't believe you for a minute. I think you've been eating your heart out for this job most of your life. I think you are inwardly doing a rain dance for glee."

"Whoopee," he said mildly. "What did you say your name is?"

"Catherine Corning," she said. "Isn't that awful? They call me Cathy Corny on the magazine because I'm always doing these sob-sister stories on the more glorious monuments of our government such as Secretaries of Labor, former Solicitors General who get appointed to the Court, and people like that. They say I have a Touch."

"No doubt," he said. "Well, I hope you'll give me the same sweet treatment you've given all the rest."

"Have you read any of my stuff?"

"Occasionally."

"Then you know I bite. Beware!"

"You bet I will," he assured her solemnly. Then he smiled, more broadly and in a more relaxed fashion this time. "As a matter of fact, to level with you, I have wanted to be a Supreme Court Justice ever since I first decided I wanted to be a lawyer. And that was about thirty years ago, now. Roughly the time you were in diapers."

"Not quite," she said. "Not—quite. Tell me the story of your climb to the Court. Our public wants to know."

"Then we can't disappoint them," he agreed, and obliged; much more fully and candidly, he realized later, than he had ever related it for any other interviewer in a career that had in large part been spent in the public arena.

It had begun sometime around age sixteen after a childhood and youth spent on the family ranch in California's fertile and lovely Salinas Valley, inland and south from San Francisco. His parents had assumed, and so had he for quite a long time, that he would grow up, go to college, probably at the University of California's agricultural school at Davis, and then come home to work with his father and eventually assume management of the property. It comprised some four thousand acres, acquired originally by his grandfather starting in 1894, and had provided the family with a more than comfortable living ever since. They raised truck crops, as did most of the valley: lettuce, tomatoes, beets, turnips, the like. The ranch's prosperity ebbed and flowed with the seasons and the weather, sometimes good years, sometimes bad, but overall far more of the former.

"It's a good living," his father said comfortably, and no one could deny it. The temptation for Tay to take the easy way and stick with it was very great, strengthened by sentimental ties, the fact that he was the eldest of two sons and a daughter and was locked into the family assumption that, naturally, he would take over the ranch. What else did Barbours do?

It therefore required some major event to pull him away. It had occurred quite by accident in high school when a civics teacher with some imagination had decided to form the class into a student replica of the federal government and take a mock piece of legislation through its various stages up to and including legal challenge and final decision by the Supreme Court.

He often reflected that if Miss Tillson had not had this inspiration, he would probably be a pillar of the Salinas Valley to this very day, president of Rotary, adviser to the Future Farmers, battler with Cesar Chavez, staunch believer in all the things his father had believed in without question or quarrel.

Instead Miss Tillson had said, "Tay, you're going to be the Chief Justice," and a life's direction had changed in a moment.

(She was in her seventies now, in a retirement hotel near Monterey. She had called him twenty minutes ago and with the persistence and determination he remembered had worked her way through the Labor Department switchboard to his office. "Tay?" she inquired without other introduction. "Do you remember Civics I and our 'Supreme Court' days together?" "Yes, Erma," he said, "bless your heart, I do." "Well, you haven't made Chief Justice," she said; "yet. But now you've got a foot in the door, you'll get there." "One step at a time," he said. She chuckled, a fading but still gallant sound. "Do us proud, now!" she admonished. "Don't let Civics I down!" "How could I?" he asked. "After all, you're the one who got me into all this." Which had pleased her very much, of course; and truly enough, she had.)

He was a thoughtful and conscientious boy, and in preparation for his role he did considerable research on the Court. He found the two weeks during which the class carried its legislation through mock House, mock Senate and mock Court not only fun, but exciting. Some glimpse of something came to him, growing stronger every day they played their educational game. It became very serious for him before it was over, and when, as "Chief Justice," he presented all his arguments with force and clarity and then declared solemnly, "Accordingly the ruling of the Supreme Court of California is reversed," the class burst into spontaneous applause.

Afterward they had to prepare a theme on their experience in "government." Miss Tillson gave him a straight A. "Some critics," his paper concluded, "find it hard to analyze exactly why the Supreme Court is as powerful in our system as it is. They say it has 'lifted itself by its own bootstraps' to acquire this power. One critic even says that the Court 'rests firmly on the cushion of its own self-esteem.' But it has been many, many years since anyone has successfully challenged its power. It is a special place."

And so it is, he thought now as he sorted out his memories for "Cathy Corny," whose quick intelligence and deliberately disrespectful

challenges intrigued him into a greater unburdening than he had intended. Their interview easily lengthened past the hour she had requested.

"You sound as though you were quite a little prig before you got this
sudden flash of light about the Court," she suggested with a smile she
knew would be provoking. "A real little Goody Gumdrops of an obedient son and heir."

"No, I wasn't," he objected, but much more mildly than he might
have with someone else. "I was just a good boy. That meant something,
when I was growing up in the Salinas Valley."

And so it had. Aside from normal childhood deviltry, such as the
time they took their three horses and decided to run away to Carmel
over on the coast at ages ten, eight and six, he and his sister Anne and
brother Carl were good and reliable kids whose parents felt that they
would all settle surely and without difficulty into the pleasant pattern of
ranch and valley life. Fortunately Carl and his wife, Dorothy Sterling,
and Anne and her husband, Johnny Gonzales, all had, so the ranch
today was still in the family, still flourishing and still a homestead for
all the Barbours. His own wife Mary didn't like it much, being the city-
girl daughter of a Philadelphia banker, but for him there was still no
tranquillity like that he felt when he stood in the furrows of a newly
plowed field and watched the gentle purple light of California evening
touch the hills along the valley.

"I'm Antaeus," he had said recently in one of his increasing arguments with Mary about that and many other things. "I get a lot of
strength out of touching foot to my own ground." She had snorted
derisively but it was true. True enough so that the last time he had said
he was going to the ranch and she snapped, "Go without me, then!" he
had.

No, not a Goody Gumdrops as a kid, just a good and generally well-
behaved little boy, who had grown up rapidly into a physically strong,
mentally sharp, steady, thoughtful and trustworthy youth. Erma Tillson
was not the only elder who thought he had much promise and tried to
steer him toward its fulfillment. She happened to be the one who got
through.

She did not realize this until the end of his senior year, when he came
to her one day and said he wanted advice. Not very many students did
this with her, because though she was a good teacher and imaginative in
her approach, she was painfully shy and inclined to run from any intimate contacts. Also, many of the valley sons and daughters, though of
good stock, salt of the earth and all the other things complacent

rancher-parents said of them, were not touched with any special genius or interest in life beyond the prospects of the next crop and what could be accomplished on side roads in the back seats of cars after school dances. Tay Barbour's interests, as healthily lively in these areas as any of his contemporaries', also had room for a great deal more. She had thought this might be the case when he had proved so dedicated to his role as "Chief Justice," but she had not been sure: it might have been just a passing fancy that would soon subside into the general level of valley living. She found out now with thrilling certainty that this was not so.

"Yes?" she said, sounding as always more quick and impatient than she was—not meaning to, but cursed. (It was not until many years later, when he came home after being named Solicitor General and accidentally met her on the street, that she had finally begun to relax with him. By then he was at last old enough to start calling her "Erma," and after that they became real friends. But the ease of years was not yet.)

"Miss Tillson—" he began earnestly, blushed, and stopped.

"Yes, Tay?" she said, resisting her impulse to flee, forcing herself to be steady, authoritative and grown up. "Can I do something to help?"

"Well—yes, I think so," he said. He paused and then plunged doggedly on. "Do you remember in civics class when you had us play government?"

"Of course. You were the Chief Justice."

He nodded, hesitated a moment, looking awkwardly at his feet, the room, out the window, anywhere but at her.

"Miss Tillson," he blurted out, "would you say I was crazy if I said—" And stopped again, overcome.

"I won't say you're crazy, whatever you say," she promised, for she realized something very important must be in the wind. "So go right ahead. What is it?"

"If I said I wanted to be a lawyer," he said, almost angrily.

"Why, now," she said with growing excitement. "Not at all! Why would anybody say you're crazy?"

"Well," he said, struggling but determined, "the—the ranch, and—and all. My sister Anne and brother Carl say I'm crazy. They say it's crazy for any Barbour to leave the ranch. They say none of us ever has. They say I've got to stay here and run it, just as my—my father—wants me to."

"Has he ever said that?" she demanded.

He looked miserable.

"It's just understood."

"But not by you."

"No," he said, forlornly. "Not by me. I love the ranch, you know that. But I don't want to stay on the ranch. Carl wants to. Anne wants to. So why can't I go away and be a lawyer, if I want to? I'd still come home to see them and help out. I'd still be part of it!"

"Of course you would," she said soothingly. "How could anybody, particularly your brother and sister, doubt that?"

"It's—it's my dad I'm worried about," he said, miserable still. "He'll raise hell."

"Oh, I don't think so," she said with far more confidence than she felt. Frank Barbour loomed a large, rough, red-faced presence in her mind, glimpsed occasionally at school functions, awesome and omnipotent in his role as chairman of the school board, which he had been for all of the seven years she had been teaching there. "I think he'll understand. After all, he does have Anne and Carl. Why don't you go and talk to him about it?"

"That's easier said than done," Tay said with a wan smile. "You don't know how determined my dad is."

"I know how determined his son is," she said stoutly. "He ought to be proud of you!"

"He'll be prouder if I take over the ranch someday," Tay said in a desolate tone. "There's no doubt about that."

"Well, then," she said, dreading the answer, telling herself desperately, I do not want to talk to Mr. Barbour, "what do you think I can do about it?"

But Tay surprised her.

"I just wanted to know," he said, suddenly looking her straight in the eye with an anguished appeal, "if *you* think I'm crazy."

She was relieved and pleased in about equal measure.

"I most certainly do *not!*" she exclaimed. "I think you have the mind for it, and the character, and I think it's wonderful you want to do something like that. Just wonderful! And if I had anything to do with it by assigning you in our little play, then I shall be proud of it for the rest of my life! And proud of *you!* So there!"

"Well," he said, relaxing for the first time and giving her the shy, easygoing grin that was one of his most attractive characteristics, "if *you* feel that way and *I* feel that way, then maybe I'm not so far out, after all . . . But," he said, reverting again to gloom, "that doesn't make it easier with my dad."

"Well!" she said, and took a deep breath. "What about your mother?"

He looked a little less glum, but still with the world on his shoulders.
"She's a Taylor, you know, from over in the San Joaquin Valley.
They're ranch people, too. She'll probably feel the same way."

"Maybe not," she said thoughtfully. She took a deep breath. "I tell
you what. Suppose I try to find a way to talk to your mother alone
about it. Sometimes when we girls—we ladies—put our heads together
we can get the men to agree to a lot of things they didn't think they
would. How would that be? Would you mind?"

"Oh, Miss Tillson!" he said, face lighting up with a great relief.
"That would be *great*."

"Good," she said, feeling quite giddy with daring and excitement and
triumph at not having failed this tall, gangling, earnest youth—at least,
not yet. "I'll do it!"

"You *will?*" he demanded, not daring to believe it or to hope that it
would really solve anything.

"Cross my heart!" she said with a giggle that sounded surprisingly
youthful for one so elderly (she must then, he estimated years later,
have been about forty). "And hope to die!"

And joined him in the relieved and happy laughter into which this
schoolyard promise plunged him.

But after she shooed him out—"Get along now, or you'll be late for
basketball practice!"—she sat at her desk in the empty classroom for
quite some time, telling herself, Erma, you're a fool. You know you
shouldn't get involved in your kids' family matters. You *know* you
shouldn't. But Tay, she realized, was a special kid of hers, not just any
kid. So presently she took a deep breath, uttered a little prayer to the
Lord above, and told herself firmly: *It is meant to be. It will be all
right.*

And so, much to her surprise, it was. Helen Barbour, to begin with,
was much more approachable than Frank, being a small, petite, dark-
haired woman with a kindly, pleasant face and a personality to match.
She also possessed considerable charity and a perception that permitted
her to empathize with old-maid schoolteachers rounding forty and becoming aware that surrogate children were probably the only ones they
would ever have. She did feel a momentary and inescapable pang of
jealousy when Erma Tillson, having driven out to the ranch to see her
on a day when she had ascertained that Frank would be away on business in Stockton, disclosed hesitantly but determinedly that her son had
turned first to his teacher instead of his mother. But Helen was a fair-
minded woman and this swiftly passed. They both, she realized, loved
Tay and wished him well; and that was more important than anything.

"Tell me about it," she said comfortably, sitting back in the porch
swing overlooking the valley and studying Erma with a kindly attention
as she sipped on the heavily scented herb tea into which Helen had
thoughtfully slipped a teaspoonful of vodka out in the kitchen. Poor
Erma needed *something,* she had told herself, she was so tense. But
Erma was quite determined enough, as it turned out, though the un-
suspected liquor did perhaps make her words a little more fluent than
usual.

"Tay is a *good* boy," she began. "And," she added firmly, "my favorite pupil. I think he has great potential."

"So do I," Helen agreed. "Is it something to do with his potential
that's involved here?"

"That and—and the ranch. And his father."

"Does he want to leave the ranch?" Helen asked, dismay seizing her
heart—but she could not, being perceptive and honest, claim surprise.

"Yes, he does," Erma said, finding suddenly that all her doubts and
hesitations had disappeared: Helen was so easy and understanding.
"You remember we had that class project a while back, when we set up
a mock government and he was 'Chief Justice'?"

Helen chuckled.

"He was absolutely fascinated. But isn't it a little early for him to
think about being Chief Justice? I believe that takes a little time and a
few more years."

"But you have to start by being a lawyer," Erma Tillson said. "You
don't do it running a ranch in the Salinas Valley. And *there,*" she
added, something making her a little more daring and blunt than she
might normally have been, "is where he's afraid he's going to run
squarely into his father. And I agree. I'm afraid Mr. Barbour strikes
me," she said, feeling slightly giddy with her daring, "as a stubborn, if
not, one might say, even a hardheaded man."

Helen Barbour smiled, evidently not at all offended.

"He has his opinions," she agreed. "But, then, so do I, and we seem
to have managed pretty well for almost twenty years."

"*I* think," Erma said, now feeling completely and delightfully free to
say whatever she pleased, "that it's obvious that he adores you. I think
he'll do anything you say."

Helen laughed.

"I'd like to think so, on both counts. But I don't carry the day *every*
time. My record is pretty good, but not perfect."

"In this case," Erma Tillson said solemnly, "I think it is extremely
important to your son's whole future and happiness in life that you do

carry the day. If, that is, you agree with me that the young, if they really find a goal in life as imperative as this seems to be for Tay, be allowed to pursue it."

"Oh, I do agree."

"Then you will persuade Mr. Barbour that Tay should be allowed to leave the ranch and go to law school?"

"I'll do my best," Helen said, "but I think first you should talk to him directly yourself." For a second Erma looked so stricken that her hostess laughed. "He won't eat you up," she promised. "Really. I know he intimidates a lot of people, including, obviously, his own son, but he's really quite amiable. Why don't you come back tomorrow afternoon and we'll have tea? You'll find it much easier than you think."

And to her amazement, as she told Tay years later, Erma did. Frank Barbour was formidable and apparently challenging at first, but this soon changed, and presently he was agreeing mildly with both of them that possibly, after all, it was time for those Barbours who wished to, to venture from the ranch.

"Of course," he said, looking so like a big disappointed lion that Miss Tillson almost wanted to throw her arms around him and comfort him, "he *is* the oldest son, and I *have* been counting on it. In fact, I never thought there would be any question. But if that's what he really wants to do—"

"It is," Helen said. "Erma's just told you how he feels."

"I think," Frank said, shooting them both a gloomy glance, "that it's time he tells me so himself. Don't you?"

"Yes," Helen agreed. "I think maybe, now, it is."

Their interview, Tay remembered while Cathy listened intently, had been initially one of the hardest things he had ever done and ultimately one of the easiest and most rewarding. For this he always thanked Erma.

"And you never thanked your mother?" Cathy demanded sharply. "That was a damned thoughtless thing, considering she was really the one who paved the way for you—"

"Just a minute!" he said with equal sharpness. "I didn't say I *never* thanked her. I often did."

"But you thanked Erma more, somehow, didn't you?"

"Well—maybe," he admitted uncomfortably. "But I did thank Mother. She knew how I felt. But I just didn't feel—well, that I should gush about it. She understood."

"Mothers like to be gushed over," she said. "Didn't you like your mother?"

"Are you kidding?" he demanded. "Cut this amateur psychology,

O.K., and let's get on with it. Anyway, how do you know what mothers like?"

"Because I am one," she said tartly. "And don't *you* get into any amateur psychology, either, O.K.?"

"Ah *ha!*" he said dryly. "So all this demon journalism, all these piercing questions, all this killer instinct is just getting back at some man, right? He got you pregnant and left you and now you're stuck with his child? What is it, a boy or a girl?"

"Talk about killer instinct," she said, putting down her pen and notebook and giving him an appraising look. She was really quite pretty, he realized, especially when annoyed—not angry, he could sense that, just annoyed. The distinction suddenly seemed quite important for some reason he didn't really want to think about.

"If you must know," she said, "and obviously you must if we're going to get any further with *my* interview of *you,* I met this boy at Columbia when we were both in journalism school. It was Watergate time and everybody was going to save the world and win a Pulitzer, no one more surely than he and I. So we lived together for a while, and then we got married, and then we had babies, Sandra and Rowland. And then I began to be successful and he began to fail and he started drinking and his fatal charm wore off and then we got divorced and then I came to Washington at thirty-three, landed on the magazine two years ago, and here I am."

"Hardly drawing a breath," he said with mock admiration. "How do you do it?"

"I'll show you sometime," she said shortly. "Now can we get back on the track, please? That must have been a tough talk you had with your father."

"Not really," he said; and looking back now he could see that it really hadn't been, although at first his father, as always, appeared massive, formidable and quite overwhelming to the nervous and genuinely frightened youth Tay was then.

"Let's take a walk," Frank Barbour suggested next night after dinner; and, "Yes, sir," he said humbly, thinking, *Oh, my God, here it comes. What will I do?* But his mother gave him an encouraging smile and a definite nod that said: *Don't worry.* That was comforting but not enough to make it an easy walk. It was a silent one, ending in the middle of the newly plowed fields when his father broke the silence with an abrupt "Let's stop here."

Tay would always remember what a beautiful spring evening it was, the air soft and warm with the smell of fresh-turned earth, the valley stretching away below as far as the eye could see, the western range falling into darkness behind them, the eastern still aglow with the gently fading purple light. He would find his private tranquillity here many, many times in the future but it was not here now. He felt frightened, miserable, terribly tense and just plain sick.

"You see all this," Frank Barbour said with a quick, almost embarrassed gesture that encompassed it.

"Yes, sir," he said.

"Four thousand acres of it belong to us. That's a mighty damned hell of a lot."

"Yes, sir."

His father stopped quickly, scooped up a handful of the rich black soil, let it dribble through his fingers.

"It's damned fine ground, too," he said harshly, as though someone were arguing with him.

"Yes, *sir!*" agreed Tay, who wouldn't have dreamed of it. Or dared to.

Frank Barbour swung around and looked him squarely in the face. *"Why don't you like it?"*

"I *do* like it!" he cried then, halfway between tears and anger. "I love the ranch! You *know* that! I *love* the ranch!"

"That isn't the way I hear it."

"Then you don't hear the truth!" He paused for a moment, everything heightened by emotion, the earth darker, the sky bluer, the mountains sharper, his heritage everywhere more lovely. "Who told you that?" he demanded finally, voice shaking. "That isn't true!"

"Your mother and your teacher say you want to leave it."

"But that doesn't mean I don't love it!" he protested, quivering with the unfairness of it. "They didn't say that!"

"No," his father admitted grudgingly. "But they said you like something else more."

For a moment he didn't answer, knowing that it would be one of the most decisive answers he would ever give to anything. Then he said, very low, "Yes sir."

A silence fell, evening deepened, night advanced. Finally his father spoke, more softly and more reasonably.

"Tell me about it."

"I like the law," he said, voice still shaking at first but growing calmer and steadier as he went along; and not deterred by his father's first derisive "Hmph!"

"Yes, sir," he said, more strongly, "I think I want to be a lawyer."

"Hmph!" his father said again, but this time in so much more reasonable a tone that Tay was emboldened to tell him, with a shaky little laugh, "And don't say *Hmph!* It can be an honorable profession."

"Really?"

"Don't you think it will be when your son is in it?" he demanded like a flash; and before he knew it his father had started laughing, and after a tentative moment he joined in, though at first he didn't quite know why.

"That's mighty sharp," Frank Barbour said, still chuckling. "Mighty quick. You turned it right back on me. Maybe you wouldn't be such a bad lawyer, at that."

"Then you'll let me—" he began eagerly. But his father held up a hand.

"Slow down, now. Slow down. I haven't promised anything yet. You do owe me and the ranch something, you know."

"Everything," he said fervently. "Everything!"

"That's right," his father said, more grimly, "and don't you forget it. First of all, you owe me an apology for not coming to me with this, first thing, instead of relying on a couple of women to do your work for you." He paused and snorted. "That mousy little Tillson woman! She got you into this!"

"Don't you hurt Miss Tillson!" Tay cried in sudden alarm. "Don't you and your old school board do anything to Miss Tillson! She's a fine lady! Don't you hurt Miss Tillson!"

"I'm not going to 'hurt Miss Tillson'!" his father said grumpily. "Probably wind up giving her a raise, when all is said and done, for helping my son discover what he really wants to do. That's the tough kind of old son of a bitch I am. But that doesn't make me any happier that you didn't come to me first. Why didn't you?"

"Well . . ." He paused and drew a deep breath, because he knew this would hurt, and probably terribly; but even at eighteen he realized that life does these things, inevitably. "Well, Dad—because I'm afraid of you. Anne and Carl are afraid of you, too. All of your kids are afraid of you. We love you, but we're—we're—just—afraid, I guess."

Then there was a silence, a very long silence, during which he did not dare look at the massive figure looming beside him. Somehow it did not look quite so massive any more; and when a strangled, savagely suppressed sound burst from it for a moment, he realized with a sort of horror that his father was actually crying. To his great relief it did not last more than a minute or two; after which the world was back in place.

"Well," Frank Barbour said in a stifled voice, blowing his nose vigor-ously, "you know that isn't what I ever intended." His voice grew stronger and he kicked the earth with a sudden savagery. In some in-stinctive way his son knew it was far from the first time. "I've fought this earth all my life," he said. "Sometimes it's been easy, sometimes it's been hard. Sometimes I've licked it, other times it's licked me. But the war never stops. Nature never gives up. You have to keep after her all the time. Maybe that's why some of us ranch types get a little tough, sometimes. Maybe that's why we scare the people we love. Maybe that's why"—his voice trembled again and threatened to stop, but after a mo-ment he went on as calmly as ever—"maybe that's why it's not so easy to see a son of mine, my oldest son, on whom I have always set my hopes, decide he's going to give up the battle and go somewhere else."

"That isn't fair," Tay said, quietly and more maturely now, fortified by the knowledge that his father knew it wasn't fair. "I'm not giving up the battle, and I'll never be far away. You *know* that. Carl and Anne both want to stay on the ranch, and when they get married, Carl will get a lot of help from Anne's husband—"

"Johnny Gonzales!" his father said in a strangled tone. "At sixteen, she thinks she wants to marry Johnny Gonzales! *That*—"

"*Yes*," Tay said, without giving an inch. "And that's great too. He's a great guy and Carl and I want him in the family as much as she does. Things are changing, Dad. We need new blood in the family. And he loves the ranch as much as you and I do. After all, he's grown up here almost as much as we have."

"That's the trouble," his father growled. "If I'd only known what was going to happen—"

"You still would have hired Martin, because he's the best foreman in the valley. And you still would have got his son along with him. And Anne would still have done what she's going to do. So why make it tough for everybody?"

"Isn't nature enough?" his father asked in a half-wry, half-bitter tone. "Do I have to fight my own kids too?"

Tay dared to laugh, knowing he had the upper hand now.

"Not at all, Dad. Just give in to 'em. It'll be a lot easier."

"Are you afraid of me now?" his father asked and again there was a long moment, and again a decisive answer.

"Not any more," Tay said quietly. "Not ever any more, I think. But now I think we can begin to love you more than we ever have, too. So that's something."

"Yes," his father said, blowing his nose abruptly again. "That's for damned sure *something.* So how do you plan to go about this law bug of yours?"

"Well, first," he said, "I was thinking Stanford for undergraduate work. And then I think maybe Harvard, if I can get in."

"You want to go *east?*" his father demanded in the disbelieving tone of any loyal Californian who knows they have everything, and better, right there. "Why *east?*"

"Because that's where the big opportunities and the big money are," Tay said crisply, in a toughly practical tone his father had never heard before, though his mother had, in the past twenty-four hours when they had talked about it at length. "And that's where the chance to help people really is. Maybe eventually I can even go to Washington and do something to help serve the country and help make our whole society better. I'd like to do that."

"That's that damned Erma Tillson again!"

"It is *not!*" Tay said flatly. "That's my idea."

"You might even want to be a politician," his father said in a tone that unfortunately was not only Californian but virtually unanimous from coast to coast.

"I might even want to be," Tay agreed in the same crisp tone. "So don't be too shocked if it happens someday . . . Anyway, I have a long way to go. Are you going to wish me well on the journey?"

And now it was his time to turn and look his father squarely in the face, though he could hardly see it in the now swiftly gathering dusk. But he could sense a smile, and presently the big hand closed firmly over his.

"I guess I'd better make it easy and give in," Frank Barbour said with a chuckle that cost him more than Tay would ever know. "Since that's what my kids want me to do."

Five minutes later they came back to the house laughing and joking together, arm in arm. Helen Barbour gave her son a big wink and a grin and kissed them both heartily.

"*There!*" she said. "That wasn't so hard, was it!"

"Hard as hell," her husband said. "But I think we both survived."

"Yes," Tay said happily. "I think we did. I think I'll go call Miss Tillson. She'll be pleased to know."

"So your mother had to play second fiddle even then," Cathy remarked. "Didn't she deserve something for—"

"Listen!" he said, suddenly genuinely annoyed. "Will you stop this phony women's chip-on-the-shoulder business? Who says I didn't? And who says there was ever any problem? Do you know that scarcely ten minutes before you came in I called the ranch and told my mother about this appointment—even before I told my wife? Do you know that she and my dad are flying back for my swearing-in? Do you know—but of course you don't. You're just jumping to conclusions, like all the media. It's so damned stupid."

"Am *I* damned stupid?" she demanded; and added quickly, "Why didn't you call your wife first? Is something wrong there?"

"Oh, for—!" he exclaimed with a frustrated laugh. "O.K., you tell me. Go on and make up your own story. I'm obviously wasting your time. I know it will make much better reading than the truth."

"You're very defensive about your wife," she remarked thoughtfully, making a note and staring at him unblinkingly. "I wonder why that is?"

"I don't know," he said, shifting to mockery for a moment. "Maybe it's because we have the worst possible marriage there ever was and I'm planning to divorce her as soon as—"

"Are you?" she inquired with the same quick earnestness that appeared to be genuine, though he seriously doubted it. It was just a reporter's trick, they all had them.

"No, I am not," he said, deciding two could play at that game, turning completely calm and reasonable. "Mary and I have a close and satisfying marriage that has lasted for twenty years now, and which we aren't about to dissolve. Sorry to disappoint you, but that's the way it is."

"Tell me about it," she said; and after studying her for a moment, he smiled.

"All right, if you'll treat it sensibly, I will. I met her in my last year at Harvard Law."

The school years, divided between Stanford and Harvard, passed very profitably and pleasantly for him. He applied himself with diligence to his pre-law course at Stanford; enjoyed the many extracurricular activities he found available; was a star of the basketball team, as he had been in high school; speaker of the student senate in his senior year; had his share of conquests on the back roads west of campus; and generally enjoyed the life of a healthy, vigorous, studious, reliable and outwardly gregarious young male. "Tay is so *well balanced*," one of his fraternity brothers who was not, particularly, remarked sarcastically as they neared graduation; and so he was.

When he was accepted at Harvard Law School and prepared to leave for the east at the end of his fourth Stanford summer back on the ranch, he took with him a thorough preparation, many good memories and a few good friends who would stay with him over the years. He did not take a wife, nor did he take the unbalancing of emotion and of views that were to warp and twist so many of the college generation that came soon after.

He completed his undergraduate years, he often reflected, just in time to escape the effects of the Vietnam war. Unlike Earle Holgren, now staring vacantly at nothing in his carefully modest cabin in the woods, who came to Harvard a few years later, Tay was not a self-conscious child of rebellion self-consciously rebelling. A character infinitely steadier than Earle's would not have permitted it, even had the timing been right. Fortunately for him it was not. The maintenance of a level head and an undeviating advance toward established goals did not become a personal battle to survive the chaos of a generation but simply an extension of an already well-ordered progression.

At Harvard his love affair with the law, which had begun rather lightly in Erma Tillson's Civics I and had grown steadily more serious at Stanford, became a final commitment. By now it absorbed him to the point where it almost seemed that there had never been any other major interest. The ranch was still a part of him—he was drawn into its affairs on many occasions by the family corporation Frank Barbour had set up, he still went back for vacations, pulled on jeans, work shirt and battered old hat, and drove tractors and trucks and plows and harrows with his father, Carl, Martin and Johnny Gonzales and the rest. He still loved it. But always his mind was at work on the problems of the law, his thoughts, never idle, were concentrated on examinations yet to come. His heart was at Harvard and, more specifically, in the law.

Aware of this—as who could not be?—Frank Barbour told Helen many times that he felt he had done the right thing to take the time to find out what the boy really wanted and encourage him to do it. She always agreed gravely that it had been one of the best ideas he had ever had.

At law school, also, Tay made several good friends whose paths crossed his repeatedly over the years as they all rose steadily in the profession. One of the first, the one who meant the most and always would, was a young Southerner of substantial wealth, political purpose and considerable personal charm who came into his life one day at the library with an amiable grin, reentered it when Tay came to Washington and now was about to become not only friend but colleague and fellow Justice. Stanley Mossiter Pomeroy was six months younger than he, a little less serious, a little more relaxed, but equally ambitious and dedicated to the law.

Their eyes had met across a study table, held, been followed after a moment by smiles.

"Hi," the other had said, holding out a friendly hand. "I'm Stan Pomeroy, except I like to be called Moss because my middle name is Mossiter and it's different. My best friends call me Moss. I expect you'll want to do the same?"

And he gave an engaging grin that Tay could not help but respond to.

"I expect I will," he said, "if you want me to."

"I think I do," Moss said. "You look like a good guy to me. Do you need any help on anything?"

"I'm making it O.K."

"So'm I, but on the whole I think a team does better."

"Probably," Tay agreed. "We can spread the headaches around."

"And boy!" Moss said. "Does this place give 'em to you!"

A team they had become, studying together, researching together, writing together, serving as practice audience for each other's oral presentations, giving each other critiques of substance and style, fortifying one another in all the rigors of the paper chase. And, cautiously at first on Tay's part, but then with increasing acceptance and ease, they became a social team as well, meeting a steadily increasing number of girls from Radcliffe, Smith, Wellesley, Vassar, going on double dates to Boston and New York, skiing in Canada, picnicking on the Cape, breaking away from the grind whenever they could.

Moss, as he explained matter-of-factly, was probably going to marry a girl down home in Charlotte, South Carolina, named Sue-Ann Lacey but, "In the meantime, I do not intend to let any virgins grow under my feet. I've got a better place for 'em." In pursuit of this he ranged far and wide through New England's educational institutions for the warm-blooded young and did not do at all badly in achieving his announced intention: even though, as he confessed to Tay from time to time, he really did love Sue-Ann and he only wished the damned law school would come to an end as fast as possible so he could marry her and have her save him from all this worthless carryin'-on.

For Tay, too, it was essentially worthless. He could not deny he enjoyed it, even if much more circumspectly and on a much more modest scale. But it soon lost its savor and before long he was beginning to look seriously for someone he could genuinely love and who could genuinely help him in his career.

He related none of this to Cathy Corning, though she did her best to pry it out of him. To hear him tell it this afternoon, he and Moss were virgin, hardworking, no-nonsense students who stayed glued to their law books until Moss went home to Sue-Ann and he found Mary Stranahan at Smith.

"That must have been boring," Cathy observed dryly.

"Dreadfully," he agreed cheerfully. "But it made us such good students that we both seem to have wound up on the Supreme Court. Don't knock it."

"Never," she said, making a note. "I thought I was to get the truth."

"Within reasonable limits." He smiled. "I set the limits. And I define what's reasonable."

"You'll make a good Justice," she said with a sudden answering smile. "You sound like one already. You're an arrogant bunch of birds, you know that?"

"I'm sure we don't mean to be," he said. "I'm sure we're not. It just seems that way, sometimes."

"Like now," she agreed. "Get on with the fairy tale."

"Well," he said, "*then* I met Mary Stranahan."

"And lived happily ever after."

"Perfectly," he said, although he knew, and by now she was absolutely certain, that this was not the case.

Yet for quite a while—more than half their years together, in fact—it had been. He had met Mary at a dance at Smith—one of his other classmates had a younger sister there and invited him to go along as a blind date. The whole thing was very conventional and clichéd—"No surprises," as he had put it once not long ago, and with a sudden bitter twist to her mouth she had echoed, "No surprises. *That's* for sure." But he could not honestly see that this was his fault. "It takes two to tango," he had snapped back, more sharply than he had intended; and then they were off again into one of those upward-spiraling exchanges that more and more often ended in angry silence, until now the angry silence was virtually unbroken save for the ordinary civilities of getting through the day.

How this had happened he was not exactly sure, because at first and for a long time thereafter things seemed to go very well. The original blind date escalated into more, and then soon into weekend trips to Mary's Main Line home outside Philadelphia. There he met her bank-president father and her fashionable party-giving mother and was gradually accepted as worthy despite his rural background—"A *farmer*, my dear, from *California*. But a good boy, and really rather sweet." Engagement and marriage soon seemed inevitable and came about on his graduation from law school.

If anything, he thought with a wry smile for Mrs. Stranahan which he
kept to himself, Mary had more trouble passing inspection with his family than he did with hers. Frank Barbour was strongly opposed at first
and did a lot of dark talking about "upper-crust arrogance" and "wa-
tered-down Eastern bloodlines." Helen, more tolerant and ready to accept whatever would make Tay happy, expressed mild reservations
about Mary's "somewhat superior manner." But eventually they came
around, as they had about the law, and when the day arrived they were
in Philadelphia to do their part as smoothly and pleasantly as he could
possibly have wished. The day ended in amicable harmony for the parents and ecstatic happiness for the bride and groom. Everything seemed
set for the rest of their lives.

He graduated third in his class—Moss Pomeroy was fifth—and went to
New York, where his grades had brought him an invitation to join a
prestigious firm that had many dealings with the government. One of its
senior partners had been in the Cabinet, some of its juniors were "on
the shuttle," as they put it, commuting frequently to Washington to
serve on temporary boards, commissions, congressional committee
staffs, corporate law cases. Washington had always been a dream of his.
He was not sure for quite a long time whether he wanted to use experience there as a springboard from which to go home and run for
Congress, or concentrate on the type of pleading before the government
that brought enormous fees from corporations and guaranteed a living
both desirable and admirable in Main Line eyes.

Mary's instincts and influence of course were all for the latter—under-
standably enough, given nature and background. She had been a little
rich girl and she intended to remain one. That, he supposed, was the
first start of the slow erosion, because his own ideas, conditioned by the
compassion he got from his mother, and perhaps more than he knew by
Erma Tillson and Civics I, moved increasingly in the direction of public
service. He had no memories of great depression such as still haunted
his parents' generation, but taking care of people and making life better
for the society as a whole seemed to him just common sense. Not only
was it right in what he conceived to be the moral sense, it was right
from the standpoint of keeping the democracy on an even keel. It was
not on an even keel during his first years out of law school, and although the reasons were not economic at that time, they became increasingly so as he and the century grew older.

Five years after joining the firm in New York he was a hardworking,
diligent and highly respected younger member who could ask for, and
get, transfer to the Washington office. From then on his life became

more and more involved with government. Inevitably in time he entered
it, not via the congressional route that he had originally toyed with but
through the administrative side, in which he felt he could perhaps contribute even more.

In a sense his decision to accept whatever opportunities might come
his way in that area was a compromise with Mary. She had been vehe-
ment in her opposition to any thought of his running for Congress.

"I will *not* be a politician's wife!" she announced, forgetting that all
public service is inevitably political sooner or later. But the idea of
holding high appointive office did not seem to bother her at all. It was
respectable, and something the Stranahans and their friends could understand and appreciate.

He continued to handle corporate cases for a while longer but presently found himself leading a group of younger partners that began to
agitate for a broader public service approach. On his tenth anniversary
with the firm he found himself appointed head of a new public service
division; and the process of transforming Taylor Barbour the likable
farm boy from Salinas Valley into Taylor Barbour the increasingly
prominent liberal lawyer was underway in earnest. It is a process that
happens with Washington lawyers if they are shrewd enough to recognize, and properly make use of, the creators of reputation. Like so
many successful careers in Washington, his was a combination of
idealism, an eye for the main chance, and strong boosts from the capital's liberal old-boy network. By the time he was thirty-five he was
firmly set on the path that in eleven more years would bring him to the
"special place" he had first become aware of in Erma Tillson's class,
thirty years before.

He had discovered in law school that he had a powerful grasp of his
own language. He could both write and speak it with a touch that was
always effective and sometimes mesmerizing. He began to contribute an
occasional article to *Harper's* and the *Atlantic Monthly* (the growth of
violence, terrorism and irrational crime), the op-ed page of the New
York *Times* (the need for judicial reform), the Washington *Post,* the
Washington *Inquirer,* the *Saturday Review, Newsweek, Foreign Affairs,*
the like. Invitations to participate in an increasing number of seminars
and public forums came his way, arranged by a steadily widening circle
of influential friends. He was invited to serve on advisory committees of
his political party. He began to work for causes dear to the hearts of
those who can make or break. Anna Hastings of the Washington *Inquirer* and Katharine Graham of the Washington *Post* invited him and
Mary quite often to dinner. His name began to pop up with increasing

frequency in columns, editorials, television commentaries. He was asked to appear, as "a rising young liberal Washington attorney," on "Face the Nation," and when that proved an easy success, on "Meet the Press."

The old-boy network labored ceaselessly in his behalf. It took no more than a year or two until its members could congratulate themselves that they had made another good choice. Taylor Barbour was on his way.

He was already considered a highly successful lawyer and one of America's leading liberals when, at thirty-eight, he received his first appointment in the executive branch of government, Assistant Attorney General in charge of the Office for Improvements in the Administration of Justice.

There had been many in this particular office, quite far down the ranks of the Department of Justice, who had not made much of it. By now, however, Tay was sophisticated enough to know that almost any sub-Cabinet office is what you make of it. His speeches and literary output doubled. He made a well-publicized call upon the then Chief Justice to discuss the administration of justice and what they could do—jointly, he gave the impression—to streamline it, speed it up and make it more efficient. The Chief was flattered by this dutiful attention from a man so much younger and already possessed of such an outstanding reputation. He promised to cooperate with Tay in every way he could.

It was Tay's first direct contact with the Court, and although, in the way of Washington, nothing much came of it but paperwork, also—in the way of Washington—his personal reputation and public visibility were much enhanced. At the conclusion of their study he received a glowing letter of commendation and approval from the Chief. At Tay's suggestion it was released to the media. The image grew.

And it was not an empty image, either, he could tell himself with justified satisfaction. He worked hard at his new assignment, spent many hours studying the administration of justice, traveled around the country to visit most of the major federal and state courts, offered recommendations that were practical, specific and, he felt, sound. If they did not do much to break the growing logjam of an increasingly litigious nation, that was not his fault. His work was diligent, thorough, constructive, farsighted. "Somebody else will have to follow through on it," he told Moss when he was moved up two years later to be Solicitor General, "but at least I've laid a good foundation." Later he was to perform equally diligent service, and gain further public acclaim, when as Secretary of Labor he was appointed vice-chairman of the President's

Special Commission on Crime and Violence. Unlike most of his politically cautious fellow members he came out strongly against the rising tide of vigilantism, which brought him much praise from major media and much bitter condemnation from his more worried countrymen. But he felt it must be said.

Only one thing galled him as he ascended the public ladder toward what he continued to hope would eventually be appointment to the Court, and that was Mary's apparent growing disaffection and dissatisfaction with their life in Washington. The political melting pot throws together the multimillionairess who has come to the capital to trade her lavish parties for the chance to call the mighty by their first names and the wife of the truck driver from New Jersey who by some fluke happens to get himself elected to the House of Representatives. It blends them into a fascinating and amicable mélange of backgrounds and interests.

The charm of this escaped Mary. She had been reared to associate with a certain class of people and that was really all she wanted to do. She was, he realized, a genuine snob; and in the extremely democratic society of the capital, where office and rank, not an individual's background, wealth or even manners, determine whatever snobbism exists, she was never entirely at ease. She was one of the few people he had ever known who did not find Washington fascinating. At the same time she had a loud and frequently expressed horror of "going back to California and just being a farmer's wife." Going back to California was of course the last thing he himself intended to do, but it had inspired quite a few dramatic scenes in recent years.

The only thing that would make her really happy, he felt, would be for him to join a top law firm in Philadelphia, buy a house on the Main Line and sink slowly into affluent desuetude as the years passed profitably, and lifelessly, by.

This was not for him; yet he could not really conceive that this alone was enough to bring about the slowly growing separation he had sensed, fought against, and ultimately found too strong to overcome. There must be something more to it; and being an honest, generous and compassionate man who often blamed himself for others' errors, he felt that it must be something in him that was lacking. They had been married six years when they were finally blessed with one child, Jane, on whom he gradually came to focus much of his time and emotion; Mary announced firmly that she was having no more. He had balked but she had been adamant. After a time he had come to accept it and had hoped that by giving Janie the best possible home and trying always to keep them a close-knit and love-surrounded family unit, he could both protect his daughter and strengthen his marriage. Because he was also a man of great tenacity and determination and because Janie obviously grew to love him considerably more than she did her increasingly cold and absentminded mother, which did not help, he had been able to pretend to himself for far longer than most that something less than half a loaf could be made to seem better than none. In the last few years the pretense had become increasingly thin.

Mary did her duty socially, entertained for him, smiled and bowed and flattered the people she thought would advance his career, and he could not fault her on that. But she made it increasingly clear that she did it not really for him but simply because that was what girls from her background were trained to do. Her private comments on his growing success and rising reputation became increasingly sharp and destructive. She did not seem to approve of ambition, and she apparently realized that he had far more than most people, observing no more than his pleasant smile, steady calm and quietly decisive manner, perceived.

It was only after he became Solicitor General, however, that she began to be really outspoken about this. He had long ago ceased to discuss his duties or his dreams with her, but with the shrewdness of the disgruntled (and, in fairness, the unhappy, because he thought sometimes—and tried not to think it—that she must be very unhappy) she knew where his ambitions lay.

"You want to be on the Court." she said flatly after his first day of arguing the government's cases before it. "You're positively glowing. I've never seen you so excited. Did they make you an honorary member?"

"I don't think anybody but you would know I'm excited," he said with the calm that seemed increasingly to annoy her. "And if I ever make it, it won't be honorary. I'll be there."

"I can't think of anything more boring. Those dowdy old men and their dowdy old wives! But I suppose you'd love it."

"I don't think you can call Sue-Ann Pomeroy dowdy," he said mildly. "She has enough glamor for—"

"For all of us? Yes, I know you like Sue-Ann, you always have. And she likes you, too. I wonder if you think Moss is fooled?"

"There's nothing for Moss to be fooled about!" he said sharply, provoked into the sort of retort he felt she was looking for, nowadays. "You know Moss and I *and* Sue-Ann are the best of friends, always have been, and always will be."

"I'm surprised it's even a threesome," she remarked as she hurried into her jewelry (they were on their way to dinner at the gracious old Spanish Embassy on Fifteenth Street Northwest, their fourth black-tie affair in that one typical week). "The way you and Moss worship each other."

"We don't 'worship each other,'" he said, putting on studs and cufflinks, keeping his voice low-keyed and matter-of-fact. "Next to my brother Carl and my brother-in-law Johnny, I expect he is my best friend, but we don't worship each other. We know each other's faults too well for that."

"You tell him things you'd never tell me!"

He gave her a level look.

"I often get the distinct feeling that you don't want me to tell you anything. So why shouldn't I tell Moss?"

"But I'm your *wife!*" she said, angrily, and as he saw it, completely irrationally.

"Really?" he said in a cold tone that only she ever heard, and that only lately. "I didn't know."

"Well, why *don't* you know!" she demanded, her voice suddenly ragged between held-back tears and growing anger. "I've done my best to be a good wife to you, all these boring years in this boring town with all its boring parvenus from all over America! And all the time I've hated it! Hated it, hated it, hated it!"

"And hated me too, I guess," he said, staring at her with a thoughtful reasonableness he knew must anger her still further, but he couldn't help it; he *was* thoughtful and he *was* reasonable. "I'm sorry I've been such poor company for you, all this time."

"Well," she said, turning back to her dressing table, adjusting her hair, voice returned abruptly to normal, "you weren't once, I guess I have that to be thankful for. We had a few good years."

"Oh, don't sound so damned elegiac all of a sudden!" he said, suddenly angered himself now. "Why haven't we got good years now? Whose fault is that, tell me? Not mine, I assure you, not mine! I do *my* best! *I* try."

"Noble you," she said, no longer tearful, no longer sounding even angry. "And I suppose I don't?"

"I don't see very damned many signs of it."

"Well," she said, gone away, dismissing it and him in one of the rapid mood changes that seemed to be increasingly frequent, "don't worry about it. I won't leave you. I'll stick around and be your dutiful little Supreme Court wife, if that ever comes."

He hesitated for a fraction of a second and then put it into words.

"What makes you so sure I don't want you to leave me? What makes you so sure I won't leave you?"

"And jeopardize your career?" She gave a hoot of disbelieving laughter. "Oh, come on, now, Mr. Justice! Never that! Never, never, *never* that!"

All he could manage was a "Don't be so sure!"—which sounded weak. And was weak, for he was certain, then, that she was right.

And yet, he told himself later as he drove in silence to the Spanish Embassy—and yet. Whatever was left of it for her, if anything, there was much still left for him. He had loved her very much once, and the residue could not be dismissed so ruthlessly. He still sought desperately from time to time for some way to re-establish it, but increasingly in these recent months he found himself gradually giving up the fight, retiring more and more into the patient uncommunicative silence he observed in so many Washington unions that gave substance to the standard aphorism, "Washington is full of great men and the women they married when they were young." Increasingly he found that this concentrated his thoughts and emotions on Janie, who gave promise of developing into a stunning young lady, beautiful, intelligent, lively and interested in a thousand things, most particularly her father's career.

"I suppose she wants to be a lawyer too," Cathy suggested, having without comment made a few brief notes on his brief comments about his marriage: "a real partnership . . . a sharing of mutual interests . . . her consistent and helpful devotion to my career . . . think you'll agree she's considered one of Washington's best hostesses, which has been of great assistance . . . always supportive, always helpful . . ."

Whatever Cathy thought about this—and she had already made clear in tone and glance that she didn't think much—she did not quite dare challenge him openly. All she did was grow increasingly silent and thoughtful as he telescoped some fifteen years of happy marriage and four or five increasingly unhappy ones into a few bland sentences from which emerged a picture of domestic partnership resting on a solid foundation of love and mutual absorption in his career.

"So you really aren't going to get a divorce after all," she said at the end, mockery muted but present. "You had me fooled for a minute there. That's *good*. There has to be *something* solid in this world, and I'm glad you and Mrs. Barbour are *it*. It restores one's faith."

"I hope so," he said, matter-of-factly, giving her an impassive gaze, which she returned with an amused and unmistakable skepticism in her eyes. But he continued to stare at her with a bland interest and after a moment her eyes dropped and she made the pretense of another note.

"So," she said, "tell me about Jane. I suppose she wants to be a lawyer, too."

"Janie," he said, eyes and voice suddenly filling with pride, "is quite a girl. She's almost fifteen—tall—blond—dark-eyed, which makes for a combination—everything in the right proportions and getting more so—charming—lovable—extremely intelligent—quick-witted—just a hell of a bright kid."

"And obviously the apple of daddy's eye."

"Obviously," he conceded with a smile. "But she deserves to be. She's at the top of her class at Madeira School right now, associate editor of the school paper, going to be editor, captain of the basketball team, head of the social committee, president of the honor society—you name it, she's got it. And she does think she wants to be a lawyer, yes. I think some astute young man is going to get to her first and change that into home and babies. But maybe not—maybe not. Maybe he'll be a lawyer, too, and they can work out a legal career together. And still have home and babies. That would be the ideal thing. Tell me about Sandra."

"Oh, you remembered," she said with a pleased smile. "Her name came up so far back in the conversation I thought you'd forgotten."

"I don't forget things of interest to me," he said; and this time his direct glance caused her to blush, which caused him to say sternly to himself: *Whoa.* But he did not stop looking at her and after a second she returned a gaze as steady as his. This time his eyes shifted first and his voice was not quite so matter-of-fact as he asked, "How old is she?"

"She's eight. Pretty much the tomboy and hoyden right now, but she's going to blossom when the time comes. I don't think she's as smart as Jane, probably, but then"—she smiled—"she probably doesn't have as smart a mother. Or father."

"I don't know the father," he said, "but I don't doubt the mother." She blushed again and gave him a little mock bow.

"Thank you, sir, you're most kind. I also have Rowland."

"Yes, I remember. Younger or older?"

"He's ten. A reflective kid, but active. Thinks a lot and then goes out and plays baseball with the rest of the guys on the block. A funny combination, in some ways. I think he's going to go places."

"I'm sure of it. You have a housekeeper?"

"Yes, during the day, until I get home. She babysits at night if I want to go out."

"Which I imagine is frequently. You must have half the males in the press corps at your feet."

She looked pleased again, but shook her head and laughed.

"We're too busy competing all the time. It doesn't leave much room for romance."

"Oh, well," he said lightly, but with a little excitement he told himself sternly was nonsense, "maybe one of your interviews will lead to something, someday."

"Yes," she agreed levelly. "That's always a possibility . . . So then, last but not least, came the Labor Department."

He nodded, accepting her lead, turning businesslike again also. "Yes, two years ago, as you know. A lot of work, a lot of headaches. Off the record, I really wasn't all that interested; I would have preferred Attorney General. But the President seemed to think I could do a good job here, so I agreed and took it on. It hasn't been dull, I can say that."

"And you've probably gained perspective from it."

"Oh, yes. The Court takes a lot of cases that are labor-related. I argued some before them as Solicitor General. This is a different perspective, as you say. I expect it's been good for me."

"And it's been good for the country," she said thoughtfully. "You've done a good job here, in a tough spot."

"I'm glad you approve," he said, intending it to be a lighthearted remark. It came out, however, somewhat more seriously. For a second her eyes widened and she gave him a quick glance, though her face remained noncommittal.

"As a matter of fact," she said with a pleasant smile, "I think you've been on the right side of nearly everything."

"Still a good boy," he said wryly.

"Always," she agreed. And added with a sudden mischievous little grin, "Have you ever had any desire not to be?"

"Never," he said with mock solemnity, a restless little excitement stirring again. "Miss Tillson wouldn't let me. To say nothing of my mother."

"I hope *not*," she said, laughing with genuine amusement. "So that's your story . . . And now you're on the Court—and you've achieved your life's ambition—and so where do you go from here?"

"Nowhere. I'm on the Court, it's where I've always wanted to be, it's where I expect I'll stay for the rest of my life."

"No presidential ambitions?"

"None, and that's the truth."

"Chief Justice?"

"Off the record, it would be nice, but essentially, aside from five thousand dollars a year more and a little better chance of getting your name in the history books, we're all on about the same level. It's nothing I'll look for. If it comes someday it'll come, and if it doesn't I'm going to be quite content where I am. I won't lobby for it."

"A contented man in Washington," she said. "There's a rarity. Maybe I'll suggest that for the title of my piece: 'He'll Be Happy Where He Is.'"

"It's true," he said, and for the first time the full impact of his appointment hit him and he realized with a sudden deep satisfaction that, yes, it *was* true. He had achieved everything he wanted now. The years opened before him full of dignity and service.

"What would you like to have said of you when you retire?" she asked. "I always find that's usually a good question with which to conclude an interview. People reveal a lot about themselves when they write their own obituaries. After all, with a little luck and good health you'll be on the Bench for—good Lord, thirty years or more. It's awesome."

He laughed.

"Yes, it is, isn't it? Frightening, too . . . Well . . . I'd like it said of me that I tried always to help the people of this land who need help—to uphold the law, and peaceful orderly process, in all disputes—to strengthen the law and make it fairer, insofar as one Justice can do that —to work amicably and well with my brethren—and Mary-Hannah and any of her sisters who may join us in the future—in trying to bring justice to our judgments and to all who appeal to us for help. I'd like it to be said that I was a fair, decent, honorable and worthy judge—that I had some consistent view of social betterment and social progress for America—and that I did what I could, as effectively as I could, to advance that view in a tough and difficult time in the life of our country . . ."

He paused and smiled. "Is that enough, or do you want more?"

"If you manage all that," she said, smiling too, "you'll be doing very well. I just want to say, quite seriously," she added, putting away pen and notebook, closing her handbag, "that as one American citizen I am personally very pleased with your appointment. I think you're a real liberal and a fine person and I feel genuinely good about having you on the Court. I really do."

"Well, thank you," he said, surprised and pleased. "I know you journalists are chary with personal accolades, so I appreciate that doubly." He hesitated and then yielded to impulse, something he almost never did, for he had become a thoughtful and careful man. "As you know," he said, and something in his tone made her look at him with a sudden close attention, "we almost never give interviews on the Court, but if you want to stop by sometime just to check and see how things are going—talk about the country or the world or whatever—feel free. I'll be glad to see you."

For a moment she did not reply, continuing to study him with the same grave expression. He felt with sudden panic that he had said too much, gone too far, been very foolish. But she showed him it was not so.

"Why," she said quietly, "I'd be delighted. I will try to do that. Soon."

"Please do," he said, and ventured further. "I'd be pleased."

"Yes," she repeated gravely, "I will do that . . . Mr. Secretary—Justice—thank you very much for your time. I think we've got a good interview. I'll send you a copy when it comes out in the magazine. I hope you'll like it."

"I'm sure I will," he said with equal formality, shaking hands as he saw her to the door. "Thank you so much."

"Good luck," she said.

He smiled.

"Thanks. I'll need it."

And so he would, he thought as he turned back to his desk, and perhaps not entirely with the law.

But this thought, for whatever it was worth—and he told himself with some impatience that it probably wasn't worth much, certainly *shouldn't* be worth much—did not occupy him for long. His secretary buzzed and he returned to his desk to pick up the phone. He assumed it must be Mary, who had not been home when he called earlier with the news. He braced himself for some sort of sarcasm, he was not sure exactly what.

"Yes?" he said, tone sharp.

"Is that you, Daddy?" Janie asked with some hesitation. "You sound awfully—awfully *mad,* somehow I thought you'd be happy. I just heard about your appointment. *I'm* happy."

"Thank you, baby," he said, tone softening immediately as he sat down and swiveled his chair around to stare out at the dull blue sky and the sunlight getting heavier as the afternoon lengthened. It would be a hot night: full summer not far behind. "I'm not mad, just busy. *I'm* pleased too. It's good of you to call."

"Everybody out here at school is jumping up and down, they're so excited," Jane said; honesty prompting her to add, "At least, *my* friends are excited. Betsy Randall says her father is going to get you through the Senate Judiciary Committee in 'jig time.'"

"Oh, she does, does she?" he said with a chuckle. "And how does she know? He hasn't told me that, yet."

"He will," she said positively. "Betsy says they talked about it at dinner last night after the President called him. Has the President called you?"

"Oh, yes," he said, remembering that quick, terse notification that assumed, as it always did, that anyone approached about anything would automatically recognize its wisdom and accept immediately without question; which in this case, of course, was true. "Yes, he called. I think it's nice of him to select me."

"He'd better pick you, silly old President," Janie said. "Who else is there?"

"Lots of people."

"Not any better!" she said stoutly.

He laughed. "Well, I can't argue with that."

"Have you talked to Mommy?"

"I called her earlier."

"Yes, I know," she said, "but did you talk to her?"

"She wasn't home. She hasn't called back yet."

"But she *must* know by now. It's on the news. Everybody knows."

"I expect she'll be calling pretty soon," he said, tone revealing nothing. "She's probably busy doing some errands or something."

"I doubt it," Jane said, sounding much older than fifteen.

"Well, I don't know where she is," he said, a little sharper. "I told you I called her and left word. That's all I can do, isn't it?"

"She ought to call you *right away*," Jane said. "I did, just as soon as I knew."

"Now, see here, Janie," he said, "just lay off it, O.K.? She'll find word at the house, or she'll hear it on the news, or somebody will tell her—"

"Not me," Janie said.

"—or somebody will tell her," he repeated firmly, "and then she'll call me. Would you like a report when she does?"

"No," she said, laughing in spite of herself. "Of course not. But I just want her to call you, that's all."

"So do I," he said calmly.

"But I expect," Janie added, "she may say something mean. I don't think she likes you to be famous."

"No, it isn't that. And you mustn't be so critical of your mother."

"She's critical of you."

"That's something else. It's also none of your business, young lady."

"Well, I don't understand it!" his daughter said flatly. He sighed.

"I think she just doesn't—like Washington too well. She'd rather I wasn't in public life."

"Well, you are," Janie remarked. "She ought to be used to it by this time."

"I know," he said. "But—maybe she never will be. We'll just have to see. Anyway," he went on firmly, closing that subject, *"I'm* glad I'm in public life, and I'm very glad I have your support. I'm very glad you called. Thank you very much for that, baby. I've got to get back to work and clear up a few things here, right now, so I'll see you later at home, O.K.?"

"O.K., Daddy," she said. "I love you."

"I love you too, baby," he said, and put down the phone with another sigh. His secretary promptly buzzed again. This time it was the call he expected.

"Well," she said, "you made it, Mr. Justice. I suppose I should congratulate you."

"I expect most people will,' he said, voice calm and, he knew, infuriating. Her voice rose sharply, as expected, in reply.

"And so I'd better not go against the crowd, hm? Well, I expect they'll congratulate me, too. In fact, some of my friends already have."

"And how did you answer them?" he couldn't help asking. "With a scream?"

"I should have. But no, as always I'm being the perfect wife. 'Thank you so much—such an opportunity for him—yes, he can be of great service—so honored the President considered him worthy—you think he will be a great Justice?—well, aren't you kind and sweet—I shall *certainly* tell him.' . . . You seem to be very popular."

"I'm getting a few calls myself."

"All favorable?"

"I'm afraid so."

"There's no possibility you'd turn it down?"

"The Supreme Court?" He snorted. "Oh, come now. I accepted two hours ago, when the President called. But don't worry. The Court doesn't have a very heavy social schedule. You won't have to play the perfect wife too many times a year."

"Then I really *will* be bored," she said, and sounded genuinely bleak. "But I think I'll go right ahead entertaining anyway. It's the only thing to keep myself from going mad."

He uttered a sound that combined protest and resignation.

"You're always so frantic lately. Why don't you just relax and take it easy? There are plenty of things to keep you busy in this town. And even on the Main Line I think they consider Supreme Court Justices worthy of some respect." He tried to be light. "I mean, there are only nine of us in the whole world, after all. Rarity should mean something."

"I'm bored," she said, "don't you see? Bored, bored, bored! As I've told you before."

"Then," he said quietly, "I can only conclude that, at the heart of it, you're bored with me. Because Washington is not all that boring a city. It is, in fact, a very exciting city. So I guess I'm the culprit."

There was silence, after which she said in a rather distant, thoughtful voice, "Yes, I'm afraid that's probably the truth. There was a time once, quite a long time, when you weren't. We had fun when we were younger and you were just starting up the ladder. And for quite a while after that. But the higher you've gone, the more absorbed you've become. The more your career and ambitions have meant to you. The less I have."

"That isn't true! That's a horrible thing to say! I have been a good and loving husband, a good father—"

"Yes," she interrupted sharply. "You've taken Janie away from me, all right, there's no doubt of that."

"I haven't taken Janie away from you! I can't help it if Janie finds you cold and me loving. You've had her with you a lot more than I have. I'm sorry if you feel left out, but that must have been your own decision. It wasn't mine."

It was her turn to cry out.

"Oh! How can you be so—so cruel! How can you be so *obtuse?* I don't think you've understood anybody's feelings but your own, or been interested in anybody's feelings but your own, for the past ten years. You've been so busy scheming how to get on that Court that you've just lost all touch with human emotions! You no longer have a heart, if you ever had one!"

"That isn't how Janie sees it," he said, knowing he shouldn't, but driven by some devil he seemed unable to control. "Now is it?"

"Oh!" she cried again. *"Oh!"* And began to cry, which he thought was probably just a trick, so far had they parted from one another in these recent years and so little did he trust the honesty of her emotions now.

"The thing I will always remember about this day," he went on quietly in words that he knew were searing, but again, he seemed unable to stop, "is that my own wife spoiled it for me with this telephone call. I thought all my family would be happy for me. The rest are, but the most important one is not. I feel a dead weight of opposition as I take up these new burdens. It doesn't make them any easier to carry, and it spoils the day that should have been one of the happiest of my life."

"You are impossible," she said in a choked voice. "Just *impossible*. So *superior*. And so *smug*. And so—so *perfect*."

"I'm sorry," he said evenly, "but if that's the way you feel, then maybe we'd better be honest about it and get a divorce."

"Oh, no," she said with a bitter little laugh. "Oh, no, I won't let you get away with it that easily. I'll stay around for a while and go right on pretending that everything's all right. You've put me in hell, but that will be *your* hell, Tay. The perfect Justice will continue to have the perfect wife. And how envious the rest of them will be. And how happy we will be."

"I'm going to hang up now," he said in a dulled voice. "I'll see you at home. We can talk about it there."

"*No!*" she said. "We won't ever talk about it again! We'll just go on, that's all. We'll just go on."

"All right," he said in the same lifeless tone. "We'll just go on."

But how they could, or how he could take up his new responsibilities with the clear head and untroubled heart he felt he must have, he did not know; and all through the afternoon as he took more calls, accepted more congratulations, answered questions from the media, taped two television segments for the evening news, a leaden sadness and worry dragged him down. Just before he left the Department of Labor at 6 P.M., after his secretary had gone for the day, he put in a call to the *Washingtonian*.

"Catherine Corning, please," he requested, holding his voice steadier than he at first thought he could.

"I'm sorry," the receptionist said, "but I believe she's gone for the day."

"Do you have a home number for her?"

The standard Washington answer came back.

"I'm sorry, but she has an unlisted number and we're not permitted to give them out. If you wish to leave your name and number, I can have her call you tomorrow—"

He took a deep breath.

"Just tell her that her friend from Civics I called."

"Civics I?" the receptionist asked in a puzzled voice. "What agency of the government is that?"

"Just tell her," he said with a sudden impatient harshness. "She'll understand."

"Is this some kind of a joke?"

"That's for her to decide," he said in the same tone. "Just do as I say, please."

"I'll see she gets the message." There was a sniff. "I only hope you know what you're doing."

I hope so, too, sister, he thought bitterly as he put on his coat and hat and let himself out, saying good night to the handful of guards on night duty. You bet your bottom dollar I hope so, too.

3

In the obscure little cabin huddled in the woods near the town of Pomeroy Station, Earle Holgren was slowly and methodically putting on his jogging shorts and shoes as the sun slanted swiftly lower through the trees and the long southern twilight began. He had just made love to Janet, who lay sprawled on the bed.

"You look like a damned sack of potatoes," he said in a contemptuous voice.

"I didn't notice you minding much in the last few minutes," she replied with an unimpressed yawn. "Or maybe you were so hot it wouldn't have made any difference."

"Don't be so damned smart," he said, suddenly threatening, swinging around and coming toward her with a menacing air.

"O.K., O.K.," she said, waving him off with an unhurried hand. "No need to get nasty about it. You must really be full of p. and v., to be going jogging after *that*." She chuckled suddenly. "I know you aren't full of anything else at the moment."

"You're so damned funny," he said. "Someday you'll die laughing."

"Maybe," she said. "Maybe. We'll see. Where are you going now, back to your precious atomic plant?"

"It isn't *my* plant," he said, "and it isn't precious. It's a damned vicious crime against all of humanity. It's a desecration of the earth and the sky and all the creatures therein. It's an abomination against mankind."

"You really sound like a hill preacher," she said with mock admiration. "I guess it's living around here for the past few months. When are we going to leave this dump and get back to someplace that's fun?"

"Soon enough," he said grimly. "Soon enough."

"Going to take me and John Lennon Peacechild with you?" she inquired, sitting up lazily and pulling on her robe; but he could tell she was really asking and really paying attention to his answer.

"Of course I am," he said scornfully. "What makes you think I wouldn't?"

"I don't know," she said, yawning again. "Sometimes I just wonder."

"Well, don't wonder!" he ordered sharply. "People get hurt wondering."

She looked suddenly alert. The dullness miraculously dropped away.

"That's the second time today you've told me about people getting hurt. What are you planning? Going to hurt somebody? Going to hurt us?"

"No, I am not going to hurt somebody!" he said furiously. "And I'm not going to hurt you! Why don't you mind your own business?"

"Have fun at the old atomic plant," she said, yawning yet again and apparently turning dull and uncaring as abruptly as she had roused. "They must think you're part of the scenery, by this time."

"They won't be there," he said sharply. "It's past quitting time. You don't catch those capitalistic two-TV bastards working any more than they have to. The day crew won't be there."

"Well," she said, looking around vaguely for John Lennon Peacechild, who was peacefully snoring in his crib in the corner, "don't get hurt prowling around. I imagine they've got guards."

"Yes, they've got guards. They're friends of mine."

"Oh, you know them," she said, and once again he had the impression that she was paying attention much more closely than she would have him know.

"Yes, I know them. Now get your ass up off that bed and start getting supper. I'll be back in half an hour."

"Yes, sir," she said, standing up and starting toward the crib. "Yes, *sir*. When are they ever going to finish that old plant, anyway? 1995? It seems like we've been here forever."

"Next Friday," he said with a grim satisfaction. "At three P.M. in the afternoon."

"My," she said admiringly as she scooped up John Lennon Peacechild and began crooning to him as he grunted and reached for her breast. "You *do* know everything about that old plant, don't you?"

"I don't know a damned thing." he said angrily as he flung open the door and stepped outside. "Not a damned thing."

"That's good!" she cried as he slammed the door. "Because I think it's best not to know about things like that!"

Instantly he flung the door open again and glared at her.

"And what the hell do you mean by that?"

"Not a thing," she said as John Lennon Peacechild nuzzled greedily at her bulging flesh. "Not a thing at all. After all," she said, giving him an innocent look over the baby's busily working head, "what could I know? You're the one who knows everything."

"You get that damned supper," he ordered grimly. "And don't ask me any more damned questions, hear?"

And slammed out again and started jogging along the lane toward the deserted roadway in the gathering dusk.

"Yes, sir," she said thoughtfully as she stepped to the window and watched him go. "Yes, *sir*."

4

In Washington, too, the long twilight began, and past the stately front entrance to the Supreme Court the stream of home-going cars passed steadily on their way to Maryland and Virginia. Skillful lighting illuminated the great white building so that its front portico seemed to glow from within. Along the main floor, obscured by trees and shrubbery, other lights burned. All of the Justices and their staffs were still at work. The day of Taylor Barbour's nomination was drawing to a close. In the chambers of the Chief Justice, following the pleasant custom he had established soon after his appointment five years ago, he and such brethren as wished to were gathered to hail the coming of the night with whatever potion pleased them.

Duncan Elphinstone, who had always been a very light drinker, was holding a glass of white wine, as were Mary-Hannah McIntosh and Ray Ullstein. Wally Flyte and Rupert Hemmelsford, veterans of innumerable similar sessions in the Senate, were both drinking bourbon and water. Moss Pomeroy was sipping a vodka and tonic, Hughie Demsted the same, Clem Wallenberg a martini. They had just filled their glasses. Turning to one another with mock solemnity, they joined the Chief in their invariable toast, originally proposed by Justice Flyte in a characteristically irreverent moment:

"To the Honorable the Supreme Court and the Honorable Us!"

"Moss," Hughie Demsted said, "tell us about your buddy Barbour. What can we expect?"

Moss looked thoughtful for a moment as they all settled down on chairs and sofas and studied him expectantly.

"W—ell," he began slowly. "I first met Taylor Barbour in the library at Harvard Law School just about"—his eyes narrowed as he calculated —"twenty-four years ago this very day. Or maybe yesterday, I'm not quite sure. Anyway, a long time ago. We racked up positively brilliant grades together and we scoured the eastern seaboard for young ladies. You all know his general record—"

"I do," Justice Hemmelsford said, "and it's too damned liberal for me. But I will say he's a good lawyer."

"He is that," Justice Demsted agreed, "and personally, I find his liberal record quite acceptable."

"*You* would," Rupert Hemmelsford said. "All you young fellows are alike."

"I don't see Moss winning any liberal ratings," Hughie demurred with a grin.

"I try," Moss said. "I try. Anyway, you know that his record is liberal, that in private practice he got away from corporate law and got more and more deeply involved in social causes, and that finally that brought him to the favorable attention of our great co-worker in the White House, who thereupon appointed him an Assistant Attorney General and then Solicitor General, which meant that he spent most of his time up here arguing the government's side. I defer to my elders as to how good he was at that."

"I thought he was very cogent," the Chief said. "Very well informed, and well prepared."

"Very effective as an advocate," Ray Ullstein agreed. Wally Flyte nodded.

"A damned good speaker. He can be very powerful when he wants to be."

"He impresses me as being very sincere in what he believes," Mary-Hannah said.

"And I'm not?" Justice Hemmelsford demanded in mock indignation. "Why, Justice McIntosh! What a thing to say about a brother!" And his eyebrows twitched and blinked and he gave her a sidelong, amiable leer. She laughed.

"Rupert, you old fraud, of course you're sincere. Sometimes you're more than sincere. That's why I always tremble when I find we're on opposite sides of something. I expect to be decimated by one of those zinging minority opinions you hand down. Positively scathing!"

"The fact that I am in the minority so often says something I don't like too well about this Court," Rupe Hemmelsford observed seriously. "I think there's entirely too much of this five-to-four business."

"You wouldn't mind if it were five to four your way, Rupe," Justice Demsted remarked. "So stop the crocodile tears."

"Actually," Duncan Elphinstone said thoughtfully, "it would please me, too, if we could find a little more unanimity these days on some things. I agree with Rupe, we're very much a five-to-four Court right now; one man—or woman—can swing it a little too easily, it seems to me. Maybe it's just foolish personal pride on my part, but once in a while I'd like to see 'the Elphinstone Court' really agree on something. Now," he added in a tone so unconsciously wistful that they all looked amused, "I suppose Taylor Barbour will bring in one more discordant note."

"One more liberal note," Justice Wallenberg said approvingly.

"One more radical note," Justice Hemmelsford responded gloomily.

"Oh, come on, now," Justice Pomeroy objected. "One more independent and self-respecting note, to join a similar chorus from the rest of us. He's a brilliant man, he's a great advocate, he's compassionate, tolerant, broad-minded and determined. What more could you ask?"

"God!" Rupert Hemmelsford snorted. "Do we need any more determined people on this Court? That's half the trouble now."

"Personally—" Justice Ullstein said quietly, and because he so rarely spoke up to assert himself about anything, saving that for his incisive, clear-cut and powerful opinions from the Bench, they all turned to him respectfully. "Personally, I think it is well that the diversity of the Court is going to be maintained. I know the Chief would like us to be more unanimous. I suppose any Chief Justice would like to have his Court speak with one voice, as John Marshall often managed to persuade his to do. But I'm afraid it won't work now as it did then. Still, I should like to see more unanimity because I should like to see more consistency. I think consistency is the key to the law; as well, I might add, as the key to the Court's continuing strength as a co-equal branch of the government.

"Some of us can still remember World War II days when Joseph Stalin inquired, 'How many divisions has the Pope?' How many divisions do we have? None, when you come right down to it. But we, like the Pope, possess a mighty army nonetheless, for our strength rests on the willing and freely accorded acceptance of a free and democratic people. But that is all it rests on. John Marshall virtually made the Court out of whole cloth, single-handedly and over the furious opposition of his second cousin, Thomas Jefferson, who fought him all the way. He succeeded and so here we are. But if we are not consistent, if we sway too much with each passing wind, if we are divided too often and for too long, then our strength wavers and we are by that diminished.

"I hope our new Justice may aid us to find a more generally acceptable ground among our differing opinions. I welcome his coming."

"Hear, hear," Hughie Demsted said, and all, even Justice Wallenberg in a rather grudging way, gave Justice Ullstein a little round of friendly applause, as they sometimes did when he delivered one of his rare personal pronouncements.

"He may do that," Moss Pomeroy said, "though actually we all know that he's going to go with the liberal side, which will just guarantee more five-to-fours. But, that's life." He uttered their closing formula. "Another, anyone?"

"Not I, thanks," Hughie said. "It's late and I've got to run. We've got guests coming for dinner and Kate will never forgive me."

"I, too," Mary-Hannah said. "Can you give me a ride to Watergate, Hughie?"

"With pleasure. Anyone else need one?"

"I'm staying to do a little more work," Wally Flyte said, and several others, including the Chief Justice, said the same. They parted with friendly good-byes. By tacit agreement it had long ago been decided that no one would take a second drink. Their pleasant little ritual simply gave whoever was free, and wanted to, a chance to meet at the end of the day—exchange news and views on whatever might interest them—relax together for a few minutes before going home or out into the nighttime social Washington—become more friendly with one another.

As he bade them all good night and returned to his own big desk to consume a hasty cup of soup and a hamburger, reopen the briefs on *Steiner v. Oregon,* up for certiorari from the Ninth Circuit Court of Appeals, and start working on into the night, the Chief congratulated himself once again that what they had unanimously christened "The Certiorari Club" had been a good inspiration on his part. The Elphinstone Court was not as unified as he would have liked but it was a friendly Court in contrast to some in the not so distant past which had housed real feuds among the Justices. He liked that and prided himself upon it. He had no doubt that Taylor Barbour would fit into it, as a person, very well.

Before getting to work again, he decided to go out for a moment to the Great Hall of the Court and, as he liked to put it, "restore myself." There in the huge echoing marble foyer lined with busts of former Chief

Justices, his habit was to stand off to the side in a niche beside one of his predecessors and, turning toward the oaken doors of the Court Chamber at the far end, simply surrender himself for a moment to the past and to the awesome majesty of the law which he and his fellow Justices each in their time embodied. He had been on the Court nine years now, Chief Justice for five, and it still was a thrill to him to cross the broad marble esplanade on First Street Northeast, climb slowly—at seventy it was becoming slower—the fifty-three marble steps to the oval marble esplanade in front of the building, go through the pair of six-ton bronze doors past the guards and the admonitory sign SILENCE, and enter this vast white chamber where tourists, law clerks, building staff, guards, newsmen, lawyers, Justices crisscrossed as they went about the business of the Court.

There was rarely an hour of the day when the Great Hall was not busy. There was always life there: the life of the law, to which he was devoted, and from whose contemplation he always drew renewed strength.

So it was on this night when the Court was about to be complete again with its ninth Justice. He looked forward with real anticipation to the addition of Taylor Barbour. The Court, as Ray Ullstein had truly said, rested on the freely given acceptance of a democratic people: over and above his other responsibilities and burdens, each Justice carried the preservation of that acceptance on his shoulders. Anything that showed undue dissension, anything that broke the solemnity of the law, anything that reduced the dignity and the stature of the institution had the potential of weakening in some measure that acceptance.

His great predecessor John Marshall, fourth Chief Justice and virtually single-handed creator of the Court as the country knew it today, had always been extremely jealous of the reputation and standing of the Court. He had fought his cousin Jefferson to a standstill on the issue of the Court's right to determine the constitutionality of the laws, and had won; and nearly all Justices from the early days of the struggling Republic on through the gathering storm of civil war, right on down to today's violence-plagued, crime-ridden nation, had been vividly conscious of that responsibility. He was confident Tay would bear it well.

The challenges had been tough before, Edmund Duncan Elphinstone reflected now, but perhaps no tougher, if as tough, as those the Court faced today. Very soon now, in some form or other, the issue of violence would come up to them. And it was very apt to be, as they had discussed with foreboding this morning, not only the violence of criminal against victim but the counterviolence of an enraged citizenry against the criminal. Then might come testings he did not really want to think about at this moment. But he knew that sooner or later he must. And so must they all.

He sighed heavily, completely unconscious of anyone around.

"Good night, Chief!" someone called cheerfully. He came cut of his reverie to see a bright-faced, rosy-cheeked young woman in her mid-twenties hurrying by with a briefcase on her way out of the building.

"Good night, counsel," he said. "I hope you've had a good day."

"Busy," she called back over her shoulder. "I work for Justice Ull-stein. *Busy!* But I'll survive!"

"Good girl!" he called after her with a smile. "So will we all." Adding to himself more grimly than he had realized he felt: *I hope.*

He waved good night to the guards, turned to the right at the end of the now almost deserted Great Hall and made his way along the corridor that ran parallel to and around the Chamber, and so to his offices and the offices of the other Justices beyond. He had a good crew with which to navigate the heavy seas that appeared to lie ahead. The bequests of three very different Presidents, they were a highly individual and in some ways, he supposed, quirky bunch. Yet all were brilliant lawyers, dedicated public servants, devoted defenders of the law and the Constitution as each saw it.

His mind ran over them as he crossed his silent office and went into the tiny kitchen that had been installed by Chief Justice Warren Burger, who loved to cook and often prepared lunch for himself or an occasional guest or two. He opened a can of tomato soup, put it in a pan and set it to heat; took two frozen hamburger patties out of the small refrigerator, unwrapped them, put them in the oven; went into the bathroom and made himself ready for the sumptuous meal that always worried Birdie, dining alone at home in Georgetown, but which he always found quite enough on the frequent nights when he stayed late working. In the mirror a wise, wrinkled, kindly little face topped by a startling upright shock of snow-white hair looked back at him with an analytical expression.

"Birdie," he had demanded not long ago after reading a profile of himself in the Washington *Post,* "do I look 'monkey-faced'? Am I a 'Roger B. Taney type'? Do I look as though I might have been 'weaned on a pickle'? Do I, now, really?"

"Of course not, dear," she had replied promptly, but with a gentle little chuckle that caused him to give her a sharp look before starting to smile himself. "At least, not *entirely.* Your expression always indicates that it was probably a *sweet* pickle."

"Now, how," he demanded, "is that supposed to help my wounded ego?"

"Well," said his companion of forty-five years with the amiable candor he always prized and always relied upon, "you must admit you aren't a blond, six-foot Viking. You are rather small, you know, which of course is fine with me, otherwise, since I'm also five feet four, I probably wouldn't ever have married you. And you aren't any Rudolph Valentino, which is also fine with me, because that means I haven't had to worry about you—*too* much—with other women. And you do rather resemble Chief Justice Taney, a bit. But, then, not all you Chief Justices can look like Charles Evans Hughes, after all. There was only one of *him*."

"If I ever heard a quibbling, evasive, pettifogging, question-dodging answer," he said with a humorous indignation, "that's it. You ought to be a lawyer."

"Oh, heavens," she said, tapping him lightly on the cheek. "It's bad enough being married to one—and the most famous one of all, at that. Anyway, dear, the children and I love you. Your face has *character,* and that's good enough for us."

"A truly flattering and ego-building commendation," he remarked. "I shall treasure it."

And, he thought, he probably did, because he had to admit he wasn't the handsomest man in the world. Sometimes he rather wished he were a little more so, particularly when the Court had its annual picture taken and here stood this wizened—yes, at seventy he supposed he could be honest and say "wizened," at least to himself—little figure in the middle, flanked by eight taller associates. But he had dignity, he would say that; nobody could summon up the awe of the law more effectively than he when he wanted to, as many an incompetent pleader, called sternly to task for rambling on too long before the Bench, could testify.

"When the Chief lays down the law," they said around the Court, "everybody snaps to."

And everybody did, he thought with some satisfaction, though he didn't mean to be too arbitrary about it. But he did respect the procedures of the Court, and he desired others to; and since he had the authority, he exercised it.

"Large certainty resideth in that small frame," Mary-Hannah once remarked in a humorous imitation of Shakespeare; and they all recognized the fact and accepted it without much chafing.

He ruled the building with an iron, if comfortable, hand, being sometimes more concerned, some outsiders charged, with housekeeping details than he was with cases. This was deceptive, for he had a mind that missed nothing and was "on top of every case before the Court, all the time," as Clement Wallenberg had admitted grudgingly not too long ago. When he became C.J. he found in the history and accoutrements of the Court a pleasant diversion from the legal problems that often involved him in sharp contention—although, in general, he tried to play an ameliorating part in the constantly shifting alliances that had of late produced some of the most closely decided verdicts in the country's history.

Back in his office as his soup came to a boil, the hamburgers sizzled to exactly the right point (he was not such a bad cook himself, if truth were known), he reflected on what he referred to privately to Birdie as "my little brood." He was disturbed by their frequent lack of unanimity, but as characters and colleagues he liked them all. There was his senior Associate, Richard Waldo Flyte of Illinois. Heavy—in fact, as he himself put it bluntly, fat—with a round, owllike face and a portentous manner broken by frequent gleams of humor, he never took himself quite as seriously as his outward aspect might indicate to the uninitiated, and was always a help in smoothing over personal animosities. His appointment, as Seab Cooley had remarked one day in the Senate Majority cloakroom, had made him as happy as a whale in aspic. His whole instinct from Senate days was to work with people as harmoniously as possible, and he could always be counted on for the friendly comment that encouraged the reluctant, the jest that eased the way. The Chief had been grateful for this on many occasions.

Clement Wallenberg of Michigan was a different matter; the Chief sometimes wondered, with a puzzled shake of the head, whether it would ever be possible to blend Clem smoothly into anything. He rather doubted it, not because he and the others didn't try, and not because Clem was really such an ogre, but just that he fancied himself to be so, and carefully cultivated the reputation whenever he could. He too was slight of build, though somewhat taller than The Elph; shrewd but casual of intellect; given to occasional free-swinging interpretations of the law but on the whole staying fairly consistently on the liberal side. He had a temper, as the Chief described it once with an upward-spiraling index finger, "that goes *zoooom* like that!" But underneath it, aside from Justice Ullstein and quite a long list of other things in the world that he professed to abominate, he was a generally amiable, if prickly, man.

Raymond Ullstein of New York had indeed been, as Justice Wallenberg often liked to point out, a corporation lawyer. But far from being "smart-assed," as Clem also liked to put it, he was one of the mildest and most polite, and also one of the most respected and universally beloved—which was perhaps what galled Clem the most—of gentlemen. On the Court he was generally liberal but considered himself, perhaps in slightly greater degree than his associates, who also shared the feeling, "the guardian of the Constitution." Clem Wallenberg fancied the title for himself and resented the media's conferring it on Ray; which also accounted for a good deal of their sometimes rocky relationship.

The middle member of the Court, fifth in seniority, brought as always a gentle and kindly gleam to the Chief's eye as he consumed his modest meal. With her short-cropped gray hair severely brushed back, her pince-nez gleaming and her dark eyes snapping angrily at some challenge to her strongly held ideas, Mary-Hannah McIntosh of California could look every inch the formidable dean of the Stanford Law School which she had been at the time of her appointment to the Court. But underneath, as she had once told the Chief with a laugh, "beats the heart of a softie." "A very *nice* softie," he had pleased her by saying, "and one we all love dearly." A lifelong spinster, the law had been her favorite, and often only, companion; and never more demanding, she had found, than when she sat on the nation's highest bench. Few, the Chief had once remarked to Wally Flyte, had ever brought to it a greater service and dedication.

And next came, The Elph thought with the amused smile with which they all thought of him, Number Six. "Old Rupe" they called him in Washington, and with a determined and not to be deflected air he went about living up to it—"Old Rupe-ing," as Wally, his former Senate colleague, put it, "all over the place." Yet under the carefully created image, Rupert Hemmelsford of Texas possessed a very sharp, very shrewd and very well-informed mind that could very quickly demolish anyone who didn't realize it. He was quick to spot pretense in lawyers coming before the Bench and quick to puncture it; and, like Wally, often contributed leavening humor, usually stories that began, "You remind me of the feller who—" The eyes would peer sideways with their exaggerated, slightly lascivious glance, the slow-as-*mo*lasses drawl would ooze over the broadly grinning lips, and the poor fellow would become completely discombobulated and have to start all over again. Both his humor and intellect had been welcome additions to the Court.

Seventh in seniority—and for both him and Number Eight the Chief's eyes held the same fond, indulgent expression that they did for Mary-Hannah McIntosh—was Hughie Dubose Demsted of the District of Columbia, a big and gentle man of forty-eight who still possessed a lingering youthful earnestness that endeared him to his colleagues and made him, next to Moss Pomeroy, probably the most publicly popular of all the Justices. He had loved the Court from the first day he came on it, and since then he had become one of the most reliable, most gentlemanly, most soft-spoken and most determined members of the "liberal bloc" of the Elphinstone Court.

He, Ray Ullstein, Clement Wallenberg and Mary-Hannah McIntosh almost consistently voted together. The Chief Justice, Rupert Hemmelsford and Moss Pomeroy generally stood together on the conservative side, with Wally Flyte occasionally on the liberal side, but, when he considered constitutional fundamentals too much threatened, moving back to the conservative. Presumably, given his past activities and general reputation, Taylor Barbour would join the liberals and be as firm in that cause as his longtime friend from South Carolina was in his.

If anybody could persuade Tay to become a conservative, the Chief reflected with a fond smile for his lively young colleague, it would be the one known up to now as "the baby of the Court," a media cliché which Tay, though six months older, would no doubt inherit.

Stanley Mossiter Pomeroy had been on the Court three years and, as The Elph had once explained in informal remarks when they were giving a reception for the members of the D.C. bar,

"Does anybody think of the Supreme Court as waterskiing? It's Moss. Do they have a mind's-eye picture of us scuba diving in the Bahamas? It's Moss again. Do they imagine us getting up every morning to jog, playing volleyball with the law clerks in the gym on the fourth floor, racing our sailboats on the Potomac? Well, it's Moss. Do we all have wives who could model for *Vogue?* There's Moss again. Thank goodness we have *him* around! Otherwise they'd think we're a bunch of old fuddy-duddies instead of the dashing group we are!"

To which Moss could only grin and say rather defensively, "Well, it's true. I'm sorry I like to do all those things, but it's true."

And so it was, and he supposed he did lend a note of rather surprising youth and agility to his associates, because every summer he did seem to pop up regularly in the magazines and newspapers doing something dashing. But damn it, he supposed he *was* dashing, though he did not try deliberately to create the image. He just liked to be active—always had—had always possessed the money to indulge it—and had also married Sue-Ann Lacey, which was a great extra in itself. He and Sue-Ann had been the darlings of Charleston in their early married years, and still were, as a matter of fact.

Since he combined all his many attractive attributes with a very astute mind and a great application to his chosen profession of the law, he had gone very far very fast, first following his father into the family law practice established by his grandfather Mossiter, then at thirty into the state attorney generalship now held (and disgraced, in Moss' opinion) by Regard Stinnet, then into the lieutenant-governorship at thirty-four, the governorship at thirty-eight and then to the Supreme Court of the United States at forty-three.

It was a nomination that had astounded a lot of people, including himself, but aided by his youthful good looks, charming demeanor and undeniable grasp of the law, he had sailed triumphantly through the Senate on a vote of 89–6.

It had meant relinquishing, at least for a time, presidential ambitions, which he and Sue-Ann did "nurse quietly in their bosoms with all the soft deception of the suckling dove," as Justice Hemmelsford put it once to Justice Wallenberg when they were discussing their newest associate. But that could wait. Others before him had clambered off the Bench to indulge other ambitions, and there would be no reason why he should hesitate if the opportunity came.

Meanwhile he was a faithful and dedicated Justice, one, he told himself proudly and with some truth, of the best; and he felt that was a fair enough bargain. With Rupe and the Chief he formed an alliance that sometimes became the basis for some of the 5–4 decisions that the Chief deplored yet to which he himself contributed. Quite often they had been able to swing Wally Flyte and Homer Dean their way. He was not so sure that they could swing Tay Barbour. Over almost a quarter century of friendship he had acquired many more diverse impressions of Tay than their associates had; and if there was one thing that sometimes stopped Moss, it was Tay's adherence to his principles and convictions. He was not impervious to reasoned argument, nor was he by any means completely unmovable, but as long ago as their first year in law school Moss could remember shouting in exasperation, "Sometimes I think it would take a damned earthquake or some other catastrophe to get you to budge one little inch when you've got your mind made up about something!"

Tay had just smiled patiently, looked up from his books and replied in a mild voice, "We ride out earthquakes all the time, in California." His mind, Moss knew, had long ago become set in the liberal pattern for which the President presumably had chosen him. He could be swayed, but short of "an earthquake or some other catastrophe," he was going to be a pretty predictable vote when he took his place on the highest Bench.

This, too, was the Chief's impression as he finished his snack, cleaned off his desk, rinsed his dishes and left them in the sink for his messenger to wash in the morning. He closed the door of his little kitchen and returned to his massive desk to resume his study of *Steiner v. Oregon*. It involved public utilities, which the Chief generally found a bore, but their rate-setting practices were more important than ever these days to an economy lurching from one crisis to another. He told himself with a sigh that he must get to it.

He could not help, however, letting his mind wander off before he did so to the new member who would soon join them. There was one area in which he knew they were in alliance already, and that was the area of rapidly growing crime and violence of all kinds.

Inevitably, demagogues were rising to profit from this. Attorney General Regard (*Reegard*, as Moss had translated it into Carolinian for them) Stinnet of South Carolina and Attorney General Ted Phillips of California were the most active so far, but they would be hearing from many more soon. It needed only some frightfulness in one state or the other, and one demagogue or the other, both or all, would be leading the pack full-cry. Vengeance is mine, saith the Lord. At the rate things were going, He would have a great many volunteer helpers, very soon.

And then would come the testing of the Court that they all anticipated with such apprehension. The Executive Branch would try to stand against the surge, but its leader was political too, and another term was coming up. He would not go over to the vendors of vengeance, but he would bend and he would waver; he would cry out against, but he would subtly and equivocally incline for. And the Congress? It, too, might not break, but it, too, would bend and it would answer. Election day—always another election day—was coming; and the pressures would be enormous, and almost impossible for any but the strongest to resist.

And so there would be left, as so often before in American history there had been left—the Court.

With a sudden start the Chief Justice drew himself up to his full seated dignity, spread his hands before him on the desk and stared straight ahead. He looked for a moment like the avenging angel himself —the avenging angel of the law.

"*No!*" he said sharply aloud to the empty office, "*No!*" to John Marshall who looked down with a quietly challenging, show-me air. "*They will not do that! They will not override the law!*"

He and his "little brood," human like all the rest—troubled and imperfect like all the rest—having but few glimpses of certainty with which to navigate the storm—given the benefit of a little more knowledge of the law, but no more certainty of right than all the rest—would not permit it.

"The Court will stand firm!" he said, still aloud. *"The Court will stand firm!"*

His voice, deep and somber for so small a man, heavy, emphatic, implacable in righteousness, rang out in the silence. The big office echoed with it for a second, shocking him: he had not even realized he had spoken aloud. Embarrassment vanished as quickly as it came. No one had heard him in this late hour in the near-deserted building. And even if anyone had, what of it? He meant it—he meant it. And he, no less, he knew, than his associates, was afraid . . .

He thought, with a heavy sigh as he looked down at his veined and knobby hands—so small to share so tenuous yet so great a power as the Court possessed—that nothing that might happen in these next few weeks and months bearing upon the issue of crime and violence would be easy. The country was moving toward some explosive lancing of the boil, some disaster that would symbolize it, epitomize it and bring it to a head. Would that the people had one neck, Nero had said, that I might cut it off. Would that crime had one neck, the Chief thought, that the Court might cut it off. He was not normally a superstitious man or one given to much foreboding about the future, but he just had a feeling —he had a feeling. Something would bring it about. Something would do it.

On a sudden impulse, he reached for his private telephone and dialed the unlisted number his secretary had secured for him earlier in the afternoon. He felt a sudden need to discuss something happy with somebody.

"Good evening, Justice," he said when the level, steady voice came over. "This is Duncan Elphinstone. It is my great pleasure to congratulate you and welcome you to the Court. We couldn't be happier to have you aboard."

"*N*ow what are you writing?" Janet demanded, although she told herself she really didn't want to know. He was always so damned busy about something, she just liked to needle him now and then to see how close she could come to making him really mad. It was a little game she liked to play, never realizing, not being really a very bright girl, how far from a game it was for him; which was her mistake.

"None of your damned business," he replied promptly, glowering up from the flimsy old portable typewriter and the scattered papers that covered his old wooden desk. "No!" he said sharply, covering them with his hands as she started to come toward him, dangling John Lennon Peacechild precariously from one hip. "They aren't for you! Stay away!"

"Well, all *right*," she said, suddenly sullen, sitting down on their one rickety old sofa, hauling the baby into her lap and staring at him resentfully. "I was just asking. And don't tell me," she added with a spiteful vigor before he could reply, "that people who ask questions get hurt. I know that's your line and I don't give a damn, do you hear me? I don't give a damn."

"You'd *better* give a damn," he said tersely, abruptly taking up a sheet of paper and holding it close to the lamp. "How does this sound?"

And with great solemnity he read:

"Whereas we live in a corrupt capitalist society bereft of hope—"

"What's 'bereft' mean?"

"*Christ!*" he said. "It means there isn't any. There isn't any hope, stupid, get it? No hope!"

"There isn't when you're around," she muttered. "That's for sure."

"What's that?" he cried, half-rising as if to start toward her. "*What's that?*"

"You heard me, I expect," she said, not flinching. "What other fancy words have you got? Is that all of it?"

"No, it isn't all of it," he said with heavy mimicry. "It goes on into a lot of stuff you wouldn't understand, stupid."

"And stop calling me stupid!" she cried with a sudden harshness. "Just because you went to college somewhere, I guess—"

"That's right," he said smugly. "I certainly did." He scowled. "Damned worthless rich man's playpen. Playpen for rich men's kids! Worthless! Nothing!"

"You aren't making much sense," she observed coolly. "If you didn't like it, why did you go there? Where was it, anyway?"

"You wouldn't know," he said. "I went there because my damned father went there and my grandfather before that and I was *expected* to. *Expected* to! I didn't go there because I wanted to. I was *expected* to!"

"I'll bet they're real proud of you now," she remarked. "*Real* proud."

"They hate my guts," he said complacently. "And I hate theirs. So we're even. Or at least"—he scowled—"maybe we are or maybe we aren't. Maybe we will be someday."

"You're crazy," she said. "You don't make sense."

"Oh, I make sense," he said, a curious half-crooning note in his voice. "Oh, yes, I make sense, all right. I make sense. You'll see. *Everybody* will see."

"With *that?*" she asked scornfully, pointing to the paper he still held in his hand, not even knowing it was there.

"It's my Manifesto," he said proudly, laying it carefully back on the desk. "They'll hear about it when—" He stopped abruptly and gave her a piercing glance.

"When what? You're nuts."

"Oh, no. *Oh,* no!"

"You sound like it to me," she said, shifting John Lennon Peacechild about to a more comfortable position. "You sound as though you're about to fly right out that window, sometimes . . . You mean," she went on idly, "that that little piece of paper is going to mean something to somebody? Is that all you mean?"

"I mean it will when I—" he blazed up. And stopped.

"Well, *what?*" she taunted. *"What* are you going to do?"

His eyes narrowed. A cautious curtain dropped.

"That's all right, what I'm going to do. You just don't worry about what I'm going to do. I didn't say I was going to do *anything.*"

"You're certainly doing a lot of talking and posing and carrying-on lately for nothing, then," she observed. "You're as nervous as a damned cat. Way you're acting, somebody'd think you were going to blow up the—the Statue of Liberty or something."

"Who said I'm going to blow up anything?" he demanded, jumping up and advancing upon her so fiercely that this time she instinctively shielded John Lennon Peacechild with her shawl. "Who said that? Who said it?"

"Nobody said it!" she shouted. The baby began to cry. *"I* said it! So what?"

"Listen," he said, seizing the shawl with an iron grip so that it almost choked her. "Don't you ever say that to anybody else, you hear?" He shook the shawl savagely so that her head rocked back and forth. "You *hear?* Don't you *ever* say that to *anybody again!* It isn't true! *It isn't true!* So knock it off! *Don't even think it! Don't even think it!"*

"Take your hands off me!" she screamed, yanking the shawl away from her throat. "Take your hands off me, you crazy! Don't you touch me like that again, ever, you hear! *Ever, ever, ever!* I don't give a damn what you blow up! I don't give a damn what you do! I don't give a damn about anything! Just leave me and John Lennon Peacechild alone!" She sank back, huddled over the baby, and began to cry. "Just go back and write on your damned paper, if you want to! *I don't care!"*

"Well," he said triumphantly, turning his back upon her with a sudden frightening dismissal of interest, "I don't care either, so that makes two of us . . . Now," he said, taking up the paper again, holding it out in front of him, examining it with a critical but approving eye, "where was I? Oh, yes. 'Whereas we live in a corrupt capitalist society bereft of hope and of the humanity, kindness and true compassion which decent people everywhere ought to show to one another—' "

"You *are* crazy," she whispered, holding John Lennon Peacechild tight as his sobs gradually subsided. "You really *are* crazy."

So, too, possibly, was the attorney general of South Carolina, although probably no one would ever formally certify him as such. He was, after all, doin' nothin' more, he said, than jes' respondin' to the

public will. And what could anybody say was crazy about *that?* Wasn't
that what a public official *ought* to do? Seemed that way to him, he said,
and if a few people got hurt in the process, well, they'd asked for it,
hadn't they? And they'd hurt other people first, hadn't they? So what
did the damned crazies expect? He wasn't a vengeful man, but society's
safety came first with him, and if the law wasn't a help to society, then
he guessed society had to help itself. That, as he conceived it, was his
job and nobody, no, sir, not nobody, was tellin' him he wasn't right
about it. The people liked it, didn't they? He was gettin' mail and telegrams and phone calls from as far away as California, wasn't he? All
over the country they were tellin' him to go to it, boy, weren't they? So
what were those damned northern liberals and that damned human-
rights bunch worryin' about? *They* weren't gettin' hurt by the crazies.
Wait until they were, and then see what they'd say about it! They'd
holler a different tune then, he'd wager! He'd bet his bottom dollar
they'd be glad he was leadin' the country in the right direction then, by
God!

Thus spoke, upon the right occasions, *Regard* Stinnet, a dark-eyed,
dark-haired, dark-minded, well-set-up thirty-six, just then concluding a
mutually congratulatory conversation with his equally strong-minded
think-alike, thirty-five-year-old Attorney General Ted Phillips of California. Like his opposite number across an uneasy continent, the attorney general of South Carolina did not, as he expressed it privately,
"talk corn pone" to his intimates. It was only when he took to radio or
television or got out in the back hollers that he really let fly with the
redneck stuff. That was for the folks back home. Actually in his office
—and sometimes, also, on the air, because a lot of high-class people
lived in South Carolina, too—he was a well-dressed, well-groomed, soft-
talking, highly intelligent graduate of The Citadel and Yale Law School
who used perfectly good English and held his accent and his temper
under reasonable control. Outwardly he could be, and often was, one of
the mildest and most civilized men around. This of course made him
doubly effective when he did let fly, and doubly dangerous to his state
and country in a tense and difficult time.

He had his eyes on several places higher up the political ladder, and
hoped by a combination of skillfully applied guile and bombast to get
there. Moss Pomeroy, who knew exactly the game he was playing,
might be his only obstacle; and he didn't think Moss would be all that
much of a problem. Moss was on the Court, and as Regard could tell
from a shrewd analysis of some of his recent opinions, his national position was giving him the opportunity to see too many sides of too many

things. Moss was beginning to have Doubts, of a kind that Regard always capitalized in his own mind. Regard did not have Doubts, and that gave him a great advantage. Regard was that type of demagogue who genuinely believes his own demagoguery. This made him an almost invulnerable politician for this particular moment in his nation's history— a man of dynamic persuasion to a rapidly growing number of his countrymen—and a genuine danger to the lumbering processes of a democratic but now increasingly inadequate system of justice.

Whether he wooed them softly or shouted from the stump, whether they were rednecks or bluestockings, more and more were paying attention and expressing agreement. Crime and violence were bringing their inevitable reaction in an era in which the courts had made retribution increasingly uncertain and, when it was attempted, either impossible to achieve, ponderously slow or almost laughably (had laughter been possible) light.

Regard was convinced that in himself and his fellow avengers, crime and violence were about to meet their match. He knew as surely as he knew anything—because letters, telegrams, telephone calls and an increasing number of editorials, columns and commentaries were telling him so—that he was riding a rising tide of popular feeling. "The hour has come!" he solemnly assured his listeners on every possible occasion; and the man for the hour—or one of them, for they were becoming many—had arisen.

Already Regard had proposed, as Moss had reminded the Court this morning with disbelief and distaste—that a whole range of moderate crimes be punished by public flogging, and that the death penalty also be made public. Being a child of his time, he had quite inevitably and without a moment's second thought proposed the logical next step: that these events be put on television. In prime time.

His proposals had been greeted with horror, outcry and scorn by human-rights organizations, the American Civil Liberties Union, the earnest, the idealistic, the decent, and the more staid and solid elements of the press and television itself.

And yet—and yet.

Even while they loudly protested and denounced, a secret, sneaking, awful but insistently tantalizing thought was beginning to creep into the minds of network executives and their advertisers.

What could possibly draw more viewers?

What could possibly assure an advertiser wider exposure and bring more money into network coffers?

DEATH IN PRIME TIME.

Deny it as they would, try to push back its horrid fascinations as they might, they knew it was a natural.

Greed, the ratchet wheel that turned far too many Americans in the closing years of a sick and savage century, was beginning to impose its own self-destructing logic in this area as well.

Surely many enterprising Romans must have advertised on the walls of the Coliseum.

It was not only for a worried Chief Justice in Washington that the ghost of Nero stirred.

It grinned, more kindly, on Regard Stinnet too.

"You know, Ted," he had just told his fellow attorney general out in Sacramento, "I think you and I may be riding something a lot bigger than we realize. I mean, man, the people are *fed up*."

"All over the country," Ted Phillips agreed.

"Got any vigilantes out there?"

"A few. The impulse is spreading."

"You encouraging them?"

Ted uttered a dry little laugh.

"Officially I'm still expressing horror and repugnance at the whole idea. But how much pressure can a public servant take without yielding to the wishes of his people?"

"Exactly my point," Regard Stinnet said promptly. "Exactly my point. Some of these do-gooders seem to think you and I are causing all this rumpus. They act as though the God damned criminals and terrorists have nothing to do with it. I haven't started this parade. But," he added with an equally knowing laugh, "I sure as hell don't intend to let it go by without me, that's for sure."

"Me, either," the attorney general of California concurred. "After all, it seems to be what the people want—and more and more of them seem to want it. It's our job to channel it into areas as law-abiding as possible, but the movement is growing so fast that I don't think we can stop it. God knows I'm against vigilantism—"

"Oh, me too!" Regard agreed fervently.

"—but if it's going to go on anyway, to the point where it would take real police action to stop it—then what's the choice?"

"The choice is," Regard said crisply, "that you only have a limited police power anyway, right? And if you pull it off the criminals to go after the good people who only want to fight the criminals, then the criminals are going to get even worse than they are already, because the police and the law-abiding public will be busy fightin' each other instead of fightin' the criminals. Right?"

"Absolutely right," Ted Phillips agreed.

"You meet yourself coming back on that argument," Regard observed. "It's a damn circle with no way out. What you've got to do is get the police power and the people movin' in the same direction, and that's what I'm tryin' to do down here."

"We've been hearing quite a bit about your ideas, lately. A lot of favorable comment."

"I'm gettin' calls from as far away as North Dakota pledgin' support," Regard said, "even though they don't have such a huge problem there as I do, and particularly you do. It's just a general conclusion all over the country, I think, that enough is enough, that's all. *Enough is enough.*"

"A good slogan."

"Be my guest," Regard Stinnet said. "I'll use it—you use it—we'll spread it all over this damned country. *Enough is enough.* Next time we have an excuse to let go with it, we'll go. I'll bet you in ten days' time it'll be on every bumper from here to Alaska and back."

"Let's consult often on this," Ted suggested. "In fact, how about trying to set up a regular round of calls about once a week with all the attorneys general all over the country?"

"Might even have a meetin'," Regard said thoughtfully. "An annual meetin'—semiannual—every month, even. Hell, the problem sure as hell isn't goin' to go away anytime soon."

"That's certain," the attorney general of California agreed. "O.K., let's get organized. Why don't we just split the states in two, you take twenty-five, I'll take twenty-five, and we'll call everyone in the next week or two—"

"Let's say two, give ourselves enough time," Regard suggested. "And let me think about the list a little bit." He chuckled. "Some places, you know, they think a southern accent means you're kind of dumb. California culture might go over better."

"If they think a southern accent means you're dumb," Ted Phillips said, "they're dumb. Do you think they'll go along?"

Regard sniffed.

"Oh, there'll be some of 'em who'll shy away and keep on cryin' for law and order. But hell, man! Don't they realize we're tryin' to re-establish *real* law and order after too many years of coddlin' criminals and lettin' our cities and towns be turned into damned jungles? You take care, now. We'll talk soon, hear?"

"We certainly will," Ted Phillips agreed, and added, half-humorously but seriously too, "Enough is enough."

"You're damned right," Regard Stinnet said with satisfaction. "Enough is sure as hell *e-nough.*"

After his new friend—they had never even met before, the call had come out of the blue from Sacramento, apparently prompted by a genuine interest in and respect for his own efforts—had hung up, Regard had remained at his desk saying "Enough is *e-nough*" quietly to himself several times with complacent emphasis. Then he had jumped up, as was his custom, and begun to pace up and down in front of the big window in his office that looked down on dim night-shapes of trees and level lawns. He was a restless soul possessed of a great energy that rarely allowed him to settle long in any one chair, room, place. And he was always thinking, as his mother had remarked when he was still a solemn-eyed baby who rarely smiled: always thinkin'.

What he was thinking now was that when Moss Pomeroy came down to dedicate the Pomeroy Station atomic energy plant, he must try to have a real talk with him.

Moss had just been up there too long in the rarefied atmosphere of the Court, Regard suspected. It was all very fine to be high and mighty and remote and above it all, as he had told Carolyn just the other day when the Justice's name had come up, but it did put you out of touch with what the ordinary folks were thinking. Regard doubted if Moss and his fellow Justices even knew there was an explosive unrest growing in the country; he doubted they even knew how deep-seated and uneasy was the popular feeling, how frustrated and how ready to explode into counterviolence. Moss should know these things, then he would understand better what was going on. They should all know these things. Maybe Moss could tell them, after Regard explained it to him.

He decided he would call Moss tomorrow and see if he couldn't set up a definite appointment, maybe after the dedication ceremony. Moss needed to know—they all needed to know because, Regard suspected, the day might not be far off when a case or cases growing out of this would go right on up to the Supreme Court. If they were as out of touch with the country as they sometimes appeared to be, then they might not render a fair judgment at all. They might listen to a lot of this liberal human-rights crap and make the wrong kind of decision. And they just couldn't afford to do that any more. They just had to help put down the criminal and the violent, otherwise the country might well turn on the Court itself. And even Regard didn't think that would be right.

He might go along with it if that seemed to be the popular will and there was no way to restore genuine law and order otherwise; but he certainly didn't think it would be right. Actually, in a detached sort of way, he felt that it would really be kind of sad.

6

"**Y**ou come to us, of course," the Chief said, "at a difficult time, Tay—if I may be so familiar."

"Please."

"Good. You can call me Chief or Dunc, whichever seems easiest."

"Chief, I suspect, for a while at least."

"Well, I keep an informal Court, as you'll find. Public dignity at all times, because I think that's important for the image, and I think the image *is* important—"

"Certainly."

"—but otherwise, reasonably informal." He laughed. "Many, including our brethren and May McIntosh, call me The Elph behind my back. I don't encourage this to my face."

"Never," Tay said gravely. The Chief laughed again.

"You sound suitably impressed with the Court already. It *is* a great honor."

"And a great responsibility. I am very well aware of that, Mr. Chief Justice."

"I know you are," the Chief said. "I didn't call to lecture you about it, just to congratulate you and warn you of the obvious, which is that, as you know, we don't face any easy decisions these days. The whole crime situation is growing much worse, the potential much more explosive."

"And our responsibility—the Court's responsibility, I should say, since I'm not confirmed yet—that much greater."

"No worry, you will be. Yes, it is. I only hope the issue comes up to us in some form in which we can stand together—some form in which it doesn't get all tangled up in Bill of Rights, human rights, grays and blues and browns and yellows and everything except simple black and white. That's so often the way." He sighed. "Things aren't clear-cut. It complicates the job so."

Taylor Barbour laughed sympathetically.

"It does indeed. And of course you know I'm one who always sees the grays and blues and browns and yellows. I almost never see the blacks and whites."

"I was afraid of that," The Elph said with a rueful humor. "I was afraid of that! More five-to-fours!"

"Yes, I expect so. I'm sorry, but—"

"Oh, no, not at all," The Elph said, more cheerily. "That's the way you see things, that's the way you'll vote. I wouldn't expect you to be inconsistent with what you believe . . . By the way, while I have you—I'm going to host a little party at the Court next Friday evening, if you and Mrs. Barbour would be free—"

"Now, just what else," he asked with a laugh, "could we possibly be doing that would take precedence over that?"

"Well, I didn't know," the Chief said. "You birds in the Executive Branch are always buzzing around the social circuit, a lot more than we do. Partly this is something I like to do each year toward the end of the term, just to send everybody off to recess on an amicable note. But it's got an added importance this time with a new member coming on. You can consider it a formal welcome for you. Eight o'clock—black tie—the dining room up here. It will be a good get-acquainted time."

"That's very kind. We do appreciate it, very much. You're again assuming, of course, that I'll be confirmed."

"My dear boy!" the Chief Justice exclaimed. "Are you kidding? You'll get two or three young loudmouths on the Senate Judiciary Committee who may look for a few headlines at your expense—may try to bounce you around a bit in the hearings—but Rupe Hemmelsford and Wally Flyte tell me the Senate is overwhelmingly on your side. They're now estimating no less than eighty-six or eighty-seven, perhaps even more, for you. I wouldn't worry, if I were you. For a man of your known—and perhaps even rigid, might I say?—views, you have surprisingly few enemies in this town."

"A somewhat backhanded compliment," Tay said with a laugh, "but I appreciate it."

"Meant," The Elph said. "Meant. Please give Mrs. Barbour my best regards and congratulations also, and tell her Birdie and the others are looking forward to having her join them. And now I've got to get back to work. You haven't heard of *Steiner v. Oregon* yet, but you will—you will."

"Are you still working? Isn't it getting rather late?"

"Not for us up here, my boy. We *work.* I'm in my office and Clem, Wally, Rupe and Moss are still in theirs, I believe. This building stays alive to all hours and Justices are often right here with it. You'll find out."

"That's all right," he said. "I like work. I do thank you for calling, Chief. It was very gracious of you."

"Not at all," Duncan Elphinstone said. "Just between you and me, the White House doesn't always send us such good material, although of course each of us in his own time thinks it does. It's my pleasure to say a private but warm hello."

"I do appreciate it," Tay said. "You know I do."

And that, he reflected as the Chief went off the line, was how a civilized human being treated another on the day of his personal triumph. He had received many calls during the afternoon—some twenty-five were waiting when Cathy Corning concluded her interview and left —and with the single exception of his wife, every one had been genuinely happy for him. Her discontent weighed down the day, weighed down the evening, weighed down the house.

They were eating at home tonight. It would have been a silent meal except for Jane and Sarah Pomeroy, who dashed in just in time, flung hats and coats on a hall chair, took their places, flushed and laughing— perhaps a little too much so, he thought for a moment, but dismissed it. These two had known each other as long as they could remember, become best friends when both had been sent to Madeira School, now were inseparable and always in and out of each other's house. He had hoped this might bring Mary more closely into his friendship for Sarah's parents, but she had remained withdrawn and grudging. She and Sue-Ann "do not get along very well," as she put it with no particular reason given; and she had made it clear years ago when she first met Moss that his irreverent banter and easygoing approach to life did not accord with what she considered a dignity "befitting his position."

"Hell, Mary," Moss had objected when she once said as much, "that's an awfully old-fashioned way of looking at things." He grinned with innocent and unconscious egotism. "I don't have to worry about my 'position.' Pomeroys and Mossiters never have had to. We've always just *been* there, that's all. As Grandfather Mossiter used to say, 'As long

as I don't ride a horse up the state capitol steps with a naked prostitute
across the saddle, I'll get along all right.' I believe one of our Revolu-
tionary ancestors did that once. Must have been quite a sensation, but
everybody's been very well behaved since. So don't worry about me. I'm
doing fine."

To this day, Tay thought, Mary always seemed to have that horse
and naked prostitute on her mind when she looked at Moss: or perhaps
it was just that he had—or certainly used to have when they first met—a
direct and challenging sexuality that made her uncomfortable. He no
longer had it now, or if he did, kept it under very good control: Sue-
Ann, Tay suspected, saw to that with a firm and unwavering hand.
Moss now was quite the dignified Justice, even though the irreverent
humor constantly popped out. That wouldn't change, and thank God
for it. He suspected it would be fun working with him on the Court: he
seemed to be an unquenchable spirit. His call earlier today had been the
first Tay had received after talking to his parents.

"You see?" Moss had said cheerfully and without preliminary. "I
told you. It was inevitable. The President decided there ought to be at
least one Justice worthy of the Court, and here you are."

"I hope I'm worthy of the Court," he replied soberly.

Moss snorted.

"If you have any doubts about *that*—"

"You're a high-powered group."

"Yes, but human—human. We don't like the country to suspect it,
which is one reason we refrain from interviews and remain generally
anonymous. But we have our quirks, as you'll find out. I warn you,
though—I may try to convert you to the conservative side. Too many
damned liberals around this place."

"That may take a little doing," Tay said. "You haven't succeeded in
all these years. If it hasn't happened by now, it isn't going to."

"Oh, you never know," Moss said airily. "Circumstances alter cases,
as they say. How's Mary taking it?"

"I haven't been able to reach her. I've put in a call, but she's out at
the moment. I imagine she won't be too happy."

"I swear," Moss said with the candor of a very old friend. "She's the
only lawyer's wife I know who probably won't be happy when her husband goes on the Supreme Court. I'll never understand your wife, Taylor. Never."

"That makes two of us," he said with a rueful humor. "How's
yours?"

"More understandable," Moss said in a lighter tone. "Doing just fine, thanks. And Janie?"

"Oh, she's fine," Tay said, voice instantly warmer and less troubled. "She and Sarah seem to be running Madeira School together, as near as I can ascertain."

"Yes," Moss said, his tone also filling with affection for his daughter. "They're quite a pair. I understand Sarah's spending the night with you tonight."

"Yes," he said, sounding troubled again. "Over Mary's objection, but Janie and I overruled her."

"Now why," Moss demanded with annoyance, "would she object? It seems perfectly all right to me."

"I don't know," he confessed. "I really don't. It 'upsets the household,' she said."

"I think she'd be very happy if she never saw the Pomeroys again," Moss said, "and all we've ever tried to do is just be friends. Very puzzling. Well, anyway: delighted to have you with us on the Court, old buddy. Whoever would have thought, back at Harvard Law—?"

"Is that a serious question?" Tay inquired, amused. "*We* thought, didn't we?"

"Hoped," Moss conceded.

"*Thought*. Nothing modest about us in those days. Or have you forgotten?"

"I guess that's right," Moss agreed with a chuckle. "We *thought* then. We've *hoped* since. And now it's all come true."

"Yes," Tay agreed, voice shaded with many things. "It's all come true."

"Well." Moss broke the mood briskly. "One thing I did want to do, while I have you, was to see if you and Mary would like to come down to South Carolina with us next Friday and help me dedicate the Pomeroy Station atomic energy plant. The rest of the Court won't go, because they agree with the Chief that it might look like endorsing a controversial subject that keeps coming before us, but I thought maybe since you're just coming on, and will just barely have been confirmed by then, you might feel free. Just for old friendship and old time's sake. I'd be very happy to have you, if you'd like."

"Well—" he said, and hesitated, "I'd love to—nothing personal, you understand—but I think maybe—for the same reason—"

"O.K.," Moss said, sounding resigned but then brightening. "I understand. I just wanted company, that's all. So Sue-Ann and I will go alone. Mary probably wouldn't want to go anyway."

"No," Tay admitted, "probably not. However, just a thought: is Sarah going?"

"She wants to."

"Fine. Take Janie. She'd get a thrill out of it."

"Good idea. I'll tell Sarah to ask her."

"Perfect. Look, I have another call coming in, but I'll see you soon, hear?"

"In chambers," Moss said. "Hot damn! We're going to have fun on the Court, old pal, even if you are a damned liberal!"

"And you a damned conservative," Tay had said, hanging up with the warm feeling a visit with Moss always gave him.

"Daddy," Janie inquired as she and Sarah settled down from the flurry of their entry, "will you have to wear your Supreme Court robes around the house?"

"That's a ridiculous question," Mary observed, ringing for Julia, their maid of ten years. "He will only wear them on the bench."

"Well, I didn't *know*," Janie said. "I just wanted to be *sure*."

"No doubt," her mother said. "You girls are late for dinner."

"I'm sorry, Mrs. Barbour," Sarah said with her quick pretty smile. "It was my fault. I wanted to stop at one of the stores over on Wisconsin Avenue on the way home, so we had them drop us off there."

"And then *walked?*" Mary demanded. "You girls should never *walk* in Georgetown. You should never *walk* anywhere in this city. You're old enough to know that."

"It's only four blocks," Jane said defensively. "It's still light enough."

"Whether it's light or not," Mary said flatly, "I don't want you doing it. It isn't safe, no matter what time of day it is or where you are. Is that why you girls don't really seem quite as confident as you'd apparently like us to believe? Did anything happen on the way home?"

They exchanged a swift glance but not swift enough to escape Mary.

"Well?" she demanded, voice suddenly harsh with concern. "Tell me this instant!"

"Well—" Janie began carefully.

"*Yes?*"

"There was this man," Sarah admitted. "Behind a bush."

"And?" Mary pursued, face white, as Tay too leaned forward, pulse accelerating.

"He didn't do anything," Janie protested.

"That's right, Mrs. Barbour," Sarah said. "He just *looked*."

"How did he look?"

"He just *looked*," Janie insisted; but Sarah added more candidly, "He didn't look very nice."

"In what way?" Tay asked, trying to keep his voice calm.

"Oh," Sarah said, blushing. "You know."

"So then you ran," Mary said, "and that's why you were so out of breath when you came in. Right?"

"Well—" Janie began.

"*Isn't that right?*"

"Yes, ma'am," Sarah said in a subdued voice. "We didn't say anything because we didn't want you to get upset."

"Upset?" Mary demanded with a scornful shaky laugh. "*Upset?* Now, why would any sensible parent get upset about an innocent little thing like that? *Upset?*" Her voice became cold and emphatic. "I don't want you girls to walk in this city ever again, anywhere, do you understand me? I don't care whether it's six A.M., six P.M., or high noon, *you are not to do it.* Is that clear?" She swung suddenly to Tay with a harsh sarcasm. "Surely your father will support me in *that?*"

"Yes I will," he replied emphatically: on this, at least, there was no disagreement. "You just *must* not do it, baby. It isn't safe. I'm sure your father and mother have told you that too, Sarah."

"Well!" Sarah said, recovering with a little flounce. "It's safe enough in South Carolina."

"I don't believe you," Mary said flatly. "Anyway, you are not to do it here, understand? If you do it again, you won't be permitted to come over and play."

"Oh, Mo*ther*," Janie said. "We're *fifteen*."

"Not quite," Mary said.

"Well, three months."

"Yes, and you act like five instead of fifteen," her mother said. Her voice rose decisively, her lips got their tight line. "We are not discussing it further. Those are the terms. Abide by them or forget it."

Janie looked at Sarah and shrugged.

"We can stay at *your* house after this."

"Janie!" Tay said. "Stop this right now. Your mother and I are agreed—"

"For once," Janie said, looking stubbornly down at her plate.

There was silence for a moment, after which Sarah began to giggle, starting from sheer nervousness and swiftly going out of control. This made Janie giggle too, and in a moment they were laughing hysterically. He came very close to joining them but he could see that Mary was actually white and trembling with anger.

"Janie," he said, forcing his voice to remain grave and steady, "one more crack from you about anything and you're going straight to bed without your supper, fifteen or no fifteen, and I'm driving Sarah home. Now, you just decide, young lady. We'll wait for you."

And putting down his knife and fork, he did so while Mary, looking a little mollified, followed suit. The giggles subsided at once, to be succeeded by a heavy silence during which Julia, taking in the situation with the practiced glance of a mother of four, served dinner with briskness and dispatch and retired rapidly to the kitchen.

"I'm sorry," Janie murmured finally. "I apologize, Mother."

"I apologize, too, Mrs. Barbour," Sarah echoed sweetly. "It *was* my fault, just like I said. We won't do it again."

"Very well," Mary said. "I sincerely hope not. The world is bad, out there." She shivered suddenly and stabbed at her food. Her husband quietly resumed eating and presently the girls, after giving one another a furtive sidelong glance, did the same. Silence ensued until Sarah gave a little sigh of repletion and looked up happily at Julia when she brought in dessert in response to Mary's bell.

"Julia, you old lamb!" Sarah exclaimed. "You're just the *best* cook. We don't have any better down in South Carolina!"

Julia, who had planned to be stern because she too considered Sarah a rather flighty little thing, a bit mite big for her britches because of being a Pomeroy and a Mossiter and a Lacey all rolled into one, found herself dissolving into a pleased smile in spite of herself.

"Thank you, Miss Sarah," she said. "It's always a pleasure for me to cook for you. Even if"—she couldn't resist with a glance at Mary that she knew would do her no harm—"we all *were* beginning to wonder where you were."

"Now, Julia," Sarah said, tone changing instantly. "Don't you go getting sassy, now. We've been all over that and have *moved on to other things*. You behave yourself, now, you old scamp."

"Miss Sarah," Julia said, drawing herself up, voice trembling a little but holding her own. "I am not an old scamp, but I surely think you're a young one. You can't talk to me like that, miss. I'm not a slave of the Pomeroys! Or the Mossiters! Or the Laceys! Those days are gone forever!"

"That's all right, Julia," Tay said soothingly, thinking: my God, the

Supreme Court will be a vacation after this. "Sarah didn't mean it the way it sounded."

"No, I didn't, Julia," Sarah said with a sudden change of mood and her sweetest smile. "You *are* an old lamb, and I *do* apologize if I sounded uppity. Nobody cocks better than you. *Nobody!* I do apologize."

"It seems to me as though everybody is apologizing to everybody these days," Janie said in a clear, detached voice; but before one parent or the other could respond, Julia fortunately decided to let it drop.

"Why, I do thank you again, Miss Sarah," she said grandly. "Anytime!" And sailed out with her armload of dishes.

Both girls broke promptly into giggles again, and Tay could not suppress a glint of amusement they both saw and took encouragement from. Not Mary: she was definitely not amused.

"Girls," she said sharply, "stop this time-wasting and finish your meal. I'm sure your father has a lot to do to get ready for the Court, Janie. And I'm sure you both have plenty of studying to do. So hurry it up."

"Actually, Mrs. Barbour," Sarah said, "we *do* have a lot to do and we are certainly going to do it. We have to get ahead in our work so that we can go on that trip."

"Oh?" Mary said, and Tay could see her instinctively digging in her heels, which of course tightened him up also. They were apparently about to do battle over the girls, even though Mary did not for the moment know why. Evidently Sarah had conveyed the invitation. "What trip is that?"

"I have been invited," Jane announced with some grandeur, "to attend a dedication."

"Of what?" her mother demanded.

"Our atomic energy plant," Sarah replied. "Well, not exactly *ours,* but it's on land we used to own, I think. A long time ago. Like before the Revolution, maybe."

"And when will this ceremony be held?" Mary inquired, her tone producing the start of dismay on Janie's face.

"Next Friday," Sarah said cheerfully, unaware of storm signals. "It's going to be at a place called Pomeroy Station, down home in South Carolina. My daddy's going to give the dedication speech, I guess. Or one of them. He was governor when they began it, and it's named after us, so he's got to be there. He said I could go, and I invited Janie." She turned a comfortable smile upon Mary. "We'll miss two days of school, so that's why we have to study extra hard these next few days."

"Jane," her mother said coldly, "is not going to miss two days of school."

"Oh, *Mother!*" Jane wailed, and Sarah echoed, "Oh, Mrs. *Barbour!*"

"Now, Mary," he said in a tone he tried to keep reasonable. "I'm sure if the girls get ahead in their work—"

"Jane is not ahead in her work."

"Three straight A's and two B's last time," Janie said bitterly. "That's all!"

"Nonetheless, young lady, you've been slipping a bit in the last few weeks. They tell me things at the school. I keep track."

"Yes," Janie said. "I'll bet you do."

"Indeed I do," Mary said, unmoved. "You are my daughter, my only child, and I have a right to inquire how you are getting along. Too many extracurricular activities for you, young lady. You can't afford any time off."

"I can't help it if I'm *popular!*" Janie said and Sarah said earnestly,

"She really is *very* popular, Mrs. Barbour. I sometimes think that old school would just *collapse* without Janie."

"I doubt it," her mother said dryly. "If you're going to be so *popular,* young lady, you have got to keep up your grades along with it. This is no time to go skipping off to South Carolina. What your parents permit you to do, Sarah, is their affair. It was nice of you to try to include Janie, but I'm afraid she simply won't have the time to go."

"But I'm *studying ahead,*" Janie protested, on the verge of tears.

"Mary," he said, as Julia popped in the door and hastily popped back out again, "be reasonable about this. If the girls get their work done ahead, I really don't see any reason why—"

"We are spending a lot of money to send her to that school. Two of the things it is supposed to teach are character and discipline. If one keeps up one's grades, that is one thing. If one begins to slip, that is another. Some people may permit their children to get by with sloppy work. I will not."

"*I* don't do sloppy work!" Sarah said, face flushing.

"I did not say you do," Mary said calmly. "I said *some people* may let their children do sloppy work. I don't, and I presume your parents do not, either. I'm rather surprised, frankly, that your mother and father would encourage you to skip school and even permit you to encourage someone else to do the same. It is not what I would have expected from a Supreme Court Justice."

"Well," Tay said shortly, "I am a Supreme Court Justice—or about to be, anyway—and I can't see any valid reason at all why Janie shouldn't accompany Sarah if she studies ahead and gets things in order before she leaves."

"Just say I am a terrible mother who wishes to protect her daughter's integrity and character," Mary said, "and leave it at that. I know it is terrible of me, but there it is. Janie," she said flatly, "will not go on this harum-scarum adventure with you, Sarah, so you both had better stop talking about it. I will not permit it, and that is final."

"It is not harum-scarum," Sarah said indignantly, also close to tears. "It is a *real occasion.*"

Mary sniffed.

"So I gather you have been told. I hope you enjoy it. Jane will not."

"Daddy—" Janie appealed, dissolving at last. *"Daddy—"*

"And appealing to your father," Mary said, showing her first signs of agitation, "will not do you any good. I see you girls have finished your dinner. Go along and study, please. *Now.*"

"Oh—" Janie said. *"Oh—"*

"Come on, Janie," Sarah said, managing a fair amount of dignity as she got up and started toward the stairs. "It's no use talking to your *mother.*"

"Or your father—" Mary began, but he suddenly cut her short.

"You girls go along," he said harshly. "I'll talk to your mother."

But their wan looks back indicated that they did not put much faith in that, nor did he as Mary called firmly, "Julia!" and Julia scurried in and began removing the remnants of the meal. Mary walked straight into the den, turned and faced him.

"Taylor Barbour," she said evenly, "I will not permit my daughter to go on this wild adventure with that—that—*little southern belle!*"

"For heaven's sake, Mary," he said, feeling suddenly tired—it had, after all, been a rather long and emotion-filled day—"Sarah is a perfectly decent child. Quite a little lady, in fact."

"She treats Julia like dirt," Mary said, "and she is *not* a good influence for Jane."

"She treats Julia southern sometimes," he said, "but you notice Julia doesn't stand for it. Julia can take care of herself. They all understand one another down there. And as for Janie, they've been friends since they were a year old. Why is she suddenly such a bad influence?"

"It isn't 'suddenly.' It's in the last year or so, when Sarah has begun to blossom out and turn into a little flirt. She's giving Janie ideas about boys."

"Well, I suppose Janie's going to have them, isn't she? That seems perfectly normal to me."

"Jane is a slow developer," her mother said. "She isn't ready for it yet. I'm sure she and Sarah are up there right now talking about the subject. I don't think Sarah thinks of anything else these days. It isn't good for Janie. And as for persuading Janie to walk home through Georgetown at this time of night—"

"We don't know who persuaded whom," he said. "They did it, and it was very unwise and I supported you in your objections, didn't I? I understand your feelings, both as a parent and as—as a victim."

"You can't understand," she said with a shudder, eyes darkening with the thought of the always haunting incident that had occurred in the supermarket parking lot one evening soon after they had moved to Washington. "Nobody can understand that except another person it's happened to. Mugged and robbed and almost raped—" She shuddered again. "*Nobody* can understand it. Certainly not a *husband*."

"I try," he said, bleakly. "I've tried all these years. I suppose it's part of why you dislike Washington so—"

"I *hate* Washington."

"—and why you're so overly protective of Janie—"

"I *can't* be 'overly protective' of Janie," she said fiercely. "*She's all we have.* And *you* ought to show some concern for her too, if you were any kind of a father!"

"Oh, my God, Mary," he said, almost literally bereft of words. "My *God,* how can you say such a thing . . . Anyway," he resumed, reverting almost desperately to the previous subject, which at least made some sort of sense, "forbid the girls to see each other altogether, then. Don't stop at just some—some occasion down in South Carolina. Put on a complete ban and see what good it does you. You'll really have Janie intrigued if you do that."

"And as for that dedication—"

"We were all invited, actually, but Moss said he assumed you wouldn't want to go. I agreed. You wouldn't."

"Well, don't put the burden on me," she said, sitting down and folding her hands composedly in her lap. "I don't think it would be fitting for you, either, would it, as a Justice who may have to pass on atomic energy matters?"

"You are right," he conceded, exasperated by her ability, still unimpaired, to analyze things with considerable clarity. "That is quite correct. He told me Sarah might be going and *I* suggested that she invite Janie."

"Are you pleased with the rumpus you stirred up?"

"*I've* stirred up?" he demanded, exasperation growing. "To me it was just a nice outing the girls could go on together—a fun thing, Mary. Not a desperate issue to get everybody upset about. I just thought it would be *fun.*"

"You just didn't think, if truth were known," she said coolly. "*I* think it is time to phase out that friendship a bit. As Sarah gets older she gets more like her mother and father. I'm not going to have my daughter associating too much from now on with that little magnolias-and-swamp-adder character, sweet as honey to your face and hard as nails underneath. You can't trust a one of them."

"Mary," he said in a tired but dogged tone, "I do not think that there is any harm at all in letting Janie go to Pomeroy Station with Sarah, and I would like you to relent."

"No," she said quietly.

"Not even if I said please?"

"Don't humble yourself," she said with a dry little laugh "It doesn't become you. Why don't you go somewhere and think about the Court? That ought to be enough to occupy anyone for quite a long time."

He looked at her steadily for a long moment. She looked steadily back.

"Oh, I'm sorry," she said, getting up with an exaggerated quickness. "This *is* the den, isn't it? And you probably want to think *here.* I'll go on up and read. Take your time. No hurry."

"No," he said, voice expressionless. "No hurry."

After she had gone he sat for some minutes staring at the floor, face weary and set. Then he sighed heavily. She was right. He should "think about the Court." Apparently there was not going to be much else to occupy his thoughts or engage his heart from now on.

He remembered that his confirmation hearings would be coming up very soon, and that he should put his thoughts on the law in order. He went to the desk, sat down, placed a blank piece of paper before him and forced himself to concentrate. After a few moments it came easily. His mind raced, his pen raced. He was far away from quarrels, trials, tribulations, Sarah, Jane, Mary—back with the law, to which, he knew she was convinced, he had always really given his deepest, most heart-felt and most lasting commitment in all their years together.

In the great white building, now almost entirely silent and deserted as the clock moved on, the Chief Justice, kindly face and shock of white hair pooled in the light of his favorite battered old student lamp from

Duke Law School days long ago, was also writing his thoughts on the current state of the laws. He had abandoned *Steiner v. Oregon* some time since. His mind had wandered for a bit through casual concerns and then had come inevitably back to crime, violence, horror, the aching and explosive burdens of a society awry—a subject he would soon have to address in his annual speech to the American Bar Association. It was almost ten o'clock. He knew he must get home to Birdie soon or she, though long inured, would begin to worry. His mind also raced, his pen too hurried over the paper.

"Confronted by such a situation," he wrote, "we must ask ourselves where can society best seize upon the problem and in what direction should our most diligent efforts go? It seems to this observer that there must be a greater determination, a more diligent safeguarding, a greater willingness to resort to stronger action and a more stringent attitude toward those who—"

"So," wrote the stocky figure hunched over the battered desk in the isolated cabin in the trees near Pomeroy Station, "what should our Manifesto be? It should be this: to say to Society—*Beware*. We must be more diligent. We must fight with greater determination. We must be willing to use strong action. We must be unforgiving and stern toward those who—"

In the tiny bedroom in back he could hear a sleeping grunt from the baby, a steady snore from its mother. An expression of amused contempt crossed his face for a moment. He glanced at his gold wristwatch, saw it was almost ten o'clock. He hid his masterpiece carefully away in his knapsack, put it under the mattress of the sagging old sofa, snapped off the light, shucked off his clothes, lay down and drew a scratchy old army blanket up to his chin.

Serene, untroubled, soothed by an absolute and absolutely sustaining conviction, he was instantly asleep.

7

The next few days went fast for the Court and its member-designate. In the marble edifice where it could be said, as the late Associate Justice Van Devanter once did say, "We look like nine black beetles in the Temple of Karnak," the term began to move into high gear as it neared its finish. Of the approximately 5,000 cases that had come up to them since last October, more than 4,300 had already been disposed of. By diligent overtime and ruthless selection, they had managed to winnow the number granted certiorari to 203, some few major, most relatively minor, but all bearing on some point of clarification or precedent. Now they were down to a handful. The end was in sight.

They were able to congratulate themselves, as they often rather smugly did, that despite the steady growth in the number of cases in recent years, it still took only 9 Justices and a staff of no more than 350 to run their entire co-equal branch of the government, whereas the Executive bureaucracy remained well over 3,500,000 and in the Legislative Branch the 100 Senators and 435 Representatives felt they had to have more than 50,000 staff members to assist them.

The Supreme Court was a tidy operation and the Chief and his sister and brethren prided themselves upon the fact and took pains to see that it remained so. "You have to have space to think in this job," Clem Wallenberg put it; and they surrounded themselves with it and preserved it jealously. Small, concentrated, powerful: they felt their impressively small size was part of their impressively enormous authority. *Multum in parvo*—much in little. It was a nice feeling.

So things moved forward briskly at the Court toward the conclusion of the term. A block away along First Street, in the Everett McKinley Dirkson Senate Office Building, the Senate Judiciary Committee also moved forward with its hearings on the nomination of Taylor Barbour of California to be Associate Justice. The chairman, Senator Henry Randall of Virginia, started things off with a courtly and emphatic endorsement, echoed by equally glowing statements from four of his colleagues and approving nods from several others. The burden of proof was obviously going to be on Tay's opponents, if any. In the face of his evident good faith and integrity they did not get very far.

It was established very quickly that he was not a "Cadillac liberal," nor a "headline liberal" nor a full-page-ad-in-the-New-York-*Times* liberal: he was the genuine article, going back philosophically to Woodrow Wilson, Hiram Johnson, the La Follettes, Burton K. Wheeler, Justices Holmes, Brandeis, Cardozo, Douglas—the "old-fashioned" liberalism rooted in the very fabric of American democracy, springing from the earth of the plains and the slums of the cities. No opposing testimony was able to dim this fact.

The hearings concluded after three days and twenty-three witnesses, eighteen of whom were favorable and only five opposed—and they, as Senator Randall remarked to him in a wry private comment, "from the outer fringes of anti-abortion, female subjugation and Love God, God damn you." Tay used the occasion to put his personal and public philosophy on the record in words no one could misunderstand or misinterpret.

"I believe in the law," he told the friendly committee and overflowing Senate Caucus Room audience. "In fact, I love the law . . .

"I have given a lot of thought in the past three days as to where a truly dedicated Justice of the United States Supreme Court should stand on all the many issues that come before him—or her—and it seems to me that the stand should be somewhere in the intelligent, balanced and reasonable middle. If one has to categorize me, as a few here have attempted, I suppose it is fair to say that I am 'liberal' in what I hope is the most reasonable and sensible meaning of that term.

"I would like—" he said, and paused. For some reason he was suddenly conscious of Cathy, seated behind him at the press table. They had greeted one another quite casually—perhaps too much so, on both sides—when he had entered the room this morning.

"I would like to give you my concept of what real liberalism is, and how a true liberal acts. Those are words which, like 'conservatism' and 'conservative,' in recent decades have become so debased by many people that they have become simply slogans, essentially meaningless. But there was an original and good meaning for all of them, and I hope I have always remained true, and always will remain true, to that original meaning.

"Within, that is, the American context. There are some forms of liberalism, or so-called liberalism, that are a long way from our generally mild home-grown variety. Them I condemn and oppose, always have and always will.

"It seems to me that American liberalism, in its truest and finest form, is a belief that society does have an obligation to assist the less fortunate; that it does have a responsibility in such areas as an adequate education; readily available, inexpensive health care; a floor under wages; the right of unions to organize and protect their members subject to the privileges and restraints of reasonable law—and that making people healthier, happier, more educated, more productive is only basic common sense and is the surest way to guarantee the security and growth of the nation.

"There are degrees in all these things, and I suppose the dividing line between 'liberals' and 'conservatives' probably comes, or should come, not on objectives but on degree. I am sure that basically all Americans believe in these things. It is only the question of how far and how fast government should go in trying to achieve them—or whether, in fact, government should intervene at all, but rather should leave their achievement to the so-called 'natural laws' of a free society and a free economy.

"It is at that point, Mr. Chairman, that I part company with the more conservative of our conservative friends. I believe government has not only the right but the obligation to intervene, and I think its interventions, subject to common sense and common democracy, are good. I think that was decided once and for all in *McCulloch v. Maryland* in 1821, when the Marshall Court declared that the Constitution comes from the sovereign hand of the people and can, virtually without restriction, 'be adapted to the various crises of human affairs.'

"You remember the basic dicta:

" 'The government comes directly from the people.' It is 'a government of the people.' It 'represents all and acts for all.' It is 'supreme . . . and its laws form the supreme law of the land.' Since it is given powers to secure 'the happiness and prosperity of the nation' it 'must also be intrusted with ample means for their execution.' At the same time, 'The powers of government are limited,' and its limits 'are not to be transcended.' Yet these must not be overly restrictive: Congress has the power to perform the duties assigned to it 'in the manner most beneficial to the people.' If the end is legitimate, it lies within the scope of the Constitution, 'and all means which are appropriate, which are plainly adapted to that end, which are not prohibited, but consistent with the letter and spirit of the Constitution, are constitutional.'"

He paused, smiled and shook his head admiringly.

"John Marshall was a *very* clever man."

Henry Randall smiled back.

"You're no slouch yourself, Mr. Secretary. Anyone who can quote *McCulloch v. Maryland* with that exactitude—"

"Mr. Chairman," Tay said, "I have read and re-read that case so many times over the years, seeking support for my own convictions and the warrant for what I wanted to advocate and do both as private citizen and as public, that I could almost recite it backward in my sleep. I'm not so sure Chief Justice Marshall understood it as 'liberal' in the context in which we would use the word today, but that's the end effect . . .

"So I think the mandate for a traditional style of liberalism is well rooted, and I make no apologies for having adhered to it throughout my career. Mine is not a far-out liberalism: it is really quite a conservative liberalism, if I may state it so. But it *is* liberal, and I am not ashamed of it."

He sat back, pleasant, calm and self-possessed, graying, handsome and distinguished; already, in mind's eye, seeming to wear the flowing black robe. There was a heavy burst of applause, the hearing ended with handshakes all around. Henry Randall announced that the committee would go into closed session in five minutes to vote on the nomination, emerged smiling fifteen minutes later to report that they were recommending confirmation to the Senate by a vote of 13–3. Over on the Senate floor the Majority Leader announced that the final vote would come immediately after convening next afternoon. When it did it was 89–9. Some Supreme Court nominations had held their surprises. His, as Wally Flyte and Rupert Hemmelsford had accurately predicted, was not among them.

In fact, it was quite universally hailed, even by those journals that might have been expected to have misgivings. His supporters fell dutifully into line. The New York *Times,* the Washington *Post,* the Washington *Inquirer,* the Los Angeles *Times,* the Chicago *Sun-Times, Newsweek, Time,* most of the political columnists and TV commentators praised his character, his integrity, his fairness, his legal knowledge, the earnest and honest liberalism of his public career, his even temperament

which, the New York *Times* said, "ideally equips him for the high and
sober office to which he has been appointed." (Clem Wallenberg passed
a note to Wally Flyte when they were on the bench hearing arguments:
"I didn't know we were *that* sober." Wally shook his head in mock
reproof and the arguing lawyer, an earnest young man from Wisconsin
presenting his first case before the Court, interpreted it as a personal
reflection, flushed, lost his place and had to start his sentence all over
again.)

Even the more conservative columnists and commentators managed
to find a lot of good words to say.

"We don't altogether like Taylor Barbour's politics," one summed it
up, "but no one can deny his excellent character and likable personality. He is known to Washington as a good, able and honest man; and
he may yet turn out to be a far more middle-of-the-road Justice than his
supporters confidently assume. It would certainly not be the first time
this has happened on the Supreme Court."

Back in his office, after he had said farewell to the Labor Department's employees massed in the building's courtyard, he received in
rapid succession calls from the President, "Very pleased and confident
that you will do a great job in helping to keep the Court on the right
track," which he answered with noncommittal gratitude; from his
daughter, who squealed with excitement and shouted, "I love you,
Daddy! I think you are just the *greatest!*" to which he responded, "I
love you, too, baby. I'll try to make you proud of me," and was answered, "Oh, *Daddy!*"; from his wife, who said only a brief "Congratulations, Tay. I know how much you wanted it and I'm glad for your
sake that you've got it," to which he replied gravely, "Thank you,
Mary. I appreciate your good wishes"; from his parents and Erma Tillson, with whom he both laughed and cried; and, toward the end of another long and hectic day, a call to which he responded—how? He was
not altogether sure, thinking back a few minutes later. During the afternoon he had argued himself so convincingly out of the hope that it
would come and had been so pleased when it finally did come that he
could not recall exactly how he did respond in the first few moments.

"My *goodness,* you're a hard man to get through to," she said with a
laugh, not bothering to introduce herself, assuming that of course he
would know who it was. He did.

"Oh," he said stupidly. "Have you been trying?"

"I certainly have. I'm up in the Senate Periodical Gallery and I've
been trying to reach you ever since the vote. Everybody in the world
seems to be on your line. May I be the last to congratulate you?"

"Anytime," he said, beginning to recover a little but still in some pleasant confusion. "Anytime. How nice of you to think of me."

"For heaven's sake," she said with a chuckle. "How could I not think of you? You're the biggest news in Washington today. We don't get a new member of the Court every day, particularly not such a fine, noble, upright—"

"All right, now," he said, feeling himself in control again and beginning to adopt an equally light tone, "let's have a little respect for your elders, if you please."

"Not so elder," she said, and for a second the lightness slipped a little. "Not so elder at all. Anyway, I think it's just great. I know how much you've wanted it, and I think it's just great that you've got it. Not that there was ever any doubt, but I know what it means to you and I know how pleased you and your family must be."

"They're delighted," he said, and he knew her call really was prompted by genuine goodwill when she let it pass and did not immediately inquire, "Including your wife?" This was not a call from Cathy Corny the Demon Reporter, he told himself wryly, but with an inescapable little thrill of excitement. This was Cathy Corning the—what? He decided rapidly that he would be very well advised to settle for "friend" and let it go at that.

"So what have you been up to since I saw you last?" he inquired, making his voice more impersonal.

"Exactly one week, two days, nine hours and twenty-one minutes ago," she said with a little laugh that was not so impersonal. "Haven't you been keeping track? I have."

"Certainly," he said with mock gravity, "but I make it one week, two days, nine hours and *twenty-seven* minutes. It seems like forever."

She laughed again.

"I'll bet. I'll bet you haven't thought of me once in the past week, with all that's been going on."

"Oh yes I have," he said quickly; too quickly, probably, because her tone became instantly more serious.

"So have I. Really. I'm not kidding you. I've thought about you quite a lot."

He hesitated for a second—thought bleakly, *What else is there?*— rushed on.

"It's been quite constant with me. I've wondered how you were coming with the interview—"

"Is that all?" she interrupted, sounding quite dismayed. He sighed inwardly and plunged ahead.

"No, that isn't all."

"What else have you thought?"

"Nothing I'm going to discuss on the telephone," he said with a sudden tartness.

"I'm sorry," she said, sounding instantly contrite. "I won't bother you any more. I just wanted to tell you how much I—"

"No!" he said sharply. "Wait a minute! There must be some other—" His voice trailed away. There was a pause.

"I live," she said evenly, "on Fifth Street Northeast near the corner of Fifth and Stanton Square. It's a little yellow house, 168 years old, neat, I like to think, with a picket fence, boxwood in front and a red-and-green fanlight over the door. I will be there in an hour. You could stop by for a drink and we could talk."

"We could," he said cautiously, a last passing bow to what he knew was best, a farewell nod to common sense.

"We could," she echoed in the same level tone.

"*Yes,*" he agreed suddenly. "We could."

In South Carolina Earle Holgren made his last run of the day, stopped once more to survey the work at Pomeroy Station, now rushing to completion on a twenty-four-hour schedule, checked once more at his secret cave. Then he turned in the gathering dusk and jogged back down the winding mountain road to his secluded cabin, his bothersome woman and hampering child, his sagging desk, his lengthening manifesto and his fierce, misshapen dreams.

8

His parents and Erma Tillson were there, Janie was there, Sarah and Sue-Ann; Mary, dressed in a severe black dress with a single rose, face composed, expressionless; and in the special box reserved for the President, to the right of the bench as the overflow audience of press and public faced it, the President himself and the new Associate Justice: two days after the Senate vote, two days after his visit to the house on Fifth Street.

Looking a little tense, a little pale, not meeting his eyes but otherwise also perfectly composed, Cathy sat facing straight ahead in the regular media section to the public's left.

It was exactly 10 A.M. when the bell rang, the red velvet curtains parted, the Marshal rapped his gavel, the President, Tay and the audience rose to their feet and the Justices in their solemn phalanx stepped through the red velvet curtain and took their places at their simple black leather rocking chairs.

The Marshal, a tall young Japanese-American who five years ago had been one of Justice Ullstein's brightest law clerks, cried out the traditional words in a firm, commanding voice:

"Oyez, Oyez! All persons having business before the Honorable the Supreme Court of the United States are admonished to draw near and give their attention, for the Court is now sitting. God save the United States and this Honorable Court!"

Duncan Elphinstone and his colleagues took their seats, with a rustle

and murmur the audience followed suit. He glanced thoughtfully out
upon them for a second, then smiled as he turned to the President.

"We are greatly honored this day by the presence of the President of
the United States, who I understand wishes to break precedent just a
trifle. The Court"—his smile broadened—"thinks this can safely be done.
Mr. President—?"

"Mr. Chief Justice," the President said with a bow and a smile,
"Your Honors. It is indeed my pleasant duty to present to you this day
the Honorable Taylor Barbour. I wish to thank you, Mr. Chief Justice,
for permitting me to usurp your prerogative and administer the Constitutional oath to an appointee of whom I am very proud."

He left his box and stepped forward, Tay following, into the well of
the Court directly below the Chief Justice. The Clerk handed him the
worn and much-thumbed Bible that Frank Barbour had brought from
the ranch in Salinas Valley, where it had occupied an honored place in
the living room ever since it had crossed the plains with Tay's great-
great-grandfather in 1851. The President took it, held it in his left hand
and raised his right.

"Place your left hand on the Bible, raise your right hand and repeat
after me," he instructed. " 'I, Taylor Barbour—' "

"I, Taylor Barbour," Tay said in a voice that trembled only slightly
with the realization that it had all come true at last; and repeated phrase
by phrase the oath required of all Americans taking civil or military position with the government of the United States, excepting only the
President, whose oath, somewhat broader, requires him to "protect,
preserve, and defend" the Constitution:

"I, Taylor Barbour, do solemnly swear that I will support and defend
the Constitution of the United States against all enemies, foreign and
domestic; that I will bear true faith and allegiance to the same; that I
take this obligation freely, without any mental reservation or purpose of
evasion; and that I will well and faithfully discharge the duties of the
office on which I am about to enter. So help me God."

"Mr. Chief Justice, Your Honors," the President said; bowed to
them, handed the Bible to Tay, shook his hand, gave his arm a friendly
squeeze; nodded to the Secret Servicemen seated along the main aisle,
entered the protective square they formed immediately for him and
walked quickly out. The Elph smiled down upon his new associate.

"It is now *my* pleasant duty," he said, "to administer the Judicial
oath. If you will place your left hand on the Bible, Justice, raise your
right hand and repeat after me—"

And in a voice now completely steady, Tay complied:

"I, Taylor Barbour, do solemnly swear that I will administer justice without respect to persons, and do equal right to the poor and to the rich, and that I will faithfully and impartially discharge and perform all the duties incumbent upon me as an Associate Justice of the Supreme Court of the United States, according to the best of my abilities and understanding, agreeably to the Constitution and laws of the United States. So help me God."

"Congratulations, Justice," Duncan Elphinstone said with a broad and fatherly smile. "You can't escape us now. This Court," he added quickly, "will now stand in informal adjournment for ten minutes to permit applause, congratulations, hand shaking, and other forms of jubilation appropriate to the swearing-in of Justice Barbour."

And he rapped his gavel sharply, put it down, stood up and led the applause which, never permitted in the Chamber save on such a rare occasion as this, now rose and filled the normally hushed and dignified high-ceilinged room.

Janie, tugging Mary by the hand, rushed up and kissed him; Mary did too, in a coolly dutiful way. He was very conscious of Cathy, caught her eye at one point, but she looked quickly away. The media, save for those regularly assigned to the Court, milled about and began to drift out. Helen Barbour laughed and cried and kissed him all at the same time. Frank Barbour shook Tay's hands in both of his, beamed and then gave Erma Tillson, whom the Barbours had brought with them from California as their guest, an exuberant hug.

"We certainly started something, didn't we, Erma?" he asked. She smiled, a tiny birdlike person now, almost a ghost from the past, who had lived long enough to see one of her most cherished dreams come true.

"Yes, sir, Frank," she agreed with a wink at Tay and Helen which Frank saw, grinned at and returned, "we certainly did, didn't we?"

"Justice!" the Chief called down. "Tay! Come on up here. You have friends here who want to congratulate you too, you know; and Court resumes in five minutes. And you're on it now. So hike up here!"

"Yes, sir!" he said with a bow and mock salute, seeing all their smiling faces beaming down upon him. "I'll be right there."

He gave his mother and Erma final kisses and hugs, shook his father's hand again, kissed Janie and Mary once more, waved to the still standing, eagerly watching audience. Out of the corner of his eye he saw Cathy picking up her coat and purse. *Don't go!* he cried inside. *My first day!* But she obviously thought it best, because she turned away without looking at him again and started toward the huge oaken doors giving onto the Great Hall. Just before she got to them she turned back for just a second: her eyes met his in the faintest of salutes. Then she turned and was gone. Behind him at the bench, Moss looked started for the smallest second. It was long enough for Mary to catch his expression, glance at him and hold his glance with a deliberately quizzical look until he turned almost angrily away and said something innocuously jocular to Wally Flyte.

In a moment Tay had come up the short flight of steps and joined them. The next minutes passed quickly with a kiss from Mary-Hannah, hearty handshakes from the Chief and his new Associates. A law clerk respectfully murmured his name. He turned and found her holding out a black robe draped over both arms. With a smile he took it; with a smile she helped him put it on. Duncan Elphinstone stepped to the bench, the Marshal raised his gavel and brought it down. An immediate respectful silence fell, during which audience and Justices rustled back into their seats. Tay found his where it is for the most junior, to the far left of the Chief, at the end of the line. He took it, drew a deep breath and smiled out upon the members of his family and the now silent and respectful audience. The one he wanted to see was no longer there, but the world, as represented by the Chamber, was watching Taylor Barbour.

It saw a dignified man who looked the part because he had always been destined for the part.

I will be good, he promised the world. *I will administer justice without respect to persons, and do equal right to the poor and to the rich.*

"The Court—the full Court," the Chief said with a note of pride in his voice, "is now in session. We have presently before us *Steiner v. Michigan.* Counsel, you may proceed whenever you are ready."

And John Marshall's institution, being once again complete, leaned forward attentively and proceeded on its patient, traditional way.

In the thoughts going through Tay's mind at that moment, Cathy and the Court were inextricably mixed. Memories of the meeting at the house on Fifth Street commingled with the many impressions he had accumulated over the years of the awesome body of which he was now a member. For a time, inevitably, the Court predominated; insistently and not to be denied, the episode of two days ago came back. Sometime, he suspected with a moody foreboding, the two would have to be reconciled.

He was glad the time was not now, for he did not know at that moment how it could possibly be done.

Almost furtively he glanced along the row of attentive faces beside him: the Chief Justice, neat little figure upright and dignified, staring down impassively at counsel for Steiner; Justice Flyte, leaning forward chin on hand, following every word; Justice Wallenberg slumped back in his chair, twiddling a pencil in his fingers, deceptively casual, ready to pounce; Justice Ullstein, hands folded in front of him, leaning forward with earnest attention; Justice McIntosh, face pleasant but communicating nothing to the pleader at the bar, making a note from time to time on the yellow legal pad on the desk before her; Justice Hemmelsford, eyebrows twitching automatically now and then, half-smile on lips that might at any moment open to utter some devastating comment to confuse and confound the advocate; Justice Demsted, chin also on hand, handsome face earnest and intent; Justice Pomeroy, expression revealing nothing, nodding from time to time in a manner the lawyer took to be supportive but might find out at any moment was not.

How different they were, yet essentially, he supposed, how much the same as the five who were serving in February 1801, when President John Adams, having failed to persuade John Jay to return to the Chief Justiceship he had resigned six years before in the earliest days of the Court's shaky and as yet undefined power, turned to his Secretary of State, John Marshall, and persuaded him to serve.

John Marshall, history showed, had not been at all reluctant, for he had been imbued from the first, apparently, with the same fierce reverence for the Constitution and desire to see it work that now infused his distant inheritors almost two hundred years later. Before he took his seat as Chief Justice on February 4, 1801, he had been a lawyer in his native Virginia, then Congressman from Virginia, then Secretary of State. Much later William Wirt, one of the most brilliant lawyers of the early Republic, summed up the Chief Justice who served thirty-four years and almost single-handedly created the Court as Tay and his country now knew it.

"Marshall's maxim," Wirt said, "seems always to have been, 'Aim exclusively at *Strength*.'" And Marshall himself, long before the great decisions that were to define and sanctify in law both the great powers of the federal government and the great powers of the Court, argued for the new Constitution in the Virginia ratifying convention of 1788 with the words, "Why then hesitate to trust the General Government? The object of our inquiry is—*is the power necessary—and is it guarded?*"

He had given a resounding and unshakable *Yes* to the first question; and despite the hatred, annoyance and constant opposition of his cousin Jefferson, he had determined—and got away with it—that the answer to the second should be a *Yes* fully as resounding and unshakable.

Altogether, as most lawyers conceded and as nearly all subsequent Justices of the Supreme Court recognized gratefully, an amazing and remarkable man, who even more than Jefferson and the other Presidents he served with and outlasted in the thirty-four years from 1801 to 1835, placed the stamp of his personal ideals, beliefs and convictions upon the American government.

The great cases thundered down the years in Tay's memory as they did in that of every lawyer who ever studied the Court:

—*Marbury v. Madison,* 1803: Marbury, a justice of the peace in the District of Columbia, had been appointed by outgoing President John Adams but denied his appointment by incoming President Thomas Jefferson. He sued Madison, Secretary of State, demanding his commission. John Marshall used the case to establish the right of the Court to declare acts of the government unconstitutional. First he threw a sop to his cousin by ruling that the withholding of Marbury's commission was legal; then he skillfully cut the ground out from under his cousin by going on to state that the law under which Congress gave the Court jurisdiction in the case exceeded the Court's original powers as stated in the Constitution, and therefore was itself unconstitutional—*as decided by the Supreme Court,* which, Marshall asserted, had the right to determine such constitutionality or unconstitutionality. It was a masterpiece of yes-and-no—or, rather, no-and-yes. From it the Court emerged, almost behind the President's back, as the arbiter of the Constitution. The dislike between the cousins grew, but the Chief Justice had claimed his ground and the President, frustrated and angry, could not decide how to dislodge him. And although Andrew Jackson was to remark spitefully in a relatively minor case years later, "John Marshall has made his decision, now let him enforce it," the Court's prestige survived and it went right on successfully exercising the power John Marshall had blandly and designedly appropriated for it.

—*United States v. Burr,* 1807: Jefferson's renegade former Vice President, Aaron Burr, was accused of treason. Burr demanded that a subpoena be issued against the President, requiring him to appear and produce his evidence against his former Vice President. Marshall, sitting as Circuit Justice for the Fifth Circuit in Richmond, upheld the request and issued the subpoena. Jefferson, furious, insisted that the President was not subject to such action. Marshall backed down to the extent that he ruled that the President's attorneys might examine the evidence and withhold anything they deemed vital to national security. Jefferson backed down by instructing his attorneys to do this, though he himself still refused to appear. Marshall felt he had vindicated his position that all citizens, no matter their station, were equally subject to the law. Jefferson, the presumed democrat, felt he had vindicated his position that the President was above the law and could defy the mandates of the courts. Both cousins realized they could push their contest no further without shattering forever the delicate balances of the American system as it then existed. It was not until 1974 that the Supreme Court ruled 8–0 that Richard Nixon must produce his Watergate tapes. One hundred sixty-seven years after *United States v. Burr,* John Marshall won his battle with his cousin. The law finally, in a much stronger nation and a much different climate, was declared equally applicable to all —but only then, perhaps, because of the personal nature of the President, which was far different from that of Thomas Jefferson.

—*McCulloch v. Maryland,* 1816: the opinion to which Tay had paid tribute in his testimony before the Senate Judiciary Committee in which a Marshall-dominated majority affirmed the right of the federal government to intervene where necessary in discharge of its constitutional obligation to secure the welfare and happiness of the citizenry.

—*Trustees of Dartmouth College v. Woodward,* 1819: which established conclusively that acts of a state are subordinate to those of the national government. The legislature of New Hampshire had passed laws against Dartmouth College. The decision held that these were repugnant to the Constitution of the United States. They "must, therefore, be reversed."

—*Gibbons v. Ogden,* 1824: which asserted the authority of Congress over interstate commerce and completed the greater roster of the Marshall cases.

Such enormous powers, created almost single-handedly by one supremely shrewd and determined individual, inherited by nine fallible human beings. Again he glanced along the bench at his eight colleagues as *Steiner v. Michigan* concluded and argument of the next case began. "Although the Court is essentially judicial," Alexis de Tocqueville had written long ago, "its prerogatives are almost entirely political. Its sole object is to enforce the execution of the laws of the Union . . ." And, prescient, wise and foresighted as always, he had concluded concerning its members that, "Their power is enormous, but it is the power of public opinion. They are all-powerful as long as the people respect the law; they would be impotent against popular neglect or contempt of the law."

And that possibility, in this unhappy time of raging crimes, everspreading violence and a citizenry increasingly restless and disposed to take the law into its own hands, was the possibility they faced now:

"popular neglect or contempt of the law." Under John Marshall they had survived the opposition of Presidents and the objections of the states. Under Warren Burger they had survived the willful obstructions of a President and finally made the law supreme over even Presidents. But what would they do if the great mass of the citizenry ever turned against them? If contempt of the law became, as it now threatened to become, a way of life not only for those who broke it but for those who felt they were defending it? If the center did not hold, and the growth of anarchy outstripped almost two hundred years of careful, patient building of the walls that held back the night?

He shivered suddenly and became aware that from the other end of the bench Moss was watching him with a casual but speculative glance. It swung away. He was left puzzled and disturbed. What was the matter with Moss? Did he know? Could he possibly—?

But it was not possible. True, Moss had seen him after he left his office in the Labor Department that day for the last time, but it had been only the most fleeting, casual glimpse . . .

His secretary had departed at five, he had remained until six cleaning away the few remaining personal items from his desk: it made a good excuse for leaving when the building was virtually deserted. Only the night guard, a personal friend from many late hours during labor troubles, saw him go.

"Good night—Mr. Justice," he had said with a broad grin.

"Good-bye," Tay had corrected. "I'm afraid this is it, Robinson."

"We sure hope you'll come back to see us," Robinson said. "Won't be the same without you. But we know you'll be good up there on the Court, too."

"I'll do my best," he promised, holding out his hand.

"You can't do any less," Robinson said, giving him a firm shake. "It just isn't in you to do any less than your best—Mr. Justice."

He smiled.

"I hope you're right, Robinson. I'll try."

"You do that," Robinson said, bowing him into the elevator to the garage with a flourish. "You just can't go wrong. We *know* it!"

But what would Robinson and the rest of the Department have said, he wondered as he got in his car, took a deep breath and started up the Hill toward Fifth Street, if they had known he was sneaking out, like a typical Washington cliché, for a rendezvous of whose ultimate outcome he did not have the slightest doubt?

What would they have thought if they had known that, in spite of many opportunities over the years, this was truly the very first time since his marriage that a strong code of personal honor and public duty had cracked enough to permit such an event? Some, no doubt, would have been astounded that it happened at all. Others would have been humorously contemptuous that it had not happened a hundred times, so numerous were the opportunities in the capital's ever-shifting, politically mobile population.

He reflected with a sudden impatience that it really did not matter what they would have thought: all that was important to him was what Taylor Barbour thought. And that, he had to admit with enough objectivity remaining to prompt a wry smile, was confused at best.

Some interior exchange had gone on during their interview, an increasingly intimate mutual appreciation that had surfaced during their telephone conversation earlier this afternoon. This had been only the second time they had talked, he reminded himself; things had no right to hurtle forward so fast. Yet the fact was that they had. Why? He could not have said, unless it was simply the accumulation of all his frustrations and unhappiness with Mary, seeking whatever outlet was available, taking the first that came along.

Yet in this he found he was genuinely afraid that he was being unfair to Cathy. He supposed many men in his situation were not that concerned about it. But his curse, as he had recognized early in life, was fair-mindedness. It was great for a public servant, splendid for a judge, but he told himself ruefully that it could certainly raise hell with one's personal life. Much simpler to be uncaring, egocentric, ruthlessly selfish and cold-blooded: then you didn't see both sides and find yourself in danger of becoming paralyzed by it. Not that he was, obviously, for here he was driving up the Hill in the soft May evening amid the still steady stream of traffic homebound to suburban Washington and the Maryland suburbs south along the Potomac. But it was not an easy journey for a decent and fair-minded man.

It challenged, as he realized, his concept of himself.

Particularly did it challenge what he had become over the years, a genuinely distinguished public servant; and what he was now, the newest member of the highest and most unusual tribunal in his own country and possibly the world. Did other public servants do this sort of thing? Yes, there had been examples during his years in Washington: but not Taylor Barbour. Had other Justices done this sort of thing in the Court's long history? Perhaps, but not Taylor Barbour. Why, then, was Taylor Barbour doing it?

He shook his head angrily, and drove steadily forward with patient skill through the slow-moving traffic. As he stopped at the light at the

corner of the Dirksen Office Building, someone honked sharply twice.
He glanced to his right toward the Court and saw Moss waving from his
dark blue Lincoln Continental. Tay waved back. Moss took both hands
from the wheel, lifted them in a puzzled gesture and gave him a humorously questioning look, as if to say, "What are you doing going out
Northeast? You live in Georgetown." Tay smiled and shook his head,
expression noncommittal: let Moss speculate. He thought uncomfortably now that maybe Moss had. Maybe that accounted for the expression Tay had just intercepted.

His thoughts returned momentarily to the bench. An older lawyer
was arguing another case. It was almost eleven forty-five. Soon they
would be breaking for lunch. He wondered what he would say if Moss
approached him with it directly. It had better be convincing, he thought
unhappily, because Moss was a shrewd and intuitive man behind the
southern charm.

Ten minutes after leaving the Labor Department, though it seemed
more like an hour as the traffic slowed him down, he had arrived at
Stanton Square and Fifth Street. There indeed was a little yellow
house, "neat, I like to think," a picket fence, boxwood, a red-and-green
fanlight over the door; no sign of life he could see at the moment. He
drove on half a block, found a space, parked and locked his car, walked
back under the trees that overarched the street, stepping carefully on
the uneven brick-paved sidewalk, probably as old as the 168 years she
had mentioned for the house.

He came to the neat little gate in the picket fence, opened it, looking
neither left nor right, walked up to the high front stoop; paused, automatically adjusted his tie, touched the bell. He heard it chime melo-
diously deep in the house, expected to hear children call. Instead a dog
yapped sharply twice and was evidently hushed. Heels clicked along the
hall. He felt a sudden ridiculous panic, took another deep breath in an
attempt to alleviate it. She opened the door, smiled, held out her hand,
drew him in. They stepped apart as she closed the door and stood for a
moment staring at one another.

"You did it," she said, trying to sound lightly humorous, not quite
making it. "I didn't think you would."

"I said I would, didn't I?"

"Oh, yes. Anybody can say they'll do something. Not everybody does
it."

"I do," he said gravely.

"I know," she said with a little gurgle of laughter, sounding genuinely amused this time. "You're Taylor Barbour. You keep your word because-you-are-a-good-boy."

"Not particularly, at this moment," he said with a sudden self-contempt that made her look genuinely concerned and half reach out for his hand, which he kept rigidly at his side.

"I'm sorry," she said after a second. "I only invited you for a drink. If you'd feel better about it, we can forget it and you can go right now." She turned and moved toward the tiny old-fashioned parlor, blinds down, that faced on the street. He followed her, took the antique rocking chair she indicated. She took a seat facing him on a horsehair sofa that must have gone back to Abe Lincoln's day.

"I didn't mean that as harshly as it sounded," she said. "I'm very happy to have you here. I just meant that if it was going to cause too many problems—"

"How can it not cause problems?"

"Then why—" she began, almost desperately.

"Because," he said quietly, "I want to. Do you?"

"What?" she asked, again sounding halfway between humor and desperation. "Have a drink? Yes, I'd like a drink. What will you have?"

"Is that all you asked me here for?" he inquired, face somber, eyes holding hers with level candor. "If so, I'll have a light gin and tonic, please." He smiled suddenly. "And we will Chat," he added, giving it an ironic capital.

"Well, heavens!" she said with a shaky little laugh. "At least we can start that way, can't we? We hardly know each other, after all."

"Well enough," he pointed out, "for you to invite me, and I to come. Where are your children?"

"Visiting friends for dinner. They won't be back until nine or so."

"Did you arrange that?"

"Who cares?" she demanded with a little blaze of anger. "Do you want them here? Are you missing something without them?"

His eyes dropped before her challenging gaze.

"I'm glad they're not here," he said quietly.

"All right, then! I'm going to get our drinks!"

"All right, then!" he said, mimicking. "Get them!"

"All right!" she said, and for the first time they exchanged tentative, but genuine, laughter. "This is no time to be stuffy."

"Get the drinks," he ordered. "I'll wait."

"You'd better," she said, rising and going into the hall toward the kitchen.

I will, he thought; *though God knows what I'm getting into. But I can't seem to stop. Not,* he added honestly to himself, *that I want to.*

"There," she said, returning in a couple of minutes, handing his glass to him. "I made it light, as you requested."

"Cheers."

"Cheers. I thought you did very well in the Senate."

"I was pleased," he said. "It was a very comfortable vote."

"Eighty-nine to nine is more than comfortable, it's overwhelming. I knew you had a good reputation but I didn't realize quite how awesome it must be to a lot of people."

"Not including you," he suggested. She started to smile, then turned quite serious.

"Oh, yes, I'm impressed. I'm *very* impressed."

"Why should you be?" he inquired with a return of bitterness. "I'm here behind the world's back, cheating on my wife—"

She flinched as though he had slapped her; responded very quietly, "You assume a great deal very fast. What makes you so sure?"

"Shouldn't I be, Cathy Corny?" he inquired, almost angrily. "Hasn't it been implicit almost from the beginning? Why was I invited here?"

"You shouldn't be so honest," she suggested. "Someday it may get you in trouble."

"It may get me in trouble right now," he said, staring into some far distance she could not fathom.

"If you don't want it to," she said, still quietly, "why did you come?"

He shook his head angrily once again as if to clear it, took a deep swallow of his drink, looked back at her.

"Because I like you," he said harshly.

For a second a gleam of amusement came into her eyes; she almost laughed.

"That's nice. You express it with great tact. You're making this a very romantic moment, you know."

"Well—" he said; and suddenly, for some reason he could not understand, he too felt close to laughter; and in a second gave way to it. She joined him and for several moments they were helpless with it.

"You are so—*something,*" she said finally. "What a Don Juan! I think we'd better keep laughing. I'm not sure I can take any more of this as a serious proposition. Small letter *p.*"

"Cathy," he said, abruptly earnest again. "I *am* serious. Believe it or not, I've never done this before—"

"Believe it not," she interrupted crisply, "I have, but believe it or not, it's only happened twice in the six years since my divorce. Neither lasted long, and it didn't matter a damn either time. But if it helps your conscience any and will make it any easier for you, I'm a Genuine Fallen Woman, Noble Justice, and you needn't worry one little bit about your morals. You can blame it on me: it's all my fault." She laughed again, quite genuinely. "What in the world are we talking about, anyway? Where's the problem? It isn't going to happen anyway, at this rate. Why don't you go on home?"

And she got up, apparently quite composed and at ease, put down her half-emptied glass and started toward the hallway. It would have been an effective gesture except that she had to pass close to him to accomplish it and her expression suddenly shattered into something quite different as she approached his chair.

He caught her hand and placed it against his cheek.

"I talk too much," he said humbly.

"Yes, you do," she said, lightly touching his head with her other hand. "But perhaps we can get you over that."

And so they had, and very happily: more happily than he could ever remember with Mary, even when they were first married. The remembrance brought a sudden stirring that caused him to shift uneasily in his chair and think: *Good Lord, here I am on the Supreme Court listening to arguments and—* He could feel himself actually blushing, and to cover it cleared his throat quickly and bent forward over his legal pad to make a note which he found later did not make much sense. But it sufficed—he thought, though when he looked up he caught Moss' contemplative glance again. He smiled and winked companionably. Moss perforce winked back. The others were listening intently to the argument and paid no attention. He too tried to concentrate, but the memories of that night, which he knew had changed his life fundamentally forever, could not be prevented.

He had left shortly before eight, not knowing what his reception would be at home and for the moment not really caring, so euphoric was his mood. He had never been, he realized, so genuinely happy before—so completely at peace with himself and the world in every way. There had been occasions when he had been quite happy physically but mentally restless; other occasions everything had seemed perfect when considered intellectually but the physical expression had not been quite right. With Cathy, everything was right: he was fully and completely happy and his doubts and hesitations, which earlier had appeared so important, seemed to be utterly and entirely gone. Until he got to Georgetown. And there, of course, conscience came back a hundredfold, as he had suspected, and dreaded, that it would.

Yet it was his own inward doing, for Mary had made no particular comment. She seemed uninterested in where he had been, having earlier accepted without demur his explanation that he would be at the Labor Department "cleaning out my things." Months ago, when he had begun to work late on the strikes, she had accepted the fact that he might often be arriving late. At first she had been suspicious, called him on his private line that remained open after the switchboard closed; at first made excuses for this, then made none. "Just checking up on you," she had taken to saying matter-of-factly, and he always said, "Well, I'm here." After a time she stopped doing even that, and presumably had not done so tonight, since there was no change in demeanor or attitude that he could see. Yet, watching her and Janie covertly as Julia served the meal and they began silently eating, he could not believe that she did not sense something different in him. But if so she said nothing about it.

"Daddy," Janie said presently, "do you think you will enjoy the Court?"

"Yes, I do," he said, pleased with the chance to get away momentarily from his thoughts. "I think it's going to be very new and exciting."

"I imagine," Mary said, making what appeared to be a genuine attempt to join in, "that it will take you a few days to really become accustomed to it."

"Justice Demsted told me it took him two years. Justice McIntosh said it took her even longer. The word they both used was 'awe'—their 'awe' of the Court. I can understand that. It is an awesome institution."

"Are the Justices nice?" Janie inquired.

"They seem to be," he said. "Very."

"Who do you like best?" she asked. "Aside from Uncle Moss, that is?"

"Yes," Mary said dryly.

"I really like all of them, so far," he said, ignoring it. "Justice Hemmelsford and I have never really seen eye to eye on things, but I think he's going to be all right as a colleague. And the others seem very pleasant. Certainly they all went out of their way today to make me feel at home. I couldn't ask for a more cordial welcome. The Chief Justice, incidentally, is giving a little dinner party at the Court Friday night, Mary, and would like us to attend."

"That's only three days away—" she began.

"Do you have anything on?" he interrupted, more sharply than he intended, but driven by nerves and guilt, he supposed. Anyway, he seemed unable to control it.

"I'll have to see—" she began.

"You know," he said shortly. "If you do, cancel it. This is virtually a command performance and I want your company."

"Would you go without me?" she inquired. He thought she was a little taken aback by his unusually harsh tone.

"It's in my honor, I understand. Indeed I would. But I think you can find your way clear, can't you?"

"Yes," she said in a martyred tone. "I suppose so."

"Good."

"Do I get to go?" Janie asked, and made a face. "Since I can't go with Sarah. It's the same day, isn't it?"

"Yes," he said. "Moss says the ceremony is at three P.M. and they hope to get away by five so that they can return here in time for the dinner. Yes, I don't see any reason why you can't go. I'll ask the Chief Justice."

"Really, Tay!" Mary said. "This is a dinner for adults. I assume. I don't see any reason why—"

"Because it's in my honor and she's my daughter," he responded sharply.

"Can't I do *anything?*" Janie demanded, abruptly close to tears. *Mr. Chief Justice and Your Honors,* he thought, *if you could only see your new Associate and his happy home now.*

"That seems to me a fair question, Mary," he said. "How do you answer it?"

"Actually," she said calmly, "I have been thinking about Sarah's invitation, and while I still think the value of it for Janie is decidedly questionable—"

"Oh, *Mommy!*" Janie said, face lighting up.

"—still," Mary went on calmly, "I think perhaps I was a little hasty in my decision. I think perhaps it was just reaction—you both were pressuring me so. On second thought and further reflection, I suppose it would be all right for Janie to go. The Pomeroys are still not my favorite people, but I suppose Janie wouldn't suffer any harm from their company. I can see it would be exciting for her."

"Oh, *Mommy!*" Janie said again, ecstastic. "Thank you, thank you!"

And she jumped up and ran around the table, almost upsetting Julia, who was just entering and exclaimed, "Ooops!" to give her mother a big hug and kiss. Mary received it with a little pat and a complacent "Thank you, darling."

"Thank you, Mary," he said gravely, thinking: it was ever thus, in bed or wherever—first the withholding and then the gracious conferral, reaping all kinds of gratitude and benefits therefrom. A mental image of Cathy, loving, unrestrained, generous, giving, rushed into his mind and was banished. Or he attempted to banish it. Without much success, he recognized with an inward guilt and sadness; but Mary, damn her, asked for it.

"May I go and call Sarah?" Janie asked, flushed and sparkling.

"Eat your pudding first," Mary said.

"I will!" Janie cried; rushed back to her seat, gulped it down in three enormous mouthfuls, yelled, "'Scuse me!" and dashed out and up the stairs to her room.

There was silence for a few moments.

"That was very generous of you," he observed dryly. "What did the Pomeroys do to suddenly refurbish themselves in your estimation?"

"Nothing," she said, almost indifferently. "I don't like the Pomeroys. It was just what I said. You and Janie were so *insistent*. I thought she needed a lesson in patience. And as her mother I thought it was my duty to give her one. It doesn't seem to have hurt her. She seems to like me just the same. Sorry, Tay."

"You are very pleasant," he said, folding his napkin carefully and placing it beside his place. "I suppose *I* should be very grateful also, that you are going to condescend to come to the Chief's dinner with me."

"'The Chief,'" she said. "How quickly you slip into the lingo. Yes, of course I'll go, although I find little Birdie a complete bore and the rest equally stimulating. Will Justice McIntosh wear her hockey boots?"

"I am not going to discuss the Court with you any further," he said, pushing back his chair and standing up, an expression of distaste on his face. "I wish you could be more enjoyable to be around but I suppose it's too late now. You make it hard for me to sympathize with you. I'd like to sympathize, if you really dislike the life here so much, but you make it very difficult."

"Maybe you should find someone else," she suggested, shooting him a sudden sharp glance that made his heart thump suddenly: *Does she suspect or is she just fishing?* Whichever, he had damned well better be calm.

He shook his head as though he could not believe it.

"Mary," he said with a fair show of patience, "shall we just stop all this discussion? It isn't getting us anywhere. I'm glad you're going to the

Chief's dinner with me. I'm glad you've decided to let Janie go to South Carolina. We both appreciate your consideration and generosity."

"Yes," she said. "Well. I just hope Janie will be all right."

"Why won't Janie be all right?" he demanded. "She'll be with Moss and Sue-Ann, she'll be perfectly safe. What could possibly happen to her?"

"There's been some talk of a demonstration, hasn't there?" she said with a sudden harshness that made him realize anew that, in her own particular difficult way, she did love their daughter. "The Pomeroys won't hurt her but someone else might."

He shook his head with an annoyed impatience.

"I'm sure there's no need to worry."

She gave him a somber look. Their eyes held. Then he straightened his shoulders as though to ward off hobgoblins and turned away.

"I'm going to the den to do some reading. Tomorrow is going to be a big day for us."

"Bigger than today?" she asked. He did not bother to respond but again came the paralyzing thought: Does she know? Instantly followed by the logical answer: *She can't possibly know anything.*

But a few moments later, deep in his old leather armchair, deciding to read once more through *Marbury v. Madison, McCulloch v. Maryland* and the rest of John Marshall's monumental decisions, the house on Fifth Street, Cathy and their time together—approximately an hour and a half—came rushing back. And with them, a growing sense of uneasiness, unworthiness and guilt.

How could he feel at ease with his new associates on the Court? How could he feel worthy of their respect and trust? How could he really rationalize his behavior, even though Mary made it easy for him with her attitude? How could he face her and Janie if the affair continued? How could he live with Taylor Barbour as Taylor Barbour had now become?

It damaged his concept of himself. For the first time, Taylor Barbour was not quite as perfect, perhaps, as Taylor Barbour liked to think he was. *And about time, too,* he supposed some of his critics might say if they ever found out. He resolved grimly that they never would. He also resolved that it would never happen again. But he was too honest for that: he knew it would . . .

And now the morning argument period was over, the red light glowed at the lectern, the pleader obediently concluded his final sentence. The Elph said, "Thank you, counsel. The Court will now recess for lunch. We will resume at one o'clock." The Marshal used his gavel, the Justices rose, turned and disappeared through the red velvet curtain, which closed behind them. Media and audience also rose, stretched, started slowly out, talking in muted, decorous voices. The stately room fell silent.

In the Robing Room, as they divested themselves of their official outerwear, Moss suggested casually, "How about a bite with me in my chambers, Tay?"

"Thanks, Moss," he said, ready with an excuse and relieved to have it, "but the Chief has invited me to join him, and I think maybe—"

"Oh, sure," Moss said cheerfully. "No problem. We'll do it sometime later in the next thirty years. How do you like it so far?"

"Are there words?" he asked, hoping he sounded light and humorous. "It's overwhelming."

"Yes, I saw you absorbing the impact," Moss said with a smile that did not entirely conceal an attentive interest. "You looked about ten thousand miles away."

Only five blocks, he thought wryly.

"It takes getting used to."

"I'm not entirely used to it yet," Moss said, "and I've been here quite a while now. Which is probably the way it should be . . ." And abruptly he asked, "Sure it's only the Court that's on your mind?"

"Yes," he said with what he hoped was his usual pleasant smile. "What else would there be?"

"I don't know," Moss said as they handed their robes to the clerks and stepped into the hall. "You looked *very* thoughtful. Where were you heading last night when I saw you?"

"Moss, old buddy," he said with a laugh, "curiosity not only killed the cat, it has also been known to seriously debilitate Supreme Court Justices." He added with an exaggerated emphasis, "I was on A Secret Errand of Great Importance."

"Oh," Moss said with a grin and a wink. "One of those."

"Absolutely," he said, continuing the laugh as they stood for a moment outside the Conference Room, which led on into the Chief's chambers. "Isn't that just like me?"

"No, it's not," Moss said, "which is why I'm going to be worried if it should turn out to be true."

"Well," he said shortly, "it won't. So forget it. It's nice of you to take Janie down to the dedication with you."

"O.K.," Moss said, dropping it as he always had when he came up against Tay's polite stone wall. "Right you are. Yes, Sarah jumped at the idea of inviting her and we thought it would be fun and an experience for them."

"You'll be back for the Chief's party, I understand."

Moss frowned.

"I'm not so sure now. They tell me they're running a little behind schedule down there these last few days. They're still planning to be ready by Friday, but now there's some talk of delaying the dedication until around six or even seven, maybe. In which case we won't make it back. But don't worry about Janie. We'll go on to Columbia, stay there for the night if we have to and come back Saturday. One way or another," he said cheerfully in a phrase they would remember in anguish later, "we'll get her back to you."

"I'm sure you will," he said, aware that the Chief's principal clerk was standing diffidently but determinedly at his elbow. "Yes?"

"The Chief's ready, Justice," the young lawyer said, "if you are. Excuse us, Justice?"

"Surely," Moss said. "Have a good meal. You'll enjoy getting to know Dunc, he's quite a guy. See you back on the bench at one."

"On the dot, I suppose," Tay said with a smile.

"You bet your bottom dollar, the dot. Right, Jim?"

"We try to adhere to a schedule," the clerk said with a smile. "It's easier that way. This way, Justice, if you please—"

Lunch passed pleasantly and quickly, the Chief's discussion of Court history banishing for a time other thoughts, and on the dot they were back on the bench.

"We come now," the Chief said after the Marshal had once more sounded the traditional call, "to *Magnuson v. Minnesota*. Counsel, you may proceed when you are ready."

And so the afternoon passed, and so the next two days passed; and on Friday, his office by now furnished pretty much as he wanted it, his favorite secretary from the Labor Department on the job, another about to be hired, one law clerk appointed and two more awaiting interviews, he was beginning to consider himself almost settled in.

He dropped Janie off at the Pomeroys' apartment at the Westchester when he drove to the Hill at 8:30 A.M. Flushed and excited, she kissed him good-bye with a fierce hug and "I love you, Daddy!"

"I love you, too, baby," he said, kissing Sue-Ann and Sarah also, shaking hands with Moss. "Take care of her and have fun, you all."

"We will," Sue-Ann said. "Don't you and Mary worry. We'll have fun."

"Mary's more worried than I am," he said, thoughtful for a moment. "She's afraid of some demonstration or something."

"Pooh!" Janie said. "I'm not worried. Are you, Uncle Moss?"

"Nope," he said firmly. "And don't you be either, pal. I'll call you if we decide to stay over. Everybody'll be at the Court, right? I'll call the dining room."

"Fine," Tay said. "You do that."

And so, not too long after 8 P.M., speaking in a voice Tay at first could hardly understand, he did.

9

Somewhere in the gentle twilight that had succeeded a golden afternoon a band was playing. He could hear it distantly, and the hum of voices. Cars passed him, grinding up the mountain road. A fair-sized crowd hiked amicably along around him, gossiping, chatting, feeling the excitement of the show to come. He spoke to no one, though his attitude was not hostile: on his face was a set, unchanging grin, so that his expression appeared to the casual glance to be good-natured, well-wishing, friendly. The lines of tension around the mouth were concealed by the heavy beard, the chilling coldness in the eyes was hidden by the grin and gleaming teeth. He estimated that by the time of the explosion it would be quite dark. It would be a pretty sight against the looming mountains and the trees. It would flower like a fountain. It would be a rose of death.

He liked that phrase: a rose of death. He said it over to himself quite a few times as he neared the natural amphitheater where Pomeroy Station Atomic Energy Installation stood in the glaring eye of a hundred floodlights. Temporary grandstands had been erected facing the entrance. A speaker's platform, back to the plant, faced the audience. Already the stands were almost full. He was among the last to arrive. But everything was in place. There was no hurry.

He neared the roped-off area where uniformed guards watched impassively as a small group, some students and some leftovers like himself from an earlier age, stomped and shouted, their placards proclaiming hatred, dire predictions and fear. He stopped for a moment and watched them with contempt. What children they were, even the older, graying ones.

He felt no community with them any more.

His methods were more direct.

They were window dressing.

He was reality.

Casually he stepped behind a tree, stood absolutely still while the remaining stragglers walked down the slight declivity and climbed into the stands facing the huge white plant. Somewhere down there were Janet and John Lennon Peacechild. He had told her to go on ahead, that he wanted to write a little on his "law study" before coming on.

"You'll miss the show," she said. "Why don't you come with us?"

"Because I don't want to come with you!"

"Well, all right!" she said. "All *right!* You sure are jumpy tonight. You'd think you were going to be part of the ceremony or something, you act so nervous."

"I'm not nervous!" he shouted, making John Lennon Peacechild hiccup and begin to cry.

"All *right,*" she repeated. "You don't have to shout. You do anything you damned well please. Johnny and I will go see the show, won't we, baby?"

"You do that," he said, "and the sooner the better. I'll be along in plenty of time."

"Plenty of time for what?" she asked, eyes narrowing speculatively, voice mocking. "What've you got in mind, mister? You going to jump up and make a speech, or something? We going to have a big demonstration, courtesy of Billy Ray? You going to start tearing down that plant block by block? We'll really have to be sure to get good seats for that, won't we, baby?"

"Listen," he said, trying to sound patient, doing a reasonably good job of it. "What makes you think I've got anything against that plant? I've never said anything, have I?"

"No, but you sure have nursed it along every day, step by step," she said shrewdly. "You've sure been interested. You've been running by that old plant every hour on the hour for the past three months like a mother hen, hovering around it and keeping an eye on everything. I expect you've even been writing about it in that old paper of yours you're always working on. Why don't you let me read that paper if it's so special?"

"*Don't you touch that paper!*" he hissed, standing up and raising his clenched right fist. She flinched and jumped back, John Lennon Peace-child letting out a startled squawk at the suddenness of her movement. *"You hear me? Don't you touch that paper!"*

"All right," she said, really frightened for once, or simulating it, he couldn't tell which: but she had damned well better be. *"All right!* I won't touch your precious damned paper! And don't you touch me or John Lennon Peacechild, either!"

"Get out!" he ordered in a disgusted tone. "Just get out! Go on to the plant and see the show!"

"Are you coming?" she asked, pausing at the door.

"I'll be there," he promised with a grim little smile. "Just you don't worry about *that!* I'll be there."

Now he stood looking down upon the scene, the jostling, excited crowd, the little group of demonstrators off to one side, the thin line of guards, the speakers' platform filling with dignitaries, the plant with its giant stacks like huge concrete lingams rising floodlit against the mountains and the rapidly darkening sky. Then he slipped quickly off to his right into deeper woods and made his way with a feral stealth like the predator he was, scarcely disturbing a branch or snapping a twig, to a vantage point off to the right from which he could still see the floodlit plant and hear, muffled but distinguishable enough for his purposes, the voices that now began to boom over the amplifiers.

Months ago he had traced the rusted tracks of the old mine railroad through the mountain and had found to his delight that the cave curved back to the face of the bluff overlooking the blind side of the plant, no more than five hundred feet away. There was another, smaller opening there which, like the other when he first found it, was completely covered with growth. He had not disturbed it until a week ago, when he had moved all of his equipment through the cave—narrowly avoiding a vertical shaft that appeared to be bottomless, about midway in the passage—to this secondary opening. Three nights ago, when there was no moon, he had persuaded Janet to drink herself into oblivion and then after midnight had returned. Waiting until the sleepy guards had convinced one another in loudly reassuring tones that there was, as usual, nothing about but skunks and raccoons and maybe a fox or two, he had made his final arrangements.

Now he took up his vigil and prepared to watch and wait, absolutely silent, absolutely still, until the moment he considered perfect arrived. It would not be very long. Press and television had been full of the dignitaries who would be there. The most fitting and suitable for his purpose would be at the lectern, he estimated, in just about forty-five minutes.

Above the enormous floodlit portico the words EQUAL JUSTICE
UNDER LAW stood sharp against the marble as the Chief and Birdie,
Tay and Mary arrived in the Chief's official limousine—the one piece of
federal folderol, as Duncan Elphinstone described it, that he permitted
himself.

When he first became Chief Justice he had made an unsuccessful attempt to abandon "the Chief's car," as being unsuited to the simple
dignity that he perceived, correctly, to be one of the Court's major
strengths with the country. He had been overruled, kindly but firmly, by
the Congress, whose leaders had their own official limousines and would
have been quite embarrassed if the Chief Justice suddenly appeared to
be more humble than they were. The Elph had threatened at first to
leave the limousine in the garage and never use it, but eventually
reached a practical compromise: he never used the vehicle except when
an occasion was truly official, or a social gathering of genuine importance to the general image of the Court and his own high office.

Tonight, he felt, was such an event. He had come to realize over the
years that a little pomp and circumstance never hurt anybody when
done with skill and at the right time. Tonight The Elph considered it
amply justified.

He also had no qualms about the expense item that would appear in
due course on the records of the Court when they went to the Appro-
priations committees of House and Senate. The committees were never
anything but friendly, solicitous and polite—most of their members were
lawyers themselves, suitably in awe of the Court and respectful of its
powers and position—but even so, the Justices liked to be very sure that
their tidy little operation never showed any waste or expenditure that
could be even remotely criticized as unwise or unnecessary.

"Living next door to the whorehouse," Wally Flyte had chuckled one
day with a gesture toward the Congress across the plaza, "we girls *have*
to be good."

This disrespectful and unexpected sentiment from an ex-Senator had
caused a startled guffaw in the Conference Room that had been heard
some distance down the corridor by several passing law clerks, two
secretaries and a guard; but the remark had never been repeated outside, so that not even the Justices' friends in Congress—and most of
them had many—knew what was meant when one of them would remark to another, "Living as we do—" and then go off into private

chuckles. It was one of their best-kept in-jokes and accurately summarized both their determination to preserve their own immaculate
image and their sternly hidden but nonetheless inescapable feeling of
superiority toward their co-equal branch of government.

Tonight, the Chief felt, was a suitable occasion for spending money
on all counts. It would be a good and deserved welcome for the new
Justice and Mary; it would be a tasteful and dignified occasion that
would receive respectful and worthwhile mention (not coverage, for this
was never permitted of the Court's social engagements) in the media;
and it would be a chance to bring them all together in a formal/infor-
mal meeting at the ending of the term. Along about Month Five, he had
observed, tempers could begin to become a little frayed and things
could get a bit itchy. Accordingly he had made it a practice to give
these little dinners at about six-week intervals. Together with the Wal-
lenbergs' brunches in good weather, and occasional at-homes held by
the others, they did quite a bit to keep things calm, even when in a legal
sense he and his brethren and sister often found themselves diverging,
as Justice Hemmelsford put it, "all ways from Sunday."

This term, the Chief Justice reflected as the limousine turned down
Massachusetts Avenue from Georgetown past the embassies, the division had been less than it had been in the past: but the day would
come. Regard Stinnet down in South Carolina had referred in a recent
television special to "the growing need for a self-help justice system in
the United States." The public response had been highly enthusiastic,
and greatly disturbing to the guardians of the law.

Duncan Elphinstone sighed and became aware that he was being addressed by his wife. She had apparently been addressing him for several moments because she now said, with a little laugh that sounded as
gently annoyed as Birdie ever allowed herself to be,

"Goodness, Dunc, but you're a long way away! Mary has asked three
times if you are going to have them plant tulips around the Court next
spring. Can't you hear her?"

The impatient thought: really, what an inane question for a Supreme
Court Justice's wife to ask, shot through his mind; followed by the real-
ization: what a genuinely *disinterested* question for a Supreme Court
Justice's wife to ask.

"Sorry," he said, "I *must* have been far away. Yes," he added politely, "I think we will have some tulips next year."

"I always think they're so *bright,*" Mary said, in her best social voice.

"Well, dear," Birdie said, "they *are* bright, aren't they? Always so
cheerful, *I* think."

"Do the bulbs come directly from Holland?" Mary asked, set on a safe course and, her husband knew from experience, trained and determined to stick with it.

"I really don't know," the Chief Justice said as his driver skillfully negotiated the Friday evening party-going traffic along Embassy Row. "The Architect of the Capital handles all our landscaping and gardening. I believe some of the bulbs do come from Holland, but I suspect they probably also have their own private stock by this time. After all," he added gently, "the building is fairly old."

"When was it built?" Mary took the opening and this time appeared to have hit the right note, for The Elph immediately brightened.

"Oh, we were built—*it* was built," he said earnestly, turning so that he could half-face them in the back seat, "between 1932 and 1935 as the result of persistent lobbying with Congress by one of my distinguished predecessors, former President and Chief Justice William Howard Taft. Before, you know, in the very first days, the Court met in the Royal Exchange Building in New York City. Then, when the government moved to Philadelphia, the Court met for a time in Independence Hall, and later in the Philadelphia city hall. As you know, the government moved permanently here to the District of Columbia in 1800 and we went through several changes of meeting place, first in the Capitol building, then for a while, after the British burned the Capitol in the War of 1812, in several private homes. After that we went back to the Capitol and from 1819 to 1860 we were in what is now the restored 'Old Supreme Court Chamber' they show the tourists over there. When the Senate moved from its original chamber, now shown as the 'Old Senate Chamber,' where all the great pre-Civil War debates were held, we moved to that room and stayed until Bill Taft decided it was about time we had our own quarters and lobbied successfully for them. The building, Number One First Street, Northeast, was dedicated on October 13, 1935, by Chief Justice Charles Evans Hughes, who said, 'The Republic endures and this is the symbol of its faith.' . . . Let us hope," he added with a rather bleak humor, "that both are still true."

"Oh, I think they are," Mary said politely. "That is *very* interesting. It's really *quite* fascinating."

"I doubt it," the Chief said, but with a gentle smile that robbed it of its sting. "I could go on half the night, of course, Court history of all kinds being one of my hobbies. For instance: the building of course is modeled upon the Parthenon in Athens and its foundation dimensions are 385 feet from front to back on the east and west sides, and 304 feet front to back on the north and south sides. It rises four stories above ground floor at its highest point and is built of three million dollars' worth of marble combined with a variety of woods, principally American quartered white oak. Vermont marble was used almost exclusively for the exterior. The four inner courts are of white crystalline flaked Georgia marble. Above basement level, walls and floors of corridors and entrance halls are principally of creamy Alabama marble.

"I might add," he said with some pride, "that the building, plus furnishings, was brought in ninety-four thousand dollars under the estimated cost of nine million seven hundred forty thousand dollars authorized by Congress, which then—and now—and I am afraid forevermore—remains something of a miracle in the history of these United States.

"Which concludes my lecture for this evening. That will teach you not to get me started, Mary."

"I'm sure there is more," Mary said in her best party manner. "Someday you must tell me much, *much* more."

"Perhaps," The Elph said with a chuckle. "It may rank under the heading of things-you-didn't-really-care-whether-you-knew-or-not about the Supreme Court. However, it *is* interesting to know about the place where we work. Right, Tay?"

"It has always interested me," Tay said, pulled up out of a deep reverie in which Cathy, the Court and his family were swirling in some sort of fandango he could not seem to unsnarl. "I've been a Court history buff for a long time."

"At his teacher's knee," Mary said in a tone that prompted Birdie to laugh quickly and exclaim,

"My, you *have* had a real interest, haven't you! Mary, we ladies of the Court have our little gatherings from time to time—nothing formal, just as the spirit moves. We do hope you'll join in."

"Well—" Mary said in a reserved tone. "I shall have to look at my calendar and see if—"

"You aren't doing that much," Tay said. "It sounds great, Mrs. Elphinstone—"

"Birdie, please."

"Birdie—and I'm sure Mary will be delighted to attend."

"I shall have to see," Mary said in the same remote tone. "You don't know all that I do, Tay. There *are* important things that take my time—"

"But just once every six weeks—!"

"Now," Birdie interjected firmly. "We won't say any more about it. Mary knows perfectly well that she's always welcome and we'd love to have her, but nobody's pressuring anybody, on Dunc's Court. I know Mary will do her very best to be with us when she can."

"I hope so," Tay said, staring out the window.

"I shall have to see," Mary repeated, still politely distant. "It will all depend."

"I hope I didn't scare you off with too much history," the Chief said lightly. "I do go on sometimes, when I get started."

"Oh, no," she said, "not at all. I'm sure you and Tay will find much to talk about in that area."

"Oh, we'll talk a great deal in many areas," the Chief said, 'won't we, Tay? Particularly," he said with sudden glumness, "about crime and violence."

"Yes," Tay agreed, forced to drop his own broodings, which he thought was a good thing, and concentrate on the kindly little face and bright little eyes peering at him from beneath the shock of white hair. "It does seem," he added suddenly somber, "that things get worse every day."

"They aren't good," The Elph said grimly. "They are not good. That fellow down in Moss' state, what's his name, that attorney general—Regard Stinnet—you probably saw him on the news last night:

" 'There may yet come a time when an outraged citizenry will take matters into its own hands to punish those the courts allow to perpetrate their execrable acts upon society. That time could be very soon. It could be tomorrow. It could be today.' His statements are getting more and more inflammatory all the time. And you know what he and your attorney general out there in California are proposing: a conference of all the state attorneys general once a month—"

" 'To coordinate and *put into immediate effect'*—emphasis mine—'the spontaneous demand for action which is springing up all across our troubled land,' " Tay finished for him. "There's a call for nationwide vigilantism if I ever heard one."

"And we're so helpless," Duncan Elphinstone said. "It's ironic. The most powerful Court in the land, maybe in the world, and here we sit paralyzed because our only power is appellate. We can't *do* anything, in any affirmative sense. We just have to sit and wait until something comes up from the courts below. We can't make things happen, we can only say they should or shouldn't. It's ironic," he repeated, "and it makes me, for one, feel both foolish and frustrated. Because I'd like to do a lot of things. I'm sure we all would."

" 'How many divisions does the Pope have?' " Tay quoted wryly. "Not enough, obviously."

"Maybe something will come before you soon," Birdie said, being comforting as always as the limousine drew up in front of the Court.

"It can't be soon enough," her husband said, a comment he would remember with a rending sadness before the night was out.

For the moment, however, all was cheerfulness, friendliness and goodwill as they emerged from the limousine into the glare of a few modest lights and a couple of hand-held television cameras. Someone in the press room had got wind of their dinner, as someone usually did. The Chief congratulated himself that security was pretty good at the Court but reporters did have their contacts and some of them would talk. As long as it was something harmless like this, however, he didn't mind. It would be good for a picture in the *Post* and the *Inquirer* and perhaps a snippet on tomorrow night's news. CASTLE STODGY THROWS A BASH, he thought to himself with an inner humor the media might have been surprised to learn he had. It wouldn't hurt the image.

The rest arrived just behind them, and on a wave of amicability they walked slowly up the steps and went in.

The Great Hall was brightly illuminated just as it always was— "white, white, *white*," as he had overheard some tourist's child remarking one day. The night guards smiled and bowed; one young newcomer even stood to attention and snapped them a smart salute. A few late-working law clerks were still in the Hall; they smiled and stepped back respectfully. From their niches along the walls the busts of his predecessors looked down upon them as they passed.

They ascended to the second floor, turned left and made their way along the corridor—again, the Chief reflected, white, white, *white*—to the dining room. He noted that the staff had outdone itself: ferns and flowers on the snowy tablecloth, the gleam of old silver, the soft glow of old china, the patina of antique chairs and cabinets, candlelight, candlelight everywhere. It seemed like John Marshall's day again, welcoming, warm, charming—and snug, for a little while, against the clamors of the angry world, from whose constant concerns this was for them a most rare and precious escape.

The Chief felt a sudden warmly sentimental glow for them all, and for the Court . . . The Court! How they all loved it, and how much it meant to them and to their country! Eight fallible men and a woman, embodying the Law—how many long centuries, how much bitter struggle, how much pain and blood and sacrifice it had taken to bring civilization to this point! And how darkly it was threatened, and how easily it could be toppled were it not constantly, constantly protected.

He was sorry Moss and Sue-Ann were missing the occasion, because they always added a charm of their own, particularly to such faintly antiquarian scenes as this; but he supposed they must be having a good time down in South Carolina. He had seen Moss on his home grounds a couple of times before. He loved to play the grand seigneur when he got to South Carolina, and nobody did it better. Right now, the Chief supposed, he was making some graceful little speech that would set them all roaring. They loved Moss, down there, and everybody was always anxious to hear him speak.

And indeed he was preparing to hold them spellbound in the palm of his hand once again as he sat patiently on the speaker's platform with Sue-Ann on one side and Sarah and Janie on the other. The girls, as he had accurately predicted, were having a grand time of it. Both were used to public life to some degree, but this trip, with its flight in the plane provided by the President, its gala reception concluded just an hour ago, its quick tour of the just-finished plant with all its fresh new smells and spick-and-span cleanness, the friendly crowd gathered to witness the ceremony, the setting in the beautiful little valley in the tree-clad hills, the floodlights, the noise, the fun, the excitement— "Your eyes are bigger than saucers," he told them and they went off, without further prompting, into gales of giggles.

"Girls!" Sue-Ann whispered, leaning over to them. "Girls! The governor is speaking. Now, you-all stop that and listen, hear?"

"Yes, ma'am," Sarah said, struggling without much success for composure. "I'm trying, I'm trying."

But it was too much for them and they began to giggle again behind their hands while Moss, smiling a little and shaking his head, commanded the amused sympathy of the parents in the crowd. There was a little murmur of laughter. The governor, puzzled, hesitated in midflight, turned around and glanced back; saw what was causing it and promptly joined in.

"You two young ladies are disruptin' my speech, you know that?" he said good-naturedly. "Now, you just hush and pay attention, because this is serious business."

"Yes, sir," Janie squeaked, voice cracking, and immediately they were off again.

This was too much for everyone, and for a moment the little vale filled with laughter, its sound rising pleasantly through the trees to the cave mouth where the only one who was not amused wished with a furious impatience that they would stop the insane yakking and get on with it. He was growing more tense by the minute. His lips now were drawn back from his teeth and unconsciously his face was set in a wolflike mask that would have frightened anyone who saw it. No one did. His hands, resting on knees that steadied a detonator, trembled and were wet with sweat. He stood up suddenly, unzipped his pants and freed himself: he knew from experience what would happen when he hit the charge. Then he leaned back against a tree and stared up unseeing into the velvet night. *Get on with it,* he told them savagely. *For God's sake, get on with it.*

After allowing the laughter to run on for a few more seconds, the governor did. His amiable banalities floated out through the soft cool air, echoing slightly from the low rolling hills all around.

"And so now," he said finally—Janie and Sarah having managed to contain themselves, everyone now listening approvingly to his words, the little group of demonstrators corralled off in a corner, silenced by police with clubs who gestured threateningly if they so much as coughed (and also silenced because the television cameras were being kept away from them)—"now, we come to our principal speaker of the evening, my great predecessor in the office of governor, a great Associate Justice of the Supreme Court of the United States, but above all"—he took a deep breath and sailed on—"above all, a great son of South Carolina, a man we all know and love, a man whose ancestors came to this state almost three hundred years ago, to this very ground we stand on, which was their first ancestral home in the New World, a man who"—he took another breath and rumbled on—"wherever he goes and whatever he does, is always and indubitably a true son of South Carolina—Justice STANLEY MOSSITER POMEROY! Of," he added almost as an afterthought as the crowd surged shouting and applauding to its feet, "SOUTH CAROLINA!"

Moss rose and stepped forward, shaking hands with the governor, lifting their joined hands high in the standard political gesture, nodding, smiling, waving with his free hand, while the generous and affectionate welcome engulfed them.

When it died down he stepped forward and started to speak. Then he stopped, grinned and turned to gesture to the girls.

"You all know Sue-Ann," he said as they came obediently forward, "but I want you to meet the two young ladies who have caused such a disturbance here tonight. This is my daughter Sarah—and this is her good friend, the daughter of our newest Supreme Court Justice, just seated on the Court, as you all know—Jane Barbour. Girls—"

And he gestured them forward and stepped back while they stood giggling and waving in the floodlights and the friendly applause surged up once more.

Above in the trees, having ceased his attempts to really listen after he had heard the Justice's name, off in a world of his own that was racing to a climax of terrible tension and almost unbearable excitement, the watcher calculated that the speaker must now be well launched; and, reaching down, touched the detonator.

Instantly he leaped up, his back arched, his body convulsed. He staggered back gasping and groaning against the tree and gave himself up helplessly to the agonizing pleasure he could not have stopped had he wanted to, which he did not.

On the platform his rose of death flowered in the soft summer night. All along the dark side of the plant that faced his shuddering oblivious body, companion roses flowered too.

"Justice Barbour," the Chief Justice was saying with a benign smile in the cozily candlelit, peaceful, eminently civilized room, "before we begin this charming repast in this charming place, perhaps it would be fitting to say a few words and offer a toast of goodwill to our new Associate, whose presence honors this Court as we know it will serve the country.

"We are glad to have you here. We wish you well. We are certain that you will perform great service.

"Perhaps we should warn you, however, that it is not only in the White House—although," he interjected with a wry little smile, "various Chief Executives have sought to take all the credit to themselves—that it can truthfully be said, 'The buck stops here.' It also stops *right here*, in this Court. There is nobody above us to appeal to. There is no way, saving only a law of Congress or an amendment to the Constitution, to change the basis for one of our rulings. There is no one we can pass the burden along to. Here we must deliberate and decide. Once we have accepted a case there is no way we can discharge ourselves of it except by a decision. We have to vote it up or down. We may delay a bit, sometimes, to permit further argument or further study; but then the day comes and the decision must be rendered. Up or down, it must be voted; yea or nay, we must give voice. And once we have, that is it—unless reversed freely and in their own good time by future Justices—for so long as this Republic remains as we now know it. Which, pray God under whom we hold our liberties, will be for quite some time to come.

"Once, in the first days I came here, I started to use the garage entrance to the building. I still do, to large degree, as do we all, because it is the most direct and most private access for us. But every once in a while I still do what I used to do quite deliberately two or three times a week then, and that is, enter from the First Street side as we did tonight, so that I can come up the steps to the main entrance. And there before me, chiseled in the marble, I see our historic charge: Equal Justice Under Law.

"*Under law*—that is the gist of it. The law that men have fought for, died for, given everything for, over so many long centuries; *the orderly process,* which in its way is almost—not quite, but very close—almost more important, even, than the substance it embodies.

"To do things peaceably and without violence. To consider all views fairly and equably. To reach agreement sensibly and patiently. To give all sides an equal hearing, and accord to each the right to state his point of view. To impose the will of one upon another only after the most scrupulously fair and honest balancing of opposing opinions. Above all, *to deal with one another in peace and without violence.*

"These, it seems to me, should be the highest aims, as they are the noblest indications, of truly civilized men. They are increasingly, terrifyingly, rare in this world we live in now. It is they that we nine in this house, and all our brethren and sisters of the law wherever they be found, are charged with preserving. We cannot enforce them, for that rests in other hands; but we can state them and we can define them and we can perfect them, so that all may hear a clear call and all may have a common standard to adhere to.

"I do not pretend"—and here his eyes became troubled, his kindly face concerned—"that in these days this is an easy task; or that all men pay attention; or even that all of us so charged throughout the land are equal to the task, or able—or even desirous—of responding with such high standards. But we must try; we must try. Above all we, *we of this Court,* must try.

"We cannot prevent the errors of others, but in our own house we have inherited from great men the power to correct them. And this we must do—imperfectly, sometimes, but always, I would hope, as honestly and diligently as we can.

"So again, Justice Barbour: we are glad to have you here. We hope you will find us congenial companions in the long, never-ending march toward the rule of law. It is not here yet—indeed it is retrogressing everywhere in these troubled times—but there is no better alternative. We must keep striving. Both the goal we hope for, and the penalty for humankind if we do not achieve it, are very great."

He picked up his glass of wine, raised it high.

"To Taylor Barbour, of the Supreme Court of the United States, Associate Justice," he said solemnly. "We wish you well. May the law always be your principle, as you are now pledged to be its servant. And may all go well with you on this Court and everywhere."

"Hear, *hear!*" Wally Flyte cried, as they all rose, took up their glasses, drank deep; even Mary, though Tay could sense her rather amused and patronizing attitude. He did not care; he was deeply moved and not at all sure, as they resumed their seats, how he would reply. He took a deep breath and straightened his shoulders. None of them would ever forget how he had looked in this supreme moment just before his world began to shatter and collapse: tall, dignified, honest, sincere; grave, handsome, self-possessed; both judicious and judicial, as became his new position.

Softly and deliberately he began to speak to these few, these precious few, his brethren and his sister who lived and worked beneath the banner that was theirs to uphold, EQUAL JUSTICE UNDER LAW.

"Mr. Chief Justice," he said, "my sister and my brethren—my friends. I would be a poor human being and a poor servant of the law if I were not profoundly moved by the remarks the Chief Justice has seen fit to address to me. They are the words of a wise and generous man, one who leads this Court with kindness, decency and compassion; one whose grasp of the law far exceeds my own and to whom I expect to look often for guidance in the days ahead. May I propose a counter-toast:

"To Duncan Elphinstone, a great Chief Justice, a great friend, and above all, a great human being."

And once again they were on their feet, glasses raised, while The Elph blushed and smiled and finally, with a hurried, abashed and touching gesture, dashed a hand across eyes that had filled, spontaneously and quite innocently of artifice, with tears.

"My friends," Tay resumed when they were seated again and watching him once more with a generous but intent surveillance, "my concept of this Court began a long time ago—and with it, I think, though I was not conscious of it at the time, my concept of myself both as a lawyer and as a person."

(*And how is that concept doing now?* a small inner voice inquired.

Now that you have gone to Fifth Street and rutted like an alley cat? But this was so unfair to Cathy that he silenced it with savage sternness, hesitating only the slightest of seconds, which Moss perhaps would have noticed. But Moss at this moment was far away, and dreadfully occupied.)

"As you know, my emphasis all these years has been on what some might call the 'liberal' side of things"—Rupert Hemmelsford stirred in his chair and Tay caught his eye and winked, which amused them and brought a reluctant grin from Rupe—"but which, I like to think, is simple compassion, decency and common sense.

"I have never been one to feel, as some who claim the liberal label do, that everyone who disagrees is a sinister reactionary whose character, career and achievements must be destroyed as ruthlessly as possible if he dares to question the accepted liberal faith. Nor do I feel, as some of them do, that any form of censorship and suppression of opposing viewpoints is justified. Nor do I feel that derogation, belittlement, besmirchment may, and should be, substituted for fair argument. I think, and have tried to practice, that it is fair to state one's own point of view as strongly as one can when one has reached what one believes to be valid conclusions, but that one should also give an equal hearing to those who disagree. One should not censor or suppress them and I do not believe I ever have. It is my belief that convictions, if honestly held, may be honestly and strongly stated, but arguments leading up to them should be fair and open to all comers.

"To me, moderation and fairness are major signs of a true liberal."

"Hear, hear!" Wally Flyte said again; and approving applause agreed.

"The whole thrust of my social beliefs is that government has the right and the obligation to exercise its powers for the betterment of the individual and the improvement of the whole society.

"But"—his tone turned somber—"it is, as President Grover Cleveland said, a condition which confronts us, not a theory. And the condition, as we are all aware, is very grave.

"I do not have to review, here of all places, terror in the streets—violence of all kinds general and political—citizens living in fear, going about their business in fear—worrying about themselves and their children—empty, senseless, pointless death occurring on a moment's whim—contempt for law, contempt for kindness, contempt for life—the whole fabric cracking at the hands of criminals, pathologues, punks. We are in a sorry state at this moment, a culmination of family breakdown, parental irresponsibility, economic uncertainty, inadequate police, overcrowded courts, excessive coddling of criminals by many greedy and overliberal lawyers and by many courts including, let us face it, this one—the whole paraphernalia of a society inexorably breaking down under an excess of its own basic principle of freedom for all—except, in recent years, the poor unfortunate victim who happens to be in the way.

"The American reaction to this—let us say the human reaction, for never was there a nation whose form of government gave it more chance to express every aspect of human nature, good and bad—the American human reaction, naturally, is to go too far the other way.

"Action and reaction, failure and result: the inevitable twins. Posing for this Court, and probably very soon, a decision or decisions we may desperately wish we were not required to make.

"So, my sister and brethren"—he paused and saw they were all enrapt save Mary, whose carefully controlled but faintly disapproving look he ignored—"how shall we meet the challenge when it comes?

"For myself, I am going to try hard—try my damnedest—to hold to the principles of fairness and justice in which I believe. I know we all are, and I am not assuming any special virtue or superiority about it or implying that anybody will do less. I am just trying to say what I think. I am going to try to be true to the Constitution and its protections for all citizens, accuser and accused, victim and criminal, individual and society.

"Maybe that can't be done, in a climate becoming as tense and frightened as the one we live in. Perhaps fairness and moderation are going to lose the battle, at least temporarily—I hope to God temporarily, if it happens. Perhaps—the Constitution being what we say it is, as some of our less guarded predecessors on this Court have been known to state—it will be impossible to maintain all of its protections for all citizens, fairly and squarely across the board. But I am going to try, because that is the way I am: try with a fairness and dispassion as determined, as unwavering and as free from hampering emotion as I have in me.

"I like to think, perhaps falsely, that that's a lot . . .

"I am afraid I have spoken too long and too egotistically, but I wanted to state to you—and maybe also," he added with a sudden disarming smile, "to myself, that I will not be found wanting or failing when the great tests come."

He started to sit down, but they were all on their feet applauding (even Mary, politely but evidently not quite daring to refrain), and then they were crowding around him, the men to shake his hand and slap him on the back, the women to give him hugs and kisses. Somewhat to his surprise, even May McIntosh participated in this, throwing her arms around him in what he knew must be an uncharacteristically impulsive gesture and murmuring in his ear, "You're *wonderful!*"

"Thank you, Mary-Hannah," he said, with a pleased chuckle. "Now I can say I have been kissed by a Justice of the Supreme Court."

She laughed.

"A few years ago it could never have happened. But now, if you live up to all you say you will, it might even happen again sometime."

"I'm going to do my best," he told her solemnly. She squeezed his arm.

"We know you are," she said, equally serious, "and we know it's going to be great."

Summoned by the Chief Justice's antique hand-bell bearing the authentic inscription *John Marshall*—given the Court a year ago by an admirer down in Virginia who had recently come across it among some old family relics—the special staff from the kitchen entered and began serving the meal; and for the next few minutes they all chatted amicably, gradually relaxing from the solemn mood induced by Tay's and the Chief Justice's remarks. Both had gone to the fundamentals of the Court and the hard realities of the times. It took a little while to move from under their spell back to the easy exchanges of ordinary dinner-table conversation.

He knew he had made a great hit. He could sense it all around the table in the warmly approving comments, the cordial glances, the new respect that he saw in all eyes but Mary's; and her reaction, he realized suddenly, did not really matter any more. He felt himself suddenly free —completely and genuinely free for the first time since their marriage. He found himself wishing—was at first ashamed of himself, then defiant, then glad of the thought—that Cathy could have been there to hear him. He knew now that whatever doubts he had harbored about seeing her again were banished. He would see her again. He would tell her about this. And they would be happy for him, together.

He felt a sudden great impatience for this to happen, and was lost in contemplation of it when he became conscious of a phone ringing somewhere in the background. Conversation hesitated a second, then resumed. One of the waiters went to get it, a moment later came to Tay and leaned down to murmur quietly,

"Justice, Justice Pomeroy is on the phone and wants to speak to you. At least," he added in a puzzled tone, "I *think* it's Justice Pomeroy. He says he is, anyway."

For a moment after he picked up the receiver and said hello, Tay was not sure himself, so husky and ravaged was the voice in his ear. But it was Moss, all right; and although Tay immediately said, "Hi, where are you, Columbia?" in an attempt to keep the world on an even keel, he knew with an awful instinctive certainty that for some reason it was not, and might never be again.

"What is it?" he asked sharply, more loudly than he intended. He was conscious of another sudden halt in the conversation, this one a full stop: his own tone had been too obviously alarmed not to bring silence. He turned toward their anxious faces, receiver to his ear, as if seeking reassurance; so that they knew as soon as he that something was terribly, dreadfully wrong.

"What is it?" he demanded again. "Moss, what is it?"

He realized with a knowledge that set his heart racing and almost, it seemed, out of control, that Moss was crying.

"Moss," he said more softly, his voice perfectly audible in the now entirely silent room. "Moss, old buddy, what is it?"

"Our—baby—girls," Moss managed to say; broke down; and started over. "Our—baby—girls—"

"What's wrong with our baby girls?" he demanded, and Mary screamed, rushed to his side and grabbed his arm. He flung it off with a glare he made no attempt to conceal.

"Moss," he said, voice trembling and almost out of control. "Moss, you must calm down and tell me. *What about our baby girls?*"

"There's been," Moss said, "there's been an—an explosion."

"What?" he cried in a dreadful voice and was conscious that somewhere almost beyond hearing Mary was screaming again and that they had all uttered sounds of fright and apprehension.

"There's been—an explosion," Moss managed again. "I guess he wanted to—get—me on the—platform, but they—they were—there." He finished in a rush: *"Oh God, I wish it had been me!"*

"Were they—" he attempted and failed. "Were they—?"

"They're in the—hospital," Moss said with careful slowness. "Here in —in—Columbia. The doctors—don't know at this—this point."

And again he broke down and Tay could only hear harsh, strangled sobbing on the line.

"Mary and I are coming right down," he said firmly, summoning reassurance from God knew where, but summoning it. "Hang on, buddy. Is Sue-Ann all right? . . . and you? . . . Thank God for that . . . *O.K., O.K. It is not your fault and you must never, ever say that or feel it, do you hear me! . . . All right! . . .* We will be down just as fast as we can. Our love to you both. *Hang on."*

And slowly he put down the receiver, gave Mary a look which he felt she did not even see, drew a deep breath and faced them.

"Someone," he said, very carefully and slowly, "apparently bombed the plant. Sarah and Janie have been—been injured." He drew a heavy breath that seemed to come from the bottom of the world. "They are in the hospital in Columbia and Mary and I must—must go at—at once."

He was aware of Mary staring at him, face absolutely white; of the silence in the room, broken only by some Justice, he did not know who, saying clearly, "Son of a *bitch!*" and some wife, probably Birdie, saying, "Oh, dear!" and starting to cry.

Then he was aware that a small, erect figure was at his side, one hand firmly and comfortingly on his arm, the other lifting the telephone receiver.

"This is the Chief Justice," Duncan Elphinstone said. "Get me the President . . . I don't care where he is or what he is doing!" he snapped, and there was no doubt that it was a co-equal branch of the government talking. *"You tell them to get him!* . . . Mr. President? Yes, how are you? . . . Yes, we know now . . . No, we didn't hear it on the news, we're having a dinner up here; Moss just called and told us. Can you have a plane ready at Andrews Air Force Base in fifteen minutes to take Tay and Mary to Columbia? Good . . . Yes, I'll tell them, yes. Thank you so much, Mr. President—thank you, Bob. We appreciate it. Good night . . . He sends his deepest sympathies and prayers," he said, turning to Mary. "Now take my car and get on out to Andrews. There'll be a plane waiting."

"My baby!" she screamed suddenly, at last bursting into tears. *"My baby!"*

"Yes," the Chief said crisply, "and we all sympathize most deeply. But there is no time to stop and think about it now. That plane will be ready in fifteen minutes. Now please *go.*"

He kissed Mary firmly on the cheek, gave Tay a firm handshake, turned them both around with a surprising strength in his small hands and walked them firmly to the door.

"Good luck and God bless you," he said as he closed it behind them. "We know everything will be all right."

But when he turned back to them in the warm, charming, civilized room, so snug and secure against the horrors of the savage world, he stood, back resting against the wood, his face a mask of profound sadness and dismay.

For a long time he, no more than they, could speak.

From the plant at Pomeroy Station, unseen in the wild chaotic confusion of those first horrified minutes, the watcher had gone home. After cleaning himself, carefully wiping any possible fingerprints off the detonator and burying it, carefully checking to be sure he had left nothing traceable lying about, he had sneaked swiftly away through the trees and vanished down a woods trail, known he thought only to himself, that paralleled the road; and so to the cabin.

There a terrified but determined Janet waited: stone-cold sober, he could see, and in the grip of a great and obvious agitation.

The moment he closed the door behind him he saw, with an instant blinding rage, that she was clutching in one hand, waving it back and forth in front of her like a shield that would somehow fend him off, the pages of his precious manifesto.

"Where did you get that!" he yelled in a frightful voice, and trembling but determined she shouted back,

"Don't you yell at me, you murderer! I found it, I found it, I saw what it says here, how that plant is a symbol to the whole world of how greed, moral corruption and decay afflict our whole society, how you hate it and wish it were gone, and all! I found it! *I found it!* I don't know what you were going to do with it, send it to some newspaper I suppose, boasting about what you did, but I got it first, Billy Ray, I got it first, and so what are you going to do about *that?*"

"What are *you* going to do about it?" he asked, suddenly soft and menacing, reflecting ironically in that weird moment that she really did think he was Billy Ray, she never had known him as Earle Holgren in the three years of their casual liaison which had soon become boring and now had obviously become extremely dangerous to him. "What are *you* going to do about it, bitch?"

"I am not a *bitch!*" she screamed, and he stepped forward, slapped her twice across the face and made a lunge for the manifesto. But she was too fast for him and jumped back, clutching it close. He could hear John Lennon Peacechild begin to squall in the bedroom, which didn't help matters any, either.

"Listen," he said, breathing hard, forcing his voice down, trying to sound reasonable while his heart pounded and his mind raced trying to decide what to do. "I didn't blow up that plant."

"Ho!" she said. "Ho, you *liar!* What kind of a fool do you think I am, you poor pathetic *liar?* It says right here how much you hate it—"

"I don't give a God damn what it *says*," he shouted, "it doesn't say I blew it up! It was just a dream. I was just play-acting. It doesn't mean anything! It was just a *fantasy!*"

"Some dream!" she cried. "Some fantasy! You carry death with you, Billy Ray, you and your *fantasies!* Where were you during that ceremony? You never came near John Lennon Peacechild and me *because you were somewhere up there in those trees getting ready to blow that place up!* And now you've probably killed those two pretty little innocent girls and God knows who else, and damaged the plant, and everything!"

"I don't care if I damaged the plant—" he began loudly but her triumphant crow interrupted him.

"You see, you did do it! You did! You just told me so! You see you did, you did, you did! And they'll get you, Billy Ray, because you probably did kill those girls too! They'll get you good! And I hope they do!"

"And what will you do?" he demanded, beginning to edge slowly toward the desk because he didn't know whether she had taken the gun out of it or not.

"I'm going to turn you over to the law," she said, and suddenly, as he suspected, she slipped the pistol out of the pocket of her granny dress and pointed it, wavering but too close to miss if she fired, straight at his face. "Now, you stand back from me, Billy Ray, and don't you come near me while I telephone. I'm going to call the cops and turn you over."

"Call the *pigs?*" he demanded, trying desperately to resurrect old hatreds and old, automatic reactions that might aid him in this moment of greatest peril in his life. "*You* call the *pigs?* Have you forgotten—"

"That's all right what I have or haven't forgotten!" she cried, and the gun, steadier now, pointed straight at his eyes. "You stand back, Billy Ray! You stand back while I telephone!"

"How can you telephone?" he demanded, desperation giving his tone believability. "Do you think I didn't think of that? I ripped out all the wires before I came in. *You can't telephone. You can't get through. There's nobody here but us, you slut, so what about that?*"

"Well—" she said uncertainly.

"Look there, see how they're ripped out!" he cried; and as she turned instinctively, he leaped; and after a furious struggle, because she was a big girl and suddenly it was she who was fighting for life and their battle did not go easily, he got the gun.

"Now!" he said, gasping for breath, holding it on her as she had held it on him, drawing ever deeper breaths, forcing himself to become calmer and colder by the second, until the gun was steady and he was again in complete command of himself as he was of her. "Now, Miss Bitch, you and I are going to take a walk in the woods."

And suddenly she was terrified, for now truly, as she had cried a moment ago, he "carried death with him," and it was everywhere: in his eyes, in his voice, in the set of his body, in the sudden stealth with which he moved.

He gestured to the door with his gun as she cried out, *"What are you going to do to me?"*

"What do you think?" he demanded contemptuously and suddenly she screamed, "You can't do it, somebody will hear you! You can't do it!"

"They'll never think to look for us where I'm going to take you," he promised, voice suddenly soft again, everything under control, a happy singing in his mind. After all, he had killed once tonight, or thought he had, and he was in the mood now. It would be easy. And she was asking for it. She had no right to interfere with the dreams and the destiny of Earle Holgren and now she was going to get what she deserved. For Earle Holgren the invincible it would be as impersonal as squashing a bug.

"Now," he said, "give me those papers!"

And when she had, shaking so she could hardly hand them to him, he crumpled them up, jammed them in the fireplace, set them alight with his cigarette lighter and, keeping eye and gun warily trained upon her, stepped back and watched them burn.

"Get your shawl," he snapped, and desperately seeing in this some frail, flimsy sign that he might really be considerate and not be going to kill her, she jumped obediently to grab it from its hook by the door.

"Now," he said, *"march!"*

It was at that moment that John Lennon Peacechild, whom his father had literally forgotten, chose to let out a sudden renewed, angry squall. Instantly Earle Holgren paused.

"No!" Janet wailed. "No, no, *no!*"

He stepped up to her, whipped the pistol twice across her face and then held it at her ear.

"Get him," he ordered.

"No!" she wailed again, but he jabbed the gun so deeply into her ear that she screamed in pain; and then, whimpering dully, steps dragging but obedient, went into the bedroom while he stood at the door and held the gun on her; wrapped John Lennon Peacechild in his blanket and, beginning now to sob softly in a helpless, abandoned sort of way,

brought him slowly out into the living room she knew with awful certainty she would never see again.

Under one arm, she could see, Billy Ray had the flimsy little portable typewriter.

"Out the door," he said and still dully, still obediently, still with the soft murmuring mutter of sobs and incoherent protests, she walked before him as he turned onto the trail and they started up the mountain.

He was gambling, and the silence as they walked persuaded him he was correct, that by now the furor would have died down at Pomeroy Station; that there would be guards, but that they would be the country boys he knew so well from his growing-up years in these hills, whom he considered not very bright, not very quick, not very brave—inclined to be superstitious, not the type to put themselves in danger if they could possibly avoid it—nervous, uncertain, not anxious to be heroes, quick to run if they could, the kind through whose loose and nervously organized cordons he could pass without fear of discovery or challenge.

But he made very sure that Janet would be still, jabbing her repeatedly in the ear with the gun when she half-stumbled or when her sobs, which she seemed unable to control, welled up again. Once when the child began to whimper he jabbed her with extra severity and she slapped a terrified hand so hard over the baby's mouth that he thought she would suffocate it. In his last act of kindness—there had not been many—toward his son, he jabbed her again and whispered savagely, "Stop that! Don't kill him!"—though why he did not want her to, since he intended to himself, he could not have explained rationally to anyone. He wondered for a second, with his ability to stand outside himself and observe his actions, usually with pleased admiration, whether he *was* rational right now. Maybe not, he concluded; but he was certainly getting away with what he wanted to, there was no doubt of that. And that was admirable enough, all right. No one could say he was not intelligent, or smart.

Meeting no opposition, hearing no sounds other than the night woods now that the horrified crowd had trailed away and all was still save for nervous guards and the team of federal investigators already at work inside the plant itself, he took his little convoy back up the trail and through the dense cover to the rear opening of the cave where he had watched and waited scarcely an hour ago.

Prodding with the gun, he directed Janet into the cave. She stumbled twice as they walked along the old mine tracks. Savagely each time he reached out a hand to grab her hair and yank her upright. She was sweating copiously, her terror giving off an animal smell. The baby could sense it and was absolutely quiet now.

Midway in the passage they came to the old abandoned well. Stepping forward he tossed in the typewriter, heard it splash, after a long moment, far below. Roughly he yanked the child out of her arms, the shawl off her back, muffled the gun in it, held it to the nape of her neck, fired and pushed her forward. She fell without a sound.

He paused for a second, started to raise the gun, thought he heard something, froze. After a moment he decided it was just imagination and shrugged. But he wiped the gun carefully and threw it after her. Then he wrapped the shawl around the baby's head, tied it tightly, and as casually as though he were tossing a football, pitched the child after its mother.

So ended the brief sojourn of John Lennon Peacechild in a world he never made and never got to know; and of his mother, Janet, whose real name Earle Holgren had never really known, any more than she had known his.

He listened carefully for a long time, heard nothing. Finally he scraped the earth smooth where they had stood, drew brush with careful casualness over the well-mouth; turned and, walking carefully on the rails, went back out to his vantage point.

He emerged into the cool night air, compulsively once more uncovered the detonator, wiped it clean and reburied it; took a deep breath, stretched—and was instantly set upon by a hundred blows rained upon him from a dozen clubs. Someone yelled exuberantly, *"Got him!"* and the woods suddenly reverberated with shouts of excitement and savage satisfaction.

And so they had—a little late for Janet and John Lennon Peacechild, a little late for Sarah and Janie—but indubitably.

For several more moments the blows engulfed him, savage—excited—happy—out of control. At first he fought back furiously but in seconds they were too much. He began to sink rapidly into unconsciousness. Before he did a triumphant thought shot through his mind.

Nobody had warned him of his rights.

Animals, enraged, had taken an animal.

Even as his mind spun down into darkness he knew with a great flash of triumph that all of this would come in very handy when his case moved through the judicial system of the United States of America. He knew he would soon have many bitter enemies but many earnest, idealistic—and some self-interested—friends as well, and they, too, would come in very handy when his case began to move, on a parallel course, through the minds of his countrymen.

In the warm, charming, candlelit room, so peaceful, so civilized, so snug and secure against the horrors of the savage world, the Chief stood silently after Tay and Mary had left, his back resting against the door, his face a mask of profound sadness and dismay. For a long time he, no more than they, could speak.

At last he said quietly, "I think, if everyone agrees, that we had best go home."

"And pray," Justice Demsted agreed quietly.

"Maybe this is our case, Dunc," Justice Flyte suggested softly.

The Chief sighed heavily.

"I pray not," he said, "for who can be objective on this? But maybe it is, my sister and my brethren. Maybe it is."

The thought accompanied them, an insistent and implacable incubus, as they went somberly through the Great Hall to the enormous oaken doors, nodded grave good-nights to the anxious, sympathetic guards and walked slowly out beneath the great white portico that promises to all Americans EQUAL JUSTICE UNDER LAW.

TWO

1

Enough is *e-nough,* Regard Stinnet was saying silently to himself, over and over, as he sat in the hospital waiting room. Enough is *e-nough.* This was too much. Just *too* much. Somehow in his mind—and he had learned from experience that he could trust his mind to mirror reasonably well the reactions of most minds in the country—the bombing of Pomeroy Station and the horrible attack on two innocent young girls was an instant symbol of everything that was wrong with the criminal justice system.

It was true that the criminal justice system had not had time to deal with the culprit; it was true that the culprit was apparently only one man, and he more a deranged ideologue than one of the haphazard violent who were terrifying the citizenry: but those facts did not matter. Somehow, psychologically, Earle Holgren was suddenly and instantaneously a symbol for the whole damned messed-up country. Regard Stinnet sensed, for he was a very shrewd politician, that his destiny was probably going to be very closely entwined with that of Earle Holgren. And, he suspected, he would not be alone in this.

Far from it.

Quickly, as he waited for Moss Pomeroy to come out of the room where Sarah and Janie had been taken, the attorney general of South Carolina reviewed what had been discovered so far about the bomber of Pomeroy Station.

He was known in the little town, where he had occupied a cabin hidden in the woods for some two years, as Billy Ray, one of many aliases: the FBI had found out already that his real name was Earle Holgren. It had established his age, his parentage, his college and post-college radicalism, his living arrangement with a woman and child. It was known that they kept strictly to themselves, which was not regarded as strange by the neighbors: mountain people did. Holgren apparently did all the shopping. The woman almost never appeared. Only two or three residents could be found who had even seen her, and their descriptions were uncertain and inconclusive.

There had been periods when Holgren had been away from his abode, sometimes for as long as a month. The FBI was working on a theory that would align his absences with certain disastrous events elsewhere. So far it had been unable to get a fix on anything. But many facts were coming in fast on Earle Holgren.

The major thing seemed to be that he was an active and inveterate protester against the society; one of those damned radicals that Regard Stinnet hoped to sweep out of the world along with all the kooks and crazies who were terrifying the good people of America. The Earle Holgrens had motives, they made some pretense at idealism and noble principles, but in Regard's mind, as in many of his countrymen's, it came down to the same bottom line: they were all violent, they were all against society, they were a disturbing and dangerous element—and it was time, and past time, to get them out.

He was too good a lawyer to be careless, however. He was already worried about one thing: he had ascertained through careful questioning of the sheriff out there that the boys who grabbed Holgren had been a little overenthusiastic and hasty and he had an uneasy feeling that Earle Holgren was very well aware of it. These types always knew their rights, he reflected grimly, and they or their damned left-wing lawyers always made the most of them. In this case it was quite apparent that the prisoner had not been notified of his "rights," and it was quite apparent that he had been brutalized pretty badly. The way was open for all sorts of trouble in trying to bring him to book.

Why there *should* be trouble, though, Regard thought with great exasperation, the good Lord and Aunt Minnie only knew. There was no doubt the man had done it—one of the best trackers in the mountains had been put on his trail and, though Earle had somehow managed, by one of those illogical flukes that often happen in such cases, to leave his cabin and return to the scene of his crime undetected, his pursuer had picked up his traces on the trail, tracked him to the cave, and then had identified him beyond doubt through simple observation of the way in which he had carefully scraped the leaves and dirt away from the detonator, carefully wiped and rewiped it for fingerprints and then covered it over again.

How did Earle know it was there in the first place? Why was he so careful about wiping it off? Why did he so carefully rebury it?

Obviously because he had put it there and obviously because he knew any fingerprints that might be on it were his.

But, as Regard recognized with a frustrated sigh, knowing something for certain and proving it in court were frequently two different things. He knew he had his work cut out for him.

There were, however, several things in his favor. The principal one was the general climate of public opinion, still only two hours away from the event and still quivering with the horror of it. Expressions of shock and dismay were coming in at a steadily mounting rate from all over the country. The identity of the victims brought it home with shattering impact. To think that it had been directed against Justice Pomeroy of the United States Supreme Court! And Justice Pomeroy's daughter Sarah! And the daughter of another Supreme Court Justice, the newest one, Taylor Barbour! It was absolutely outrageous. It was unbelievable. It virtually guaranteed a verdict of guilty—inevitably so in South Carolina but also, he was sure, in any court in the land.

This time the very citadel of law and order itself had been attacked, no matter if the reason might have come from some twisted misdirected idealism concerned with something else. When *he* got through with it, he promised himself grimly, there would be only one motivation anyone would remember: Earle Holgren had been trying to destroy the Supreme Court, the protector of our liberties, the guardian of our laws, the precious inheritance that keeps us and our children free! No, my fellow Americans, this was no petty, mean, sneaking, skulking crime prompted by the misbegotten twisted idealism of a sorry specimen of humanity—*this was an attack on the Supreme Court of the United States itself!*

Beat that one, you shabby two-bit bastard of a no-good tramp, Regard Stinnet advised Earle Holgren with silent savagery. If—you—can!

There was a stir down the corridor and he jumped up to look, but it was not the Justice or any member of his family, only a couple of nurses and an orderly wheeling some elderly man along. Regard turned back to the waiting room which he was sharing with a sizable crowd of reporters, and shook his head.

"Nothing yet," he said. One of the men who covered the statehouse regularly demanded,

"Regard, damn it all, when you goin' to give us a statement on this thing?"

"When we know what's happened," he said. "Now you all know that, I've told you a dozen times."

"We know what happened to the plant," the reporter said.

"Right!" he said. "Right! But we don't know the outcome yet of this egregious and dreadful attack on the Supreme Court of the United States in the person of our own Justice Pomeroy! We don't know what's happenin' to his lovely little daughter or to that other lovely little girl who just happened, God bless their poor sweet innocent souls, to be in the way when this foul murderous perpetrator unloosed his evil deed upon them! We do not know yet what—"

"Are you saying this was an attack on the Supreme Court rather than an attack on the Pomeroy Station plant?" another reporter inquired, this one a hard-bitten old bat who had been covering the statehouse when Regard Stinnet, he often told her with relish, was still wettin' his diapers.

"Henrietta-Maude," he said, "now, you just use your imagination a little bit, will you please? You know very well that this was no ordinary attack on some ordinary old atomic energy plant. God knows we've had enough of that crazy sort of thing in recent years, but this was a cold-blooded, deliberate attack on Pomeroy Station when *Justice* Pomeroy was there, and it was deliberately designed to destroy *Justice* Pomeroy *as a symbol of the Supreme Court of the United States!*"

"How do you know that?" Henrietta-Maude inquired, unimpressed. "The guilty party tell you that before your men slugged him into unconsciousness?"

"They weren't 'my men'!" he snapped, "and I don't know anything about their 'slugging him into unconsciousness'! And neither do you, Henny, you weren't there. No more was I!"

"Then how do you know?" she persisted with the doggedness he had come to know and hate. "He leave you a written statement or something?"

"I'm not sayin' we have a 'guilty party' yet, and if we do, he didn't leave us anything as far as we know now," Regard said.

"Then this 'attack on the Supreme Court' business is all your own idea?" Henny's male colleague inquired in the same skeptical tone she had used. He snorted.

"Great God Almighty, great balls of fire in the mornin'!" he exclaimed. "If you folks aren't the most skeptical, disbelievin', down-puttin', unhelpful—"

"Well, is it?" Henny reiterated, unimpressed. "Did you dream up this so-called 'attack on the Supreme Court' just to rouse up the country, Regard Stinnet? Wouldn't put it past you one minute. Sounds just like you."

"I don't *need* to dream it up," Regard said with an impatient sarcasm. "It's right there plain as the nose on your face, which is some plainness, believe me, Henrietta-Maude. It's as obvious as you are, which is some. Do you mean to tell me you're out defendin' bombers and murderers and all—"

"*Is* anybody dead?" one of the other reporters demanded quickly. They were suddenly eagerly alert.

"Now listen," he said, telling himself he'd got to watch his temper, sometimes it got a little ahead of him. "Now listen, y'all. You saw me come in that door ten minutes ago, y'all were already here. You know I've had exactly the same sources you have in the last ten minutes, which is nil. Why do you think I'd be waitin' here if I knew anything? I'm waitin' for news just like you. And here," he added as a bustle began down the hall and they all jostled out to greet it, "it may be comin', right this minute."

And so it did, and it was obvious before he reached them that Justice Pomeroy had nothing but further tragedy to relate. Sue-Ann, face muffled in handkerchief, was sobbing on his arm, a doctor was steadying her on the other side, the head nurse hovered about them both. Moss hardly seemed to see them at all as they surrounded him with questions, respectful, but urgent.

"Governor—Mr. Justice," somebody started it going, "can you tell us—?"

He took a deep breath and tried to speak. His voice broke and he started over.

"I—have to tell you," he articulated with difficulty, "that our—our daughter—Sarah—is—is gone."

There was a shocked intake of breath, protests, curses, sympathetic sounds; several of the women, including Henrietta, began to cry softly even as their pens scribbled busily.

"And Jane Barbour?" Henny asked, managing to sound both sympathetic and true to duty.

"Janie is—alive. But the doctors say her condition is—is very—uncertain—at the moment."

"You mean that she—?" someone asked. Moss shot him a look in which anger and despair commingled.

"I mean," he said harshly and clearly, "that the doctors say that she may not—come out of it." Sue-Ann uttered an anguished cry and Moss added bleakly, "I do not know which—which—is worse, the certainty or the—uncertainty."

For several seconds there was an appalled silence, broken only by the quick scurry of their pens.

"Are Janie's parents—?" someone asked finally.

"I talked to Justice Barbour an hour ago," Moss said, more calmly. "He said they were flying down at once. They should be here soon, and then—then—you can talk to them. It seems only fair to ask you to put all this under embargo until you have."

"We are so sorry, Governor and Mrs. Pomeroy," Henrietta said clearly. "We hope the guilty person is suitably punished."

"He will be," Regard Stinnet spoke up before the Pomeroys could reply, "if the sovereign state of South Carolina which I represent has anything to say about it. And by God, we *will!*"

"What if it comes up to the Supreme Court, Mr. Justice?" a voice inquired, its owner sounding unhappy at having to ask but doggedly doing his duty. For a very long moment, there in the hushed, brightly lit hospital corridor, Moss stared at him without expression. Then he sighed, a deep and infinitely tired sound.

"That depends," he said. "First—if it comes. And secondly, on the courts below."

"Will you disqualify yourself in such an event?" the voice persisted, if possible unhappier but knowing, as did they all including the Pomeroys, that it had to be asked.

Again there was a long silence before Moss replied.

"That, too," he said at last, "depends."

"So you may *not* disqualify yourself," Henrietta said flatly, and for a second it seemed likely that only her weatherbeaten years around the statehouse, her sex and gray hair prevented Moss from actually striking her. But his furious look passed as instantaneously as it had come and he only said again with a heavy sigh,

"I know you-all feel you have to ask these questions, Henrietta, but Sue-Ann and I are really very tired now, and I think you can excuse us if we just go along back to—our—our—baby . . . Regard, you come with us and then you can tell these folks later about the—the arrangements."

And with a dignity that no one now dared challenge they turned and walked slowly back down the long bleak corridor, Regard taking Sue-Ann's arm and accompanying them with a subdued and suitable gravity.

Ten minutes later he was back, face strained but in command of things and obviously savoring the feeling. Sarah's funeral, he said, would be held on Monday at "High Pillars," the Pomeroy plantation. Interment would be in the family plot on the plantation. Family and close friends only would attend. No media coverage would be allowed.

"And as for that—that—*being*," he added with a sudden furious anger, "he will get *justice*. I swear by everything peace-loving, law-abiding Americans hold dear, *he will get justice*."

"What's his name?" someone demanded, but Regard only shook his head impatiently. He wasn't ready for that yet.

"Hanging justice?" Henrietta inquired. He almost snapped, "I sure as damned hell hope so!" but thought better of it just in time.

"Justice to the full extent of the law," he replied instead; and slid smoothly into where he intended to go.

"When an attack so savage," he said, "so unprincipled, so deliberately designed to strike at the Supreme Court of the United States and at the fundamental liberties and orderly processes of this country, takes place, then the severest of all penalties must be sought. I can tell you flatly that it will be. I call upon all good Americans everywhere to support me, and to support the forces of law and order everywhere in securing justice—justice *now!*—for the individual responsible, and for all such individuals wherever they may be in this land, who strike at the institutions, at the safety—*at the very lives*—of all decent, law-abiding citizens. The law must act. The law *will* act. *And the law will prevail*.

"Enough," he concluded, voice dropping to a stern, emphatic note, "is enough!"

And that, he told Earle Holgren savagely, will take care of *you*. And also, he thought in his far-ranging, clever mind, it should pretty well take care of any lily-livers on the Court when the question of securing *real* justice in these troubled United States of America came up before them. They wouldn't be able to duck it; they would have to rule for the utmost penalty. He was determined to make sure of that.

In the limousine as it raced toward Andrews Air Force Base, Tay had tried to take Mary's hand. With a savage half-animal sound she had yanked it away. He did not try again.

Nor did he try to speak to her as she sat sobbing quietly in the corner of the seat, crowded back against the upholstery as far as she could go. That, too, he had attempted when they were walking in a daze out through the Great Hall of the Court, guards hurrying before them, the few remaining law clerks and staffers making inarticulate sounds of sympathy as they passed.

"Mary—" he had begun tentatively. "Mary, I—"

"Don't say *anything!*" she had snapped through her sobs. *"Don't say anything!"*

So he had already abandoned that.

Now he did not know when, if ever, they could communicate again; but he knew that if they did it would be agony for him, because events had proved her all too tragically right; and she was not one to let the advantage go. He would be hearing from it as long as he lived.

Or as long as they were together.

He wished with a sudden searing feeling that was part emotional, part physical, all-encompassing, that Cathy were beside him now. He had never known Cathy in a time of testing—he really hardly knew her at all, as yet, though he promised himself once again that this would soon change—but he felt he knew instinctively how she would react. She would be steady, compassionate, forgiving, sustaining: *kind.* She would not hold against him forever a decision, made from the best of motives, to give his daughter an opportunity to experience, and to grow, in the company of her friend.

His daughter! God Almighty, *Janie!*

He could not believe it.

He just could not believe it.

When Moss had called, his mind, overwhelmed with a thousand things, had yet leaped instantly to the implications of his new position. This was not surprising: he was a lawyer, thought as a lawyer, reacted as a lawyer. *What if Sarah or Janie dies? What if the case comes up to us as so major a case must almost inevitably do? What if I have to help decide it? What will I do?*

Fantastic though it might seem to outsiders that he would be able to consider this at such a moment, yet it was his training, instinctive and inevitable. He did not dwell on it, there was then no time; but instantly and inescapably it was in his mind. And now, as they rode in silence toward the waiting plane and—what?—it was coming back: perhaps as a defense mechanism against the dreadful possibility his mind was not yet ready to accept or even really contemplate.

Like Moss—indeed like all his colleagues as they sat and brooded now in their various abodes—he simply did not know at this point what he would do. His first reaction was that he must of course disqualify himself and so must Moss. But then he hesitated. Was that not running away? Was that not abandoning his responsibility to the Court and the law? Was that not taking the easy, duty-evading way out, even though some might hail it as an example of "ethics"?

And if he did not disqualify himself, would he not then be voluntarily submitting himself to the most agonizing battle between what his heart and emotions wanted and what his training in objective law might tell him he must do?

He felt at that moment more alone than he had ever been in his life. He knew the feeling would not diminish. If things progressed as seemed possible in the case of the Pomeroy Station bomber, his private purgatory would become lonelier still.

He was a long, long way from the Salinas Valley now.

He uttered some involuntary sound of protest and anguish, so deep and wrenched-up that it startled him. It also startled Mary, who stopped sobbing for a moment and gave him a bitter, skeptical glance.

"Don't tell me," she said, "that you're actually *feeling* this."

"My God, Mary!" he said in an unbelieving tone. "My *God! How can you say such a thing?*"

"Oh, it comes easy," she said in the same bitter way, "when you've lost a daughter."

"We don't know yet—" he began in a voice that trembled; and went on carefully, "we don't know yet that this is the case. All we have to go on is what Moss told me. And that wasn't conclusive."

"No," she said, "but *you know*. You feel it in your bones, just as I do. We've lost her."

"No!" he cried sharply, thankful for the heavy glass that shut off their conversation from the driver as the car surged through Washington's near-deserted nighttime streets. "No, I will not believe that! I will not believe that! You have to have some hope. You can't just abandon everything!"

"You abandoned Janie," she said in a cold, tired voice, sobs forgotten now in this harsh contest. "You let her go down there when I didn't want her to. You encouraged her. The two of you beat me down and overrode my objections—"

"That is completely and utterly unfair," he replied in a tone suddenly as flat and cold as her own. "You changed your own mind, we didn't change it for you. We both accepted your decision, although neither of us liked it. You know that very well."

"You never liked anything I did for Janie," she said, starting to cry again. "You were always jealous, you never liked what I did for her."

"Stop putting it in the past tense!" he demanded loudly, with a sudden almost superstitious vehemence. "She isn't"—his voice faltered—"yet."

"We don't know. *We don't know.*"

"Then don't tell me we do know!"

"I know we've lost her," she repeated bleakly between her sobs. "I just *know* we've lost her."

But how they might have lost her, neither was prepared for; and when they arrived at the airport, to be met by a gravely solicitous Regard Stinnet, they did not at first find out. Regard introduced himself, produced four state troopers, rushed them quickly through the waiting crowd of reporters who got nothing and photographers who managed to snap a satisfactorily ghastly picture of parental anguish, and whisked them away in an official limousine to the hospital. They ran the media gauntlet silently again and were ushered at once into the office of the director.

There they found two grave doctors, one older, gray-haired, fatherly, the other young, high-strung, obviously capable. Regard and the director withdrew, the door closed. A lingering sob or two from Mary—a constant silent repetition on his part of the phrase *I will not break, I will not break, I will not break*—and the older doctor began to speak.

"Mrs. Barbour," he said in a kindly voice, "Mr. Justice: I am afraid we may have sad news for you, but not"—he held up a hand sharply as Mary cried out—"not fatal news. Your daughter is alive and holding her own. She is a strong, healthy child and we think she will survive. Unlike"—he shook his head sadly—"poor little Sarah Pomeroy, who encouraged us for a few minutes and then—just—failed."

"How are the Pomeroys?" Tay asked, hardly recognizing his own voice. "Are they all right?"

"Justice and Mrs. Pomeroy are brave young people," the doctor said. "They will manage. My question is"—he paused and gave them a keen look—"will you?"

"Why?" Mary cried in a terrible voice. *"What is the matter with her?"*

"I am deeply sorry to have to tell you that there is a possibility of damage to the brain—"

"She's a vegetable!" Mary cried in a tone of such absolute horror that the younger doctor instinctively started up and came toward her. Tay took her hand and this time she permitted it, but it was cold—cold—and totally unresponsive. Perhaps, he thought, she did not even know about it. She gestured the younger doctor aside and he returned to his chair, watching her intently.

"There is a possibility," the older doctor said quietly. "I must emphasize that: at this moment, only a *possibility*. But it is one I want you to be prepared for. There is a good chance that she will recover completely and perhaps much faster than we can imagine now—but I must tell you frankly that the possibility of brain damage is there. You must be very brave, because she needs you now perhaps more than she has ever done. She is your baby again, and you must take care of her."

"We will," he said, barely able to articulate. "Is she—is there any chance—that she can—know us?"

"She drifts in and out," the doctor said. "She may not recognize you for days, or it may happen very soon. There is a chance. But you must not build your hopes too high. That can only hurt you further."

"Nothing can hurt me further," Mary said in a faraway tone. "Ever again."

"Mary," he said harshly, "life has to go on. Stop dramatizing. You are hurt. I am hurt. Above all, Janie is hurt. It isn't going to help her at all to have you—"

"Nothing is going to help her at all," Mary said with a terrible conviction, and something remote and unreachable seemed to freeze in her expression forever. "Nothing . . . May we," she said in a tone that was suddenly almost impersonal, "see her now, doctor?"

"You may," the doctor said. "But don't expect too much. She is heavily sedated and, as I say, there may be no sign of recognition at this point."

"Or any point," Mary said in the same remote, impersonal voice. "Nonetheless, I suppose we must satisfy ourselves that she is still in existence."

"Mary!" he cried again, "Mary, *for God's sake*—!"

But she said nothing further, nor did she so much as glance at him: simply rose gracefully, as she had been taught to do, turned, head high, and walked out into the corridor ahead of them, glancing neither right nor left.

He was thankful to see that all media had been banned from the floor now; down the corridor only two figures, clinging together, awaited them. They broke apart, hurried forward. Sue-Ann, face ravaged with tears, started instinctively to extend her arms to Mary. Mary drew back. Sue-Ann recoiled as though struck.

"I hope you are all very happy," Mary said in a clear, distinct voice, "now that you have destroyed my child."

There was a moment's stunned silence; then he and Moss spoke together, but Moss was rightfully the most outraged and it was his voice that overrode, and shouted down the hall.

"*Our* child is *dead!*" he cried, face contorted with sorrow and rage. "How *dare* you say such a thing to us!"

"I am sorry for that," Mary said, face white but unyielding as Sue-Ann stared at her with disbelieving eyes. "But I am even sorrier for my child, who very likely will have to live on in darkness. Perhaps the Lord was the more merciful in your case, if that was the way it had to be. Except," she added bleakly, "that I do not think it had to be that way. I do not agree they had to be here at all. I thought it was unwise from the first. I know that I was alone in this. Now"—and for the first time her voice threatened to break—"I am really alone." A ghastly sardonic humor crossed her face for a second. "But, then, so is Janie."

And she gave them a tiny little bow and brushed past, leaving him to face them while the two doctors, faces revealing great concern for Mary's condition, hurried forward to accompany her.

"I'm—sorry," he said brokenly. "Oh, I am sorry."

"That's all right," Sue-Ann said, putting her arms around him and beginning to cry again. "That's all—right, Tay. Don't you worry about it —for—for a minute."

"No," Moss said, taking his hand between both of his. "Don't you worry, Tay. I'm sorry, too, I never should have said that, even if she— even if she is—"

"I know," he said, his own eyes filling at last. "I know. I don't know what's the matter with her. I think maybe this has made her a little—a little crazy—right now."

"It's a crazy night," Sue-Ann said with the ghost of a tremulous little laugh. "Hadn't you noticed? Really crazy."

And turned to Moss and dissolved again into tears.

Over her head Moss gave him a long look.

"You'd better go on with Mary, buddy," he said quietly. "You'll want to see your daughter. We've reserved a room for you at the Carolina Inn. We're going back now ourselves, since there's nothing"—his voice sagged, then steadied—"more that we can do here tonight. We'll see you there and we'll talk. Maybe everything will be calmer then."

"Yes," he said thankfully. He started forward, stopped. "Oh. One thing. Have they got him?"

Moss nodded.

"Alive?"

"Yes."

"Then he'll stand trial."

"Yes," Moss said. Their eyes locked and Moss nodded slowly. "It may very likely come up to us."

He nodded too, face blank.

"Yes . . . and what will we do then?"

Moss sighed and shook his head as though trying to clear it of almost intolerable weight.

"I can't think about it now . . . I just can't think about it now.'

"No," Tay agreed. "But we will . . . we will."

He turned and walked slowly down the hall toward the doorway, his whole being crying out against his entering. But inside were only Mary, the doctors and his little girl. Her head was bandaged, her face bruised, but otherwise she looked quite normal—just his little girl, sleeping. His mind would not accept then that she might never wake up. She looked so natural. He could not believe it.

He just could not believe it.

2

Elsewhere in Columbia, fully awake after several hours of heavy sleep, hurting all over but cold mind racing, the bomber of Pomeroy Station appraised his situation. It was, all things considered, good.

So far, he was confident, there was no absolute evidence to connect him to the crime. And while he fully intended murder when he set off the charge, being on the other side of the plant where he could not see the result he was not at all sure that he had achieved it. There had been no opportunity to hear news so he did not know whether he had killed Justice Pomeroy or how much damage he had done to the plant. But one thing he did know with certainty, and that was that the evidence, if any, on which he found himself obviously inside a jail cell was circumstantial at best. All he needed was a clever lawyer—dozens of the right persuasion, he was confident, would flock to his side, eager and earnest to "challenge the system" and "preserve human rights"—and he would be home scot-free. His trial was not a worrisome prospect. It promised, in fact, to be rather fun.

He was absolutely sure that no one had observed him prior to the bombing; they were all too preoccupied with the ceremonies below. He knew that there were no fingerprints left on the detonator: he had wiped it clean a dozen times. He knew that the mere fact that he might have been observed doing so after the fact proved nothing in the hands of a clever lawyer: he could hear him now.

Had he been seen actually using it? Could anyone prove it was actually his? Were his fingerprints on it? No to all three? Well, then, so what? Maybe he did have it in his hands after the event—what proof was there that he had it before the event? What proof was there that he had used it? Could opposing counsel offer such proof? If so, please share with the jury any special knowledge he might possess on this point. We do not want to keep the jury and this honorable court in the dark on matters so vital, do we, counsel?

Circumstantial, that's all they had—circumstantial! And Earle Holgren had learned long ago, through careful study of many pertinent cases during the Sixties and early Seventies, as well as advice from his lawyer in New York, that shrewd lawyers, juries whose nervous consciences could be played upon, and determinedly "enlightened" judges could wreak havoc with circumstantial evidence. He wasn't worried about that.

He felt very good about what he had done this day. It wasn't everybody who could make his statement in as bold and dramatic a fashion, not everybody who could focus the attention of the whole nation, as he knew it must be focused right now, upon himself and his cause. He had done it just right, and what he had done would be remembered for a long, long time.

And he had 'em. *He had 'em!* The damned hillbillies had been so anxious to get him, so desperate, so out of control, that they had never even told him about his rights. They had *denied* him his rights. They hadn't warned him, they hadn't asked him if he wanted a lawyer, they'd just been so damned hot to climb all over him and club him to death that they hadn't even stopped to think about it.

Well, more fools they.

He was confident there wasn't a court in the land would convict him, after that. He was home free and there wasn't a damned thing anybody could do about it.

It was at this point, when he still hurt like hell but when his mind was happily and jubilantly at peace, that he became aware of a blur of shadow outside his door and a softly menacing, utterly contemptuous voice that said:

"What you smilin' for, you worthless piece of murderin', two-bit human slime? What's so God damned funny in this world of yours, funny boy? Let me know. Me and the folks of the sovereign state of South Carolina, we want to know, so's we can join right in and have the big hee-haw with you. Tell me about it, shit-face, O.K.?"

He could hear the door being unlocked and through eyelids that could barely open, eyes that still could barely see, he became aware that the shadow, tall and lanky and looming low over the bed where he lay helpless—physically, but not mentally, oh, never mentally, not Earle Holgren—had pulled up a chair and was seated by his side not a foot away.

"Now," Regard Stinnet said again, still softly, "tell me about it, Earle Holgren. Isn't often I got a right smart, clever man like you in here. You got us all fooled and where you want us. Tell me how you did it."

For several seconds he just lay there; then huskily but with great determination he whispered:

"Give me my rights."

"Hell, man," Regard said dryly. "You don't want your rights *now*. It's too late to give you your rights *now*. You know *that*. The boys messed up a bit, you know *that*. You got what you wanted as far as rights are concerned, out there at the cave by Pomeroy Station when they didn't warn you. What you want with rights *now?* You're a lot better off legally without 'em, you know it."

"You're assuming," Earle Holgren whispered with painful slowness, "that I'm smart enough to know that. Maybe I'm just dumb."

"Oh, no!" Regard said. "Oh, no, son of a bitch, you're not dumb! I know your type and you're not dumb. You're just dumb in thinkin' this society is goin' to let you bastards get away with this kind of stuff forever, that's where you're dumb! Because, shit-face, it isn't. It isn't!"

"Better get me a lawyer," Earle Holgren whispered, "before you say too much yourself, shit-face. Who the hell are you, anyway?"

"My name is *Re*gard Stinnet," Regard said, "and I'm the attorney general of this whole shootin' shebang of South Carolina. Doesn't that make you feel important, Mr. Earle Holgren? You want to feel important, don't you? That's why you bombed Pomeroy Station plant and tried to kill a Supreme Court Justice and *did* kill his daughter—"

For a split second Earle Holgren looked blankly surprised. But he was too smart to give Regard the response he had hoped to provoke.

"You're assuming an awful lot, Mr. Stinnet," he whispered politely. "Saying all those things about me, including I bombed Pomeroy Station. Were you there?"

"—tried to kill a Supreme Court Justice and *did* kill his daughter," Regard repeated. "I'll bet that makes you proud, killing a fifteen-year-old girl! Mighty brave stuff, *Mr.* Holgren!"

"I'm sorry," Earle whispered, still politely, "if any innocent person got hurt. Who on earth would want to do such a horrible thing? What kind of people do you breed down here in the whole shootin' shebang anyway, Mr. Stinnet?"

"Not as bad as what wanders in here," Regard said grimly. "Not as bad as what wanders in here, that's for sure! And not only that, but you know what else you did? Do you know?"

But again Earle Holgren only smiled patiently and responded in the same polite way.

"Why do you keep saying what *I* did, Mr. Stinnet? You haven't proved I did anything, and I"—he could not entirely suppress an ironic little expression, more grimace than smile through his greatly swollen lips—"*I* haven't said I did anything, either. So, what else did the bomber of Pomeroy Station do?"

"He got at *two* Justices of the Supreme Court," Regard said, "which isn't going to do him any good if his case ever gets up there. In fact, if I was him I'd be damned worried about *that*. He got at two of 'em."

"Oh, were there two of them there?" Earle Holgren inquired with a mild interest. "I don't remember reading about that."

"I'll bet you read everything else about it you could get your hands on!" Regard snapped.

"I like to read," Earle Holgren said thoughtfully. "I learn a lot, reading."

"Yes," Regard said. "Well. You'll be interested to know that not only did you miss Justice Pomeroy *but* kill his daughter Sarah, but you also hit little Janie, who's the daughter of the new Justice, Justice Barbour, and it looks as though you may have paralyzed her and turned her into a vegetable for life. That's what you did!"

"That is horrible," Earle Holgren agreed gravely, "but again, I have to point out that this is all speculation on your part, Mr. Stinnet, and not very clever speculation at that. Don't you think maybe it's time now that I had a lawyer? Since apparently you aren't going to have them beat me up again, to try to make me talk."

"I didn't have them beat you up in the first place," Regard said angrily. "I wish to hell they either hadn't done it at all, or finished the job."

"Don't you think," Earle Holgren asked, returning to his air of almost disinterested politeness, "that maybe if you had them torture me enough, you could get me to confess? Wouldn't that be real American justice, Mr. Stinnet? Wouldn't you like them to try?"

"No, I wouldn't like them to try!" Regard grated out. "I know your type. You fanatics are all alike. We don't know enough in this country to make you break. Maybe where your friends are and where you get your orders from, they could do it, because they're bloodthirsty monsters and they've had nothing but practice, but we can't because—"

"I don't have any friends and I don't take orders from—" Earle Holgren interrupted angrily, words blurting out through bloated lips in a sudden surge of genuine anger that made Regard hopeful for a second. But right on schedule, it ended. Abruptly Earle Holgren stopped, went through an obvious internal struggle, won it and lay back with gingerly care upon his cot.

"Mr. Stinnet," he said politely, "I really think I'd better have a lawyer now. Otherwise you may say something that will really prejudice your case against me, since you seem to think you might have one. We wouldn't want that to happen, would we? I don't care about me, I can take care of myself, but I think for your own protection I'd better have a lawyer now. Don't you think?"

For several seconds Regard Stinnet stared at him while he, looking like a battered teddy bear but perfectly self-possessed under the blood and bruises, stared impassively back.

"Who do you have in mind?" Regard finally asked in a perfectly matter-of-fact and unemotional voice. Two, he told himself, could play at that game, and from now on, he would. Earle Holgren looked thoughtful.

"There is one possibility—" he began slowly. Then he shrugged, just as Regard thought he might be getting somewhere. "But to choose him I'm afraid would only encourage your wildest fantasies in this matter, Mr. Stinnet. It would just be too pat. No. I don't know of anyone. Why don't you have the court appoint somebody?"

"Perhaps your parents will have someone in mind," Regard suggested; and for just a second the shot went home. A fleeting look of protest?—anger?—pain?—went across Earle Holgren's face. But it too was instantly gone.

"Perhaps," he agreed indifferently. "Do they have to be told?"

"Do they have to be told?" Regard echoed. "My God, man, you're a national case already, don't you know that? It's hardly four hours since you bombed that plant—"

"Please," Earle Holgren said, lifting a polite, protesting hand.

"—since that plant was bombed," Regard corrected himself.

"That's better," Earle Holgren said placidly.

"—and already it's a national—no, probably already a worldwide—sensation. How *about* that," Regard said heartily, "*you,* Earle Holgren, a worldwide sensation, and all because you bombed a plant down here in little old South Carolina! Imagine that!"

"I think you're imagining it," Earle Holgren said with perfect gentility. "Really, Mr. Stinnet, do get me a lawyer, now, before you say things you'll be sorry for Please?"

Regard gave him a long quizzical look. A grim little smile touched his lips.

"All right, boy," he said. "you've had your chance. If you think you can escape justice in today's climate in this country, you're goin' to have another think comin'. But I'll get you your lawyer. There's one out there waitin' right now, as a matter of fact. I don't know anything about her—"

"'Her'?" Earle Holgren echoed with a mildly intrigued interest. "What's she look like?"

"She's not a beauty," Regard said accurately, "but she looks as though she might have brains."

"I think that's the important thing, don't you?" Earle Holgren inquired, and for the first time Regard laughed, quite genuinely.

"You know it is, Earle," he said. "Do you ever! Shall I send her in?"

"You sure you want her to see me like this?" Earle Holgren asked dryly, and Regard turned quite cheerful.

"Hell, man! Best she see for herself right now. If we waited until we had you patched up it'd take a little time and you'd have an even bigger story to tell about police brutality. Plus the fact you'd probably make it a lot worse than it is."

"It isn't exactly comfortable," Earle Holgren pointed out.

"I'm sure sorry," Regard said. "I sure am sorry. But I guess we'll just have to go with it, as is. Make yourself pretty, now."

"What's her name?" Earle asked.

"Deborah Donnelson," Regard said. "Calls herself Debbie, I believe."

"Deborah Donnelson," Earle Holgren mused. "Sounds like a movie star. Where's she come from?"

"The Lord sent her," Regard said, "just when you need her most. Isn't that providential? Every murderer should be so lucky."

"Fuck off," Earle Holgren said, sounding quite unamused. "Send her in."

Regard Stinnet stalked out, slammed the iron door behind him, nodded to the court stenographer seated in the hall hidden from the prisoner. The stenographer got up and stepped into an adjoining doorway, out of sight: she would be back for the next visitor.

Earle started to smooth down his hair with two swollen paws, then stopped with a sardonic grin and messed it up again. He was helping the wrong team there, for a minute, trying to make himself look more presentable. The grungier the better, as he knew very well, not only for his own case but for his potential lawyer: women loved that sort of thing from teddy bears, the grungier the better. He rolled over on his side facing the wall, groaning with pain as he did so. He was faking the disinterest but he didn't have to fake the groan. He really did hurt like hell.

"They beat you up," she said, a worried, sympathetic voice behind him. He started to roll back and she said sharply, "Don't move if it hurts you!"

"Of course I will," he whispered with some impatience. "I have to see what you look like."

"Well," she said when he had accomplished the move to the accompaniment of more groans, each of which made her wince. "Here I am."

He had an impression of dark eyes, dark complexion, a thin, pale, earnest face, big spectacles, dark hair rolled tight in a bun, a taut, intense expression. Jesus, he thought tiredly, one of those. But he was perceptive, and the overall impression, as that South Carolina yahoo had said, was brains. And brains were what he needed on his side. He had plenty but he couldn't do it alone. Maybe she had the kind he needed. He was too smart to dismiss her without finding out.

"How did you happen to find me?" he asked. "Somebody send you?"

"Yes," she said. "You know him. He called me and asked me to come."

"You live down here?" he asked, surprised. She nodded.

"For the time being. My husband comes from here. I just got divorced."

"You were married?"

She blushed, he guessed; some darker infusion seemed to darken her already dark skin. What was she, part black, Hindu, Jewish, Russian, middle European? He didn't know: interesting, anyway. He lifted a paw, dismissing his own question. "Sorry, didn't mean to sound surprised. Lots of people get married."

"True," she said, stopped looking offended and smiled: really quite attractive if you liked women, which he really didn't, all that much. Needed 'em sometimes, used 'em sometimes, but didn't really like 'em, he guessed. Earle Holgren, he told himself with pride, never really *liked* or *needed* anybody.

Except of course, right now, he did need a good lawyer. And maybe, just maybe, this uptight type would be just the ticket. She'd be a novelty, anyway. Joan of Arc and Little David, taking on Goliath, the System.

"Where'd you go to school?" he asked, shifting his position and wincing, at which she winced sympathetically too, so that he laughed in a shaky, whispery way, which was all he could manage right now.

"Listen," he said, "don't mind me wincing once in a while. I *hurt*, lady. They really worked me over."

"Yes," she said; and added with a sudden blaze of anger, "And we'll work *them* over, too."

"You bet," he agreed. "But first I want to know where you're coming from. You go to Harvard?"

"I went to Vassar," she said. "And then to Columbia Law School."

"Your folks have a lot of dough?"

"Enough," she said. "I don't see them much. And yours?"

"Likewise and likewise," he said. "They may come fluttering around now, though. Try to ignore them if they do. They'll just get in the way of what we want to do."

"What do we want to do?" she demanded, suddenly sharp and shrewd, taking him aback a little. But that's good, he thought, that's good: she's a sharp lady. "Where are *you* coming from?"

"I want you to get me out of here," he whispered with an attempt at a pixie grin that he knew probably looked awful from the outside though it felt cute inside. "It's not so much where I come from as where I want to go. Which is out O-u-t."

"Are you guilty?" she asked, fixing him with a sudden intense gaze. "If I'm to represent you, I've got to know."

"You aren't representing me yet," he pointed out, but amicably. "We can talk about that later."

"I have to know!" she repeated. "I have to know!"

"Well," he whispered comfortably, "maybe someday I'll tell you, how about that. Meantime, I want to know what your reasons would be for taking me on. I couldn't afford to pay you much money, you know. What would you get out of it?"

"The satisfaction of seeing justice done!" she said with a fierceness that surprised him.

"And that would be getting me out?" he inquired in a quizzical whisper.

"Yes!" she said with a humorless intensity. "Yes! I see you as a martyr to this whole corrupt system, a victim of our times, a sincere protester against greed and corruption and the awful danger to our society represented by the construction of poorly conceived, poorly built dangerously operated atomic energy plants, a sincere and valiant fighter for the cause of human justice, human freedom, human—"

"Whoa, whoa, whoa," he whispered, half smiling, holding up a hand, "whoa, *whoa!* You don't have to stump-speech me. We aren't in court yet."

"But don't you agree?" she demanded fiercely. "Don't you agree?"

"Yes," he whispered, "I agree, I agree. But I'm not saying I'm the same guy you seem to have in mind. You seem to think I did the bombing, instead of being in here on a bum rap."

"*They* think you did," she said. "You ought to see the papers and hear the television and radio. They've got you condemned and in the chair already."

"So much the worse for them," he said with a sudden scowl that was startling after his apparent good nature up to now. "False arrest, defamation, trial-by-media—we've got 'em where we want 'em. Let the stupid bastards rave on. So much the better for me."

"They caught you with the detonator," she said. "They caught you coming out of the cave. They can't find your wife and baby, they think you sent them off somewhere—"

"Oh, I did," he said with a sudden attempt at a smile that she couldn't quite analyze, it looked so distorted on his cracked and swollen lips. "I wanted 'em to have a good time, for a change. They were getting tired being cooped up with me in that little cabin."

"Where are they?" she asked. He made a feeble attempt at a shrug but had to stop with a grimace of pain which she mirrored in her sympathetic look.

"They went off to the seashore someplace," he said. "They'll be back when they're ready. Meantime it's best to have 'em out of this, I think. She wasn't my wife, anyway."

" 'Wasn't'?" she echoed quickly and he smiled and shook his head, as much as he could with a patient and indulgent air.

"There you go," he said, "there you go. So I got my tenses mixed up, couldn't anybody? 'Wasn't.' 'Isn't.' Anyway, they aren't here, so who cares, really?" His face darkened suddenly. "Good riddance to bad rubbish, if you want the truth."

"You had a fight, then," she said, frowning. "That's too bad. She could be a good witness for you if she were friendly."

"She isn't friendly," he said with a sudden little laugh she couldn't fathom; except she knew it left her uneasy. "Don't count on her. She won't testify for me. We'll just have to go on what we've got."

"Which is what?" she asked, giving him a sudden penetrating look that he was beginning to think was characteristic.

"Well," he whispered with a sudden wry grimace that she too was beginning to consider characteristic, "not my good looks, that's for sure."

"They'll improve," she predicted with a smile; and on a sudden impulse added, "Suppose you tell me what your defense will be. I get the feeling you know some law. You didn't take law, did you?"

"Nope," he said. "But I've absorbed some, here and there. Well, to begin with—"

After he had outlined his theory about circumstantial evidence and how it could be turned in his behalf, he stopped and looked at her with a satisfied expression. "Isn't that a pretty good defense?"

She studied him for several moments before replying.

"I think you're guilty," she said quietly. "I think you're guilty as hell."

"I didn't say so!" he whispered sharply. "They can't prove it! What the hell makes *you* so sure?"

"Because," she said, still quietly, "I agree so much with what you want to do and with the point you're making. I could have done the same thing myself if I had the opportunity. I suppose that's why."

There was silence while he studied her in return. Then he laughed as much as he could and rolled again to the wall, groaning once more as he did so.

"Am I to represent you or not?" she demanded.

"Suit yourself," he whispered over his shoulder. "Do you want to?"

"Yes," she said fiercely. "Yes, I do! I want to join your statement!"

"Be my guest," he said with the wracked ghost of a chuckle.

"Shall I tell Attorney General Stinnet?"

"I said, 'Be my guest,'" he whispered impatiently. "What more do you want?" Again he chuckled. "I'd like to hear what that pompous son of a bitch has to say to that."

"Don't underestimate him!" she advised sharply. "He's one smart son of a bitch and he's going to turn you into a symbol of everything this country is afraid of. I've watched him coming up these past couple of years I've been living down here and I know what he plans and how he operates. I'm not underestimating him and don't you, either!"

"Have faith, sweetheart," he told her over his shoulder. "Truth and justice are on our side. Righteousness forever!"

"I think you're crazy," she remarked, quite impersonally, "but I think we can make you a symbol too—*our* symbol. So I'll take the case, thank you very much."

"Thank *you*," he whispered with an ironic politeness. "Welcome to the evening news."

"That's where we're going to be fighting it," she agreed. "So I'd better get started right now."

And ten minutes later down in the prison lobby, facing Henrietta-Maude and the rest who had come over from the hospital, while Earle Holgren lay painfully on his side and slept again after his long and busy day, she did. Earle Holgren, she said, was a symbol of all Americans who truly believed in democracy, a dedicated fighter for the people, an enemy of all the corrupt reactionary fascist forces in the country that were always seeking to—

"He'll plead not guilty, of course," Henrietta interrupted dryly.

"Of course," Debbie Donnelson replied.

"Is he?" Henrietta inquired, wise old weatherbeaten face as shrewd, sharp and tenacious as the intense dark one facing her.

"Have you proof otherwise?" Debbie snapped. Henrietta smiled with the smile of one who, in forty years of newspapering, has seen it all.

"The proof is your job, girlie," she said. "I just report it to the folks. Right now, they're going to take a mighty lot of convincing if you're to make them believe he's not."

"They still can't convict him unless they've got proof," Debbie said.

"Regard Stinnet thinks he's got enough," Henrietta reminded. Debbie snorted.

"Regard Stinnet," she said, "thinks he has a lot of things he doesn't have."

Actually, while Earle Holgren continued to sleep peacefully in his cell the dreamless sleep of one both physically exhausted and mentally satisfied, Regard presently found that he had quite a bit more than she thought he did. The sheriff at Pomeroy Station was a tenacious and intuitive young man, too; and after he had thoroughly studied the deserted cabin for quite a while he had a hunch and an impulse, and followed them through.

He went back to the plant, aglare with lights as the inspection team continued to sift carefully through the debris; spoke for a while with the guards now ringing the site in a state of determined, if somewhat belated, alertness; and presently faded away unnoticed into the woods above. There he entered the cave and began patiently traversing it inch by inch, going very slowly, reading leaves and twigs and misplaced stones with all the skill of the mountain-trained.

Midway in the cave, covered over with branches and not too noticeable to the hasty eye, he found the mouth of what appeared to be an old abandoned well. Carefully he removed the branches, stretched full length on the ground to anchor himself, inched slowly to the rim and cast his flashlight beam into the depths below.

Apparently snagged on a ledge he estimated to be no more than ten feet below, he saw a jumbled heap of what appeared to be clothing; a tangle of what appeared to be long black hair, covering what appeared to be a bloody, shattered face; and, staring up at him with apparent intensity but without expression of any kind, what appeared to be, and indeed were, a pair of open eyes.

And even then, Regard Stinnet told himself disgustedly at three in the morning, he still didn't have the bastard. He had what might be his dead woman and his dead child. He had a crumpled sheet of paper so soaked in blood and waterlogged as to be almost illegible, found in one of the dead woman's pockets. But he didn't have his gun—they had tried to dredge the well but it appeared to go off into one of those bottomless fissures characteristic of the hills. He didn't have his fingerprints, he didn't have anything on him, really, except his presence outside the cave, his proximity to the scene of the crime—crimes—and dried semen on his pants. He would probably claim he was in the cave making it with some local babe, Regard thought with a disgusted snort, when suddenly the world just blew up around him. And that slick little sharpie who had wandered in out of nowhere to represent him might just be able to make it stick, too.

Well, Regard told himself with grim determination, not if *he* had anything to do with it: and he'd have plenty, Mr. Smart-Ass Holgren could be sure of that, *plenty*. Debbie Donnelson and her client weren't the only ones who saw that it would be played out on the evening news. He decided he would begin seriously right now to organize the campaign that would make of the Pomeroy Station bomber a symbol of all that was terrifying the country. He would make of Earle Holgren a lever whereby he himself and the millions of worried citizens who agreed with him might get the criminal justice system off its dead ass, as he put it to himself, and *get it moving*.

Debbie, he was sure, was going to try all the delaying tricks she could think of: but she wasn't the attorney general of South Carolina, an operator with a great deal of influence and a great many IOUs to cash. There were ways to speed up a trial as well as delay it, and in this instance he was quite confident he could do it. *His* judges, unlike some of the kooks Ted Phillips had to contend with in California, were *reliable*. They could be *counted on*. He didn't know which one would get it—he hoped Perlie Williams, who was a boyhood chum and agreed with him

absolutely on what needed to be done in the country—but they were all
good friends and they would all cooperate.

He didn't want any of this two-, three-, four-year lag on this one.

He wanted justice and he wanted it *now*.

"Justice NOW!" he muttered to himself. "*Enough is enough*. Justice
NOW!"

The two thoughts made a nice combination.

Hell, they made a damned good pair of slogans for a nationwide organization.

Rapidly he sketched his ideas for its seal on a memo pad:

That, he told himself with satisfaction, made a mighty effective sign.
Harassed men and women throughout the nation could rally around
that one. They could also rally around its founder and leader, who suddenly saw himself in mind's eye standing on endless flag-draped plat-
forms stretching into infinity while millions beyond number roared their
approval and in gratitude began to talk, in a great ground swell that
would not be denied, of higher things.

Well—he snorted and stopped himself short. There's a long way to
go yet, Regard, boy, he thought dryly: y'all better stop sellin' those
chickens before their mammies have even laid the eggs. Right now
you've got to organize. And you've also got to send that boy Earle
Holgren right back to his Maker the fastest possible way you know
how.

And that, he reminded himself in sudden glumness, is not going to be
easy.

He picked up the eavesdropping stenographer's notes, which he had
read already several times, and ran through them once again. Illegal as
hell, he couldn't use a damned bit of it in court, but it was enlightening
and helpful, anyway, even if it did leave a lot of things unanswered. At

least he knew the nature of his opponents better. One of them was a cold-blooded killer absolutely beyond conscience and morality. The other was a wide-eyed, tensed-up female ideologue, innocent and idealistic on the one hand and on the other a shrewd, sharp, calculating little legal whiz kid who would be like a terrier in her defense of what she saw as her client's "statement."

"You want to 'join it,' sister," he said aloud with another snort. "You want to 'join it'! Well, by God, aren't you the one, though."

But that didn't mean the calculating part of her wouldn't be a damned tough legal barrier. Particularly when, as he knew full well, she would have behind her the support of a number of famous well-heeled people and organizations and very likely a substantial share of major media as well. Not that any of them would condone outright or even indirectly what Earle Holgren had done in taking three lives and possibly destroying a fourth: but they would be inclined to sympathize with what he had done to the plant, and they would be very anxious that his "legal rights" be protected, and they would be very hypersensitive to anybody who seemed to be critical of what they conceived to be a sincere, if misguided and possibly even extreme, social protester.

Who was this mysterious guy in New York Debbie mentioned who had called her in? She hadn't named any names, but Holgren obviously knew at once whom she meant. His personal lawyer, maybe? Some left-winger who kept an eye on cases like Holgren's and stood by to help out when needed? Maybe even some Commie, which wasn't beyond the realm of possibility at all according to the FBI reports Regard had received in the past three hours, covering the Sixties and Seventies when Holgren had been getting in deeper and deeper. Or maybe even Holgren's rich old man, who feared and despised everything Holgren stood for and abhorred what he had done but nonetheless might have answered the call of parenthood in an emergency, as so many of the poor pathetic abandoned bastards did when their kids who hated them got into trouble.

A lot of possibilities. So far the FBI hadn't come up with it and maybe they wouldn't; but it was something to hammer on, anyway; something to throw Miss Deb off balance, perhaps. Something to speculate about in the media, most of whose members might despise what *he* was doing, but could be trapped by a clever man into using their own news channels to distribute his claims and allegations nationwide.

Yep, the evening news was where it was going to be fought out, equally with the courtroom: because he was going to make damned sure that the evening news came right inside the courtroom. He had his move on that all planned. The evidence so far might be all circumstantial but the conclusions to be drawn by the public could be crushingly decisive if he played them right. He damned well intended to.

He looked for a thoughtful moment at his freehand seal of Justice NOW! Any able draftsman could whip it into shape in ten minutes. By nightfall of this very day coming up, stickers, decals, T-shirts, ashtrays, banners, placards, you name it, could be streaming off assembly lines. He had a friend right here in Columbia who was in the novelty business: they saw eye to eye on the crime situation, and Regard bet he'd be willing to contribute most everything at a quarter cost, if not even right-out free. And he'd also bet that his friend Ted Phillips in California knew or could quickly find similar resources out there. In a week they'd have the country blanketed from one side to the other. Given the state of mind people were in about the situation, Justice NOW! could very well be the fastest-growing organization ever dreamed up in America. The confirming thing was that there had been no necessity to dream it up: it was there full-blown, a natural, a child of the times.

He glanced at his watch: three-thirty. It was half-past midnight in Sacramento. He dialed the home number Ted Phillips had given him. A drowsy young female voice answered. In a moment Ted came on.

"I've got me an idea," Regard said without preliminary. "Listen to this."

"That's great!" Ted Phillips enthused when he finished telling him about his plans to make Earle the symbol, and about Justice NOW! "That—is—*great!* I don't see how it can miss."

"Want to be vice-president?"

There was a pause of several seconds: Regard knew what was happening. Ted Phillips was calculating all the political angles, just as he had himself. He was confident of the outcome. Popular concern was so great that there could only be one.

"I think it's the best way to channel this threat of vigilantism into constructive and useful channels," Ted said slowly. "This is the compromise solution we have all been seeking, between unbridled public vengeance and the slackness and inadequacy of the present criminal justice system. This is the answer. This is the middle ground. Justice NOW! will lead the way."

"Save that," Regard said jovially, "and use it. The answer, in other words, is yes."

"The answer is yes," the attorney general of California said, "and I couldn't be happier to sign on. What about a national convention? The sooner the better, I'd think."

"That's a damned good idea," Regard agreed. "We'll tie it right in with the case. I'm not standin' for any delays in this matter. He's got him a shrewd little biddy who I have the feelin' is a pretty good little lawyer, but I'm not puttin' up with any nonsense. We aren't goin' to drag *this* case out for the next five years. We're goin' to move and *move fast*. The whole country is goin' to demand it—except that, God damn it, I've got my work cut out for me to prove he did it. Wish me luck."

"I do that," Ted Phillips said. "If I think of any way to help, I will. It's good to get *moving*."

"Justice NOW!" Regard remarked.

"Enough," Ted rejoined cheerfully, "is *enough*."

And enough of this damned hectic night is about enough for me this very minute, Regard told himself as he sent his compliments to Mrs. Phillips and bade his new friend and colleague good night. It was now nearing 4 A.M. and he had been up for almost twenty-two hours straight, the last eight of them on the merry-go-round of what he was already capitalizing mentally as *State of South Carolina v. Earle Holgren*. He had damned well better get on home and get at least three or four hours' sleep. The new day was going to be equally busy.

First, though, he decided he had better draft his formal statement to the media while everything was still fresh in his mind. He decided he would call a formal conference for 10 A.M. to start the ball rolling and at that time would put the whole thing in perspective. Wearily, yet with a final surge of strength that came from an iron constitution and an iron will, fortified by genuine indignation and an unwavering ambition, he began to write in the silence of his book-lined office.

"Ladies and gentlemen, my fellow Americans and friends of justice:

"As you all know, there occurred in South Carolina last night a dastardly horrible crime against lives and property.

"The property was the atomic energy plant at Pomeroy Station.

"That can be rebuilt.

"The lives were those of two young girls, a young woman and a male child of approximately six months in age.

"They can never be rebuilt.

"A possible suspect is being held pending further investigation.

"There is substantial indication that the attack was not only upon the atomic plant per se, but upon the institution of the Supreme Court of the United States. In addition to disrupting the plant, it seems clear there was a clear intention to assassinate Supreme Court Justice Stanley Mossiter Pomeroy and through his death do grievous damage to the faith and confidence Americans have in their judicial system.

"Unhappily, as many Americans recognize with alarm and dismay, that judicial system is at the moment in substantial disarray. This episode makes that sad fact even clearer. Will we now have endless delays, endless legal quibbles, devious and dilatory obstructionist tactics by unprincipled lawyers—" Ah, there, Debbie! he thought. How y'all, gal? "—and a complaisant tenderness for an obvious murderer on the part of too-lenient, too-'liberal' judges?

"Not in South Carolina. Not in an America whose people cry out more desperately than ever in the face of these latest awful crimes, *'Enough is enough! We want Justice NOW!'* Not when the Supreme Court, the very cornerstone of our laws and our liberties, has been directly, viciously, wantonly attacked with consequent loss of one beautiful young life, the possibly permanent damaging of another, and who knows what dark reasons for two additional deaths?

"It is time now to change all this once and for all. It is time for America to return to the concept not only of 'Equal Justice Under Law' which is the great motto of the Supreme Court, but to equal justice under law *swiftly rendered and speedily carried out.*

"America has been patient too long.

"America has been lax too long.

"America has freed her criminals and punished their victims too long.

"Enough is enough!

"America wants Justice NOW!"

And in a separate statement, which he would dictate to his secretary first thing in the morning and release simultaneously with his spoken word, he would announce the formation of Justice NOW! Immediately after that would come Ted Phillips' endorsement from California, and they would be off and running.

Earle Hogren, you murderous psychopath, he thought with satisfaction, you've started something a little bigger than you planned, boy. We're going to use you to hang the whole kit and caboodle as high as we can haul you. From now on this country is going to be on the march. At last we're goin' to clean up this criminal mess from coast to coast and border to border. At last all you worthless murdering bastards, you scum of the earth, are going to meet your match. Enough is *Enough.*

He picked up the phone, called the jail and told them to rouse Earle Holgren immediately.

"He'll just be restin' nicely," he said. "You go in there with all lights blazin' and start poundin' him with questions the minute you get him awake. Don't give him time to collect his thoughts, just go after him.

Then let him sleep again. But don't let him sleep more than an hour or two at a time. Keep up the routine as long as it takes. He'll break one of these days. Or he'll be damned sorry he didn't."

No more rough stuff whose results people could see, for Earle Holgren; but there were, as Regard Stinnet had learned in the terrifying three months he had been a prisoner of the communists in Vietnam, other ways.

He got up from his desk, started to snap off the lights. On a sudden impulse he returned to the desk, took a book from a shelf behind it, opened to a familiar picture. Across the stately white pillars and EQUAL JUSTICE UNDER LAW he slapped the hand-drawn seal of Justice NOW!

"We'll see, friends," he said with a grim little chuckle. "We'll see."

Then he roared off home in his armored Mercedes and fell into a heavy sleep for four hours, rising fresh as a daisy, as he proudly told Carolyn, to face the excitement of the day on which Justice NOW! would be born.

In Washington, those who lived and worked under the banner Regard had thus, in his own mind, improved upon, arose in more troubled mood. It was a Saturday morning and normally not more than three or four would have gone to their offices. Today, drawn by a compelling and irresistible urge to seek the reassurance of one another's company, they were all in the building by nine o'clock. Shortly thereafter the Chief called them to the Conference Room.

He had ordered a wide-screen television. He adjusted the picture, reduced the sound to inaudibility and turned to face them.

"Good morning," he said quietly. "Mr. Stinnet of South Carolina is going to be performing in a few minutes. I thought we should watch."

"By all means," Justice McIntosh said. "Have you heard from—?"

"Neither," The Elph said, "and aside from my first call expressing our condolences, I haven't tried to reach them. I didn't think we should intrude until they want to contact us."

"Oh, certainly not," she agreed. "I just wondered."

"I'll admit my impulse has been to call every hour on the hour," he said with a sad wryness, "but I suppressed it."

"I expect we've all felt that way," Wally Flyte said. "I still can't believe it happened. The national evil has landed on our doorstep now, all right."

The Chief Justice nodded unhappily, and gestured to the television screen. A reporter was mouthing something as the camera opened on a crowded press room and a tall, lanky, well-dressed individual appeared on the podium. "I think Mr. Stinnet is about to tell us everything he wants us to know."

Hughie Demsted, seated nearest the machine, got up and increased the volume. Then they settled back attentively as the commentator said in a hushed voice, "Ladies and gentlemen, Regard Stinnet, attorney general of South Carolina . . ."

In a voice he made deliberately heavy and emphatic, Regard ran through his prepared statement. He had made only one significant change. He had awakened with the conviction that this really *was* the big chance. He had decided that if he was going to gamble he had better gamble and gamble big. It was time to throw the dice or call the game. He disclosed the identities of Janet and John Lennon Peacechild and he had revised the key paragraph so that it now read:

"A suspect is being held pending further investigation by the FBI, by my office and by the district police and local government officials at Pomeroy Station. The name of this individual is Earle Holgren, though he has used numerous aliases over the past few years. He is a former resident of Greenwich, Connecticut, thirty-six years of age. He was a student radical in college and has since been engaged in various underground activities and protest movements of a radical nature. There appears to be sufficient evidence to link him to the crimes at Pomeroy Station. We believe we will have enough to obtain an indictment before the day is out. Should conviction occur, I am serving formal notice now, according to the laws of South Carolina, which require thirty days' notice of such intention, that the death penalty will be sought."

He raised a peremptory hand to still the clamoring questions that immediately arose and went firmly on with his planned peroration concerning the sad state of the criminal justice system, the attack on the Supreme Court and, finally, the demand for Justice NOW!

He began folding his notes at the lectern as the questions, surging and insistent and featuring now famous national names and faces, rushed there from far beyond the familiar statehouse crowd in Columbia, began to besiege him. For a moment or two he appeared about to answer, his expression still earnest, open and sincere, eyes thoughtfully widened, but just then (Right on schedule! he thought with satisfaction) a telephone rang at a table off to one side of the platform and behind him an aide leaped to get it.

"Mr. Stinnet!" he cried excitedly. "It's for you, Mr. Stinnet! It's Mr. Ted Phillips, the attorney general of California!"

"What the hell—?" a famous voice among the media inquired. But the networks knew, for instantaneously there appeared before the Justices in Washington and before all their many millions of countrymen and women who were watching that day, a split screen: Regard to the left, Ted Phillips to the right.

Solemnly Regard offered the vice-chairmanship of Justice NOW!

Solemnly Ted accepted.

"Thank you, my friend," Regard said. "I know that you agree with me that *all* states should be represented on the board of this organization, as all states and all citizens are directly involved in the war against violent crime. Therefore I shall appoint all of our fellow attorneys general to serve as associate vice-chairmen of Justice NOW! Very soon I shall convene a meeting of all who desire to come.

"I think," he said in a tone that would, he knew, make it very difficult for any to refuse, "that most of us care enough about lifting terror from the backs of our citizens and restoring true justice to America to attend. Together we will plan how best to organize to bring that justice back to America.

"Meantime"—he looked once more earnestly, directly into the cameras, "meantime, what can the honest men and women of America do? You can join us, I say to you, my countrymen and women! You can join Justice NOW! We don't need your money—except maybe no more than a dollar apiece to help defray expenses of a small secretarial staff, because I know there are going to be so many, many millions of you that a dollar apiece will be more than ample. The main thing we need is your support—your strong, articulate, loyal, patriotic, law-loving, law-abiding, law-strengthening support, which will give us literally the strength of millions from all across this beloved, worried land.

"Send your names to me, Regard Stinnet, Attorney General, Columbia, South Carolina. *Do it today!* Together we will raise a mighty army to strike the shackles from the law! Together we will smite the transgressors and drive them from our streets and cities! Together we will do battle for the Lord and for the safety of ourselves, our children and our society! Join us! *Join us!* Together we will be invincible! *Enough is enough! Justice NOW!*"

And, face aglow with mission and purpose, he replaced the telephone receiver on its hook. On the other side of the split screen, his face also appearing enrapt in vision, Ted Phillips almost reverently did the same.

For a long moment there was utter silence in the crowded press room in Columbia, in the Conference Room of the Supreme Court of the United States and indeed in most places across an entire continent within sound of Regard Stinnet's voice.

"Whooo-eee," Justice Demsted said softly as he got up and went to the machine. "That's some attorney general. May I, Chief?"

"Yes, turn it off," Duncan Elphinstone said with a little shudder of distaste; and when Hughie had done so and returned to his seat, the Chief drew a long, thoughtful breath, gave them a moody glance and said, *"Well."*

"It doesn't look good, does it, Dunc?" Wally Flyte remarked softly. Clem Wallenberg snorted.

"It looks like bloody hell and damnation for everybody," he said. "This is exactly what we've been afraid of, and now it's come. What do we propose to do about it?"

"What can we do about it?" Ray Ullstein inquired. "It hasn't come up to us, and it won't for a while yet. Maybe never, if some clever advocate gets hold of it and gets this individual released."

"I don't think anybody will be released from this one," Hughie Demsted said. "I think this Stinnet has the country's mood analyzed perfectly. There's going to be enormous pressure for a fast trial and a fast conviction, unless I miss my guess."

"And the death sentence," the Chief Justice said gloomily.

"And an appeal to us," May McIntosh predicted. "And there—we—are."

"You shouldn't object," Justice Hemmelsford remarked tartly. "That will give you and Clem a chance to write more brilliant opinions pointing out how awful the death sentence is. Those of us who happen to believe in simple justice won't have a chance to be heard in all the approving uproar."

"I don't know that it will be all that approving," Justice McIntosh retorted with some asperity. "If the public clamor is as heavy as Hughie thinks it will be, then we may find ourselves very much in the minority, not only here but nationally."

"This is an anti-death-sentence Court—" Justice Demsted began. He paused. "Or is it?"

"I know you were counting on picking up Tay Barbour's vote," Rupert Hemmelsford said with some spitefulness in his voice, "but where does Tay Barbour stand now? It suddenly isn't an academic question for him and Moss, is it?"

"It suddenly isn't academic for any of us," Justice Wallenberg growled. "And maybe it's a good thing. We get entirely too removed and Olympian on this Court. We tend to be pretty arrogant and self-righteous sometimes. Maybe it's good to have real life yank us down off the bench and rub our noses in the filth and unhappiness of this world once in a while. One of our brethren almost lost his life yesterday; his child did. The child of another is apparently hanging between life and death. Maybe it's good for us to have to live with reality for a change. Not, of course, that I'm happy it happened the way it did, you understand me. But maybe it's time we were humbled. We play God too much in this building."

There was startled silence for a moment. Mary-Hannah adjusted her pince-nez and looked at them thoughtfully.

"I quite agree. Here we sit in our nine separate chambers like little tin gods, above the law, above the people, even, thanks to John Marshall"—she smiled wryly—"and may he preserve us from the ebb of public support as he has for so many long, long years—above the Congress and above the President. We *are* too Olympian sometimes. We *are* guilty of too much righteousness. But how can we feel that way now, when 'law and order' is suddenly taking on a very grave and potentially lawless aspect? I'm dreadfully worried, myself. One unbalanced murderer is starting to shake the whole fabric of American justice —indeed the whole fabric of American society. If he's the type he appears to be, I'm sure he's enjoying it thoroughly. And his case *is* coming up to us sooner or later, of that I'm sure. Probably sooner. How do we reconcile our sworn duty to the country and the law with the problem he poses?"

"How do we deal with the problems Stinnet and his sidekick in California pose?" Rupert Hemmelsford inquired gloomily. "That's the immediate issue. Like you, May, I'm worried as hell. This 'Justice NOW!' bit is not a very happy idea, in my estimation. They're going to have the whole country riled up by nightfall."

"It is already," Duncan Elphinstone said with equal gloom. "I wish there were something we could do. I'd like to issue a statement deploring it, but that would be too much of a shock, I suppose."

"It would only bring great criticism," Justice Flyte said, "and anyway, how could you? Their ostensible purpose—in fact, I don't have any reason to doubt them, I think their genuine purpose—*is* law and order. They *do* want to re-establish and strengthen it. They *are* genuinely appalled by the spread of violent crime. I'll grant you Stinnet is using it to make political hay, but the bottom line is still violence, lawlessness and wanton disregard for life. That's something every decent citizen can relate to, and millions of them are doing so, right now. And as you say, Hughie, it's going to bring enormous pressures.

"*Convict and kill:* that's all the majority wants to do to this guy right now. There're going to be some very fundamental issues raised by this case, I'm afraid; and I'm afraid it won't be at all clear-cut." He sighed heavily. "Sister and brethren, thanks to little Mr. Earle Holgren, we, like everybody else, face one hell of a problem."

"And the biggest problems of all, of course," the Chief said sadly, "are those faced by Moss and Sue-Ann and Tay and Mary. I only wish we could help them." His eyes were sad and far away. An answering sadness fell upon them all as the law sank suddenly into the background and the full import of the human tragedy rushed back. "I only wish we could . . ."

But whether anybody could was a question to which, Tay decided as the day wore on, there was as yet no answer. Certainly he did not seem able to find one: it was all he could do to keep on an even keel himself. He received no help from Mary. She remained closed off in her private world, and though he tried several times, he could not break through.

After their interview with the doctors and their brief talk with the Pomeroys, they had returned to the room where Janie was sleeping. A nurse hovered, and at first he suffered this, uneasily but with some patience. Mary did not.

"Would you mind getting out?" she snapped suddenly. The nurse, a kind-faced woman whom he judged to be in her later fifties, responded with a startled look.

"I'm here on doctor's orders, ma'am," she said politely; and added, more firmly, "and here I intend to stay until ordered otherwise."

"I'm ordering you otherwise," Mary said harshly. The nurse did not flinch.

"Indeed," she said. "I meant doctor's orders, Mrs. Barbour. Those are *my* orders."

"Not against the wishes of the family," Mary said crisply. "Do I have to go and get the doctor and make a scene of it?"

The nurse started to respond on the order of, "You are already," visibly caught herself just in time.

"I shall go and talk to him myself," she said with dignity.

"Please do," Mary said. "And take your time about it. There's no need for you to hurry back."

"Whatever he says," the nurse said coldly and went out, lips tightly pressed, hostility and disapproval in every step.

"Why did you have to do that?" he inquired automatically; he was really too tired and emotionally exhausted to care. But it seemed something should be said.

"Because I am in torment," his wife said in a dead voice. "I am in hell. I have to let it out somehow. Would you rather I turned on you?"

"I'm more used to it than that poor woman," he said with a sad indifference. "Go ahead."

"Sometimes, Taylor Barbour," she replied in the same desolate tone, "I think you have no feelings whatsoever. Sometimes I think you are composed of the law, of ambition, a reasonably large endowment of brains—and nothing. Nothing at all. There is no heart. Somewhere it got left out."

"Mary," he said, voice trembling, looking at her with a sad patience across the comatose form of their daughter. "I understand how you feel. I am—trying to be patient with you, under great provocation. But I am not going to take it much longer. I warn you. Not much longer."

"What can you do?" she asked. "Certainly you can't leave me now. Not when my child lies at death's door because of your indulgence and irresponsibility toward her welfare. That would not fit the image of the great Mr. Justice Barbour, now, would it? To abandon me and Janie in this, our time of extremity?"

"You are so dramatic," he said with a sigh. "So dramatic. I too am having my 'time of extremity.' Don't you think it would help us both—and help Janie—if we tried to be friends and help each other through it, instead of your being so grossly unfair? I have done my best with this marriage. I have been a good husband, I have been a good father. This I know, and this I cling to. You can't destroy that knowledge, though God knows you are trying hard enough. And the awful thing to me," he added quietly, "is that I don't know why. I just don't know why."

"Perhaps there is no reason," she said, the ghastly ghost of a smile crossing her face for a moment, "except your own perfection. It may be too much for those around you—or for me, at any rate. Others can admire it from afar. I have had to live with it."

"But I'm *not* perfect," he protested, thinking even as he did so that this was an insane conversation, and perhaps that was the answer, perhaps she truly was insane. "God *knows* I am not. I have never claimed to be. I have never thought to be. The idea is absurd."

"Oh, no," she said. "Oh, no. Perfect Taylor Barbour, the perfect lawyer, the perfect man, the perfect husband and father—so good, so kind, so dignified, so *superior*. Always *superior*. And I suppose, if the case of the destroyer of your daughter, perhaps even yet the murderer of your daughter, ever comes before you, you will be superior then. I can see you now—weighing all things, balancing all things, being thoughtful, considerate, compassionate, *forgiving* to a piece of human filth who doesn't deserve a second's forgiveness from anyone—being Taylor Barbour, the perfect judge, calm, judicious, above it all—*inhuman.*"

"Don't be too sure," he said, voice harsh with strain, "that I will be the perfect judge if this case ever comes before me."

"Your character won't permit you to be anything else," she said with a sigh. "These are the things on which you pride yourself. They comprise the entity known as Taylor Barbour. You cannot betray them, for that would be to betray yourself. And you wouldn't do that, even for your own daughter."

For a long moment they stared at one another, passed beyond hostility into some other world of utter truth; and finally he sighed and rubbed his eyes with his hands.

"No," he said, voice low. "You are right. I could not betray the objectivity and fairness I believe in—I could not betray the law as I see it. I should have to be fair, because that is what I am. Without that there wouldn't be any Taylor Barbour."

"Not even for your own daughter," she repeated bleakly. "Not even for her."

"No," he replied, as one damned—and thought then that it was true. "Not even for her."

"Well," she said, "at least you don't prevaricate or attempt to dodge the issue or try to hide behind words, I'll say that for you. At least you're honest in your inhumanity."

"Mary—Mary—leave me alone, O.K.? *Just leave me alone.* We should never have a discussion like this under conditions such as these. We should never have it any time. I don't want to talk about it any more. I swear in the presence of our poor little"—his voice broke for a second, but he forced it on—"of our daughter, that I have tried to be a good husband to you and a good father to her. I have tried to be a good human being, a good lawyer, a good public servant. I shall keep on trying to be so. I hope the facts may permit me to do what you want, but if they don't, then I must be true to what I believe. I cannot do otherwise, for that is the way I am. Now, please, let's leave it at that. I beg of you. Since you force me to beg."

She gave him a long, contemplative look, a strange mixture of contempt and cold amusement in her eyes.

"Even now," she said softly. "Even now, the perfect image, the proper sentiments and the proper words. Even now, Taylor Barbour. You need a humbling, Tay."

"And you need *something*," he said, bitterly at last, "though God alone knows what it is."

"Look!" she cried suddenly in a voice that made the hairs rise on the back of his neck. *"Her eyes are open!"*

And so they were; but there was nothing in them, and after what seemed an eternity, though it could only have been a moment or two, they closed.

He stood up abruptly.

"I am going to see Moss and Sue-Ann," he said harshly. "I shall be back very shortly. You may come with me, which would be the decent thing, or you may use the excuse you have and stay away."

"My child is not an excuse," she said bleakly. "She is a necessity to me if not to you. Go along to them."

"I shall convey our sympathies," he said with a savage politeness.

"As you like," she said, and turned back to stare again, stricken and intent, at their daughter's face.

Outside in the hall he found the nurse, seated on a bench reading a magazine, an expression of stern disapproval still on her face: within call, as he knew she felt she must be.

"I must apologize for Mrs. Barbour," he said. The nurse glanced up, then back to her magazine, expression unchanged.

"Don't," she said. "She doesn't deserve it. Why should you lower yourself to defend her?"

"I'm her husband," he said simply. The nurse sniffed.

"Too bad you don't have someone else," she said, snapping over a page with a slap that dismissed him. *"That* one doesn't deserve you."

He started to retort, to put her in her place, to relieve tensions by berating her for insolence, disrespect, unkindness—then he stopped. She had given voice to the impulse that had been in his heart ever since their arrival. He did have someone else. Why not let her comfort him?

"Thank you," he said abruptly and turned away, leaving her looking after him, speculative.

There was a phone booth at the end of the corridor. He closed the door, dialed, gave his credit card number, waited. The phone rang three times in the charming little house off Stanton Square; her recorded voice requested name, number, message; a beep-tone sounded.

"This is Taylor Barbour—" he began, and at once she broke in.

"Yes, Tay," she said quietly. "I'm here. I've been wanting to call you but I thought I'd better wait. How are you getting along?"

"Managing," he said, amazed at the flood of relief and calmness that swept over him at the sound of her voice.

"And your daughter?"

"Still unconscious."

"What do you think?"

"Fifty-fifty," he said, voice suddenly shaky. He forced it steadier and went on. "They think she's going to live, but there's some possibility of —of brain damage."

"Oh, I hope not," she said in a hushed voice.

"I'm trying not to believe it," he said, and realized suddenly that he was not only trying not to, he was succeeding. He was absolutely certain that Janie would come out of this safely and be Janie again. Only that certainty, he knew now, permitted him to keep going: only that certainty enabled Taylor Barbour to defend what he believed, and continue to be what Taylor Barbour thought Taylor Barbour ought to be. *Help me, Janie,* he prayed silently in his mind. *Don't let me down now. I couldn't stand it.*

More firmly he said:

"I am convinced she will be all right. You know doctors. Sometimes they try to prepare you for the worst a little more than necessary. They're basically confident, I think."

"How is Mary taking it?" she asked.

He hesitated a second, then told the truth.

"Poorly."

"She's blaming you."

"Yes."

"Ah, darling," she said, sounding for a second close to tears. "I am so sorry."

"That's all right," he said hastily, anxious that she not falter also but remain his strength. "It's just the way she is. She probably can t help herself."

"Oh, I think she can," she said, voice stronger with skepticism. "I think she knows what she's doing, all the time."

"No," he said, and in all fairness meant it. "I don't think so. She really is devastated by this. It makes her more—more extreme than she normally is."

"She shouldn't be extreme at all," she said with a complete, flat honesty that forced him to agree.

"No . . . but she is."

"I wish you were here," she said suddenly. "Or I there. It's too hard to be apart at a time like this."

"Yes," he said, and abruptly it was true and he no longer worried about consequences. "It won't happen again."

"How can it not happen again?" she inquired bleakly. "She isn't going to let you go, is she? Furthermore, we've known each other a couple of weeks. How can we be sure of anything, yet?"

"I'm sure," he said; and was.

"Well, I'm not."

"Why not?" he demanded sharply. It was desperately important to know.

"Just because I'm not. It doesn't happen this fast—and last. Or so I've found." She laughed, somewhat shakily. "On my few excursions out."

"I hope this is more than an excursion," he said gravely.

"I think so," she said, tone instantly grave in response to his. "But I want to wait a little longer before I become a back-street romance."

"You won't ever be that!" he declared, hurt and angry. "I don't—I'm not like that."

"What are you like? You see, that's what I don't know."

"Am I—inadequate in some way?" he demanded. "Is that it?"

"Heavens, *no!*" she said, and this time laughed more naturally. "Far from it. You're quite man enough for me to handle, thank you very much."

"Well, then—" he began indignantly, but again she stopped him with laughter.

"You're so *male*," she said. "'*Am I adequate? Very well, then, isn't that sufficient? What are you complaining about? What else is there?*' Well, my dear: quite a bit. Anyway, we're getting rather far away from your tragedy, aren't we? How are the Pomeroys taking it?"

"Cathy—" he began, but she only repeated levelly, "How are the Pomeroys taking it?"

"All right," he conceded, "I'll stop. But we'll talk about this."

"Please," she agreed. "When you're back."

"Yes . . . The Pomeroys are taking it very hard, but bearing up. I'm just on my way to see them now."

"If they knew me I'd say give them my love. But of course they don't and probably never will, so—"

"Oh yes they will," he said flatly. "I'll tell them I talked to a friend in D.C. who sends her love, and that they will meet her one of these days and appreciate the thought even more when they have."

"That will allay their curiosity, all right . . . Will this case come up to the Court?"

"I expect it may. But don't ask me now what I'll do, because I don't know." In spite of himself his tone became bitter. "I've just been accused of being smug, superior, obsessed with the law to the exclusion of my own daughter, and having no heart and nothing inside. So I really couldn't tell you. Anyway, I don't want to talk about it further now."

"I'm sorry," she said quietly. "She picks a good time to be unfair. It must be very helpful to you both."

"It seems to help her," he said; then some lingering trace of loyalty brought a halt. "But I don't want to discuss all that right now, any more than you do the other. Maybe when we see each other again—"

"Which I hope will be soon," she said. "Very soon. Though I know it will probably be many days."

"Yes. There's no indication yet of when we can move Janie, and of course that imposes a further worry, too, because I've just come on the Court, I know how busy they are, and suddenly Moss and I aren't there to keep up our share of the work. Ah, the whole thing is so damnable, such a waste for everybody. Except, I suppose, the psychopath who did it. People like that never care how many they hurt or they wouldn't do it in the first place."

"I know," she said. "I'm against the death penalty, but I begin to wonder, now . . . I begin to wonder."

"I don't want to think about that, either," he said; and added with a bitter irony, "There'll be plenty of time. I must go to see Moss and Sue-Ann now. I'm glad you're home. I didn't know whether you would be, but I just wanted to touch base—I wanted to be in touch with reality again."

"I hope I represent that to you," she said quietly.

"More so every day."

"I'm glad. Call whenever you can."

"I will. I wish—"

"I know," she said. "I, too. Good-bye and God bless."

"God bless," he said and hung up, aware as he left the booth that the nurse was studying him with a curious look. He returned a cold one that made her drop her eyes hastily again to her magazine. He glanced quickly into the room, saw the tableau unchanged, Janie sleeping and Mary leaning forward above her, chin in hand, face white and strained, endlessly studying; and turned and strode on out. Under a tree nearby a driver sprang up, jumped in a car, brought it quickly to him.

"Compliments of Mr. Stinnet, sir," he said, hopping out to open the door. "Where'd y'all like to go?"

"The Carolina Inn," he said and sank back into the seat, closing his eyes and rubbing them deeply. The car swung out and away.

"Mighty sorry to hear about y'all's trouble, Mr. Justice," the driver said with a hearty and excruciating friendship as they entered traffic. "And Governor Pomeroy's too, of course. Terrible, terrible, terrible, *terrible!* I think they ought to hang that no-good bastard in front of the state capitol and declare a national holiday while they're doing it. I think they ought to do that with all these murderous bastards who are turnin' America into a jungle, then maybe we'd get somewhere with restorin' law and order the way they ought to be in America! Yes, sir!"

"Maybe we would," he said, hoping agreement would stem the flood. Of course it only encouraged it.

"But I guess Mr. Stinnet has the answer all right, don't you think?" the driver asked, swinging half around to glance over his shoulder.

"Does he? What's Mr. Stinnet's answer?"

"You mean you haven't *heard?*" the driver demanded, disbelieving, turning back just in time to narrowly avoid an oncoming car. "You mean you didn't hear him and the attorney general of California on television this morning? But no, of course you wouldn't, you've been with your little girl. I'm sorry, Mr. Justice, naturally you wouldn't."

"Tell me about it," he suggested, warning instincts alerted. The driver obliged. Tay offered no comments, though a heavy concern began to grow in his heart.

"I guess that'll show 'em," the driver concluded with satisfaction. "News says they're getting so many phone calls and telegrams for Mr. Stinnet it's practically shut down the statehouse switchboard. That'll show 'em! Don't you agree, Mr. Justice?"

"It certainly indicates there's a great deal of public interest," he answered cautiously. The driver snorted.

"It indicates a damned sight more'n that. It indicates that this country is determined to have Justice NOW! And by God we're goin' to get it! They're goin' to start distributing buttons and bumper stickers at the statehouse this afternooon, and I'll bet you by today week this whole damned country'll be plastered with 'em from one end to the other. People are just fed up, Mr. Justice, they're just God damned *fed up!*"

"Maybe so," he replied and for a second the driver looked blank.

"Aren't you?" he asked in an odd tone. "God knows if *any*body ought to be, *you* ought to be."

"I am," he said with a sudden savage emphasis. "You have no idea how *many* things I'm fed up with at this particular moment."

"Well," the driver responded uncertainly. "Well, all right. I was just

tryin' to be friendly, Mr. Justice. I didn't mean to get you riled up. I
thought all decent folks would agree with Justice NOW! and what Mr.
Stinnet is tryin' to do. I was *just* tryin' to be friendly."

"I know you were," he said with a sigh, "and I'm sorry I snapped at
you. I'm just under—a lot of strain, I guess."

"And naturally enough," the driver said, mollified. "Naturally
enough. Maybe I'd better shut up and concentrate on my drivin' for a
while. We're almost there, anyway."

"Thank you," he said, and repeated: "I'm sorry."

"Quite all right," the driver said, recovering. "You give Mr. Stinnet
my very best. You tell him I think he's doin' a great job and we all
think he's goin' to be a real national figure in no time, the way he's
goin'."

"I'll tell him," Tay said, "but I'm sure he knows already."

And indeed there was a certain indefinable glow about the attorney
general of South Carolina when the car finally reached the Carolina Inn
and his tall, lanky figure hurried forward, hand outstretched. Here, Tay
recognized, was A Man With A Purpose. It was quite obvious the purpose was being achieved very rapidly and in all ways pleasing to its pro-
prietor.

"Mr. Justice!" Regard said with a suitable mixture of cordiality and
respect for tragedy. "Mr. Justice, I can't say it's nice to have you here
for the reason for which you *are* here, but in any event I hope you feel
that you're among true and sympathetic friends who want to help you in
every way we can."

"I do feel that, Mr. Stinnet," he said, shaking hands gravely taking
the occasion to give his host a quick but encompassing glance. A
smooth talker and a gentleman in one aspect, he thought, a demagogue
and fanatic in the other. Shrewd, quick, adaptive, ambitious, determined
and not to be deflected: a formidable character, seized now of a formidable crusade to which even Supreme Court Justices, he thought wryly,
might find it hard not to bow.

But not yet awhile, he promised himself. If ever.

"Mr. Stinnet," he said, "how are Moss and Sue-Ann, and can I see
them?"

"Of course you can, Mr. Justice," Regard said, hurrying him past the
reporters and photographers who had gathered from around the lobby.
"They're bearin' up. Pomeroys and Laceys are good blood, Mr. Justice,

good blood. It's a terrible shock and tragedy for them, but they're takin'
it like a true son and daughter of the Old South. Like South Carolina
would want them to; like South Carolina *expects* them to. And they *are*.
Quite remarkable, Mr. Justice. Yes, sir. Quite remarkable. Not that y'all
aren't, too," he added hastily. "I must say from what I hear, and what I
can see right now, both of you are takin' this tragedy with the greatest
possible courage and fortitude. Especially when things are so—so uncertain, you might say."

"Uncertain, yes," he agreed grimly, "but I am convinced my daughter will recover completely from this senseless and wanton act."

"So am I!" Regard assured him as the police pushed back the media
and they began to ascend. "So are we all! There's no doubt of it! And
you surely are right, Mr. Justice, to describe this as a senseless and
wanton act. Isn't that what most of them are, these days? And isn't this
exactly an example of why all decent, law-abiding Americans must
unite in a great crusade against the tide of lawlessness that is sweeping
the land? Doesn't it prove we need an organization such as I've just
founded to coordinate and direct the campaign?"

"Yes, I've heard about your organization. How is it going?"

"Wildfire," Regard said with satisfaction. "Plain wildfire. I'm glad
you approve of it, Mr. Justice. It's good to have your endorsement."

"I haven't endorsed it," he said sharply, "and you know very well
that in my position I neither can nor will. So be very careful how you
quote me to the media, Mr. Attorney General. Bear in mind that you
may ultimately come before me on the Court, and don't antagonize me
with unfounded reports."

"No, sir," Regard Stinnet said, looking crestfallen for a moment.
"That's the last thing I would wish to do, believe me. All I want to do is
convict this worthless piece of human excrement and at the same time
encourage and unite all decent law-abiding Americans who want to see
their country restored to safety and security for themselves and their
children."

"You're taking quite a responsibility on yourself," he observed as the
elevator stopped and the door opened upon another small group of
police standing guard at a room halfway down the hall.

"Somebody has to," Regard responded smoothly, "particularly if the
sworn custodians of the law shirk their trust."

For a moment he almost uttered an angry retort, then prudence intervened.

"Sometimes what appear to be good ideas initially can get badly out of hand," he remarked as they came to the guarded room and the police stepped aside for them to enter. "You should watch yours."

"Everybody's goin' to be watchin'," Regard told him happily. "Everybody's goin' to be watchin' because *everybody* has an interest. Yes, sir," he added with satisfaction, "everybody's goin' to be watchin' who's for us. *And* who's against us. '

And composing his face quickly into a suitable mask of sorrow he rapped gently on the door and called softly, "Moss. Y'all in there, Moss? Mr. Justice Barbour's here."

Moss appeared, haggard and exhausted but composed. Tay held out his hand. Moss gripped it hard, their eyes held for a moment. Then Moss stepped aside and gestured him in. Sue-Ann, her fine beauty drawn taut by tiredness, pain and the ravages of recurrent weeping, but also composed, rose from a sofa and kissed him gravely on the cheek.

He started to turn toward Regard. The attorney general anticipated him.

"Now if y'all will excuse me," he said, "I've got to be gettin' back to my office. They're goin' wild over there with the response to Justice NOW! It's comin' in from all over the country and it seems to be growin' bigger by the hour. I think we've really got somethin' goin'. Apparently this dreadful crime has suddenly just coalesced everything. Things are goin' to change in America from now on." His face turned grim. "I've also got a date with that despicable no-good restin' over there in the county jail."

"What evidence have you got?" Moss inquired somberly. "Any?"

"Mostly circumstantial," Regard admitted. "But enough to convict the bastard in today's climate—the climate he's created for himself. When we get this thing really organized—"

"You can't win the case with a circus," Tay said bluntly. Regard gave him an indignant look.

"A circus, Mr. Justice!" he exclaimed. "I shouldn't think you'd be the one to cry 'circus,' when your very own little baby is—"

"That's enough!" Moss snapped, face white. "You get on back there and tend to this case, Regard. And just remember that if, when and if it comes up to us, public pressure isn't going to have much effect."

"You haven't seen the kind of public pressure that's goin' to build around this one, Moss," Regard said softly. "You fellows on the Court just don't have any concept of what's beginnin' to build. It's been a mighty long time—maybe back as far as Dred Scott—since the Court has had to face the public outcry it may have to face on this one. And while I'm sorry I put it on a personal basis, Justice Barbour, sir, and I do apologize for that, still it seems to me there's a question that ought to be concernin' you two: just how *will* you handle it, if it does come up to you? There's never been a case before where individual Justices have been so directly and *personally* involved. How will you handle that?"

There was silence while he and Sue-Ann studied their somber faces. Again their eyes met.

"We are sworn to uphold the law," Tay said gravely. "To 'administer justice without respect to persons, and do equal right to the poor and to the rich.' And so I intend to do."

Moss gave a heavy sigh and nodded as his eyes sought his wife's.

"And I," he said at last, voice low.

"I respect your intentions," Regard said, still softly, "but it may not be so easy when the man who destroyed your daughters comes before you."

"Oh!" Sue-Ann cried. Her husband put his arm around her and nodded toward the door with a sad and tortured expression.

"Get out of here, Regard!" he ordered. "You just get on out! Right now."

"Yes, sir," Regard said calmly. "I will go back and make my case and tend to Justice NOW! You gentlemen be thinking, meanwhile."

And he bowed gravely, turned and left, closing the door gently but firmly behind him.

Sue-Ann returned to the sofa. Moss remained standing in the center of the room. Tay stared out the window.

"He seems very confident," he said finally, turning to them. "He must feel he really does have the country behind him."

"I suspect he does," Moss said. "Right now, anyway. Long enough to carry him through the case, maybe . . . Taylor"—he rubbed his eyes hard, sighed, sat down next to his wife—"what *are* we going to do?"

"Not anticipate," Tay replied, taking a chair opposite. "Perhaps that's the best thing we can do, at the moment."

"How can we not anticipate?" Moss inquired. "He's right. It'll come up to us. If there's a conviction and a death sentence, there'll be an appeal to stay execution and remand for re-argument. And that will come directly to me as Circuit Judge for the Fourth Circuit Court of Appeals. And, Tay"—his face looked tortured again and his voice dropped to a near whisper—"I just don't know how judicial I can be if I'm confronted with the—the murderer of my daughter."

"But you must be," Tay protested, realizing even as he said it how glib and trite it sounded, yet driven by his own rigid concept of the law. "You must be if you—if you stay on the case. If there is error in the courts below, if reasonable doubt exists—you have to be, Moss. You have no choice."

"Easy for you to say," Sue-Ann observed in a small voice that passed no judgments but chilled him with its remoteness, "when Janie still lives."

"Even if—" he began, lowered his head in his hands, took a deep breath, started over. "Even *if*—and even if *I* were the Circuit Judge being appealed to, I still would feel that I must be true to my oath and to my concept of the law. I just couldn't do otherwise."

"You don't think so now," Sue-Ann said, "and I pray you won't ever have to find out. But if you did, I think you might feel differently. Even you, Tay, who have always been perfect."

"But I'm *not* perfect!" he protested bitterly, for here was the damnable word again, the damnable misunderstanding of himself. "God knows I am not! I'm just a stumbling, awkward, inept, imperfect servant of the law who is weak like everybody else, *not* possessed of any special knowledge, *not* possessed of any exceptional abilities. Just *myself*. Not perfect, as God is my judge. *Not perfect*."

"But capable of—objectivity," Sue-Ann said, as though he were a complete stranger she was contemplating for the first time. "That's where you are different, maybe. I'm not sure Moss can be so—so objective . . . any more."

"But the law—" he began; and stopped, for suddenly his words seemed enormities to himself as he realized for a second how they must sound to his friends. But the perception was gone in a second. He realized only that further discussion now was fruitless, though he knew with an unhappy certainty that it would come back when they returned to the Court.

"Moss," he said earnestly, "this certainly isn't something you need to decide now. It will be months before the case comes to trial—"

Moss shook his head.

"He wants to ram it through just as fast as he can, and I think he's going to be able to do it. It'll be three months at the most; much less if the courts here cooperate. And since I am who I am," he said, quite simply and without egotism, "they'll do it to oblige me as well as him. Oh, we'll get it through fast, I think I can predict that. And *then* we'll see what happens."

"All right," Tay conceded. "But wait until then. Nothing at our level has to be decided about it right now. You're not in shape to do it, I'm not in shape to do it. Let's don't fight about it, for God's sake."

"I don't want to," Moss said. "You're the one," he pointed out, but

not unkindly, "who's talking about his duty to the law, at the moment."
A ghost of his old humor came back for a second. "I'm just trying to
get through the day. Is there—any change? With Janie?"

"No," he said, brought back with a crash to concerns far more desperate at the moment than the law. "But," he added firmly, "the doctors are optimistic and I'm optimistic too."

"How optimistic are they?" Sue-Ann asked quietly.

"They say there is some possibility of brain damage," he admitted,
"but—" he hurried on, "it is only a possibility. The chances are equally
good that there will be none. That"—his head came up in challenge—"is
what *I* believe. She is a strong and healthy child, as the doctor put it,
and the chances are excellent that she will come through entirely unscathed and be herself again."

"I pray every minute," Sue-Ann said gently, with a generosity of
spirit and soul so instinctive, kind and complete that his eyes filled with
tears.

"I'm sorry," he said, voice unsteady. "Sorry—sorry—*sorry*—when you
two have so much to bear—"

"That's all right, buddy," Moss said, barely steady himself. "That's
what friends are for. Don't worry about us. We've had as much as the
Lord can throw. He can't do any more to us now."

"How is Mary?" Sue-Ann inquired, again a kind and genuine concern in her voice.

"Mary is Mary," he said. "I can't begin to tell you again how sorry I
am about her behavior when we first arrived. It was inexcusable. Just
simply inexcusable."

"She was under great strain," Sue-Ann said. "Don't you fret yourself.
I can understand it."

"I can understand it, too," he said bitterly, "but I can't forgive it. It
was inexcusable."

"You must forgive it, Tay," she said. "It does no good to harbor
these things. She'll be better as the crisis passes."

"You don't know what she's said since," he responded, still bitterly.

"We don't want to know," Sue-Ann said, "but I'm sure, again, that it
was just because she's under such a strain."

"You've known Mary for a long time," he said. "If it's strain, then
she's been under it for many years."

"Perhaps," Sue-Ann agreed; but to his sudden sharp glance her voice
and expression were noncommittal. "Still, you must be patient. You
have too much to face together to let things separate you now."

"What would you say—" he began; and then abruptly stopped. These

were his oldest and best friends; for just a second he had been on the
very verge of blurting out something about Cathy. A last-minute caution, the inward secrecy of Taylor Barbour, "a very private man," to
use one of the media's pet clichés about him, had intervened. Someday
soon, perhaps. But not yet. "Nothing," he said with a careful smile to
their puzzled glances. "Nothing at all . . . Is there anything I can do to
help you?"

"Thanks, pal," Moss said, sounding more himself for a moment.
"Just coming over has been a help. Everything's pretty much under
control, I guess. We'll have the"—he took a deep breath—"the services
tomorrow at the plantation. We want you and Mary to come if you
can."

He nodded.

"If we can. *I'll* try, at least. A lot depends on how—if Janie is—is
making progress."

"Of course," Sue-Ann said. She stood up, held out her arms, gave
him a kiss. "Thank you for coming, Tay. We appreciate it . . ." Her
sad eyes filled with tears again. "All this horror, all these people involved, you and us and the girls and all these people down here and the
Court up there and Regard Stinnet and his Justice NOW! and people
reacting all over the country—and all because of one cruel, sick, twisted
being. It doesn't make sense. It just doesn't make sense."

But they could not know then how far the lack of sense would spread
before it was over; or exactly what results would ultimately flow from
the devious and deadly mind of the bomber of Pomeroy Station, even
now conferring once again with his intense and idealistic counsel as the
flood that would presently overtake them and many others rose ever
higher in the offices of the attorney general of South Carolina.

4

Not, of course, that the knowledge would in any way have intimidated Earle Holgren, who by now was beginning to feel considerably better. He would have enjoyed it, in fact—all except its ironic conclusion, which not even he in his wildest dreams could at this moment have imagined. As it was, he could imagine some of the turmoil going on outside. It pleased him immensely.

Faithful to Regard Stinnet's orders, his captors had subjected him to alternate rest and interrogation; but being of a nature that permitted the instant sleep of the just and the righteous whenever he had a moment's chance, he had not found it too much of an ordeal.

During his waking periods he had been bland, uninformative and scornfully abusive. "Slob-Face" was the mildest epithet he had addressed to the two deputies assigned to interrogate him, and he had several times come so close to provoking them to strike him that it had been, as he told Debbie delightedly now, "a real turn-on."

"I don't think you're very funny," she said coldly. "I also think you are a psychopathic murderer. I think I should drop your case and get as far away from you as I can."

"You are absolutely right," he agreed promptly, shifting position with an exaggerated wince that brought an instant look of concern to her angry face. "You never said a truer word. Tell me why, though. It's interesting. I want to know how you think."

"Why did you kill that woman and child?" she demanded.

He gave her a look of bland surprise.

"Oh, did I? I didn't know there was any proof of that. In fact, that's your main defense for all of this, isn't it? No proof of anything. How come you're accusing me of it?"

"I thought you were someone with a Cause," she said bitterly. "I believed in you because I thought we agreed on this whole rotten society and all its works. Now you turn out to be just a cheap murdering psychopath—"

"Stop calling me that word!" he demanded, with a sudden fierce anger, grabbing her wrist in a grip so tight that she gave a little cry of alarm and tried to rise and yank away. But he was too strong for her and inexorably forced her back down again.

"Now," he said, contemptuously throwing her arm back at her, "you sit still and be quiet. And don't you call me a psychopath again. *I know what I'm doing!* I've always known what I'm doing and *I know now.* So lay off the smarts and act like a lady. Otherwise," he said with an abrupt sunny smile, "I really may have to dismiss you as my counsel."

"I want to know why," she persisted, breath coming in little gasps, dark clever face contorted with pain and alarm. "I want to know why, after making a perfectly good statement by bombing that atomic plant, you had to spoil it all by killing that woman and child."

"Listen," he said, shifting again, and again grimacing in the exaggerated way that he calculated would enlist her sympathies in spite of herself, "nobody has any proof that I bombed that plant, let alone that I killed anybody—"

"You killed Justice Pomeroy's daughter," she interrupted, "and nobody's sure yet just what you did to Justice Barbour's."

"I didn't do *anything* to *anybody,*" he said with a deliberate recurrence of anger, "and don't you keep talking as though I did! Nobody can prove anything—"

"They won't have to prove anything!" she snapped. "Do you have any idea what's going on outside? Do you have any idea of the pressure that's beginning to build on this case?"

"My two big sweet interrogators gave me some gobbledygook about something called Justice NOW!" he said scornfully. "All about that yahoo Regard Stinnet and some sort of vigilante group he's whipping up out there. Do you think the media is going to stand for that?"

"Do you think you're the media's darling?" she demanded. "What makes you so sure 'the media' gives a damn about you?"

"Because they'll think I'm being railroaded," he said triumphantly. "Because I got beaten up and didn't have my rights protected. Because I'm against atomic energy. Because I'm raising hell with the established order and they love anybody who shits on America. And that," he predicted, "is why they'll love me."

"The sooner you understand what's going on, the better for you," she said, rubbing her wrist to help the circulation. "This Regard Stinnet is no yahoo and Justice NOW! is no minor vigilante group. He's starting a nationwide law-and-order movement and it's already catching hold like wildfire. He's going to try to ram this case through just as fast as he can, and with judges and juries the way they are down here, particularly when you attacked their darling Mr. Pomeroy and killed his daughter—" He started an angry protest but she held up her hand sharply and raised her voice—"*You listen to me!* Because they *think* you did, whether you did or not, they're going to crucify you if they can. He's demanding the death penalty and he'll get it. Then maybe you'll realize what's going on!"

"And where will my brilliant legal counsel be, all this time?" he inquired softly. "Won't she be doing anything? Won't she be trying to help me? Won't she be raising all sorts of clever points and thwarting this dastardly plot?" He paused, shook his head. "Oh, I'm sorry," he said elaborately. "I forgot, you've dropped the case. You're not with me any more. You're going to run away and let the wolves have me." He sighed and turned his face to the wall, groaning and flinching as he did so. "Ah, well," he said, voice muffled over his shoulder. "So be it. If I'm doomed, I'm doomed. But I did expect better than this from a sister who seemed to understand what it is really all about."

"I understand what it is really all about," she said, voice tart but with an undercurrent of uncertainty that amused and did not surprise him, "but I'm damned if I understand what you're all about. I still don't know why you killed that woman and child—"

"Drop that!" he demanded furiously, turning over and half-sitting up, grimacing with a pain genuine this time because of the swiftness of his move. "Just God damned drop it, do you hear me? Nobody can prove I killed *anybody,* so God damn you, *drop it* or get OUT! And decide damned fast which it's going to be!" And he rolled over again to face the wall, back rigid and unyielding.

There was a long silence during which Regard's secretary, sitting at the receiving end of the bug that had been placed in the cell during one of the suspect's sleep periods, had time to check her shorthand notes and correct a couple of haste-induced errors. Debbie finally spoke, in a low, intense voice.

"All *right,* Earle Holgren! All *right!* I'll stay with your case but it's only because—only because—"

"Only because what?" he demanded, rolling back over with another carefully calculated wince. "Because you agree with my ideals or you love my big hairy macho bod, or what? I'd really like to know, so I can understand our relationship. It's got me damned puzzled at the moment."

"*Oh!*" she exclaimed "You are so—so—"

"I'm just me," he said with an amiable grin. "Just poor little old Earle Holgren, fighting the people's battles and holding off the dragons of greed and exploitation. That's who *I* am. And who are you, Debbie Superstar? What keeps you hanging around?"

"Well, it isn't your big hairy macho bod!" she said angrily and his grin broadened.

"Oh, now? But you don't get very many of those, do you, Deb? There's always a chance with me, though. I'm available any old time. Maybe we can have a legal conference sometime soon without the room being bugged—" he stopped and shouted, "WITHOUT THE ROOM BEING BUGGED" and Regard Stinnet's secretary, fifty yards away, yelped and yanked the earphones off "—and then, Deb old girl, we'll see what happens."

"You're impossible," she said, but with a sure instinct he could hear the first intimations of an agonized excitement growing in her voice. "*Just simply impossible!*"

"And I forgot also," he agreed amicably, "I'm a psychopath and a murderer and a dreadful, dreadful person. To hear you tell it. So that wouldn't do at all, now would it? Plus the fact you shouldn't sleep with your lawyer, it just causes complications. Which reminds me," he added with a sudden dark scowl, "my folks tried to send around some smooth-talking legal fat cat from New York during the night. I guess they want me to accept *him* as my lawyer."

"And are you going to?" she asked, hating herself for the sudden anxiety in her voice, but, he noted with delight, evidently unable to stop it.

He shook his head scornfully.

"I told him to fuck off," he said. "And I told him to tell them to do the same. Hell, I haven't seen them in fifteen years. Why the hell do they want to come crawling around now? What have they ever done for me, except disapprove? It's a fine time for them to be sucking up to me now."

"Maybe they love you."

He snorted.

"Do yours?"

"Well—" she began, paused and flushed. "That's neither here nor there."

"I thought so," he said with satisfaction. "They made us what we are today and now they want to come crawling back to beg forgiveness when we're in the trouble they created for us. At least that's what the fashionable theories say." He grinned suddenly, a cruel expression without humor. "And I don't mind telling loudmouth Stinnet," he added, raising his voice again, "that that's sure as hell a mighty good defense nowadays. Especially when it's true. Right, Debbie Superstar?"

She gave him an alarmed look and said primly, "It is something to consider."

"You bet it is," he said, "and so's this." And fixing her with his jolly Santa Claus stare, he ran his hand abruptly up inside her leg until it could go no farther, where it then got very busy.

"*Oh!*" she cried and jumped up and away, blushing furiously.

"Don't say, 'how dare you'!" he suggested with a chuckle. "You know how I dare, right, Superstar? Oh yes," he added dreamily, "we'll have a lot of things to consult about, one of these days. Won't we now?"

"If I take this case—" she began breathlessly. "If I take this case—"

"Well, God damn it," he said impatiently, "are you or aren't you? I'd for sure as hell like to know."

"I—"

"*Are you?*"

"Well," she said, voice trembling. "I—yes, I guess I am. Yes. I am."

"All right, then," he said, rolling back to the wall again. "I think they're going to indict me tomorrow—or maybe it's the next day—I'm beginning to lose track of time—anyway, soon—so I think you'd better go now, and get everything in order. Maybe you'd better talk to the press, too. Get the thing rolling. If old Regard is playing for the headlines with his Justice NOW! maybe we'd better start our backfire. Justice for Earle Holgren NOW!—that's us. Right?"

"You still," she said from the door to his impassive back, "don't realize what we're up against. 'Justice NOW! for Earle Holgren' for a hell of a lot of people is *hanging* Justice NOW! So don't kid yourself. It isn't going to be easy."

"Fuck 'em," he said drowsily, either feigning or actually drifting off to sleep even as he talked. "Got a good case and we're going to win it, Superstar. We're . . . going . . . to . . . win . . . it . . ."

"We're going to try," she said, dark little face suddenly ablaze with determination. "We're going to do our damnedest."

"That's good . . ." he said in a muffled voice; and in a moment as she stood earnest and intense by the door, the sound of a faint snore reached her ears.

"Oh—!" she said angrily, but the only response was another.

She stood for a moment irresolute, convinced that the snoring was play-acting. Her eyes widened in thought. For a second she looked genuinely afraid. A sudden involuntary shudder, prompted by genuine fear, passed over her body.

"What am I getting myself into?" she whispered to herself. "What am I getting myself into?"

But then, true to her beliefs, her idealisms, the "culture" she had belonged to ever since college, she raised her head in a rigid challenge, stepped out, nodded curtly to the guard and walked briskly down the hall to the room where the press was waiting. She flung open the door and strode in, head high, expression stern.

The handful of reporters who had greeted her at her first press conference on the night of Earle's capture had grown substantially.

"May we call you Debbie?" Henrietta-Maude suggested. "After all, we're probably going to be seeing a lot of each other."

"Certainly," she said. "I will have to apologize if it takes me a little while to remember you all by name. You have me a bit outnumbered. But it will come. What can I do for you?"

"Tell us about your case," Henny said. Debbie smiled, rather bleakly, and seated herself on a table crowded with microphones, one leg dangling casually, the other drawn up under her.

"It is a case based on the obvious, I suspect," she said, while the forty or so reporters in the room, some of whom she did recognize by name from national television, watched and scribbled intently. "It is based on (a), lack of proof; (b), the potential dangers to human life and society posed by atomic energy; (c), the First Amendment, which guarantees the right of the citizen to protest those things he believes to represent such dangers; and (d), the personal background and upbringing of the suspect, which may conceivably have some bearing if the state is able to prove that he actually committed the crimes which the attorney general of South Carolina is attempting to claim he committed."

"Aren't you being unusually candid in tipping off opposing counsel about your strategy?" someone inquired. She shot him a scornful look.

"We have nothing to hide," she said flatly. "It's all right out in the open. I will never lie to you."

"Are you satisfied in your own mind that your client did not commit these crimes?" someone asked. She did not hesitate for a second.

"I am satisfied no proof has been produced, or will be produced, that will link Earle Holgren directly with these crimes."

"That wasn't the question," someone else pointed out, persistent but not hostile. "The question was—"

"I know your question," she said crisply. "Would I be defending him if I did not believe in his innocence?"

"You might," Henrietta remarked. "Lawyers often do. You're different?"

"I haven't made up my mind yet," she said, immediately gaining further points with her candor. "My inclination is to abide with traditional American jurisprudence which holds that a man is innocent until proven guilty. Do any of you ladies and gentlemen have proof that Earle Holgren is guilty? I would certainly like to know it, myself. And so, I assume, would Mr. Stinnet."

There was laughter and someone said dryly, "Yes, I expect he would . . . So at the moment you're taking the case on the assumption that you have an innocent client. How did you happen to come into the case, anyway?"

"I live in the area," she said, "and since the controversy seemed to revolve around opposition to atomic energy, to which I am also personally opposed, I decided to offer my services to Mr. Holgren. He accepted them. It was as simple as that."

"Oh, really?" Henrietta inquired. "That was very fortunate for him, was it not? Is he paying his own fees, or is somebody else helping to finance his case?"

"We have not discussed payment."

"At the moment no one is paying you?" someone asked in a surprised tone.

"At the moment we have not discussed payment," she repeated. "I assume we will in due course."

"What is your impression of your client?" a feminine voice, which she recognized as that of one of television's larger luminaries, inquired from the back of the room. "Is he defiant? Depressed? Upbeat? Downbeat? Sullen? Happy?"

"I think," she said carefully, laying the groundwork for what she knew already would be one of the most difficult problems of her case, "that he is responding alertly and well to the various aspects of the matter. He is, as you have already ascertained from the academic record that has been released by Mr. Stinnet's office, a very highly intelligent individual. As such he is sensitive and reflective of the pressures around him."

"Moody and unpredictable, in other words," the television luminary remarked. Debbie permitted some annoyance to enter her answer.

"He is naturally under great pressure at the moment," she said severely. "His reactions are strong and positive. When he considers a subject serious and important, he reacts in such a manner. When it is amusing, he laughs."

"He laughs," the television luminary repeated thoughtfully. "Does he find a lot to laugh at in this matter, which involves partial destruction of important property, the death of a Supreme Court Justice's daughter, the very serious harming of another Supreme Court Justice's daughter and the death of a woman and child, possibly his? These things amuse him?"

"I did not say *these* were the things that amuse him," Debbie said coldly, "and I hope for the sake of future amicable relations with the media that such words will not be put in my mouth. Actually I have had two brief talks with him and he has not laughed very much. He has been severely beaten, he was denied his constitutional rights to warning and counsel upon his arrest, and life on the whole is a very serious matter for him. As," she said thoughtfully, "I should think it would be for the state of South Carolina and the official who has taken it upon himself to justify those actions."

"How does Holgren look?" a male voice asked and in a quick change of tone she replied,

"He looks like hell."

"Badly beaten?"

"Badly beaten."

"But his spirits, on the whole, are good."

"His spirits on the whole are good. He is sustained by his determination to prove his innocence and his certainty that he can."

"Prove his innocence or keep someone else from proving his guilt?" Henrietta inquired. Debbie smiled.

"The burden of proof is on his accusers, is it not?"

"And you don't think they can do it," a famous columnist from New York remarked.

"If proof does not exist," Debbie said calmly, "how would you suggest they go about it? Manufacture some? I thought those days were gone, even in the—I thought those days were gone."

"Do you expect to confer with Mr. Stinnet regarding plans for the trial?"

"Of course I am available for any consultation Mr. Stinnet wishes. If, that is," she added dryly, "Mr. Stinnet is not too busy with his extra-curricular activities to tend to his primary responsibility, which is this case."

"Don't underestimate Mr. Stinnet," Henny said. "He'll take care of this case and his 'extracurricular activities,' as you put it, both, and still keep you hoppin'. I suppose you mean by that, Justice NOW!"

"I mean this reactionary, anti-democratic, so-called 'law-and-order' crusade that he seems to have pulled out of his hat in the past twenty-four hours," Debbie said sharply. "I mean his vigilantism, with all its harsh and ominous threats to our democratic society and the rule of law. I will admit he's come up with a name for it that may be appealing to many people impatient with the orderly processes of the law, but that doesn't change its essential repugnant nature, repugnant to our whole democratic way of life."

"Strong words," Henrietta observed. "You realize that as of half an hour ago his office had received over ten thousand telegrams and phone calls, and that the number is apparently increasin' by the minute. And they haven't even started counting the mail, yet."

"That doesn't make it right," Debbie said calmly, "and one must hope that the genuinely democratic elements in this country, the com-mon-sense democracy of this country, will soon put it in perspective and reject the extremism which it represents. When you of the media make clear to the country the dangers that are inherent in it, I don't think there will be any doubt of its rejection."

"You may not find," the television luminary said, "that all of the media is going to be quite so unanimous against it as you seem to as-sume. And you may find that your client is in more trouble because of it than he might otherwise be."

"If I have to fight this case on the TV channels and the front pages," Debbie retorted, "I shall do so."

"Where else can you win it?" Henrietta-Maude inquired; and stared back unimpressed as Earle Holgren's lawyer flashed her a look that would have done credit to her client himself.

"Listen!" she said. "Listen, all of you! If you think for one minute that I, or any other decent, law-abiding American is going to sit idly by and let a corrupt and decaying criminal justice system railroad Earle Holgren to his death without proof and without a fair trial, then you have another think coming. That isn't the way America works! Mr. Stinnet talks about Justice NOW! All right, we're going to *have* justice now—and it won't be his kind of vigilante justice, either! It will be real justice, which is what all decent, law-abiding Americans want! It will be *real* justice for Earle Holgren! I appeal to all decent Americans to HELP EARLE HOLGREN! That's the slogan *I* want to see, because it fits the facts!"

"La Pasionaria of Pomeroy Station," a male voice remarked in the background and amid a flutter of laughter Henrietta said clearly,

"Isn't it *amazin'* how people can start from exactly opposite poles and arrive at exactly the same place? I thought Regard had the decent, law-abidin' people on his side, but accordin' to this young lady, they're all over there with her. Well, we'll see."

"You certainly will see," Debbie said, more calmly. "If Mr. Stinnet thinks we're going to lie down and let him walk all over us without a fight, he'd better reconsider, because that isn't the way it's going to be. And I don't care how many 'Justice NOWS!' he fabricates."

"Well, I guess that tells Regard," Henrietta said, closing her notebook with a snap. "How often do you plan to hold these performances for us?"

"They aren't 'performances'!" Debbie retorted. "And your comment expresses exactly the state of mind I had expected to find here regarding this defendant. It is going to make it extremely difficult to find a fair judge, a fair jury and a fair trial. This atmosphere is highly prejudiced and highly hostile."

"Will you try for a change of venue?" someone asked.

"I may, though I doubt if anywhere in the state would be any better. It is something I shall have to consider carefully, however. The main thing I want to do is appeal to all fair-minded citizens all over the country to assist us with their contributions and their support. I am counting on the basic traditional spirit of fair play in America. Those who believe in it will assist. Those who do not will of course go their own way. But I don't think we will lack for help."

And in this, as the day drew on, she proved to be correct, for it was not long after her press conference had ended with one more defiant blast at the criminal justice system, one more appeal to "decent, law-abiding American citizens," that the first tentative questionings began to appear.

By some happenstance on the evening news, the battle between the founder of Justice NOW! and the defender of Earle Holgren somehow became transformed into a contest between a big, menacing, overbearing figure and a gallant little wisp of a woman as she bravely sought to save a possibly innocent suspect from the forces of evil in a corrupt and unfair system. There were no flat assertions that the suspect was innocent, nobody was able to deny that the response to Justice NOW! was indeed unprecedented and overwhelming, but it was stressed that as nearly as could be ascertained so far, the attorney general's case against Earle Holgren appeared to be based heavily on circumstantial evidence. It was conceded that Justice NOW!, though not yet twelve hours old, was already a major political phenomenon that inevitably would have effects "reaching far beyond the immediate case of Earle Holgren." But there was also a genuine and openly expressed concern that it might well lead, as Debbie had asserted, to rampant vigilantism that could well upset the whole fabric of American jurisprudence.

This was not the case, however, among the viewers and readers, as the rising response to Justice NOW! continued to prove. There might be high-level discussions of circumstantial evidence and potential vigilantism among those who prided themselves on being above the battle, but gut instinct in the country seemed to be that the bomber of Pomeroy Station was guilty as hell, and that the sooner he was strung up, the better—not only for the sake of retribution but for the sake of society as a whole. Somehow a large, insistent and apparently overwhelming majority seemed to agree with Regard Stinnet that this case summarized the whole frustrating, frightening, infuriating increase in wanton crime that had plagued the country in recent years.

It was as though many millions had suddenly and finally decided that enough was indeed enough; and no voice of caution, restraint or detached intellectual weighing of pros and cons was going to be able to stem the irresistible popular decision that there must be a time to stop it, and the time was now.

5

S arah Ann Pomeroy was buried at "High Pillars," the Pomeroy plantation southeast of Columbia, on Monday. In the soft late-spring afternoon, the old house, built by Pomeroys in 1821 and inhabited by them ever since, had never looked more beautiful or serene. The service, arranged by Sue-Ann with the strength that women find within themselves on such occasions, was the same. Only one thing marred it for the family, the plantation and house workers and the little handful of old friends from across South Carolina gathered on the lawn beneath the oaks: the minister's inability to stay away from the topic that was arousing and agitating the country.

"Everyone here," an old aunt remarked to an old uncle as they drove away after tearfully kissing Sue-Ann and Moss good-bye, "is just as upset about this awful crime, and wantin' that Stinnet boy's plans to succeed, and all, as anybody else. Why did the preacher have to drag it in over poor Sarah's grave? We surely didn't have to be reminded!"

But remind them he did. It seemed he could not stay away from it, try as he undoubtedly did to keep his brief remarks free from everything but the terrible loss of a happy and promising young life.

"Now we have seen," he intoned, and in spite of his best intentions a rising indignation entered his voice, "that beautiful young life wantonly destroyed by the actions of an evil being who, apparently moved by some perverse quarrel with society, has brought directly to our beloved Pomeroy family the savage sickness that afflicts the land. Vengeance is mine, saith the Lord! May He find a million, yea ten million, yea hundreds of millions, to do His work for Him! May justice indeed be restored to the land, and may this crime and its swift, inevitable punishment serve as a beacon to restore America to goodness, to sanity, to security and to truth. Only then will our dear Sarah be at rest. Only then will we know that she has not died in vain!"

Even Regard, rapidly repeating several of these phrases to himself so that he could remember and use them in later speeches, squirmed uncomfortably; and for a few seconds the serenity and peace of the lovely old homestead were invaded by the ravening horrors of the world outside. The minister went on and concluded without further reference to them, and afterward Sue-Ann and Moss thanked him gravely and told him what a wonderful job he had done. But later Sue-Ann also protested bitterly, and cried again even though Moss said gently, "But, honey, how can we escape it? It's true, what he said. The very reason for our being here reminds us; we can't forget it for a minute. Nobody can."

At the hospital in Columbia, to which Tay returned immediately after the service, it was equally inescapable. He had accepted Regard's offer of a ride out, and on the return journey in his armored Mercedes—Regard did not specifically describe it as such, but the moment Tay slipped inside he realized he was surrounded by gadgetry of a particularly specific kind—the attorney general could not resist his own comments on the ceremony they had just been through.

"I could wish that old preacher had been a little less blunt about it," he remarked as he skillfully negotiated the deserted back-country roads at a speed that sometimes caused his passenger to tense, "but I guess after all it was what everybody was thinkin'. And I can tell you," he added with satisfaction, "they're sure thinkin' it out around the country. Did you see the New York *Times* this mornin'? No? Well, I tore it out to show Moss and you, because I thought you might miss it."

JUSTICE NOW! SWEEPING COUNTRY, the headlines said. LAW-ORDER GROUP WINS SWIFT SUPPORT. MANY THOUSANDS JOINING.

A picture of Regard and a secretary holding up sheaves of telegrams and letters accompanied the story, which was written by the correspondent who had been sent down to Columbia. His text had a distinct undertone of uneasiness.

"He seems to be worried about you," Tay remarked, handing the article back.

"Ah, shucks!" Regard said. "Those Northerners up there in New York can be counted on, you know that, Mr. Justice. You can just count on 'em. They're right there every time, expressin' their doubts and fears about anything spontaneous and law-abidin' that happens in this country. But that isn't goin' to stop Justice NOW! We're rollin', man! We're really rollin'!"

And inspired by this he cheerfully trod harder on the gas and the sleek car shot along through narrow lanes and under overhanging trees a-drip with Spanish moss.

"Regard," Tay said, "would you mind? I'd like to get back to the hospital as a visitor, not a patient. One patient in the family," he added with some grimness, "is enough."

"I'm sorry, Mr. Justice," Regard said, slowing down so abruptly that only a strong seat belt kept Tay in place. "I really am. I get to goin' along thinkin' about Justice NOW and how it's racin' ahead all over this great land of ours and *I* get to racin' ahead." His tone changed to a genuine solicitude. "How is your little girl? I couldn't tell much from that story—he doesn't dwell on it."

"He doesn't know. I'm not talking to the media right now, and neither is Moss, as you know. Janie is—holding her own, thank you."

"Is she—?" Regard began delicately. "Are there any signs of—?"

"She doesn't know us yet, no."

"Still in a coma," Regard said thoughtfully. "That's a for-damned shame, I'll tell you."

"We aren't happy about it."

"How is Mrs. Barbour taking it? Like a real gallant lady, I imagine."

"She's a strong woman," Tay said in a noncommittal tone that Regard filed away for future reference. "We're both managing, although"— he suddenly uttered a deep sigh—"it isn't easy."

"No, sir," Regard agreed emphatically. "That it isn't."

"Have you uncovered any further evidence?"

"A few little things," Regard said, starting to drive a little faster. "The main thing is, we've got such a ground swell started that it's goin' to be easy to get a fast trial. I've already talked to friends of mine in the courts and they're willin' to shove it right along. I knew a lot of it would depend on who it went to for trial, and I've taken care of that, I think. I've also arranged for trial to be held here in Columbia instead of out there in the hills. The attorney general's got a good deal of power in this state if he's got the right friends. You can arrange a lot of things by mutual consent."

"Oh," said Tay. "That's interesting."

"Yes," Regard agreed, abruptly cautious. "Well, I wouldn't want you to think, Mr. Justice, that we're goin' to do any railroadin' here, so don't make a note of that to worry about if it comes up to Washington. We're goin' to abide by all the rules, you can be sure of that. We're just goin' to abide by 'em *fast,* that's all, because that's what we want and that's what the country wants. I think the day is fast comin' to an end for take-your-time justice in America. I think this case is goin' to mark a turnin' point. I think from now on people are goin' to demand *and get* swift and effective justice."

"If you can figure out how to clear dockets all over the country so that we can have this speed you want," Tay said, "well and good. But how are you going to do that?"

Regard looked scornful.

"We're goin' to tell 'em to God damn *get movin',*" he said, tromping down on the gas again. The car shot across a tree-blind intersection, narrowly missing a farm truck coming in from the right.

"Please," Tay said. "Save your speed for the courts, O.K.?"

"Sorry," Regard said with a smile, again slowing as abruptly as he had accelerated. "I just get excited thinkin' about what a revolution we're goin' to bring about in the criminal justice system, that's all. It's goin' to be *sensational.* I mean, we've got hold of somethin' here, Mr. Justice, we really have. It's all comin' together, thanks to that bastard Holgren. Justice in America," he said with a satisfied certainty, "is never goin' to be the same again."

"It does need reform," Tay conceded as they began to enter the outskirts of the city and his host, of necessity, began to adopt a more leisurely pace. "My only concern is with the orderly processes of the law. Interfere with those and you're in trouble with us on the Court, as you know. So watch it. "

"I most certainly will," Regard said solemnly. "I may talk like a hick sometimes when I'm out in the boonies where they want to have you talk like a hick, but I'm not a hick, Mr. Justice, as you know very well."

"Indeed you're not," Tay agreed. "You're one hell of a smart man. Which, in some minds, makes you a dangerous one."

Regard gave a contemptuous snort.

"To their complacency and their phony-liberal attitudes and their casual disregard for justice if it doesn't suit their narrow ideologies, and their eternal coddlin' of criminals who are the scum of the earth—yes, sir, Mr. Justice, you bet I am. And I'm goin' to be even more dangerous to those things, too, now that I've roused up the country and started gettin' the people behind me. A million, yea ten million, yea hundreds of millions, as that old preacher-man said. They're comin' to me, Mr.

Justice. They're flockin' in from all over. They want Justice NOW! And they're goin' to get it. They're not goin' to be denied."

"Just remember," Tay said again, "that the Court does not take kindly to manhandling of the law."

"The Court," Regard said crisply, "is goin' to do what the country wants, or the Court is goin' to regret it."

"Are you threatening the Supreme Court of the United States?" Tay demanded sharply.

"No, sir," Regard said as he pulled smartly into the hospital drive. "I'm just sendin' the Court a message about the way things are. I hope it'll get through, Mr. Justice, as it would be too bad if the Court stood in the way of the popular will. Its members have been pretty shrewd about avoidin' any such showdown in the past, and I suspect present members will be equally shrewd. I don't anticipate any real trouble." He gave Tay a bland glance. "Do you?"

"I hope not," Tay said evenly.

"So do I, Mr. Justice," Regard said calmly, "because if there *is* trouble based on tightenin' up the criminal justice system, then I'm not so sure the Court will emerge on the popular side of it . . . Now, what the hell," he said abruptly as he parked, "is that bedraggled little swamp-hen of a gal doin' draggin' her sorry tail in here to your hospital?"

Debbie Donnelson was standing on the stairs.

She started toward them at once.

"Mr. Justice!" she called. "Mr. Justice!"

"Miss Donnelson," Regard said in a tired tone, "Miss Donnelson—Debbie—now, why do you want to bother the Justice? You know his little daughter is still in grave danger, you know he's tired out and exhausted, you know—"

"If you will stop telling me what I know and get out of my way, Regard," Debbie said curtly, "I believe I am old enough to convey to the Justice myself why I am here, and I believe he is old enough to comprehend it. Or am I mistaken, Mr. Justice?"

"I think you have made a reasonable assumption, Miss Donnelson," Tay said, amused in spite of the heavy weight that seemed to settle upon him every time he approached the hospital. "What can I do for you?"

"You can talk to me," she said in the same crisp way. "Or allow me to talk to you, rather. Is there somewhere here where we can go?"

"I don't know—" he said uncertainly. Regard, with an elaborately suffering sigh, said, "There's a small sun room I think we can get for you privately if you really want to talk to this person, Mr. Justice. I'll go in and arrange it."

"Thank you, Regard," he said, and Debbie nodded in a businesslike way. "And thank you for the ride."

"You've been to the funeral," she said. "How was it?"

"Tell your client it was sad," Regard snapped. "He'll enjoy that, psychotic that he is."

"Please continue to dislike him," she remarked in a cold tone. "It will hopefully affect your judgment."

"I despise him," Regard said calmly, "but I assure you it won't affect my judgment. If you'll excuse me—" and he brushed on by and went in. They stood there without speaking until he reappeared: there was not, after all, much to say at that point. He returned and gestured them in. "It's all yours. They'll show you the way."

"Thank you," Tay said.

"Let me know if there's any change with your daughter."

"I will. Perhaps I'll see you again before we go back to Washington."

"I'll make a point of it," Regard said. "Enjoyed your company, enjoyed our talk. My best to Mrs. Barbour."

And brushing past Debbie he loped off to his car, jumped in, slammed the door, backed out with a flourish and zoomed off.

"Damned reactionary," Debbie said, watching him go. "Damned *misuser of the law*. But he'll pay for it before I'm through with him. He'll pay for it."

"You're a rather fierce young lady," Tay observed. She gave him a sudden quick smile that lighted up her usually somber little face.

"I can be," she said as they walked in and a nurse directed them to their impromptu conference room. "If necessary."

"With such a client," he remarked, "it may be. Now," he said, forestalling retort by gesturing her to a chair and taking one himself, "what is it you want to talk to me about?"

"First of all," she said with evident sincerity, "I want to tell you how delighted I am with your appointment. I think it's a marvelous thing to have such a truly dedicated and proven liberal on the Court. I believe every progressive, right-thinking American had a lift of the heart when she or he heard about it. I know I did. We expect great things of you, Mr. Justice. Your appointment is cause for real hope and genuine rejoicing."

"Well, thank you," he said, flattered in spite of the warning knowledge that of course she wanted something or she wouldn't be there. "You're very kind and very generous."

"I mean it. I don't say things I don't mean."

"I saw your press conference on television. Does that apply to statements about your client?"

For a split second she hesitated; but she looked him straight in the eye.

"On the evidence now before us," she said calmly, "I have no grounds for believing him to be other than innocent."

"Mmmm," he said. "And what do you think?"

"What I think is immaterial, Mr. Justice. You know that. You're a lawyer."

"I've found in my own practice," he said with some irony, "that a certain amount of personal conviction helps in mounting an effective defense."

"I do have convictions!" she exclaimed angrily.

"I'm sure. But not so many about Earle Holgren."

"About what Earle Holgren stands for," she said in the same harsh tone. "What he represents. His ideals, his dreams, his belief in what is best for America—"

"Injuring my daughter is best for America," he said with a sudden release of tightly held bitterness. "Killing Justice Pomeroy's. Murdering a woman and child. These are things that are best for America."

"If you feel that way," she said swiftly, "and if he does, then you should disqualify yourselves if this case comes up to the Court. Obviously you are not objective. Obviously you cannot be judicious. Obviously your honor as a liberal demands that you step aside."

"You're conceding your case," he said, and knew he had struck home. "You're jumping 'way ahead. How can you give him a good defense with that state of mind? You're beaten before you start, Miss Donnelson. Your client would be wise to get another lawyer."

"He has chosen me to represent him," she said, flushing but standing her ground, "and I intend to do so to the best of my ability."

"Then perhaps you will secure his freedom and our whole discussion will be academic. What is the purpose of it, in any event? The matter has not come before us, it may not. You know I cannot comment one way or the other about it, or about what I would do in such an eventuality. Why are you here?"

"Because I want to tell you—" she began. "Because I want to beg of you to remain true to your instincts and your reputation. Because I want you to fight for justice on the Court as you have always fought for it all your professional life, in government and out. I don't know whether I can win this case in these courts or not, but if it does come up to the Supreme Court, then I just want you to know that I, like all who believe in real justice and the rule of law in America, will be looking to you to fight the battle as you always have."

He studied her for what seemed to her a long time, gaze disbelieving, moody and inward-turning.

"Miss Donnelson," he said finally, "do you realize that a few yards from here my daughter is lying in a coma from which she may or may not recover, as the result of the crime of your client?"

"No one has proved he did it!"

"No," he said quietly. "But you know, and I know, that he did. And we also know that the climate in this state and in the country is such—"

"Thanks to Regard Stinnet!"

"No, not thanks to Regard Stinnet!" he said harshly. "Thanks to the American people getting damned well fed up with senseless crime and violence. Regard Stinnet couldn't ride this wave if it weren't already about to break. He's not a genius, except at capitalizing on public opinion. And he's got a great deal of it with him on this. So leaving aside the question of the facts entirely, there's enough emotionalism building up to carry this case against your client just on the grounds of circumstantial evidence, let alone what anybody can or can't prove about the facts."

"That's exactly why it's up to you and other fair-minded members of the Court to stop it if it comes up to you," she said promptly.

"Miss Donnelson," he inquired, "have you been listening to what I've said? I said that my daughter is lying in there in a coma because of this—this individual of yours. How do you expect me to be objective about it?"

"But you're *Tay Barbour!*" she cried, seemingly almost in tears. "People *expect* you to be objective and fair! You can't do anything else! It wouldn't be *you!*"

He shook his head as if to clear it of demons, then rested chin on hand, staring down at the floor with eyes that were far away and bleakly unhappy.

"Miss Donnelson," he said finally, "everybody tells me that. I tell myself that. I tell them that. But if you want to know the real truth, in my heart of hearts I *just don't know*. I just *don't know* what I would do if Janie—if Janie doesn't recover . . . I admire your spirit and your guts, to come to me at such a moment and make your appeal. It takes more courage than I would probably have, if the positions were reversed. But I can give you nothing definitive, nothing you can depend upon—you shouldn't anyway. In the job you have to do, the immediate issue is all that should concern you and the ultimate future should be left to take care of itself. That's the only way to commit yourself entirely to a case, as I presume you know. Don't look to me, at least right now, for any certainties beyond what happens today and tomorrow. All I can promise is that I will do my best to be fair, should it come to me, because that is my nature. But whether I can or not, at this moment I simply do—not—know."

"Thank you," she said gravely, standing up and holding out her hand. "Thank you for leveling with me. Taylor Barbour's fairness is worth the equivocations of a thousand other men, and I'm not worried. I know you will be honest and you will be fair. *You will guard the law.* That is all I can ask."

He stood up too, ignoring her hand.

"But we can't ask that of you, can we?" he asked with a sudden savage bitterness. "You are determined to set a murderer free."

She retreated a step, face suddenly white.

"Only through the law," she said, voice quivering but determined, thinking, then, that she meant it. "I am determined to exhaust all the resources of the law. I, too, wish to guard the law."

"'The law'!" he echoed, almost in a whisper. "How much it twists people, and how much they twist it."

There was silence while they stared at one another, no longer in the tenuous shallow intimacy of a discussion between strangers but truly strangers now. At last she gave him an odd, jerky little bow.

"Thank you, Mr. Justice. I appreciate your taking the time."

He nodded, seemingly not even seeing her. He said nothing. After a moment she said, "Well—good-bye," turned, clutching her enormous cloth bag to her as if it were some protective shield, and walked away.

He remained for several moments motionless. He had revealed his true uncertainties to her as to no one else, not even Moss and Sue-Ann to whom he had appeared adamant and unyielding, the perfect servant of the law. At this odd moment, before this odd witness, he had suddenly stopped trying to convince himself and others by bluster and insistence, and told the truth.

He could not say why. Perhaps because she was so determined and demanded so much of him. He did not know.

He became aware that a couple of nurses were staring. He took a deep breath, straightened his shoulders, braced himself and turned down the corridor toward Janie's room.

You're Taylor Barbour, he told himself with a bitterness more devastating than any he had turned upon her. Don't forget that. It's very important.

To somebody.

It was important to the Chief Justice for one, as that decent soul sat in his quiet office and thought of the day's just concluded Monday session and the cases announced for argument and review. Seven Justices had come through the red velvet curtains when the Clerk cried, "Oyez! Oyez!" All eyes in the audience kept returning to the two vacant chairs. Their silent emptiness made him and his colleagues distinctly uncomfortable. He could feel the uneasiness along the bench even as they were matter-of-factly setting down their work for the term's concluding days.

Finally he said something about it.

"I might take official recognition of what everyone knows: Justice Pomeroy and Justice Barbour are—unavoidably detained—and cannot be present at today's session of the Court."

A little murmur rippled across the audience, upset and angry, with a distinctly personal note that said disturbingly much about the mood of his countrymen.

"It is likely," he went on, "that they may be absent for several more days. I think I can say on behalf of my sister, my brethren and myself, that we send our absent brethren our deepest sympathies and condolences and hope that the Lord may restore them to us and to as much peace of mind and comfort of heart as may be possible under the circumstances of their absence."

"And let's hope the law wipes out the maniac who did it, too," a male voice said clearly from the audience, and immediately there was consternation in the chamber, where such demonstrations simply do not occur. The Clerk and the Marshal jumped up and glared out sternly over the audience; several of the uniformed guards stepped through the side curtains and stared about importantly; members of the media in the press section also stood up and looked around; and suddenly, here and there through the assemblage, perhaps seventy-five in a group of about two hundred, lapels were turned over, handbags were held up, and the red-and-black shield of Justice NOW! appeared.

For a split second the Chief Justice considered ordering the chamber cleared. As instantly instinct said No! Nothing would have been more inflammatory at such a moment. Nothing would have played more directly into the hands of those leading the movement.

He turned to the Clerk and the Marshal, the guards and the media, and waved them down with a quick, decisive hand.

"The audience is reminded," he said with a smile of gentle reproof, "that demonstrations of any kind whatsoever are forbidden by the rules of the Court. However, I think it safe to say that my sister and brethren and I can appreciate the depth of public feeling which this event has created in the country, for it has created equally deep emotions here. Though this Court has no jurisdiction in the matter," he added with deliberate slowness and emphasis, "like all Americans we too wish to see justice done and hope that it may be swiftly accomplished . . . And now if we may return to the agenda—"

And smoothly he proceeded with the session's business, net daring to glance at his colleagues, though he heard both Wally Flyte and Clem Wallenberg alongside him expel tensely held-in breaths of relief as the audience obediently settled back and resumed respectful attention.

Later when they adjourned and disrobed an impromptu post-mortem took place in the Conference Room.

"Dunc," Wally said, holding out his hand, "congratulations. That was a tight moment and you handled it exactly right."

"Superbly," Mary-Hannah said while the others expressed agreement. "Did you notice how *many* of those labels there were? It's scary."

"Terrifying," Ray Ullstein agreed soberly. "I didn't quite realize—"

"I didn't think it would get here so fast," Hughie Demsted said.

"I got about thirty letters this morning," Clem Wallenberg said. "There'll be more."

"Got some myself," Rupert Hemmelsford said. "I'm glad you explained we have no jurisdiction, Chief."

"I tried," The Elph said, "but whether it will receive sufficient prominence in the media to do any good—"

"Oh, I think it will," Justice Flyte said. "I'm sure your whole statement will be run, plus explanations of just what our jurisdiction is. People are reasonable—"

"Not any more," Justice Wallenberg said dourly. "This fellow Stinnet has his finger on something. He started it forty-eight hours ago or such a matter, remember, and already it's here at the Court. If the fallout is here now, imagine what it's going to be like if the case itself comes here. Sister and brethren, we're really going to be on the hot seat then."

"Personally I'm not afraid of it," Justice Demsted said. Justice Wallenberg shot him an annoyed look.

"Who the hell said *I'm* 'afraid'? I assume none of us is *'afraid.'* It's just not going to be very pleasant, that's all. We're going to need all of Dunc's grace and diplomacy to see us through."

"Plus our own guts and character," Justice McIntosh said. Her expression became thoughtful. "I wonder what Moss and Tay will do if he's convicted and the case comes here."

"By rights," the Chief Justice said, "disqualify themselves."

"Yes, by rights," Hughie Demsted said. "But I'm not so sure if it were one of my kids that I'd be so noble. I might be tempted to hold my seat and sit in judgment. And it would not be a gentle judgment, I'm afraid."

"It will be a terrible dilemma for them," Justice Ullstein agreed gravely. "And its early coming, I think, probably inevitable. Almost every major death sentence eventually gets appealed here. One of this notoriety almost certainly will."

"Well," Justice Hemmelsford said, "let's hope it's delayed awhile. In the normal course of things it may not reach us until next term and by then maybe the novelty and the impetus of Justice NOW! will have worn off. It may be easier to decide a lot of things by then."

"I think you're very optimistic, Rupe," Wally Flyte remarked. "I think this case is going to go through the courts down there and be on our doorstep before we know it. Vengeance is stalking this country—vengeance for a thousand—a million—crimes of pointless and inexcusable violence in these recent years. Something has snapped, with this case. Maybe it's the instinct of thirty years of public life, but I can just feel it. This isn't going to be your ordinary slowpoke case this time. This is going to be justice—if you'll excuse the expression—NOW! The country's out for blood, and Regard Stinnet is its shepherd. Mark my words. You'll see."

And as the next few days unfolded, they did.

There seemed to be no stopping the apparently irresistible growth of Justice NOW! Wally Flyte appeared to be correct.

The country really was out for blood.

Something really had snapped.

Regard's thesis had apparently been adopted by a majority of his countrymen: when all was said, this was indeed an attack on the Supreme Court. It seemed to have coalesced everything.

The tired shrug, the hopeless shake of the head, the saddened and frustrated "What can you do?" suddenly were gone. An apparent majority had decided that they knew what to do and were rap_dly proceeding.

There were some on the other side seeking what they regarded as balance and reason. They might as well have been talking to the wind.

The television networks sought desperately but almost without success to find disagreeing voices. Nearly everyone interviewed persisted in talking about "this horrible crime against America . . . time to put a stop once and for all to this mindless crime and violence . . . they ought to string that bastard up without a trial," and the like.

In editorial offices as distant, removed and above-the-battle as the Court itself had been until that chilling moment of revelation. earnest pleas were addressed to readers who no longer paid attention. The pleas began to sound a little hysterical as their authors realized how few of their countrymen gave a damn for their cautionary admonitions.

Equally alarmed—and equally futile—were certain famous figures of pulpit, academe, the legal profession, the literary world; certain Hollywood activists noted more for dramatic ability than social perception; certain professional advocates of fashionable right-think; certain organizers of protests and demonstrations; certain compilers of full-page ads in the New York *Times* and mailing campaigns to Senators and Congressmen.

They too cried loudly for due process of law, warned of vigilantism, spoke, with a tenderness they had rarely shown before, of law and order.

They, too, clamored in vain.

There were, it seemed, far more small and medium-sized newspapers in the country than there were large, powerful newspapers; and out there in what some scornfully regarded as the boondocks, a much more responsive appreciation of the mood of Main Street. Papers that lived off Main Street and were not responsive to its needs had long ago discovered that they did not do very well with advertising and circulation, which were the names of the game. Accordingly there was a noticeable inclination on the part of the non-metropolitan press to give strong support to Regard's brainchild.

Similarly, local television stations, like local newspapers much closer to the country and much more aware of what was actually going on, did the same. There was a definite note of respect for Justice NOW! from the very beginning. It grew as the movement grew. When local mayors, officials and leading citizens appeared on local shows to endorse and defend the purposes of the movement, the desperate advice of the major national commentators faded out.

Even more direct and disturbing evidence of the majority mood occurred. A bomb exploded in, and heavily damaged, the press room of the New York *Times*. A picket line at the Washington *Post* overturned the car of the publisher, injuring that individual seriously enough to warrant hospitalization. Bombs destroyed parts of the reception areas of two of the networks, and part of the newsroom of a third.

A shudder ran through the ranks as it began to sink home:

The people mean business.

Rightly or wrongly, they were on their way.

The first fruits of this were not long coming in South Carolina.

THREE

1

Earle William Holgren was indicted shortly after 10 A.M. Wednesday in the State Court of General Sessions in Columbia for the murder of Sarah Ann Pomeroy; the attempted murders of Hon. Stanley Mossiter Pomeroy and Jane Margaret Barbour; the murders of a woman identified as Janet Martinson of Pomeroy Station and a male child aged approximately six months, name unknown; and the wanton and deliberate destruction of property at the atomic energy plant at Pomeroy Station, South Carolina. Defendant's lawyer entered a plea of not guilty and bail was set at one million dollars. *South Carolina v. Holgren* was underway.

Outside the courthouse as the trial began a crowd estimated by local police and the experts of national press and television to be well over ten thousand had gathered, as ugly and hostile to the defendant as might have been expected. Encouraged and in many cases led by members of rapidly growing Justice NOW! the angry spectators waved banners and held signs that summed up the general mood. STRING EARLE HOLGREN FROM A SOUR APPLE TREE, one said. SWIFT DEATH TO ALL MURDERERS, said another. CONVICT HOLGREN, SOUTH CAROLINA'S ENEMY, said a third. YOU HAVE KILLED OUR BEAUTY, HOLGREN: YOU WILL DIE— FAST, promised a fourth.

Everywhere the shield of Justice NOW! danced and shimmered from poles and placards waved rhythmically back and forth above the crowd. A loud, ominous hum filled with a vindictive hatred that appeared likely to erupt at any moment came clearly over the nation's airwaves and television screens.

"This is a crowd that wants to kill Earle Holgren," NBC's man said while Justice NOW! banners, thrust before the cameras, almost obscured his somber face. There was no doubt of it.

Nor was there any doubt that the nation was going to be kept well advised of every step of the proceedings. All major media were represented. Television anchormen and commentators, leading columnists and editorialists, top feature writers were all on hand. The Carolina Inn overflowed with their noisy gossip and cluttering paraphernalia, and out along Interstates 20 and 26 all the major motels were equally crowded.

Limited space in the courtroom excluded the general public, but no one could say, in view of the ominous motley gathered outside, that it was not part of the trial.

A solid wall of humanity crowded the approaches to the entrance, shouting out its sentiments as each new group appeared.

Tay and Mary Barbour were the first. The Justice, face drawn and obviously strained with emotion, gave only the briefest of nods to acknowledge the cry that went up—not exactly a cheer, but rather a sound of universal sympathy and concern. His wife stared straight ahead without expression, her face also white and strained, set in a rigid mask of pain. The crowd's sympathy seemed to waver, uncertain in the face of her apparent refusal to acknowledge it; but in a moment she and the Justice managed to muster slight but appreciative smiles. The sounds of sympathy rose again as they disappeared.

Two minutes later a limousine drew up, the excitement increased to a new and warmer pitch. South Carolina's own were arriving. Again there was a cheer, filled with deep affection and support, as Moss and Sue-Ann, both looking desperately tired but composed, stepped from the car and started toward the entrance. They, too, barely acknowledged it at first, but when they reached the entrance they turned, smiled with obvious gratitude, and waved. The sound surged higher, solicitous and protective.

A moment after, almost unnoticed at first in the excitement of the Pomeroys' arrival, another chauffeured limousine drew up and a couple in their late sixties stepped out, gray-haired, pale, tense, faces drawn with sorrow and unhappiness. Their pictures had appeared very seldom in the papers or on the television screens and at first no one recognized them. Then it dawned on the crowd that they must be the parents of the accused. At first there was a tentative wave of boos, quickly stilled by the sight of their obviously unhappy faces as they hurried toward the entrance. A low murmur of sympathy replaced the boos as they disappeared inside. "It isn't their fault they have an ungrateful, worthless son," someone said loudly. The comment seemed to be generally accepted as a wave of almost gentle concern followed them in.

Five minutes after that all gentle sounds abruptly ceased. An ugly roar went up, filled with hate. The defendant, walking in a square of armed police who glared sternly at the nearest watchers as they threatened to break across the ropes and engulf the prisoner, stepped out of an armored van and started for the entrance. His head was bandaged (a protection no longer necessary medically, but with an eye to television he had insisted upon it when his counsel had visited him soon after breakfast). He held his right arm awkwardly against his body and walked with a definite limp, particularly in his left leg. "Stop faking, you phony bastard!" some woman screamed at him, but he only tossed her a contemptuous smile and walked on. The roar swelled, multiplied, became more ominous.

Behind him came Debbie, eyes straight ahead, face expressionless. Rotten eggs, two rotten pumpkins, several small rocks, a brick, gobs of spittle flew after them as they were hurried to the entrance. As he reached it, Earle Holgren turned and gave them a jaunty finger, his contemptuous grin broadening into a sardonic grimace that plainly said, *I am superior to all you poor, pathetic bastards*. The ugly roar surged to fill the world. Across America, as his jeering face and gesture reached millions of his countrymen from their television screens, many and many a watcher grimly echoed Justice NOW!: *Enough is enough*.

Inside the courtroom he sobered somewhat but there was still an air of unrepentant defiance about him that communicated itself instantly to those he had hurt as they glanced, trying not to glance, at his stocky, bearded figure. He turned and surveyed the room with the same contemptuous expression in his eyes, though his face now was not jeering but suddenly watchful.

"I feel as though I am looking at an animal," Mary whispered to Tay with a shudder he felt in his arm alongside hers.

He nodded grimly.

"Treed," he whispered back, "but not yet cornered."

Next to her Sue-Ann Pomeroy drew in her breath sharply and seemed to flinch away a little as Earle's slow and careful gaze swept across hers; but Moss stared back at him with a somber and expressionless appraisal that for just a second seemed to disconcert him. Then the second passed and quite deliberately, taking his time and letting them feel his contempt and superiority, he let his eyes wander on across the room until he had completed his examination. Then he turned his back on them and leaned his shoulder against Debbie, who had been watching his performance with tightly compressed lips.

"Stupid bunch of jerks," he muttered.

"Don't get too smart for them," she remarked. "They might not like it."

"Hell," he said, "that's what you're here for, sweets. You'll get me out of it."

"Not if you act like a God damned preening egomaniac," she told him savagely. She pulled away from his intimately pressing shoulder and began to go through her papers. He studied her for a moment, then snorted and turned with an again-contemptuous smile toward the bench.

"The court will be in order," the bailiff announced loudly. The audience stood up, the judge came in. Last to rise, with an elaborate show of boredom and disinterest noted in a sharp quick glance by the judge, was the defendant. He did, however, finally manage it; and after studying him for a moment with an amused little smile and an intent gaze that alarmed Debbie, the judge said, "Please be seated." Quickly the audience obeyed. Slowly, so did Earle Holgren.

The judge, carefully chosen, was Regard Stinnet's friend, Perlie Williams—James Perle Williams in full, a transplanted Yankee from Pennsylvania who had been a South Carolinian since his parents had moved there when he was ten. His handling of the proceedings was crisp and to the point. Like Regard he was a hick only in season and this was not the season. He was a smart man and a judicious one and he tolerated no nonsense in his court. He too was aware of the publicity aspects of the case. His opening move caught both counsels off guard, though not for long.

"The court is cognizant," he said into the silence that abruptly descended over the standing-room-only audience of family, legal attendants, media, "that because of the nature of the crimes alleged against this defendant and because of the personal and emotional aspects of the matter insofar as this particular state is concerned, the selection of an unbiased jury may be an almost insurmountable task. However, it can be accomplished, providing counsel show a reasonable and equal determination to expedite. Will counsel approach the bench, please."

"Watch out for tricks!" Earle Holgren hissed. Debbie gave him an impatient look and hissed back, "Certainly!" But it was with considerable inner perturbation that she went to the bench.

Regard, apparently not at all perturbed, gave her an ironic little bow and then turned, impassive, to Perlie Williams.

"Now, I just want to tell you, young lady," the judge murmured confidentially in his pleasant voice, "and you, too, Regard, that I am not standing for any frivolous challenges or any deliberate stalling. The state, and I think the nation, demand and expect a speedy trial and a swift conclusion. I realize that this may seem to be playing into the hands of opposing counsel, Miss Donnelson. On the other hand, if you must rely, as I think you largely must, on such public sympathy as you can muster for your client, your cause will not profit if it is generally perceived that you are deliberately delaying things. It is to everybody's advantage to move right along; not to the endangerment of a fair trial, Miss Donnelson, but in the interests of justice and also of your own cause. Does that seem a reasonable conclusion?"

"Suits me fine, your honor," Regard replied briskly. Debbie hesitated.

"The court is only asking reasonable restraint and prudence, after all," Judge Williams pointed out. "I am determined not to have a circus."

"Very well, your honor," she said at last. "In that understanding I shall certainly do what I can to speed it along—always reserving my just rights and those of my client, however."

"Certainly, counsel," Perlie Williams said with some impatience. "No one is going to try to take them away."

"I hope not," she said, giving Regard a sternly quizzical glance.

"Absolutely not," he agreed. "That's the best way I know to get reversed on appeal. And," he added grimly, "I don't intend to get reversed on appeal on this one. Not by anybody, no time, no way."

"Very good," Judge Williams said. "Court will be in order, please." He turned to Regard. "Proceed, counsel."

But before Regard could speak, Debbie was on her feet.

"Your honor," she said, "I would like to request a change of venue." There was a ripple of startled sound across the room.

"Dear me," Judge Williams said dryly. "Why is this, counsel?"

"It is nothing personal, your honor," she said hastily. "You appear to be scrupulously fair and my client and I are much heartened by this. My request is for transfer to the appropriate court in Charleston, South Carolina."

"It is indeed a charming city," Perlie Williams conceded, and many in the audience laughed, "but is that sufficient reason for going there? Perhaps counsel can enlighten me."

"Your honor," she said earnestly, "my reasons for this request are, I think, self-evident in view of the situation that prevails around this courthouse at the moment. It is no secret that we are in a very hostile climate here. Displays of hostility were so great when we entered that for a moment I actually feared for the life of my client"—a hoot of scorn came from somewhere, and Judge Williams rapped his gavel sharply—"and I certainly fear for any chance of a fair trial in this area. Not where your honor is concerned, as your honor knows. But simply because popular sympathy is very strongly on the side of Justice Pomeroy, perhaps to the exclusion of any possibility of a fair trial. That is the ground for my request, your honor."

"You will find," Perlie Williams remarked, "that Pomeroys are fully as popular in Charleston as they are in Columbia, Miss Donnelson. And as for hostility toward what has happened and toward the one who, rightly or wrongly, is held responsible by many citizens, I am afraid that it is not only statewide but nationwide. Therefore, while I sympathize with your concern about demonstrations of hostility outside the courtroom—which," he added, looking sternly about—"will not be tolerated inside it—I am afraid I must reject your request for change of venue. Now, if we might proceed with the selection of a jury—?"

"We are bitterly disappointed, your honor," Debbie said, and looked it, "but must bow to your decision."

"Thank you," Judge Williams said with some irony. "Bailiff will call the first prospective juror, please."

"Your honor," Regard said smoothly, "before we proceed to that, the state would like to suggest most respectfully to your honor the possibility that television be admitted to these proceedings as well as the printed media."

"We agree, your honor," Debbie said quickly.

"Do you, now," Perlie Williams said.

"Yes, sir," Debbie replied. "We believe the public interest, both here and throughout the nation—"

"Throughout the world," Regard interjected. She nodded.

"—and in all probability throughout the world, would make it most advisable, or certainly most considerate of that interest, if television could be admitted. It would be an education for the public, we feel. And, I might add," she said with a glance at her opponent, "a good protection for my client in case anyone tries to pull any tricks."

"Does counsel for the state agree with these arguments?" Judge Williams inquired with an amused expression to which Regard decided to respond with equal amusement.

"Not entirely, your honor," he said with a fatherly chuckle, "because counsel is obviously quite alert enough and determined enough to protect her client without help from television or anybody else. In addition to which, of course," he remarked, less amicably, "nobody is goin' to try to 'pull any tricks' on one who obviously, considering everything, deserves the most tender and solicitous treatment from the law—at least equal to the tender and solicitous treatment he has given others."

"Your honor," Debbie said sharply, "I object to the implications of counsel's remarks and counsel's tone and I ask that his last sentence be stricken from the record."

"I think not," Judge Williams said. "Mr. Stinnet did not object to counsel's reference to 'tricks' and just now he did not name anyone in his own comment. I take it you both are agreed on television. The court has no aversion to it. Our space here is limited and it will have to be done on a rotating-pool basis, but it is perfectly agreeable to the court. The court will accept whatever arrangement the networks agree on. Now if we could return to the selection of a jury, bailiff will call the first prospective juror, please."

"Before that, your honor—" Regard said. Perlie Williams smiled rather wryly.

"Yes? What is it now?"

"Well, your honor," Regard said earnestly, "there's a lot of mighty fine folks outside there who have a great interest in what's goin' on in here, and it just occurred to me that maybe it would be a kindly act to string up some loudspeakers and broadcast the proceedin's directly to them. I'm just wonderin' if your honor's tolerance would extend to that?"

"Your honor," Debbie said, "we really must object. The temper of that crowd out there is already inflamed enough. I think it would be entirely too prejudicial to my client and entirely too much of a handicap to me. I think it would make a three-ring circus out of these proceedings and create a constant hostile pressure on my client and me which would be most deleterious—"

"Miss Donnelson," Perlie Williams said in a kindly voice, "these folks, as counsel for the state accurately says, are vitally interested in what is going on here. I don't really think an arrangement such as Mr. Stinnet suggests is going to create any more hostility to your client than obviously already exists. We don't want it to be said that anybody tried to curtail their First Amendment rights to receive all the information they can, and receive it instantaneously and directly, now, do we?"

"Your honor," Debbie said, "you know and I know, with all respect, that the First Amendment has nothing to do with it, since it covers the dissemination, not the reception, of information. Loudspeakers would be a most strained interpretation of—"

"Ah, but Miss Donnelson," Judge Williams said. "Ah, Miss Donnelson, *somebody will say so*. Somebody will argue that loudspeakers *do* disseminate information and that they cannot be curtailed, under the First Amendment. And God knows we have enough problems with this case already, don't we, without that? No, I think we will accept your suggestion, Mr. Stinnet. It won't do any harm, in the court's estimation, and it might do some good in moving things along. And now if we could return to the jury? Bailiff?"

"Your honor," Debbie was on her feet before the bailiff could respond, "we wish to announce that we waive all rights of selection and challenge."

There was a startled stir from the audience. Regard was also on his feet like a shot.

"Your honor!" he protested, for a moment looking genuinely, even comically, dismayed. At Debbie's side her client poked her arm with an audible chuckle and said, quite loudly, "Good for you!"

"Your honor," Regard said, recovering rapidly but still obviously taken aback, "this is most irregular!"

"I don't know of any law that says we *have* to select or challenge prospective jurors," Debbie remarked. "It is a right, not an obligation. Am I not correct, your honor?"

"You are," Perlie Williams agreed. "You intrigue me, counsel. I'm interested in the reasoning behind your decision. Would you care to share it with the court? You don't have to, but it would be interesting."

"Gladly, your honor," Debbie said crisply. "Because our point that the climate here is such that it is highly prejudiced against the defendant has been brushed aside; request for a change of venue based upon that obvious prejudice has been denied; television has been admitted; loudspeakers have been approved; and now I want the country to see exactly what I was talking about. Therefore it is obvious that counsel for the state must have a completely free hand in selecting exactly the type of jury he wants—prejudiced, biased, completely unfair—the only kind that can possibly be selected in this jurisdiction given the atmosphere I objected to. My perfectly valid and soundly based objection was dismissed. Very well, let him have his way. The country can judge for itself."

"Your honor," Regard said, breathing hard but managing to keep his temper. "I object most strongly, both professionally and personally, to opposing counsel's remarks. They themselves are prejudicial to me, prejudicial to a fair public judgment of this case, prejudicial to potential jurors themselves. I object, your honor. I object!"

"The court will admonish counsel for the defendant to be perhaps a little more polite in her references to counsel for the state," Judge Williams said, "but I don't see what else I can do. She doesn't have to select or challenge if she doesn't want to, counsel. What would you suggest?"

"But she is simply, deliberately, laying the groundwork for an appeal!" Regard said angrily.

"What else would you have a good lawyer do, counsel?" Judge Williams inquired. "Isn't that part of her duty as defense attorney?"

"I am also, your honor," Debbie said blandly, "making my contribution to opposing counsel's, and your honor's, desire for a speedy trial. We're going to save a great deal of time for you, here. I should think counsel for the state would be gratefully applauding my action, instead of puffing up like an indignant catfish."

"I will suggest to counsel for the defense again," Perlie Williams said, "that she restrain her tendency to indulge herself in that kind of verbiage. There *is* an atmosphere here which is not friendly to her client, as she truly says, and she will not make it more friendly by such tactics."

There was a burst of applause, long and loud, which caused Earle Holgren to swing around angrily. An immediate hail of boos responded and Debbie yanked hard at his arm. He gave her a glance but turned back. She stood up with dignity.

"I thank your honor for his generous suggestion," she said, "and I shall try to abide by it. Meanwhile, jury selection may proceed without us."

And after a few more moments of grumbling from Regard, endorsed with further applause from the audience but not in the slightest moving Debbie, it did. Regard recovered his poise, took his time, by noon had dismissed twenty of the sixty-seven called. Judge Williams recessed court for an hour, a much-diminished crowd again applauded its favorites and harassed the defendant as they made their separate ways to lunch. After lunch the process resumed. By 3 P.M. Regard had dismissed thirty of the forty-seven remaining, went carefully back over the seventeen left, dismissed five, got his twelve. He made very sure that all were college graduates, professional people: six men and six women; six whites and six blacks; one twenty-three, one twenty-seven, one sixty-five and one seventy, the remaining eight ranging between fifty and fifty-five.

"I intend to get a balance," he remarked at one point to Perlie Williams, "and since counsel for the defense will not help me, I intend to make sure it *is* a balance."

At the end of the process Judge Williams congratulated him and Debbie stood up.

"Your honor," she said, "I wish to congratulate counsel for the state on the good job he has done in selecting his jury. I, too, believe he has selected a well-balanced panel that will very adequately discharge the task he desires it to perform."

"I repeat to counsel for the defense," Perlie Williams said with some sternness, "that she does herself no good with that kind of remark. Counsel had her chance and refused it. Now whatever happens is at least as much counsel's responsibility as anyone's. I think that is quite clear on the record. No appeal can be based upon the nature of this jury, I believe. It has been selected with scrupulous fairness by Mr. Stinnet. Would counsel not agree?"

Debbie gave him a cool look.

"I will leave that judgment to others."

"I admire your tenacity, Miss Donnelson," Judge Williams said. "I don't think it helps your client very much; but it is, in its own rigid way, admirable. And possibly more effective than seems likely at the moment. Time is the only possible judge of that . . . Speaking of time, it is now almost five P.M., and it has been a long day. Court will be in recess until nine A.M. tomorrow, at which time counsel for the state will open his case."

And with a quick rap of his gavel and a pleasant nod to the audience, he left the chamber. A comparatively quiet opening day appeared to be coming to a quiet and routine close. For several minutes all was orderly and as expected.

The Pomeroys and the Barbours moved slowly out as the rest respectfully made way for them. The elder Holgrens had already gone, slipping out a side door of the courthouse to avoid the crowd. The defendant was being taken out in his square of police—four instead of the previous eight, which for a second puzzled him a little; but no sounds came from outside so he supposed the crowd had mostly gone, now that the novelty had worn off. The remainder of the audience was slowly moving out. The defendant just had time to call over his shoulder to his counsel, "You know, you're damned good!" in a surprised and admiring tone that brought a wry smile to her tightly pursed lips, when he and his guards came out of the entrance into the late afternoon sunshine.

At once things began to happen, very fast.

First came a sudden roar of sound. It was instantly apparent that the crowd, far from dispersing, had regathered during the afternoon, very quietly, to almost its morning strength.

Then came the tossing of several tear-gas canisters at the prisoner, his guards and the group of reporters and cameramen that preceded them, which swiftly had them all gasping, choking, and staggering blindly about.

And then came another great roar of "Justice NOW!" and with it a flying wedge of perhaps twenty men, dressed in what appeared to be black jump suits, the shield of the organization emblazoned on their chests, carrying rifles and wearing gas masks, charging through the helpless group around the prisoner with a ruthless determination that shoved aside the few police who had been stationed along the edge of the crowd. The rush took the attackers, virtually without opposition, straight to their objective.

Within thirty seconds from his appearance on the steps Earle Holgren, blinded and gagging, was captured. His arms were swiftly roped at his sides, his stocky form was carried like a sack of potatoes to a waiting blue van. It roared off. Behind it the crowd broke and began running for its cars, apparently heading for some prearranged rendezvous.

A final great shout of animal satisfaction, happy, exultant, gratified, expectant, filled the world. Inside the entrance the Pomeroys, the Barbours and Regard shrank back stunned while out front the tear-gas victims continued to stagger, gasp and vomit, and in their midst Debbie, managing by some feat of sheer willpower to remain on her feet, screamed, "Save him! Save him! Save him!"

For a long, bitter moment the Justices stared at Regard and he stared back. Finally Tay ground out, "You created this monster. Now do what the lady says and save him!"

Regard's face was a study. But finally he nodded.

"Yes, God damn his worthless, evil soul, I suppose I'll have to. But," he added grimly, "I can't do it alone. You'd better come with me, Mr. Justice. And you too, Moss, it's goin' to take the three of us, with this crowd."

Again there was a bitter moment while the two Justices looked at one another. Moss was wavering, Tay could feel it. He grasped his arm desperately.

"Moss, we must. It can't end this way. We'd never recover from it. The Court wouldn't recover. The *law* wouldn't recover. We've got to try. We've *got* to."

And at last with a deep, deep sigh, Moss inclined his head.

"Come on!" Regard yelled. "Put your handkerchiefs over your noses and run like hell!"

And stopping only to scoop up Debbie, whom he grabbed around the waist with a cry of "Come on, gal, we're goin' to get your worthless baby!" he led the way through the still staggering tear-gas victims and the remnants of the crowd to his blue Mercedes, unlocked and yanked open the doors, shoved her in and, after Tay and Moss had scrambled into the back seat, started the engine, turned on the siren and flashing red light that he had clapped on the roof, and shot onto the street.

"Where—?" Debbie began and started to retch. "Where—?"

"Don't you puke on my leather!" Regard roared. "You hang your head out the window if you have to! But NOT ON MY LEATHER!"

"I am not," she gasped, after an obviously titanic and successful struggle, "going to *puke* on your precious leather! Where are we going?"

"I know where we're goin'," Regard said, his face beginning to gleam with the excitement of the chase as the speedometer passed sixty. "Just don't try to get out, sweetheart. Stay with me and I'll get you there. O.K., *counsel?*"

"Yes, *counsel,*" she said, sounding more herself by the moment. "Is it the usual place where you have your lynchings?"

"And don't be God damned smart, either," he snapped, "because unless we get there in time, this really is goin' to be one and you'll *really* have somethin' to tell your friends up north. Now, hang on!"

And as they all did, he gunned it up to eighty and shot through the outskirts of the city while cars and pedestrians scattered desperately in all directions.

Ten minutes later they began to be blocked by other cars, but with the siren and the constant use of his horn and the recognition that instantly came as they saw his familiar vehicle, he managed to eel on through at a still rapid pace and presently they were on the edge of a large open field. In its center stood an enormous oak and under one of its branches, from which dangled a rope, a blue van with a ladder against its side.

On its top stood four of the black-suited squad from Justice NOW!, still wearing their masks. In their midst, tightly pinioned, the rope around his neck, stood Earle Holgren. He was cold sober now and white as a sheet but the look of arrogant defiance was still there. It was obvious that if they killed him he had no intention of giving them the satisfaction of seeing him break first. With a roar of engine, squeal of brakes, scream of siren and a final long, steady blast on his horn,

Regard swung in alongside the van, cut the motor, reached under his seat, grabbed a bullhorn and jumped out.

At once a deathly silence fell over the crowd, which already numbered perhaps two thousand with more arriving constantly at its outer edges.

"Listen to me!" Regard shouted through the bullhorn. "Listen to me, you good people! I want to talk to you and I've brought two other men who want to talk to you." Abruptly he leaned down to the window and hissed to Debbie, "*You* stay in there, you bothersome woman!" Then he turned again to the crowd, which had begun to murmur uneasily. "Jenkins!" he shouted up to the top of the van. "Jenkins Terwilliger, is that you? I'd know you anywhere, you hotheaded bastard! Help me give a hand up to our two distinguished visitors here!"

And with an elaborate gesture he turned back, opened the door of the car and bowed low as he whispered urgently, "Make it good, now, you two! You're dignified as hell, remember. Be that way!"

As Tay emerged, obediently straightening to his full six feet three and looking out upon the crowd with a gravely challenging air, he was greeted with a shout of surprise—not hostile, but, as Regard was pleased to note, uncertain. When Moss followed and stood for a moment surveying them with equal gravity, face almost expressionless, the shout was louder, warmer—and increasingly uncertain.

"Come on!" Regard whispered "Upsy-daisy!"

And with Jenkins Terwilliger pulling above and Regard giving a helping shove from below, first Tay, then Moss climbed up the ladder to the top of the van.

"Now, Jenkins," Regard ordered, using the bullhorn so that his voice boomed over the field, "it's gettin' mighty crowded up there. I want you and your friends to come down here and guard this van while I go up there with my friends from the Supreme Court of the United States and say a few words to these good, law-abidin' folks."

There was a movement of protest from the four black-suited men, a turn toward ugliness in the murmur of the crowd. Regard was ready for them.

"I want you to stand guard, I said! I didn't say I wanted you to run off and leave this—this *individual* alone. He can't escape anyway, you've got him tied like a hog at bacon-time, but the Justices and I will vouch for him, I can promise you that. So y'all just come on down, now, and let us handle it. All right, Jenkins? This isn't doin' anybody any good, and you know it. Come on down, now! *Right* now!"

For what seemed an interminable time but could only have been a few seconds, the four atop the van hesitated while the crowd grew very still. Tay and Moss, staring out with determined calm, did not dare move. Behind them the prisoner was equally still. Regard said nothing, just continued to stare up with an air of impatience; and in a moment the gamble worked. Slowly and reluctantly, but obeying, the four black-suited figures clambered down. As each reached the ground Regard shook hands with vigorous and elaborate approval.

"Thank y'all," he said when all were down. "Thank you for complyin' with the law, which is what Justice NOW! is all about, remember. Now I'll just get myself up there"—which he did with several grunts that he was careful to utter over the bullhorn, so that first a few, then many, began to laugh, and with their laughter began to dissolve the tension.

"Whooo-eeee!" he exclaimed when he finally stood on top. "That's too much exercise for a country boy who doesn't get any except mebbe liftin' a jug and chasin' women or mebbe I should say chasin' women and liftin' a jug."

This time many more laughed and the tension eased still further. Tay began to realize that his respect for Regard Stinnet was rapidly going up. He glanced sideways at Moss and saw that he, too, was relaxing just a little; and although he did not dare turn and look at the prisoner, he could sense that even he was less tense. He was, in fact, Tay knew, becoming watchful. He hoped fervently that Regard knew what he was doing. He did.

"Now, first of all," he said through the bullhorn in a familiar but still emphatic tone, "I want y'all to understand that you've got friends here who sympathize with how you feel—not," he added quickly as Tay stirred a little at his side, "with the methods y'all seemed gettin' ready to adopt to do somethin' about it. No, sir, I've got to tell you honestly that all three of us up here represent the law—even though," he added sarcastically as four or five television vans and half a dozen automobiles screamed to a stop off on the edge of the crowd and their occupants began to scramble frantically through the crowd with their gear—"our good friends from the media who are just arrivin', a little late as usual" —there was a scornful hoot from the crowd—"may not give us much credit for law and order, down here in South Carolina. Whether they do or not," he declared, his voice rising emphatically, "that is the sole point and purpose of Justice NOW!, that great movement to which many of you belong, and to which I hope many, many millions more soon will belong. We're growin', friends, we're growin'! And they aren't goin' to be able to stop us, because all across this great land our strength is as the strength of millions, yea hundreds of millions of good,

God-fearin', law-abidin', *law-respectin'* citizens. And that's why I'm up here right this minute talkin' to you, and why our two great friends from the Supreme Court of the United States are goin' to be speakin' to you shortly, too. Because we, like you, *respect and abide by* the law; and what some few folks might have been contemplatin' here before we arrived just doesn't have any place in the law, or any place in a decent, God-fearin' America or any place in this great state of South Carolina. We don't need that! We've got our strength in Justice NOW! Justice NOW! wants law and order! Justice NOW! *is* law and order—a great, spontaneous outpourin' of love and respect and *obedience* to the law! That's what you want and I want and these whole great United States want. Isn't that right, now, my friends? *ISN'T THAT RIGHT?"*

With a great shout the crowd responded *"RIGHT!"* Under its cover Regard dashed a hasty hand that Tay and Moss could see was trembling across a forehead that they could see was beaded with sweat. Tay's respect continued to rise.

"Now," Regard said, his voice becoming steadily more assured, "let me just warn you one thing about our friends from the media, here. Their whole job is to get you riled up again, you know. They can't be content with folks just quietin' down and behavin' themselves, that doesn't look good on the evenin' news. They want wild-eyed people and wild-eyed statements, that's what they live on. So I'd suggest, for the sake of Justice NOW! and for the sake of the dignity of the sovereign state of South Carolina which we all love, that y'all just refuse 'em any interviews out there when they stick their damned microphones and writin' pads in your faces. You tell 'em to pack up and *git!* Right?"

"RIGHT!" the crowd shouted and there was much laughter and applause. They were with him one hundred percent now, and the famous commentator who audibly exclaimed, "Damned rabble-rousing son of a bitch!" was promptly shoved around and had to be rescued by nearby police.

"Now," Regard said, gesturing scornfully over his shoulder toward the prisoner. "I'm goin' to get this worthless piece of human junk back to jail where he belongs, so if you and your friends will assist me, Jenkins—I'm trustin' you now, and bear in mind the world is watchin' and we want to do things right, for all our sakes, so you help me out, now—I'm goin' to untie his legs so he can walk, and then we'll get him down the ladder. And then I want you and your friends to put him in the back seat of my car and stand guard over him until I get down there, at which time we're goin' to form us a little escort-party and get him back to jail in the style to which he's accustomed. How about that?"

Again there was a wave of laughter, applause and approving shouts across the crowd; and Regard, though the sweat was starting again on his forehead and his hands were once more trembling slightly, turned and moved firmly and with absolute outward assurance toward the prisoner.

For a second Earle Holgren's eyes glared, his head came back, his mouth began to pucker.

"You spit on me, you piece of shit," Regard hissed, so low that only Earle and Tay and Moss, instinctively moving to help him, could hear, "and you'll be torn limb from limb so fast you won't have time to turn your head before it's off. Now, *stand still!* Gentlemen, you keep an eye on him while I do this."

"I can barely stand to look at him," Moss murmured in a voice of such contempt that even Earle Holgren's endless insolence appeared shattered for a second. Tay nodded.

"But we'll help," he said. And they moved closer to the prisoner while the crowd again became deathly still as Regard knelt down and swiftly untied the rope around his ankles.

"Stomp your feet," he ordered in a low voice. "Get the circulation goin'. And hurry it up, because I don't know how much longer we can keep these good folks from cookin' your evil flesh for dinner . . . Now, move!" And he gave Earle Holgren a savage shove toward the ladder as the Justices stepped back and watched with expressions that justified Moss' comment: they really could hardly bear to look at him.

Carefully, with Regard steadying his shoulders from above and Jenkins Terwilliger reaching up with conspicuous roughness to grasp his legs from below, they eased the defendant down: and again, as he reached the ground and Jenkins and his friends stepped forward to surround him, the crowd became deathly still. In the stillness Regard said calmly through the bullhorn, "I'm trustin' you boys. For Carolina and Justice NOW!, get him into that car and close the door on him. *Fast.*"

Once again they hesitated for a moment and the crowd, if possible, became quieter. But Regard continued to stare down at them with apparent complete assurance that he would be obeyed; and he was. Aside from a startled "What the *hell!*" from Jenkins when they saw Debbie sitting rigidly in the front seat, her eyes carefully turned away from them, there was no disruption or outcry. Before there could be Regard turned again to face the crowd.

"And now," he said, his voice becoming hushed but still carrying clearly, "I'm goin' to call on two famous men to speak to you very briefly for just a minute, because you know how sad things are for them and we don't want to keep 'em here long. Justice Barbour—?"

"Yes," Tay said, accepting the bullhorn as Regard thrust it into his hand and stepping forward a little, though at the moment he had no idea exactly what he would say. But it came naturally enough.

"First," he said, "I want to pay tribute to a pretty remarkable fellow, I think, and that's your attorney general." There was a wild burst of applause and approval. "We've already disagreed on a lot of things, and quite possibly we're going to disagree on a lot more before this case is finally disposed of by all the courts that may ultimately be involved. But he's a brave man, that's for sure, and I congratulate him fully on that."

There was a roar of approval from the crowd.

"I want to congratulate you, also, for responding so wisely and effectively to his appeal for calm and reason. I think the three of us up here are agreed one hundred percent on one thing: the law *is* the issue, and the law must be preserved. You are doing this when you peaceably accept the fact and go peaceably about your business, confident that Mr. Stinnet fully shares your feelings and will faithfully follow them as his guide when the case resumes in court tomorrow.

"I congratulate you on your patience, your restraint and your respect for the law. Justice will be done, in whatever court this case may come to. I think I can give you my word on that. Moss—?"

He held out the bullhorn while applause, full-hearted and friendly, rewarded him. It trailed off uncertainly when Moss at first made no move to accept the horn but simply stood unmoving for what seemed a very long time. His face was set and far away, his eyes tortured and unhappy as he stared out over them; and finally all sound died away.

"Moss—?" Tay said again quietly, gesturing with the horn. "Moss, these are your people. They want you to talk to them."

Applause agreed; and suddenly it welled up into a roar, sympathetic, welcoming, overwhelmingly responsive, as Moss seemed to come out of his sad reverie and reached for the horn.

For several more seconds his gaze traveled moodily from side to side across the crowd, which swiftly quieted again to the point where only the whir of cameras and the occasional indignant cry of a reporter, jostled by some competitive colleague out of his vantage point, broke the stillness.

"My dear old friends of South Carolina," he finally began, "you know what a—" his voice trembled a little but he went on, "what a heavy sorrow Sue-Ann and I have had to bear in these past few days—in fact, will always bear, for nothing can take the place of our bright spirit who is—is gone. But, life goes on, as it must—a cliché one doesn't appreciate fully until one has to . . .

"I think what has happened here today illustrates the truth of what Justice Barbour has said. My good, close friend Regard Stinnet (Tay felt a slight tingling of alarm, but kept his face expressionless) deserves the highest compliments for his courage and common sense, as you deserve equal compliments for your willingness to follow his lead. Your organization Justice NOW! is indeed devoted to law and order, and only if it abides by them can it hope to hold and increase its already astonishing membership. I sincerely hope it will proceed in the spirit in which it was founded and so be able to do the great job of restoring law, and respect for law, which it has so effectively begun."

No, Tay cried out in his mind. *Not you, Moss.*

But the crowd went wild with cheers and applause and Moss concluded gravely.

"It is true, and I think we on the Supreme Court recognize it to be true, that the criminal justice system as it now stands needs very drastic revision and speeding-up. This case may well be the symbol and the beginning of that process. It is, as Justice Barbour says, the purpose of all three of us standing before you now to uphold, defend and strengthen the law; and so it is of the Supreme Court. Justice NOW! may not be the means some of us would have chosen to do this, but it exists and in its very short life it has already become a major constructive force throughout the country looking toward the strengthening of law and order. We will ignore the sentiment it represents, I think, at our peril."

Again a great approving shout went up; and Tay thought with a desperate sadness, *Moss, oh Moss. What a mistake, what a terrible mistake.*

"Sue-Ann and I," Moss concluded, voice again close to breaking, "have already expressed our gratitude to our dear friends of South Carolina in the statement we issued two days ago. But let me reaffirm it to you now. Dear friends, your love is our great strength; and your great strength has the gratitude of our love."

Another swell of sound, this time respectful, sympathetic, almost tender. As it died away Regard said quietly over the bullhorn,

"And now, friends, we'll be on our way. We will be back in court tomorrow morning to get this distasteful but necessary job done just as fast as we can. Have faith. We are not going to disappoint you. Thank you for your patience. Good-bye and God bless."

And he gestured Moss and Tay before him as the crowd, with a last flurry of shouts and handclaps, watched them go. Carefully the Justices descended, Tay first; and when they reached the ground, shielded from the crowd for a second as Tay turned toward Moss to give him a helping hand down the last rung of the ladder, their eyes met and Tay shook his head sadly.

"You shouldn't have, buddy," he said in a near whisper.

"You don't have a dead daughter," Moss replied in a choked voice with a look as though he had never seen him before. "It charges one."

"Into the car as fast as you can, gentlemen," Regard whispered urgently behind them, "and let's get out of here before the mood changes again. I'm sorry you have to sit beside that bastard but I don't dare let anybody else drive him and I don't dare let the two of them sit together. She might cut his ropes and slip him a gun to turn on us."

"You don't really think so!" Tay exclaimed as they hurried toward the Mercedes.

Regard shook his head grimly.

"No, not really, I suppose. But you never know with her type. They can get pretty damned intense sometimes, particularly if she wants to get into his pants, as I expect she will sooner or later. Anyway, I'm not takin' any chances. In you go."

Moss hesitated. Tay said quickly, "It's all right, Moss, I'll do it," and slid in beside the defendant, who drew away from him as much as possible as Moss followed and closed the door.

"Don't worry," Tay said savagely. "I don't want to touch you either, Holgren."

"It's the stink I got from his jail," Earle said, nodding toward Regard as he started the motor, turned on the siren, backed the car around in a wide, screaming half-circle and rocketed out onto the road back to Columbia, followed by Jenkins Terwilliger and his friends, two police cars, and, trailing and complaining, as many of the media vans and cars as could get organized to follow them.

"You couldn't possibly get as much stink from that jail as you brought into it," Regard told him as he pushed the speedometer up to seventy and shot ahead of the procession. "Why don't you just close your big, smart, clever mouth and let us get along without the benefit of your wise-ass remarks for a little while? Pretend you're back on the van about to be lynched. I noticed you were pretty quiet then."

"I must protest—" Debbie began primly, and Regard half-swung toward her, which prompted Earle to yell, "Keep your eyes on the road, you damned jerk! Do you want to kill us all?"

"Only you, sweetheart," Regard said savagely, but complying. "Only you."

"Well, that's too bad, man," Earle said with elaborate cheerfulness, "because I was just about to thank you for saving my life back there. That was a brave thing you did and we appreciate it, don't we, counsel?"

For a moment no one said anything: the sheer effrontery of it was too much. Then Debbie said cautiously, "I think perhaps you had better not say anything more, Earle."

"So why shouldn't I 'say anything more,' counsel?" Earle demanded, mocking her tone. "And why are *you* mad at me, man? I just wanted to thank you for a real great thing, that's all. You saved my life, man. You saved an innocent soul. Can't I thank you for that, man?"

Again for a moment no one said anything; but up the back of Regard Stinnet's neck a red flush crept, and on the wheel his hands grew knuckle-white. Abruptly he slowed the car. Squealing brakes behind indicated that his startled caravan was doing the same.

Deliberately he reached up and adjusted the rear-view mirror so that he was looking straight into Earle Holgren's eyes.

"Listen, *man,*" he said with a softness much more impressive than rage. "Don't you thank me, you worthless son of a bitch. I'm going to see you dead if it's the last thing I do. But it's going to be in the right way, at the right time and in the right place. I'm not goin' to see poor old South Carolina pinned to the wall for a lynching one more time just because of you, you murderous piece of slime. You've done enough damage to this state and her fine people already. I'll meet you and your smart little lady here in court and we'll talk about it then. I don't want to hear one more word out of you about anything until you're up there on the witness stand. So shut *up,* hear?"

And with a sudden vicious distaste that rocked them all back against their seats he stomped on the gas and got them the hell out of there; and neither the prisoner nor his counsel said another word to anybody all the rest of the way.

2

Once again they ran the jeering gauntlet, somewhat smaller today. Police stationed every five feet faced the crowd on each side, hands on guns. Regard was taking no chances from now on. The defendant arrived in an armored van accompanied by ten motorcycle outriders, disembarked in the center of a sixteen-man square of guards and was hurried forward at a near run to the door. Again obscene insults were shouted, rotten eggs and plastic bags of cow dung thrown. None struck him or Debbie, hurrying after. He was still ostentatiously limping but had no choice but to keep the pace set by his protectors. At the door he half-turned as though to repeat his gesture of yesterday. The nearest guard shoved him roughly forward before he could complete it, and, almost stumbling, he disappeared inside to a final yell of contempt. An expression of naked animal hatred crossed his face for a moment as he was hurried down the hallway but by the time he entered the courtroom he had recaptured his normal amused, superior air.

Tay and Moss were in place, their wives absent, Sue-Ann at home forcing herself to begin answering the thousands of messages of condolence that had flooded in, Mary still grieving over her daughter's comatose form at Richland Memorial Hospital. The elder Holgrens were also there, and today on entry had ventured a shy, sad, tentative half-nod toward the two Justices. Moss stared straight through them, unforgiving, but this time Tay managed a meager but not unfriendly smile in return. This seemed to ease them somewhat and he felt better for it.

Court was called to order, Judge Williams walked briskly in and took his place. The writing press leaned forward expectantly, and from their newly built platform along the wall to the judge's right, the pool television crew kept its camera moving restlessly from face to face.

"Before we return to counsel for the state," Perlie Williams said—as he had been requested to do in a private phone call an hour ago—"is there anything either counsel wishes to say to the court?"

"Yes, your honor," Debbie said, standing up and bowing to him. "If your honor please, I should like to have placed in the official record front pages and editorials from the Washington *Post,* the New York *Times,* the Chicago *Tribune,* the New Orleans *Times Picayune* and the Charleston, South Carolina, *News* and *Courier.* They are representative of many other journals, all paying high and deserved tribute to the personal bravery and decisive intervention yesterday of Mr. Regard Stinnet in what could have been a most unfortunate happening for my client and for everyone concerned with the preservation of law and order in America.

"I wish also to congratulate the members of his organization, Justice NOW! who were willing to respond so promptly and with such a sense of responsibility to his appeal for law and order. This speaks well for the constructive work that Justice NOW! may be able to do in the future."

For a second Regard's face was a study. Earle shot her a sideways quizzical look and both in the room and outside there was a sound of hesitant puzzlement: such words from such a source were the last things anyone had expected to hear. Then Regard bowed low.

"I thank counsel again," he said, though with just the slightest trace of a sardonic wink that only Perlie Williams and Debbie could see. "She is most kind to my poor self and to a great spontaneous grassroots movement which does indeed seek to strengthen law and order . . . In regard to which, your honor," he added casually, "I would like to place in the record a letter from a lawyer in New York who does not seem to agree as wholeheartedly as Miss Donnelson with either Justice NOW! or its stated purpose of strengthening the criminal justice system in America. It is apparent from this letter that there are some in the legal profession who are not quite so enthused about it all as she and I evidently are. If it please the court—"

"Your honor!" Debbie said sharply as Earle leaned forward, suddenly intent. "I feel I must object, your honor, because I really don't see what an extraneous expression of opinion concerning Justice NOW! by some unknown lawyer in New York has to do with this case. Whoever this lawyer is, he has nothing to do with this case."

"Does he have something to do with this case, counsel?" Perlie Williams inquired of Regard—pursuant to the second private phone call he had received prior to today's convening.

Regard studied the letter and then looked up blandly directly into the television cameras.

"I am not sure, your honor," he said thoughtfully. "However, opposing counsel seems to be genuinely concerned about it, so perhaps if she *insists—*"

"Your honor," Debbie said calmly, though she could see from the stirring in the media that it was too late, Regard had their interest, he'd give it to them and they'd have it nationwide within the hour, "possibly I *am* making too much of this. Let counsel go ahead and put it in, if he wishes. I don't see the pertinence, but—" she turned away indifferently and began going through her own papers. Something about the set of Earle Holgren's shoulders, however, betrayed them both.

"Who is this letter from, counselor?" Judge Williams inquired.

"Shucks!" Regard said. "It may not be the one Miss Donnelson thinks it is, at all. She's probably right. Let's just forget it."

"You have *me* intrigued, now," Perlie Williams said with a smile. "Let me have the name, counsel, and I'll decide."

"Well," Regard said with some reluctance, "if your honor insists, it's Harrison Aboud." Earle said distinctly, "Damn!" There was a stirring from the audience, a sudden chorus of heavy booing from outside. "Never heard of him much, myself."

"Counsel is being disingenuous now, I'm afraid," Judge Williams remarked. "Harry Aboud has defended virtually every dissenter, protester, left-wing bomber, murderer, terrorist, communist, social disrupter in the United States for the past twenty years." Suddenly his voice changed. He was for a moment no longer the amiable presider but abruptly the cold probing inquisitor. "Why isn't he here, Miss Donnelson? Why are you representing this defendant instead of Harry Aboud, who is obviously interested?"

"Because this defendant asked me to, your honor," Debbie said, calmly still though her tightly clasped hands showed strain.

"How did the defendant know you, Miss Donnelson?"

"As I have told the press, and as your honor may have read," Debbie said carefully, "I happen to agree with the many millions in this country and the world who fear and abhor atomic power. Even though wrongly accused, as I believe we will be able to show, I felt that this defendant also shared those views. Therefore I felt that someone who felt as I do was being falsely accused and needed help. So I offered my assistance to him and he accepted."

"Was this at Mr. Aboud's suggestion?"

"I had never discussed this matter with Mr. Aboud."

"I didn't ask if you had discussed it with him, I asked if he suggested that you offer your services to the defendant."

Debbie's chin came up defiantly.

"No!"

"Your honor," Regard said, "I suggest counsel be put under oath."

"I am judge in this court, Mr. Stinnet," Perlie Williams said calmly, "and I intend to let counsel do it her way. She prefers to say that Mr. Aboud did not suggest her defense of Mr. Holgren. That is the way she wants it to stand and that is the way we will let it stand. Unless counsel wishes to amend her answer."

"No, your honor," Debbie said, breathing a little faster but otherwise seemingly unperturbed. "I do not."

"Very well. Does counsel for the state wish to read Mr. Aboud's letter into the record?"

"No, thanks, your honor," Regard said. "It is the usual cr—it's the usual stuff about how impossible it is for a defendant to get a fair trial in America and how awful Justice NOW! is, and how dangerous it is to our free, liberty-lovin', democratic way of life, to whose preservation Mr. Aboud is of course so notoriously dedicated. It mentions the defendant, but only as a case in point. I'll have copies for the media. Like I said, it really doesn't need to go into the record."

"Well, by now, counsel," Perlie Williams remarked, "I think it might just as well, don't you? Miss Donnelson has said she doesn't object. And I don't object. So in it goes. Does counsel have any other exhibits at the moment?"

"Not at the moment, your honor. But as my first witness, I'd like to call Sheriff William Lanahan of Pomeroy Station, if you please."

"Your honor," Debbie said as the young officer who had found the bodies of Janet and John Lennon Peacechild stood up. "Your honor, I request that further proceedings in this case be delayed for one month."

"Now, why," Perlie Williams inquired gently, as the room and media erupted in a babble of urgent whisperings and a great boo rose from outside, "would you request that, Miss Donnelson?"

"Because I submit, your honor," Debbie said, lips pursed and expression grim, "that in the general hurly-burly of trying to rush this defendant headlong to perdition, the matter of his psychiatric condition has been entirely overlooked. We do not know what it was at the time of the alleged crime committed at Pomeroy Station by person or persons unknown"—there was an angry hoot from outside, but she went defiantly on—"we do not know what it has been in the past—we do not know what it is now. I am not even sure that he is mentally able to stand trial. If this trial is to be fairly conducted, it seems to me a month is not too much to ask for expert and qualified individuals to determine these things."

"Miss Donnelson," Judge Williams said patiently, "you will recall that in conference at the bench prior to start of trial, I remarked that if you were perceived by the public to be deliberately and unduly delaying these proceedings, it would not do your client any good. Now are you very sure you wish to pursue this tactic? Particularly for such a length of time?"

"Other defendants in other cases undergo psychiatric tests for months, your honor," she observed with a show of indignation. "Is my client to be denied *one* month, simply because of the hysteria whipped up here by counsel for the state and his organization?"

"Both of which counsel was praisin' to the skies not fifteen minutes ago!" Regard exclaimed indignantly. Outside the boo rose again.

"Yes, I was!" Debbie said angrily. "And I think yesterday *you* showed courage and *they* showed good sense in following your advice. But good qualities are not being shown in some other aspects of this case, and this is one of them My client has a right to psychiatric examination—"

"Oh, the state will admit he's a psychopath!" Regard shot back.

"I object, your honor!" Debbie snapped.

"Objection sustained," Perlie Williams agreed promptly. "Counsel will restrain himself, if possible. Or I'll restrain him. Miss Donnelson, tell the court why you think an entire month is necessary for psychiatric examination."

"Because, your honor," Debbie said earnestly, while her client and everyone else studied her dark, determined little face and listened carefully to her clear, incisive voice, "Earle Holgren at this moment is an unknown quantity to all of us here. All we know is that he was seen in the vicinity of the bombing at Pomeroy Station: there is no proof that he did it. We know that he was brutally set upon and beaten by so-called 'peace officers.' We know that he was denied his right to be informed of his rights, and we know that he was denied his immediate right to be represented by counsel. We know that yesterday he was almost lynched by a mob of South Carolina citizens. We know that he is the object and the victim of a concerted drive to rush him through trial with such speed that there is very grave danger that he will in no way receive a fair hearing. We know that he must be defended in an atmosphere of bias, prejudice and hatred. But what is Earle Holgren really like? That we do not know."

Distantly came another angry hoot. Many obviously thought they did. She went on, chin a little higher, expression still more determined.

"I have talked to my client, your honor, and of course those conversations are privileged communications between defendant and lawyer. But I can tell you that out of them I have formed a picture of a product of a luxurious but oppressive home"—the elder Holgrens looked at one another with a startled dismay that brought murmurs of sympathy from their neighbors and a quick, contemptuous glance from their son—"who early became convinced, most sincerely and idealistically, that much needs to be changed in America; who has devoted his life to date to trying to bring those changes about; and who is motivated always by the highest ideals and dreams for his country and his people—"

"Miss Donnelson," Judge Williams interrupted dryly, "if you don't mind, I must ask you again why you consider it necessary for your client to have a psychiatric examination."

"Because he has been hurt by life!" she exclaimed angrily. "Because his ideals and dreams have been thwarted, warped and frustrated! Because who knows what damage has been done inside to a highly intelligent, perceptive and sensitive mind! Because the very life of a valuable human being is at stake! Because—"

But this time her words were drowned in a wave of booing that swept not only the crowd outside but the audience in the courtroom. It was several moments before Perlie Williams, vigorously pounding his gavel, was able to restore order.

"The court," he said when he had finally secured it, "will remind the audience once—just once—that order is to be maintained in this courtroom. If the audience cannot be in order it will be directed to leave and the room will be cleared of everyone but the principals in the case and the media. This warning will not be repeated. Miss Donnelson, you do not, in my estimation, seem to be getting much of anywhere. However, since the court does not wish to either endanger—or enhance—your chance for appeal if you should ultimately wish to make one, I am willing to go through the process of psychiatric examination of the defendant. But I am not willing to take forever to do it. The public interest in a swift conclusion of this matter is too great, as you yourself are well aware. I will not give you one month. I will give you one week."

"But, your honor—!" Debbie cried in what appeared to be genuine dismay.

"Today is Friday. Over the weekend you will appoint one psychiatrist; the state will appoint one; the court will appoint a third. They will have full access to the prisoner between the hours of ten A.M and five P.M. beginning next Monday and terminating one week from today. They will present their report to the court at ten A.M. on the following Monday.

"Court will now stand in recess until ten A.M. next Monday week."

And with a last decisive rap of the gavel he stood up, turned his back on them all, and went out.

Again the elder Holgrens slipped away, the audience moved quickly out. This time security was absolute. The crowd had been ordered back fifty feet on either side. The guards virtually ran the prisoner to the van, hurried him inside, scrambled after him and slammed the door. The van roared away in the midst of its motorcycle escort.

More leisurely, Tay and Moss stood up, nodded to Regard and Debbie as they gathered their papers, ignoring each other but taking time to smile good-bye to the Justices, and went out together into the drowsy afternoon.

"What are you going to do for the week?" Tay inquired. Moss sighed.

"I'm going back to D.C. There's nothing I can do here. Sue-Ann may stay a few days but the Court goes on, you know. The work is piling up. I feel I've got to get back, until I'm recalled here to testify, which I suppose I will be. And you?"

"I'd like to," Tay said, "but I just don't see how I can leave Janie at the moment."

"No change?"

"No change. And Mary would never forgive me if there was a change, either good or bad, and I wasn't here. I'd never forgive myself. I'll just have to hope the Chief and all of you understand."

Moss gave him an impatient but affectionate look.

"Oh, of course. I won't be going up until Monday morning. Why don't you come out to the house on Sunday for a few hours, just to get away? I don't suppose Mary would come, but—"

"No," Tay said with a sigh. "I'm sure she won't. But I will, if all's calm."

"Good. Call me around ten and I'll come get you."

Tay nodded. He hesitated for a second and then decided to risk it. "I want to talk to you anyway. About—yesterday."

"What about yesterday?" Moss demanded, immediately defensive.

"You know what about yesterday," Tay said, "so don't play innocent. That's a no-good organization, Moss, and you know what the media are already doing with your support of it."

"I didn't support it!"

"You came damned close. And it just isn't good—it just isn't fitting or proper. And what's more, I'll bet the Chief tells you so, too."

"I'm not a child," Moss snapped, "to be lectured like a child."

"No, but you are a Justice of the Supreme Court, and that imposes some obligations. Anyway," he said as Moss' expression became even more set, "I'm not going to stand here in front of the courthouse and argue with you about it. We'll talk about it Sunday—if you'll let me."

"Oh, I'll let you," Moss said as they reached his car, "but it won't do any good. Get in, I'll drop you at the hospital. How do you think things are going so far?"

"Skirmishing," Tay said, obediently abandoning the subject. "No hits, no runs, one or two minor errors on Miss Debbie's part. Regard remains the hero of the hour so far, I'd say, but even he hasn't moved things much. Too early. But a lot can happen in a week."

"And not in Earle Holgren's favor," Moss said grimly as he put the car in drive and started off. "I hope to God."

"You see?" Tay said, trying to make it light. "That's what I mean."

"You worry about your own problems," Moss said shortly. "You've got enough."

And so he had, he thought as they arrived at Richland Memorial without further conversation and Moss dropped him off with a quick handshake and "See you Sunday." The moment he entered the doors the head nurse hurried toward him. Oh God, no, he prayed. Don't let it be. *Don't let it be.*

But the nurse, to his dazed relief, was smiling; and her voice when she spoke held a lilt of happy excitement.

"Mr. Justice!" she called out from halfway across the lobby. "Mr. Justice, you're wanted at once in your daughter's room. Hurry on up, now!"

"Is it—?" he began, not daring to really ask. "Is it—?"

"It's good news!" she said, and he became aware that other nurses were looking his way, smiling, beaming. "Good news! But you just hurry on up! Mrs. Barbour will tell you all about it. Hurry on, now!"

"Yes, ma'am," he said, a great happiness beginning to grow in his heart. "Yes, *ma'am!*"

And, almost boyishly, he did 'hurry on'; and outside Janie's room he saw other nurses smiling, the older doctor from their first interview waiting, an air of excitement and encouragement. With tears in his eyes he opened the door and went in. Instantly a cold hand seized his heart. Janie was still lying apparently comatose, unchanged in any way he could see. But Mary looked up, face alight.

"She spoke to me!" she exclaimed. "She spoke to me! I was going to send for you at the trial but it was just a little while ago and they said you'd be back soon."

He nodded, his impulse to go to her and put his arms around her. But there was something in the set of her head and body that warned him off, even now. So he simply stepped forward to the other side of the bed and looked down at his daughter's sleeping face.

"What did she say?" he asked, aware that the doctor had come into the room and was quietly watching them.

"Not much," Mary said, "and rather slurred and hurried, but clear enough. Her eyes opened, quite wide, and focused on me for a moment as though she were trying"—her voice trembled, then steadied—"trying, very hard. Then she said, 'Mommy, how are you, Mommy?' And then, 'Where's Daddy?' And then her eyes closed and she went back—back to sleep. But she recognized me, Tay! She remembered us! She isn't gone, after all. She's in there somewhere and the doctor thinks she'll be waking soon again." She turned and appealed directly to him. "Don't you, doctor?"

"Yes, ma'am," he said, coming forward to stand at the foot of the bed. "Indeed I do. When Mrs. Barbour cried out the nurse hurried in and also heard Janie speak. *She* feels it was quite distinct." He smiled. "She's a little bit more optimistic even than Mrs. Barbour is, I think. I agree with them both. I believe there are grounds for optimism."

"How much?" he demanded; and ignoring Mary's upset, impatient movement, repeated sternly: "How much?"

"That," the doctor said, giving him a candid look, "I could not say with any assurance at this moment. I would say there are more grounds for than against, let's put it that way. She has roused once and spoken: the history of these cases is that this is usually a good sign. It is usually followed with reasonable rapidity by further arousals, further speech, a gradual restoration of normal responses. She has already recognized her mother and asked for you. That is a long way on the road, Mr. Justice. You mustn't be too impatient. Her system received a terrible shock, after all. But if things progress on a rising curve, I should think you might be able to take her home in a couple of weeks—certainly not more than a month. Back in Washington, she would have to remain mostly in bed but with increasing activity every day as recommended by your doctor or doctors up there, for perhaps another month or two. But say three months at the most and she should be reasonably recovered. Not racing about, perhaps, for a while, as I'm sure she used to do; but in time—in time . . . providing, as I say, that everything goes forward as we hope."

"Will you go back to Washington and leave me all alone here?" Mary inquired.

"I don't like the way you say that, Mary," he responded gravely, while the doctor looked uneasy, "but yes, I will have to go back before she can, and presumably you will remain here. I'm sorry if that seems unfair, but I have barely yet put my toe in the water as far as the Court is concerned. The work is piling up and they need me to carry my share of it and that's where I have to go. Providing, as the doctor says, things are proceeding as we hope and Janie is making comfortable progress."

"Will you have to testify at the trial, Mr. Justice?" the doctor asked before Mary could make some retort both he and the doctor were afraid would be unpleasant.

"I don't know," he said. "I really won't know until it resumes, I suppose. Since Mary and I were not at Pomeroy Station—"

"Only Janie," she said.

"Yes," he agreed, again gravely, "only Janie—I don't know quite what we could testify to, except, perhaps, her condition. If that is improving as we hope, then my testimony and Mary's might be of some use to the defense, in that Miss Donnelson could elicit testimony that might, she would hope, tend to lessen the defendant's culpability in the minds of the jury."

"I would never give testimony that would do that," Mary said flatly. "You might, but I wouldn't."

"If you were under oath on the witness stand you would testify in response to the questions defense counsel asked you," he said patiently. "You might not want to, but I think you would be required by law. Or be held in contempt. Whichever."

"I would expect some such wishy-washiness from you, Tay," she said, while the doctor looked as though he wished he were somewhere else. "But if I were called, I would speak my piece regardless of the consequences. I would say what I thought of that monster and no one would be in any doubt where I stood. I would not crawl to *Miss Don-*

nelson"—she spat out the name—"or that two-bit country judge, or any-one else. I would have that monster's head, if I could."

"I think most people in America agree with you, Mrs. Barbour," the doctor said mildly, "although I must say Judge Williams is rather highly thought of in these parts . . . So, we have to expect you to leave, then, Mr. Justice, sometime in the next few days?"

"In a week or so, probably. I'll fly down for the weekends, but during the weeks, barring something unforeseen, I'll be at the Court."

"And I'll be here," Mary said.

"Thank you, Mrs. Barbour," the doctor said politely. "That will be a real help. Now, if you will excuse me, I'll be on my way. But I'll be back later this evening, and of course if anything happens in the mean-time, they'll let me know and I'll return at once."

"Thank you, doctor," Tay said, holding out his hand. But before the doctor could take it, Mary cried, "*Look!*" and they all froze, as what Tay would ever after refer to in his own mind—when he could bear to think of it—as "Janie's brief miracle" took place.

There was a slight moan from the bed. Her eyes opened, quite clear and quite alive. She looked around, saw Mary. Her eyes moved on, saw the doctor, saw him. Her expression, tense for a second, relaxed and a perfectly natural smile, the most beautiful smile he thought he had ever seen, flooded across her face.

"Hello again, Mommy," she said, and beside him the doctor mur-mured, "'*again*,'" with a hushed and thankful intonation. "And hello, Daddy."

"Hello, my darling!" Mary said, and began to cry.

"Hello, baby," he said softly, though his eyes were filling with tears and he could barely articulate. "How are you feeling?"

"Oh," she said, considering. "Pretty good, I guess. Kind of headachy and fuzzy, but—you know. Not too bad."

"We're very thankful for that, Janie," the doctor said, and she smiled again.

"I suppose you're the doctor," she said, not moving her head or body, only her eyes. "You look nice."

"He is nice," Tay said, managing a little better. "He's been very good to your mother and me and extra *specially* good to you."

"That's good," she said. "Thank you."

"You're welcome," the doctor said. "You *are* welcome, Janie. Is there anything we can get for you?"

"I feel a little hungry."

"Good," he said. "I'll go find a nurse and we'll see what we can whip up for you."

"Daddy," she said when the doctor had gone, looking pleased and humming slightly to himself, "when are you going to take me home?"

"In a while, baby," he said. "It won't be right away, but as soon as you're able we'll get you back."

"Will you stay with me?" she asked, and Mary shot him a look.

"Yes," she echoed, "will you, Tay?"

He took a deep breath and met it, as he had to, head-on.

"I have to get back to my work, baby," he said. "You've probably forgotten, but I've just been appointed to the Supreme Court—"

"Oh, yes," she said. "I do remember."

"—and they need me there. But Mommy will be here, and I'll be here on weekends. At the rate you're going it will only be a couple of weeks, probably, before we can move you right back up home to your own bed. Then you'll be all well again in no time."

"I'd like that," she said, yawning suddenly and beginning to sound drowsy. "What happened, anyway?"

"We'll tell you about that when you feel better," Mary said.

"Was it somebody bad?"

"Very bad," he said gravely.

"I hope they shoot him dead," she said, sounding drowsier. "Don't you, Daddy?"

Again Mary gave him a quick look. He ignored it and spoke very slowly and carefully, for a moment hardly seeing his daughter as he concentrated on how best to answer.

"I hope he will get what he deserves," he said, "because he is a very, very bad man. But I don't know whether it will be best to shoot him or to put him in jail for the rest of his life so that he can never, never do anything to anybody again. Maybe that would be better. We'll just have to decide that after there's been a trial and—"

"She's asleep," Mary interrupted harshly. "She isn't even listening any more. She's asleep! So you can stop trying to rationalize everything for yourself and wait until another time."

"So she is," he said, almost stupidly. "So she is."

And when the doctor returned immediately after with the nurse carrying a tray with soup and crackers, they decided it would be best to let her sleep for a while. The doctor increased the intravenous feeding slightly and left them with confident assurances that things were now moving very well, and that they could expect her to have increasingly frequent waking periods.

That evening, and twice again on Saturday, she did. Each time she went through much the same procedure, starting alert and herself, gradually becoming drowsy, without warning dropping off to sleep again. Saturday afternoon she stayed awake long enough to eat soup, crackers and a couple of spoonfuls of mashed potato. Their optimism increased.

It was with rising hopes and growing confidence that he called Moss Sunday morning and prepared to visit "High Pillars." Mary, their truce holding as her own hopes rose, went so far as to send her best wishes. He decided he would make it warmer than that when he told them. Not "her love," which wasn't true and which they would hardly believe, but something more in accord with the steadily rising happiness and excitement he was beginning to feel as the enormous weight of recent days appeared to be lifting slowly but surely from his heart.

On the lawn where Sarah's services had been held, under the stately old trees in front of the lovely old house, they ate a pleasant light lunch served by the Pomeroys' family cook who had been with them, Moss told him, since he himself had been five years old. Her face was grave and still touched with sorrow for the family tragedy, but the meal she prepared was delicious, and even Sue-Ann was able to eat a fair portion of it. When she had finished she stood up, brushed a hand across eyes still tired from weeping, gave Tay a quick kiss and smiled.

"I know you two want to talk before Moss goes back to the Court tomorrow," she said. "I'll run along and see if I can take a nap. I could use one. I'm so glad things are working out for you, Tay. It's wonderful."

"It's a miracle," he said.

"You deserve it," she said, again with the simple generosity that had touched him so when they had first met after the tragedy. "Please give our warmest wishes to Mary, too." Her eyes filled abruptly with tears. "I know how happy she must be."

"Yes," he said, "I'll tell her. Try to have a good rest."

"I will," she said; kissed her husband; and then turned back for a moment to Tay.

"Dear Tay," she said. "What would we have done without you all these years?"

"Managed somehow, I suppose," he said, trying to make a small joke of it. "It wouldn't have been easy, I know, but I expect you could have."

"That's right," Moss agreed gravely. "It wouldn't have been easy . . . Sleep well, honey, and come on back out whenever you feel like it. We won't be talking too much heavy stuff."

"Oh, I expect Tay will want to," she said, but trying to smile too. "He's a pretty serious fellow . . . I'll see you later, you two."

And she turned gracefully and walked across the lawn, head high, stopping for a moment to pick a couple of camelias from a plant by the door, then going on up the whitewashed stone steps and into the stately house as though this were the same as any afternoon before the world went mad.

"She's a gallant lady," Tay said softly. Her husband nodded.

"She is that . . . sit down, buddy. Tell me about Janie."

They sprawled side by side in canvas lounge chairs, and when he had completed his story Moss said, "That's great," in a firm voice as though he had determined to put everything else behind him. "You'll be back at the Court soon, then, won't you?"

Tay nodded.

"As soon as we see what happens when the trial begins again a week from Monday. I suppose there's a chance we may both be called as witnesses—certainly you, I should think."

"Yes, I expect so. I'm planning to come back next weekend. I just want to check into chambers for the week and get some work done." He smiled sadly. "Life does go on, you know . . . or so they say. I don't want them to forget my face up there . . . What's your gripe about Justice NOW!?"

"Not a gripe," Tay said, a little startled by this sudden introduction of the subject he had been wondering how to tackle. "Just a concern, let's say."

"You didn't like what I said the other day?"

Tay took a deep breath as a couple of hummingbirds darted by and a jay screamed off in the trees.

"No, I did not. I thought it was inappropriate, unbecoming and quite prejudicial to your position if the case comes up to us."

Moss grunted.

"Well, that's laying it on the line."

"I hope so, because that's what I intend to do. It's a long way from what you said when we discussed the subject of vigilantism, up in Washington."

"*I'm* a long way from what I was then," Moss said somberly, pulling up a piece of grass and starting to chew on it absentmindedly. "Or weren't you aware?"

"But you *can't*—"

"Can't what?" Moss inquired moodily. "Support my own people? Support, if you will, the people of the entire United States? Because that's almost what the movement is coming to represent now. What do you mean, I *can't*? So far I don't see any reason why I shouldn't."

"They were about to lynch Earle Holgren Friday afternoon, you know," Tay said quietly.

Moss gave him a somber glance.

"Maybe that would have been the best solution for everybody."

"*No!*" Tay exclaimed, genuinely shocked. "You don't mean that!"

"No?" Moss said, shifting in his chair, biting savagely at the piece of grass. "Why don't I, Tay? What has that bastard done to give me any cause to be charitable to him? He killed my daughter, you know. *He killed my daughter.* He almost killed yours. He wanted to kill me. What has he earned from me, except my eternal hatred? Why shouldn't I want to see him destroyed?"

"But not like that!" Tay protested. "Not without the full functioning of the law, Moss! You can't *possibly* advocate that."

"Why can't I? Why must I pretend I'm not what I really am underneath here"—and he slapped his sports shirt, hard, over his heart—"an animal, so filled with the instinct to hate and maim and kill and destroy that I can hardly see straight when I think of that—that—" He choked up and had to stop for a moment. All around, the gentle afternoon lay golden on the lawn. He shook his head violently as if to clear it, then dropped it in his hands and rubbed his eyes. "I'm sorry," he resumed in a lowered voice, "but you're in a different position, you see. Things are working out, for you. Lucky Tay is lucky again: Janie's on the way back. You don't have a daughter lying—lying—under—under six—six—" And suddenly he started to cry, sobs wracking his body in a flood of agony that he tried to muffle but which continued to shake him for several minutes while Tay, almost equally shattered, stared unseeing at the serenely peaceful trees and tried to think, without success, of words of comfort that refused to come because, perhaps, they did not exist.

At last Moss said brokenly, "I'm sorry, pal, I'm sorry. It—it—isn't easy. I didn't mean to call you 'Lucky Tay,' you know that. Sue-Ann and I are as happy for you as we can—can possibly be. We're so thankful for you . . . and for Mary, too, though she probably—wouldn't—wouldn't—believe it. I'm sorry . . ."

"I know," Tay said; reached out and clasped Moss' arm hard for a moment; then rested his own chin on his hands, stared moodily out across the lawn and sighed with a heavy sound that seemed to come from somewhere infinitely deep inside. "I know . . . I'm afraid I must sound awfully pompous and awfully smug—" Moss made a little gesture of protest. "Oh, yes," he said bitterly. "I know I sound that way sometimes. But I don't mean to. I *really* don't mean to. Mary tells me I'm so superior all the time, and maybe that's how I seem to other people, but I'm not—not really. And it *is* easier for me, now that Janie seems to be . . . getting along. But even if she weren't, Moss, I think—I *really* think —I would still feel the same way . . .

"At least," he said, as Moss watched him intently through reddened eyes, "I hope I would. I don't really know. That odd little person who's defending him came to me the other day and begged me to be 'true to myself' and to my 'great liberal principles' if he gets the death sentence and it comes up to us on appeal. I told her I'd try, but that I just didn't know—I just didn't know . . . Even if Janie is really all right, I still don't know . . . because I hate him too, Moss. Oh, how I hate him! But," he said, and his eyes darkened with the struggle of it, "we're supposed not to have those feelings, on the Court. We're supposed to be insulated from everything—above it all . . . aren't we? I've only been there ten seconds compared to you and the rest of them, but I do conceive of that as being my charge and my obligation. I can only try to remain true to that . . . and I think you should too, awful though it is and terribly hard—*hard* . . ."

He sighed.

"We've *got* to protect the law, Moss, it's what we're sworn to do. It's what we've been pointing toward ever since we were kids together in law school. It's the summation of our lives, really—the Law. That's what we hold in trust for the future, just as others in the past have held it for us. Somehow it's got to give us the strength to remain true to it, otherwise the whole thing goes down. We can't betray it—we *can't*. At least I can't—and I don't think you can, really, either. You may feel like it now, God knows I'm not the one to blame you. But I think when you're back on the bench it will be different. The obligation will reassert itself and the law will prevail . . . At least," he concluded, almost in a whisper, "I hope it will for you . . . and for me . . ."

But Moss made no comment, continuing to stare moodily into some far distance; so that he did not know, then, whether he had made any impression. They were silent for what seemed like quite a long time, though it may have been only a few minutes. The afternoon drowsed, the shadows began to lengthen a little under the trees and across the lawn. A peaceful, gentle hum of birds, insects, the first stirrings of a little breeze seemed to hold the world. Finally Moss turned, looked at him squarely and said perhaps the most surprising thing, to Tay, that he had ever said in all their long friendship.

"Have you met someone in Washington?"

His first instinct was to dissemble. Then suddenly it seemed wrong and unnecessary in the presence of his oldest, closest friend at such a moment of trust and mutual dependence in a time of sorrow.

"How did you know that?" he asked, returning Moss' look with honesty as direct as his.

Moss frowned.

"I don't know, exactly . . . little things . . . something different . . . a more openly harsh attitude toward Mary . . . a little underlying excitement . . . maybe even happiness . . . a sense of something that I seemed to feel . . . maybe just because after all these years we have an instinct for each other . . I don't know." He half-smiled—distracted, Tay noticed with relief though it was at his expense, from his heavy sadness. "I don't know . . . but do you know when I began to suspect?"

"Sure," Tay said. "The very first night, when you saw me driving out Northeast."

"That's right. I thought, Now, what the hell is he doing going out that way? He lives in Georgetown." He grinned suddenly: the old bright, blithe Moss reappeared for a moment. "I almost followed you, you know that? I almost became a sneak and tried to catch my old buddy *in flagrante delicto,* that's how startled and intrigued I was. It was so *unlike* you, particularly after having just been appointed to the Court. I thought, How *could* he. *That* isn't Tay! And then I thought, Why, the crazy bastard! He's human, just like everybody else!"

Tay winced but Moss didn't notice.

"And I gave a big chuckle and said right out loud, 'Go, man, go!' And turned left onto Independence Avenue and went on downtown and safely home . . . So. Is it good?"

Tay hesitated; and decided again to be honest.

"I don't know yet," he said slowly. "It is for me. I hope it is for her."

"You want it to last."

"Yes," he said simply, "I do."

"And knowing you, you don't want it to stay on this basis. You want to get a divorce and marry the girl. Right?"

"Yes."

"And you don't think Mary will let you go without a hell of a fight no matter what she feels about you. Does she suspect?"

"I don't think so," he said. "Mary is"—he smiled wryly—"Mary-oriented. She usually senses anything that really threatens her security, but she hasn't seemed to sense this yet, maybe because of—of Janie. She's never seen us together—probably never will. And after all, this was only a couple of weeks ago, you know. She hasn't had too much time to suspect, what with one thing and another."

"Tell me about it," Moss suggested. "If you want to."

"I don't mind," he said, and did so, while Moss again listened intently, making no comment as the afternoon moved gently on toward its inevitable close.

"So that's it," he concluded. "Very brief, very ordinary, very standard for such things—I guess. I've never done anything like this before."

"Well, I have," Moss said. "For a while after we were first married and I was proving to myself that I was still in there pitching and could still stay the course. But I stopped it before too long and fortunately never got caught. I realized what I had and decided I'd better not risk it." He smiled without much humor. "Sue-Ann isn't Mary."

"No," he agreed, and sighed. "Sue-Ann isn't Mary."

"It's amazing to me, frankly, how you've stuck it out this long. But I guess that went with your concept of yourself."

"Yes, it did," he replied sharply, "and I'm not very proud of myself now, if you want the truth."

Moss smiled again.

"Don't you think I know that? I haven't known you twenty-four years for nothing. But I think you should be, because apparently she's a nice girl, and she really does love you—or," he added as Tay moved in his chair, "is beginning to—and obviously you're falling in love with her so—why not? You're going to have to get a divorce one of these days, inevitably, and you know that; so why not just face up to it and make the fight? When you're both really sure, that is."

"When we're both really sure . . ." he echoed, and his expression darkened. "And what about the Court?"

"Then you're obviously not sure, if you're going to let that inhibit you."

"It's got to inhibit me to some extent, Moss," he said earnestly. "How can it not? I've just been appointed, I can't go around bed-hopping—"

"Oh, come *on*," Moss exclaimed. " 'Bed-hopping'! You sound like the horniest Congressman who ever hit the Hill. One little affair that quite soon, probably, is going to become entirely respectable, and you're 'bed-hopping'! Stop exaggerating! If that's the kind of language you use I hate to think what your opinions will be like. People will think there's a revolution coming in the law every time you open your mouth."

"Well, anyway," he said, laughing, as Moss intended, in spite of himself, "I don't feel that it's at all appropriate."

Moss snorted.

"Now you sound like a real stuffed shirt. 'Not at all appropriate'! Well, get you, Aunt Mabel! Now, look," he said firmly, "you just want me to help you argue yourself into it. You keep on with that little gal and you do what your heart tells you and don't you worry about the Court or anything else. For once, Taylor Barbour, you do something spontaneous and what's best for *you*. All right?"

"But," he said, still going through the motions of fighting his conscience, though he really knew the battle was already firmly won, "there's Mary—and there's Janie. I just can't walk out on them. Particularly Janie."

"If this Cathy is as great as you obviously think she is, then she's going to be the best thing that ever happened to Janie. And as for Mary, it seems to me she's forfeited most of her right to be worried about. So just cut it out."

"Well—"

"Listen! Knock it off. Have you talked to her lately?"

"Only from a public phone at the hospital. I rather think one of the nurses eavesdropped."

"They won't eavesdrop here," Moss said, getting up. "Come on in and give her a call."

"I can't," he said, suddenly feeling shy and awkward as a teenager. "I haven't anything particular to say."

"Just say hello," Moss suggested, sounding again for a moment quite like his old self. "That ought to start something." He held out his hand. "Come on. Off your duff."

"Well—all right," he said, allowing himself to be pulled out of his chair. "She probably isn't home, anyway."

"Probably waiting breathless by the phone every minute of every day," Moss said as they started toward the house. They were halfway there when Sue-Ann came out on the veranda. Her face was tense, expression alarmed. An answering fear shot through his heart. The peace was gone. The lovely afternoon had reached its ending.

"What is it?" Moss asked sharply. "Something wrong?"

"It's Mary. From the hospital."

Tay began to run, took the steps two at a time.

"Where—?"

"To the right," she said, standing aside. "In the library."

"Hello?" he said. "Hello?"

"Come back," she cried in a voice of terror and anguish he knew was genuine. "Oh, come back!"

"Yes," he said, beginning to shake all over. "Right away."

"I'll get the car," Moss said behind him, and raced out to the garage and did so, not even stopping to change from sandals to shoes.

"Good luck," Sue-Ann said, giving him a desperate kiss. He returned it, nodded, jumped in, slammed the door. They were off like Regard, he thought crazily as Moss trod on the gas. Off like Regard, off like Regard, off like Regard. They said nothing on the drive though it seemed to take forever to reach the hospital.

Mary looked at them with haggard, almost unseeing eyes.

Doctors and nurses stood about.

His daughter lay still and white.

Even whiter than he was.

"Oh, my God!" he said, as he felt Moss' hand steadying his arm. "Is she—is she—"

"She is alive," the older doctor said, taking him gently by the other arm and walking the two of them out into the corridor. "All her vital signs are good. However—"

"However *what?*" he demanded, feeling as though he were far down in a deep well somewhere, looking up and shouting to a tiny little figure above, though the doctor was at his side, his hand still gentling his arm.

"However, she has had a seizure—a grand mal, or epileptic, seizure—and I am afraid the encephalogram indicates—" his steady voice faltered for just a second, then resumed its level pace, "that brain function has been almost entirely lost." He tightened his grip and so did Moss as Tay swayed a little, then steadied.

"And it will not—" he said, trying to articulate and managing just barely to be understood. "It will not—"

"We think in all probability it will not come back," the doctor confirmed gravely. "These things happen, we do not know why. It happened. Everything possible was done. Your wife screamed immediately, med-alert was sounded, everybody came—and we were helpless. Everything possible was done, and we were helpless." For just a moment he lost his professional calm and looked like what he was, a man who knew, in the fashion of doctors, a little more about his fellow beings than his fellow beings knew, but still did not know the answer to the ultimate question he now asked aloud.

"Why does God do these things?" he demanded of the impervious universe with a sudden savage vehemence. "Why, why, *why?*"

"I know why," Tay said in a ghastly voice. "To humble me."

"Oh, *buddy,*" Moss said. "Oh, buddy, *don't.* Ah, *don't.*"

"I've got to go back in there," he said, suddenly wheeling about, shaking them off, almost running toward the room that held his daughter and wife, both now gone from him, in all probability, forever. "I've got to go back in there!"

"Mr. Justice," the doctor said as they watched him go. "I think you had better stay with them for a while. If you can bear it."

"Yes," Moss agreed, white and shaken but mustering from somewhere the strength he had to have. "Yes. I can bear it."

And for two or three hours, until Tay asked him to take him and Mary back, exhausted, to the hotel, he did; and never by slightest word or look suggested reproach or drew comparisons of any kind, but was steady, supportive, loving, patient and kind, even when Mary retired into some private world of her own. It was not until he got home that he and Sue-Ann wept again; and when, around 9 P.M., he called the Chief to tell him the news and report that he would be back in time for the session tomorrow, he too could barely articulate. Across Washington in six more homes when the Chief telephoned to pass on the news, renewed sadness fell. It was a somber Court indeed that reconvened next day at 10 A.M.

Only the bomber of Pomeroy Station, in fact, enjoyed himself during the week his trial was in recess, and that was because, being, as he had known from an early age, a superior individual, he seemed to possess a resilience not granted ordinary men.

He was fortified in this by the fact that in some segments of the media he was not doing so badly. Many editorials, news analyses and commentaries in smaller journals and local stations continued to praise Regard for his courage, Perlie Williams for his evenhandedness and Justice NOW! for its astonishing vigor and continued phenomenal growth. But considerable praise was accorded by the major media to Debbie for her stout defense of her client and for her insistence that he be given psychiatric tests to determine his fitness to stand trial. There seemed to be a substantial feeling in some major news outlets that somehow he was gaining ground and might, after all, turn out to be innocent of the charges lodged against him.

There was no such divergence of opinion among the general public, or at least among that still rapidly growing sector of it represented by Justice NOW!

The organization was up to almost five million members and still the letters, telegrams, pledges of support and monetary contributions continued to flow into national headquarters in Columbia. Forty-one additional attorneys general had formally endorsed the organization and the few who still remained aloof were under heavy pressure to conform. Many members of Congress had also signified their approval, some by actually joining, others by statements indicating support and encouragement. Of the nation's fifty governors, thirty-eight had already issued endorsements. Most of the other twelve were expected to follow very shortly.

Surveying his explosively expanding political domain, Regard was well content. And although the jury had been directed, upon their release to go home, not to read or view anything during the week that might prejudice their opinions, he knew he could count on human nature to take care of *that*. He felt his case was in good shape.

For her part, Debbie spent the week carefully drawing the picture of herself and her client as two small, almost helpless figures overwhelmed by an unprincipled juggernaut. She and Regard were invited to appear together on "Today," "Tonight," "A.M. America," "60 Minutes," "Meet the Press" and "Face the Nation," and on each she showed herself adept at both irritating her opponent and gathering some sympathy for herself—at least from their questioners, who by and large were friendly toward her, critical toward Regard, and alarmed by the continuing rapid surge of Justice NOW! By week's end she had received and put into an Earle Holgren Defense Fund the sum of almost $200,000 from around the country, much of it from Hollywood, antinuclear groups and a few anonymous but heavy contributions from such overseas sources as Libya, South Yemen, Angola and smaller conduits whose interest had nothing to do with the personalities and issues involved but was simply to stir up trouble in America. The American Civil Liberties Union, as she had expected, offered assistance, and from Harrison Aboud in New York she received two telephone calls, both monitored by Regard's people, offering advice and instruction. Aware that her phone was probably bugged, she was circumspect, polite and noncommittal during the course of these, and at the end of the second asked Harry to stop calling.

"I understand," he said in the expansive jovial way that had helped earn him such a good press over the years. "I certainly understand!"

"I certainly hope so," she had replied tartly and rung off; but it was good to know, she told herself, that support was gathering for her client. She was confident there would be more as the contrast between his lone figure and the onrolling behemoth of Justice NOW! became more obvious.

She only saw him once during the week, and that was Friday afternoon when the psychiatrists canceled their final interview. She had chosen a famous and very fashionable young doctor from New York; Regard the older, equally famous head of psychiatric studies at Emory

University in Atlanta; and Judge Williams a similarly well-known teacher at the University of Chicago. The media referred to them as "a blue-ribbon panel," and they were, but Earle Holgren was a match for them—so much so that even the young New Yorker, disposed to be friendly, concluded the week as frustrated and annoyed as his colleagues.

There was no doubt in their minds that he was sane, highly intelligent, completely competent to stand trial, and an infuriatingly arrogant and egotistical being.

"I don't see what the bastard needs a lawyer for," the young New Yorker said. "He could handle it himself with both hands tied behind him."

"He does have an interesting mind," the doctor from Atlanta agreed.

"Which is going to trip him up in due course," the doctor from Chicago predicted.

"Which is not our problem," the New Yorker noted. "It's Miss Debbie's, and I wish her joy of it."

They decided to cancel the final interview, retire to the Carolina Inn and begin drafting their unanimous report to the court. Earle Holgren, being left with nothing much to occupy the afternoon, sent for his lawyer, whom he had carefully kept at arm's length for the entire period of interrogation.

Despite her valiant attempts she could not escape an insidious and unsettling excitement. She was disgusted with herself to realize that her breath was coming faster, her heart pounding more rapidly, as they brought him into the room where she was waiting and then withdrew and shut the door. A guard still watched every couple of minutes through a peephole, however, and she wondered if he could sense her hateful agitation. Her client could. The moment he saw her he gave his most cheerful Santa Claus smile and said loudly, *"There's* my superstar sweetie! How are you, Superstar?"

"Be quiet!" she said, blushed furiously and hated herself the more.

"Why?" he demanded, and looked over his shoulder. "Because of *him?* They can't understand English down here. Don't worry."

The guard said, "Son of a bitch," clearly, and Earle gave him his favorite gesture. The guard hit the door hard with the flat of his hand and Earle, grinning, turned away and dropped his voice to a whisper as he sat down at the table opposite her.

"You've been damned good this week," he said with a genuine admiration that made her blush again, this time with a pleasure she found as degrading as the excitement. "I like the way you've kept that red-necked yahoo on the defensive on all those programs. You must be building up quite a head of steam for us."

"Not anywhere near the head of steam he's building up with Justice NOW!" she said. "If you've seen the programs you must have seen the news about that, too."

"Oh, yes. Old Yahoo is being pretty good to me, for some reason or reasons unknown. I'm getting TV, newspapers, the works. I think maybe that *is* the reason—he wants to scare me with his crummy outfit. And," he added as she made a gesture of protest, "don't tell me that it isn't crummy just because it has a hell of a lot of people in it. There are a hell of a lot of fools in this world who will join anything, particularly if they think they're going to wind up getting somebody's blood with it."

"What makes you think they aren't? Do you know something I don't know?"

"You're going to save me, sweetheart," he said, grinning expansively and cupping her hands in his. "You're just plumb going to work a miracle and pluck this poor innocent child right out of the jaws of death, that's why."

"Stop that," she said sharply, yanking her hands away. "You act like a fool yourself, sometimes. What's the matter with you, anyway? You'll be lucky to get off with life, the way the country's feeling right now."

"Hell!" he said, and suddenly he wasn't grinning any more. "They're not going to prove anything! There's nothing they *can* prove! And supposing they do convict me, we'll appeal it, won't we? We can keep this thing going for years before they even come close to getting me. Which they can't do," he repeated, "because they haven't got the proof."

"I think you really are crazy," she said. "I think you really think you can bluff your way through this thing. You say you've seen the news but you certainly haven't absorbed it. I wonder what the psychiatrists think of you. They must have had a field day."

"*I* had the field day," he said, relaxing into a triumphant chuckle. "They never laid a finger on me."

"What do you mean, 'never laid a finger on you'? They were *supposed* to lay a finger on you! They were supposed to be convinced that you have psychiatric problems and can't stand trial. Do you mean to tell me—"

"Listen!" he said, clamping his hand on her wrist as he had once before, so tightly that she almost cried out in pain. "I'm not going to act like an idiot for anybody, anytime! I'm not an idiot and I'm not going to pretend to be. Maybe *you* don't respect my mind, but I do! I gave those bastards such a rough time it made their heads spin. They'll certify me sane, all right. I'm saner than they are."

"Well," she said with a bleak humor, "that shoots that. And now," she added in a level voice, *"take your hand off my wrist and don't you ever touch me again unless I say you can.* I mean it. *Now!"*

For a second he looked startled. Then he burst out laughing and released her wrist.

"Oh, boy," he said. "Oh, boy. You really do have spirit, don't you? 'Don't ever touch me again unless I say you can'! Well, you will, sweetheart, you will. Too bad the Jukes and the Kallikaks are peeking in the door or I'd take my clothes off right now and we'd find out about it right this minute. Oh yes," he said, and his tone was completely confident, "you'll say I can one of these days, Superstar. The old bod is about ready to burst. I want a little help. You wouldn't say no to your favorite client, would you?"

"Maybe you should blow up another plant," she suggested. "That seems to do it."

He gave her an angry glare.

"Nobody can prove I blew up *any* plant," he said. Then he grinned. "Anyway, you'd be a lot cozier."

"You are impossible," she said. "Absolutely and completely impossible."

"But you like it," he said airily. "Oh, yes, Superstar, you like it. The bod, incidentally, is feeling a lot better now. I think I'll stop limping when I come into court again Monday."

"You'd better," she said dryly. "I think you've made your point. Plus the fact that they took plenty of pictures of you at the time of your arrest and if Stinnet doesn't offer them as exhibits, I will."

"Good," he said cheerfully. "What else are we going to do to delay things?"

"We aren't going to do anything. You've seen enough of Williams, you know how he is; he isn't going to permit any more delays. From here on in we're driving right straight through to the end, I'm sure, just as fast as he can decently move things along. And he will be decent; he strikes me as a decent man. But he isn't going to tolerate any monkey business, particularly with the whole country, practically, crying for your scalp."

He gave her a sudden sharp, shrewd look.

"What's your overall strategy? Don't you think it's about time we discussed it?"

"I think so," she agreed, and in a few swift sentences sketched it for him. He smiled.

"I like that. Yes, I like that. I'd suggest a couple of other things also—"

When he had concluded, she argued with him vehemently, but when he refused to be moved, she shrugged.

"It may or may not work," she said, "but what have we got to lose?"

"Just my life," he said, but he didn't sound as though he really believed it was that serious. "Just my life. A mere nothing, in the opinion of many, but important, in a minor way, to me."

"Have a good weekend," she said, standing up and nodding to the guard, who opened the door and started in. "Read lots of newspapers. Watch lots of TV. Get lots of rest. Monday starts the real battle."

"I'm ready for it," he said grimly. "God *damn* it!" he added fiercely to the guard. "Take your God damned hands off me! I'm *coming!*"

And as the guard glared at him but obeyed, he made her a mocking bow, gave her an airy wave, and started off down the corridor, solid, stocky, apparently supremely confident and in control of all he surveyed.

She wondered, as she went thoughtfully out to her car, whether he really was or whether it was just a well-managed bluff. She was sure the psychiatrists would certify him sane but she wondered in what sense the word could here be applied. She suspected, herself, that he was far from the normal meaning of the word as most people used it. And once again she shivered, in spite of the sunlight, and wondered what it was that she had allowed Harry Aboud to get her into.

4

The three psychiatrists submitted their unanimous report to the court on Monday. It found Earle William Holgren to be sane and, in fact, well above normal intelligence, perception and comprehension. It did not presume to judge his mental state at the time of the crimes at Pomeroy Station but it did declare him to be, in the respectful opinion of respondents, fully capable of standing trial and participating in whatever inquiries might be directed to him by counsel.

"The report will be accepted and filed," Judge Williams said without other comment; neither counsel demurred; and the trial moved on. Under the pressures of national insistence and Justice NOW! it lasted just four days more.

Regard's first witness, as he had earlier announced, was Deputy Sheriff William Lanahan of Pomeroy Station.

Sheriff Lanahan, a dark, intense young man of perhaps twenty-seven who obviously took himself and his duties very seriously, spoke in a backwoods drawl that at first seemed to indicate a slow and cautious mentality. It developed that, while cautious, it was not slow. His testimony was detailed, specific and damaging to the defendant—as far as it went. He was obviously too honest to push it any further.

Yes, he said in response to the attorney general's questioning, he had returned to the plant after the explosion and begun an intensive search. Presently he had come to the cave, the tunnel, eventually to the well and so to the dead woman and child. No, he did not recognize them of his own knowledge.

When he emerged from the cave, he had been just in time to see the defendant wiping off the detonator that Regard had offered in exhibit, and to join up with the others who had surprised the defendant and were even then taking him into custody. Had he participated in any unduly brutal or excessive attacks upon the defendant? No, sir, he himself had not. Had anyone? He thought "one or two of the boys" might have been "a little too enthusiastic," but he did not think it had been done with malice, only in the excitement of the moment. Did he consider it a normal, understandable human reaction when confronted by such a heinous crime, aimed at the Supreme Court of the United States and in fact resulting in the death of Sarah Pomeroy? Opposing counsel objected, but not before Sheriff Lanahan agreed that, yes, sir, he supposed that was how you could state it. Did he himself consider the defendant guilty? Opposing counsel objected that this was supposition, Judge Williams agreed, and cross-examination began.

"You did not observe the defendant actually using this detonator"—gesturing to it—"or any other explosive device?"

"No, ma'am."

"And you did not at any time observe the defendant actually engaged in any activity that could logically be claimed to be part of the alleged crime for which he has been indicted?"

"No, ma'am, but the whole thing was certainly mighty suspicious."

"Oh, was it," Debbie demanded. "And why was that?"

"What was he doing there at all?" the witness retorted, unabashed. "Why was he fooling around with a detonator right after a bombing? Just likes 'em, maybe, for a hobby?"

There was a stir of laughter in the courtroom, and outside, where the forces of Justice NOW! were once again in place, a distant, derisive hoot.

"Your sense of humor is not the issue here, sheriff," Debbie said tartly. "A man's life is the issue."

"Yes, ma'am," the sheriff agreed politely. "And Miss Sarah's, and those other two, and the Supreme Court, and all."

Again the bitter hoot; and for a moment Debbie stared down at her papers, lips pursed, jaw set. At her side her client sat, chin on hand, never taking his eyes off the witness, who from time to time stared back as ostentatiously unimpressed as Earle was ostentatiously challenging.

"And after your 'instinct' led you back to the cave and you had discovered the bodies of a woman and a child, you quite inadvertently came out just at the moment when the defendant was being seized, and joined in his arrest?"

"Yes, ma'am."

"You were not involved in the brutal treatment given the defendant by his captors?"

"No, ma'am."

"But you observed it."

"Yes, ma'am—*no,* ma'am, I did *not* see any brutal treatment."

"Well, did you or didn't you, sheriff? There seems to be some doubt in your mind."

"Like I told Mr. Stinnet, one or two of the boys may have been a little too enthusiastic, but that's understandable, seeing as how it was such a terrible attack on the Supreme Court. To say nothing of the deaths of that sweet little girl Sarah, daughter of our great former governor and now Associate Justice of the Supreme Court, and those other two."

"Yes, Mr. Lanahan," Debbie said dryly, "we know all about who they are. And I submit to you that no matter who they are, there is no excuse for 'one or two of the boys' being 'a little too enthusiastic' when their enthusiasm is of a nature so violent as to result in the type of injuries to my client which are disclosed in these photographs taken by the Associated Press just after his arrest"—she held them up toward the bench—"which, your honor, I request be placed in exhibit at this point in the record."

"The country has seen the photographs, Miss Donnelson," Judge Williams reminded. "But you have permission to place them in the record if you wish. Please proceed."

She hesitated a moment and then said, "Thank you, your honor," as her client muttered, "For nothing," under his breath. "I would like to ask the witness now if he observed the manner in which the defendant was taken into custody."

"I've already said I was there," the sheriff said, looking a little surprised.

"And was the defendant advised of his rights at that time?"

"I was somewhat on the outside of the group, ma'am. There was a lot of noise. I couldn't hear everything that was said."

"Sheriff Lanahan, stop being disingenuous. You know whether or not defendant was advised of his rights at time of arrest. Was he?"

"He may have been, ma'am, I really don't know."

"He says he was not."

"Well, ma'am, he may have some interest in presenting his own variation of the facts."

There was a snicker from the audience as Debbie flushed and snapped:

"Those are the facts!"

"If you say so, ma'am," the sheriff said with gr̶
wouldn't know."

"*I* don't say so!" she said angrily.

"Well, ma'am," he said, "neither do I."

Again the audience was audibly amused and from outside
derisive sounds.

"No more questions for this witness, your honor," Debbie s̶
sat down. Her client leaned against her shoulder and muttered, "̶
ass bastard." "They'll all be alike," she responded. "There's no poi̶
calling any of them. They've got their story all lined up."

"So have I," he reminded her, "if Old Yahoo puts me on the stand.̶

"Well, just stick to it," she advised, "and don't get too smart-ass
yourself."

"The only good thing is, we're getting on record that Stinnet *does*
have his witnesses all lined up. Right?"

"Right," she agreed; and added, as Regard released the sheriff and
turned toward the bench with a portentous air, "Now what?"

"Mrs. Marion Holgren," he said. The audience craned forward, the
pool television camera swung in on the small, well-dressed, dignified
woman who stood up and proceeded, looking neither left nor right, to
the stand. Her son remained absolutely motionless in his seat as she was
sworn. She only looked at him once in all her time on the stand.

"You are Mrs. James Holgren—Mrs. Marion Holgren?" Regard said.

"I am," she replied in a small, clear voice.

"You have one son."

"I did," she said in the same soft but distinctly carrying tone. A little
stir ran through the room.

"Mrs. Holgren," Regard said gently. "I can understand your answer,
I think, and the emotion that prompts it. However, it is not sufficient in
a court of law, or for the purposes of this case. You do, in fact, presently have a son."

"Yes. May God help him."

"Do you see him in this courtroom?"

"I have seen him in this courtroom."

"Mrs. Holgren," Regard said, still gently but with a trace of growing
firmness, "please respond directly, painful though it may be. Remember
it is painful for all of us. Is it your son who sits beside Miss Donnelson,
counsel for the defense?"

For the briefest second her eyes flicked across Earle's face as he

nce. Then she looked away and did

christened Earle William Hol-

Holgren. Was he a good

of a mixed-up, bloody
golden haze. Her lips

ny. "His father and I had no
everything."

nt in grammar school and high school?"

ady? Reliable? Truthful? Dependable?"

ose things. He was a *good* boy."

where did he go wrong, Mrs. Holgren?" Regard asked. Debbie was
on her feet.

"Your honor, I object. That question is—"

"Objection sustained," Perlie Williams said.

Regard nodded.

"Very well. Let me rephrase it. When, in your opinion, Mrs. Holgren, did your son become less steady—reliable—truthful—dependable—
and good?"

"I would say," she said with a certain objective thoughtfulness,
"when he was about a sophomore in college."

"Now ask her what college I went to," Earle whispered sarcastically
to Debbie. "Might as well play on all the prejudices." But Regard, too
smart for that, had other plans.

"How did you become aware of this?"

"When he came home for holidays and vacation he was—different."

"How 'different'? In dress? In manner? Habits? Beliefs?"

"Pretty much all of them. Though it took his father and me a while
to realize how much he had changed."

"Was there dope?"

"Some. But we felt that was an effect, not a cause—something he felt
he had to do to satisfy some—some peer group that was watching him.
To look big in their eyes."

" 'Watching him'?"

"Telephoning. Calling him away to meetings. Keeping an eye on him. Encouraging him."

"Encouraging him to do what, Mrs. Holgren?"

"Hate us. Hate his country. Hate everything we had reared him to be."

"Did you feel that this came from his college?"

"It centered there. Where it came from, we didn't know. Maybe just" —her lips trembled again, again she steadied them—"maybe just—from us."

"From you?" Regard asked with genuine surprise. "How could that be?"

She made a vague gesture, brought a tightly clutched handkerchief to her face.

"I don't know," she said, and began to cry. "He just began to—to hate us. Just hate us. He told us he—he despised us and everything we— we stood for. He never gave us any real reasons why. I'm not sure he even knew."

The defendant stirred in his chair and the television camera obediently zoomed in on his face. It wore a scowl of moody contempt, unmoved and unmovable, untouched and untouchable.

"And this went on until he left college?" Regard inquired, voice gentle again.

"Left college and left us," she said bleakly. "He came into a substantial inheritance from his grandfather when he graduated, and he took it and just—just disappeared. We never saw him again until we entered this courtroom last week."

"Did you have any idea where he was?"

"Your honor," Debbie said, "I object. What has her guess got to do with the case here?"

"Anything that throws light on the character of this individual is pertinent to this case, your honor," Regard remarked with some asperity.

"Objection overruled."

"Did you have any idea where he was, Mrs. Holgren?"

"We had suspicions," she said, more calmly, "but we never knew. We never knew. We advertised. We advertised a lot, wherever we could think of. We hired private detectives, we tried to track down people we thought might be friends who had known him—" She gave a wan little smile. "We did lots of things. But we never found out."

"And he never contacted you, in all these years."

"No," she said, starting to cry again. "He never contacted us, in all—these—years."

"Where did you and Mr. Holgren really think he was, Mrs. Holgren?" Regard asked softly, and again Debbie was on her feet.

"Your honor, I really must object. Any answer to that would be entirely suppositional, prejudicial—"

"Let her answer it, Miss Donnelson," Perlie Williams said quietly. "The perception of this defendant that people have is important, I think you will agree. Let us find out what two decent, loving, puzzled people, the closest people to him by virtue of blood, thought about this. If you don't mind."

And after she had returned his unyielding gaze for a long moment she looked away, shrugged and sat down.

"Now, Mrs. Holgren," Judge Williams said, "if you can, or care to, please answer Mr. Stinnet's question. Where did you and his father think your son really was?"

"We thought," she said, still crying, "we thought he was in some—some kind of life where he might—might be doing—awful things. And I guess," she concluded with a sob, "I guess maybe—maybe this—shows—that we were right."

"Your honor!" Debbie cried, on her feet once more. "I really must object! In all fairness, your honor!"

"Are you through with this witness, counsel?" Perlie Williams inquired. Regard nodded.

"Yes, your honor," he said quietly. "I would just observe, however, that this is yet another example of the kind of human damage that this individual seems to spread around him wherever he goes. All the misery, all the unhappiness, all the pain. It is a great tragedy, your honor. A great tragedy, all around."

"Your honor!" Debbie cried again, but Perlie Williams, face stern, said only, "Your witness, counsel, if you care to cross-examine."

"Very well," Debbie said, a sudden vicious sharpness in her voice, "I will. Mrs. Holgren!"

"Yes?" Earle Holgren's mother said in a tired voice, staring at her with ravaged eyes that brought murmurs of sympathy from the audience. "What can I tell *you* about my son?"

"Not about your son, Mrs. Holgren," Debbie said, unmoved, "but about two parents whose overprotective, domineering, smothering, devouring love—if such it could be called"—the witness gave her a strange look and a murmur of angry protest rose in the room—"destroyed the

capacity of a carefree, laughing, happy, outgoing child to enjoy life and
participate in it as he wished to do and was fully equipped to do."

"Your honor—" Regard began. But Mrs. Holgren did not need his
assistance.

"I do not know you, Miss—?"

"Donnelson."

"Donnelson," she said quietly. "But I think you would be quite offended if I were to describe you as prejudiced, biased, twisted, unfair—"

From the ranks outside came a growing sound of approval. Debbie
flushed but remained silent.

"—and totally mistaken in your assumptions and whatever it is you
are trying to prove. Isn't that right?"

"It is my place to ask the questions, Mrs. Holgren!"

"I don't believe it is your place to ask the kind of question you have
asked," Mrs. Holgren said, "and I don't think it is necessary for me to
answer it. Is it, your honor?"

And she turned directly to him. Ferlie Williams smiled in a comforting way and looked at Debbie.

"I think it might be well—assuming counsel wishes to pursue this line
of questioning—if she were to restate it in terms less prejudicial and
offensive to the witness. Otherwise, the court would suggest that she
drop it and pursue some other inquiry."

"Your honor," Debbie said, "this matter is pertinent, because it is
designed to prove that my client did not have a normal childhood and
was, indeed, crippled to a considerable degree emotionally by the
smothering effects of—"

"Counsel is concluding, then, that her client has committed some
crime that needs excusing on these grounds?" Judge Williams inquired
blandly.

There was a stir of gleeful excitement in the audience.

"No, I am *not,* your honor!" Debbie said angrily. "I simply wish to
show that while my client is innocent of the charges brought against
him, it is due to the fact that he has a strong innate character, not because anything in his childhood or upbringing prepared him adequately
for the stresses of adult life."

"Oh, that is it," Judge Williams said softly. "I was getting a little lost
as to where you were going, counsel, but that makes it all clear. In any
event, if you wish to proceed, do so without too many adjectives and
adverbs, please. Otherwise the court may have to respond favorably to
objections from the other side."

"Mrs. Holgren," Debbie said, "did you have a governess for your child?"

"We have two children. Our daughter Melissa is three years younger than—than Earle. At the time she was born, yes, we did employ a governess to take care of the two children."

"Why was that, Mrs. Holgren? For their convenience? Or for yours, because you were rich and too busy with your own lives to give your children adequate attention?"

"Your honor—" Regard began but Perlie Williams held up a hand and he subsided.

"Is being rich a crime, in your mind, Miss Donnelson?" Mrs. Holgren asked quietly. "Because if so, I think you should know that for the first few years of our married life, my husband was quite poor—poor enough to satisfy even you, I imagine. It was only after Earle was born that his business career began to rise at a rapid rate. Thanks to his enterprise and ability, it never faltered. By the time of Melissa's birth we were very comfortably off. We are now quite, quite rich, Miss Donnelson. If that is permissible, in your world."

"I don't know what you mean by 'your world,' Mrs. Holgren."

"I am sure you do, Miss Donnelson."

"No!" Debbie snapped. "I do not! You are evading my question, in any event. Was the hiring of a governess for the children's welfare or for your own selfish convenience so that you could lead a carefree and idle life—"

"Oh, Miss Donnelson," Mrs. Holgren said, by now quite composed, "if you knew how silly your clichés sound. We devoted as much time as we possibly could to the children. I made a point of being with them every afternoon when they were little, their father always spent an hour with them when he got home from business. When they entered school we saw them at breakfast and after dinner. We were not ogres, Miss Donnelson. We were good parents. We are not the excuse. Though I wish"—for a second her composure cracked—"it were that simple. Or that easy to understand."

"You saw them at set times during the day, as convenient to you as possible, 'at breakfast' and 'after dinner.' Did it never occur to you that this arm's-length regimen might have had a harsh, adverse and crippling effect on them?"

"It did not disturb Melissa," Mrs. Holgren said, to the audience's amusement, echoed from beyond the walls. "She grew up a perfectly stable young lady and is now the happily married mother of three in

Montclair, New Jersey. Would you like her to come and tell you about it? She would probably be quite happy to do so, if you wish."

"No," Debbie said with frigid politeness. "I do not think that will be necessary. Did you and your husband ever try to influence your son's thinking politically during his formative years in high school and college?"

"We made our views known to him. They did not agree with his."

"Is it not a fact that you threatened to withhold his allowance, and at one time refused to give him an automobile he had been promised for his birthday, because he would not abandon what you regarded as 'unhealthy associations' with certain student protest movements?"

"Did he tell you that?" Mrs. Holgren inquired. "He always was good at fabricating reasons for things."

"Mrs. Holgren, I am not asking you your opinion of his veracity—"

"Oh?" the witness said quickly. "I thought that was one of the issues here."

Again there was amusement, and at Debbie's side her client moved restlessly, scowled and reached out and tugged at her dress. "Yes?" she whispered in an annoyed tone, leaning down. "Drop the bitch," he whispered. "She's too fast for you."

"But—" she began.

"I know her," he said dryly. "After all, I'm her son. Drop her."

For a moment Debbie's face was a study. Then she shrugged and turned to the bench, ignoring Mrs. Holgren, who was staring down at her hands and ignoring her.

"Your honor," she said, "this witness obviously has no intention of being cooperative. I have no more questions."

"Your honor," Regard said, "I do. Just one. In your opinion, Mrs. Holgren, as his mother and knowing him as only you and his father can, would this defendant be capable of the crimes with which he is charged?"

"Your honor—" Debbie protested, but Perlie Williams again held up a cautionary hand.

"Would you like me to repeat the question, Mrs. Holgren?" Regard inquired softly. She gave him an anguished look, her hands working at her purse. She shook her head. Tension rose sharply.

"No," she said. "I—I understand it . . ." Her voice dropped to a near whisper. "It is an awful question to ask a mother . . . a terrible question."

"But necessary," Regard said gravely, "I believe."

"Then I would have to answer—" she said, so low it could hardly be heard beyond the immediate area of the bench—"yes." And, composure shattered, began again to cry.

"Thank you, Mrs. Holgren," Regard said quickly. "That will be all."

5

ime seemed to jump: the next two days of the trial went fast. Regard put on the stand most of the members of the group that had captured the defendant, Debbie cross-examined them diligently to no avail. Like Sheriff Lanahan, their memories were dim as to exactly what had transpired. They simply could not remember whether the defendant had been informed of his rights though they did concede that they might have "roughed him up a little bit." Townspeople testified that they almost never saw Janet, remembered her really hardly at all. Construction workers and guards testified to the daily, sometimes twice or even three times daily, visits of the defendant to the Pomeroy Station plant. A couple of them said they had the feeling that he was "around the place a lot," particularly in the last few days before the dedication. One said he "thought I saw him in the woods a couple of times quite apart from his jogging. He stopped by to visit with two of the guards rather late at night." Forensic experts were called, the detonator was examined, studied, analyzed.

It was all inconclusive.

Nothing quite tied Earle Holgren beyond reasonable doubt to the crimes.

No one was quite able to link him inescapably with them.

Circumstantial evidence piled up.

Absolute, irrevocable facts seemed to elude the prosecution.

For most of the country and an overwhelming portion of the media, this did not seem to matter much. In the ten days since the trial's beginning, Justice NOW! had continued to grow, its membership now up to almost eight million. Its effects began to be felt far beyond the confines of the courtroom in Columbia, though that remained the focus of national attention and the prime symbol employed by the movement's organizers. Many courtrooms throughout the land suddenly found themselves the objects of vigils, "citizen watches" as they came to be called, impatient and insistent that the processes of justice be speeded up. Some judges, resentful but nervous, began to shorten recesses, telescope time, do away with lawyers' deliberate delays. Many more, glad to have the excuse, jettisoned cases right and left, sometimes with more fervor than fairness. A noticeable quickening and toughening began to be obvious everywhere, encouraged by the governors, the attorneys general, the growing number of speeches in the legislatures, the constant proddings of the local press, the increasingly vocal and organized insistence of the citizenry.

There was also a grim tightening-up of the war against street crime. In seven days Justice NOW! managed to produce and distribute nationwide a pamphlet, *How to Organize Your Block Against Street Crime*. Already, in a hundred thousand neighborhoods and more, citizens were meeting, practicing with guns, being taught how to arrest and disarm, forming street patrols, launching around-the-clock surveillance, indulging themselves, and encouraging the police to indulge, in swift and violent reaction to the slightest sign of criminal activity.

Already at least ten would-be robbers and half a dozen rapists had been violently roughed up.

Five did not survive.

The mood was furious and savage. The reaction had finally come, and it was terrible.

Bewildered and dismayed, some of the major media sought desperately to denounce, caution, soothe. Further bombings and attempted assassinations of some of their leading figures were the only responses. CHAOS IN THE STREETS! cried the worried television specials. AMERICA RUNS AMUCK! proclaimed the anxious news magazines. LAW BECOMES LAWLESSNESS! said the somber editorials.

Hardly anybody paid attention.

In such a climate, the initial popular presumption of Earle Holgren's guilt rapidly became an accepted article of faith. Some major newspapers and the networks might expound frantically on vigilantism and try to point out that the facts did not yet warrant such a judgment but their desperate concern was dismissed with impatient contempt by the overwhelming majority of their countrymen, and even by some of their own.

"We think," the New York *Post* editorialized on the third day of the resumed trial, "that Earle Holgren is guilty as hell."

And this, a few protesting voices to the contrary, summarized the prevailing conclusion.

With such support, the attorney general of South Carolina, never one to doubt his own capabilities and potential, felt a comfortable confidence as the trial entered its fourth day and he prepared to put on the stand his four concluding witnesses. Each day at recess he and Debbie, faithful to their promise to the media, had held separate press conferences. Hers, despite a valiant determination to put a good face on things, sounded increasingly uncertain under the sharply probing questions of Henrietta-Maude, her colleagues from the statehouse, and the glittering and gossipy luminaries of national TV and journalism. Many of them were not partisans of the attorney general, many of them in principle favored Debbie's cause, but her insistence that the facts were not there to convict her client seemed increasingly wan and defensive as popular clamor grew. There was an air about the jury, too. As any seasoned trial lawyer could tell from looks, expressions, set of body, tilt of head, sharp attention or yawning lack of it, their minds were beginning to be made up.

"We're home free," Regard told Ted Phillips exultantly when the California attorney general called to check on progress, "and that murderous bastard is seeing his last days, or I miss my guess."

Under heavy guard, but at Regard's orders still permitted to have magazines and newspapers, listen to radio and TV and keep fully current with his progress in the public estimation, the defendant was hardly ready yet to concede his prosecutor's jubilant conclusion. He was convinced of the motivation for the attorney general's generosity—"to make me scared as hell," he told Debbie scornfully—but he was not about to let it succeed. If anything she thought it made him, outwardly at least, more self-confident and more defiant.

"Hell!" he said, in a talk they had on the eve of what they knew (Regard did not) would probably be the last day of the trial. "He isn't *proving* anything."

"You read the papers and watch TV," she said in a tone she hoped would prod him into being more serious. "This country has gone mad. You know he doesn't have to prove anything."

A contemptuous expression crossed Earle's face.

"Oh hell. 'Reasonable doubt.' Well, there *is* a reasonable doubt, isn't there? If those rednecks on the jury convict me, what court in the land will uphold them?"

"Plenty," she said shortly and shook her head, baffled. "You must feel *some* concern, for God's sake. It's your neck."

"They haven't really heard from *me,* yet," he said with a calm confidence that to her seemed almost bereft of sense. "I have a little support myself. And even if we lose here, we'll take it on up. If the state supreme court licks us, we'll take it to the U.S. Supreme Court. They won't dare uphold the death penalty. Under South Carolina law they can't even give me the death penalty anyway, unless there's a unanimous jury verdict in favor of it. And who says Old Yahoo is going to get that? He isn't even going to get a verdict of guilty at all, with the flimsy stuff he's got."

"He isn't Old Yahoo. He's exactly the same age you are, thirty-six. And he knows his jury. Putting your mother on came pretty close to wrapping things up as far as unanimity goes."

He scowled.

"That bitch! I'll cut her to pieces when I'm free to talk."

Debbie shrugged.

"I hope so, because she certainly didn't do you any good."

His scowl deepened.

"Is Stinnet going to put those Justices on the stand?"

"I'm sure of it. He'd be a fool not to, wouldn't he? And he's nobody's fool."

"More cheap shots for sympathy."

"And he'll get it, too," she said tartly, "unless you can find some way to overcome the impact of one dead girl and another in a coma."

"Is she still in one?" he asked with an odd sort of detached interest, as though it were something entirely separate from his concerns. "There was a rumor on last night's news that she had come out of it."

"I don't know," she said somberly. "They're being very close-mouthed. The rumor *I* heard, from somebody who got it from one of the hospital staff, is a lot different from that."

"Well, no doubt her father will try to pin me to the mast with it, whatever it is," he remarked scornfully.

"Don't you knock her father!" she said with a sudden fierceness. "He may be the only hope you have, when all is said and done."

He snorted.

"That phony liberal?"

"He is *not* a phony liberal!" she retorted with the same blazing anger, "and don't you ever say that about him! You aren't worthy to lick his boots, you with your phony pretensions to be some sort of world-saver!

You're as empty of purpose and devoid of reason as any punk out there on the street. You're all alike!"

And suddenly once again his hand was on her wrist, and his grip was so tight that she almost screamed for the guard as his eyes bored savagely into hers.

"Listen," he said, very softly. "Don't you ever say anything like that to me again, you hear me? I *do* have a cause, I *do* have a purpose, I *am* better than that trash! *What I do means something. And don't you forget it.*"

"So you say," she said, breathing heavily, simultaneously frightened and angry but having sense enough not to try to pull away as the guard looked in, snorted in derisive misinterpretation, and walked on. "So you say. But it isn't going to do you a damned bit of good if you blow it all with your God damned crazy ego. Now, I told you not to touch me again. And I mean it!"

And she aimed a vicious kick under the table that caught him just where she hoped it would. He howled and dropped her wrist, clutched himself and rocked back as the guard, responding to his yell, rushed up, looked in and started to unlock the door. She held up a hand and shook her head.

"We're fine, thank you, officer," she said calmly. "Mr. Holgren just injured his hand a little."

"*Mister* Holgren shouldn't be so free with his hands," the guard said, locking the door again, "and maybe he wouldn't get himself hurt."

"That's what I tell him," she said cheerfully. "Thank you, guard."

"Yes, *ma'am*," the guard said sardonically and walked off down the hall, whistling.

"I'd suggest you be damned careful what you say about the Justices," she said as though it had never happened, "particularly Justice Barbour, when you get on the stand. He may well be the swing vote on the Court if your case ever gets up there. You may need him." She gave a sudden derisive chuckle. "You may actually *need* somebody, Earle Holgren! How about that?"

He gave her a long thoughtful look that for some reason sent a sudden chill down her back.

"What's with you and this guy Barbour?" he inquired with a deliberate lazy insolence. "Have you been sleeping around with Supreme Court Justices, Superstar? Tut, tut."

"I talked to him," she said, ignoring his ostentatiously sly grin. "On your behalf, believe it or not. He didn't have to tell me anything: he told me he would try to be fair. If you want to ignore potential help like that from such a source under circumstances like these, then the hell with you. You don't deserve to be saved."

He gave her a sudden, sharp, shrewd glance that again she found oddly disturbing.

"That's what you *really* think, isn't it? Well, let me tell you this, Superstar: They're all out to get me, your precious Justices along with the rest. So let 'em come at me. Their minds are made up. It's all a farce, just like this whole worthless fucking country. But I'm ready for 'em, precious Tay and all the rest! If he has to agonize that much about it, then the hell with him too."

"He only wants to be fair!" she protested, sounding closer to desperation than she had anticipated, much closer than she liked.

" 'Fair!' " he echoed sarcastically. A sudden profound bitterness settled over his face. "Shit! Nobody's fair, in the world I live in."

But as his trial moved toward its conclusion, and as the rising tide of civil unrest came closer and closer to the citadel itself, there were nine who knew desperately that they, above all, must try to be fair. One in particular found the terrible weight of fairness almost more than he could bear. And he was aware that it would not stop. Long after the event, he supposed, he would still be trying to decide whether he had really been fair in the case of the Pomeroy Station bomber.

In a few terrible moments, in one terrible afternoon, he had apparently lost beyond recovery both his daughter and his wife. Janie's seizure had lasted, they told him, not more than a minute and a half. Mary's reactive and apparently permanent withdrawal had begun almost immediately after. When he and Moss had rushed into the hospital after their tire-screeching dash from the plantation, it was already obvious that his wife was moving off into some territory where he could not find her. Her anguished cry over the telephone, calling him back, was the last show of real emotion. From then on, nothing but a frigid and uncommunicative politeness had been her only response to his desperate pleas for support, help, understanding, love.

To her almost psychotic bitterness over the fact that he had been largely responsible for permitting Janie to go to Pomeroy Station there now was added a monumental resentment created by their daughter's loss of mentality. That this loss was permanent he refused, for several days, to accept. Mary had accepted it at once; it had simply confirmed her worst imaginings. When the doctors finally persuaded him that he too must abandon hope he had gone through such a night of pain and agony as he had never thought to experience. It was then that he realized that Mary, too, was gone forever. He remembered with a terrible self-mockery that he had wanted this, and would soon in the course of things have actively sought it: but not for such a reason, and not at such a price.

The ultimate jest came, however, when he learned that, though gone from him in any emotional or caring sense, she apparently had no intention of leaving his roof and board. She was going to punish him, he realized. The helpless body of their daughter was to be the means.

"I suppose," he said, on the day after his long night, "that we will have to start thinking about—about Janie."

"What about Janie?" she had asked, not turning to look at him, continuing the blank staring out the window that now occupied most of her time whenever they were alone at the hotel.

"Well, obviously, there are some serious things to plan for. How much longer we should keep her here. How we get her back to Washington. What we do—then."

"I can't stand the thought of her in an institution," she said, and a sudden sob, unexpected and seemingly startling her as much as him, broke through. It was quickly stifled and she repeated firmly, "I can't stand the thought of her in an institution. I won't have it. I simply won't have it."

"Mary," he said with a sinking heart as he realized the full import of her concluding words, "we have to be practical—*I* have to be practical."

"You!" she said, swinging suddenly to face him for a moment, eyes haggard but unyielding. "*You!* Were you ever anything else? What has practicality got to do with it when Janie's peace of mind is concerned?"

"Mary," he said as gently as he could, "Janie doesn't—doesn't—have a mind—any more. You know what the doctors say. It's a matter of her physical comfort, now."

"I'm talking about *Janie!*" she said fiercely. "*Janie*, I'm talking about."

"Yes, and so am I!" he said harshly. "We could provide nurses and attendants at the house but I'd rather pay the money to a good institution and be sure the care was absolutely top-notch than take a chance on what we might be able to hire at home. At least we'd know everything was being done right. There are good places near Washington. We can always visit."

"But *I want her home*," she said in the same fierce way. "Not in some 'good place near Washington.' Not in some '*institution*.' Not where 'we can always visit.' But *home.* Home, home, *home!* I want my daughter *home.*"

"My daughter, too," he said, trying to speak more calmly, "and I want her where the care will be best. And I want her there for another reason, Mary." He took a deep breath, paused, went on: it had to be said if one was a mature individual. He hoped he was.

"I want her there because there is no longer anything we can do for her, other than provide good physical care; and because neither of us, I think, could stand the strain of having her with us all the time in her present condition. There comes a time when mature people, having done all they can, have to go on and live their own lives; and I'm afraid that's the point where we are now. Oh yes, I know," he said as she swung back furiously toward him once more. "I'm sure it appalls you, but the whole situation is appalling; and I don't think we can make it any better by refusing to handle it in the most sensible, realistic, practical sort of way. And that doesn't mean," he added, suddenly choking up and almost breaking down, "that I don't love Janie."

"Love!" she said. *"Love!* What do you know about love, Tay Barbour, except love of yourself and love of the law? I despise your law," she cried harshly. *"I despise it!* And I despise what it's done to you. And now what you want it to do to our daughter. The law is a great monster. It has eaten you up."

"Nonetheless, Mary," he said, and his voice now was harsh too because he felt it had to be, "we must face up to what has to be done for Janie's sake and her best welfare." He stood up abruptly. "I'm going in the bedroom and call my family. I want to hear some kind words from people who really love me. I've had enough of this."

"Call then," she said more calmly but also unyielding. "Get your solace, if you can. But don't forget Janie. And don't forget we have to solve her problem when we get back to D.C. And don't forget *I want her home.*"

"Yes, Mary," he said as he shut the door firmly behind him. "I won't forget anything you say."

Nor could he, even when the loving and anxious voice of Helen and Fred Barbour came over the line from the Salinas Valley, which was basking now, he knew, in the slanting golden afternoon light of California spring as it fell across the level fields and tumbled, tawny hills he knew so well; or when he then called his sister Anne and her husband Johnny Gonzales and his brother Carl and his wife, all living now in nearby Soledad while the folks remained at the home place; or when, on a sudden impulse, he called Erma Tillson in Carmel.

No word of Janie's condition had been allowed to reach the media: the news hit them with devastating surprise. All the women cried. His father, Carl, and Johnny had difficulty speaking. Love and affection poured to him across the continent. He felt somewhat better, though nothing could take away the terrible ache of his daughter's misfortune or his wife's unyielding response.

And nothing, he knew, could take away the terrible responsibility he might soon have to face as a member of the Supreme Court of the United States. After the near lynching and the public mood it symbolized, he was absolutely certain that Earle Holgren, whatever the proof or lack of it, would be convicted and sentenced to death. He was equally sure the sentence would come up to the Court on appeal. How would Taylor Barbour face the challenge? What would Taylor Barbour do?

Decision was coming closer. How did he propose to meet it?

Impulsively, again, he dialed an unlisted number that he had been given along with six others when he took his seat. This time a phone rang in Georgetown, in a comfortable study walled on all sides with books. Reserved but friendly, the Chief's voice said politely, "Yes?"

"This is Tay," he said. "Taylor Barbour."

"Oh, yes, Tay," Duncan Elphinstone said with an instant concerned cordiality. "My dear friend, how are you? And your daughter?"

"Not—very good, Chief."

"I don't have to tell you," the Chief said gently, "how much sympathy and love there is for you and Mary here . . . How is Mary? Is she managing all right?"

"No," he said with a rush of candor that surprised him yet seemed perfectly natural with this decent, considerate man. "She is not managing at all well. In fact, very badly."

"Tell me about it," the Chief suggested. "If you feel like it. If it would help."

"Yes," he said gratefully. "I think it would."

There was silence while he spoke. At last the Chief sighed.

"Very difficult," he observed. "Very difficult . . . and nothing anyone can do to help, except be sympathetic."

"That helps . . . How are things on the Court? I feel very bad about not being able to be there right now, when I know—"

"Nonsense!" the Chief said. "Nonsense! We're getting along without you very well." He sounded amused for a moment. "I don't mean that quite the way it sounds, you know. I mean that we are managing quite comfortably without any undue strain on anybody. Except that we all have a constant burden in our hearts about you and Moss, of course. He seems to be bearing up pretty well this week, but he dreads coming down there when the trial resumes. I suppose you'll both have to testify."

"He will, I'm sure. I don't know quite what I can contribute, having arrived after the bombing."

"Unless I miss my guess about young Mr. Stinnet, you will be expected to testify about Janie."

"What is there to testify about Janie?" he asked bitterly.

"Exactly," Duncan Elphinstone said gently. "What do you think of young Mr. Stinnet's crusade these days? Going rather well, isn't it?"

"Too damned well," Tay said in a worried tone, diverted for the moment as the Chief had intended. "It's frightening."

"Indeed. But inevitable, perhaps. In a sense I suppose all of us in the law are guilty. We've either actively engaged in the law's delays for purposes not always worthy, or we've passively accepted the delays and connivings of others. A heavy reckoning seems to be underway. We're having silent demonstrations almost every day in the chamber, now; more orderly than the first one, but a lot of Justice NOW! buttons and ostentatious head-shakings, lip-pursings and disapproving frowns. Or approving, as the case may be." He chuckled somewhat ruefully. "Not so many of the latter, I'm afraid. They seem to want us to set a fierce example."

"And are we?"

"We are doing exactly what we have always tried to do, I believe," The Elph said in a firm voice. "Uphold the law. Provide equal justice. 'Do equal right to the poor and to the rich.' Keep the system on an even keel. It seems for the moment, at any rate, that this is not enough to satisfy our impatient and angry countrymen."

"Can we satisfy them, I wonder?"

"It isn't easy," the Chief said. "And it particularly won't be easy when the case of Earle Holgren comes up to us, as I am certain it will."

"Oh, yes," Tay said grimly, "it will. I've already had a talk about that with the young lady who is handling his defense."

"Oh?" The Elph said, and Tay hastened to add, "It was her idea. She waylaid me and I couldn't escape. She demanded that I be fair. I said I'd do my best. But," he added honestly, "I told her I was damned if I knew whether I could be. And I'm damned if I do."

"Of course—" the Chief Justice began; then paused, coughed delicately and went on—"possibly there might be a situation in which you might not have to be—put to the test. You might consider that the more advisable thing to do."

"Disqualify myself? Do you think I should?"

"I'll admit it has crossed my mind."

"Oh, mine too. But again, I'm damned if I know what's best. What do you really think?"

"It would avoid a good many problems."

"Have you discussed it with Moss?"

"We had a little talk about it. He doesn't seem to look too kindly on the idea of disqualifying himself. Even though I pointed out that he could under no circumstances be considered objective or disinterested in judging one who is very likely the murderer of his daughter. I said he *could* make an objective choice and stay out of it. He said Earle Holgren had the choice of whether or not he would be the murderer and he had made his choice, 'so I don't see why I shouldn't feel free to make mine.' "

"Yes, that sounds like Moss, all right. And you see, Chief, I'm just about in the same boat."

"I know you are," Duncan Elphinstone said. "I'm not minimizing the dilemma, and I can't criticize the two of you one little bit. God knows I'd probably feel the same way myself. How could any father feel otherwise? But we're supposed to give up those human elements when we take the oath here."

"None before has ever had the problem facing Moss and me."

"True. As you know, the law says that if a Justice or any member of his family has so much as a single share of financial interest in any case coming before the Court, he *must* disqualify himself. *Absolutely every other kind of case is entirely within his own discretion.* All I can do is state my own opinion, which you asked for. I think both of you should withdraw and let the rest of us handle it. But if you won't, you won't, and that's that."

"I haven't said I wouldn't," Tay said slowly. "I'm still thinking. And I have a hunch Moss is, too, for all the strong talk . . . Sometimes I wish I'd never gotten involved with the God damned law," he said with a sudden savagery. "Sometimes I think I should have been out there leading that lynch mob, stringing that worthless bastard up or frying him alive. He doesn't deserve anything more."

"But you *are* involved with the God damned law," the Chief remarked quietly. "And thereby hangs a difficult decision."

"Terribly difficult," Tay agreed somberly. "I don't know at this point. *I just don't know.*"

"Well," the Chief said in a comforting tone, "you don't have to decide tonight. Or for some nights to come, so don't let it bother you too much, if you can help it. Let it work itself out, if you can. Sometimes things do in one's mind, I've found, if one can just leave them alone."

"Easier said than done," Tay said unhappily. "But thank you, Chief. You've been a help."

"I hope so," Duncan Elphinstone said. "How much longer do you think the trial will last?"

"Not long, I imagine."

"And the verdict there is a foregone conclusion, I suppose."

"I don't see how it can be otherwise," Tay said, "given the public pressure that exists."

6

Boomer Johnson was sixteen and it was a great big world out there. His eyes looked twice as large as usual, his normally earnest, slightly worried expression seemed to have grown into a single frightened frown and he appeared to be barely breathing, so tightly was he holding himself in. He was visibly shaking when he walked to the witness stand. A little titter of amusement, not unfriendly, rippled through the room. Regard surveyed him quietly for a moment or two.

"Boomer," he said suddenly—so suddenly that Boomer jumped—"I'll bet you had grits for breakfast."

"Yes, sir," Boomer said cautiously, though the question was so friendly and unexpected that he couldn't help but smile a little.

"I'll bet they were good, too."

"Yes, sir," he replied, his tentative smile widening as he began to relax a little. "Real good."

In the front row of the audience his mother, who had been brought in with him from Pomeroy Station at the state's expense, smiled encouragingly. Regard gave her a friendly nod.

"Did your mama make them?"

"No, sir," Boomer said. "Not today. We ate in the hotel. Usually she makes 'em, though. And they're real good, too. A *lot* better than the hotel."

"I'm sure they are," Regard said, giving his mother another big smile. "Now, Boomer, that nice man alongside you, there, is going to show you a Bible, and you put your right hand on it and repeat after him what he says. O.K.?"

"Yes, sir," Boomer agreed, feeling calmer and more confident all the time. "Goin' to try to, anyways."

"Good," Regard said and paused while the bailiff swore Boomer in. "Now, Boomer," he said, "you take a look at that man with the beard there and tell me if you've seen him anywhere before."

Boomer looked at the man, who was sitting next to a funny-looking old lady with half-glasses on, and the man looked at him—pretty fierce, Boomer thought, with a big scowl and eyes that seemed to go right through Boomer, or try to, anyways. But Mr. Stinnet was smiling at him with *his* eyes and so Boomer tried to ignore the bearded man's eyes and just concentrate on him personally, what he looked like, and all. He knew him, all right, and he knew the man knew he did. The man was trying with his eyes to will Boomer not to say so but Boomer wasn't scared of him, with Mr. Stinnet and his mama there, and all.

"Yes, sir," he said stoutly. "I surely have."

"Good," Mr. Stinnet said. "Now, you just tell us about it, in your own words." He shot a sudden glance at the funny-looking lady. "We won't let anybody interrupt you," he said, and the lady looked mad for a moment and then shrugged. But she obviously wasn't happy. Both she and the man, Boomer felt, were just willing him not to say anything. He went right ahead, though. He realized the whole audience was listening very carefully just to him, Boomer Johnson, and he was beginning to enjoy it. He didn't look half so worried, now, and he had totally stopped shaking.

"Well, sir," he said, "Mr. Stinnet: I was going up to the big old plant at Pomeroy Station—"

"Just one interruption. You do live in Pomeroy Station, and always have?"

"All my life," Boomer said. "It's a good place. We have a nice little old house there, and my mama works in the laundry—"

"So you pretty well know everybody there?"

"Just about everybody," Boomer said. "I seen *him* a hundred times, I bet."

"Good," Regard said. "Now, just go on with your story."

"I been to the old plant a lot, too," Boomer went on. "All us kids been there quite a bit while they building it. And I see *him* visitin' there a lot, too. Not doin' anything," he added as Mr. Stinnet made as if to ask something. "Just lookin', just like us kids. That is, until the day of the de—de—"

"Dedication."

"That's right," Boomer said, "until the day they de-di-cate it. Then I see him doin' quite a few funny things."

"Let me just ask you," Regard said. "How come you were able to see him, Boomer? Weren't you with the rest of the people, down in front there while they were speech-makin'?"

"No, sir," Boomer said. "I got a independent mind."

"That's good," Regard said with a chuckle as the audience chuckled too, and from the big crowd that had gathered on the outside as if knowing, or expecting, that something climactic would happen, came a distinct sound of amusement.

"Yes, sir," Boomer said. "I like to mosey about and see things. I like to see what's really goin' on."

"And what was goin' on with this man here?"

"Well," Boomer said, "I was up there on the hill, see, 'cause I could get a good view up there and it kind of give me a different slant, you know? Not like everybody else. I had me my own perch. I like to do things like that, ask my mama. She tan my hide sometimes—used to, anyways, before I got to be a man—'cause she said I find a perch that get me in trouble someday. Well, it didn't this time. But I sensed they was trouble, even so. Somethin' funny goin' on. With *him.*"

"How so, Boomer?" Regard inquired softly.

"First of all," Boomer said, "he was up there with one of them bomb-blowin' things—"

There was a hiss of excitement from the audience and the small press section, a rumbling outside. The pool television camera swung in on Boomer's face, as candid and open as the day was long.

"—like you use to set off dynamite. They had a lot of 'em around the plant when they was first buildin' it, you know. Lots of rock they had to move, did a lot of dynamitin'. I don't know whether this was one they left from that or whether he brung it himself. Anyways, he had it, there he was, big as life, foolin' around with it."

"How do you mean, 'foolin' around with it'?"

"Oh, fiddlin' and fidgetin'. You know, sort of feelin' it and testin' it, you might say—"

"I object, your honor!" the lady with the glasses said sharply and Boomer gave her a look of blank surprise. It had looked like testing, to him.

"The court will advise the witness—" Perlie Williams began. Then he changed course and leaned forward man-to-man. "Look, Boomer," he said, in a friendly voice. "When you tell us these things, you just tell us what you saw, O.K.? You know you're just kind of guessing when you say this man was testing the bomb-blowing thing, isn't that so, now?"

"Looked like testin' to me," Boomer said stoutly. " 'Course," he conceded as the judge continued to smile down at him, "that might have been just my idea. Maybe it just *looked* that way."

"Now you've got it, Boomer," the judge said encouragingly. "That's the difference, you see. That's what we have to stick to, in a court like this one. We want to know what you actually saw, not what it *looked* like you saw. O.K., Boomer?"

"Yes, sir," Boomer said. "I see what you mean, now."

"Good man," Perlie Williams said, and both Boomer and his mother looked proud. "You just keep right on, now. But just remember that difference, all right?"

"Yes, sir," Boomer said obligingly. "I surely will, Mr. Judge . . . Well, anyways, he was fiddlin' and fidgetin' "—he looked questioningly at Perlie, who nodded—"and when things began to step up down there, the band playin' and everybody gettin' excited and all, he seemed to get more and more excited himself."

"How did you know he was excited, Boomer?" Regard asked. "Remember we just want what you saw, now."

"Well, he was pullin' at himself," Boomer said. *"You* know."

There was a burst of startled laughter in the courtroom, a scornfully amused sound from outside.

"Were his"—Regard paused for a second, considered and discarded several phrases, decided to meet it head-on—"were his pants unzipped?"

"No, sir, they wasn't," Boomer said. "He was just gropin' around, was all."

Again laughter swept the room. The defendant swung around to give them a contemptuous look. An answering contempt came back.

"What happened then?"

"Well, he didn't actually pull it *off*," Boomer explained carefully. "Leastways I couldn't *see* that he did—"

"O.K., Boomer," Regard said hastily, "I think we get the picture. So that's why you thought he was excited, I take it."

"Yes, sir," Boomer said. *"I* get excited when I—" He suddenly remembered where he was, in front of his mama and all these people and all, and stopped, stricken, while laughter, this time full-out, rocked the room. "What I mean is," he cried desperately, "what I mean *is,* you got to be pretty excited to do that, don't you? I mean, don't you?"

"Yes, Boomer," Regard agreed gravely, "you're right on that . . . So you saw this man and he was acting excited—you thought, on the basis

of what you saw he was doing and what you know about how excited it
makes a person feel. I think we can concede, your honor, that Boomer's
conclusion was probably correct, can we not?"

"I object, your honor," the lady with the glasses said angrily. "I object to this down-home clown act we're getting here in a matter as serious as this! That testimony should be stricken from the record!"

"It's not a clown act, Miss Donnelson," Judge Williams said mildly.
"It's an honest account by an honest young man of what he honestly
concluded from the defendant's actions. The way he describes them
seems to tie in pretty well with the evidence adduced by examination of
the defendant's clothing after his arrest. I think we'll let it stand. Go on,
Boomer. Then what?"

"Well, it was heatin' up like I said," Boomer resumed with dignity,
though he was sure he was going to catch hell from his mama later for
what, certainly not meaning to, he'd blurted out about himself. "And
that man was actin' excited and then they started the speakin'."

He stopped and Regard gave him a surprised look and said, "Yes?
And then what?"

"Then I had to take a—I had to go behind a tree," Boomer said,
"and after that I decided it was about time to go down and check my
friends Tad and Willie, Simpson, you know, they was in the crowd in
front there, so down I went. And next thing I knew there was this big
bang and—"

"And you weren't up there when it happened, and you didn't see
what the defendant did," Regard finished for him, trying to keep the
disappointment out of his voice while Debbie looked triumphant and
Earle Holgren gave him a wry, sardonic grin.

"No, sir," Boomer said. "I wasn't, and I didn't." He realized how
happy this made the lady and the man with the beard and suddenly felt
very bad because he seemed to have let Mr. Stinnet down. "I'm sorry,
sir," he said lamely. "I truly am sorry. I would of stayed up there if I'd
knowed. I—I'm really sorry, sir."

"That's all right, Boomer," Regard said, recovering rapidly because
there wasn't anything else to do. "You couldn't have known what was
going to happen, otherwise I'm sure you would have stayed and
watched the defendant use the bomb-blowing thing and cause the
expl—"

"Your *honor*," Debbie cried, and Perlie Williams nodded.

"Exactly so, counsel. Mr. Stinnet, we will strike that, if you don't
mind. Now let's be in order and move on. Does this witness have anything further to give us?"

"Yes, sir," Regard said with a pleased expression while the jury murmured back and forth amongst themselves. "What did you do after the explosion, Boomer?"

"I went back up to where I'd been."

"Why did you do that?"

"Because," Boomer said firmly, "that man had made me mighty suspicious, the way he was actin', and I wanted to see what he was up to next."

"I object, your honor," Debbie said.

"He's describing his own state of mind, Miss Donnelson," Judge Williams said. "I think it's a fair statement. Go on, Boomer. Was he still up there?"

"No, sir," Boomer said, "he'd left by then. But I saw him later."

"Oh? How was that?"

"Well, by that time, later on that is, everything was pretty wild around there, you know? Police and cops and sheriffs and everybody runnin' all over the place. So I went down and hung around for quite a while—not gettin' in the way," he said hastily, "just watchin' and observin', like I like to do—and after a while, oh, about an hour, I guess, I went on back up there one more time. And this time I see him again!"

"And what was he doing this time?" Regard asked softly, while the room became very still and the jury leaned forward intently.

"He was walkin' along the hillside hidin' in the brush."

"Alone?"

"No, sir," Boomer said, conscious of his effects now and dragging them out a bit. "He wasn't alone."

"Who did he have with him?"

"He didn't exactly have 'em *with* him," Boomer said. "It looked to me more like he was almost draggin' 'em. Like they was bein' *forced* to go."

"And who was it, Boomer?" Regard asked patiently, while the room became even quieter.

"A girl," Boomer said, "or maybe a little older than a girl, maybe you might say a young lady. She was carryin' a little baby."

There was a gasp of released breath from somewhere in the room, tense scribblings in the press section. Regard, too, was conscious of effects.

"Were they walking along freely with him? Did the young lady seem happy? Was the baby laughing?"

"No, sir," Boomer said. "They was scared-to-death, the young lady was, anyway. I guess the baby was asleep or didn't know, or somethin'.

Like I said, they was bein' dragged—I thought," he added, with a glance at Perlie Williams.

"How could you tell that?"

"Well, he was stickin' real close behind the girl—the young lady—like you do when you want to make somebody *march*. She was real white and shakin'. I think he was holdin' a gun on her."

"Your honor!" Debbie cried. Regard interceded smoothly.

"Did you actually see the gun, Boomer? This is important, now, so think carefully and try to remember exactly what you saw."

A look of great concentration settled on Boomer's face for several seconds. Then he leaned back.

"I can't say as I exactly *saw* a gun," he said, while an audible dismay ran through the audience, "but he was holdin' his right hand under her shawl up against her head and *they was somethin' in it*. I could see *they was somethin' in it*."

"But you can't say exactly, for sure, and no mistake, that it was a gun?"

"No, sir," Boomer said, his honest face heavy with concern and regret for again, apparently, letting Mr. Stinnet down. "It was *somethin'*, but I can't honestly say that."

"Thank you, Boomer," Regard said with obvious regret. "You *are* an honest young fellow and your great state of South Carolina appreciates that. So what happened then?"

"Well, then," Boomer said, "I kept real still, of course, because there was somethin' about him and the way he was pushin' them along and he seemed so *excited*—"

"Not in the same way, though," Regard suggested with a smile and Boomer returned a tentative smile of his own.

"No, sir, not in the same way. It was just the way he looked—just somethin' *about* him. He was real excited. I could *feel* it. It just came out of him like—like a swamp fog, you might say. It was all around him. It scared me to death. I tell you, it really did. I didn't want no part of him, no way."

"And then?"

"Then they just disappeared—just like that. Just—pow! I think I know what it was, though. It was that old mine cave up there. I think they went into it."

"You didn't follow?"

"No, sir, Mr. Stinnet, I did not follow. I told you, I didn't want no part of him. He scared me to death. He was in a killin' mood, Mr. Stinnet. He was in a mind to kill."

"Your honor!" Debbie protested, and this time Judge Williams nodded.

"Boomer," he said, "I think you're drawing your own conclusions again. You don't really know what this man was thinking at that moment, do you?"

"No, sir," Boomer said. "But," he added fervently, "I sure know what I *felt* he was thinkin'. And I got right out of there. Yes, sir. Right out!"

"I think we'll strike your last two answers from the record, Boomer," Perlie Williams said. "If that's agreeable to the state."

"Oh, yes, sir," Regard said amicably. "I think the jury has a pretty good idea of what the situation was. I think it has a pretty good idea of the situation right from the first moment the witness saw the defendant. Boomer," he added in a fatherly tone, "you're a fine young man and a fine witness and I thank you very much. That's all the questions I have, but I think the young lady may have some for you."

"What young lady?" Boomer asked, looking about in honest innocence. The audience snickered. Debbie flushed but proceeded.

"Boomer," she said, "you're a good boy, aren't you?"

"Yes, ma'am."

"And an honest boy."

"Yes, ma'am."

"You did not see the defendant—this man whom you saw on the mountain before the explosion at Pomeroy Station—use the bomb-blowing thing."

"No, ma'am."

"You did not see him use the bomb-blowing thing or in any way—*to your personal knowledge*—do anything to cause the explosion at Pomeroy Station."

"No, ma'am."

"You did not see him threaten the young lady or the baby?"

"No, ma'am, but—"

"You did not see him threaten them, Boomer."

"No, ma'am. I didn't see it."

"And you did not follow them into the cave."

"No, ma'am."

"And you have no way of knowing what, if anything, occurred inside the cave."

"No, ma'am."

"Thank you, Boomer, that will be all. Enjoy your grits tomorrow morning. You've earned them."

"Thank you, ma'am," Boomer said as she indicated he should step down. "I didn't mean," he added politely, "to say you were an *old* lady, ma'am."

"That's all right, Boomer," she said, with a sudden smile that lighted up her face and made Boomer think maybe she might perhaps be almost sort of young, after all. "I fool a lot of people."

"Yes, ma'am," he said; and wasn't quite sure why everybody, including the lady, laughed again as he started toward his mama. But it was a friendly sound, so he guessed he had done all right with everything.

"Your honor," Regard said gravely, "it is my intention now to call the Honorable Taylor Barbour, Associate Justice of the Supreme Court of the United States."

7

An hour before, when he had telephoned Cathy from a public booth in the courthouse lobby, he had wondered aloud whether he could go through the ordeal of public testimony along the lines he knew Regard would pursue.

"I'm one of the sympathy witnesses," he told her with some bitterness. "Moss and I are supposed to reduce the jury to tears."

"Will it be hard?" she asked quietly. "I shouldn't think so after what you've just told me about Janie."

"No," he agreed, instantly sobered. "I didn't mean to sound like that. I just resent—"

"You resent everything right now," she said, "and why shouldn't you? The world is not a happy place for Taylor Barbour at the moment. I'd be resentful too. But it has to be done if that individual is to be convicted and given what he deserves."

"They'll give him death."

"So?" she demanded with a sudden fierceness. "What else does he deserve, for what he has done to you?"

"Do you mean that?" he asked, genuinely shocked. "I thought you were opposed to—"

"Oh, I was, I was. But I find that when it's my man that is involved—"

"Oh, is that what I am?" he inquired, a sudden small but persistent happiness beginning to grow in his heart in spite of everything. "Is *that* what I am?"

"I'm thinking about it," she said. "Anyway, it makes it all different when it's somebody you love. Somehow all the smart, fashionable objectivity goes out the window."

"Yes," he agreed, not daring to push it further at the moment. "I suppose that's true."

"You know it's true. I don't see how you can look at your daughter and not know it's true."

"It's very hard not to feel that way," he admitted.

"Don't you feel that you would just like to abandon all your earnest civilized ways and literally tear him limb from limb? I do."

"Of course I do," he said gravely, "but I can't afford to let myself feel that way. I don't dare even start down that road. That isn't what I'm here for. I'm here to keep a level head, if I can. I'm here to keep the balance. I'm here to provide justice. And that," he said quietly, "is the ideal I have to cling to, no matter what the provocation."

"You're almost too noble," she remarked. "Hate a little. It might do you good."

"Oh, I hate," he said grimly. "I hate. But what good does it really do me? What good does it do Janie? It might satisfy something in me but it can't bring her back. At least I don't see how it can."

"Strong emotion can sometimes do remarkable things."

"Yes, but not that kind of emotion. Love, maybe, which God knows I feel for her; but not hatred for somebody else. He's of a nature that might be destroyed by compassion and pity, because he isn't capable of them and doesn't understand them. But hate he understands. He thrives on hate. He *is* hate."

"And shouldn't he be removed from the world, then? Wouldn't it be a much better place without him?"

"There you challenge the concepts of a lifetime. It isn't that easy to overcome them."

"Mine, too," she said. "But I find I'm managing to overcome them, as this thing unfolds. I'm coming pretty close to abandoning them permanently, which is something some of my friends will howl me down for when they find out. But they don't know what it means to suffer what you're suffering and what the Pomeroys are suffering. Basically, like many of that type, they have no imagination; and since it hasn't yet happened to *them*, God help them, they can still afford to be arch and all-knowing about it. But now it's happened to me—or to you, which is close enough so it's almost the same thing—and I'm not arch and all-knowing any more. I hurt inside. I feel savage inside."

"God!" he said. "You think I don't? But I can't afford to give in to it, Cathy. I just can't afford it."

She was silent for a moment. Then she sighed.

"No, I suppose you can't. So, my dear, what now?"

"We'll bring Janie home as soon as possible and then we'll see. Mary wants her at home; I think she should be where she can have proper full-time care. I also," he said, took a deep breath and decided to be completely honest, "think it would be too much of a strain to have her at home. It would be a constant wearing, a constant hopelessness and helplessness, a constant—"

"A constant distraction from the law," she interrupted, "which is your wife, mistress, friend, love, lover, obsession and curse, I suspect. Is that right?"

"Do you love me?"

"I said, 'Is that right?' " she replied harshly.

"And I said, 'Do you love me?' " he said, his heart pounding so hard it hurt, but determined to find out once and for all.

Again she was silent for what seemed an infinity to him, though it could not have been more than half a minute or so.

"It's defeated Mary," she said at last. "How do I know it wouldn't defeat me?"

"Because you don't resent it, I think," he said carefully. "You don't regard it as competition, but as something I have to do to justify my life and make me happy . . . and to serve my country, as I have been selected to do, which also makes me happy."

"I love you," she said slowly, "but whether I can love the law too, that much, even for your sake, I don't know, Tay . . . I just don't know. We'll have to talk about it some more when you get back. Maybe I'll have had time to do some more thinking by then."

"It will probably be sometime next week," he pointed out, more lightly. "Think fast."

"Yes," she said, her tone lightening in response to his. "I'll try . . . And now," she said, suddenly brisk, "good luck with the testimony today. I know it will go well. After all, you just have to tell the truth."

And the truth, he could sense now as he took the oath and seated himself in the witness chair, was what Regard was after: the truth about Janie, which was not yet public knowledge, and which Regard obviously hoped would stun, shock and enrage the jury. He had no doubt that Regard was right, and testified as fully and matter-of-factly as he could: because after all it *was* the truth, and hate, though nobly denied, is not all that easy to suppress.

"Mr. Justice," Regard said respectfully, "I shall try to make my questions brief because I know this is a very painful matter for you and for all of us. Or at least," he added thoughtfully, turning to stare at the defendant, "most of us."

Debbie made as though to rise but with a wry little smile Earle put a hand on her arm and pulled her back.

"Mr. Justice," Regard said, "I believe you arrived in South Carolina after the bombing of Pomeroy Station?"

"I did."

"Why did you come here at that time?"

"Because my daughter Jane," he said in a tone as level and unemotional as he could make it, "had been injured in the explosion. She had severe lacerations and bruising of the body."

"Principally in what area?"

"The cranial area."

"How did the severity of the injuries display itself?"

"She was in a coma when her mother and I arrived," he said, and there was a clucking of sympathy from the jury and throughout the room. He caught Moss' eyes and received a sad but encouraging look.

"She did not know you."

"No, sir, she did not."

"How long was it before she emerged from the coma?" Regard asked. "Or," he added quickly, "did she?"

"Oh, yes," Tay said, struggling to keep his voice steady. "A week ago last Saturday."

"Did she know you and her mother at that time?"

"Yes."

"Was she fully comprehensive of your presence?"

"Yes."

"And of her surroundings?"

"Yes."

"And of what had happened to her?"

"She knew that something bad had occurred."

"Was she responding normally, would you say, except for some understandable weakness and drowsiness from sedation?"

"Yes," he said, reflecting that Regard had certainly done his homework and bracing himself for the next question. It was exactly what he expected.

"And is she now?"

The room became deathly still.

He hesitated for a second, glanced again quickly at Moss, who nodded his head almost imperceptibly, looking both sad and grim. He took a deep breath and said clearly,

"No, she is not."

Again the sympathetic sounds, the shocked, horrified reactions.

"Would you care to tell us what has happened, in your own words, Mr. Justice," Regard asked gently, "or would you like me to elicit it with further detailed questioning?"

"Oh, no," he said, though it cost him much, "I will tell you . . . She lapsed back into coma after our short initial conversation with her and then roused again, three times, during the course of Saturday afternoon and evening. On Sunday, believing everything to be progressing well, and being assured by the doctors of this, I accepted an invitation to visit Justice and Mrs. Pomeroy at their home outside the city. Shortly before I was preparing to return to the hospital I received a call from my wife, who had remained with our daughter."

"What did she say?" Regard asked.

" 'Come back, oh, come back!' " he said, and despite his firm intention to keep it unemotional, something of the terror of Mary's anguished cry crept into his voice. His audience became, if possible, even more hushed.

"And you did so."

"As fast as Justice Pomeroy could drive me," he said, "which was very fast . . . At the hospital"—he stopped, mastered himself with a visible effort that made his recital even more moving—"at the hospital I found that my daughter had—had suffered a massive seizure—"

There was a sympathetic cry of "Oh, *no!*" from somewhere in the room, but he ignored it though sorely tempted to cry out savagely, "Oh, *yes!*"

"—and had again lapsed into coma, this time—this time, so the doctors have told her mother and me—for—for good."

He paused and heard some woman, possibly Mrs. Holgren, actually sob.

"Do you mean to say," Regard said gently, "that your daughter—"

"I mean to say," he said, and this time the savage desire to shock, in some sort of blind impotent protest against fate, did come out in his voice, "that we are informed on the best of medical authority that our daughter Jane has permanently lost all mental capacity and for the remainder of her life will never be more than a—a living corpse. A human vegetable. A nothing. A *nothing!*"

And his eyes, filled with the rage and horror of it while the audience burst into shocked incoherent sounds of sympathy and protest, came to rest at last squarely on the defendant, who stared back defiantly. But for the first time his face was white, his defiance was obviously and unmistakably an act of sheer will, and his eyes, after holding Tay's for a moment, shifted and looked desperately—or as close to desperation as he would allow himself—away.

"Your honor," Regard said softly, "I have no further questions of this witness. Counsel—" he added with grim politeness and gave Debbie a slight, sardonic bow.

She stood up and a low, rumbling boo swept through the audience, echoed a hundredfold outside. Judge Williams rapped his gavel sharply and spoke in a voice that showed a little tension but was, as ever, reasoned and firm.

"The audience has been warned," he said. "I want no further disturbances or demonstrations of any kind. *Stop that!*"

And crashed down his gavel a second time, so hard that it seemed it might break. Absolute silence ensued. He let it run on for a good long time before he finally said:

"Counsel, do you wish to question the Justice?"

"Yes, your honor," she said in a low voice. "Just two questions. First, Justice Barbour: do you believe in, or do you oppose, the death penalty?"

"Your honor," Regard began, "I must object to that kind of philosophical question in this proceeding. It has no place—"

"Oh, yes it does!" Debbie cried, even as Perlie Williams turned upon his old friend and said firmly,

"Counsel is overruled. The question is entirely legitimate, in the court's estimation. Your honor, would you care to answer?"

"Yes," Tay said, voice still tense but relatively back to normal after his bitter outburst. "Philosophically and in principle, I am opposed to it and always have been. However—" he said, holding up a hand as there was again an uneasy stirring in the audience despite Judge Williams' dictum, "however, I would not now, or ever, prejudice my judgment of future matters that might come before me as a jurist. Nor would I foreclose myself arbitrarily from whatever judgment the facts of an individual case might call for." And there, Cathy, he told her in his mind, *I am meeting you halfway, at least, and I hope you appreciate it.* "Does that answer your question, counsel?"

"If that is the best you can do, Mr. Justice," she said. He looked straight at her and replied quietly, "It is."

"Very well," she said. "My second question is: If the matter here should ultimately come before the Supreme Court of the United States and you should not disqualify yourself, will your daughter's condition affect your judgment concerning this defendant?"

"Your honor," Regard said, "now I really must object. Will counsel and her client never cease tormenting these poor people who have in the one instance lost a child from life, and in the other lost a child from all sentient being? Will they never have the common decency, your honor, to refrain from—"

"Counsel!" Perlie Williams said sharply, in his first show of real anger in the whole trial, the tensions surrounding the case apparently getting even to him at last, "I will rule you both out of order, and I so do. Counsel for the defense asks an impossible question which should bring its own reward and create exactly the prejudice she claims to be fearful of. Counsel for the prosecution is indulging in maudlin self-serving. You will both be in order or we will have a recess and let you think about it. Justice NOW!" he added sarcastically, "or no Justice NOW!"

For several moments after that the courtroom was again very quiet. Hardly anybody dared cough, move, whisper or even look directly at the judge. Finally, he shifted position a little and sat back slowly in his chair.

"Justice Barbour," Regard ventured to say in a very quiet, circumspect voice. "I believe you may be excused, sir, if that is agreeable to opposing counsel—?"

Debbie nodded with equal care and Regard said,

"Justice Pomeroy, if you will please take the stand."

There was a muted stir of deep sympathy and warmth as Moss came forward; yet though his testimony was perhaps even more tragic than Tay's, it was in a sense anticlimax. There was, after all, nothing much to add to the implacable, unchangeable fact that Sarah was dead. Nor could there be at this point much more sympathy than had already come to him and Sue-Ann in the past three weeks from all over the state and the nation. The Pomeroys were much admired and much loved; their tragedy was South Carolina's and it had already been expressed in a hundred editorials and television and radio commentaries, many thousands of letters, telegrams, telephone calls.

He testified quietly, with obvious emotion but without the open and uncharacteristic bitterness that had momentarily overwhelmed his old friend; and although what he had to say was devastating, it basically covered old ground and no longer carried quite the same emotional impact.

When the trial was reviewed and recapitulated, as it was in almost every area of the media all across the country in the week immediately following its conclusion, it was recognized that the two witnesses most responsible for the conviction of Earle William Holgren were Boomer Johnson and Justice Taylor Barbour; and of these it was the Justice, with his heavy burden of living tragedy that he would most likely have to carry with him as long as he lived, who was generally conceded to be the final factor.

To Moss, also, Debbie put her two questions and from him elicited answers both more direct and more damaging to her client's hopes. Although Regard again tried to protect him, and Perlie Williams sharply reminded her of his statement not an hour ago concerning her second question, Moss brushed them both aside with thanks and said he would be glad to answer.

To the question, "Do you or do you not believe in the death penalty?" he replied calmly,

"I do."

There was the start of applause, hastily quelled in response to Judge Williams' monitory glance, inside the room. Outside a triumphant roar of approval came from members and friends of Justice NOW!

Debbie waited patiently, if with some obvious annoyance, until it quieted. Then her second query:

"If the matter here should ultimately come before the Supreme Court of the United States, and if you should not disqualify yourself, will your daughter's death affect your judgment concerning this defendant?"

"Miss Donnelson," Perlie Williams began sharply, "I warned you—"

"Your honor," Regard said simultaneously, "I thought we had been all over that—"

Moss interrupted. "That's all right," he said again. "I don't mind."

He sat for a moment considering. The room again became very still. Finally he spoke slowly and thoughtfully, looking directly at his fellow Justice, who looked somberly back.

"If you bring this case before us, Miss Donnelson, as it is quite obvious you intend to do should the jury render a verdict of guilty upon your client and should the verdict be upheld by the supreme court of the State of South Carolina, then I would have to be honest with you"— he paused and the room if possible became even quieter—"and say that, yes, if I remained on the case, I could not help but be influenced by my emotions. However—" he said, holding up a hand, very much as

Tay had done in response to the immediate murmur, "however, I hold an office for which I have a great regard, in an institution for which I have a great regard. I certainly am not prepared to say at this time how *much* I might be influenced, or whether you could count on my vote one way or the other. To expect me to say that now—or even, in fact, Miss Donnelson, to *know* that with any certainty now—is a little naive, it seems to me."

"Would you disqualify yourself?" she asked, and again Judge Williams and Regard both started to protest. But again Moss stopped them with a mild "I don't mind . . . Miss Donnelson," he said, as though he were querying a child, "do you really expect me, at this moment, to give you an answer to that question?"

"I would appreciate it, your honor," she told him crisply. He shook his head as if in disbelieving wonderment and said, "Miss Donnelson. Oh, Miss Donnelson! How naive can you get? Again, I don't know. It isn't one of those things you just decide on the spur of the moment or with a snap of the fingers. I can't tell you until I actually face it. And although you were precluded from asking this same question of Justice Barbour, which I guess you intended to do"—she nodded—"I expect if you had asked it of him that his answer would have been exactly the same as mine."

He looked at Tay, and the audience turned and looked at him, too; and Tay also nodded, expression grim.

"There you have it, Miss Donnelson," Moss said softly, and for the only time his hatred for her client came into his voice. "You and your friend just don't know, do you? You just don't know what might happen, if you get up to the Supreme Court of the United States. You'll just have to guess, won't you? You can't really plan, you just won't know 'til the time comes. I feel sorry for you both, Miss Donnelson, I really do. But there it is."

"Your honor," she said to Perlie Williams, "I have no further questions of this witness."

"Probably wise, counsel," Perlie said dryly, prompting sarcastic, approving laughter from courtroom and Justice NOW! "Probably wise . . . Justice Pomeroy, thank you very much, sir, you are excused." He turned to Regard. "Counsel?"

"Your honor," Regard said, "the State of South Carolina rests its case, reserving summation until the defense has also completed its case."

The courtroom seemed to relax for a few moments. But when Debbie stood and addressed the bench, something in her rigid back and tone of voice brought an immediate hush again.

"Your honor," she said, sounding strained and unhappy, "as counsel for the defense I have an announcement to make to the court. I wish to emphasize that while the first portion of what I am about to announce is my decision, taken in consultation with my client, the second portion is solely and entirely his own idea. It is a decision taken by him over my strenuous and repeated objections. But he is determined upon it, your honor, and this being so I have no choice but to abide by his wishes. I just want to emphasize that it is not my doing and the results are not my responsibility."

"I think you've made that clear enough," the defendant said in an impatient voice that carried clearly in the excited hush. "Just get on with it now, O.K.?"

"Yes, your honor," Debbie said with sudden anger. "I shall 'get on with it.' Firstly, the defense will call no witnesses—"

There was a gasp of surprise, followed by a murmur of voices despite Perlie Williams' stern looking about. Several reporters half rose, poised to dash out with bulletins. The pool television camera swung in upon her tense, determined face.

"—since we believe the prosecution has not proved its charges beyond a reasonable doubt and because we rely on the good sense, honesty and integrity of this jury and the traditional American principle that a man is innocent until proven guilty. No such proof has been produced here and we do not believe any witnesses from our side could give additional force to what the record already clearly shows."

She paused, took a drink of water and resumed, looking if possible even more tense.

"At his request, however"—her audience, if possible, growing even quieter—"the defense will put one person on the stand. I have here a written notice, addressed to the court, of his desire to waive his constitutional right against self-incrimination. I now hand it to the court."

She stepped forward, handed a paper to Judge Williams and stepped back while he took it, read it without expression, and handed it to the bailiff, who handed it to the official reporter. Then he looked down for a long, thoughtful moment upon the defendant.

"Earle William Holgren," he said. "This is your own decision, made without coercion from this court or anyone else?"

"It is."

"Please come forward and be sworn."

"He's crazy," Moss whispered to Tay as the room and the crowd outside exploded, as spectators gabbled, reporters dashed and the television camera swung wildly from Debbie's grim face to Earle's triumphant expression to the elder Holgrens' anguished dismay to the two Justices' own startled disbelief.

"He has a monumental ego," Tay responded, "which I guess is craziness. And it's going to be the death of him."

"By God," Moss said, voice rising savagely against the hubbub. "I hope so."

8

The testimony the defendant gave under the questioning of his counsel and the cross-examination of the state received substantial praise from some of the major media, but in the minds of the great majority of his countrymen it really had very little to do with the crimes at Pomeroy Station. Very little—or everything, as Moss murmured to Tay as they listened to the destroyer of their children duck, dodge, defy and orate. Very little about the specific things with which he was charged—everything about the state of mind that had made them possible. The clichés of that small but much-publicized segment of a generation that had lived outside reality, and now was frozen in time with nothing for company but its own twisted misconceptions of the world, passed in review. Along with them went a contemptuous disregard for human life, the law and the ordinary decencies by which most people live as the simple price of survival, which linked the defendant directly to the rising tide of street crime, murder, rapes and robberies throughout the land. Those who had regarded Earle Holgren as a symbol of all that was wrong with the public safety felt more than justified in making his case the focus of their organized efforts.

"They're all alike!" was the general reaction.

And at heart, they were: animals, no matter if they were as sophisticated as he or as cretinous as the stabbers in the street—lost, abandoned, bereft—outside the pale of society and the necessary restraints of organized living.

Not, of course, that the defendant would ever admit this. He clung tenaciously to his lifelong conviction that he was something different and something special, because to admit otherwise would have been to shatter his very being. The attorney general, who had studied him with great care in the past three weeks, realized this and concentrated on the ego that challenged him with bitter venom. The defendant's counsel did what she could, with little help from him, to protect him.

For several minutes after Earle took his seat on the stand, Regard went through an elaborate charade of searching through his papers, conferring with the two junior aides who had been with him throughout the trial, apparently for the purpose of carrying his briefcase since he had never before sought their opinions on anything; and generally consuming time. On each occasion when Debbie thought he was ready and started to ask her client a question, Regard would raise a supplicating hand and burrow into his papers again. Presently a little titter began to run through the audience as Debbie became more and more openly annoyed and on the stand a deep and frustrated scowl settled on the face of the defendant. Finally he could stand it no longer and turned to Perlie Williams to say sharply,

"Your honor—"

"Yes," Perlie said in an icy voice. "For what purpose, and on what excuse, does the witness directly address the bench?"

"For the purpose of getting this show on the road," Earle snapped, "and because I am getting damned well fed up with the antics of that clown over there—"

"Your honor!" Debbie and Regard cried together, she in genuine alarm, he in genuine anger. Judge Williams was ahead of them.

"Do you wish to be held in contempt of court, Mr. Holgren?" he demanded. Earle shook his head and, in one of his lightning changes of mood, grinned amicably.

"No, *sir,* your honor," he said expansively, "how could I be? I feel no contempt for *you,* sir, only for *him.* And he isn't the court, I don't believe. He just happens to be here."

"He is here for the purposes of the court," Perlie Williams began, "and therefore—" Then he shook his head in disbelief and broke it off. "If counsel for the state is ready," he said, "suppose we proceed."

Regard flushed, the crowd stirred, Earle beamed with elaborate complacency.

"Your honor," Debbie said in a shaken voice, "if I may begin with a few questions for the witness—"

"He's your client, Miss Donnelson," Judge Williams noted. "And your problem. You handle him any way you like. But I will say to him"

—and he stared at Earle, who ignored him and stared out into some distance that prompted him to keep on smiling—"that if he wishes to avoid citation for contempt he will refrain from too much cuteness. What he does to his own cause is his business, but respect for the law is my business. Remember that!"

"Yes, your honor," Earle said, still not looking at him but smiling now at the jury. "I'll remember that."

And the members of the jury, curiously enough, were suddenly leaning forward intently, paying little notice to anyone else, concentrating all their interest and attention upon him. "Score one for the bastard," Moss muttered. "He has them where he wants them, already."

And from then on, until Regard finally succeeded in prying them loose, he did not let them go. As far as he was concerned, there was no one in the world but that jury. He courted them, he frightened them, he wooed them—he fascinated them. "It's as though he were a snake," Tay commented at one point, and they a flock of hypnotized birds. Debbie gave him his openings and away he went. Within a few minutes it was almost—almost—conceivable that if they had been required to vote then, they might have failed to achieve unanimity and thrown the case. That they finally did not was a tribute to Regard but even more, perhaps, to the insistent demands of Justice NOW! whose members, outside and free from his hypnotic personality, kept up a distant but continuing reminder that a new era had dawned in American justice.

"Mr. Holgren," Debbie began, "what was your interest in the atomic energy plant at Pomeroy Station?"

Earle considered.

"I really had none, counsel, aside from sharing the views of millions of concerned Americans that atomic power is a dangerous, and dangerously unnecessary, enterprise for us to be engaged in. I'm against it, because it is so dangerous and as such, in a general way, I was against—still am against—the Pomeroy Station plant. But I had no desire to hurt it or in any way to interfere with its operation. It just made me sad. I hated to see it, but"—he sighed heavily—"what can a citizen who wants to protect himself and posterity do?"

"It didn't occur to you to do anything specific?" Debbie inquired. "Such as blow it up, in the manner mentioned in the indictment entered here?"

"No, ma'am," Earle said in the same respectful tone. "Why would I want to do such a thing?"

"It is so charged," she said.

"Has anyone proved it?" he inquired like a flash, and several members of the jury couldn't keep from smiling a little.

"Not to my knowledge," Debbie said and paused to let it sink in. "Tell me, Mr. Holgren, why you were, as one of the workers at Pomeroy Station put it the other day, 'around the place a lot'? Were you there so frequently as that would indicate, and if so, why?"

"First of all," Earle said reasonably, "I really wasn't there all that much. I used to jog past there quite a lot before"—he looked straight at a couple of ladies on the jury and smiled—"before I got slowed down a bit in the last three weeks. It's healthy." He stretched and spread his legs a bit. "I like to be healthy." The ladies, in spite of themselves, smiled back.

"Did you live alone, Mr. Holgren?"

"Nope," he said. "I had a girl friend—we weren't married, but we'd been together awhile. We had a little boy, too. They were about the same ages as those poor folks they found in the cave." He shook his head, grieved by the enormity of it. "That was a very sad thing," he said gravely. "Very sad."

"Where are your girl friend and the baby now?"

"Took off," he said. "Just took off. Someplace. Up north, maybe—down south—out west. Who knows?" Again he shook his head sadly. "That's the way it always seems to happen with me. I just don't have any luck with love, that's all. Never have had."

"I don't see why not," one of the jury ladies whispered to another. "He's the *cutest* thing!"

"Except for the eyes," the other lady, more level-headed, replied. "Look at the eyes." She shivered suddenly. "He gives *me* the creeps."

"Mr. Holgren," Debbie said, "were the young woman and the baby boy found in the cave your girl friend and your baby boy?"

"Has anybody identified them as being such?" he inquired in surprise.

"You heard two witnesses day before yesterday testify that they thought they might be. They couldn't be sure."

He shrugged.

"Oh, well. 'Might be.' If apples were peaches, lots of things might be. But then, they aren't." He smiled at the jury again, a confidential, skeptical look. "No, I'm afraid not. They showed them to me—*he* did"—he nodded toward Regard without looking at him—"but it wasn't anybody I'd ever seen before in my life. I just didn't know them." He did look at Regard. "Sorry about that."

Regard gave him a long look, quite expressionless. Earle, unmoved, stared back.

"Did you see the witness Boomer Johnson up in the woods above the plant prior to the explosion?" Debbie asked, suppressing an inner shiver but telling herself that he was her client, and Harry Aboud had asked her to do it, and that was what lawyers were for.

"Boomer?" Earle repeated, and his eyes came to rest for a moment on the big round saucers of Boomer, sitting with his mother toward the back now that his part of it was over. For a moment Earle stared straight at him and instinctively Boomer shivered too and clutched his mother's arm. She tried defiantly to stare back but Earle wasn't interested in her. It was almost as though he were memorizing Boomer. Then he smiled and turned his terrible eyes away—leastways, *Boomer* thought they were terrible and he was scared-to-death, and so was his mother.

"Boomer?" Earle said again. "No, I don't remember seeing any Boomer up there. Because of course," he added smoothly as there was a catch of breath through the room, "I wasn't up there, you see, so how could I see any Boomer? And how could any Boomer see me?"

"He says he did," Debbie said.

"Oh, I *heard* him say it," Earle said indifferently, "but you know kids, particularly black kids. They're always imagining things . . . No, I didn't see any Boomer because I couldn't have, not being there. And he didn't see me."

Yes, I did, Boomer cried in his mind. *Oh yes I did, you awful, terrible man.* But he didn't dare say anything aloud, of course, and his eyes just got a little bigger, if that was possible, and he clutched his mother's arm a little harder, and she got even more frightened of that terrible man, and his thoughts about Boomer, than she was already.

"What is your opinion of the Supreme Court?" Debbie inquired.

"The U.S. Supreme Court?" Earle said. "Why—O.K., I guess. I haven't had much to do with it"—he grinned at the jury and more of them than expected to found themselves grinning back—"but I guess it's all right. I certainly don't wish it any harm, even though *he*"—and again he tossed a nod toward Regard—"seems to have some bee in his bonnet about it. I couldn't care less, really. They do their thing, I do mine. I mean, isn't that true of most Americans, the way they feel about the Court? I mean, they're just"—he flung his left hand in the air—"up there. I mean—that's it, right?"

"Then you don't bear any particular animosity toward Justice Pomeroy?"

"How could I?" he asked, puzzled. "I don't even know the man. I never even saw him until this whole stupid mixup began."

"Even though you have testified strongly that you are completely opposed to nuclear power, you did not blow up, or attempt to blow up, the Pomeroy Station plant with the added objective of killing or injuring Justice Pomeroy, who was to be principal speaker at the dedication?"

Earle looked amazed, and disgusted as well.

"Now—now, look. How ridiculous can you get? Why would I want to do that?"

"That isn't what I'm asking," Debbie said. "I'll get to the why in a minute. I just want to know if you did."

"Has anybody proved it?" Earle inquired blandly and Regard said, "Christ" sotto-voce but quite audibly enough for Perlie Williams to give him a look—not unsympathetic, but a look.

"No testimony has been adduced," Debbie said.

"Good," Earle said. " 'No testimony has been adduced.' Well, good for me, then. I guess the answer to your question must be No, then, right? Absent testimony adduced, that is."

"It isn't my place to make judgments," Debbie said. "That's the jury's job."

"And I certainly hope," Earle said, turning upon them a sudden dazzling smile, "that they will do their job to the *very best* of their ability. In fact, I know they will—fairly, honestly, without fear or favor, not yielding to public clamor or pressure, but upright, objective, compassionate and honest, like true sons and daughters of old Carolina. I *know* that."

"I can hear 'Dixie,' " Tay murmured. "He's unbelievable." "And getting away with it, or close to it," Moss agreed grimly. "Look at them!"

And indeed most members of the jury were, for the moment at least, obviously enthralled. Only two or three continued to look skeptical, including the lady who was disturbed by the defendant's eyes.

"You say, then, that you did not intend or inflict any harm upon the Pomeroy Station plant, and that you did not intend or inflict any harm upon the person of Justice Pomeroy. And that you have no animosity toward the Supreme Court of the United States and no desire to do harm to it through the person of Justice Pomeroy."

"I couldn't have stated it better myself," Earle said admiringly, and again turned directly to the jury. "Isn't she wonderful? You see why I selected her to be my lawyer. I knew she was good. But she's *really* good."

"You are too kind," Debbie remarked, and her client shot her a sudden sharp look that momentarily changed his face entirely; but it was gone as instantly as it came when she went on calmly, "When did you break off relations with your parents, Mr. Holgren?"

"About age twenty," he said, his eyes flicking quickly and impersonally over the sad, strained faces of the two distinguished old people sitting in the front row. "I just couldn't take it any longer."

"Take what?"

"Being smothered to death. Having my life lived for me. Being told what to do all the time and being disapproved and punished when I did what *I* wanted to do. Being ruled. And overruled."

"You heard your mother's testimony."

"Oh, yes," he said indifferently. "I heard it."

"You heard her say that your parents detected a noticeable change in you about your sophomore year in college. What was that?"

"I think I found out about girls," he said dryly. "Or maybe it was boys. I don't know *what* it was!" he added with sudden savagery. "*I* thought I was doing all right!"

"Not according to her," Debbie said, referring to the transcript. "She says you came home 'different'—in dress, manner, habits, beliefs. I quote from the attorney general: 'Was there dope?' And from Mrs. Holgren: 'Some. But we felt that was an effect, not a cause—something he felt he had to do to satisfy some—some peer group that was watching him. To look big in their eyes.' And the attorney general: 'Watching him?' And Mrs. Holgren: 'Telephoning. Calling him away to meetings. Keeping an eye on him. Encouraging him.' And the attorney general: 'Encouraging him to do what, Mrs. Holgren?' 'Hate us. Hate his country. Hate everything we had reared him to be.'"

She laid down the transcript and turned again to her client.

"Did you change in all these ways, Mr. Holgren?"

He shrugged.

"Maybe. Kids do. Everybody grows up sooner or later, much as some parents hate to admit it. I think I probably just grew up."

"What was this 'peer group' your mother talked about?"

"There wasn't any 'peer group,'" he said patiently. "That's just an inadequate mother's rationalization."

In the audience, Mrs. Holgren clutched her handkerchief to her mouth to stifle some inarticulate, anguished sound. Earle gave her an impassive, appraising glance as though he had never seen her before. Some members of the jury began to look a little upset.

"Why do you say she was 'inadequate'?" Debbie demanded sharply. "I'm sure she was doing her best."

"Oh, yes," he agreed, taking the cue, suddenly amicable. "I'm sure she was. I don't know that I was all that easy a kid to understand, either. Maybe it was partly my fault. It's hard to assess these things fairly. I'm sure we've all had similar problems, either as kids or parents." And he smiled once more directly at the jury, whose members appeared mollified.

"So there was no 'peer group,' then," Debbie said quickly.

"Of course not," he said with a dismissing smile. "What would that mean, anyway?"

"I don't know. I'm asking you."

"Well, I don't know either," he said, smile broadening. "I took to running around a lot, but again, lots of kids do. And I was critical of my parents, probably, and what kid isn't at that age? And they were pretty conservative and I guess I was pretty liberal, and again, what's so unusual or unnatural about that kind of generation gap? But I didn't 'hate' anybody. I didn't 'hate' them or 'hate' my country. That's absurd!"

This time it was Mr. Holgren who uttered some muffled, protesting sound. But Earle just continued to smile, not looking at his father, and no further sound came from him, and presently the jury relaxed again.

"How were you treated at the time of your arrest?"

"I was savagely beaten up," he said, a note of genuine anger entering his voice. "His thugs set on me—"

"Your honor," Regard said sharply. "I must object to that description of the law officers and good citizens of Pomeroy Station who apprehended this man. They are not thugs, nor are they mine. They are law-abiding citizens seeking to capture a man who had just blown up the plant and murdered three—"

"Your honor," Debbie said with equal sharpness, "now I object."

"The defendant's remark and that of the attorney general will be stricken from the record," Perlie Williams said. "Please proceed, Mr. Holgren. In order."

"Yes, sir, your honor," Earle said, not yielding much, "but I can't help but feel indignant still at the way I was brutally treated. The jury has seen photographs of me taken after the arrest, they're in exhibit here, and some of them were in the papers and on television. I wasn't such a pretty sight, thanks to those who did it. Frankly," he said, again addressing the jury with an intimate directness, "I felt like holy hell. I *hurt*. I *really hurt*. And when I get around to suing the state for false arrest, I'm going to include as many of the bast—as many of those who did it as we can find. Furthermore, counsel," and he swung back to

Debbie, "I was denied my rights as well. Nobody notified me of them and as you know it was not until early morning of the next day that you were permitted to visit me and I was permitted to have myself a lawyer." He turned and glared at Regard for a moment. "That will be taken into account, too."

"It most certainly should be by the jury," Debbie said as Regard ignored his look; and added thoughtfully, "And by any other jurisdiction that may consider the matter."

"That means us, kid," Moss whispered wryly, "and don't you forget it." "We can't, Moss," Tay responded seriously. "We have to take those things into account." "Maybe," Moss said grimly. "Maybe." "You know we do," Tay replied, "and no 'maybe' about it."

"Why do you think it is," Debbie inquired in a puzzled tone, "that you got involved in all this, Mr. Holgren? Why would workers at the plant testify that you were around there a lot? Why would Boomer Johnson testify that he saw you in the woods above the plant just prior to the explosion and then just after in the company of a young woman and an infant whose general description tallies with the bodies found in the well? Why would your mother testify that some sort of 'power group' was putting pressure on you to hate your parents and your country, and that you responded? Why were you apprehended near the entrance to the old mine shaft? Why would these things happen to an innocent man, Mr. Holgren?"

"Well, you know," he said, hunching forward confidentially in his chair and looking straight at the jury, not at her, "I have asked myself these questions many times while I have been under false arrest during the past three weeks. I'm glad you're playing devil's advocate for me, Miss Donnelson, because I know these are things that are very puzzling to me, as they must be to everybody, and I want to answer them as best I can." He paused and shook his head, baffled. "I've been giving it a great deal of thought and all I can come up with is that there must be some conspiracy, some sinister plot which has selected me for its target in the hope that I can be made a symbol and a rallying point for an organization devoted to the political ambitions of some individual or individuals who feel they can profit from framing me . . .

"I was up in the woods above the plant"—there was a startled excitement in the audience, sharp looks from the jury; he smiled calmly and waved a monitory hand—"don't everybody get excited now, this was *after* the explosion, *after* the time when our young friend Boomer claims he saw me and some unidentified young woman and child up there—I *was* there *after* because I, too, was looking for the individual—

or individuals—responsible for the dreadful crimes that occurred there that day. Prior to that time I had been mingling in the outskirts of the crowd—the honorable attorney general can probably find a dozen people who saw me, if he *really* wants to look—but after the explosion I decided I would do what I could to help, because I did do a lot of jogging around there and I am pretty familiar with the area. So I went on up and started looking. I knew where the old cave was—"

Debbie looked at him through narrowed eyes, face expressionless but mind whirling: was he really so egotistically unbalanced as to push his luck this far? He was. "—because I had stumbled on it one day when I was exploring around just out of idle curiosity, and because I like to know the lay of the land." He grinned suddenly. "I'm like young Boomer. I too like 'my own perch'—I too have 'a independent mind.'" Audience and jury joined him in a small, patronizing chuckle for Boomer's grammar. Then he resumed his narration seriously again. "So I knew the cave. It occurred to me that if somebody else knew it, namely the guilty party, he might consider it a good place to hide. I had just stepped into it to explore when I realized I didn't have a flashlight, so I started back out—and just then the good, law-abiding citizens of Pomeroy Station, as he calls them—and I'm not saying they aren't, your honor, I'm sure they are, they were just kind of excited at the time— jumped me and beat me and took me into custody without so much as a by your leave, or my rights, or anything. I was only trying to help, and look what happened!"

He gave the jury an injured look and shook his head in wonderment.

"As I said," he concluded solemnly, "I can only figure that somebody must have decided that I was to be made the scapegoat for an organization intended to further somebody's political ambitions. As to why certain people have testified to certain things, well"—he shrugged— "it's always possible to suborn witnesses."

"Your honor," Regard said with a dangerous glint in his eye, "is this individual charging me with suborning witnesses?"

"Oh, no," Earle said airily. "I just said it was possible to do that, I didn't say anybody *did* it. I just said it was *possible.*" His tone became suddenly vicious. "Surely the great attorney general isn't denying that *some* time, at *some* place, at *some* point in history, witnesses *have* been suborned by *some*body, is he? It *is* a humanly conceivable act, isn't it? It *has* been done, right? It *could* happen again, right? *Some* place, *some* time, by *some*body?"

"Your honor," Regard said, breathing a little heavily, "I will not dignify talk like that by replying. Are you through with your client, counsel? Because I'd like to get at him."

There was a rather nervous laugh in the room, followed by vigorous applause. But the jury was not amused. They all looked grave and concerned. Earle had shaken them and Debbie decided to let it go at that.

"Your honor," she said, "unless my client wishes to add something of his own—"

"Oh, no," Earle said complacently, leaning back with his expansive air, "I think that pretty well states the case as *I* see it."

"It's been a long afternoon so far," Perlie Williams said, "and likely to get longer. The court will stand in recess for twenty minutes, after which we'll resume. It is my intention to go right on as long as it takes to wind this matter up today."

"That murderous little bastard is a complete phony," Moss said glumly as he and Tay headed for the men's room, "but I'm afraid he's made some points." "Which we will have to consider, if and when," Tay said with equal glumness as they queued up. "He's one clever, amoral son of a bitch." "He hasn't got away with it, yet," Moss said, not too hopefully. "I don't know," Tay said, and sighed. "I just don't know."

When court reconvened the attorney general stood for several moments simply looking quietly and intently at the defendant. Presently, though his eyes never left Regard's and his defiant and sardonic look never changed, this began to get to Earle Holgren. He shifted in his chair, put one arm up on the back of it, thoughtfully felt his beard with his other hand, began to look more and more sullen and angry. Finally he spat out:

"*Yes?*"

"Are you questioning me?" Regard said softly. "It's really my job to question you, you know. I thought that was what you wanted—you've offered yourself here, when you didn't have to."

"Get on with it, then," Earle said angrily. "Just get on with it."

"Oh, we've got plenty of time," Regard said lazily; and then, since Judge Williams also appeared to be getting a little restive, he dropped it and became serious.

"Your name is Earle William Holgren, otherwise known as—?"

"A lot of things," Earle replied with an insolent grin, quite himself again now that battle had been joined. "I think you probably have them all written down there."

"Oh, I do," Regard said. "I just wanted to see if you could remember them. As you remember all the back roads and wood paths of South Carolina. You have, in fact, known South Carolina since the age of ten, have you not, since your parents purchased a small estate near Pomeroy Station? You are entirely familiar with the area, aren't you, Earle?"

"I came here as a boy, yes," Earle said; and added in a tone that brought an uneasy stirring in the audience, "And if you want to address me, my name is *Mr*. Holgren."

And he lolled back, amicably insolent, his younger-Santa Claus resemblance quite pronounced this afternoon. Only the eyes were alert, shrewd, always hooded, always moving, darting here and there to sweep his opponents' faces from under the bushy salt-and-pepper brows.

"What were you doing with this exhibit," Regard inquired, pointing to the detonator, "when Mr. Boomer Johnson saw you?"

"*Mr*. Boomer *Johnson?*" Earle echoed, amused. "That *is* playing for the down-home vote, isn't it, Mr. Stinnet?"

"Just answer the question, please," Regard said patiently.

"I collect them," Earle said. "I love funny things."

"Go right ahead and hang yourself, *Mr*. Holgren," Regard suggested with an amicability of his own. "I don't care if you want to give me smart-aleck answers. It only antagonizes the jury more. Please continue."

"I found it in the woods," Earle snapped, suddenly scowling.

"You didn't bring it with you."

"No, I found it, I said!"

"After you had already put it there on a previous occasion?"

"Your honor—" Debbie began, but her client shot her an impatient look and she subsided.

"I've told you I found it," he said, more quietly. "Did *Mr*. Boomer *Johnson* see me put it there on a previous occasion? Did anybody? I don't recall any testimony."

"There is none," Regard agreed calmly. "I just wanted to see what kind of lies"—Debbie moved, Judge Williams frowned—"what kind of testimony you would give about it. We are to take it, then, that you just happened to find it there, and that when Mr. Johnson saw you, you were just fondling it, as it were?"

"And myself, too," Earle reminded with a cheerful grin. "Don't forget that part of his testimony. Pretty racy stuff. No, Mr. Attorney General, I wasn't doing anything with it. I just found it and examined it, that's all. And then Mr. Johnson took a leak and things began to get lively down by the plant and he left to go down and check on his friends Willie and Tad Simpson, and there the record stops. Right?"

"There the record stops," Regard agreed again, "until Mr. Johnson saw you return with the murdered woman and the murdered child."

"They weren't murdered then!" Earle shot out and there was sudden tension in the audience. Regard nodded.

"But soon to be, Mr. Holgren," he said calmly, "soon to be. According to Mr. Johnson's testimony they disappeared in your company; and when they were found a couple of hours later, they were dead."

"So. Obviously somebody killed them, I'd say."

Jury and audience tensed suddenly.

"My point exactly," Regard said.

Earle frowned thoughtfully.

"I wonder who it could have been? Who would do such a dreadful thing?"

"Whoever used the detonator and blew up Pomeroy Station, killed Sarah Pomeroy and destroyed Jane Barbour's life, I'd say," Regard replied. "Any guesses, Mr. Holgren?"

"In a court of law?" Earle responded dryly. "Oh, come now, Mr. Stinnet! Incidentally," he said, smiling at the jury, "before everybody gets all excited thinking I've slipped and forgotten something—Mr. Johnson did *not* see me return with, and I quote Mr. Stinnet, 'the murdered woman and child,' because I wasn't *with,* quote, 'the murdered woman and child.' Mr. Johnson did not, in fact, see me at all because I wasn't there, as I have already testified. Mr. Johnson tells a mighty good story, I'd say: some kids *do* have a great imagination. I didn't see him because I wasn't there and he didn't see me because I wasn't there. I was only there much later when I was trying to find the murderer, or murderers, and got beaten up and had my constitutional rights violated and—"

"All right, Mr. Holgren," Regard said patiently, his accent becoming broader, drawl accentuated, "I think we've all heard that sad tale and we all get the picture. I'm not defendin' it, we'll accept it, that's the way it was. I will say you're very clever, though, to lead us on about that woman and child. You almost had us believin' for a minute that you'd slipped up on somethin' real important. You *are* clever, you know?" he added admiringly. "Real clever."

"I try," Earle said with some complacency.

"And very successfully, too," Regard said in the same admiring tone. "But you've always been a brilliant fellow, haven't you? Very bright in school. I mean, very quick and perceptive, quite superior to most minds you meet. Isn't that a fair statement?"

"I'm adequate," Earle admitted, complacency increased. "That's about as far as I'd go, Mr. Stinnet." He chuckled suddenly. "I'm modest."

"That, too," Regard agreed. "But seriously, now, isn't it true that you graduated with highest honors from Phillips Exeter, that you graduated magna cum laude and Phi Beta Kappa from Harvard—"

"I knew we'd get to Harvard."

"Nothin' wrong with graduating from Harvard," Regard said. He too chuckled, a cozy, companionable sound. "Though I like to think Duke is better. Anyway, it's quite somethin' to graduate magna cum laude and Phi Beta Kappa, from wherever it is. Not very many do that. And not very many are as shrewd, as quick and sophisticated about things as you are, or I miss my guess."

"I manage," Earle agreed, more complacently still.

"I know you do," Regard said, his voice becoming still more slow and drawly, seeming almost to reach out physically and pat Earle admiringly on the back. "And I suppose that's why you decided to waive your Fifth Amendment rights and testify here today, because you figure that you can do a better job, probably, than even that smart young lady you have defendin' you, there. From what I've heard so far, I guess maybe you were right."

"I think so," Earle agreed. "Nothing personal, you understand," he added with a comfortable smile at Debbie, who did not return it. "And after all, Mr. Stinnet," he went on in a patronizing way, "the Fifth, you know, protects a witness against self-incrimination. And how could I be incriminated? I haven't done anything to be incriminated for. There's no proof of anything on the record. You haven't got a case. Why should I be afraid to testify and tell the truth in my own behalf?"

"Not a reason in the world, Mr. Holgren," Regard said in the same comfortable, just-pals voice, casually taking from his pocket the crumpled sheet of paper he had been hoarding against this moment. "That appears to be a very smart decision by a very smart man. Why is it, then," he asked in a casual, almost absentminded way, "that a mind like yours could produce such almighty infantile, stupid, idiotic, mindless, worthless blither as this? What do you call it, a man-i-fes-to, is that it? Shucks! It just 'pears to be a big pile o' childish drivel to me."

And he made as if to read it to himself, an amused, contemptuous expression on his face, while on the stand the defendant reacted exactly as he had hoped he would.

His face literally turned white with shock and rage for a moment, his whole body swung into action. His arm came off the back of his chair in a flash, he stopped caressing his beard, he crouched forward tensed like a wound-up spring and actually looked as though he were about to leap from his seat and land bodily on his interrogator. His lips drew back in a feral grin that drew a gasp from the audience, his eyes got a strange fanatic light that really scared the perceptive lady on the jury and quite a few others. He uttered an odd hissing sound of indrawn and explosively expelled breath. He was suddenly, and apparently uncontrollably, a fearsome sight.

"Did a man as smart as you actually write this piece of crap?" Regard shouted, stepping close and waving the paper in his face. "This ridiculous—infantile—stupid—baby-shit piece of *crap?* This poor—*pathetic—*"

"God damn you," Earle yelled, lunging at it and almost toppling from his seat as Regard stepped nimbly back, "give it to me! God damn you, *give it to me!*"

"*No—*" Debbie started to shout, then crushed a hand against her mouth to stifle it as somewhere in some distant dream, through the courtroom uproar and the great excited roar outside, she heard Perlie Williams furiously using his gavel.

Too late, she thought. Too late.

"Oh, it *is* yours, Mr. Holgren!" Regard cried triumphantly. "Then why is it, Mr. Holgren"—and his voice dropped to a low and menacing note, each word coming like a sledgehammer—"why is it that it was found in the well with that murdered woman and child, *Mr.* Holgren? You just tell me about *that,* Mr. Holgren, because *we want to know.* The whole wide world is listening, *Mr.* Holgren, so"—his voice abruptly became very soft and very savage—"you just go right ahead and tell us all about it, *Mr.* Holgren, *if you please.*"

There ensued an obvious and mighty struggle in the figure on the stand. Willpower triumphed, slowly at first, then more rapidly, as he sat, still crouched, chest heaving, breath coming in agonizing gasps. Presently, probably not more than a minute, though it seemed much longer to them all, he was in control of himself again. From somewhere, amazingly, he managed to extricate an almost normal expression and the beginnings of a contemptuous, sardonic smile.

"I swear," the jury lady who had thought him cute whispered excitedly to the lady who had thought him ominous, "it's just like that werewolf movie I seen last month! I swear it is!" The skeptical lady snorted. "Don't be so melodramatic," she advised in a satisfied voice. "We've just heard him hang himself. That's good enough for me. Who needs werewolves?"

But the defendant was not prepared to admit this yet.

"Mr. Stinnet," he said, voice still shaking with emotion but a controlled and coldly angry emotion now, "you just prove that, please. You just prove that piece of crap belongs to me. You just prove—"

"Mr. Holgren," Regard interrupted softly, "you just told us that." And started to add, "Have you forgotten?" and caught himself just in time. There would be the only defense that might hold up—temporary insanity. And he had almost given it away free. He shuddered inside . . . then his eyes met Debbie's for the briefest of seconds, and although he glanced immediately away, he knew that she had perceived it too. God *damn,* he told himself. God damn, God damn, God *damn.*

But his voice was as calm and matter-of-fact as though he were discussing the time of day when he concluded quietly:

"Your honor, I have no further questions of this witness."

"Your honor," Debbie said in a clear and level tone, "I do. First of all, does counsel intend to place this piece of paper in the record as an exhibit, or does he just wish to use it to try to entrap the witness? How do we know there is anything on it? We haven't seen it."

"A point well taken," Perlie said. "Mr. Stinnet?"

"Your honor," Regard said, "*I* have no intent to conceal anything. Certainly I offer it as an exhibit." He stepped over and handed it to Debbie. She scanned it without expression and handed it back.

"We have no objection, your honor, although, as your honor can see, it is so stained as to be illegible."

"The stains are blood, however," Regard said, and there was a little gasp from the audience. "And it was found in the pocket of the dead woman, who apparently secreted it there in some last, pathetic, futile attempt to implicate the man who was about to murder her."

"Your *honor,*" Debbie said sharply, while through her client's mind there shot the thought *The damned bitch tricked me,* followed instantly by *But it's illegible, so what difference does it make?* His expression, shaken for a split second, instantly recaptured its rigidly controlled impassivity.

"I am quite content to let the record stand," Regard said. "I will leave it to the jury to decide the import of the witness' violent reaction to this blood-soaked piece of paper."

"Your *honor,*" Debbie protested again and Perlie Williams nodded. "Objection sustained. Question your client, Miss Donnelson."

She made an instant decision to drop the issue of the paper, which she considered to be damaging enough, in its uncertainties, to Regard.

Her client, now excessively wary, showed no further inclination to flaunt his cleverness. He was, in fact, as Tay murmured to Moss, scared to death. "I hope to hell *to death*," Moss replied grimly. It was something not everyone perceived. Outwardly, particularly in the eye of the watching television camera, he seemed fully restored and back in complete command of himself and the situation. His counsel knew he was suffering a mortal wound. But she did her best.

"Mr. Holgren," she said, "have you ever been subject, as a child or later on, to sudden seizures of temper—to what might be called, quite accurately, blind rages?"

"Your honor," Regard began and she quickly amended, "to bouts of anger when you did not remember afterward what happened?"

Earle gave her a quick look and took the cue.

"How did you know that?" he asked, amazed. "Yes, I have."

"Times when you had *no recollection whatsoever* of what had occurred?"

He nodded solemnly.

"Right."

"And so could not be really considered responsible for what occurred during those periods?"

"Your honor—" Regard said, but Perlie Williams gave him a look that said, *Drop it*.

"For instance," she said, "do you remember Mr. Stinnet a few moments ago producing a piece of paper which he displayed to you?"

Her client looked puzzled, thought hard for a moment, finally shook his head.

"No . . ." he said uncertainly. "I—don't—think so."

"Do you have any recollection at all of what counsel for the state, the judge and myself, have just been discussing?"

Earle shook his head, still puzzled.

"No," he said in a wondering tone. "Not the slightest."

"*God*," Moss whispered. "Give him enough rope," Tay replied. "He's not fooling anybody."

But it was obvious the jury, even including the skeptical lady, was shaken. Debbie pressed on.

"You have absolutely no recollection of being shown a piece of paper, and of an outburst of apparent temper in which you demanded that it be given to you?"

"Absolutely none whatsoever."

"Now, Mr. Holgren," she said, "let me take you back three weeks to the dedication of the atomic energy plant at Pomeroy Station. What is the last thing you remember on that occasion?"

Earle frowned, very thoughtfully.

"I remember," he said slowly, "that I was absolutely enraged by the dedication itself, by the fact of this extremely dangerous and frightening installation being formally opened and about to be put into operation; that I thought of all the hundreds of thousands, maybe millions, of people, who could be hurt or even killed if something should go wrong; and I was frustrated and even more enraged by the thought that there was absolutely nothing that could be done to save these innocent thousands. Maybe millions."

"Did you remember thinking of anything you might do?"

"No," he said firmly. "I do not. I just remember a sudden blinding flash—of rage," he added quickly, and the audience subsided—"at my own helplessness. And then I don't remember anything more until I was scrambling up there onto the hill to look for whoever had attacked the plant. I had—come to, I guess you might call it—a couple of minutes before, to hear somebody shouting, 'They've bombed the plant and hurt Sarah Pomeroy!' and that just got me out of that crowd down there like a shot and up on the hill to do what I could to help. I mean, I'm against atomic power, but Moss Pomeroy's a great man whom I've always admired, and when I heard that"—he shook his head. "Well, that just did it. I just *moved,* that's all. You couldn't have stopped me."

"*Why, you absolute son of a bitch,*" Moss whispered savagely. Tay put a quick hand on his arm. Moss shook it off: Tay clamped it back. "You be quiet, buddy," he whispered with equal force. "You just calm down and let him hang himself." Moss gave him a glare as though he didn't recognize him for a second, but subsided.

"So you don't remember anything at all between the time of the start of the dedication and the time you found yourself on the hill?"

"I'm trying, counsel," Earle said with a helpless little smile, "but I swear to God I don't remember one single thing."

"Thank you, Mr. Holgren," Debbie said calmly. "I think that will be all."

"Do you wish to re-cross-examine, Mr. Stinnet?" Judge Williams inquired.

Regard looked at Earle, earnestly and helpfully smiling now, and shook his head with a disgusted expression.

"Your honor," he said, "I think it is obvious to the jury and indeed to the whole country as represented by the media and the pool television camera that if I spent another hour with this individual I would only get more fairy tales, and since our purpose here is to ascertain the truth—"

"Your honor," Debbie said in the same calm tone, "I object."

"—since our purpose here," Regard repeated firmly, "is to ascertain the truth and not fairy tales—"

"Counsel," Judge Williams said.

"—I of course have no further questions of this witness. As far as I am concerned, he is excused."

"And as far as I am concerned, your honor," Debbie said.

"Guards," Perlie Williams said, "you may remove the witness . . . Miss Donnelson," he said after Earle, still smiling in an interested, attentive and cooperative fashion, had been taken out, accompanied by the distant savage roaring of the crowd outside, "is it your intention to change your client's plea to not guilty by reason of insanity? Is that what this is all about?"

Debbie looked up from her papers, which she had begun to go through with a studied indifference. She looked quite surprised.

"Oh no, your honor. We are quite content to stand on a plea of not guilty. After all, while opposing counsel may arrange dramatic stunts for television, no facts have been adduced on the record to prove that he is."

"Very well," Judge Williams said. "Does counsel wish to make any summary statement?"

"No again, your honor," she said calmly. "The facts speak for themselves and they do not convict my client."

"That is for the jury to decide, Miss Donnelson," Judge Williams said, "as you very well know. Mr. Stinnet, do you wish to make a summation?"

The audience became abruptly quiet and for several moments Regard stared thoughtfully off into space. Then his eyes came back to the audience.

"Mrs. Holgren and Mr. Holgren—Boomer—Justice Barbour—Justice Pomeroy—no, I think I shall refrain from a summation also. I too believe the facts speak for themselves, and I happen to believe that they do convict the defendant. He is as savage and ruthless, though better educated and more intelligent, as any murdering street thug. He is one of them. He is part of the deep sickness of this country that Justice NOW! is trying to correct. But as your honor says, that is something for the jury to decide.

"The state awaits its verdict with every confidence that it will both convict and, pursuant to the laws of South Carolina and in the fashion set forth therein, approve and order a sentence of death."

There was a ripple of applause, a distant shout of agreement. Perlie Williams turned to the jury.

"Members of the jury," he said, "I too shall refrain from indulging the sound of my own voice to give you any lengthy instructions. The matter is in your hands. We seem to be in a new era of American justice at the moment in which undue and unnecessary delays are increasingly unpopular with our fellow citizens, as well they should be.

"Accordingly you will begin your deliberations at nine A.M. tomorrow, and it is the court's hope that you may well and justly—and swiftly —bring forth your verdict."

Afterward Regard and Debbie held their press conferences and made their countering claims of victory. The two Justices, polite but grimfaced, refused all media comment and were whisked away together in the chauffeured limousine provided for them by the attorney general.

The jury was locked away for the night and the case of Earle Holgren moved on to the evening news, the headlines, the editorials, the columns and the bitterly held and strongly expressed opinions of his countrymen—toward the day, increasingly likely now, when it would reach the chambers of the Supreme Court of the United States.

The jury's first day of deliberations, Friday, lasted eight hours; the second, Saturday, seven and one-half; the third, Sunday, ten. At 7 P.M. Sunday the foreman called Perlie Williams and said, "Judge, I think we have a verdict."

"Congratulate everybody for me," he said, "and be ready for court at nine A.M. tomorrow."

For the last time in Columbia, the crowd was large, restless and near unruly as the defendant, his lawyer, his parents and the two Justices arrived. Boomer Johnson and his mother were not there. "We're goin' to get us as far away from that man as we can *git!*" she had declared when the bailiff asked if they wanted to stay for the finish. He couldn't say he blamed them. The defendant was a strange man and not only Boomer and his mother were made uncomfortable in his presence. The bailiff suspected a lot of people felt that way. Certainly he did.

For instance, look at the man now. Here he was, about to be sentenced, probably to death, and he appeared as insolent and jaunty as he had on the first day he entered court. His whole attitude coming in had been as contemptuous of the crowd as ever, which had of course provoked the crowd to even greater imprecations than usual on this, their last chance to let him know what they thought of him. Now he was giving the audience his usual long, slow, contemptuous look, sweeping his parents and the Justices with a swift, impersonal glance that appeared entirely at ease, entirely unconcerned. Only the very slightest tremor in his hands and a spasmodic and apparently involuntary flickering of the eyelids betrayed the fact that Earle Holgren was human after all, and probably, as Justice Pomeroy had observed before, scared to death. And to death, as he told Justice Barbour once again, Moss continued to hope it would be.

In the media section Henrietta-Maude, her statehouse colleagues and all the national luminaries of print, tube and airwave waited in tense anticipation. Their gossip and guessing abruptly ceased as Judge Williams entered, took his seat and stared for a moment, calm as ever, around the room.

"Will the foreman please rise and approach the bench?" he requested. A great tension occurred. Earle Holgren continued to lounge in his chair but the lounging suddenly was no longer fluid: it seemed he lounged in ice. At his side Debbie became rigid, across the way Regard was very still. The two Justices leaned forward, the elder Holgrens seemed to shrink back. The media, immobile and momentarily silent, made no movement, uttered no sound. The jury was somber. With an air of determined dignity their handsome old black foreman approached the bench. The clerk of the court cleared his throat portentously and intoned,

"Have you considered the case of Earle William Holgren and the charges entered here against him?"

The foreman bowed.

"We have."

"And have you reached a verdict or verdicts upon these charges?"

"We have."

He handed the clerk a copy of the indictment. The clerk took it solemnly and turned it over. On the back were written the verdicts on each of the four counts, each verdict signed by all twelve jurors. Solemnly the clerk read them out.

"On the first count of the indictment, that the defendant did murder Sarah Ann Pomeroy"—the clerk paused dramatically for a second and the tension if anything grew greater—"the unanimous verdict of the jury is—Guilty."

There was an explosive release of pent-up breath and held-in emotion, from outside a long, triumphant, savage shout. There was a short, sharp cry from Mrs. Holgren, instantly smothered. Earle did not move. None of the principals moved. The clerk cleared his throat and continued gravely,

"On the second count of the indictment, that the defendant did attempt to murder the Honorable Stanley Mossiter Pomeroy, the verdict of the jury is—Not Guilty."

Again the rush of release and emotion, again no movement from audience or principals. The only response came from Moss, the slightest whisper that only Tay could hear, reluctant but honest—"Fair enough."

"On the third count of the indictment, that the defendant did murder Janet Martinson and unidentified male child, the unanimous verdict of the jury is—Guilty."

Again the release of emotion in the room, the savage triumph outside. The reporters were poised now, ready to leap and run.

"On the fourth count of the indictment, that defendant did wantonly and deliberately destroy sundry property at the atomic energy plant at Pomeroy Station, South Carolina, the unanimous verdict of the jury is—Guilty."

There was a last explosion of sound, a mad scramble as members of the media tumbled over one another to get out and away to the telephone. Judge Williams patiently watched a tide he could not stem and when it ebbed, rapped his gavel and restored order.

"Pursuant to Section 16-3-20 of the South Carolina Code," he said, "when a defendant is convicted of the crime of murder, a separate sentencing procedure to determine whether he shall be sentenced to death or to life imprisonment must be held. The statute states that this proceeding shall be conducted by the trial judge before the trial jury 'as soon as practicable after the lapse of twenty-four hours unless waived by the defendant. This waiving of the jury proceeding must be agreed to by the state. If defendant wishes to waive and if the state agrees, hearing on the sentencing is to be held in open court.'

"Does the defendant wish to waive this right of jury proceeding?"

"Your honor—" Debbie and Regard began together. Regard deferred.

"The defendant definitely does not want to waive this proceeding," Debbie said.

"And the state will not agree to his doing so," Regard said promptly. "So that, I would say, is that."

"The jury proceeding will not be waived. There remains the phrase 'as soon as practicable after the lapse of twenty-four hours' from time of conviction. It is now nine twenty-three A.M. I do not know the mood of the jury"—he looked at them and they all nodded vigorously—"but the mood of the court and I am sure the mood of the state, and certainly of the country, is that there is nothing to be gained by further delay. In this second phase of sentencing, both sides may present arguments concerning the death penalty if they so desire.

"The jury, the defendant and opposing counsel will reconvene here at nine-thirty A.M. tomorrow. When a decision has been reached the court will reopen to the public to hear it announced.

"Again, I am empowered to instruct the jury. My only admonition, given the popular mind, is that speed is of the essence.

"The court stands adjourned until further call."

Next day, the jury met for three hours. Debbie spoke for ten minutes against the death penalty, Regard for fifteen for it. Earle, though he had the right under the statute to speak in his own defense, said nothing. When Regard concluded Debbie spoke for approximately two minutes in rebuttal. Regard waived reply and everyone looked expectantly at the judge.

"Any further arguments?"

"None, your honor."

"Mr. Holgren? This is your last chance to address the jury."

"What good would that do?" Earle inquired in a spiteful tone.

"Probably none," Perlie agreed crisply. "Nonetheless, you have the right."

Earle gave him a contemptuous look.

"I waive it."

"Miss Donnelson and Mr. Stinnet," Perlie said matter-of-factly, "you and I will retire. Guards, remove the prisoner. Ladies and gentlemen of the jury, the room is yours for as long as you need it."

An hour later the foreman sent a messenger to his chambers. Five minutes after that he announced that court would reconvene at 4 P.M. to hear the jury's instructions on the sentencing of the Pomeroy Station bomber.

For the last time the room filled to capacity. For the last time Debbie and Regard took their places, the defendant's eyes made their slow chilling tour of the audience. The elder Holgrens and the two Justices were there. The pool television camera moved from face to face. Judge Williams turned to the jury as politely as though they were meeting at some social function and in a quiet voice inquired,

"Does the jury have any recommendations to the court concerning the sentence or sentences to be administered to this defendant?"

The foreman stood up.

"Yes, your honor."

"Please step forward and state them," Perlie said and settled back, chin on hand, eyes intent upon the foreman's face. Tension rose once more to almost unbearable limits.

"On the fourth count of the indictment of which we deem the defendant guilty, namely the destruction of private property at Pomeroy Station atomic plant, the jury is of the unanimous opinion that the court should impose such sentence as is fitting for a crime of this nature."

"Thank you," Perlie Williams said. "Are there other recommendations?"

"Yes, your honor," the foreman said gravely. "Two more." And the tension rose further.

"On the third count of the indictment of which we deem the defendant guilty, namely the murder of Janet Martinson and unidentified male child, it is the recommendation of the jury that the defendant be imprisoned for the rest of his natural life.

"On the first count of the indictment of which we deem the defendant guilty, namely the murder of Sarah Ann Pomeroy"—all other sound seemed to vanish from the world as the foreman paused, straightened his shoulders, took a deep breath and began to read carefully from a piece of paper that shook noticeably in his heavy-veined old hand—"as directed by the law of the state of South Carolina, which requires that such a recommendation be made by the jury and that it be unanimous, it *is* the unanimous recommendation of the jury that Earle William Holgren be put to death in the manner prescribed by said law, namely electrocution in the facility provided for that purpose in the Central Correctional Institution in Columbia, South Carolina."

Again the release of breath and emotion, the long wild yell from outside, Mrs. Holgren's anguished quick-stifled cry, the press rushing out to phone bulletins, the television cameras darting back and forth across the principals; and Judge Williams leaning forward, face somber, to say quietly,

"The court thanks the jury for its recommendations, unanimous and therefore binding upon the court according to the law of South Carolina. The court is required by law, after receiving such recommendation and prior to delivering sentence, to find as an affirmative fact that the death penalty is warranted under the evidence of the case and is not a result of prejudice, passion, or any other arbitrary factor."

He paused and the room became absolutely still.

"The court," he said, still very quietly, "does so find as an affirmative fact and accordingly sentences Earle William Holgren to be put to death in the manner prescribed by law."

Again the wild surge of emotion, the yells, Mrs. Holgren's cry, the tumbling tumult of the media.

And his final words, delivered in the same grave tone:

"Said sentence to be carried out at a time set by the court if, in accordance with the law of South Carolina, the supreme court of the state of South Carolina, after being automatically appealed to, upholds the verdict."

Once more, for the last time, cameras swung wildly over the faces of the principals:

Earle again sitting as in stone, a strange bitter smirk on his face—Debbie, drained of color, taut and tense—a slow smile spreading across the face of the attorney general—and, an image that would remain with their countrymen because it was photographed from the screen and spread across a thousand newspapers and magazines—the face of Justice Pomeroy, nakedly and savagely triumphant.

And the face of Justice Barbour, sad, brooding, deeply troubled and uncertain.

Automatically, as with any death sentence under South Carolina law, the case was appealed to the state supreme court. Its five members, who normally might have met at a casual lawyers' pace in a week or two, took cognizance of the fact that Justice NOW! organized an enormous DEATH TO HOLGREN rally that night at the statehouse, and of the further fact that as if on command an enormous tide of telegrams and telephone calls immediately began to flood in from all over the state and nation demanding action.

Prudently the justices came to the unanimous conclusion that they would meet at ten the next morning.

Promptly on the hour they convened in closed session and Regard and Debbie presented their arguments. Both were brief, both repetitive. By eleven-fifteen the justices were able to dismiss them and go into conference. Again cognizant of the public mood—"Action, action, no more pettifogging and delays!" as the Columbia *State* put it in a front-page editorial—they made no attempt to fake any lengthy discussion. For appearance's sake they did delay their verdict for twenty-four hours but there was never any doubt in their minds or anyone else's what it would be:

STATE COURT REJECTS APPEAL! HOLGREN DIES!

And next morning, Thursday, true to his desire and pledge to "move things along," but at the same time allowing in his usual evenhanded way for a fair time for appeal:

WILLIAMS SETS HOLGREN DEATH TWO WEEKS FROM TODAY!

And two hours later, following Debbie's hastily called press conference:

HOLGREN TO APPEAL TO HIGH COURT. COUNSEL WILL "SEEK JUSTICE IN THE HOME OF JUSTICE."

And the case of Earle Holgren moved on inexorably toward the moment, now only hours away, when it would finally reach the Supreme Court of the United States and there be decided by earnest but fallible human beings forced to contend, on their own doorstep at last, with the sickness of an age.

FOUR

1

It was hot in Washington and getting hotter. The capital's suffocating summer, starting tentatively in May, now lay heavy, humid and implacable on the city. It was the time of stifling days and breathless nights; the time when, after sundown, the fortunate scurried swiftly in air-conditioned cars from air-conditioned homes to air-conditioned gathering places and scurried nervously back; when the less fortunate— the frustrated, the empty, the wandering—took to the streets and shadows; when the sinister underbelly of the beautiful troubled city came to life; when many, particularly the young, roamed aimless, hopeless and murderous under softly overarching trees through silent alleyways along eyeless ruined houses, and when even on brightly lighted thoroughfares in what the media described as "fashionable [i.e., white] Northwest," their frightened fellow citizens thought long and hard before venturing even the shortest of distances on foot.

It was a time that could be used to justify the existence and activities of Justice NOW! and cause it to flourish. And it was a time for those who tended the law to look to their task with deep unease and grave foreboding.

Tay did not know, returning to Washington at such a time, whether the reserves of character he felt he possessed were sufficient to carry him safely through the testing that now lay immediately ahead. Whatever the outcome he knew he could not emerge unscathed. But like his sister and his brethren, he knew that he now had no choice.

Given the national mood that surrounded the case of Earle Holgren, he had not been surprised by the jury's verdicts nor had he been surprised by the prompt acquiescence of the supreme court of South Carolina. The reaction in the media centers of the north had been predictable: the customary expected voices in both Washington and New York had denounced the "national hysteria" which they blamed for "the obvious railroading of a defendant who has not yet been clearly shown in law to be guilty of the crimes with which he is charged." The mood elsewhere was much more grim and much more vindictive.

The national consensus, he knew, had its elements of hysteria, but there was something deeper underlying, a cold, determined decision to "stop this thing," as the attorney general of South Carolina put it, "once and for all." The reference to "this thing" was vague but it was clearly understood by his countrymen. It meant all that complex and conglomeration of crime, whether born of economic uncertainty, emotional instability, dope, greed, envy, terrorism, thrill-seeking or whatever, that plagued the nation. Earle Holgren had become the symbol and it was undoubtedly true that his being so had done much to inspire the swift and absolute nature of his sentences despite the circumstantial nature of the evidence. But Tay knew, as everyone directly involved in the matter knew, that he was beyond question guilty, and that Justice NOW! in its insistence upon absolute justice had perhaps given a decisive assist to the cause of a decent, law-abiding, safe society.

But there, of course, was the problem for him and his colleagues, he thought as he stared moodily out into the garden of his house in Georgetown and dabbled halfheartedly with the scrambled eggs, bacon, toast and coffee that Julia had put before him. They were not very good today. Her usual skills had deserted her in the face of the family tragedy. She could scarcely mention Janie's name without retreating to the kitchen in floods of tears and her meal did not do much to distract him from the gloomy thoughts that accompanied him in his echoing, deserted dining room. "Law-abiding" was the crux of it. How could you be law-abiding if the laws were stretched, no matter how just the cause?

Mary was still in Columbia: it was not yet possible to move their sleeping child. He had returned late last night to be in time for today's regular Friday conference of the Court. It was the last conference of the term. Adjournment was expected sometime in the next two weeks. So far Debbie had not moved to file her appeal but he suspected it would not be long delayed. It was now a matter of strategy. He was as certain as he was of anything that he would be the key to it.

He sighed, a heavy sound, as the kitchen door opened and Julia appeared with a coffeepot.

"Yes, I know," she said gently, putting a worn hand on his shoulder with the familiarity of ten years in the household. "It's hard, Mr. Barbour, it really is. Why don't you have some more coffee and see if that won't make it better?"

"Thanks, Julia," he said, pushing aside the half-eaten eggs. "Maybe it will. I mustn't burden you with it, in any case."

"We'll all be burdened with it, Mr. Barbour," she said sadly, pouring the coffee, "for a long, long time to come."

He smiled wanly.

"I expect so. But you have troubles of your own, Julia. How's Bubba?"

"That boy is no good, Mr. Barbour," she said vehemently, distracted, as he had hoped, by the mention of her oldest. "He just is *no good.* I try to keep him in line but it doesn't help. He's out there in the streets all the time runnin' wild, and there just isn't much I can do about it, workin' and all. They try to make him stay in school, he won't stay. They warn him and warn him, but he won't pay attention. Sometime soon," she said somberly, "he's goin' to do somethin' real bad, Mr. Barbour. Real bad. I'm scared for him but I don't know what I can do. I just don't. He turned eighteen yesterday. He's as big as an ox already. And strong. And stubborn. He's the hardest-headed child I know. And I have to work, I can't do anythin' for him but give him clothes and put food on the table. That's not enough, with children runnin' wild like they do nowadays."

"Do you suppose he'd like some work with me on the Court?" he inquired with a sudden inspiration. The long-playing saga of Bubba going downhill had become increasingly insistent in the past three years and he had often wished there were some way to help. Now that Bubba was old enough, perhaps he could. Every Justice had a messenger, by custom black, and if that didn't suit, there were other modest but respectable jobs around the Court that might be filled by a Bubba determined to make something of himself—if Bubba were. Julia brightened noticeably.

"Mr. Barbour," she said, "that would be wonderful!"

"I'll speak to the Chief Justice," he promised, distracted for the moment from his own desperate troubles, pleased to think that he might be able to do something constructive for a fellow being. There was also a certain substitution in his mind, in a curious, bittersweet way: he couldn't do anything more for his own child. Perhaps he could help Julia's.

"Mr. Barbour," she said solemnly, "I can't thank you enough for that. I just can't. Bubba will thank you too when he realizes what a chance you're givin' him. The Court: they must be nice people on that Court if they're all like you."

"Yes," he agreed, "they're quite nice. As much as I have been able to see of them so far," he added with a rueful little smile.

"I know," she said. "It's awful. Just plain awful. What're you-all goin' to do to that murderer that killed Miss Sarah and hurt Miss Janie, Mr. Barbour? I hope," she said with a matter-of-factness that he knew expressed the feelings of the majority of their countrymen, "that you're goin' to kill him dead."

"Well, Julia," he said carefully, "I know a lot of people feel that way—"

"Everybody I know," she said in the same matter-of-fact tone. "Don't you, Mr. Barbour? Doesn't seem to be much doubt he did it, is there?"

"Perhaps not," he said, still carefully, "but the law requires that certain safeguards be observed when someone is brought to trial—"

"Safeguards!" she said with a sniff. "He didn't worry much about safeguards for Miss Sarah and Miss Janie, did he?"

"No," he agreed somberly. "Apparently he did not."

"Well, then."

"I know, Julia, but the law isn't that simple. The law says—"

"Who cares what the law *says!*" she demanded with sudden bitterness. "He killed Miss Sarah and hurt Miss Janie so bad she's like never to recover. What does the law do for *them?*"

"That's right," he echoed bleakly. "What does the law do for them? That's what I have to reconcile, Julia. That's what all of us on the Court have to reconcile. It isn't going to be easy."

"You'll do it," she assured him confidently. "Just remember what's right and you'll do it, Mr. Barbour. You can't miss, long as you do what's right."

"And that is?"

"Kill him dead," she repeated calmly. "There's nothin' else, in a case like his."

And there, he thought as he got in the car ten minutes later and started through the heavy morning traffic to the Hill, you have it, stated in the simplest possible terms: do what's right and kill him dead. Too bad, he reflected wryly, that the law is not that clear-cut. By rights it should be, but unhappily for many it is not.

The beautiful building shone softly under a leaden sky, its glistening marble dulled by the rising heat. Sightseeing buses were already parked alongside, first groups waited impatiently for the public tours to begin. Law clerks, secretaries, reporters moved quickly up the sweeping steps and through the great bronze doors. EQUAL JUSTICE UNDER LAW stared down, seemingly as commanding as ever. Within, nine troubled people began to try to come to terms with Earle Holgren and the challenge he represented to the noble sentiment in whose spirit they strove to live and adjudicate.

"Conference will be in order," Duncan Elphinstone suggested in a somewhat perfunctory tone. Wally Flyte, seeking to inject a lighter tone, remarked, "Well, Dunc, it isn't as though we're being riotous."

There was a murmur of amusement down the table, a stirring of coffee cups, a straightening of papers. Clement Wallenberg cleared his throat.

"We really don't have much left to do today, do we?"

"No," the Chief said. "Everything is pretty well set for the next couple of weeks—and then adjournment on the fourteenth—and that's it."

"Except for one thing," Hughie Demsted pointed out, "symbolized by the presence here of our two brethren who have been absent."

They exchanged looks with Moss and Tay. A little silence fell. Finally Rupert Hemmelsford spoke.

"Tell us about him, gentlemen. If you can stand to."

Tay started to speak, hesitated, deferred to Moss. Moss stared moodily down at the table and appeared to be, for several moments, far away. At last he looked up.

"He is a murderous, unrepentant, irredeemable psychotic," he said evenly, "who is guilty as charged and deserves exactly what the jury asked for him. That does not mean, however," he added quietly, "that there are not points of law that we will have to meet . . . if, that is, a majority here wishes to confirm the verdict."

"Which is something of an assumption," Wally Flyte observed softly. And again a silence fell.

"Tay?" the Chief Justice asked finally. He came out of a brown study to find them all looking at him save Moss, who had retreated again into his contemplation of the tabletop. He started to speak—paused—took a deep breath—started over.

"I agree with Moss," he said in the same dispassionate tone Moss had adopted. "He is a worthless human being, not excused by any social deprivations or insurmountable psychological obstacles—a genuine embodiment of evil—a *really evil human being,* of which there are some in this world. He is one. There are, as Moss says, issues of law. But the basic facts of the matter are entirely clear. At least in my mind."

"Of course," Clem Wallenberg said, "with all respects to the two of you, you are not the most objective of witnesses."

"No," Moss said sharply, all trace of his old bantering relationship with his colleagues gone, perhaps forever, "we are not. But you asked us, Justice. And we have told you. Do you expect us to apologize for it?"

"I expect you to be judicial," Justice Wallenberg snapped and Moss rounded on him so quickly that Hughie Demsted on his left instinctively interposed himself for a second before relaxing.

"Look," Moss said, voice low and shaking with anger. "You be just as superior and smug as you like, Clem, but it isn't going to bring my girl back—and it isn't going to make his girl well again—and it isn't going to do anything but make you out to be the ass you are. Now I'm telling you—"

But this was too much for the Chief, who slapped the table, hard, with his hand and reared back in his chair.

"If you don't mind, Justice," he said to Moss, voice like ice, shock of white hair quivering, *"we will conduct ourselves like gentlemen in the chambers of this Court.* Or I shall terminate this conference and adjourn the Court for the summer right now, if need be . . . Moss and Tay: no one here lacks any human sympathy for what you two have been through. I do not think, Clem, that it does any good to be—as Moss quite accurately said—smug and superior. It is a wonder our brethren are able to be here at all, so soon after this tragedy; objectivity may not yet be entirely possible. But I would hope that in due course, as we discuss this matter more deeply, a reasonable amount of it may be re-established in all of us. I would remind the Court that that is what we are here for."

Justice Wallenberg scowled and did not answer. Justice Hemmelsford leaned forward.

"I am wondering, Chief," he said quietly, "whether perhaps it isn't asking too much of our brethren, who have suffered these terrible tragedies, to participate in this matter. Shouldn't they perhaps consider removing themselves from consideration of the issue? If objectivity is not possible—and perhaps it isn't really for any of us, but at least more for us than it is for them, I am sure—then would not withdrawal be the most judicious act?"

"I've expressed my opinion on this to both of them," the Chief said promptly. "Perhaps others would care to, so that they can at least have the benefit of some consensus here—if there is one. You're clear enough, Rupe. Wally?"

One by one they did so: Wally remarking that their withdrawal would not mean "any shame or disgrace or loss of public interest. On the contrary, I think it might be seen by many as the most honest and honorable thing to do" . . . Clem saying flatly that while he sympathized with their emotional situation, "they ought to disqualify themselves. Don't expect they will, but they ought to" . . . Ray Ullstein remarking thoughtfully that he wouldn't presume to give advice but "will simply make the assumption that has to be made about this Court by everyone if we are to survive as the powerful institution we are—and that is that each of us makes his individual judgment as honestly and honorably as he can on the basis of the facts as he sees them. Therefore I know that whatever Moss and Tay decide, it will be their best decision and their most honest one" . . . May McIntosh expressing similar sentiments and concluding that "whatever you decide, my friends, it will be the most honest and honorable decision you can make. Good luck" . . . Hughie Demsted, saying he could sympathize as a fellow parent with their conflict between regard for the law and desire for vengeance and concluding that "Nobody can tell you what to do and nobody really has a right to judge what you do unless he sits in the same place. All I can do is join in wishing you luck."

Moss gave them a small, wry salute: Tay said, "Thanks, all." Silence again descended on the Conference Room.

"Well," The Elph observed finally, "that wasn't much help to you, was it, boys? Or to us either, except as it indicates arguments to come."

"Chief," Wally Flyte said, leaning forward, "let me think out loud for a minute and see what you all think of an idea that's just struck me. I said, more or less flippantly several weeks ago before this all began, that perhaps we could delay the issue of violence and the public reaction to it for a while in the hope that it might cool down—that perhaps we could sidestep it, at least temporarily. Now, one way or another, this appeal is obviously coming here. The young lady has announced her intention. If we are in session, there's going to be a great demand, which I think under these circumstances we would be well advised to respond to, for us to grant certiorari, hear the case and rule on the merits. I'm not so sure we want to be in that position in the present climate of public opinion. A majority of us might not vote in such a way as to satisfy the general clamor."

He paused and the Chief Justice said, "So?"

"So," Justice Flyte said, warming to his argument with all the zest of an old Senate hand working out a deal, "what we do is, we quit this coming Monday. Everybody is expecting us to quit two weeks from now. We fool 'em. We just go home. Any opinions still pending can be filed with, and released by, the Clerk.

"The appeal then becomes an appeal to a single Justice for stay of execution to permit review. If Moss does not disqualify himself, it comes to him as chief judge of the Fourth Judicial Circuit. Supposing for the sake of argument that he grants a stay of execution and refers it to the full Court, the presumption might be that we would have to come back into full session and review the case. But, again, nobody can make us. The Clerk can simply poll us by long-distance phone or telegram, we vote a flat yes or no, and we don't have to go into the merits or get ourselves entangled in the national controversy."

"Very clever, Wally," Justice McIntosh said, "but—"

"Just a minute, now," he said, wagging a cautionary hand. "Hear me out. If, on the other hand, Moss denies the appeal, the young lady is then free to Justice-shop for one more who she feels might give her the best deal. This, unless I miss my bet, and if he does not disqualify himself, is the other party at immediate interest"—he smiled to forestall any sarcastic implication—"that famed liberal and newest member, our Brother Barbour."

Tay nodded ruefully.

"Right," Wally said, as they followed him intently. "So then it comes to Tay as the second and final choice. Not wanting to pass on the merits either, but also not wanting to take full responsibility for denying stay, as I imagine none of us really would, he either grants stay himself and refers it to the full Court or, as permitted by the rules of the Court, makes no ruling, steps out of the way and passes it directly to the full Court. Again, we can follow the procedure I've outlined and simply vote it up or down long-distance, ignoring the merits and giving no explanation.

"Or, if a majority decides to grant stay and grant a hearing we can put it off until the fall term begins in October. By which time, hopefully, a lot of this Justice NOW! clamor will have died down and we can consider in a much less heated atmosphere what should be done with the defendant and with the underlying issue, which is of course the death penalty."

He paused and beamed around the table like some white-haired old pixie who has just pulled the plum out of the pudding. "How does that grab you?"

"It grabs me fairly well," the Chief said slowly, "except that I don't entirely agree with your assumption that the country will let us get away with it."

"And I don't agree," Clem Wallenberg said, "that the death penalty is the only issue. There are questions about the conduct of the trial that I intend to go into. I'm not so much against the idea of a delay, though, if we can manage it. I agree it might assure a less hectic climate to work in."

"I disagree with that, I'm afraid," Hughie Demsted objected. "I think this country is on the rampage. I don't think Justice NOW! is going to slow down over the summer just to suit us. Summer is when the crime rate rises, you know, not when it goes quietly away. I think the pressure's going to keep right on growing and it's going to be heavy—heavier than it's probably ever been, thanks to the obvious intention of Justice NOW! and its organizers to keep it that way. So I'm with you, Chief. I'm dubious, too."

"I thought we were agreed," Ray Ullstein said quietly, "that sooner or later we would have to meet the issue head-on. Why, then, try to be clever and dodge it now? It will only be waiting for us in an even more oppressive atmosphere in the fall. I say face it now."

"Perhaps we should have a show of hands, Chief," Mary-Hannah suggested. Clem said, "I second that."

"Very well," the Chief agreed. "If there's no further discussion, those in favor of adjournment—" Justices Flyte, Wallenberg, Hemmelsford and—to his colleagues' surprise—Barbour raised their hands. "Those opposed . . . Four to four again!" he exclaimed with mock dismay. Then his expression sobered.

"I am very doubtful about this," he said slowly, "so I think I will reserve my vote for a while. I can see good arguments either way. I'd like to assess public opinion a little more closely, I think. Perhaps if we wait until after the weekend—"

"Stop equivocating, Dunc," Clem Wallenberg said tartly. "Nothing's going to happen over the weekend."

But that, as they now found out, was his mistake.

There was a hurried rap on the door leading to the Chief's office. Tay, occupying the junior Justice's role at conferences of being the general errand boy and go-fer, stood up and went to answer. The thin prim face, large glasses and high-piled gray hair of the Chief's longtime secretary peeked around the door's edge.

"Yes, Elizabeth," he said with what for him was a rare impatience, "what is it?"

"I'm sorry to interrupt everybody, Chief," she said, obviously agitated, "but he just refuses to wait. He says he has to talk to you *right now.* I've hung up on him *four times* but he's called me right back each time. I—I just don't know what to do. It's so—so—*un-Court-like!*"

"That's a good word, Elizabeth," the Chief said with a chuckle, good nature quickly restored. "Relax, it's all right. We forgive you. Who is it?"

"A Mr. Stinnet," she said. "From South Carolina."

There was a stir around the table and the Chief frowned. Obviously this kind of interruption was definitely not all right, in his view.

"Oh?" he said coldly. "What does he want?"

"He demands to talk to you," she said. And repeated in a forlorn voice, *"Right now."*

"I'll go choke him off," Moss offered, rising. But The Elph held up his hand.

"No," he said thoughtfully. "Considering everything, maybe we'd better listen. Put it on this phone in here, Elizabeth, and also put it on the amplifier."

"Yes, sir," she said, adding as she went hurriedly out, "He's so *persistent.*"

"He is that," Tay murmured. In a moment there was a click and the cheerful voice of the attorney general of South Carolina boomed into the room.

"Mr. Chief Justice, sir? Is that you, Mr. Chief Justice?"

"It is," the Chief said. "Why are you interrupting our conference, Mr. Stinnet?"

"Oh, now!" Regard said, sounding genuinely contrite. "I *am* sorry, Mr. Chief Justice, sir. I really didn't know." An eager innocence came into his voice. "Would you like me to call you back in about ten minutes?"

In spite of himself The Elph smiled. Regard remarked in the same earnest tone, "I could, you know, sir. I really could."

"No," the Chief said. "You've got me now, you'd better hang on. Though I must say I hope you have a good reason."

"This is pretty important, Mr. Chief Justice," Regard said fervently. "It really is!"

"I've no doubt of it," the Chief said. "Why don't you tell me about it? Incidentally, this is the last place on earth where I want a caller to be overheard without his knowledge. You should know that I have you on an amplifier and the entire Court is listening in."

"Well, sir," Regard said, sounding genuinely pleased, "I am delighted with the honor, Mr. Chief Justice and you-all, de-lighted. Hello, Moss! And you, too, Tay—Justice Barbour!"

"I'm the only one who can answer," The Elph said, smiling at his colleagues, who were in various stages of amusement as Regard burbled on; except for Moss and Tay, who knew very well that he didn't burble without a purpose.

"They listen," the Chief went on. "I answer. Fire away, Mr. Stinnet. You have the rare privilege of addressing the Court-in-chambers in complete privacy. Assuming you're not bugging me at the other end, that is."

"Oh, *no,* sir!" Regard exclaimed, shocked. "I wouldn't do that, sir, no way! You just ask Moss, he knows me. He'll tell you. Isn't that right, Moss?"

Moss nodded.

"I think it's probably all right, Chief. He's not a fool."

"No, indeed," the Chief said with his hand over the mouthpiece. "That I gathered some time ago . . . Very well, Mr. Stinnet, you're well vouched for by your fellow Carolinian. What is this earth-shaking business, now?"

"Shucks, Chief," Regard said, "it isn't all that earth-shakin', really. It's just a rally I'm plannin' to hold that I want to invite you-all to attend. As my honored guests."

"And those of Justice NOW!?" Duncan Elphinstone inquired. Delighted laughter burst from the amplifier.

"You *know* us!" Regard exclaimed. "You've *heard* of us! We're not *strangers* to you!"

"The word has gotten around, Mr. Stinnet."

"Then you'll come!" Regard declared in a pleased voice.

"Now, Mr. Stinnet. Suppose you just tell us about it and we'll think about that later. I take it this *is* a rally of Justice NOW!?"

"Oh, yes, sir," Regard said earnestly. "I wouldn't think of speakin' anywhere else. From now on, all my speeches are under the auspices of Justice NOW! After all, it's my baby, isn't it?"

"Indeed it apparently is," the Chief agreed. "I suppose you're to be congratulated on its phenomenal growth."

"It's plumb out of hand," Regard confided. "Even with computers, we're fast losin' count. We must be pushin' ten million law-abidin', indignant, active and *aggressive* people, Mr. Chief Justice, who are out to get *anybody* who stands in the way of *true justice* in this great land of ours!"

"You're a mighty force, all right," the Chief agreed dryly, while down the table his sister and brethren exchanged glances. "When is this rally going to take place?"

"This Sunday. High noon."

"Very dramatic. In Columbia?"

"No, sir," Regard said proudly. "Right there in the capital of the United States, sir. We have permission. Right there in Washington, D.C. Right there on the Mall, where so many foul, worthless, flag-desecratin', democracy-betrayin', liberty-killin' pieces of human junk have had their demonstrations in the past. For once, Mr. Chief Justice and you-all, we're goin' to have a rally on the Mall that stands for America! For democracy! For true democracy—the *people's* democracy! For justice! For Justice NOW! I've invited all the state attorneys general and most of 'em have accepted. Plus thousands and thousands of good folks from all over this land. It *is* goin' to be a mighty thing, Mr. Chief Justice. A mighty thing! And I called you *first thing* because it's only fittin', it seems to me, that our great Supreme Court of the United States, the great defender and bulwark of our liberties, should be there. Particularly since two of your members, two good friends of mine, have just been the victims of the terrible sick violence in this country—which is all the more reason why you-all should be there. To show that you're all standin' together in the battle against crime and violence—to prove to the country that you're *really* seekin' equal justice under law—and *swift* justice too. Sure and swift and *final*. Isn't that right, Mr. Chief Justice? Sir?"

"I think it should be apparent to the country where we stand by looking at our votes, Mr. Stinnet. Is there really doubt that we are opposed to crime and violence? We are opposed to any kind of crime, even in the name of ending crime. We are opposed to any kind of violence, even in the name of ending violence."

"*All* of you?" Regard shot back and again there was a silence.

"Mr. Stinnet," the Chief said finally, "I have not consulted my colleagues on this, but I think I can speak for all of them when I say that the Court as an institution will not attend your rally." He glanced down the table and they all nodded acquiescence. "Now, as to whether individual members might wish—"

The negative head-shakes were unanimous.

"I have just been informed by my colleagues," Duncan Elphinstone said with satisfaction, "that none of them will attend on an individual basis, either, Mr. Stinnet. But thank you for thinking of us."

"Well," Regard said, "I am disappointed, Mr. Chief Justice. I really am. Another thing, too, you know—if you-all were there, might be it would prevent anybody from sayin' anything nasty about you. Not that anybody will and really mean it," he added hastily, "but sometimes folks get carried away in the heat of the moment. Sometimes when people start speechifyin' you can't be entirely sure what they're goin' to come out with."

"We'll just have to take that chance, Mr. Stinnet."

"Don't say I didn't warn you, Chief," Regard said in a cheerfully patronizing tone. "Don't say you-all didn't have fair warnin'."

"We'll take our chances," The Elph said calmly. "I would suggest, however, that if you persist in the methods you are using in trying to achieve justice you may quite inevitably run head-on into the methods we will *approve* to achieve it."

"Oh, sure, Mr. Chief Justice," Regard said quickly. "But the way things are goin' in the country, you know, it may not *matter* what you approve or don't approve."

"Good-bye, Mr. Stinnet," the Chief said crisply, and hung up.

"Why, that impudent little squirt!" Rupert Hemmelsford said into the silence that followed. "He's got a hell of a nerve! Somebody ought to tan his hide."

The Chief sighed.

"Even though he may be right?" he inquired softly; and the silence returned and deepened as they all stared moodily at one another and then, responding to some instinctive, unanimous impulse, turned to look at John Marshall, gazing down at them with a calm impassive challenge in his dark, intelligent eyes.

"If you like," the Chief said, "we can gather here on Sunday to watch the proceedings on television. I'll have them set up the big screen and prepare some sandwiches and coffee." He smiled without much humor. "We'll have a hang-the-Supreme-Court-in-effigy party."

"It's been done before," Justice Flyte pointed out with a jaunty bravado.

"Not in a long, long time," Justice Ullstein said quietly. "And never before quite like this."

To the triumphant blarings of Justice NOW! over the car radio—news of the rally seemed to be everywhere, aided by paid invitations to attend which were repeated every half hour, apparently nationwide—Tay drove slowly home to Georgetown late in the sweltering afternoon. The conference had broken for lunch, resumed for three more hours while they went over the last few remaining cases and items of Court housekeeping that had to be disposed of before adjournment. They were reminded that work would be flowing to them, as it always did, all summer long during their so-called "vacation."

"It never stops," Ray Ullstein said. "Never. So be prepared, Tay."

"I am," he said, ". . . I think. Although, do you know, I haven't even had time to fully organize my staff yet. I've got interviews with two more would-be law clerks for later this afternoon before I go home. I've really got to get going."

"Nobody's complaining," the Chief pointed out with a kindly smile. "You've had reason."

They fell silent again, contemplating the reason and the point to which it had brought them at this moment: about to be condemned at a public rally in Washington, D.C.; about to be put under enormous popular pressure to rule for vengeance, whatever the law; about to be faced with a testing from which, whatever they might decide, none of them or the institution they served, revered, and fiercely defended, could emerge unscathed. This, among other things, Earle Holgren had accomplished. Earle's thinking had probably not gone this far in the beginning, Tay reflected, but he knew he must be pleased with their discomfiture now.

Later he found time to hire his prospective law clerks, told them that he expected them to report for work in one week's time. They could not say enough in praise of him, their great hopes for his work on the Court and their deep admiration, amounting almost to reverence, for his "disinterested, compassionate and unblemished liberalism," as the young woman put it.

If you only knew what I hold in my heart for Earle Holgren, he thought, *and how hard I am going to have to fight myself to keep from giving in to it—and how easy it would be to give in to it—you might not be so fulsome.*

But he congratulated them, praised them, encouraged them and sent them on their way, floating on air. Why trouble them with all that? They would realize it soon enough.

As he drove out of the garage onto Second Street he thought for a moment of turning right at the corner and heading for Stanton Square. Some delicacy, some uncertainty—some cowardice, really, he told himself, despising himself for it—held him back. He had not spoken to Cathy since he had told her of Janie's permanent disability. Their talk, hasty, gloom-ridden, inadequate, had depressed him even further, loving and sympathetic and trying to be helpful though she was.

"It isn't the same as having you here," he had protested bitterly and she had sighed.

"Or you here. But soon, I hope."

"Soon," he had promised fervently. "Oh yes, soon."

And now here he was, five blocks away and too timorous to venture. But she might not be home—the kids might be there—the neighbors would notice—and it wouldn't be dark until almost 9 P.M.

Still too light for that sort of thing, he told himself with a sudden self-contempt. Too bright. Too honest.

Well, he promised himself grimly as he turned left and started down the Hill toward the Potomac and the quickest route home to Georgetown, that would change before much longer. Mary might not want to let him go, though as he saw it she had finally destroyed all reason for staying; but he would go, nonetheless. He would have to wait a decent interval after Janie came home, a decent interval after he had settled in on the Court. Possibly it would not be until a year from now, until the end of the next term that would start the first Monday in October: but it would happen. Somewhere in the last few days, amid all the terrible tension of Janie's deterioration, the trial, the steadily growing power of Justice NOW! and its triumphal advance upon the last citadel of the law, the conviction had come to rest in his mind and heart and could not be shaken now. His first marriage was over—he was committed to the second—and there would be no turning back.

The conviction was not shaken, only strengthened every time he talked to her, as it was now when he reached home and Julia told him with a sniff, "Mrs. Barbour wants you to call, Mr. Justice. She's soundin' upset."

"*Really* upset, do you think, Julia?" he asked; and they exchanged a glance to which Julia did not reply but only sniffed again.

Dutifully—his duty to his daughter, now, not his wife—he went to his study, shut the door and put through a person-to-person call to Richland Memorial Hospital. He had only been away from it twenty-four hours but already all that seemed like another world.

"Yes?" he asked sharply when Mary came on the line. "What is it?"

"*I want Janie home* and they won't let her come home!" she said on a rising note. "I asked them to meet with me this morning and see if we couldn't speed it up and all they would say was, 'Mrs. Barbour, we'll do our best. Mrs. Barbour, we'll do our best.' Their best! She's improving steadily, physically all the signs are good, she's obviously able to be moved. But they just keep repeating, 'In about two weeks. In about two weeks.' They're like little white-suited wind-up mechanical toys. I don't think they've ever intended to deviate from their timetable one little bit."

"Probably not," he said. "But that's their job."

"You won't call and insist, then," she said in a flat tone of voice.

"No," he said, drawing a deep breath. "I won't call and insist. Actually, it may be better this way—allow more time to make arrangements here."

"And cause less inconvenience to you while you make up your mind about the precious rights of your daughter's destroyer! That's one of the main reasons I want her there—so you'll be reminded every single second while you make your great decision. Will you vote to reverse his conviction, Tay? It would probably suit your concept of yourself."

"I don't know," he said, fighting down the savage answer that almost escaped his lips. "I just don't know, yet."

"You've said that before so many times, it's getting to sound rehearsed. You'd know if you were any kind of a father." And suddenly she said what he had been expecting to hear her say for many days now. "Are you seeing someone else, Tay? Is that why you don't want us to come home right away?"

"Mary—" he said, in spite of anticipation taken aback, fighting for a few seconds to gather his defenses.

"Well, is it? It seems to me it's a simple question, needing only a simple answer. Yes or no, Tay? You pride yourself on honesty. Tell me!"

"Mary—" he began again, and stopped. *In for a dime, in for a dollar,* he thought crazily, and said what he had to say in a voice he forced to stay level and calm. "Mary, I don't know what has put this nonsense into your head."

"It isn't true, then," she remarked in a voice heavy with disbelief.

"It isn't true," he said, his voice becoming stronger as the lie became more practiced. Yet it was impossible to be honest now. It couldn't be done over the telephone. He would have to tell her, but in what he considered her present unstable condition it had to be done face to face, otherwise there was no telling what wild things she might do.

Or so he justified himself to himself, hating the lie even as he spoke it. Even Taylor Barbour was human after all, he thought bitterly. And maybe Mary was right in her other accusation too. Maybe he didn't want the "inconvenience" of his daughter's presence while he was deciding what he would soon have to decide.

"You're very silent, Tay," Mary noted dryly. "Doesn't the lie sit well?"

"It isn't a lie!" he burst out angrily; and as abruptly forced his voice back to its normal calm level. "I shan't dignify this with any further discussion. I'm sorry the doctors won't release Janie as soon as you want them to, but they know best. You'll just have to reconcile yourself to being patient."

"I won't leave my daughter," she promised grimly. "My duty is here with her."

"Yes," he said, too emotionally drained to argue that one further. "All right, then. Take care and I'll call you in a couple of days."

"Only if it's convenient, Tay," she said, and hung up before he could frame an answer.

He sat for a long time staring out into the thick green trees, the lush azaleas and camellias that bordered the small lawn off the den. As in so many southern gardens there was a feeling of the jungle looming, ready to spring, ready to swallow up: gorgeous but overwhelming. Julia fed him cold cuts and salad; he returned to the den. Later he heard her turn off the air-conditioning and open the upstairs windows to the gradually receding but still breathless heat, as Mary had taught her to do. Soon she would leave to catch the bus across town to her home in Northeast. She lived only a couple of blocks from Stanton Square, a little farther beyond Cathy where the neighborhoods became mixed, then gave way to solid color. Another reason for caution there, although he suspected she would not censure, report, or be anything but happy for him if she knew. A momentary sadness for Mary touched his heart: she defeated the world, and so the world defeated her. It was a draw but she, he knew, suffered the more.

Presently, in the silent house, the phone rang. He knew who it would be before he picked it up. Julia was off for the weekend, the time until the gathering of the Court to watch the rally at noon Sunday stretched ahead with relatively little to do. He had no excuse and wanted none. Five minutes later, doubts and hesitations finally resolved by the sound of her voice, he was in the car and on his way.

"How did you know I was home?" he asked after the door had been shut, the world banished, and they had kissed for a long time with a desperate hunger.

"I checked," she said with a smile. "I'm a good reporter. It just took one phone call to your chambers. Very difficult."

"I was going to call you earlier, but—"

"You lost your nerve."

"Yes," he admitted with an almost boyish grin. "How did you know *that?*"

"I know you pretty well, I think," she said, serious for a moment, taking his face in her hands, studying it carefully.

"Where are the kids?"

"Gone with friends for the weekend," she said, and smiled again. "Otherwise, *I* wouldn't have had the nerve. Or the opportunity."

"Thank God you did."

"Yes," she said gravely.

He took her hand and led her, in a dream from which neither wished to waken, up the narrow stairs.

So Friday night passed into Saturday, and Saturday, in time, into Sunday, sometimes tempestuously, sometimes gently, always as in a dream.

At 5 A.M. on Sunday morning he dressed fully for the first time in thirty-three hours, kissed her softly as she lay smiling up at him from the bed and went quietly out. First light flushed the east, the tall thick trees stirred gently in the little breeze that would soon give way to heat. Down the green-tunneled streets with their charming old high-stooped houses and lovely old worn-brick sidewalks no cars or people passed. He saw no one, thought no one saw him, as he walked swiftly to his car, started it up and drove quickly away.

The city lay before him stately and white, just touched with pink, as he started down the Hill. Already, he noted as he passed the Mall, the first few faithful were beginning to gather for the rally. He shivered and drove on; reached home, let himself in, set the alarm for 11 A.M. and fell instantly, heavily, happily to sleep.

2

By eleven-twenty, when the Chief became the first to arrive at the Court, the crowd along the Mall was so dense that traffic had to be diverted to Independence Avenue on the south side. He decided when he came down along the river to Lincoln Memorial that he would exercise his prerogative and use jammed-up Constitution Avenue on the north. He had decided to eschew the limousine and drive Birdie's small black Buick, to be less conspicuous for just such a contingency. He was determined to test the mood of things for himself.

When he came to the first police line and identified himself quietly to the officers, one white, one black, who stood guard, he was waved through with a somewhat dubious "Well, Mr. Chief Justice, if you really want to take a chance—"

"I do," he said calmly and drove on. Behind him he heard one of them communicating to his next colleague down the avenue. "Legal Eagle"—which was the way the Secret Service and the police presently referred to him, somewhat frivolously, he thought—"is coming through. Watch for him and extend all assistance required. Pass it on." "Roger," he heard the recipient respond, and to himself said firmly, "Nonsense!"

Nonetheless he could not deny that he was glad to have the protection, for the crowd was intimidating both in temper and in size. He estimated that close to half a million people were converging on a large flag-draped platform set up midway between the Lincoln and Washington memorials. It took all his concentration to get safely through without hitting any of the individuals and family groups, many complete

with children on down to babes in arms, who surged along the avenue
toward their goal, many walking in the street. There were many state
and city banners, some from as far away as Hawaii and Alaska. The
crowd seemed to be mostly young, with a fairly even mix of black and
white. Apparently Regard had struck a universal note: the nation's
blacks, victimized too often by their own people, seemed to be as anxious as anyone for Justice NOW! The capital's population, not always
easy with one another, seemed united and aggressive on this.

"Aggressive," in fact, was the word he felt he might apply more aptly
than any other. Excited—united—and aggressive. Expressions were fes-
tive to some degree but basically they were determined. There was an
underlying grimness, a single-minded purposefulness that seemed to em-
anate with an almost physical impact from all who trudged along. He
sensed that these were people with a mission; and like Tay, he too shivered at the thought of what they might be whipped into by sufficiently
impassioned oratory playing on their fears and their disgust.

He could only hope, he thought uneasily as he came to the last police
line and was passed on through with a relieved smile and a "Glad you
made it, Chief!" that Regard Stinnet would be as restrained and responsible as he had been when confronted by the potential lynch mob in
South Carolina. Of course there had been a different motivation then:
Regard wanted to convict his culprit by law, not rope, and he was
working in the shadow of the Court and the appeal he was convinced
would be forthcoming. Now the matter was about to come to the Court
and he might have a different motivation that would cause him to
inflame rather than restrain. Now was the time to put all possible public
pressure on the Court; and while The Elph did not feel that he and his
sister and brethren would actually be hanged from a sour-apple tree if
they did not perform as Justice NOW! desired, still he felt it best to take
some precautions.

The minute he reached his chambers he put in a call for both the
chief of the metropolitan police and the head of the Secret Service.
Both, he was told, were at the rally, but would call back as soon as they
could be reached. Within fifteen minutes both did. They agreed immediately that the Court might need additional protection, at least today and
possibly for the next few days, and promised to send extra men as soon
as the rally concluded.

Feeling somewhat more secure, he called the kitchen and ordered up
refreshments. Then he went into the empty Conference Room, snapped
on the lights, closed the blinds, checked the big-screen television set that
had been installed yesterday. Then he took his place at the head of the

table and sat for a few quiet moments awaiting his colleagues. Inevitably his eyes strayed to those of John Marshall, calmly dominating the room. As always the man who was referred to around the Court without other identification as 'the Great Chief Justice" returned his usual strong and challenging look.

"You expect so much of us, Chief," Duncan Elphinstone said aloud. Then he smiled and added with a wry grimness, "Well, we're going to do our duty. It ain't gonna be easy, but we're going to do it."

The Great Chief Justice, impassive as ever, made no comment. He simply *expected.* And with very few lapses over the years, his heirs had lived up to his expectations—in large measure simply because they were *his.*

Such was the strength of an individual whose physical being had been dead almost 150 years. The personality, Duncan Elphinstone knew, would never die as long as there existed a United States and a Supreme Court to house it.

There was a resounding rat-tat-a-tat-tat-*tat!-tat!* on the oaken doors; they popped open and Justice Flyte bounced in with a cheerful "Hi, Dunc!" He was followed in the next few moments, more sedately, by Justices Wallenberg and Demsted, Ullstein and Hemmelsford, Pomeroy and McIntosh. Soon after, five minutes before noon, Justice Barbour came in. He looked, the Chief thought, somewhat tired; but, then, he had many problems.

"May," the Chief said, "my brethren—welcome to Regard Stinnet's Justice Hour. Draw near, because the Hour is about to begin. Oyez, oyez, *oyez* and you betcha "

It turned out they had all done exactly as he had on the way up, which provoked a general wry amusement around the table.

"I wonder what those D.C. cops made of us," Rupert Hemmelsford remarked, "this parade of Supreme Court Justices coming through one by one. 'Oops, who's that? Another Justice, by God! Is there no end to them?' "

"I wanted to get the feel of it," Hughie Demsted said, "as obviously we all did. I wouldn't say it was exactly encouraging to law and order. At least, as we see them."

"They're not unruly," Mary-Hannah observed.

"Yet," Clem Wallenberg amended.

"The potential's there, all right," Wally Flyte said. "Most of them looked pretty grim to me.'

"But orderly," Ray Ullstein said.

"So far," Tay remarked.

"They won't get too far out of hand," Moss predicted. "Don't underestimate Regard. He's a smart boy and he knows all the potentials. He'll keep it down to a reasonable level."

"If he can," Clem Wallenberg growled. "I'm pretty damned skeptical of these smart fellows who like to play with crowds. Crowds don't stay hitched all that easy."

"It will be a great temptation to demagogue," the Chief agreed. "We'll just have to see how it goes."

For the first few minutes it went very calmly. Despite the hardworking efforts of the television crews roaming the crowd to incite something violent for their viewers' edification, nobody took the bait. After the sixth or eighth attempt to encourage a provocative answer to a provocative question and stir up a little excitement, one of the roving reporters was told flatly by a black father of three, on-camera before the reporter had a chance to turn it away, "Look, man, why don't you fuck off? We're here to establish law and order and get us some justice, not get into a riot for you two-bit sensationalizing bastards." This seemed to put an abrupt and lasting damper on the television crews, because their coverage of the crowd instantly stopped and the smooth voices of their anchormen took over, describing the weather (stifling), the throng (orderly) and the platform (filled with dignitaries and the bustle of great events about to begin).

There was also a lengthy and basically pro-Holgren recapitulation of the case. Then the cameras swung to the flag-draped platform and the temporary chairman said what everyone was waiting to hear:

"Ladies and gentlemen, Regard Stinnet!"

In the quiet, high-ceilinged room with its beautiful wood paneling, its antique furniture and oriental rugs, its portraits of early Justices, its book-filled shelves and air of infinite civility and civilization, there was a sudden sharp increase of tension among his nine most important and most concerned listeners. As if he realized this he looked straight into the camera for a second and a quick, triumphant smile flashed across his face.

"That's for us," Wally Flyte said as the smile was immediately succeeded by a grave and earnest expression.

"Yes," Rupert Hemmelsford agreed. "A little private message not to get too big for our britches."

"Which he isn't," Hughie Demsted remarked.

"In South Carolina we just call that being friendly," Moss said with a bit of his old flippancy, and Clement Wallenberg said sharply, "Whose side are you on, anyway?"

"I don't know yet," Moss replied with equal sharpness. "Suppose we have the courtesy to hear him out first."

"Gentlemen," The Elph said in a warning tone. "I can't hear. Subside, please."

Regard's head came up, his expression of gravity deepened, he began to speak in an intimate, almost conversational voice to the now silent crowd. Only the distant clacking of a couple of television helicopters broke the stillness that gripped the vast throng on the Mall.

"My fellow believers in American justice!" he began (no dropped "g's" or excessive drawl today. Regard was speaking to the world). There was a great roar of shouts and applause. "We are here today to make sure there *is* justice in America—that it is fair—that it is honest—that it is quick. We are here today to demand Justice NOW!"

Again the obedient roar responded.

"You see before you on this speakers' stand forty-three of the fifty state attorneys general of the United States. You see thirty governors. You see members of the United States Senate and the House of Representatives. You do not see—"

"Oh, oh," May McIntosh said. "Here we go."

"You do *not* see," Regard repeated, and his voice became suddenly heavier and more dramatic, "any of the nine members of the Supreme Court of the United States"—a wave of boos began to run through the crowd, starting simultaneously in many places and seeming to converge in one huge expression of disapproval just in front of the platform—"even though—even though, my friends"—and his voice rose suddenly to a near shout—"I called them personally two days ago and invited them to attend!"

The rolling wave of boos grew in volume and there was a quick cut to one of the cameramen in the crowd. This time he had found some cooperators. Directly in front of him a small group had turned to face down the Mall, its members shaking raised fists in the general direction of the Hill and the Court. Wally Flyte snorted sardonically and Clem Wallenberg said, "What crap!" in a loud voice.

"My friends," Regard said, raising his arms to quiet them. "My friends, I would not want you to take this refusal by the Court as anything personal to me or to you. But I think it does show a somewhat interesting disregard for the very evident desire in this country for a fundamental change in the way the laws are enforced and adjudicated. It does show that the Court may perhaps be a little remote from the real concerns of the nation at this moment. It does show a certain arrogance.

It does show, perhaps, that the law's ultimate guardians consider themselves to be above the law."

The boos grew still louder.

"This, my friends," he said earnestly, "is a disturbing development for America. It makes even more important and imperative *your* participation in the judicial process. It makes even more necessary and vital that you show *by your own actions* what you want our courts—*all* our courts—to do. Let there be no mistaking where you stand! Let there be no doubt what Justice NOW! demands! Let it be made clear to *all!*"

"And let us storm the Court!" Hughie commented dryly. "Yaaay!"

"My friends," Regard said, and now his mien was sober and judicious, "there will soon come before the Court a case which will be, in a sense, a litmus test of its willingness to respond fully to the great demand for real justice that is sweeping all across this troubled land of ours. That is the case of the convicted murderer, Earle Holgren, with which you are all familiar.

"Yes, my friends, Earle Holgren!" he repeated as the booing took on an uglier, personal note. "Bomber and murderer! Twice convicted by the courts of South Carolina, about to come up on appeal to the Supreme Court of the United States. *Earle Holgren!* The individual who symbolizes everything that is wrong with our criminal justice system today—the individual who has been sentenced to die and *who must die,* because to reverse his sentence or even to soften it would say to the whole world: There is no justice in America! Criminals are free to pillage and plunder and murder as they please in America! No one dares enforce the law in America! There *is* no law, there *is* no justice in America! There is only justice that is injustice—law that is mockery— and crime unchecked and uncontrollable, everywhere in America!"

He paused dramatically.

"Is *that* the kind of message America wants to send the world?"

Dutifully the great throng roared back:

"*No!*"

"Is *that* the message we want to send to our own decent, law-abiding, desperately frightened citizens?"

"*No!*"

"Is Earle Holgren to be the symbol of American justice, the emblem of American democracy?"

"*No!*"

"Should his appeal be denied by the Supreme Court of the United States?"

"YES!"

"Should Earle Holgren die?"

"YES—YES—*YES!*" roared the crowd, falling into a rhythm. "YES—YES—*YES!*"

"And should he die swiftly as ordered by the courts of South Carolina?"

"YES, YES, *YES!* YES, YES, *YES!* YES, YES, *YES!*"

"Then, my friends," he said, his voice suddenly dropping and theirs instantly hushed in response, "here is how it will be done . . .

"I hold here in my hand"—he took it from his coat pocket and brandished it high in the steamy heat—"an order signed by the Honorable James Perle Williams, judge of the Court of General Sessions of the State of South Carolina. It says, and I quote: 'Pursuant to request of the Attorney General of the State, and by virtue of the authority vested in me, it is hereby ordered that the execution of the convicted murderer, Earle William Holgren, be held on July 4 in the city of Columbia, South Carolina; that said execution be conducted in such a place and under such circumstances that all who wish may attend and bear witness to the swift and just carrying-out of the law; and that in order further to strengthen justice, reinforce the laws and serve as a warning to all who might wish to transgress against the law-abiding citizens of this country in any way, shape, manner or form hereafter—*and to protect the public's right to know under the First Amendment of the Constitution of the United States*—said execution shall be conducted in the presence of television cameras and shall be freely broadcast throughout the nation and the world by any and all who wish to do so.

" 'Given under my hand and seal on this twenty-third day of June in Columbia, South Carolina. Signed, James Perle Williams, Judge.' "

There was a wild triumphant shout, interrupted only when Regard once more raised his hand and waved for silence.

"I am further pleased to tell you," he said, "that I have been informed by many of my fellow attorneys general, led by my good friend the co-chairman of Justice NOW!, Ted Phillips of California, that they intend to ask their judges and legislators to adopt the same procedure in their states. Thus will justice be served throughout the land!"

And now the enormous crowd was wildly jubilant, the television anchormen were too stunned and too uncertain of what their networks' official position would be to do much but stutter, and in the Conference Room of the Supreme Court nine grave faces looked at one another in stunned surprise.

"Son of a bitch," Justice Wallenberg said softly at last. In a jail in Columbia, South Carolina, a stocky bearded figure, glued to a television set, mouth drawn back in a sardonic smile—because now he thought he had them—said, with different intonation, the same.

"The final triumph of our technological progress," Ray Ullstein remarked with a rare bitterness. "The crowning achievement of our age. The apogee of American civilization."

"And what, pray the Lord and John Marshall," Justice Flyte inquired of no one in particular, "are we going to do about *that* one?"

"My friends," Regard concluded in an earnestly thoughtful tone, "it is clear that you agree with this order of our good friend Judge Williams."

Again, more excited than ever, the chanted triple YES.

"We hope and expect that the great majority of our countrymen will also agree with it."

And yet again the triple YES!

"And we hope and expect that the Supreme Court of the United States will not dare to interfere with the people's sovereign will."

This time the response was overwhelming, an elemental cataract of sound that burst from the screen: "NO—NO—*NO!* NO—NO—*NO!* NO—NO—*NO!*"

"So let us make our wishes, and the wishes of America, known. Let us make very sure that the will of the people is carried out. Let us continue to agitate, to insist, to keep watch. Let us remain vigilant—let us stay on the job—let us never weary or slacken in this great crusade to give America Justice NOW!"

A last volcano of sound—a last panorama of the tumultuous throng, stretching into the far distance toward the Lincoln Memorial—a last picture of a triumphant Regard, surrounded by crowding, congratulatory dignitaries on the platform—and Tay stepped forward and turned off the set.

For several moments no one said anything. Then the Chief spoke in a thoughtful, analytical tone.

"He's very clever, very shrewd. He's not only put us on the spot and guaranteed that we'll probably have around-the-clock vigils up here until the matter is decided, but now he's enlisted the networks on his side—"

"Oh, surely not!" May McIntosh exclaimed, shocked.

"You wait and see," The Elph predicted. "You just wait. He and his friend Perlie have wrapped them in the First Amendment, which makes it respectable; and now the venality can begin. Who will make the first request for advertising time, I wonder? Mobil? Exxon? IBM? It will be the most prestigious show since 'Masterpiece Theatre'—more so, because this will be *real. Real* life. *Real* death . . . unless," he said, and his tone hardened, "we stop it . . . Moss"—his voice took on a hard-boiled practicality they did not often hear from their gentle leader, "I hate to stick you with this as Circuit Justice of the Fourth Circuit, but I think I'm going to cast that vote for early adjournment that I withheld on Friday and leave you alone to handle the appeal. I agree with Wally now—I think our best strategy is to get out of town and play for time in the hope that these inflamed passions will diminish a bit before we have to hand down a decision.

"I don't presume to tell you what to do, Moss, but I think it would be helpful if you could delay things a bit. A stay of two or three weeks—even one, if that's all you can manage conscientiously. Then when it comes to the full Court we can delay still further, using the excuse of the need for intensive study of a case so complex and issues so far-reaching—maybe a month or more. And by then things may be a little quieter and the decision a majority may vote for may be a little easier to get past Mr. Stinnet and his impatient millions . . . Does that make sense to the rest of you?"

"It does," Hughie Demsted said slowly, "except that you're making two fundamental assumptions, Chief, that may or may not be correct. One is that the majority may make a decision Stinnet won't like."

"And the other?"

"You're assuming that Moss is going to grant a stay," Hughie said, staring at their colleague. "Maybe he isn't. Maybe he's going to go for the Roman carnival. Right, Moss?"

But Moss only gave him a long, moody stare, face expressionless, and said nothing.

"Well," Duncan Elphinstone said finally, "in any case, I cast my vote for adjournment now." He smiled wryly and repeated, "Adjournment NOW! Has anybody changed, or does that make it five to four?"

No one spoke.

"Very well. Moss, it's up to you. For now."

And still Moss said nothing, and still no expression crossed his face; nor did he in any way indicate what he would do as they bade one another good-bye until tomorrow at 10 A.M., and went down from the Hill.

"You know what I think, Superstar?" her client said as Regard's triumphant face, the solemn reverent crowd and the last strains of "The Star-Spangled Banner" faded from the screen. "I think you'd better get your pretty little tail up there just as fast as you can and file that appeal before those lily-livered old ladies—of whom," he added scornfully, "I think there are nine, not one—let Yahoo scare them to death to the point where they can't give me a fair decision based on the law."

"I'm going this afternoon," she said with some asperity, "as you very well know. It's taken a little while to frame the appeal. I haven't been sitting around doing nothing!"

"Well, well," he said with a chuckle. "There's real spirit for you. I know you haven't. I just think we've got to *move,* now, that's all. Particularly when he's handed us the perfect issue on a platter. Kill me on TV, will they?" His face darkened. "He's a damned fool. He won't kill me anywhere, let alone on TV. All that'll do is give the Court one more excuse to strike down the death penalty and reverse the decision. Not that they'd need any, if they had an ounce of guts. But I suspect they haven't."

"I have more faith in them than you do," she said. "Your arrest was illegal, the trial was a farce, the evidence is all circumstantial, the verdict was obviously rendered under hysterical public pressure. They don't need the TV angle."

"They don't need it," he said, "but they're damned glad they have it. You wait and see. Some of them will hide behind it. It's convenient."

"What do you care, if it gets you off?" she inquired dryly. "I didn't know you had any principles about how it's done."

"I don't," he said with a cheerful grin. "I just want to see those bastards be honest with themselves and the country, that's all. They're supposed to uphold 'equal justice under law,' aren't they? O.K., let's see 'em do it—if they have the guts. Anyway"—he shrugged—"I'm home free."

"I'm glad you're sure of that. Maybe I shouldn't bother even going up there. Maybe I should just mail in the appeal with a stamped, self-addressed envelope."

"Don't be smart," he said with a sudden sharpness, eyes darkening again. "People get in trouble, being smart."

"Was that what happened to Janet?" she inquired like a flash, and though he made as if to grab her wrist she snatched it away and stood up, just as the guard looked in.

"Any trouble, miss?" he inquired.

"No more than usual," she said with a tight smile. "Thank you, guard. I'll call if I need you."

"I'd suggest you plain holler, miss," he said, giving Earle a contemptuous look. "With this one."

"Fuck you," Earle said calmly. Then he dismissed him and turned back to Debbie again. "Don't be smart," he said again, softly. "Just don't be smart. Who do you appeal to up there? The whole Court?"

"First to Pomeroy," she said, remaining on her feet, well away. "He's presiding judge of the Fourth Judicial Circuit, which includes South Carolina."

He made a grimace.

"If he rejects it, and I'm not so sure he will, then we go to whoever I think will help us the most. There are at least four liberal possibilities. I'll pick the one I think is likeliest to grant stay and turn it over to the full Court for review."

"Well, steer clear of your hero, Barbour. He strikes me as a wishy-washy pantywaist. And he's certainly no friend, either. Since he thinks I hurt his daughter."

"Which you didn't."

He gave her a bland, ironic look.

"Nobody's proved it."

"I'll choose whom I please," she said sharply, feeling the hairs rise on the back of her neck as in the presence of something alien, which she now felt beyond question he was. Any attraction she had felt initially was gone, she told herself. He was simply a legal problem now. "You needn't worry. It's my job to protect your interests. Though," she could not resist adding, more for her own reassurance than anything else, "God knows why."

"Because you love me, Superstar," he said sardonically. "It's one of the great romances of the age. But unless you get me out of this place," he added with a mock sigh, "I'm afraid we're just never going to be able to do anything about it. And that would be a pity, wouldn't it?"

"You're weird, you know that?" she said. "Really weird."

"Have a good flight, Superstar," he said, turning away with a hearty yawn he made no attempt to conceal. "Have a good flight and give 'em hell."

Quite absurdly considering what she had just so confidently concluded, she felt a sharp pang of dismay at his apparent indifference. Stop that, she told herself furiously, *stop that!* But she didn't seem to be able to; and realized with a sudden chilling certainty that he very probably knew it.

Next morning at ten she was waiting at the bar when the Court convened, having paid the filing fee and filed with the Clerk the forty copies of petition required by Court rules. (Regard had been present also, filing his response immediately, though under Court rules he had thirty days in which to do it. They did not speak.) Her strategy was to seek recognition of the Court and announce the filing in person—thereby, she hoped, winning substantial initial publicity from those among the media disposed to be friendly to her client.

Her excitement was intense, her heart thumping heavily, as she prepared to perform this irregular and likely to be censured act. But she was not to have the chance. Instead she was as taken aback as everyone when the Chief Justice, as soon as the Court was seated, looked down calmly upon an audience filled with the little flags and lapel shields of Justice NOW! and said quietly,

"It is the consensus of the Court that the Court's business for the term is sufficiently concluded so that an immediate adjournment is possible. Accordingly the Court stands adjourned until the fall term starting the first Monday in October."

There was a startled gasp from audience, media and Court officials but he gave it no time to grow. His gavel came down with a sharp, deci-

sive *thunk!,* he rose, his sister and brethren rose, they turned without
expression and disappeared. The red velvet curtains fell softly together
and that was that.

COURT QUITS IN FACE OF HOLGREN CASE! the headlines
said. JUSTICES DUCK IMMEDIATE RULING ON TV DEATH!
HIGH COURT SIDESTEPS "ROMAN HOLIDAY" ISSUE. POM-
EROY GETS FIRST CRACK AT DAUGHTER'S ALLEGED
KILLER.

"We cannot condemn too severely," the New York *Times'* editorial
said, "the transparent way in which the Supreme Court of the United
States has turned tail and run in the face of the major challenge to
human decency and constitutional safeguards posed by the proposed
'death by television' of Earle Holgren, the alleged South Carolina
bomber.

"This craven flight ill becomes the heirs of Chief Justice John Marshall and other illustrious jurors who have preceded present members
on the nation's highest bench."

And so agreed the Washington *Post,* the Washington *Inquirer,* the
Los Angeles *Times,* the Boston *Globe* and others holding the same
view.

But from the headquarters of Justice NOW! in Columbia came a
statement signed by Regard, Ted Phillips and forty of their fellow attorneys general, urging Moss to remain on the case and upholding the proposed televised execution of Earle Holgren as "a needed and salutary
warning to criminals who in recent years have terrified America's decent
citizens and run rampant through all our cities and neighborhoods."

And a hastily taken Gallup poll stated that 63 percent of their countrymen felt that both Moss and Tay should remain on the case; and that
74 percent approved of the television proposal.

In certain luxurious—and pragmatic—network offices in New York
and Hollywood the conviction was growing, with an outward show of
reluctance but an inward rapidity, that the First Amendment—"the people's right to know"—and possibly a certain amount of monetary profit
might, after all, go very logically together.

The crowd had begun to gather almost as soon as news of the Court's
adjournment came over tube and radio. After lunch it grew rapidly in

size. By 3 P.M. it surrounded the building on all sides, particularly heavy on the front steps, at the side entrance and at the garage entrance on Second Street. All the Justices but one had departed almost immediately, well aware that some sort of demonstration might occur. The extra District police assigned on Sunday were back on the job, and the Court police, usually called upon to do little more than chide tourists politely for trying to carry cameras into the chamber, stood nervous but determined at their posts. Law clerks and staffs had been dismissed for the day and had departed almost as soon as their bosses. The great bronze doors had been shut and locked in daytime for the first time in many years: no one, in fact, could remember when the last time had been. Reporters and television camera crews circulated through the crowd picking up random quotes and clips for the evening news. The signs and banners of Justice NOW! were everywhere in the suffocatingly hot afternoon. The sky was a lowering gray. One of the District's frequent summer thunderstorms threatened to let fly at any moment.

Inside the anteroom of the Marshal's office, Regard and Debbie sat side by side on a leather sofa. Debbie had left the Court after adjournment to meet Harry Aboud for an hour's consultation and then had eaten lunch with him at Maison Blanche. Pledges of support had been received from quite a few distinguished fellow guests. Regard had stayed at the Court at Moss' invitation to eat lunch with him in his chambers, but despite earnest arguments and importuning had received no indication from a taciturn Justice what he intended to do, only that he expected to have an announcement by 4 P.M. This information had been given the media by the press office soon after lunch. Its publication had greatly increased the crowd. Now the two counsels had come together again, waiting. They still had not spoken.

Outside Moss' chambers a lone policeman stood guard. The corridor was empty, as was virtually the entire building. The library was closed, the Great Hall deserted, the press room abandoned. Everything waited on one man.

Alone in his office he sat at his desk and doodled on a yellow legal pad, his mind going over and over conflicting arguments, back and forth, back and forth, until he finally told himself that he must do something or go mad.

There were no rules binding on Justices, only on lawyers appearing before them. No one could prevent his sitting on the case and he was under no obligation or requirement to justify his ruling. A simple *Granted* or *Denied* would be entirely sufficient. But he felt he owed it to himself, to his wife and above all to Sarah to state his reasons. He was glad he had set himself a deadline, otherwise he felt he would never decide.

Once he called Sue-Ann at the plantation, asked what he should do. She told him she didn't know, but whatever it was, she would support him. "I love you," he said. "I love you," she said. The cute laughing ghost of their daughter came into both their minds. He hung up, more saddened and confused than ever.

Finally at three-thirty he gave a deep sigh, tore up the doodles and tossed them in a wastebasket. Outside, tension was rising in the crowd; through his window he could hear its uneasy murmur. There would be critics waiting to pounce, whatever he did. They would charge him with easy decision, easily made, but he knew what he had been through. He began to write, with a hand that noticeably trembled.

Finished, he called the Marshal and dictated. Two minutes later the Marshal called in his secretary and dictated also. Five minutes after that, Debbie and Regard were handed identical pieces of paper. The Marshal, moved by some hearkening-back to the past that made it seem a natural thing to do, walked firmly out through the Great Hall, had the guards open the bronze doors for him, and stepped out on the top step. Abruptly the crowd became silent. For a few seconds the only noise came from the slow, curious passage of traffic in the street.

"Appeal to stay the verdict in *Holgren v. South Carolina* to permit review by the Supreme Court of the United States," the Marshal read in a clear, steady voice, "has been received by Justice Pomeroy as Circuit Justice, Fourth Judicial Circuit. After deliberation Justice Pomeroy has decided not to disqualify himself. Arguments will be heard in chambers at ten A.M. tomorrow."

A great shout went up.

Regard gave Debbie a triumphant look as they left the Marshal's office.

Debbie turned on her heel, expressionless, and walked away.

4

Justice NOW! was back next morning: obedient to its leader's demand, it was not relaxing. The crowd was smaller, the atmosphere less hectic, but the bronze doors were still closed to all but authorized entries and the extra police were still on duty all around the building. Outside Justice Pomeroy's chambers a dozen officers now stood guard. Media only were allowed in the corridor, and they were held back thirty feet by temporary wooden barriers. Through them Debbie and Regard passed just before 10 A.M.

"What's going to happen, Regard?" Henrietta called—her office had sent her up, to her surprise and delight, to be "in at the kill," as she put it to her colleagues.

"Justice is goin' to be upheld," he said calmly. "What else could happen, here?"

"What do you think, Miss Donnelson?" someone else inquired.

"It's just a rehearsal," she said with studied indifference. "I don't expect any surprises."

"You don't expect a stay, then."

"I would be very much surprised."

Regard swung around.

"Now, I'll say," he said, "that I am not so ready to dismiss a fine Justice as counsel is. I don't know how Justice Pomeroy will rule—"

"Have you asked him?" someone inquired. He shook his head in mock dismay.

"Man, I've been on my *knees!*" Everybody laughed. "But he just isn't talkin', and he shouldn't be. The one thing I do know is that whatever he decides will be *decided on the law,* because that's the kind of Justice he is, Miss Donnelson to the contrary."

"I didn't say anything to the contrary," she retorted sharply. "I just said I don't expect any surprises. And I don't."

"The Justice is ready, counsels," the public information officer said from the door in a disapproving tone. "Please come in so we can start the proceedings."

"Yes, sir," Regard said smartly.

"Certainly," said Debbie.

At three twenty-three exactly the door swung open and they reappeared. Both looked tired, both were uncommunicative.

"How did it go?" the New York *Times* asked.

"We presented the arguments," Debbie said.

"Do you feel you got a fair hearing?" CBS inquired.

"He's a good Justice," Regard said.

"He is that," Debbie agreed, sounding faintly surprised.

"Come along, gentlemen," the public information officer urged as they rounded the corner, disappeared from view and went their separate ways. "The Justice won't have anything for you for a while, so if you want to wait it might as well be in the press room."

"Can't you give us any clue as to when it will be?"

"I haven't the slightest idea," the public information officer said.

"If we could only be sure of a time," the AP said, rather wistfully.

"Tell him Henny wants to know whether she has time to go to the hotel, take a nap, powder her nose and have a couple of drinks and a steak," she suggested. The public information officer, with a sudden humanizing grin, turned back, knocked discreetly on the door and was admitted. In a moment he reappeared.

"He says nothing until tomorrow morning. He hopes to have his printed decision for you by ten o'clock."

There was a general groan of protest but everyone quickly accepted it and took off. Outside, the crowd gradually dispersed, the extra police went home, the bronze doors were locked once more. Lights burned for a long time in Moss' office, but no one, now, kept vigil. Shortly before midnight the lights went out and five minutes later he drove out of the garage and went swiftly off through the still-sweltering night streets to his empty house.

He made one telephone call after he reached home. It lasted approximately ten minutes. Tay argued with him but could not claim to be surprised. And he did not argue very vehemently—so halfheartedly and uncertainly, in fact, that Moss finally dismissed him with an impatient "I don't think you know what you really *do* think." He could not deny it as Moss hung up and left him staring bleakly into the darkness above his lonely bed.

SUPREME COURT OF THE UNITED STATES

Earle William Holgren, Petitioner
v.
State of South Carolina.

On Writ of Certiorari to the Supreme Court of South Carolina.

JUSTICE POMEROY for the Court.

This application for stay and review comes here on appeal from certiorari to the Supreme Court of South Carolina. At issue are the deaths of Sarah Ann Pomeroy, a minor; a mature female, Janet Martinson; an infant boy, name unknown; and the destruction of certain property at the atomic energy plant at Pomeroy Station, South Carolina. The verdict against applicant imposed by jury in the Court of General Session of South Carolina and upheld on automatic appeal by the South Carolina Supreme Court is death by electrocution.

Subsequently on petition of the attorney general of South Carolina, the presiding judge in the trial directed that said execution be held in Columbia, South Carolina, on the Fourth of July, in a public place and before television cameras designed to broadcast it to continental United States and presumably by satellite to other nations.

Applicant's principal arguments presented by his counsel were the nature of his arrest, in which his right to be informed immediately of his rights was violated; the nature of his trial, in which he claims certain errors of procedure to have been present; what he terms "the undue amount of public interest and pressure" exerted upon the trial and upon jurors by the activities of an organization known as Justice NOW!; the fact that the death penalty was imposed, thereby subjecting him to what he terms "cruel and unusual punishment" within the meaning of the Eighth Amendment to the Constitution; and the fact that what the media have chosen to designate "execution by television" has been added to the penalty, thereby subjecting him further to what he terms "cruel, unusual *and monstrous*" (italics added) punishment.

The attorney general of South Carolina, appearing for the State, replied in essence that the circumstances of applicant's arrest were "subject to error in the heat of the moment" and "were not deliberate, willful, malicious or pre-calculated" in their interference with his right to be informed of his rights; that procedural errors if any in applicant's trial were "so inadvertent and minuscule as to be virtually nonexistent"; that this case drew enormous national and international attention from the very beginning by the nature of the crimes themselves, and that the effect of Justice NOW! if any, was subsequent, superfluous and ancillary to the publicity and pressure already generated by nationwide concern about crime in general and these crimes in particular; that South Carolina's laws provide that the death penalty cannot be imposed except by unanimous vote of the jury so instructing the trial judge, and also provide that all death sentences be automatically appealed to the state Supreme Court for review; that such unanimous vote of jury was forthcoming, that said appeal was made, and that the state Supreme Court did thereupon unanimously uphold the verdict; and that making the execution public and providing for its broadcast by television simply verifies the public's right to know under the First Amendment and does not thereby transform a carefully restricted application of the death penalty into a wide-open imposition of "cruel, unusual and monstrous" punishment as alleged, but rather makes of the penalty a warning and a needed cautionary event for all others who may wish to transgress similarly or in part the laws of the several states and of the United States.

In ruling upon the application for stay of execution and review of the case by this Court, particular notice is taken of the heinous nature of the crimes committed; of the fact that the death sentence was imposed only after exhaustion of all procedures provided by the carefully structured laws of South Carolina; and that neither of the courts below saw fit to question the circumstances of applicant's arrest, the conduct of his trial or the final judgment rendered thereon by a free and independent jury, upheld after due deliberation by the state's highest court of review.

Application for stay and review therefore is

Denied.

POMEROY ORDERS DEATH FOR DAUGHTER'S KILLER!
REJECTS STAY, HIGH COURT REVIEW! HOLGREN EX-
PECTED TO SEEK "FRIENDLY" JUDGE FOR SECOND TRY.
JUSTICE NOW! AND PRO-LAW MOBS CLASH AT COURT.
WORLD PROTESTS FLARE.

And sure enough, on the grand old principle of *Embarrass America
whenever you can,* the mobs were in the streets of many major cities
around the globe. Very few demonstrators had the slightest idea what it
was all about but that made no difference. The defense of Earle Holgren was ready-made for protest and it did not matter much whether
demonstrations occurred in nations with some vestiges of legal tradition
or in nations where public executions were the rule. Mobs were organized and sent into the streets with a gleeful perception that this was
one more easy weapon with which to belabor America.

Similarly in his own country Earle Holgren's case was suddenly the
focus of actual physical violence (fortunately not yet fatal) between
Justice NOW! and its critics, whom the media instantly dubbed "pro-
law." "But *we* are pro-law, God damn it!" Regard said furiously when
he saw the first such reference. His protest was futile. War by semantics
had many skilled practitioners and now they employed it once again
with the practiced ease acquired in many successful battles.

One unfortunate aspect of all this, known only to his counsel, was its
effect on the defendant: an ego already almost out of control became
even more arrogant as the reports flooded in. Another aspect was its
effect on television. As if by magic sympathetic network support for the
"pro-law" group at home and the excessive attention paid to the demonstrators abroad suddenly dwindled away. As if some giant hand had
come down and wiped it from the screen—as indeed several giant hands
had done—the pro-Holgren movement virtually disappeared overnight
from the tube.

The editors and managers of the printed media suddenly realized that
they were alone in their extended coverage of what Regard steadfastly
described to all his callers and interviewers as "a small over-publicized
minority" favoring Earle's case and opposing the proposed televising of
his death.

Debbie flew back down to Columbia after the ruling and saw Earle that evening. She had not thought it possible for him to become more complacent, more arrogant, more certain of his own superiority and uniqueness. His attitude dispelled her illusions immediately. An almost psychotic—why "almost?" she asked herself suddenly, finally admitting what she knew to be true—euphoria seemed to surround him as he called her "Superstar" and crowed over his enemies.

"They've shot their wad," he predicted scornfully, "Pomeroy's ruling was the high-water mark. From now on there's going to be a return to sanity. The Court isn't going to stand for that kind of nonsense. The law is going to prevail. The TV bit puts the cap on it. Pomeroy has his gripe—"

"Just a dead daughter," she remarked again, this time with a real bitterness, and he said, "Hey, whose side are you on?" in a tone that for a moment sounded genuinely aggrieved. Then he shrugged.

"He has his gripe," he conceded lightly, "and everybody knows it. So he's had his chance. So now we go to somebody else and get a sensible ruling—the full Court reconvenes and takes it up—and then we'll get somewhere."

"You really think the full Court will reverse your sentence?" she asked in a tone of such skepticism that he gave her a sudden angry glare. "You really are in a dream world!"

"Then why don't you get out of it?" he demanded with sudden naked savagery. "Why don't you just get the hell out, Miss Superstar, and stop bothering me? I'll get Harry Aboud or somebody else. Or I'll do it myself! I don't need you!"

"You need something," she said. "God knows what it is or who can give it to you, but you do need something, all right."

"Go on!" he said. "Out!"

But she did not move, nor did her eyes flinch from his nor did she indicate in any way that she was both frighteningly angry and frighteningly panic-stricken at the thought that he might really banish her from his life. It must be like training a cobra, she thought with a wild, helpless wryness: it's deadly but it must be fascinating to see if you can keep it from striking you. Particularly when, unlike the ones you see in sideshows, this one was neither sedated, milked of its poison, nor yet fully defanged.

"You aren't going," he remarked presently; and a pleased, knowing smile that she hated but knew she deserved spread across his face.

"Why, Superstar," he said softly, "I believe you really do like my hairy bod, after all. Or is it my scintillating wit and great brain? It could be, you know! I've all three."

"You haven't got as much of anything as you think you have," she said, finding it hard to breathe but forcing her voice to stay steady, even though his smile suddenly deepened and with a mocking gesture he made as if to start unzipping his fly to prove her wrong. "You're one step—two steps, maybe—away from the electric chair, and you act as though you're still on a picnic where everybody bows down and says how smart Earle Holgren is. Well, you're not smart. You're dumb. You're just plain dumb!"

But at this, which she fully expected would goad him into some word or gesture that would at last solve her dilemma for her and force her away for good, he only smiled; and leaning back in his chair with his hands behind his head, his legs spread wide, crotch outthrust and an insolent grin on his face, he watched her steadily while a flush slowly mounted her face and she felt as though her legs would collapse beneath her. This man was a psychopath, a murderer, a strange lost being outside the bounds of normal living—but she was helpless. So she rationalized it as she had to, hating herself for it but using the only excuse that retained even the slightest hold on rationality: she was a lawyer, he was her client, and her duty still lay with him until all channels that might preserve his life had been exhausted.

She patted her severely drawn hair with a hand that trembled ever so slightly—he saw it, of course, he always saw everything—and managed to make her voice matter-of-fact.

"I think I should file the next appeal not later than tomorrow morning."

His eyes suddenly narrowed, he dropped his insolent pose and tone and sat forward intently. "Who are you going to go to?"

"Taylor Barbour is the junior Justice, and according to Court custom—"

"According to Court custom, at this point you can choose anybody you damned please," he snapped. "I want Wallenberg, he's supposed to be the great liberal around there."

"Taylor Barbour is the younger man," she said, standing her ground. "He's more flexible, he's not so crotchety, his liberal reputation is even stronger—"

"And he has a daughter in a coma and he thinks I did it. What is it that makes him so perfect for my case?"

"Because he's an honest man!" she snapped in a tone as angry as his. "And his daughter *is* in a coma! And if *he* rules in our favor in spite of that, then *his* words will carry a lot more weight with the country and with the Court itself, and we'll have a lot better chance to win a reversal from them and get it remanded back to South Carolina for further hearing. *That's* why I want to go to Taylor Barbour! Can your ego permit you to grasp any of that?"

"Oh, yes," he said, "I can grasp that. But"—he looked at her sharply —"suppose we go to Taylor Barbour and he *doesn't* rule in our favor. That exhausts it for us, doesn't it?"

"He will," she said flatly.

"How do you know?"

"Because he's an honest man," she repeated stubbornly, "and a genuine liberal, not a media poseur like Justice Wallenberg."

He frowned.

"All I can say is, if we're going to take this kind of gamble you'd better be God damned sure of what we're doing."

"I have faith in Taylor Barbour," she said simply. "I believe in him."

"Well, goody for you. But it's my neck."

"Goody for *you,*" she retorted. "At last you appear to be realizing it."

He was silent for a few moments, only rousing to glare at the guard and give him his favorite gesture as the man looked in the peephole and then went on. Finally he spoke in a moody but grudgingly acquiescent tone.

"O.K.—O.K. We'll go with your precious Taylor Barbour. But I tell you, Superstar"—an ugly light came into his eyes that made her shiver involuntarily as she watched him staring grimly off into space—"if you're wrong—if that bastard lets us down—"

"Yes?" she inquired, deliberately unimpressed and deliberately sarcastic, since that was her only way to reassert herself. "What will you do? Die gracefully?"

"I won't die at all!" he said with a sudden furious anger. "Earle Holgren won't die at all!"

"I wish I were as sure of that as you are."

"You'd better be," he told her in the same fierce way, and again she shivered. "You'd God damned well better be!"

"I'm flying back tomorrow morning," she said, trying to ignore his tone and keep her own matter-of-fact. "I'll file it with him by nightfall."

"Good," he said, staring at the floor, chewing on his knuckles, off in some inward world of his own. "Then we'll see what that phony-liberal bastard is made of."

5

"I don't think you know what you really *do* think," Moss had told him near the midnight of his own decision; and now as he sat in his chambers looking across his desk at Debbie and Regard, for the second time met in battle before a Justice of the Supreme Court, he wished he had more certain guidelines in his own mind to follow.

With little variation, they had repeated the arguments they had presented to Moss. This time Debbie expanded her emphasis on the "cruel and unusual" nature of the death penalty and the "cruel, unusual and monstrous character" of the proposed public execution and proposed television broadcast. Regard placed his stress upon the frightening increase in general crime, the need for public example as a deterrent, "the public's right to know under the First Amendment," and—a new argument—"the proven fact that television is a basic part of American life, that many polls and surveys have shown that the majority of Americans look to television to form their opinions and attitudes on matters of grave import to the nation, and that therefore the proposed televising of this event transcends the mere punishment of a convicted criminal and raises it to the status of a major public educative act, vital to the reaching of a national consensus on the necessity for controlling crime with promptness and finality."

When they had finished he stood up and they perforce did the same.

"It is now almost noon," he said. "If you wish to tell the media, who I suppose are waiting outside and will want to know, you can say that I will either have my opinion in this matter by six o'clock this evening, or, if I don't make it by then, I will certainly have it by ten tomorrow morning. Thank you both."

He held out his hand to Debbie, who gave it a quick, hard, almost embarrassed little handshake, and then to Regard, who lingered a bit more fulsomely but presently relinquished it and followed her out. He could hear a sudden stir in the hall as the media descended upon them but it quickly died away. Apparently he had been taken at his word and the reporters would not return until six.

He called the kitchen, ordered a sandwich and a glass of iced tea; consumed them rapidly; told his secretary to have the switchboard turn away all calls and gave her and his clerks the afternoon off; heard them leave; went out and locked the door to his chambers; came back and sat down at his desk.

And faced himself.

Nothing he had heard had changed his basic blind rage against the individual who had destroyed his daughter. On the other hand nothing had changed his basic concept of himself as a decent, compassionate, liberal servant of the law who must, if he possibly could, rise above such feelings. Moss had not been able to: human vengeance had overridden his duty to the law. Or so Tay thought, and so, to judge from the bitter reaction in editorials, news stories and commentaries, thought many of the media's most prominent figures. He had argued with Moss that night, but although he expressed strong regret at what Moss intended to do, his old friend could sense his uncertainty. "You're arguing with me just because you think you *ought* to be arguing with me," was another thing Moss had said to him then. In the hours after midnight, when his mind was still churning their conversation, he had known that Moss was correct.

Now the burden had passed to him; and he knew that this was only the first stage of the testing he would have to go through before the Court reached its final decision. He was well aware, as Debbie had told Earle, that what he said in his opinion would have a major influence on his sister and brethren when they came to pass judgment. It would have a major influence on national opinion as well. He had suffered almost as much as Moss and was apparently destined to go on suffering with the same intensity, unrelieved by time's passage.

If he disqualified himself, the Court would very probably vote 4–4, South Carolina would be upheld and the death penalty-TV verdict would stand.

For this reason alone, if he was to remain true to his lifelong beliefs, he could not disqualify himself.

He was the only hope for balance.

But by the same token, if he remained on the case he could not abandon himself to vengeance or a heavy weight would be put upon the Court and there would be a drastic effect upon public opinion. If he refused to let himself be swayed by his emotions, the Court's tasks would be somewhat easier and the effect upon public opinion more calming.

A verdict from him denying stay would only encourage Justice NOW! and inflame all the angry emotions it had coalesced in the hearts and minds of so many millions of his countrymen. If he granted stay, the organization would receive at least a substantial setback and there might be some reversal of the blind drive toward indiscriminate vengeance that was now sweeping the country . . .

It was easy to state, infinitely more difficult to adjudicate when you were the only one concerned and the burden rested, at least temporarily, on you and you alone. He too had his doubts about the circumstances of Earle Holgren's arrest; he too had some questions about the conduct of the trial, even though he was convinced that Perlie Williams had leaned over backward to be fair to everyone. He still had his profound and instinctive misgivings about the death penalty, made more agonizing rather than reduced by his daughter's tragedy. And the idea of public execution compounded by television was as repugnant to him as it was, he hoped, to most who considered themselves civilized.

So there were many grounds for granting the stay. Against it, in the last analysis, lay only his own human reactions, the anguish of a parent, the thought of Janie sleeping away her life, permanently and beyond recall, bereft of all the laughter, the gaiety, the sweet personality, the good heart, all the bright promise of a life that now would never be lived. It raised doubts so fundamental about the death penalty, and about "the law" as a concept that was supposed to rise above the honest reactions of decent people, that it shook his whole life and being to their foundations. Justice had always been an abstract before to him and, he suspected, to his colleagues as well. Never before had tragedy struck directly at the Court. Never before had the challenge passed through the bronze doors beneath EQUAL JUSTICE UNDER LAW and come squarely *to them.* Always before it had been at least at one remove, more often several.

In a sense they had always been spoiled. They had always had it easy. No issue ever really came home to them in the immediate human way this one did. No one ever said them nay, nothing ever really, deeply, fundamentally and beyond escaping, challenged them. Thanks to Earle Holgren, now it would. Between them and the hour of what would be a truly wrenching decision for them all stood only Tay Barbour, who had every reason in the world to give in to his vengeful emotions—except his concept of himself and the concept that those whose opinions he valued had of him.

He thought for a very long time; drew up several tentative opinions on his yellow legal pad; read them . . . re-read them . . . polished them here and there . . . tore them up.

Nothing seemed right, nothing seemed adequate to the case or to the mental and emotional turmoil he was going through. Finally, around 4 P.M., he reached a decision. Some, he supposed, would call it cowardly, even though it followed recent Court custom that by now was virtually automatic. He was not happy with it himself. It moved things forward but it gave no guidance. It only put off the day of reckoning and did nothing to help solve the law's dilemma and that of the nine who were its ultimate guardians. It would be called—and he supposed it would be —a cop-out.

But he could not force himself, try as he might, to do other.

He wrote swiftly, called the printer and told him to rush it out immediately. At 6 P.M. it reached the media.

SUPREME COURT OF THE UNITED STATES

Earle William Holgren, Petitioner ⎫ On Writ of Certiorari to
            v.   ⎬   the Supreme Court of
State of South Carolina. ⎭ South Carolina.

JUSTICE BARBOUR for the Court.

This application for stay of execution and review by the full Court comes here for the second time, having been rejected by Justice Pomeroy.

Arguments were presented by counsel for applicant and counsel for the State of South Carolina. The arguments were largely repetitions of arguments heretofore summarized in Justice Pomeroy's opinion. Little can be gained by reviewing them. The matter obviously is of sufficient importance not only to applicant but to the country as a whole to warrant further hearing.

Accordingly the case is referred to the Court for review and stay of execution for thirty days is

Granted.

He was on his way out of the office when the phone rang. He hesitated, then picked it up.

"Justice," the switchboard operator said, "I'm sorry to disobey your request that calls be held, but I have the Chief Justice on the line. And your wife is waiting."

"Yes," he said, sitting slowly down at his desk. "I'll take them both. The Chief first."

"Good boy!" Duncan Elphinstone said. "You did the right thing. You gave us time, which is what we need most, at the moment."

"I suppose I should have stated my reasons and given some argument—"

"Not at all," The Elph said reassuringly. "Why should you?"

"Moss did."

"Moss gave in to his emotions and I can't blame him. But I think he made a mistake in letting them show. He should have done what you did: there it is, and that's that. Fortunately our rules permit another appeal and you could reverse him."

"You think it's best for us to consider it, then," he inquired, sounding dubious. The Chief responded with a vigorous,

"Yes! Of course I do. I wish you could have given us more than thirty days, but that's about all the country will stand for, I think."

"Maybe it won't even stand for that."

"No," the Chief agreed grimly. "Maybe it won't. We'll just have to see about that. I think every bit of delay helps to calm things down a bit."

"I hope you're right."

"I hope so too," Duncan Elphinstone said, sounding not at all sure.

Mary's call was equally brief. It was not as pleasant.

"I just heard what you did."

"Yes?" he said, bracing himself.

"I think it was a cowardly betrayal of your daughter, your responsibility as a Justice, and yourself. Why didn't you say what you really feel about that monster? *Why didn't you defend Janie?*"

"In my way, Mary," he said with a sigh, "I am. In my way."

"Well," she said, "it isn't *my* way, and it isn't the way of the millions and millions in this country who won't be able to understand why you gave him a stay at all, let alone why you didn't take the opportunity to describe him as what he is, that *monster*. He's *destroyed your daughter*, and you won't even call him murderer. At least Moss was honest. He said the crimes were heinous. I never admired him before but I do now."

"I'm sorry you don't admire me, but Moss has his concept of the law and of himself and I have mine. He's doing what he thinks best and so am I."

"You'll probably even vote to reverse the death sentence," she said bitterly. "That would fit your 'concept of yourself,' all right."

"I don't know what I'll do," he said for what seemed to be the hundredth time.

"You don't know what you'll do about anything," she cried, "except be soft on the criminal who destroyed your daughter!"

"How is she today?" he inquired, trying to change the subject for a moment before terminating the conversation.

"You don't deserve to know," she said, and hung up.

He sat for several minutes in his silent office, chin on hand, staring unseeing into some distance he could not really discern or understand. At last he lifted the receiver and dialed a number.

"Hello," she said.

"Can I come over?"

She hesitated.

"The kids are here." Then she uttered a little laugh. "But they might as well get to know you. They'll go to bed later."

"Whatever," he said. "Whatever. I just—I just want a little comfort. That's all."

"Yes, my dear," she said quietly. "I know. Hurry."

Another call from Columbia came north, put through after the warden checked with Regard and Regard said, "Sure, but bug it." "You're bugged," the warden told the prisoner and the prisoner told him what he could do with it. But he was so enraged that he went ahead with the call anyway.

"So that's your great liberal Justice!" he shouted when Debbie came on the line. "That's your fucking compassionate humanitarian precious Taylor Barbour! Of all the lily-livered, turn-tail, half-assed excuses for a two-bit, cowardly, sidestepping—"

"Listen!" she yelled in return, shouting him momentarily into silence. "Listen, you crazy man! He gave you your stay, didn't he? He's given you your chance, hasn't he? Why the hell can't you ever settle for what you get and be thankful? He could have denied it. He could have let his emotions run away with him like Moss Pomeroy and sent you packing. But he didn't, you ungrateful bastard! He was a decent enough man to *give you a chance.* Now *God damn you,* be thankful!"

("My, my," the warden said to his deputy as the tape spun on. "Gracious, such language." "They deserve one another," the deputy said. "Too bad they can't both fry in hell." "You're a little rough on her," the warden demurred mildly, "but *he's* a bad, *bad* boy.")

"He could have given an opinion!" Earle cried. "He could have said what a phony rap this is! You said he could have had a lot of influence on the Court if he'd had the guts! Why didn't he do it? What's the matter with that half-assed, lily-livered—"

"You said that before," she shouted back, *"and I don't want to hear another word against Taylor Barbour!* He's still on our side, I'm convinced of it! You'll see! You'll see!"

"I'd better see," he said, voice dropping abruptly to an ominous softness that made the warden glance at the deputy as they both leaned forward intently. "I'd better see, or I'll have a date with that fucking weak-kneed bastard someday! I'll have a date!"

"You'll be lucky if you have a date with anything but the electric chair!" she told him, starting to cry from sheer anger, tension and frantic frustration with him. "He may be the only chance you've got on that whole Court. And you talk about him like this." Her voice trailed away on a despairing note. "And I have to defend you. I have to defend you . . ."

"Yes," he said, quite calm now, with an odd fleering relish that again made his listeners exchange glances. "Apparently you do, Superstar. Apparently you do."

On Thursday night the headlines said:
HINT COURT MAY DELAY HOLGREN CASE THREE WEEKS.
On Friday morning they said:
JUSTICE NOW! CONDEMNS HOLGREN DELAY, DEMANDS IMMEDIATE ACTION. THOUSANDS PROTEST ACROSS NATION. COURT SIEGE THREATENED.

On Friday afternoon they said:

HUGE CROWD GATHERS AT COURT IN ANTI-HOLGREN RALLY. JUSTICE NOW! PLEDGES NON-STOP VIGIL UNTIL CASE DECIDED. SLOGANS PAINTED ON BUILDING.

Without comment at 8 P.M. Friday night, after several hours of hectic private telephone consultation, a brief statement was issued through the Marshal's office:

"Pursuant to call of the Chief Justice, the Supreme Court of the United States will convene at 10 A.M. on Monday next in closed session to hear arguments in the case of *Holgren v. South Carolina.*"

But the crowd, faithful to Justice NOW!'s promise, did not disperse over the weekend; nor did public pressure decrease on either side of the issue; nor did overseas demonstrations diminish very much; nor did the road ahead become any clearer or easier for the nine who lived and worked under the banner EQUAL JUSTICE UNDER LAW.

6

"Well," Wally Flyte said as Clem Wallenberg, the last to appear, came from the Robing Room to join them in the Conference Room where they always formed their little procession to the chamber, "lead the lambs to slaughter, Dunc!"

But it was a feeble joke and he knew it, and after a moment when all any of them could muster was a rather feeble smile in response, he gave it up and spoke more somberly. "I never thought I'd see the day when the Court bowed openly to public pressure."

"Nor I," Hughie Demsted said. "But here it is."

"I think," Mary-Hannah said, "that I could take everything else but the paint on the building. It makes me feel—violated."

"Yes," Ray Ullstein agreed, "that's the word. I think that bothers me most, too."

"And me," the Chief said; and suddenly an emotional note he obviously hadn't expected overtook him. "I *like* this place." He cleared his throat vigorously as Rupert Hemmelsford nodded.

"I'm glad to see we have extra police protection."

"We've got them all," The Elph said. "Our own, the District, and the President called a little while ago and said he'd assign a couple of Army units if we needed them. I told him I didn't think we needed to be quite that dramatic yet. Although"—he sighed—"it could happen."

"It wouldn't have happened," Clement Wallenberg growled, "if our two junior brethren had seen fit to do their duty and dispose of this case before the Court became a public spectacle."

"I did my duty!" Moss snapped. "I denied that—individual's stay. What more could *I* do?"

"Well," Justice Wallenberg conceded grudgingly, "Tay didn't. He just passed the buck to all of us. It only delayed what we're going to do."

"And that's what, Clem?" Hughie Demsted inquired dryly.

"Remand it to South Carolina for further trial," Justice Wallenberg said defiantly.

"I don't know about that," Justice Hemmelsford said, and Justice Wallenberg snorted.

"You wouldn't! If there's any reactionary, conservative way to approach things—"

"Oh, crap!" Rupert Hemmelsford exclaimed, voice rising angrily. "Stop giving me that old standard bullshit, Clem, if you don't mind. I've had it up to here with your pious posturings."

" 'Pious posturings'?" Clem Wallenberg cried, while behind his back Mary-Hannah could not resist a wink at Hughie Demsted, who winked back. " *'Pious posturings'?* Why, you two-bit reactionary bastard, I'll—"

"You won't do anything," the Chief Justice interrupted in a voice that commanded silence, "except shake hands with everybody like we always do, and get on into that courtroom and do the job you're here for. You're not such a bad Justice. Clem, if you'll just stop play-acting and get on with it."

At this unexpected attack from his flank, Justice Wallenberg was temporarily speechless. His face turned red, he looked as though he might pop. If the issue before them had not been so serious, if they could not hear the uneasy murmur of ten thousand pressing voices outside affirming the fact, Justice Flyte or someone might have made a joke and started a laugh to break the tension. As it was, no one seemed to have the heart. And presently Clem "decompressed," as Mary-Hannah put it to Tay later, without making any rejoinder other than a fearful scowl.

For several moments no one else said anything either. Then Ray Ullstein spoke in his usual reasoned way.

"I was wondering if perhaps we shouldn't extend the usual half hour for hearing arguments to a longer period for this case? It's of such interest that I think it might be wise."

"That's my inclination if the rest of you agree," The Elph said. "I think it might be well to grant an hour at least, maybe even two or three. It's not a simple case, God knows. We want to give both sides plenty of time. Plus the fact that we have a couple of *amicus curiae* briefs just filed this morning."

They all looked surprised.

"Really?" Ray Ullstein asked. "From whom?"

"The American Civil Liberties Union, for one—"

"Naturally," Justice Hemmelsford remarked.

"—and a group known as *CBS et al.*"

"*Really,*" May McIntosh said. "How interesting."

"Very," the Chief agreed.

"Probably just as well we're meeting right away," Rupert Hemmelsford observed. "Better get it over with, I think."

"Yes," the Chief said. "I'm glad you all talked me into it last night. I had some idea that extra time would calm things down out there"—he gestured toward the window, through which came the restless sounds of the crowd—"but very likely it wouldn't. Our friend Stinnet really has them stirred up."

Solemnly then, mutual annoyance momentarily forgotten, they turned to one another and shook hands around the circle, a custom started by Chief Justice Melville Fuller in the late nineteenth century, faithfully observed ever since at the start of all sessions. It was generally interpreted to mean, "We may have our differences, but we are all servants of the law."

Then the bell rang promptly at ten and they moved forward through the red velvet curtains in their stately little parade: the Chief in the center, flanked by Wally Flyte on his right, Clem Wallenberg on his left, the others following two by two, taking their seats according to seniority on each side of the central group. The Marshal cried out his customary "Oyez! Oyez!" and admonished all persons having business before the Honorable, the Supreme Court of the United States to draw near and give their attention.

"God save the United States and this Honorable Court!" he concluded, his plea noticeably more fervent than usual. Faces impassive, the Justices took their seats. Looking deeply impressive and immensely powerful, outwardly at one in the majesty of the law, they stared down upon a nervous Debbie, a jaunty but secretly nervous Regard, the two lawyers who represented the American Civil Liberties Union and *CBS et al.* From outside came the distant murmur of the restless crowd.

Debbie, as lawyer for petitioner, spoke first. She was brought to the heart of her argument when Rupert Hemmelsford pointed out that in spite of her abstention from jury selection Regard had scrupulously chosen six jurors opposed to the death penalty "who still voted unanimously when all the evidence was in to sentence your client to death. Shouldn't that tell us something?"

She looked taken aback for a moment but rallied.

"That goes exactly to the heart of petitioner's challenge to South Carolina, your honor. What it tells us is that the jury was so overwhelmed by the prejudicial emotion generated statewide and nationwide by the organization of opposing counsel, the organization known as Justice NOW! that *it did not matter* what the former perceptions and beliefs of jurors were. They were overwhelmed into voting as they did by the sheer tide of emotion generated by opposing counsel and his organization—emotion which at this moment"—she paused and gestured dramatically toward the windows, beyond which the restless murmur of the crowd could be distantly heard—"still tries to warp, influence and determine the judgment on this case—which at this moment challenges even you on this highest Court, your honors.

"Thus do the judgments rendered in South Carolina, and the actions of this organization both there and here at this very moment, fall directly athwart the position of this Court as set forth in *Gardner v. Florida*, 430 U.S. 349, 357-358, as stated by Justice Stevens for the plurality:

" '*It is of vital importance to the defendant and to the community that any decision to impose the death sentence be, and appear to be, based on reason rather than caprice or emotion.*'

"Caprice or emotion, I submit to your honors, are what have informed this case from beginning to end. Caprice or emotion are what dominated the state of South Carolina. They are what presently dominate this nation. They are what stand outside your own walls, your honors. Listen to them and ask yourselves whether they should once again control the fate of this defendant!"

She paused, color heightened, face excited, breath coming fast, mien triumphant. For a moment there was silence. Then the Chief spoke in a dry voice, yet no more harsh, challenging or personal than Justices of the Supreme Court often are to lawyers who come before them.

"You are to be commended on dramatics, counsel. Now let us get back to the facts."

Debbie flinched as though he had struck her; flushed deeply; but recovered, as lawyers before the Court must on such occasions, for they have no choice. The only consolation was her perception that they would probably be equally rough on Regard.

"Yes, your honor," she said, voice trembling a little but managing. "Here we come to what is perhaps the most damning and distressing feature of all—caprice or emotion not only dominated trial and verdict but they then apparently came to dominate a judge who theretofore had been scrupulously fair, I believe, in his conduct of the trial. At the request of the attorney general of South Carolina and on order of Judge Williams, it is proposed that the death sentence, if it be done at all, be turned into a public circus, a great media event, a televised bloodletting so far beyond the bounds of decency, justice and reason as to make a mockery of the law and a mockery of every pretense to decency that America ever had.

"Cruel, unusual—and *monstrous*. That is what is proposed by South Carolina. This attempt makes a mockery of the entire trial and a mockery of American justice in entirety. The verdict of guilty rests only on circumstantial evidence. The death penalty is cruel and unusual punishment not justified in any way by the facts on the record, which are the only things this Court is legally bound to consult. The addition of a proposal for a televised public execution lowers it to the level of abysmal barbarity.

"Petitioner requests, therefore, that the verdicts of the courts below be reversed, that the sentence of death be thereby voided and that the proposal for a public, televised execution be condemned so roundly and inescapably by this Court that no jurisdiction in this nation will ever again dare even to suggest it.

"I thank your honors."

She bowed, picked up her brief, and started to turn away. The Chief Justice stopped her with a lifted hand.

"Miss Donnelson," he said, "you have more time. Did you wish to have the *amicus curiae* brief of the Civil Liberties Union argued before us?"

She glanced at her fellow lawyer, who shook his head and then stood up and came forward.

"If the Court please," he said, "and with counsel's concurrence, I do not think that will be necessary. She has made our points concerning the death penalty and the public television proposal and made them very well. As your honor knows, our brief has gone to the media along with hers, and we thank the Court. In the interests of saving your time, we will rest at that."

"Thank you, counsel," Duncan Elphinstone said. "The Court appreciates your consideration. The Court will hear counsel for the state."

Regard came forward, not glancing at Debbie, placed his brief on the lectern, placed his hands on it and leaned forward earnestly.

"Your honors," he said, "as I look around this courtroom"—and he did so, turning to survey the beautiful high-ceilinged room where so many historic cases had been argued and decisions handed down—"I see

on the friezes above us the faces and figures of the great lawgivers of all
time. I see such men as Menes, first pharaoh of Egypt, three and a half
millennia before Christ. I see Hammurabi, almost two thousand years
before Christ. I see Moses and Solomon—Solon and Confucius—Draco
and Augustus. To my left"—and he turned, raising an arm to them
reverently—"I see lawgivers of the Christian era, Napoleon and Black-
stone, King John and Charlemagne, Muhammad and John Marshall.
Above the main entrance"—and he continued to turn so that his back
was now to the Court, whose members were glancing at one another
with amused and skeptical looks—"I see the figures of Justice, Divine
Inspiration, Wisdom and Truth, and flanking them on the one side, Security, Harmony, Peace, Charity, and the Defense of Virtue. While on
the other"—his voice dropped dramatically—"I see the powers of Evil,
Corruption, Slander, Deceit—and Despotic Power."

He turned back to face them fully once again and as he did so, The
Elph inquired mildly,

"Do you see the figure of Calvin Coolidge, counsel?

"Calvin Coolidge?" Regard asked blankly.

"Yes. He was noted for brevity."

There was a guffaw from Wally Flyte, quickly suppressed but enough
to break them all up. For several seconds there was not much decorum
on the Supreme Bench as Regard, flushing to the roots of his hair,
struggled desperately to recover his balance and his dignity. For a moment he obviously did not know whether to explode into anger or swallow his feelings and behave. Prudence and common sense made the decision and with a dignity that cost him much he bowed his head in
deference.

"I stand corrected, your honor, and I apologize to the Court if I have
violated some rule or spoken too elaborately for your honors' taste."

"Just try to stick a little more to the facts," Duncan Elphinstone
suggested. "We know all these gentlemen you mention better than you
do: we have a vantage point several feet higher than yours and we see
them almost every day of our lives. You come here in opposition to the
plea for stay and review entered by Holgren."

"I do, your honor," Regard said. "I oppose it, and the state of South
Carolina opposes it, with all the strength that is in us."

"You and your mob also come here, I take it, to threaten the Supreme Court of the United States," Clement Wallenberg grated out with
a sharp hostility that took them all by surprise. Regard flushed again
and this time responded in kind.

"Your honor may choose to use whatever nasty words he likes about the decent law-abiding citizens of this nation," he snapped, "but their concept of the law is as valid as yours, I think. And perhaps more so."

"I despise what you are trying to do to this country, Mr. Stinnet," Justice Wallenberg said, "and I make no apologies whatsoever for saying so."

"Nor do I apologize to your honor," Regard said in an equally harsh tone, calculating, inaccurately, that his audience would be largely with him where their Brother Wallenberg was concerned, "for characterizing your approach to this matter as unfair and unjudicial. Now perhaps," he added icily, "if I may be permitted to continue—"

"You may continue," the Chief said, equally icy, "but you will refrain from attacking members of this Court personally or the end effect will be to sadly damage your case, I'm afraid. And you, Justice Wallenberg, will kindly refrain from using your superior position to bully counsel. It does not become you and it does not become the Court. Proceed, counsel."

"Well—" Clem began, but The Elph rounded on him so sharply that he actually flinched back a little in his chair alongside.

"Your honors," Regard resumed after a long moment of silence, during which the tension increased and the other Justices looked solemn and wary, "I suppose this is an indication of the passions which surround this case, both in my state and throughout the nation—indeed, throughout the world. I do not deny that emotion does surround this matter, as petitioner's counsel states. But I do deny 'caprice.' There is no 'caprice' about it. We who seek the death of Earle Holgren do so coolly, deliberately, in full knowledge that we are dealing here with the life of a human being. And with full knowledge that we are also dealing with a symbol and a sign of all that is wrong with the American criminal justice system today.

" 'The life of a human being'! Yes, your honors, that is what we are dealing with when we deal with the fate of Earle Holgren. And what did Earle Holgren deal with when he removed the lives of three human beings and permanently destroyed the life of a fourth, I ask your honors? And what will be the point of those deaths, that maiming, what will be the point of his own death, if it is not brought home to the entire world and to all would-be criminals everywhere in this unhappy, troubled land, that crime in America *simply must not pay?*"

"How do you respond to petitioner's plea, counsel?" Justice Demsted inquired, sounding unimpressed. "Why don't you take up his counsel's points *seriatim?* That may help to get us back on the track."

"I was not aware I was off the track, your honor," Regard said, flushing again. "I thought my points so far quite pertinent. However, your honor wishes me to answer counsel for petitioner *seriatim*. That should not be hard to do." He glanced over his shoulder at Debbie, sitting composed and expressionless. "Since they are grounded in so little logic . . .

"To begin with, the matter of Holgren's arrest. If his 'rights' were 'violated' by the circumstances of his capture, then it was not deliberate, willful, malicious or calculated. It was simply human error sparked by the great abhorrence and repugnance his captors felt for him and for what he had done. The law must make some allowance for human error, your honors, otherwise it becomes not a safeguard for the decent but a straitjacket for the decent. And the criminal goes free on technicality . . .

"Counsel for petitioner talked about public pressure and made a great point of waving her arm dramatically out there and calling your attention to the sound of the good citizens who have come here because of their desire to see justice done. Well, let me wave dramatically toward them too, your honors"—and he did so with a sarcastic expression —"and let me, too, call your attention to their impatience for justice, their demand for justice, *their desperate need for justice!* It is out there, your honors, make no mistake! They want justice *and they will get justice!* They cannot be denied, *they will not be denied!* They want—"

"Counsel," Justice Flyte interrupted in a deliberately bored tone, "will you refrain from stump speeches? They don't do you any good, you know, not any good at all. And they simply antagonize this Court. This Court—"

"This Court," Regard said harshly, interrupting him, "had better pay attention to the will of this people! Otherwise this Court is going to be in big trouble!"

"Your effrontery," Mary-Hannah McIntosh said, her pince-nez quivering on her nose, her square, honest face suffused with indignation, "absolutely appalls me, counsel. How you can expect us to give adequate weight to your arguments when you come here and attempt to threaten the Supreme Court of the United States? How you can expect us—"

"Because you *are* the Supreme Court, your honor," Regard said softly, "and you are supposed to be above all that . . . *Are you?*"

There was stunned silence for several moments, broken only by the continuing distant murmur of the crowd. The size of the big marble room seemed to close in on the little handful of people at the bench and gathered just below it. Above them the ancient lawgivers looked down. No one spoke for quite a long time.

"Mr. Stinnet," Duncan Elphinstone said at last, "will you return to the issue or shall the Court go into recess and reach judgment without hearing your final arguments?"

"You cannot do that, your honor," Regard said with a respectful but adamantine firmness, "without inviting the certain wrath of an enormous number of your countrymen. It is checkmate."

The shocked silence enveloped them again. Hughie Demsted shifted in his chair.

"Chief, it is obvious that this man intends to fight this issue now, as he has throughout, on the front pages and on the television screens. He is apparently taking the gamble that his mobilization of public opinion is so effective that it can override any antagonism he may arouse here. He is in effect daring us to disagree with him, no matter what the law may be."

"As far as I am concerned," Wally Flyte said with an indifference that sounded quite genuine, "my vote will not be influenced one iota by either his bombast or his bluster—or his ubiquitous Justice NOW! If he makes his case, he has my vote. If he doesn't, he doesn't. And the hell with him."

"And so say I," said Ray Ullstein quietly.

"And I," said May McIntosh. "And I," said they all, while Debbie watched wide-eyed and almost breathless and Regard stood before them searching thoughtfully from face to face; not looking particularly threatening, but embodying one of the gravest challenges the Court had ever faced.

"Counsel," Duncan Elphinstone said softly, "it does appear to be checkmate. Now, would you like to continue?"

"Very well, your honor," Regard said, as though there had never been any interruption, "the matter of the jury, the alleged 'caprice or emotion' of South Carolina and the bearing of these upon the fairness of the trial in the courts below. Counsel opposite refrained from the jury-selection process. It was her free choice. As the transcript shows, I went to extraordinary lengths to be fair in my selections, absent her participation. I don't think I could have been any fairer, even choosing six avowedly opposed to the death penalty. And still, as Justice Hemmelsford noted, when the verdict came in it was unanimous for guilt and for death. So I think that issue might well be dismissed . . ."

He paused and took a drink of water, straightened his coat, his shoulders and his lanky form.

"So we come to the death sentence and the order by the Honorable James Perle Williams that the execution be public and televised. Petitioner pleads that the verdict of death is cruel and unusual punishment within the meaning of the Eighth Amendment, and he pleads that making the execution public and putting it on television would constitute 'cruel, unusual and *monstrous*' punishment. Apparently this is a voluntary and individual refinement of the Eighth Amendment which is based upon the same sort of emotional reaction that is charged against the state. We don't accept it, your honors, and I will tell you why.

"There is one simple, fundamental argument for putting the execution on television: to be a lesson and a warning. So dramatic—and so emphatic—that it cannot be ignored by criminals either actual or potential. A major and decisive deterrent to crime. A major turnaround to start this nation back on the road to a safe and secure society . . .

"That concludes my argument, your honors. I would now like to introduce my colleague representing *CBS et al.* to present, *amicus curiae,* the final argument for dismissing petitioner's plea against the televising of this execution. If it please the Court."

"Here comes the First Amendment," Wally Flyte murmured to the Chief. "And a shrewdly clever choice for it," the Chief agreed.

"Counsel," he said politely, "if you will come forward. Substantial time remains, but if possible we would appreciate your keeping it relatively short in the interests of speeding this matter along. Haven't we seen you here before? Mr. Eldridge, isn't it?"

"Eldridge, Muggridge, Pockthwaite and Thistle," said the kindly looking old lawyer who now stood before them comfortably relaxed, down-home and old-shoe, naming one of the most famously liberal—and profitably pragmatic—firms in the District of Columbia. "Yes, your honor, I have been here before; several times, in fact, the last being *CBS v. United States,* the so-called Haig Memorandum case."

"And we ruled against you," The Elph recalled.

The kindly old lawyer laughed.

"Not this time, I hope . . . Your honors: *CBS et al.,* which comprises Columbia Broadcasting System, the National Broadcasting System, the American Broadcasting System and a total of sixty-three independent cable television channels, appear here today *amicae curiae* to oppose the plea of petitioner in *Holgren v. South Carolina* insofar as it relates to a reversal of the order of Honorable James Perle Williams directing the televising of the public execution of petitioner. We address ourselves to this point only.

"We base our argument squarely upon the solid and impregnable foundation of the First Amendment to the Constitution, bolstered and underpinned by the principle, sanctified by custom in recent years to the point where it is now virtually a matter of law, 'the people's right to know.'"

"You think that extends to the people's right to see a fellow being die in their living room?" Justice Wallenberg inquired.

"Your honor," Mr. Eldridge said easily, "the people see probably a dozen fellow beings die in their living rooms every night of the year. Why should one more affront them? Especially when he has been convicted of the heinous crime of murder and has been condemned to death by due process of law?"

"In other words," Justice Wallenberg shot back, "television has created so casual an attitude toward violent death that the state may impose it willy-nilly in the assurance that it will be accepted casually no matter what the circumstances?"

"Especially when it is applied to a real-life murderer convicted of actual real-life crime by due process of law," Mr. Eldridge said blandly. "That should arouse even less protest. Few, aside from those with a special interest, protest violence on television nowadays. Why should they protest a death thus sanctified?"

"Expand on your argument for the First a little," Hughie Demsted suggested. "How do you stretch it?"

"Your honor!" Mr. Eldridge said with a fatherly smile. "Need I comment in *this* chamber that the Amendments are as elastic as a rubber band? Stretch them, indeed! Does anyone ever do anything else? The First says that Congress shall make no law abridging freedom of speech, or of the press—of which subsequent decisions here and elsewhere have confirmed television to be a part, for the purposes of the Amendment. Further it says that Congress shall make no laws abridging the right of the people peacefully to assemble, and to petition the government for a redress of grievances, which they now in great numbers"—he nodded toward the distant sound—"appear to be doing.

"To deny television—and the printed media, of course—access to the death of this individual would, in our humble opinion, be a direct, flagrant and insupportable abridgment of freedom of the press in the sense of the Amendment as broadened by subsequent interpretation. It would deny to the people that *intimate* and *immediate* knowledge of events which only television is equipped to bring them—that *actuality* which only television can provide. It would rob them of something vital to their welfare and peace of mind, namely the certain knowledge, *because they will have seen it with their own eyes the moment it happens,* that a criminal convicted of heinous crimes has indeed paid his debt to society and that justice has indeed been served quickly, decisively and without the endless delays so characteristic of our courts today.

"To deny television access to the death of this individual would be to deny perhaps the greatest of all of television's functions—its educative function.

"Poll after poll, survey after survey has shown decisively that a majority of the American people get their knowledge of events from television, with other forms of communication increasingly subsidiary and peripheral. The great majority learn all they know from television.

"It educates their minds.

"It forms their opinions.

"It molds and shapes their way of living, their attitudes toward their neighbors and themselves, their view of their own country and others, the very fabric and framework of their society and being.

"Television *is* America.

"America *is* television.

"Without it, where would we be?"

"I can see it's really great," Hughie Demsted said dryly, "but as one who has three kids who are exposed to this monster far more than their mother and I want them to be day in and day out, I am not so sure I want them to see a man actually die in front of their eyes on television."

"It happened in Vietnam, your honor," the kindly old lawyer said blandly. "It happened in Dallas and Atlanta and Los Angeles. Anwar Sadat went down in everybody's living room. El Salvador and Lebanon became as familiar as the house next door. Death after death, murder after murder, suicide after suicide, all, all, your honor, occurring in the intimacy of your own living room! Brought to you by television, the nation's greatest educational medium! Brought to you by television, the living heart of America! And now it is proposed to deny the people the right to see that justice indeed prevails, that crime is truly punished, that law does, after all, rule their land. Would you deny them that? That would indeed be an abridgment of the people's right to know!

"Nothing does it like television, your honors! Nothing!"

"How much do the networks expect to make off this?" Wally Flyte inquired.

"Your honor!" Mr. Eldridge exclaimed. "If I detect your meaning correctly, I can only say on behalf of my clients that we resent—"

"How much?" Justice Flyte repeated patiently. "Lots of big ones? Lots of bread? Millions and millions, maybe, in return for this great educational service they're so anxious to perform?"

"It would be a public service broadcast," the kindly old lawyer said stiffly, not looking so kindly.

"But somebody would sponsor it," Wally said. "They always do. How many contingency contracts already signed, counsel? How many big corporations already lined up? How many takers for Death in Prime Time?"

"I know nothing about that," the kindly old lawyer said, not at all friendly now, "nor do I consider it pertinent to our brief, your honor."

"No?" Justice Flyte said. "Well, I do."

"Perhaps you had best sum it up, counsel," Duncan Elphinstone suggested. "I think we get the drift."

"*CBS et al.*," Mr. Eldridge obliged in a coldly formal tone, "speaking *amicae curiae* in the case of *Holgren v. South Carolina,* oppose that portion of petitioner's plea that would seek to ban television from reporting the circumstances of his death at the moment of its occurrence. We base this on the First Amendment, freedom of the press and the people's right to know. We are adamant in our opposition to anything that would curtail and abridge our right to televise this execution, ordered by the court below and placed rightfully in the public domain for the public education by order of Judge Williams."

"Thank you, counsel," the Chief said, "and thank you all. I believe that concludes oral argument on briefs filed. The Court stands adjourned."

Businesslike and once more impassive, he and his sister and brethren rose and disappeared through the red velvet curtains, pausing in the Robing Room only long enough to disrobe, exchange head-shaking comments on the events of the morning, and agree to meet again at 10 A.M. Wednesday to start what they knew would be their long and heated discussion of the decision, or decisions, to be handed down in the case of *Holgren v. South Carolina.*

7

There ensued for them all one of the most intensive periods of searching precedents, reviewing law, reading briefs and transcripts that any of them had ever known. The work filled their days and extended late into their nights. The Chief and Birdie canceled out on the White House dinner for the Prince and Princess of Wales. Clem and Maidie Wallenberg abandoned plans to host a small party at the Jockey Club. May McIntosh and her fellow Watergaters, Hughie and Kay Demsted, even abandoned plans to share potluck one night in May's apartment. The Hemmelsfords and the Ullsteins, who had tickets together for a new play at Kennedy Center, turned them back. Tay and Moss, both still temporary bachelors, had planned to dine together at "one of those great little seafood restaurants" on the Potomac, but gave it up in favor, as Moss said, of "hitting the books just the way we used to." Wally Flyte, who had planned to attend the latest party of the newest hostess, called regretfully and begged off.

They were secluded all day in their chambers and on both Monday and Tuesday nights they all remained until well toward midnight. Few saw one another, though in customary Court fashion phone calls and memos flew back and forth between chambers in attempts to influence votes and change opinions. The public was allowed to resume visiting the building, in small numbers tightly controlled because of the Chief's concern for possible trouble from Justice NOW! But on the private corridors of the Court the hush of intense mental concentration fell.

Outside "in the real world," as Justice Flyte put it, the vast juggernaut of public opinion ground on. The pros and cons of both sides were debated extensively in the media, in public places and private homes everywhere. The major newspapers professed to be horrified by the position of *CBS et al.* but moral indignation seemed to be inspired basically by a fear of being outscooped by the competition. Self-important churchmen and academicians issued denunciatory statements, earnest movie stars agreed. Demonstrations for and against Earle Holgren disrupted campuses from Stanford to Harvard. Justice NOW! bombarded the Court with letters, telegrams and telephone calls until the staff finally gave up trying to cope and simply bundled up the messages and put the calls on hold. The big mob outside was gone but a picket line on regular two-hour shifts kept vigil entirely around the building and entirely around the clock.

The matter was being decided in nine hearts and minds in the inviolable privacy of their awesome, lonely power. Everyone, it seemed, had an idea of how they should decide, and everyone made his or her opinion vociferously known.

Only silence came from the great white building.

Nothing would be known until its inhabitants were ready.

No power on earth, despite Justice NOW!'s bluster, could really influence them, hurry them or control them in any way.

During these hours before conference, which seemed endless to them all, Tay's time passed even less easily, perhaps, than it did for the others. Moss obviously knew what he was going to do. Two or three others were leaning already in one direction or the other. The rest could probably distance themselves from it with some success regardless of their sympathy for him and Moss and achieve a relative objectivity. But it would be a long time before Tay could think of his daughter's destroyer with anything other than revulsion and hatred.

This was a fact of life. Somehow he must fight his way through it and attempt to reach the law on the other side. It was probably best that the Chief had set a deadline. Otherwise he could go forever and never really come to grips with it. Now he must.

Twice he called Cathy on his private line, each time seeking reassurance he felt only she could give. Each time he received it, not so much in the words as in the all-embracing, unquestioning, non-judgmental acceptance and comfort. He did not ask her advice and she did not offer it. She showed an innate delicacy and sense of fitness—and, he thought, respect for others' feelings—that only made him love her more.

He did love her now, fully and without reservation. He could hardly wait until it became possible to bring about the break with Mary and announce publicly his intention to marry Cathy. There was a certain pace that had to be followed for the sake of public opinion, the Court, Mary, Cathy, himself. But it was inevitable: a year, he thought. With good luck, perhaps less.

He did not call Mary but she called him, five times in two days. The theme was the same. He must vote to kill the monster. If the law stood in the way he must brush it aside. He could never look her in the face, never again consider himself worthy to be Janie's father, if he did not.

He asked, and this time was told, her condition. Being a healthy child, she was recovering fast in a basic physical sense. Otherwise, no change. There were dreadful moments when he wished the Lord would stop it all and let her go. He got over these but they left their scars. Try as he might he could not keep them from haunting his decision as he slowly and painfully began to inch himself toward it over those two endless days.

Eventually—a very long time, it seemed to him—they ended. He found himself again approaching the Conference Room, greeting his sister and his brethren, as in a daze taking his place, as the junior, at the foot of the table nearest the door. At his side his new law clerks had rolled up a book caddy containing the law books he wished to refer to, the notes and papers he wished to use in presenting his opinion to this jury of the only peers a Justice of the Supreme Court has. Along the table others were similarly equipped. He knew that in a sense his own symbols of preparation were only shadow play, for it was in the shadows somewhere, still unrevealed to him, that he knew he would ultimately find the words he would be called upon to speak when he voted on this case.

The Chief began it, as traditionally he always did with every case they considered. One by one in descending seniority they followed him. After the junior had spoken they would reverse the order and begin the voting from the junior up, although after the expression of views there usually was not much doubt where everyone stood.

Perhaps by then, the junior thought, seeming to draw up and away to some dream-place high above where he could look down, curiously, upon himself, he would know better what to do.

"You are familiar," Duncan Elphinstone said, "with the basic outlines of the case against petitioner and of the verdict and sentences rendered in the courts below. Let me review them briefly before we open discussion . . ."

Hear the stately words roll out, he thought to himself even as he almost automatically continued them until he had slowly, patiently and thoughtfully encapsulated all of the opposing arguments. How noble is The Elph and how mightily doth he pontificate! And how little doth he really know, when all is said and done, about what lies behind the law, the endless pain and clash and struggle of human beings back to the mist-lost centuries, as they have striven, with only feeble success at best, to bring their weaknesses—strengths—passions—prejudices—desires—ambition—hopes—dreams—amazing good, appalling evil—within the confines of the law . . .

He could see himself in mind's eye, twenty years old, just graduated from the University of Kentucky, arriving at Duke University Law School wide-eyed and bushy-tailed, ready to save the world . . . meeting Birdie almost at once, falling in love, very soon getting married . . . graduating third in his class, entering general practice with an old established firm in Louisville . . . moving along with growing success for a decade, fathering three . . . becoming a senior partner at what they told him was a remarkably early age, although in his impatience, which amused him now, he had expected it to happen virtually the moment he stepped in the door . . . becoming city attorney, county attorney, district attorney . . . serving in the state legislature for two terms . . . abandoning that to accept appointment, through the efforts of the late Senator Alben W. Barkley, as an assistant attorney general of the United States . . . resigning that to return to Kentucky as a member of the Kentucky supreme court . . . returning to Washington, again at the Senator's insistence, as Solicitor General . . . being appointed Associate Justice of the United States Supreme Court . . . subsequently being elevated to Chief Justice . . . still trying as best he could to make some sense of the human story . . . believing in the law, defending it, upholding it . . . *trying to determine what it is and what it should rightly be* . . .

"In general," he concluded, "I find myself inclined to agree with respondent on the facts of the case. Petitioner has not yet convinced me, though I am keeping an open mind for the moment. I grant you there are gaps."

That made one. "Open mind" or no, they were sure they knew where he stood.

"Gaps!" Clement Wallenberg snorted, out of order—Wally Flyte as senior Associate should have come next but Clem was too full of it to keep still. "I'll say there are *gaps!* This case stinks to high heaven from beginning to end! I think you've given your usual excellent summation, Dunc, but you're also giving us your usual disingenuous approach to it. 'Open mind'! What's to be open about? This individual was denied his rights—he was tried in an atmosphere so hectic that any other verdict was probably impossible—he was made a symbol and a scapegoat—he was given the death penalty which I will *never* support under *any* circumstances. Then some little two-bit judge who probably wanted to get his name in the papers agrees to the suggestion of somebody we *know* wants to get his name in the papers and orders this God-awful public-execution-on-television circus. My God, they probably cooked up the whole thing between them as a way to give this so-called Justice NOW! a boost! And you say you're *in doubt?*" He glared up and down the table, daring anyone to argue with him. "I say that's so much crap! The whole thing is a farce and an insult to the law!"

So he went on for perhaps ten more minutes, hashing and rehashing, while they patiently heard him out, elaborating and re-elaborating, while through his mind, too, went memories of a logger's son in the Michigan north woods who dreamed of being a lawyer someday . . . who went to a little one-room school for eight years, a tiny rural high school for two more . . . completed his studies himself at home because his father died of a heart attack and he had to drop everything to support his mother and two younger brothers . . . finally was able to go to the University of Michigan and from there to Northwestern University Law School . . . met Maidie, married, had a son and a daughter, both now tragically gone, the son in an auto accident, the daughter of breast cancer . . . became fired with the New Deal vision, plunged into social work in Detroit's ghettos for a time, became a defense lawyer for many activist groups in many genuinely humanitarian causes . . . ran for state attorney general, made it, held the job for eight contentious years battling "big business" and anyone else who happened to arouse his evangelistic ire . . . was appointed by the then President to be solicitor of the Department of Labor . . . was appointed to the U.S. Circuit Court of Appeals for the Sixth Judicial Circuit . . . was appointed Associate Justice of the Supreme Court and confirmed by a vote of 53–43, which, as he took pleasure in recording in his biography in the Congressional Directory, was "one of the closest confirmation battles in the history of the Supreme Court" . . . and fought, and continued to fight, for things as he saw them, which, as Hughie Demsted once wryly remarked, "makes it easy for him, because he only sees them one way" . . . never had qualms or hesitations or uncertainties . . . and never doubted, or ever would doubt, that his views on all subjects were the only ones possible to rational men . . .

"You know where I stand," he rasped out in conclusion. "This was a crappy case, and it's a crappy verdict. I never have and I never will support the death penalty and I certainly won't support it tied up in a little blue ribbon of prime time television!"

And that made one, on the other side.

"I, too," Justice Flyte said, "if I may now be permitted to speak," he added dryly—"have been struck, like my Brother Wallenberg, with the denial of petitioner's rights at time of arrest and with the general atmosphere of universal pressure which surrounded the case in South Carolina and, of course, has surrounded it here. But I wonder, really, if denial of rights is really all that important when the denial was undone and rights conferred within an hour—I believe we have heard it was about that—of time of arrest. As long as rights were granted within a reasonable time of arrest, I wonder if initial denial was really all that important to petitioner. I wonder if he was really hurt by it."

"You would!" Clem said. "If there's ever a weaselly way out, Wally, you'll find it."

"That's my Senate training," Justice Flyte said cheerfully, being used to this type of attack from his Brother Wallenberg. "Rave on, Clem. But I think I have a good point. Furthermore, while the pressure was great, it seems to me that it was not an insupportable burden. It's made *us* speed up things a bit, and it made *them* speed them up a bit down there, and I'm not so sure that's been a bad thing for either of us. As for the television bit, I find that abhorrent too, and I think we're going to have to handle it very carefully . . ."

And he went on in his owlishly cherubic, half-kidding, half-serious way as always, the little boy who grew up in southern Illinois, scion of an extremely well-to-do, for those days, railroad family, quite the cutest, brightest, roly-polyest little boy his teachers had ever seen . . . who got straight A's in everything all the way through grammar school, high school and college (Dartmouth), and then went on to graduate first in his class at law school (Yale) and move immediately into one of the three biggest law firms in Chicago . . . who then went on in quick succession to state senate, U.S. House of Representatives, United States Senate, was thrice unsuccessful candidate for President whose needed support for another was finally won by the promise of an Associate Justiceship on the Supreme Court . . . childless survivor of the late Marie, whom he had wed quite late, at thirty-five, loved dearly and with great devotion for twenty years, lost to cancer and grieved quietly

but intensely to this day with a depth of feeling very few were perceptive enough to realize he possessed . . . bon vivant, inveterate party-
goer, amiable, easygoing, extremely popular survivor in Washington's
ever-tossing social sea . . . frequent brooder—although, again, very few
ever realized it—about the law, who, like The Elph (who did realize it)
often reflected humbly on the enormous power the nine shared, and frequently felt that he really was not worthy to help exercise it . . . but
did, with a lively flair and a jaunty spirit because, as he once confided to
Dunc, "Somebody has to do this peculiar job, and we're it, so onward
and upward!" . . . never complained, rarely argued, always accepted
without demur the opinions assigned to him to write, receiving thereby
the media sobriquet "the workhorse of the Court"—to which he responded amicably, "Thanks, but I'd rather be in Philadelphia" . . .
Good Old Wally, the eternal reliable . . .

"Therefore," he concluded, "I'm like Dunc, begging your pardon,
Clem: I'm keeping an open mind at the moment, too. And I must say
you haven't convinced me of anything yet, for all your bluster."

And that, they thought, made two—on that side.

"Given the errors below and the general hectic atmosphere that has
surrounded this matter from the beginning," Justice Ullstein said
gravely, "I find myself constrained to agree in large part with my
Brother Wallenberg. I too find the death penalty abhorrent, and as you
know have consistently voted against it here as I always did in New
York. Putting aside my instinctive and very deep and genuine sympathy
for the human tragedies suffered by our two junior brethren—which has
not been easy for any of us to do, I am sure—I yet feel that the basic
thrust of the plurality's decision must come down on the side of petitioner if the law and constitutional guarantees are to be preserved . . ."

And in the same grave tone he went thoughtfully and precisely on,
the beautifully behaved, strikingly handsome little boy whose extremely
wealthy parents had given him every possible advantage and every possible loving encouragement to follow wherever his obviously brilliant
mind would take him . . . who had thought at first he might be a great
doctor, then had come to the conclusion, somewhere along the way in
his undergraduate days at Princeton, that he would rather be a great
lawyer . . . who had gone on to Harvard Law School, finishing first in
his class . . . who had instinctively felt something of Clem Wallenberg's
sympathy for the underdog, though above and forever insulated—
prompted by an innate goodness of heart that everyone who knew him
well could recognize beneath the shy, almost cold, exterior . . . who
obediently had entered corporate law in response to family desires and

family expectations, never imposed upon him outright but just with that gentle, insistent, inexorable and inescapable family pressure that at his economic level of Jewish culture substituted for shouts and tears and wildly emotional demands that he not disappoint his parents . . . who yet retained in his mind and heart the feeling that somewhere, someday, he should seek the opportunity to do more for his less fortunate countrymen . . . who eventually found this when five of his major clients came to him one day and asked him to run for state attorney general . . . consulted with Hester, whom he had met and married at twenty-four and with whom he had three daughters and a son, all now in the law, to his delight; and was asked in return, "Why not?" . . . ran and won and, free of corporate restraints, began to speak out more and more vocally on social issues . . . was about to run for governor when the incumbent appointed him to the state supreme court . . . was appointed an Associate Justice of the United States Supreme Court, a total surprise to him but not to Senator Jacob Javits, who had been his chief and most active sponsor for years . . . had served with rigid integrity and quiet distinction ever since, a generally "strict constructionist"—on the liberal side—which had always galled Clem Wallenberg, who felt threatened because Ray had become something of a quiet hero to much of the media . . . one of the rocks of the Court, "good to have around," as The Elph had told him once, which pleased him, since The Elph did not freely hand out compliments . . . troubled by the law's injustices and inconsistencies many times but always able to find a sustaining faith in it, nonetheless . . .

"And so," he concluded, "while I too am still open to persuasion, it's fair to say that I'm leaning toward petitioner, particularly insofar as relates to conduct of the trial, denial of rights, violation of constitutional protections and the television proposal . . ."

And that made two on that side.

"Two to two," Justice McIntosh remarked with a smile. "We're up to the halfway mark and I'm going over the mark." She adjusted her pince-nez, ran a quick hand over her close-cropped gray hair, clasped her hands in front of her and leaned forward earnestly as she used to do when addressing her law classes at Stanford. The gesture, so characteristic and instinctive, took her back immediately, even as she cleared her throat and began in her even, precise "decision voice," as Moss used to call it in his more lighthearted days.

"Petitioner," she said, "comes here carrying a heavy burden. Circumstantial evidence grounds the verdict of guilty; it does not, it seems to me, excuse the errors and inadvertencies, if one can accept them as such, that seem to surround his capture and trial. Nor does it, in my estimation, excuse the attempt by Judge Williams to turn this into a mindboggling television extravaganza. As a matter of fact, this in itself puzzles me: the transcript shows him to have been such a fair-minded, level-headed man. It is as though all whom petitioner touches seem to undergo some change. He must be a strange individual, to cause such reactions. I wonder if that is sufficient to excuse them . . ."

Curiosity about other people's reactions, she supposed, was what had underlain most of her life and brought her finally to the high eminence she now held. She had always been a curious child, a restless and dominant mind constantly searching for a proper channel. She was the fourth child of five born to a lawyer turned professor; and when he came presently to the Stanford Law School faculty, she felt that she had found her way at last. Not for her the placid routines of marriage, childbearing, housewifery followed by most of her contemporaries in those days: she was going to be a lawyer like Daddy. She was going to show Daddy, whom she worshiped but felt some impelling, never-articulated need to excel. And so she did, graduating with highest honors from high school in Palo Alto . . . going on to complete her pre-law course at Stanford magna cum laude . . . graduating second in her class at Stanford Law . . . applying for and immediately receiving a position on the faculty at Duke, where she stayed for ten years, then moved to Northwestern where she became, after a five-year stay, assistant dean of the law school . . . returned triumphantly three years later to Stanford at the personal request of the dean of the Law School, who had big things in mind for her (though not, as he confessed in an affectionate letter from retirement when she was appointed to the Court, quite *that* big) . . . began to settle into the comfortable groove, as assistant dean, where she fully expected to stay for the remainder of her professional life . . . was promoted quite unexpectedly to dean . . . was, amazingly, nominated to the Supreme Court . . . took it in stride, though not without a secret inescapable thrill when her father, long since retired, her mother, her two sisters and two brothers and their respective husbands and wives and a joint total of sixteen nephews and nieces came to Washington to see Aunt May sworn in . . . assumed her duties with a diligence, vigor and decisiveness that won her the immediate admiration of her brethren and a consistently good press—"Very important," as Clem Wallenberg assured her approvingly soon after she got there, "as a lot of it is image, you know; a lot is image" . . . extremely bright, hardworking, fairminded, "liberal" in the main, though sometimes wandering, as they all did now and then, confounding critics who wanted to put them in immovable categories . . . married to the Court as she had been married to the law all her adult life . . . and never missing, except in the long hours of lonely nights that sometimes shook her more than her brethren ever dreamed or she would ever admit to anyone, the routine of marriage, children, housewifery that in her day had been the eagerly sought and joyfully accepted lot of so many of her contemporaries . . . Good Old May—like Good Old Wally and Good Old Ray—a workhorse, a reliable, a rock . . . resting sometimes on shaky emotional foundations but always managing to restore them to stability before they tipped too far and anyone could suspect . . .

"Petitioner," she said, leaning back with both hands now outstretched before her, firmly grasping the edge of the table—another characteristic gesture when she was about to conclude—"undoubtedly *is* guilty, in my estimation, and certainly, based on a reading of the transcript, needs deep psychiatric treatment and confinement, probably for life. Like my Brother Ullstein and my Brother Wallenberg, I too am opposed to the death sentence as a matter of lifelong principle, and I certainly am opposed to any TV extravaganza. It seems to me the plurality might be able to find some middle ground in all this. At any rate I am leaning toward such a solution."

"Which makes it three to two?" Justice Demsted inquired with a smile. "Or is it two to two and a half?"

"Three quarters, maybe," she said with an answering smile. "I haven't quite decided yet."

"Very enlightening," Justice Hemmelsford said with a good-natured grumpiness, twitching his eyebrows and peering along the conference table in mock severity. "Women! I must say. It reminds me of the story—"

"No time for stories, Rupe," she said. "This is serious business."

"Yes," Moss said in an expressionless voice, breaking an impassive silence heretofore. "Yes, it is."

There was a moment's uncomfortable pause. Then Justice Hemmelsford cleared his throat and began in a straightforward manner, eschewing the twitchings and twinklings, the leers and the Old Rupe-ings.

"I find it difficult to see," he said, "how my Sister McIntosh and my Brethren Wallenberg and Ullstein manage to skirt so neatly around the nature of petitioner's crimes and their very horrendous, heinous nature. These were cruel and monstrous crimes and I think they deserve the condemnation of all decent people."

"Which they have," Justice Flyte said calmly. "Mush on, Brother."

"Well," Justice Hemmelsford said, not mollified much by his old friend and fellow ex-Senator, "my position, I am afraid, is not quite so noble as some. Nor do I feel that it is a position unsupported by law. I think the law is completely on the side of the death penalty, providing it is surrounded with safeguards such as those carefully delineated in South Carolina law. While I have considerable qualms about the television aspect, still I think that, too, lies within the discretion of the court below. I think that if we attempt to pass on it we would be stepping into an area that does, as *CBS et al.* argues, go to the heart of present-day American civilization."

"If such it can be called," Justice Demsted said dryly. His Brother Hemmelsford peered down at him at the other end of the bench and said, "Bah!"

"I am not going to indulge in whimsical sophistries with my Brother Demsted on this issue I think this Court, to put it bluntly, would be well advised to duck the television issue altogether. Far from condemning it or entering into the controversy, as that little biddy who represents petitioner wants us to do, I think we should stay far and away the hell out of it. I am not afraid of controversy, God knows, but we have reached a situation in the country on this issue where we are in danger of running head-on into a majority of public opinion."

"That stops Senators," The Elph said calmly, "but when was it ever supposed to stop a Justice of the Supreme Court?"

"Oh, Dunc, stop being holier-than-thou!" Rupe said in an annoyed tone. "Particularly when you're the one who caved in to public pressure and rushed us into this early session, hardly giving us time to read the briefs!"

"Yes," The Elph admitted, "I was the one. But I didn't detect any great ground swell of protest when I called you all and consulted about it before making the announcement. I did it because I was thinking of the Court. I thought it was wise to tack with the wind a little. I don't think we're really going to bow to our friends out there"—he too gestured in the general direction of the faithful picket line—"when it comes to the decision. Do you?"

"Certainly *I'm* not,' Justice Hemmelsford said. "I say we should react like decent human beings to this worthless thug and treat him the way decent human beings should treat him. And I'm not forgetting the law, either! I find plenty of it on my side . . . Now," he said, more calmly, "I want to tell you how I see it."

And, a bit flamboyantly, he did, with the gestures and the orotund language befitting one who, born and bred a Texan, had started orating at age ten and discovered then that he possessed the innate ability to hold and sway an audience . . . who had honed and improved the talent as he moved on through his grammar school and high school years to seek and win one elective class office after another, so that he wound up in his senior year in high school as president of the student body . . . who went on to attend the University of Texas, where he played football, made Phi Beta Kappa, was president of the debating society, and once again president of a student body in his senior year . . . by then had determined that the law, and very likely politics, would be his ultimate destination, and was sent off to Harvard Law School by his modestly fixed parents who had long ago determined that they would give their only child every possible advantage that they could, and scraped and saved to do so . . . applied himself with fierce ambition and determination, aided by "Miss Sally" Ingraham, whom he met and married at twenty-three and who possessed an ambition for him as fierce as his own . . . graduated second in his class and within two weeks had a job in Washington as assistant to his local Congressman, an easygoing soul of great wealth in oil and land who did not pay too much attention to his constituents and left "most of that borin' stuff" to Rupe and within four years found himself ousted by his young protégé, who served three terms in the House and then ran successfully twice for governor . . . and then moved on to the United States Senate, where he soon became part of the inner circle whose members really run the Senate . . . proved himself to be a shrewdly brilliant and practical mind, basically conservative on most social issues, dissembled behind a deliberately cultivated "typically Texas" flamboyance . . . elevated to the Supreme Court by a President who felt the Court needed a little more conservative balance . . . a "strict constructionist" but one who on some issues showed a surprising liberalism . . . generally considered, even by his strongest initial critics, to be "one of the better members" of the Court . . . quite set in his opinions by now and basically as intolerant as Clement Wallenberg of everybody else's . . . rather more typical than most of the rather odd grab bag of differing Presidents' beliefs, impulses and political necessities that the Court, in essence, is . . .

"So it seems to me," he said in conclusion, "that counsel for the state is essentially correct in what I consider some of his most telling points: that the infringement of petitioner's constitutional rights at the time of his arrest was inadvertent and occurred in the heat of battle, so to speak; that denial was a natural human reflection of the abhorrence felt toward the crimes committed—an abhorrence that should not be too glibly overlooked here, it seems to me; and that denial was speedily rectified within an hour or so when tempers had a chance to cool a little. As I said, I think we had best stay out of the television issue. There is no compulsion upon us to get involved in that. Prudence would indicate silence, in my estimation."

The tally at this point appeared to stand three to three.

"I am afraid," Justice Demsted said, leaning back thoughtfully, "that I cannot agree with my Brother Hemmelsford, or with others who have indicated a desire to evade the clear-cut challenge to human decency, to the right of privacy, to the very fabric of Western civilization inherent in the television issue. Such evasion, it seems to me, would be a craven abdication of our implicit duty to uphold certain norms and decencies of society. I think we have a duty to stand against it. It is a simple matter of human decency. To me it is one of the fundamentals of this case."

And as he had done all his life, he went earnestly ahead; not as witty and coruscating as some perhaps, not as brilliant as others, but sound, solid, good-hearted, compassionate and above all, as Mary-Hannah had once murmured to Clem during one of Hughie's opinions from the bench, *good* . . . *good* as a child, when as the oldest of four in Northeast Washington he had helped his widowed mother every morning take care of the younger ones before she went off to her job as secretary to one of the top officials of the Department of Justice . . . good as a boy when he began to bring home better and better grades from school and apply himself, where many of his contemporaries did not, to improving his knowledge, improving his grammar, improving his appearance, improving *himself* . . . good as a youth when, with his mother remarried to a bright young lawyer from the Solicitor General's office and the family in better financial shape, he was able to concentrate on his studies and conclude high school with high academic honors and a growing interest in the law prompted by his stepfather, who was perceptive enough to recognize Hughie's potential and generous enough to push it in every way he could . . . good as a student at Howard University, where he finished his pre-law course with top honors . . . good as a student at Howard Law School, where his work was outstanding and where he graduated fourth in his class . . . good in practice with one of the capital's leading black law firms . . . good as a husband and father after he met equally bright Katherine Bastian, a fellow lawyer, married her, and broke away to establish their own small firm dealing principally in cases arising under civil rights laws and statutes . . . good as a father when Kay had a son, a daughter and a second son in quick succession and decided to be a housewife, though always at his side with invaluable advice and support as he became more actively involved in the civil rights and social areas, more and more deeply involved in politics in the District of Columbia . . . deciding to run for public office, becoming successively city councilman, mayor of Washington and finally, for two terms, the District's nonvoting delegate in the House of Representatives . . . being appointed assistant secretary of the Department of Housing and Urban Development, elevated two years later to Secretary when his predecessor resigned to seek a Senatorship . . . nominated and confirmed six years ago by a vote of 83–16 an Associate Justice of the Supreme Court . . . voted one year to be "most valuable member of the Court" by the American Bar Association, which he knew was an example of self-conscious reverse discrimination, but also knowing that he genuinely *was* one of the best . . . in love with the Court and still, in his heart, in awe of its enormous breathtaking power and his own share in it, and humbly and deeply grateful for the opportunity . . . aware, like all of them, of the law's difficulties and inadequacies in the face of a doom-threatened, chaotic age . . . but determined, as they all were, to try to make some sense of it and help to hold some kind of line against all the forces that threatened to send the world spinning out of control, off the edge, into the final nothing . . .

"I would like to be able to agree with my Brother Hemmelsford," he concluded, "and with my Brother Flyte and my Brother Elphinstone, but I cannot. Not only on constitutional grounds but on the television issue, I am afraid I must part company. The state has not convinced me. Petitioner may be worthless as a human being, and indeed in this privacy I am prepared to concede that he is. But the law is the law, and as I read it, his arguments have not so far been successfully refuted."

And that, according to their individual calculations, as they came finally to Moss, was four to three. They were all sure it would soon be four to four. What it would be after that, when the most junior spoke his piece at last, none of his colleagues at that moment would have ventured to say.

Nor was he yet prepared to say himself, he realized with something close to panic, as Moss cleared his throat and spoke very briefly in a calm and level voice that did not invite, and clearly would not accept, interruption:

"An obviously psychotic petitioner is before us. He has committed heinous crimes. Society would obviously be better off without him. Which is the greater good, the 'rights' of an individual who cares nothing for law or human life and has by his own deliberate act forfeited all claim to charity, or the good of the society which has already suffered deeply from his twisted evil, and could suffer much more if swift and final punishment is not visited upon him?

"This is, quite simply, a *bad man*—born bad, apparently—victim of some twisted turn in his own nature for which his parents are not responsible, nor society, nor anyone but the Lord in His mysterious wisdom. But that does not mean that the rest of us should have to suffer as"—his voice hesitated, almost broke, resumed and went steadily on— "as my wife, my daughter, myself, Tay and Holgren's hapless woman and child have suffered.

"We cannot be our brother's keeper on every possible occasion, though that has been fashionable philosophy in recent years. There is a limit.

"This petitioner, in my estimation, has gone far beyond it. It is time, I think, to forget the precious niceties of the law, the extreme straining after gnats that has plagued our jurisprudence in these recent decades, the general emphasis on further punishing the victim by letting the criminal either go free altogether or escape with chastisement that is not only inadequate but is, in a grim, ghastly sort of way, outright laughable.

"I stated my view basically when I rejected the appeal for stay. I intend to expand upon it further in a separate opinion when decision is rendered. I think it is clear enough where I stand."

He sat back and for several moments no one spoke. Sarah Ann Pomeroy supported him and in her presence there was no possible counter argument anyone could offer her father. Fond as they were of him, and sympathetically as their emotions were bound up with his, no one tried.

The division now apparently stood four to four.

"And what say you, our Brother Barbour?" the Chief inquired softly, and the room became very still as they all turned at last to await the evidently now decisive view of their newest member.

For what seemed to him a very long time he did not look up or acknowledge their gaze or in any way respond to the Chief's gentle question, which was also, in some degree, command. He remained motionless, face somber, staring down the length of the table, which by now was covered with a sprawl of books and papers, half-empty cups of coffee, half-drained glasses of water and yellow legal notepads scrawled with notes. He was not yet ready. Something still held him back. Slowly he looked along their worried, sympathetic faces until his eyes met those of Duncan Elphinstone, facing him at the other end of the table.

"Would it be entirely out of order and too offensive to the Court," he asked in a voice that showed considerable strain, for he did not know how they would take it, "if I were to request that I be allowed to pass at this time and state my views and my vote at the conclusion of the tally?"

Again there was silence. Finally the Chief smiled.

"No. For lawyers here we have rules but for Justices we have only customs: we have no binding rules. Constitutionally there can be none, since we are each of us a part of a sovereign branch of the government and therefore sovereign in our own right. If our Brother Barbour needs further time, he has it."

There were murmurs of assent and with a matter-of-fact air softened by the archaic language he liked to affect on such occasions, he turned to Moss as the next most junior and inquired,

"How say you to the petition, Brother Pomeroy?"

"I say no," Moss responded quietly, "reserving the right to express my views on certain aspects of the case in a separate opinion."

"And you, Brother Demsted?"

"I say yes," Hughie said, "with similar reservation."

"Brother Hemmelsford?"

"I say no, with similar reservation."

"Sister McIntosh?"

"I say yes," she said, "with similar reservation."

"My goodness," The Elph remarked with a smile, "we're going to have opinions to end opinions, on this one. Brother Ullstein?"

"I say yes, with similar reservation," Ray said quietly.

"Brother Wallenberg?"

"I say yes," Clem said bluntly, "and I don't have any reservations. I reject the state's whole damned proposition."

"Brother Flyte?"

"I say no, with similar reservation."

"I too say no," the Chief said, "with similar reservations . . . and so, our Brother Barbour, we come back to you. Are you ready to state your views and vote?"

Twice he started to reply. Each time he felt a choking sensation as though a hand had closed over his throat. He realized his heart was beating rapidly, his face felt flushed, his skin hot. He was actually physically uncomfortable, in an odd but perhaps not surprising reflection of his inner turmoil. Now that the moment had come he again felt completely uncertain and adrift as though he were floating somewhere out beyond the edge of reason.

"I—" he began; stopped; swallowed. "I . . ."

The Chief studied him for a moment with a kindly expression.

"Would you like more time, Tay? We really aren't under all that much of a deadline. If you want another day or two—"

"I could take ten," he said, finding his voice with a wry bitterness, "and still be no surer. Why don't you give me overnight, if"—he looked along the table: sympathetic looks responded—"if that wouldn't inconvenience the rest of you too much."

The Elph nodded.

"If you're sure that's enough—?"

"It's got to be," he replied, something close to desperation in his voice. "I can't keep myself from facing this any longer."

"Very well," the Chief said. "We'll meet again at ten tomorrow. Will you be in your chambers most of the time?"

"Except when I go home to sleep, I expect. If I can sleep."

"Good," the Chief said. He smiled. "No doubt some of us will want to communicate with you to help you make up your mind . . . since you're the swing vote, now, and the final decision is up to you."

And so it was, with no possibility of equivocation or evasion any longer. Now the twistings and turnings, the balancing of arguments, the battle of pros and cons that had occupied most of his active hours and underlain all his days and thoughts since his return to Washington must cease. There was no more hiding place down here. Now he was about to find out what it could mean to be a Justice of the United States Supreme Court with everything depending, and the attention of his country and the whole world focused, inescapably, upon him.

For an hour or so after he returned to his chambers he simply sat, hardly thinking at all, while time drifted, his mind drifted, the universe, it almost seemed, drifted.

He hoped for a while that out of the drift would come some sudden revelation, some blinding answer that would make it all clear. It did not. He would still have to work it out for himself. There still was no easy way.

Slowly and painfully he began to review the arguments of both sides . . . measured against Janie, against whom all things seemed now to be measured . . .

And this, of course, was where it all broke down, and where, each time he thought he had reached some sort of compromise with conscience and conditioning, it all fell apart as the hours dragged slowly on through afternoon and into evening.

Janie . . . Janie . . . *Janie.*

Mary need not worry that his daughter was too far away to influence his decision.

He did indeed, as The Elph had predicted, hear from his sister and brethren, in some cases several times, as the long hours passed. Memos and phone calls always flowed back and forth between chambers on any important case; sometimes personal visits were included if friendships were particularly close. In his case he had not been in office long enough to develop any, except of course with Moss; and Moss, knowing very well from student days that there came a point where it was best not to push Tay any further, called him once, said, "You know what I think, but you do what you think is right," and hung up without waiting for an answer. All the others either sent memos or telephoned, and in some cases, such as Justice Wallenberg and the Chief, did both.

Tay fended off three memos and four phone calls from Clem as best he could, finally terminating the discussion by saying in a tone of cold exasperation, "Justice, give me some credit for having *some* brains, if you don't mind! All right?"

"*Well,*" Clem said. "*Well!*"

"Thank you," Tay responded crisply. "I appreciate that," and hung up.

The Chief, as was his nature, was more sympathetic, more diplomatic and obviously working toward some purpose of his own over and above convincing Tay to go with what the Chief hoped would be the majority. Duncan Elphinstone was an astute man and he had given considerable study to his new Associate.

He felt by now that he knew him pretty well and, like Moss, did not pressure him overmuch.

"I wonder if you would be offended if I suggested that possibly you could let me know what you've decided as soon as you have decided it? I can then tell the others and assign someone to write the majority opinion—as the Chief does, you know, when he is in the majority—if I *am* in the majority—instead of reconvening a formal conference to hear your views. If you want us to meet formally, of course we will, but I thought maybe in the interests of saving time . . ."

Tay thought for a moment, then said slowly, "I don't see why not."

"Fine!" the Chief said with a satisfaction that seemed a little greater than the occasion warranted. "That's just fine! Then you'll let me know as soon as—"

"I can't promise how soon that will be," he reminded. "It's only eight
P.M., at this point."

"I'm going home pretty soon," Duncan Elphinstone said, "but if you
reach a decision anytime up to midnight or even one A.M., call me and
I'll pass the word. And thank you."

"I will," Tay said, "and you're welcome."

And hung up, a little puzzled. He didn't quite see what Dunc was
driving at, though for a moment an uneasy suspicion crossed his mind.

He turned back to his desk, his legal notepad and his tortuous broodings that always came back to the same points. In front of him lay five
other memos to go with Clem's, and with Moss' and the Chief's verbal
communications. The split was still four to four. No miracle had occurred. The burden of final decision still lay on him.

Around 10 P.M. he thought he had reached a conclusion, began tentatively to draft an opinion. Within fifteen minutes he had torn it into
fine fragments that he pitched into his wastebasket, and began another.
Twenty minutes later that also followed.

On the one hand stood the law. On the other stood his human feelings and emotions. He was not supposed to have them any more, in his
new eminence.

Janie . . . Mary's shy announcement, far, far back when the world
was young and his wife was capable of shyness and of spontaneous,
genuine, untortured love . . . the arrival of something tiny, red and
squawling which, with some incongruity but with more accuracy than he
as a new parent could then realize, reminded him of the motto of the
United States: "In this year was born a new order of things" . . . the
new order taking over their lives, their household, their dreams and
hopes for the future . . . becoming even more precious when Mary refused to have more . . . growing before they knew it into a precocious
little toddler, blond and chubby, always laughing, with a gurgling
chuckle that cut through his heart like a knife as he heard it again right
now . . . passing unscathed through the standard childhood diseases,
bouncing back quickly, almost always in excellent health . . . suddenly
a schoolgirl, somewhere around seven or eight, dressed in something
blue and frilly, solemnly helping her mother serve coffee and cookies to
her grandparents when they came from California for a visit . . . recit-
ing a poem in school, probably aged ten or eleven, stumbling, blushing,
looking as though she might cry but suddenly getting a second wind and
going on triumphantly to the end, with a happy beam at her parents,
both of whom misted over . . . moving on through the school years increasingly popular, increasingly active, growing steadily prettier, grow-

ing out of gawkiness toward the promise of real beauty . . . beginning to develop a questioning, independent yet intensely practical mind of her own that delighted him with its frequent challenges to his own ideas, its ability to understand and handle the increasingly complicated concepts it encountered at school and at home . . . the first dance, the first boy, the first intimations, thrilling him and dismaying Mary, that she might follow him eventually into the law . . . the realization, as he and Mary drifted apart, that his daughter and his dreams, hopes and plans for her were now becoming most of what he meant when he talked proudly about "my family" . . . all the bright dreams, the bright laughter, the bright promise, gone—gone—into darkness and, apparently, endless night . . . because of "petitioner," a word he had clung to because it served to keep at one reserve the smugly arrogant face, the savage eyes and deceptively smiling countenance of the only being in his life he had ever really, genuinely hated and would always hate, as long as breath remained: psychopath—murderer—monster . . . Earle Holgren . . . "Petitioner" . . .

Janie!

The great white temple of the law was silent and deserted in the night.

He put his head on his arms and gave way at last to the grief he had managed to control in reasonably good order up to now.

When the storm had passed a cold calm settled finally on his mind. Slowly and methodically he set aside his emotions, went once more point by point over everything he knew and had experienced of the law. Then he carefully placed his notes neatly at his left hand; took a fresh legal pad out of his desk and placed it squarely before him; took up a pen and began to write.

Shortly before midnight he called the Chief and told him all that he had decided. The Chief was matter-of-fact, brief and to the point.

"Yes, I think that is the logical way out. I believe you are doing the right thing. How soon can you write your opinion?"

"Tomorrow, if you like."

"That's too soon. It is not going to be easy."

"No," he agreed with a heavy sigh. "It is not going to be easy."

The Elph became fatherly.

"Go on home and get a good night's sleep. You need it."

"I doubt if I'll sleep much."

"You'll be surprised. Good night."

Before he left chambers he made one quick call on his private line.

"I'm glad," she said. She, too, thought he had done the right thing.

Half an hour later, after a quick drive through the almost entirely deserted streets past all the mighty monuments and buildings of his native land, he was home and in bed. He had just time to be surprised that his mind was no longer in turmoil when all thought ceased and he fell instantly into deep, exhausted, dreamless sleep.

HOLGREN DECISION DUE MONDAY. HIGH COURT SETS SPECIAL SESSION TO DECIDE FATE OF ALLEGED KILLER. RIVAL LAWYERS CONFIDENT. JUSTICE NOW! RESUMES 24-HOUR VIGIL. "EXTREME SECURITY" PLANNED FOR MEETING.

8

Again the steamy heat—the leaden sky—the threat of thunderstorm later—the picket line stretching all around the building—the metropolitan police and the Army on guard outside—the Court's own security force alert and nervous inside. Very few were allowed to pass through the great bronze doors and the ground-floor entrance this day: regular staff, law clerks, media. All others were barred.

Around the Court, stretching out from the picket line on all sides to the adjacent streets, an enormous crowd shoved and jostled. Their unceasing gabble rose now and again to crescendo as slogans, exhortations and shouts, unintelligible but clearly menacing to the Court, burst out. Facing the pickets, backs to the building, rifles at rest but pointedly ready, a line of soldiers, sent up by the Pentagon at the President's order, stood impassively sweating in the rising heat.

"Aren't we overdoing it a bit?" Justice Flyte inquired of The Elph when they arrived in the Chief's limousine shortly after 9 A.M. and were hurried in the garage entrance. A quick look around convinced him that they were not. All the makings of chaos were present. In a way the Court had not known for many decades, it was in the eye of the storm.

In the Robing Room a few moments later everyone was sober and grim: no jokes, no laughter, no old, accustomed ease. Even Wally was serious now. The traditional handshake held an extra fervor, a deep and almost desperate pressure, a feeling of "We're all in this together"—a feeling that they just might not come out of it this time . . . although of course they knew they would.

They were the Court.

They had to.

It would be an unthinkable blow to America if they did not.

But it was a grim-faced eight men and a woman who stepped forward through the red velvet curtains when the Marshal cried his "Oyez! Oyez!" The chamber was full to overflowing. In every last inch of space members of the media from all over the world were crowded. The room had been scoured for bombs inch by inch for two solid hours. Everyone who entered had passed through a metal detector and been thoroughly searched. All precautions would seem to have been taken. But it was a strange time, in all lands: and one never knew.

"We are armored in the law," the Chief had reminded, in a voice more serious than joking, when the ten o'clock bell rang and they began to move forward to their chairs. They told themselves this would be enough. But one never knew.

When all in the chamber were seated, the Justices stared out with an impassivity a little more set and determined than usual upon the restlessly stirring media. The Chief began to speak in a quiet, almost conversational tone.

"The public information officer informs me that there has been considerable disgruntlement among our friends of the media because on this occasion we have not published the opinions of the Court"—the plural was hastily jotted and underlined on several hundred notepads—"simultaneously with their delivery. Nor are we publishing the customary 'syllabus,' as it has come to be known in recent years, which is a headnote containing a summation of the case and opinions for the easy reference, understanding and convenience of the media.

"The custom of simultaneous publication has been abandoned on this occasion after consultation among all members of the Court. Although we are not agreed on everything about this case"—he smiled slightly and in his audience the Associated Press murmured to UPI, "Oh, come on! For Christ's sake stop being cute and get on with it!"—"we were agreed that the utmost of discretion must be exercised to make sure that no advance intimation of our decision should reach the public. The reasons for this," he said with a sudden sharp glance at Regard, sitting attentively in the front row, "are obvious in what you all passed through outside on your way in here.

"In this case, the vote stood four to four at the conclusion of conference. The deciding vote was cast, and the majority opinion—at his own request—will be delivered by"—he paused and the tension shot up a hundredfold—"Justice Barbour."

There was an instant expulsion of pent-up breath, an excited stirring and whispering, "a quiet tumult," as Ray Ullstein had once put it to his seatmate Rupert Hemmelsford on another tense Court occasion. Decorum held, but only just.

Within the heart of the junior member quiet tumult also prevailed. But though it cost him more than anyone but Cathy, possibly, would ever know, he forced his voice to its customary grave and measured level and began to read, looking up from time to time for emphasis, not seeing anything in particular when he did . . . just history, perhaps— and himself, caught in its endless ironic twistings.

He began in straight narrative fashion, having discovered from many perusals that there is no set pattern for opinions in the Court, style and manner of presentation being as diverse as the personalities of the Justices who deliver them. After reviewing the circumstances of Earle's arrest, the trial, the verdict and the television proposal, he came to the nub of it:

"All of these complex issues might be addressed by the Court. The plurality has chosen to address itself to three only: whether petitioner's constitutional rights were violated in the manner of his arrest; whether his trial was fairly conducted in view of substantial popular outcry for a verdict of guilty; and whether the death penalty was properly imposed according to the laws of the state of South Carolina in conformity with prior rulings of this Court."

("And no ruling on the merits of the death penalty itself?" the New York *Times* inquired blankly of no one in particular. "And whether it is proper to televise—or to ban television?" *TV Guide* murmured in similar puzzlement. An uneasy stirring began to transmit itself, by a sort of journalistic osmosis, along the close-packed benches of the media. "Sidestep!" the Washington *Post* whispered scornfully. "Cop-out!" charged the Los Angeles *Times*. Ever-ready suspicion changed the mood instantly from excited anticipation to sarcastic put-down. Anticipating this, the tone of the Justice hardened.)

"There may be some who may wish the Court to address a multiplicity of issues, including the merits or demerits of the death penalty itself, or the propriety and moral defensibility of the proposal that the execution, if it be held, be televised. The plurality feels that these issues are secondary to the constitutional questions raised by the main burden of petitioner's defense and the main thrust of his appeal."

("How can he *say* that?" Debbie demanded in whispered dismay of Harry Aboud who, burly and jovial and visible at last, had decided to come down from New York to lend, as he put it, moral support. He was sitting beside her a couple of spaces along the front row from Regard, who from time to time gave him a contemptuous glance.)

"In any event," Tay went on, a certain dryness entering his voice, "the plurality has no doubt that these questions will be more than adequately discussed by the minority.

"I may say," he interjected in a tone suddenly more personal and informal, looking down directly at the mass of attentive faces raised to his, "that it was my own decision to request the Chief Justice that I be permitted to deliver this opinion. I thought it fitting, since"—he hesitated for just a second but a sudden harshness he apparently could not control overrode it—"since I have an interest. I felt that if I could do anything by my direct participation to give greater weight to the majority, I wanted to do it. The Chief Justice concurred.

"Query One," he resumed, his tone formal once again: "Were petitioner's constitutional rights violated in the manner of his arrest?

"On this point the majority agrees with the argument of South Carolina that there was nothing calculated or deliberate about either denial of rights or the brutality which evidently did exist. The majority feels that both were almost inevitable outgrowths of the very inflamed and extreme emotions which petitioner himself had in fact created when he committed the crimes which, in the judgment of the jury and the two courts below, he did indeed commit.

"Furthermore, we accept the argument of South Carolina that within an hour or less of his apprehension petitioner was fully advised of his rights against self-incrimination and was given free and full access to the lawyer who still represents him. The issue then turns on whether a prisoner must be advised of his rights *at the very instant of his detention,* or whether advice *within a sufficient and reasonable time* adequately meets the protections of the Constitution.

"For too long, in the opinion of the plurality, justice in similar cases in this country has turned on the nicety of the situation—on, as it were, the tyranny of the clock. Apprehended criminals known to be guilty of equally heinous crimes have actually been freed on this technicality. The majority of the present Court believes it is time to end this extreme exaggeration of the law. It is time to base the law on common sense and reduce to some degree the dependence of justice upon whether advice was given at Minute One or Minute Forty-five, *as long as advice is adequately given within a time that reasonable men, using reasonable common sense, can reasonably regard as reasonable.*

("*Christ!*" the New York *Times* whispered. "Does *that* set us back a hundred years! There goes *Miranda!*" "Damned reactionary bastards!"

the Boston *Globe* spat out. "And Tay Barbour, of all people," the Minneapolis *Tribune* remarked, more in sorrow than in anger. "Is *that* ever
a betrayal of everything he's always stood for!")

"Therefore," Tay said, aware of some stir in the media but expecting
it and ignoring it, "the majority finds itself in agreement with South
Carolina on this point and rejects the contention of petitioner that he
was subject to undue *and damaging* delay in advising him of his rights.
The delay was human and excusable and no undue or uncorrectable
damage, in our opinion, was done."

He paused and took a drink of water while Clem Wallenberg glowered down the bench at Ray Ullstein and shook his head in obvious
and exaggerated dismay. Justice Ullstein, while not so dramatic about
it, also looked unhappy and shook his head sadly in reply. Debbie,
white-faced, her eyes never leaving Tay's face, looked as though she
had lost a lifetime idol.

"On the second point," Tay resumed, "whether petitioner's trial was
fairly conducted in view of substantial popular outcry for a verdict of
guilty, the plurality once again finds itself constrained to side with South
Carolina."

(A groan, quickly stifled but loud enough to guarantee the attention
desired for it, came from somewhere in the media. Regard leaned forward deliberately and gave Harry Aboud and Debbie a triumphant
look. Harry, momentarily losing his amicable air, glared back. Debbie,
eyes unmoving on Tay, never even knew Regard had looked.)

"It is true that there was substantial popular outcry for a verdict of
guilty. But charges of 'popular outcry' and 'public pressure,' although
they too have been used in our courts to justify the overturning of verdicts and the freeing of convicted criminals, are not, in the opinion of
the majority, sufficient in and of themselves to warrant overturning the
verdict in this case.

"There is admittedly a vast and overwhelming impatience in the
country with the way the criminal justice system presently performs.
This impatience is already beginning to lead down dangerous pathways
no member of this Court and no responsible citizen of whatever station
in life can condone. Yet the impatience itself, we believe, has ample
grounds for existence; and the fact of it must be taken into account in
rendering justice.

"Otherwise popular attempts at cure may get so far out of hand as to
become, in and of themselves, dangerous to the rights and freedom of
all citizens who may, for whatever reason great or small, come afoul of
the law.

"The plurality feels that while popular pressure was very evident during petitioner's trial, and while it is very evident today, it did not unduly influence the verdict rendered. Again, the test of reasonableness applies. By any reasonable standards, the trial and verdict were fair; and popular pressures cannot be blamed for a trial well conducted and a verdict honestly and unanimously arrived at."

He paused to take another sip of water. Below, Harry Aboud nudged Debbie and whispered, "So much for you, from your great hero. What do you think of him now?" But she only looked at him, face white and strained, and then looked back at Tay. He did not see her nor note the steadily growing mixture of desolation and bitter anger that was beginning to come into her dark, clever eyes.

"We come finally to the third issue, whether the death penalty was properly imposed according to the laws of South Carolina in conformity with prior rulings of this Court. Here the majority would like to quote from the banner case that is always quoted here whenever the death penalty comes under discussion, namely *Gardner v. Florida,* 430 U.S. 349, 357–358, opinion of Justice Stevens. Omitting citations available in text, its pertinent passage states:

"'. . . death is a different kind of punishment from any other which may be imposed in this country . . . . From the point of view of the defendant, it is different in both its severity and its finality. From the point of view of society, the action of the sovereign in taking the life of one of its citizens also differs dramatically from any other legitimate state action. It is of vital importance to the defendant and to the community that any decision to impose the death sentence be, and appears to be'— and here I give what seems to the majority a pertinent emphasis—*'based on reason rather than caprice or emotion.'*

"It is here that the plurality parts company with the State of South Carolina. South Carolina's law governing the imposition of the death penalty was written to conform to decisions of this Court, and it does so conform. But while it is obvious that due deliberation and due process were had at every stage, and that 'caprice' can be completely ruled out, still the question of 'emotion' remains.

"We do not believe such unanimity for the death penalty, or the unanimity of the Supreme Court of South Carolina in upholding it, would have been present without the very great emotion generated initially by the crimes committed, and then by the carefully orchestrated action of the organization known as Justice NOW! and its leaders, to maintain, increase and further inflame that already great emotion.

"Therefore it is the opinion of the Court that the death penalty in

this instance should be set aside; and to that extent the judgment of the
South Carolina Supreme Court is *Reversed.*

"However," he said, holding up a warning hand as many members of
the media obviously tensed and got ready to move—"it is the further
judgment of the plurality that the verdict of guilty, while based largely
on circumstantial grounds, is the correct one; and it is our opinion that
the petitioner, Earle William Holgren, should be imprisoned in a federal
facility, under conditions of maximum security, with permanent denial
of parole, for the rest of his natural life.

"The death sentence being thus void, we see no need to comment
upon it or upon the television proposal.

"In this opinion I am joined by my Brethren Elphinstone, Flyte,
Hemmelsford and Pomeroy.

"It is so ordered."

("They can't just arbitrarily set aside one sentence and impose another!" gasped the young lady from the Des Moines *Register,* a new reporter at the Court. "Who says they can't?" the Washington *Post* responded tartly. "They're the Supreme Court of the United States, aren't
they? Who's to stop?")

For several minutes all was confusion as many members of the media
tried to rush out. They were barred by a line of guards, arms linked,
stretching all around the chamber, who had unobtrusively assumed position while attention was riveted on Tay's concluding words. The result
was a great deal of violently whispered profanity and a great deal of
pushing and shoving. But the guards, while tense, were neither impressed nor belligerent; and the members of the media, though frustrated and furious, were basically well behaved and in considerable respect of the Court. Nobody got hurt and a great deal of tension was
relieved. Presently the reporters were back in their seats and the chamber was in order.

The Justices, who had remained deliberately impassive, noticeably
relaxed. May McIntosh took a drink of water and murmured something
to Hughie Demsted at her left that caused them both to smile; both then
murmured congratulations to Tay on his delivery of the majority opinion. Ray Ullstein and Wally Flyte also smiled to him from along the
bench, Rupe Hemmelsford gave him a thumbs-up and Moss, with a
look in which old friendship and shared pain were intermingled, did the
same. The Chief Justice, too, smiled and nodded his approval. Only
Clem Wallenberg, face flushed with anger, lips tightly pursed, eyes glowering, stared straight ahead and gave not an inch.

"If the chamber is now in order," Duncan Elphinstone said quietly, "we can proceed. I would suggest to our friends of the media that there is a minority decision to come. There is also a matter of respect for Justice Wallenberg, who will deliver it." He turned to the rigid figure at his left and gave him a pleasant smile. "Justice, if you are ready—"

But Clem wasn't having any pleasantries. His angry expression did not change and when he spoke it was for the most part in staccato phrases sharply bitten off. "He's as mad as a wet hen," Wally Flyte whispered to Ray Ullstein. "I hope he isn't going to spoil your opinion with a temper tantrum." "Oh, he'll come through," Ray replied, "but nobody is going to mistake how he feels about you fellows in the majority."

"My distinguished brethren on the other side," Justice Wallenberg began with a scathing sarcasm, "have engaged in so much tergiversation —in its meaning of 'to use evasions, or subterfuge; to equivocate'—that one who respects the Constitution and the law can hardly know where to begin. Copies of the minority opinion will be furnished you in a few moments along with the text of my Brother Barbour's majority opinion, so I will not bore you with language you can read for yourselves. Informally, though, I'll make our points as we see them, free from his well-polished rhetoric that conceals such a poor grasp of the facts and the law."

("Wow!" the Denver *Post* whispered to the San Francisco *Chronicle*. "The old boy's really on the rampage, isn't he?" "Barbour deserves it," the *Chronicle* said shortly. "The whole majority does.")

"I'm not going to recite the facts again," Clem said, "except to remind that petitioner was brutalized when he was arrested; his rights were denied; his trial was a constant charade of trying to appease a rabid and ill-informed public opinion stirred up by a worthless organization put together for the political advantage of a few minor ambitious officials who want to become major ambitious officials; the guilty verdict was similarly a sop to rabid public pressure; the death sentence likewise; and the monstrosity of the television proposal simply an attempt to stir up a national blood lust utterly alien to the United States of America. It's a degradation to have it even mentioned. It's a worse degradation to have it deliberately evaded by the majority in their opinion. *Somebody* has to keep standards going in this country! When all's said and done, that somebody is us. The majority has failed us, in a sad way on a sad day for America. For shame! For shame!"

He paused to glare up and down the bench, while his three colleagues of the minority sought to catch his eye, shake their heads, warn him against such bitterness. It was useless, as they all knew. A glum expression settled on the faces of his Brethren Ullstein and Demsted and his Sister McIntosh, as he plunged ahead while the media scribbled gleefully in their notebooks.

"Two members of this Court should have disqualified themselves from the very beginning, and you will find we state as much in the minority opinion. We are fully sympathetic to their problems but we think it has been impossible for them to judge fairly. However, they are here, and because they are, we have the majority opinion with all its flimsy rationalizations and its skillful evasions of the issues that are really vital to the country. It is too bad, very much too bad. They would have relieved themselves of much anguish and the country of much poor law and much potential future trouble as a result of this decision, if they had just withdrawn. It will always be one of the historic mistakes of this case that they did not."

He again glared down the bench at Moss, who, genuinely angered, glared back. Then he swiveled his head like some furious old turtle in Tay's direction. Tay looked straight ahead, chin on hand, eyes, by a deliberate act of will, unresponsive and far away. Justice Wallenberg snorted and went on.

"The minority has its opinions on the probable guilt of petitioner; in general we agree with the majority on this point. But the Constitution and the laws derived therefrom are supposed to apply to *all* citizens, no matter how worthless. They are not supposed to be suspended simply because of a fair presumption—and we consider it fair—of guilt. Rights are rights. You don't split them up and divide them and turn them into fragments, a little bit applied here and a little bit applied there. You give them to everybody, or you rob all. The worthless as well as the worthy deserve the full protection of the law. Temporary public hysteria can't be allowed to change that. Otherwise we are all lost.

"Any apprehended person has certain rights. Those rights *are in being at the moment of arrest.* When a majority of this Court accepts the idea that it doesn't matter when they are granted, as long as they are ultimately granted, then it opens the door for them to be granted in an hour—ten hours—a day—two weeks—two months—whenever. Eventually it opens the way for them to be granted never.

"That is not how the minority reads the Constitution. It is not how America is to be safeguarded. It is not how our democratic rights are to be preserved. It is terribly dangerous law. It is, in the final analysis, no law. It is the anarchy that this so-called Justice NOW!"—and he gestured with a grand contempt beyond the walls, where the distant cacophony came clearly—"seeks, wants, demands.

"Consequences always spread far beyond this courtroom, never let us forget that, far beyond the language used here in handing down decisions. What we do grows and grows and grows, whether the case be large like this one or as small as ever comes here. Because nothing really small ever does come here. Everything we do is large in its ultimate effect. Nothing we do stops here. It goes beyond—far beyond. We regret the majority has forgotten this. We condemn their opening of doors that may not, perhaps, be closed again.

"The majority carefully skirts the merits or demerits of the death penalty. We of the minority are not afraid to say flat out that we are against it. We believe it does not inhibit, it does not prevent, it does not reduce. It simply sacrifices one life for one or more already gone. It does not restore lives lost. It does not reform criminals, except as it removes them. It does not prevent other murders by other people. Sometimes the threat of it does not even prevent further murders by the same person. It is murder itself, self-defeating and also barbaric, no matter how sanctified by the state. The majority dismisses it, though I understand several members of the majority will take the mealy-mouthed path sometimes followed here, of joining in an opinion and then putting in a supplemental statement that they still are opposed to the death penalty, nonetheless.

"Well: the majority has canceled the death penalty in this case, but it has done so by indirection. It has not met it head-on—"

("What does that matter," the new young lady from the Des Moines *Register* whispered anxiously to her companions, "when they've *done* it?" *"Hush!"* one of her older colleagues ordered severely and she never did find out.)

"—it has not seized the opportunity to condemn it as it should be condemned. It has evaded the issue.

"Nor has the majority addressed itself to the broader constitutional aspects, the nature of the trial, the improper place of public pressure, the monstrosity, I repeat once again, of the television proposal. We cannot agree with the majority. In our opinion the case should have been remanded back to South Carolina for re-hearing. The trial should have been vacated, given a really honest and objective jury, kept genuinely free from the hysterical taunts of this so-called Justice NOW! that besmirches America with its rabid ravings and demonstrations and—and—" he spat out the word, "*allies* designed to try to twist the laws and blackmail this Court into becoming a star chamber! . . .

"I am joined in this opinion by my Sister McIntosh and my Brethren Ullstein and Demsted."

He paused; blinked; thought for a moment; concluded in a quieter, more reasonable tone.

"I am not sure all of my colleagues of the minority join me in some of my references to the majority or in some of my language. Now and again, sometimes, I get a little carried away: a little harsh, perhaps. I don't really mean to, but I feel these things. *I feel these things! They are important to me . . .* as, I suppose," he acknowledged with a glance along both sides of the bench that brought wry but basically friendly nods from all but Moss, still angry, and Tay, still staring far away, "they are important to all of us. They have to be."

And he sat back as the Chief looked down at the media, smiled and said,

"*Now,* ladies and gentlemen. All opinions, of which there are the two major and seven dissenting or concurring in some degree, are available to you in the press room. The Court stands adjourned until the first Monday in October."

FIVE

The Court had spoken. The media split between metropolitan and small-town along easily predictable lines.

"A sharply divided Court has stood the Constitution on its head," remarked the New York *Times.* "Justice Barbour's opinion is very clever, but it is a clear evasion of responsibility."

"There is equal justice under law for somebody," observed the Washington *Post,* "but apparently not for Earle Holgren."

"Justice has been rendered fittingly on a convicted murderer," said the Porterville, California, *Recorder.*

"The Court was wise to adhere to the law and skip the diversions that might have been lavished on the death penalty and the television aspect," agreed the Fort Myers, Florida, *News-Press.*

And so it went across the country, and, indeed, across the world.

Television's general emphasis was anti-Court, since from neither majority nor minority had it really received any consolation. "Where does this leave the networks?" CBS' sage-in-residence inquired, looking into the camera with an earnestly offended expression. Echo answered, "Where?" and from the offices of Eldridge, Muggridge, Pockthwaite and Thistle came only silence.

Neither the major media nor Justice NOW! were satisfied with the performance of the Court's newest member. Critics in the media were savage in their condemnation of his "wishy-washy reasoning," his "almost cowardly evasion of responsibility," his "willingness to allow an understandable human repugnance toward the petitioner to overcome a lifetime's dedication to the finest standards of the law."

"A fine reputation (so averred the *Times*) has been shattered and a long shadow, from which he will be a long time emerging, has been cast over his value to the Court."

Justice NOW! was more direct. The first reporter who emerged from the Court after the decision was bombarded with questions. As soon as he had given his answers an ominous angry chant began to rise:

"Down with the Court!"

And on alternate beats, heavier and more insistent:

"DOWN WITH BARBOUR!"

By the time the Justices departed half an hour later via the garage entrance, the hostility had become organized. Banners had materialized and numerous straw figures labeled "The Court" and "Two-Faced Tay" suddenly dangled together from lampposts around the building.

It was not comforting for the Justices to see, as their cars were sped swiftly away in the midst of police motorcycle escorts, that many of the figures had already been ignited and were beginning to send up heavy puffs of smoke; nor to hear on the car radio as their convoys took them fast but skillfully through the noonday traffic to their respective homes, that Justice NOW! was already out with a strongly hostile statement.

"Justice NOW! cannot condemn too strongly," its concluding sentences read, "the way in which the Supreme Court of the United States has chosen to override the just conviction and sentencing of a murderous criminal. And we specifically deplore and condemn the part played by Justice Taylor Barbour, who should know, if anyone does, how deserved and how right were the conviction, the death penalty and the television proposal for the man who destroyed his daughter."

"Poor Tay," Justice Ullstein remarked to his passengers Mary-Hannah and Hughie. "He can't win."

"Clem would probably say he doesn't deserve to," Hughie said. "I was disappointed in him myself, to tell you the truth. But I can see his reasoning. I think."

"He has to live with it," Mary-Hannah observed. "I don't envy him. It will take him a while."

He had already learned that it would take him a while, though his sister and his brethren could not know it. When he left the Robing Room and returned briefly to his chambers before leaving the building, he found a lonely figure waiting for him in the corridor, otherwise deserted save for a guard seated in his usual position far along toward the center of the hallway in frcnt of Rupert Hemmelsford's door. No one else was in its empty echoing marble expanse.

Her face was drawn and st-icken; she looked, as Regard had remarked in what now seemed a long-ago moment when they had seen her waiting at the hospital in Columbia, like "a bedraggled little swamp-hen of a gal." But her eyes were blazing with anger, her expression was one of cold contempt, her voice trembled with a consuming and implacable rage.

"How could you!" she cried in a tense whisper, modulated enough so the guard would not hear but carrying clearly to Tay as he approached. "How could you? How could you betray everything you've always stood for all your life? How could you betray everybody who believes in you? How could you betray us? How could you be such a clever coward? *How could you?*"

"Miss Donnelson," he said, trying to keep his own voice low and calm, though suddenly all the accumulated tensions of recent hours—his desperate unhappiness for Janie—his hatred for Earle Holgren—his terrible struggle with his conscience—his innermost, devastating thought that perhaps in many eyes whose respect he valued he *was* only a "clever coward"—seemed to boil over inside him and threaten a rage as explosive and vindictive as her own. "I do not care to defend my decision to you or to anyone. I have rendered it, I have been supported by a majority of the Court. The matter is closed. Now please get out of my way and let me enter my office. *Get out of my way.*"

"I won't!" she cried, louder now, spreading her arms across his door. Down the corridor the guard, aroused from his customary amiable lethargy, rose and began to come toward them. "I *won't!* You owe me an explanation, Taylor Barbour! You owe the whole world an explanation! The great liberal! The great lover of mankind! The great, compassionate—"

"Miss Donnelson," he said, his own voice rising sharply in spite of his determination to hold it down, "go back to your murderer and leave me alone! You ought to be thankful we left him alive, monster that he is. He deserved nothing from us—nothing from me—*nothing! And I let him live.* If you haven't got sufficient gratitude to realize *that*—"

"Gratitude for what?" she demanded. "Gratitude for your ducking the death penalty? Gratitude for your betraying yourself? Gratitude for betraying all who believe in you? Gratitude for—"

"Justice," the guard said, sounding tough—Supreme Court guards had never had to sound tough up to these last few days, the pace was pretty slow most times, but he found he rather enjoyed it, actually—"Justice, do you want me to remove this woman? Shall I put her in jail?"

"Not in jail," he said, icily calm as she became more frantic. "All she's doing is talking. It's still a free country. Just remove her from my door and put her out of the Court. That will be sufficient."

"You'll see if all I'm doing is talk!" she screamed with a sudden violence that startled them. "You'll see! You'll see!"

"*Guard!*" he said sharply.

"Yes, sir!" the guard said hastily, grabbing her arm and yanking her, still screaming, obscene and unintelligible now, down the hall. "Get along out of here, now, you!"

And in a moment they were gone, her voice screeching quickly away into silence; and the corridor was deserted and still again. He stood absolutely rigid for several moments calming his whirling thoughts, resting his hand on his door as though to protect it from some mysterious, unexpected assault; presently tried it, found it locked, unlocked it, opened it and went in. His secretary and law clerks, he was thankful to note, had gone to lunch. The office was as silent and deserted as the hall. He walked through to his inner chamber, tossed his copy of the majority opinion on his desk, started to pick up the latest appeals for certiorari that he would take home to begin his work for the summer; paused suddenly and returned to his desk.

Picking up the majority opinion again he wrote on it in a firm hand that did not tremble, though he was still breathing heavily:

"First opinion delivered by me in the Supreme Court of the United States"; dated it, signed it, replaced it, neatly this time, on his desk.

"I'll have to send that to the Library of Congress for my 'Court papers,' " he said to the empty room with a strange ironic bitterness he couldn't quite understand. "Probably won't be anything else worth saving."

Then he too left the Court and went, in his police-escorted car, past the jeering crowd and the burning effigies of "The Court" and "Two-Faced Tay," back to the house in Georgetown and the call that he knew would inevitably soon come.

When it did it was similar in tone and general thrust to the berating he had just received. He took very little of it before he put it, finally and forever, to rest.

"I can't seem to satisfy anyone, can I, Mary?" he inquired with a wryness that only seemed to provoke her further.

"No, you cannot!" she said with a harsh anger she could barely control. "How you could be such a weakling as to sidestep the death penalty I'll never know! How you could be such a clever coward when your own daughter lies ruined forever by that monster! Why you didn't—"

"Mary," he interrupted, voice calm and certain at last because the eerie repetition of "clever coward" did it, suddenly everything fell into place. "I want a divorce. Now."

"I'm not going to give you one!"

"Then I'm going to sue for one," he said calmly.

"On what grounds? Have *I* been a poor wife? Have *I* had a sneaky little affair? Have *I* betrayed myself and my own daughter with a cowardly opinion from the Supreme Court—"

"That's not a ground for divorce," he said with a ghastly sort of humor, "and the rest you can't prove. I'll sue you, Mary, and I'll win somehow, if it takes me all my money and the rest of my life. So make up your mind to a hell of a messy public fight, or give it to me. Yes or no."

There was silence for a time, frozen and complete. She did not sob or cry or outwardly indicate emotion, though her voice when she spoke did tremble a little. He supposed that somewhere, in some part of her being that still possibly treasured him or her earliest memories of him, it did hurt her; as, to his profound surprise now that it was actually here, he found it hurting him. Not enough to stop him, however. It was far too late for that.

"What about Janie?" she asked at last.

"She'll be taken care of. That's our joint responsibility, now and always."

"I can have her, then."

"Mary," he protested, "you don't know what you're taking on. I beg of you, *please* don't start that again. She'll be so much better off in a place that's really equipped to take care of her. Really she will."

"I'm not going to have her in an institution—"

He sighed.

"I'm not going to argue that with you now. We'll have to work it out as we go along. For now, the question is divorce. Do I get it without a battle or do I have to make a public fight for it?"

Again there was a long pause. Finally she too sighed, a deep, dragging, infinitely weary sound, and surprised him utterly.

"If it will really make you happy, Tay—"

"It will," thinking, astounded, Whatever made her change her mind and give in so easily? And telling himself quickly, Don't ask, don't hesitate, accept it and be thankful, *fast*. He repeated firmly, "It will."

"Then I suppose," she said in a remote tone he mistook for disinterest, "it will have to make me happy, too."

"Thank you, Mary," he said gravely. "I think you'll find it will."

"I hope so," she said; and added in an odd forlorn little voice, "There never has been a divorce in my family."

"Mine, either."

It was only then that she began, at last, to cry, awkward, agonized, wracking sounds that seemed to come from the depths of her being.

But it was too late now.

A few minutes later, while he was puttering about in the kitchen getting himself a cup of soup he didn't really feel like eating, the phone rang again. He knew who it would be but the last thing he felt like now was talking to her or seeing her. He tried not to sound brusque when he answered, but must have because she responded quickly in an alarmed tone,

"What's the matter?"

"I'm sorry," he said. "I'm just tired, I guess. It's been a big day."

"I think you did the right thing," she said, accepting his explanation at once without comment. "It was the best possible compromise, it seems to me; the only thing you could do, under the circumstances."

"I didn't strike down the death penalty, though," he said; and must have revealed uncertainty because she replied immediately,

"Nonsense! Why did you have to? You set it aside, didn't you? You vacated it. And you still put Holgren away where he can't bother anybody any more. What more could any reasonable person ask?"

"Nobody's reasonable about this case," he said. "Maybe I wasn't myself."

"The majority went with you," she objected stoutly. "What are you brooding about?"

"I'm not 'brooding.'"

"It certainly sounds that way to me."

"Well, I'm not," he said, sounding a little amused and more relaxed.

"And the majority *did* go with you, right?"

"Oh, yes, they were glad to do so. The Elph lined them up. Anyway, they wanted to. They were as relieved as I was to find a way out—a middle ground. That's always best for the Court and the country, if it can be done."

"So why are you upset? I don't get it."

"A lot of things I want to tell you about, but not—right now."

"Oh," she said, trying not to sound disappointed, not succeeding. "I was hoping you would come over for dinner tonight. I've parked the kids with friends of mine in Alexandria and I thought now that it's all over, we could—"

"I'm sorry," he said; and repeated with a sudden urgency—"*I am sorry.* But for a while—a few hours, anyway—I think maybe—if you can understand and forgive me—I just want to be alone. I just want to think about it some more and come to terms with myself about it."

"I thought you'd done that when you made your decision," she said, but gently.

"I did but—I didn't. I need to be at peace with myself. Can you understand that?"

"I understand," she said, and he felt that she wasn't just saying so, she really did. "I wish I were able to help you, but I guess maybe—I can't. That makes me unhappy, because it destroys part of my concept of what I can be to you, but if that's the way it is, then—that's the way it is, I guess."

"I'm sorry," he said humbly. "I need you—I want you—I love you. This is just something where nobody can help me but myself, I'm afraid. I'll be over just as soon as I can, if—if you still want me."

"Try me," she said with a shaky little laugh. "Just try me . . . All right then, Mr. Justice; I love you too. Just give a holler: I'll be standing by. Fair enough? Just don't be too long."

"I won't," he promised.

"Good. As long as I know you'll be here eventually, I guess I can wait."

"I'll be there. And it won't be 'eventually,' either."

"Tomorrow night?" she asked, trying to make it light, not quite succeeding.

"Tomorrow night," he said firmly. "And that's for sure."

"I'll hold you to that," she said, still lightly but with a desperate earnestness underneath that she could not quite conceal. "So don't let me down."

"I won't let you down," he said gravely. "I could never do that."

But when they had hung up he sat for a long time staring out unseeing upon the lush overpowering garden.

You can have your divorce, said the second voice.

I love you, said the third.

Clever coward, said the first.

He spent a long, unhappy afternoon and a long, unhappy night before he finally fell asleep.

Clever coward, clever coward, clever coward.

Little Miss Debbie, he thought bitterly, was doing him just as much damage as she had obviously intended.

2

"**S**uperstar," he said when she flew down at his request to see him late that afternoon, "I guess your friend let us down a bit, didn't he?"

She thought he looked suddenly older, and tired, but still as strangely serene and confident as ever. His arrogant tone and chiding words incited her to immediate anger as they had so often before.

"He isn't my friend!" she said fiercely. "I don't consider him my friend or the friend of anyone who believes in true liberalism in America!"

"Well!" he said with mock concern. "I don't know about that. But he sure as hell isn't my friend, that's for sure. I thought you told me he was going to set me free."

"I didn't tell you any such thing," she retorted. "I told you consistently that you'd be lucky to get off with a life sentence, and that's just what you got. But I did think the least he could do would be to condemn the death penalty."

"Almost promised you as much, didn't he?" he asked, studying her closely.

"I thought so," she said, aggrieved.

"Yes. So much for one shifty bastard. And the television thing, too," he added. "Don't forget the television thing. He's a real fraud, isn't he? All these big liberal pretensions—and then it's Wallenberg who comes out and says it right. I told you to go to Wallenberg in the first place."

"What did it matter? You got your delay and you got your hearing by the Court. At least Tay Barbour did that for you, even though he did let us down later."

"The whole damned majority let us down," he said, suddenly genuinely angry. "I didn't deserve any damned life sentence! I deserve to be free! Yahoo and his phony witnesses including my old lady didn't prove one damned thing! A lot of noise! A lot of circumstantial evidence! No proof! No proof at all! In addition to which," he added as the guard, attracted by his rising voice, looked in for a moment and then moved on, "your precious Tay and his friends didn't even stand by the Constitution they're supposed to be such big-deal upholders of. They didn't even protect my rights. They had grounds to throw out the whole damned thing, the way I was treated, and they ducked it. They ducked *it* and they fucked *me,* I'll tell you that. They sure did that, Superstar. And your precious friend led 'em on."

"He isn't my friend," she cried again angrily, "so will you stop repeating that damned nonsense, please? You should have heard what I said to him after the decision. I really let him have it." She paused and looked into some far distance of lost ideals; and when she spoke it was with a cold and final contempt. "I hate him now as much as you do."

"Do you, now!" he said with a softness that broke in on her mood and made her shiver suddenly; and suddenly he was very quiet, and in his eyes was the light that had made Boomer Johnson's mother, back there in the courtroom, so glad to get Boomer safely home. "Well, do you now! Then I tell you what, Superstar: I tell you what."

"What?" she asked, afraid though she could not say exactly why: he just looked so *intent,* somehow.

"I have me an idea, Superstar," he said, dropping abruptly into a cautious whisper, no longer the amiable bearded teddy bear of the surface but now the coldly calculating inhuman force that lay, always waiting, fearfully exciting, just underneath. "You want to help me, don't you? You've always wanted to help me?"

"I wouldn't have come here in the first place," she said, voice trembling a little, "if I hadn't wanted to help you. And I did help you. I helped you all I could. It isn't my fault that the Court didn't let you go. I did *my* best."

"Oh, I know you did," he whispered, leaning forward. "I know you did, and I'm grateful for that, I really am. But now you can help me some more, Superstar, you really can. Will you do that for me now? Will you help your client a little more?"

"I don't see what—" she began; but suddenly his voice had sunk to a crooning whisper and his hand was taking on a life of its own as it moved swiftly and surely to where it had been once before.

"Oh, I'll tell you," he whispered. "Just listen to me, Superstar, and I'll tell you all about it. After all, we both hate the bastard Barbour and all the other bastards, don't we?"

"All right," she gasped. "All right, all right, all right—" while his hand kept moving, moving, moving, ever so gently, and he told her, quickly before the guard could return, all she needed to know of what he had in mind.

And that, the attorney general of South Carolina told himself that evening with a happy satisfaction as he surveyed the front pages of a dozen of the nation's leading newspapers spread before him on his desk at home, was how victory could be snatched from the jaws of defeat, to coin a phrase. Here in front of him was the proof that Justice NOW! had become *the* major organized political force in the United States of America at this particular time, and if he had his way, for a long time to come.

DIVIDED COURT GIVES HOLGREN LIFE! DUCKS DEATH PENALTY, TV ISSUE, RIGHTS. MINORITY CHARGES BETRAYAL OF CONSTITUTION, FLAYS BARBOUR OPINION. JUSTICE NOW! BURNS COURT IN EFFIGY. STINNET PLEDGES FORCES WILL CONTINUE FIGHT FOR TOUGH CRIME CRACKDOWN.

And all the front pages featured pictures of the burning, some of them, such as that in the Washington *Post,* completely filling the front page above the fold. "The Court" and "Two-Faced Tay" danced from half a dozen lampposts in their shrouds of smoke. At their feet triumphant citizens of the great Republic cheered and jeered.

It was enough to make some people shiver but it disturbed Regard not at all; because he knew, just as he knew the Justices and all members of the legal establishment knew, what lay behind the pictures and the headlines. The practical fact of it was that while the Court might have denied Justice NOW! the death penalty for Earle Holgren, it had also carefully shied away from criticizing the death penalty as such; and far from condemning the television proposal, the majority had simply avoided it. What is not specifically condemned, Regard had discovered long ago in law school, is implicitly approved; and what is not specifically denied is by implication allowed. There would be a death on prime time yet. The Court, while pretending to decide and in actuality closing its eyes, had made this inevitable. Of this he was certain.

Justice NOW! had done exactly what its creator and its now well over ten million members had intended. It had greatly speeded up the judicial process. It had cut through a swamp of circumstantial evidence to force guilt and conviction upon the individual who in obvious common sense deserved them. And it had imposed upon the Supreme Court itself a popular discipline such as that proud body had not known in many a long decade. The Court might pretend differently, it might render its opinions with all the majesty of the High Bench, but in actual fact it knew, and the whole world of politics and jurisprudence knew, that it was running scared. Essentially, it had yielded; and through this first crack in the facade Regard was certain he could lead his millions to the eventual triumph of what he and they believed to be true law and order.

And why shouldn't he? he asked himself. It was a goal the overwhelming majority wanted. It was an aim worthy of the United States of America. Swift, certain, no-nonsense justice—the execution of murderers —the ruthless elimination of the criminals who were terrorizing every city and most neighborhoods in America—what was wrong with those objectives? And what was to prevent him from riding them in due time all the way to the top?

He thought for a contemptuous moment of Taylor Barbour. Poor old wishy-washy Tay, who would have loved to give in to his instincts and join in the elimination of Earle Holgren, yet whose lifelong dedication to the law—and to his own reputation, Regard thought spitefully—had forced him instead to seek the clever, evasive way out. And it was clever, Regard gave him credit for that: it was a sidestep but it was a plausible one. It could be justified; it made sense. It removed Earle Holgren from society, even if it did not make him the decisive public example Justice NOW! had hoped. Tay might even believe in it, for all he knew. But it was a patch-up, a stopgap. They would meet again over the issue of death and television, of that he was quite sure.

In fact, he decided on the spur of the moment, he would call an impromptu rally here in Columbia tomorrow and review the whole thing, give it another push, exhort his followers, keep up the pressure. The television networks, chagrined by the decision, were on his side now: they'd give him all the exposure he could possibly desire. He knew this because several discreet telephone calls from New York during the afternoon had told him as much. It was time to announce regional councils, open an office in Washington, hire full-time lobbyists, start putting the pressure on Congress, begin preparations for the congressional elections next year when Justice NOW! and its millions could be focused on many a shaky seat. Justice NOW! could actually be a major force in deciding control of the House, where the Administration's hold was paper-thin. Calculating swiftly as his mind ranged the national map, Regard thought it might even decide as many as fifteen Senate candidacies . . . of which his own might well be one.

He was dreaming happily of the possibility, which suddenly did not seem at all outlandish, absurd or impossible, when the phone rang and he received the news that was to change the lives of a good many people involved with the case of the Pomeroy Station bomber. It would also, he realized instantly, furnish an ideal springboard from which to launch his upcoming rally. It might even launch his candidacy. And it would certainly give him another crack, not under such restraints this time, at Earle Holgren.

With a grim expression for the news but an inner exhilaration at what it could mean for all his prospects, he went into action with all the decisive skill and shrewd planning of his clever, ambitious mind.

At roughly the same moment in Georgetown, having finished an early supper with Birdie, the Chief Justice was getting out maps and travel guides and beginning to think about the driving trip to the Grand Tetons, the Grand Canyon, New Mexico and California that they had promised themselves earlier in the term. This year, instead of simply holing up in Eleuthera or some other pleasant place to study new appeals for certiorari, he had decided to take a complete break away from the Court for about a month and "get out and see the country," something he felt he should do every two or three years. Birdie had strongly encouraged this, both for his reason and for her own, which included some worry about his health if he spent all of the recess, as he usually did wherever they were, preparing for the next session.

They all did this, he knew, and the thought brought an affectionate smile to his face. It was a good Court: they were good people, even if the major media *were* giving them hell at the moment and even if Justice NOW! had burned them in effigy. You couldn't please everybody, though this time the majority seemed to have come down neatly in the middle and pleased no one. He was confident the furor would die; and he was confident that in time the majority's wisdom would be vindicated and that it would do much to appease the national clamor symbolized and used by Justice NOW!

The problem had been simple, essentially: public pressure must not be allowed to force the death penalty in all instances irrespective of whether the evidence justified it or not; the death penalty must be neither affirmed in all cases nor denied in all cases, for each was different and stood on its own feet; public pressure must not be allowed to link up with television to put execution in the realm of popular entertainment, however noble the professed motives of "example" and "public education" might be. And finally, of course, a criminal must not be allowed to go free or remain unpunished for crimes of which simple common sense knew him to be guilty.

All of these objectives, he thought, had been skillfully encompassed in the majority opinion, and because he knew it came out of the very considerable mental and emotional anguish of Taylor Barbour, he respected it the more. Tay too was being damned by both sides but the Chief felt that he deserved much credit for finding the solution that had eluded the rest of them. He had not thought middle ground to be possible but Tay had discovered it and stood by it when it would have been so humanly easy to follow Moss' lead and find in the law excuse for vengeance. The Chief and Wally and Rupert had been able, not easily but after long, highly emotional arguments, to persuade Moss to join them. And the majority had been put together.

Tay had done it, by being a man of the law and a man of character and by drawing on some deep reserve within himself of steadiness, decency and balance. He was the real hero of the decision, Duncan Elphinstone felt, though he knew Tay—for Tay was that kind—must be suffering many second thoughts and self-doubts about it at this very moment. Moved by an impulse of warmth and generosity he picked up the phone and dialed the Barbour house; only to be told by the gravely concerned voice of his respected junior that he had just heard a news flash that the Holgren case had suddenly exploded again, and that quite possibly all their work had been in vain.

"Ah jes' don' see!" the warden kept saying, shaking his head. "Ah jes' don' see how that bastard done it!"

"I'll tell you how he did it, you asshole!" Regard snapped. "He did it by getting that poor little sex-starved piss-hen of a lawyer to smuggle him in some dynamite and a gun, that's how he did it, and you stupid assholes let them get away with it! And stop shaking your God damned head or it's going to fall off! There isn't much there to hold it on!"

He had not seen the headlines yet, there hadn't been time, but he knew damned well, with a searing annoyance, that they weren't going to be so flattering now.

HOLGREN ESCAPES! undoubtedly, first off. Then, KILLER MAKES BREAK AS GUARDS CHANGE SHIFTS. And then, STINNET'S OFFICE BLAMED FOR LAX SECURITY. And finally, no doubt, a cutesy, DEBBIE AND EARLE IN ESCAPE PLOT. MANHUNT SPREADS AS LOVERS (?) FLEE.

Well, by God, you son of a bitch, he told the fugitive in his mind, the next time a lynch mob sets out to get you I won't be around to save you, you worthless piece of crap! You're on your own this time, pal, and I hope to hell somebody gets you *fast*.

And presently, of course, someone did; but not before Earle Holgren had time to do several things that to him—and to several others—were important.

3

*W*hat *am I doing here?* she asked herself; and there was no more rational answer for her than for anyone else who had ever asked the question, in strange and unforeseeable circumstances, in all the millennia before.

She was just *there;* and as she lay on the bed in a dingy little motel in a dingy little town outside Columbia and watched Earle carefully shave mustache and beard, rub artificial tan thoroughly into his suddenly exposed white jowls and hack off large portions of his hair with the help of her scissors and a hand mirror, she found herself hardly able to think coherently. It had all happened so fast and it was all so alien to what she had ever thought she would do when her life, at the suggestion of Harry Aboud, had first come into contact with that of the Pomeroy Station bomber.

Not that the idea of aiding a prisoner to escape repelled her, or that she did not sympathize with most of Earle's complaints against society: those were things she could handle. She had been a rebel herself for a while, done her bit for protest, in her heart of hearts still believed in many of the causes for which she had actively worked in college and for several years thereafter. In fact, she still worked for them: her acquaintance with Harry and her defense of Earle were proof enough of that.

Nor did the question of legal ethics bother her, since, as with him, her beliefs about the society, and her concept of her own responsibility in changing it, overrode everything else. He was, she believed, sincere in his beliefs, genuine in his concern, devoted to a vision they and many others had shared in the Sixties and Seventies. He had convinced her of this during their many talks in the jail. He had inspired in her a strange sort of repelled yet fascinated idealism about himself that she told herself now was beyond all reason. In some sort of hypnotic way he had made her *believe;* and so had tied her to himself for better or ill.

And she was honest enough—honest and, now, fearfully excited too— to admit to herself that he had also managed to create a powerful sexual attraction; more powerful, she acknowledged, than she had ever felt for anyone. It was a sickness that left her limp, which was why she had fought so hard to stay away from it during their talks; *that,* she felt, she could not handle. Yet when it had come to the test, when he had asked her help in making his escape, she had let him make implicit sexual promises that she believed—and despised herself, yet was helpless—were part of a bargain.

So she had kept her part of it, and ever since, humming softly to himself as he went busily about erasing one identity and adopting another, he had acted as though the bargain had never existed. He had let her bring him the means of escape; together they had used them. They had fled in her car until they abandoned it for a rental, which she signed for. She had taken the motel room. She had purchased the new clothing. She had drawn $100,000 out of the Defense of Earle Holgren Fund (they didn't dare take more, even that had made the bank reluctant and suspicious). She had purchased the silencer for the gun late last night on a downtown street corner where such things were available as they were all over America. She had even bought him the makeup.

He had remained as impersonal as though they were still sitting in the jail under the eye of the guard. At first she thought this was simply the calculated tactic of an old campaigner. But gradually, as the hours passed and he made no move to come close to her or show her anything but a meticulous courtesy, she had begun to wonder. And now, fighting steadily against it but feeling herself slip faster and faster into vortex, she was sliding down into a sick miasma of regret and despair that was doubly awful because it was so humiliating and so destructive of her self-respect.

She was, in other words, exactly where he wanted her to be. And the awful thing about it was that she suspected it and realized that if it were true, it once again opened up that appalling vista of himself that was very likely, she knew, the real Earle Holgren.

So she asked herself what she was doing there and had no real answer except her own debasing desire to be with him on whatever terms he might dictate even though she knew that the terms had the potential of being frightful. Again the analogy of the cobra came to her mind, and with it, suddenly, the first stirring of really overwhelming fear, the first beginnings of a desperate urge to get out, away, anywhere that would put her safely beyond his reach. She knew from studying psychology that there was a glib and obvious correlation of the snake with sex; but suddenly, with a cold certainty that had never quite come home to her in the way it did now when she realized that she herself might be in jeopardy, she knew that this snake was Death.

She was suddenly fully alert. He was not looking at her, he was looking at himself, with approval, in the mirror. Yet though she tried with all her might to refrain from abrupt movements, any revealing tenseness, she knew instinctively at once that he, instinctively, had sensed it.

The humming stopped abruptly and with an amiable grin he turned and peered into the room.

"Hey, there, Superstar," he said easily. "How you doin'?"

"I'm doing fine," she said, her heart beating fast but her voice, with a great effort, natural and easy. Or so she thought.

"That's great," he said. "So am I. How do you like this getup, anyway?"

"I'd never know it was you."

He gave a deprecating laugh but sounded pleased.

"*You'd* know," he said, "because you know me. But maybe people who don't know me that well wouldn't."

"They wouldn't dream it was you," she said, sitting up and casually slipping on the sandals she had kicked off when she lay down to rest. "It's a great disguise."

"Well, thanks," he said, coming a little further into the room. "Going somewhere?"

"I noticed a little grocery store across the road when we came in," she said, trying desperately to sound casual. "I thought I might go over and get us something. I'm getting hungry."

"Me, too," he said approvingly. "That's a *good* idea. But why don't you wait a minute and we can go together?"

"You'd better lie low for a bit, don't you think?" she asked, trying to sound matter-of-fact and reasonable. He smiled.

"I've got to get out and be seen sooner or later. Got to take a chance, get used to it. I can't stay cooped up here much longer. We've got to get moving."

Or rather, he told her ironically in his mind, *I* have to get moving. You, Superstar, must stay behind. You know too much—I don't really trust you—you represented me reasonably well but you weren't all that great—you never really *believed* in me, you took my case because Harry Aboud asked you to—you went to Barbour instead of Wallenberg—you messed up on a lot of things. And besides all that, they're after me and I've got to travel light if I'm to do all the things I plan to do. I've got *several* things planned, Superstar, and you, old girl, are the first.

Sorry about that.

But none of this showed in his eyes, though he knew that with some animal instinct she sensed it. He only repeated again, with a sudden thoughtfulness that chilled her even more,

"We've really got to get moving."

"Yes," she said eagerly, "we've got to be on our way. But first let me get us something to eat. You stay here and rest, you must be tired. And we do have a long way to go."

"I've got a better idea," he said softly, and she froze, sudden terror in her heart.

"Oh?" she said with difficulty. "What's that?"

"Relax," he said, chuckling and sitting down on the bed beside her. "*Relax*. It's just *this* idea, Superstar. And there isn't anybody around to stop us now, is there?"

"No!" she said sharply as his hands were suddenly swarming, he was yanking at her clothing, his body was beginning to press down on hers. "*No!*"

"Ah, yes!" he said, suddenly breathing hard. "Yes, Superstar! It's what—you've—wanted and what—I've—wanted—and—"

"Stop!" she cried, hardly aware that no sound emerged because he had his hand firmly over her mouth. "Oh, stop!"

"Too late, now, Superstar," he gasped. "Too late now."

And suddenly she abandoned all resistance, first as a tactic and as a desperate gamble for what she now knew was her life—then, beyond conscious volition, as something she could not, and did not want to, stop. *Maybe it will all work out* was her last coherent thought as the world began to whirl away into an even more powerful vortex. *Maybe— it—will—all—work—out—*

He gave a sudden groan, her eyes opened and stared for the last time into his, which were almost opaque now, strange and agonized and inward, burning with the strange light that had scared so many.

His body began to lunge convulsively, hers to respond. She realized, but could do nothing, that his hands, hitherto so busy elsewhere, were suddenly harshly, firmly around her throat.

"Superstar—" he gasped, "I just—couldn't let you—go out and tell

—somebody, now could I? . . . Oh, *Jesus!*" he cried suddenly. *"Oh, Jesus! It's never been like this!"*

It never had for her, either; and never would again.

Presently he got up, washed himself, dressed carefully in his new clothing, took the car and motel keys and the money from her purse and tossed it, half-open, pathetic contents spilling, on the body. Then he opened the door a crack, glanced cautiously out; stepped through with a relaxed air, closed and locked it behind him and sauntered casually to the car.

He got in, gunned the engine for a moment, swung out and away.

Something they had heard that morning on the radio had told him where he must go next. He left the motel entrance and turned right, back toward Columbia.

By now, Regard thought, the bastard and his no-good floozy—a *lawyer,* for Christ's sake!—must be halfway to Texas, or maybe Florida.

He had already concluded that they were no longer in South Carolina, for nothing had been reported.

Airports had drawn a blank. Hastily established roadblocks hadn't been able to cover a lot of back roads but he calculated that neither of them would know any country shortcuts; now the roadblocks, maintained all night, were pretty much over, but as much as could be done on short notice had been done. They had had maybe half an hour's jump before the two guards were discovered. Regard was confident that the dragnet would have pulled them in if they had been anywhere within a hundred-mile radius of Columbia. Police were still checking all hotels and motels but nothing had been reported there, either. And the all-state bulletins hadn't turned up anything yet. Quite successfully so far, Earle and Debbie had gone underground.

Once he had mobilized the nationwide network of Justice NOW!, he promised himself grimly, they'd be taken. And when they were, good-bye Earle and good-bye Debbie. There wouldn't be any carefully handled trial this time. They'd be disposed of so fast they wouldn't have time to do more than wet their pants.

It was almost 8 P.M., 5 P.M. on the West Coast; great broadcast time, both places. He told his secretary and her girl friend to come along if they wanted to, left his office, hustled them into the armored Mercedes and roared off to the park where he had arranged the rally. He was pleased to see that there were a lot of parked cars and a lot of people, maybe twenty, twenty-five thousand, he estimated, which wasn't bad for a weekday. He turned on the sirens and came to a roaring halt. A great cheer went up as he hopped out, jumped on the platform, grabbed the microphone set up for him and waved to the waiting throng and the bank of television cameras that zoomed in respectfully as he began to speak.

"My friends!" he shouted. "My fellow workers in our great crusade of Justice NOW! Today we made a mistake, but we're goin' to correct it, my friends! We're goin' to correct it! And it wasn't anywhere near the mistake our greaaaattt Soo-preme Court made the other day, was it?"

"NO!" they cried, and a happy excitement began to course through his veins and give his voice extra power.

"No, sir, my friends, it wasn't as bad as what those poor pathetic fellows up there in Washington did! They weaseled and they wobbled and they backed away from *giving Earle Holgren what he deserved!* And as a result of that, Earle Holgren was left to escape, and now we've got ourselves a little problem. But we're goin' to solve it, my friends, we're goin' to solve it! We'll get him back in no time and don't you fret yourselves about that! We're goin' to do it, my friends! We're goin' to do it! And how are we goin' to do it? *With your help!* With your help and with the help of all you good folks all over this nation who may hear my voice, all you good, law-abidin', decent folks who've flocked to the shield of Justice NOW! from all over this great land and have joined me in this great crusade to get rid of crime once and for all, everywhere in America!"

Again there was a great shout and a roll of applause.

"My friends—" he said, striking an expansive pose. "My friends, let me tell you how we're goin' to go about it—"

It was just at that moment that he heard the last thing he ever heard, which was Henrietta-Maude, somewhere down in the press section, suddenly screeching, *"Regard, Regard! Duck! Duck!"*

He didn't know what she was hollerin' about—never did know—but for just a moment he paused and peered down trying to find her in the crowd. From somewhere to one side, possibly from a small clump of trees in back of the press section—accounts differed, that being Henrietta's, who thought she had "seen something" a split second before—there came two small, quick spurts of light.

He felt as though his head were blowing up, as indeed it was; staggered and fell backward off the platform; and knew no more.

So he had been right in his prediction: there *was* a death in prime time, though not exactly the one he had intended.

Yet that did not, of course, stop Justice NOW! Ted Phillips issued an immediate statement in Sacramento, taking over the chairmanship and pledging to "follow in the footsteps of our great fallen leader"; and another two million joined the next day.

The movement had its martyr and nothing short of a miracle, the nation's pundits agreed that night, could stop it now.

After that, Boomer Johnson was easy: that stupid little ape that all the media had said was "the most devastating witness" against him—the one who had placed him unmistakably at the scene of the bombing—who had linked him unequivocally with Janet and John Lennon Peacechild—the one whose testimony had undoubtedly given the final push to the death penalty—the one whose innocent damaging goodness called forth his strongest contempt.

Earle drove half the night, taking back roads and detours he knew from his youth in the area, and pulled into Pomeroy Station shortly after 2 A.M. He had snaked his way out of the wild disorganized pandemonium of the horrified crowd in nothing flat, easy and casual but fast, reaching his car and driving quietly away before anyone could recover enough to begin seriously looking for the assassin.

Once again he was ahead of the roadblocks. Once again, he told himself with a complacent confidence that by now was losing its last tenuous hold on sanity, Earle Holgren had shown his superiority to the lesser minds who sought to stand in his way . . .

Pomeroy Station was sound asleep.

He drew off the road into some thick bushes alongside a creek and slept also, awakening just as first light and first birds announced the dawn.

He knew where the Johnsons lived and he knew their habits, Pomeroy Station being a very small village and he having lived there for almost two years with Janet and John Lennon Peacechild, who now seemed long ago and far away. A happy singing was in his heart as he cleaned the pistol, adjusted the silencer, locked the car and crept, with a woodsman's silence, along the path where Boomer, a good boy, came to get the milk every morning for his mother.

He was whistling, a carefree, innocent sound as he swung along in the steadily growing light. It was still too early for anybody else to be about and he expected no one. Thus it was that for a moment, after Earle stepped out of the woods perhaps ten feet ahead, he did not really see him or realize that anyone was there. When he did he stopped abruptly and said in a hushed, frightened tone, "Who that?"

"You know who it is," Earle said, standing there smiling for a moment, allowing himself time to enjoy the horrified look that spread across Boomer's face. Then he fired twice in rapid succession and watched with impersonal care while the body fell. He hauled it off the path down to creek's edge, pushed it in the slowly moving water and jammed it under an old submerged log where it would not be found for a while. Then he faded away into the woods again.

When Boomer's body finally broke loose from its log and was found late the next afternoon, his mama was brought sobbing and wailing to identify him.

"I knows who did it!" she cried again and again. "I knows who did it! That Holgren! That Holgren!"

And suddenly she lifted her head and let out a long-drawn howl that sent shivers up and down the backs of the sheriff's posse whose members stood helplessly by.

"He's a ha'nt!" she screamed. "He's a ha'nt!"

By then he was far away, gone north to keep his final two appointments.

4

The great white building stood serene and untroubled in the hot, steamy night, once more looking as majestic and pure as it had before the throngs of Justice NOW! had seen fit to desecrate its lampposts and paint graffiti on its outside walls. All traces of its recent riotous days were gone, removed by crews from the Capital's Department of Buildings and Grounds, working around the clock until the task was done. Now the edifice seemed the same as ever. Softly lighted, stately and beautiful, it stood again as it had stood for five decades, the high and impressive citadel of the law, its dignity jostled for a second or two in history's long passage but not, seemingly, in any fundamental way dislodged.

All was peaceful around it now, on this typically breathless late June evening; and never had the words EQUAL JUSTICE UNDER LAW seemed more impressive, or more unassailable, to the casual passers-by.

Of these there were not many as the last shreds of Washington's slow twilight faded finally into night. An occasional tourist couple sightseeing arm in arm, careful to walk close to the streetlamps whose pools of light shone down comfortingly through the thickly bending trees; an occasional slow-moving taxi, its occupants on the same sightseeing mission; a few late students and researchers hurrying nervously to their cars from the neighboring Library of Congress, feeling fortunate if they had been able to find parking space in a lighted area, walking with an extra quickness if they had not; an occasional late-working law clerk emerging from the building itself to make the same quick, uneasy progress to

car, taxi or bus. Not a very good area to be in at night, for all the building's beauty; and deserted accordingly. Not many people . . . not much
traffic . . . not much doing at the Court, this night.

The guard at the desk just inside the tall bronze doors was half-sleep-
ing out his shift, from time to time leafing idly through the pages of the
final edition of the Washington *Post,* which he had already perused a
dozen times. Things were back to normal again. The big excitement was
over and everybody at the Court, thankfully, could go back to the routine as usual. It was a good routine, he reflected, and he liked it: not
too fast, not too slow, just enough to keep a man interested, not make
him too bored but not ask too much of him, either. These last few days
had been exciting, he couldn't deny that, and it had been fun for a little
while to have everything tensed up so you didn't know from one minute
to the next but what some crackpot might try to break in the door or
cause an uproar in the chamber. But that wasn't right, for this place;
that wasn't the Court. He liked it just the way it always had been as
long as he could remember, and that's how it was once again, right now.
He hoped they'd seen the last of the hectic times. A few days of that
were enough to last a long, long while, as far as he was concerned.

Tonight, for instance, had been typical so far of what he usually
found on this shift, now that it had all simmered down and things were
back to normal again: a few outgoing law clerks and staff people; a few
incoming, to catch up on piled-up work; now and again a late researcher to use the library, authorized by a Justice or sometimes, in a
courtesy occasionally granted by the Court to its fellow branch, by a
member of Senate or House. This evening he had admitted two or three
of those, a couple of women and one fellow who said he had a pass
from one of the North Dakota Senators. The Congress was out of town
for the Fourth of July recess and there wasn't any way to check
this. The fellow had looked reliable and seemed to be intelligent and
knew what he was talking about, so the guard had waved him on in.

Usually there were two or three of the Justices, sometimes more,
working late; last week they had all been in, at all hours, working on
the Holgren case. But now they were in recess, too, and he didn't know
how many were actually still in town. Most times they cleared out as
soon as the term ended and skedaddled for their summer hideouts;
nobody saw 'em until sometime in mid-September when they began to
drift in to get ready for the October term. Right now, as far as he knew,
the only one left around was Justice Barbour, and the only reason he
knew that was because the Justice had come in, not very long ago—

about half an hour before the last researcher, as a matter of fact—and
had stopped to chat a bit before going to his chambers.

"Thought you'd be on vacation, Justice," the guard had remarked
with respectful familiarity, and the Justice had smiled, though in a
rather preoccupied way. He must still be burdened down with the Holgren case, the guard thought.

"Don't worry," the Justice said. "I'm going to be on my way just as
soon as I can get everything cleared up in my office. I still have some
things to take care of."

"Hope it won't take you long, in this weather," the guard observed.
The Justice nodded.

"It's a bear, isn't it? But then, Washington in summer always is. I
think about a week more, and then I'm going to get out of here. Anybody else still around?"

The guard had told him that as far as he knew, there wasn't.

"Not tonight, anyway. You've got the building to yourself, almost."

"Good," Justice Barbour had said. "Then I can really get a lot
done."

He had gone off along the Great Hall, past the busts of the Chief Justices, and disappeared around the corner. In mind's eye the guard could
see him going along the empty corridor that paralleled the chamber and
then around to the back corridor, and so along to his own chambers. He
was going to be a good man on the Court, the guard thought and
chuckled. He'd certainly started out with a bang!

Twenty minutes later there had been this researcher, and he too
seemed pleasant: a youngish sort of fellow, clean-shaven, with a good
tan, carrying a couple of yellow legal pads under one arm; curious himself about who was in the building, after he'd explained that his North
Dakota Senator had sent him. The guard didn't see anything wrong in
his curiosity, it was a natural thing in such a famous place, but he'd
shrugged it off with an easy smile and a "Nobody of any importance."

"Oh," the researcher said, sounding disappointed. "I thought I saw
Justice Barbour come in a few minutes ago."

"Must have been a look-alike," the guard said comfortably. "No Justices tonight. Sorry."

"Oh, that's O.K.," the researcher said. "I've got a lot of stuff to dig
out in the library, anyway. Shouldn't stand around sightseeing. Which
way," he added politely, "is the library?"

"You haven't been here before?" the guard asked, a little surprised
though he shouldn't have been, they got a lot of strangers in all the time

to use the Court's more than 200,000 volumes. "I'll call somebody from the guardroom to come and show you up."

And he started to pick up the intercom, but the researcher smiled and said, rather quickly, "Oh, no, don't bother anybody. Just tell me. I'll find it."

"Afraid we have orders," the guard said with pleasant firmness, and put in a call. But that was just the moment, he found out later when it had happened and the Court was again the focus of the world's shocked attention, that his buddy had decided to go to the men's room. So after the phone had rung a couple or three times he shrugged, turned and gestured and said, "Well, you go down to the end there, turn right, and just around the corner there's a little elevator you can take up to the third floor, which is the library floor. There'll be a guard there who can direct you on in."

"Thanks a lot," the researcher said, and added casually,

"Where are the Justices' offices?"

"They turn left where you turn right to the elevator," the guard said. "But the public isn't allowed back there."

"Oh, I know," the researcher said amicably; and casually asked one last question:

"Many guards on duty tonight?"

"One or two on each floor," the guard said. He smiled. "We had eight or ten last week in the midst of that Holgren business, but it's all calmed down now."

"I hope they catch the bastard," the researcher said. "I see where he's got out. And they think he maybe killed that Regard Stinnet, too."

"Yes," the guard said somberly and added with some vehemence, "I hope they catch him. He deserves everything he gets!"

"He sure does," the researcher said with a sudden smile. "He sure does. Well, thanks a lot. See you later."

It was only after he too had disappeared at the end of the Great Hall that it occurred to the guard to wonder idly why, if he had been close enough to the building to see Justice Barbour enter, he had asked about him; and why it had taken him twenty minutes before he himself had come in. Then he dismissed it with a shrug and forgot about it. It didn't seem to have any significance at the time. Nor did he call up to the third floor, as he was to regret bitterly later, and alert the guard there that a researcher was on his way.

Official Washington, even now, is not really a very careful city. It is still an essentially good-natured and trusting place in which an Earle

Holgren, comfortably presumed to be fugitive in the South, can enter a casually guarded Supreme Court without arousing alarm.

At his back, and all around him, the guard had the comfortable feeling of the silent building: its interior lights burning low, its atmosphere hushed, a few people working, the night lengthening on, the powerful atmosphere of the law going forward at its own inexorable pace—a sense of power, serenity, stability, peace.

"I hoped you might be home," he said over his private line, "but I didn't dare think I'd be so lucky."

"And why not?" she asked, sounding very pleased. "Actually, I ought to bawl you out and refuse to speak to you. You said you'd call me for sure *last* night, not tonight. Have you any concept of what I've been through in the past twenty-four hours?"

"I'm sorry," he said, quickly serious. "I really am. I do know, because I've been through it too. But it hasn't exactly been my fault. That is, it has but it hasn't, if you know what I mean."

"Well, not exactly, no," she said with a chuckle. "Am I supposed to?"

"If you're going to be a Justice's wife," he said. "It's really taken me all this time to come to terms with myself and really decide once and for all that I did the right thing. Now I'm sure."

"Do you mind," she said carefully, "if we back up for a minute? Did you say, 'If you're going to be a Justice's wife'?"

"That is what I said."

"I thought that's what you said."

"It *is* what I said. Really, now, what a ridiculous conversation!"

"I am going to be a Justice's wife?"

"Well, of course," he replied lightly, "if your honor wishes to reject appellant's request—"

"How come appellant is in a position to make the request?" she asked, an excited amusement beginning to run under her words. "Is she actually going to give you a divorce?"

"She is actually going to give me a divorce."

"I don't believe it!"

"Believe it."

There was a pause. For just a panicky moment he wondered if for some wild unknown reason she might say No. He dismissed it at once but decided he had best plunge on.

"Therefore, as I say, appellant *does* request, if your honor pleases—"

"Yes," she interrupted with a shaky little laugh, "my honor does please. And so does all the rest of me."

"Good," he said, sounding so relieved that she began to laugh, whole-heartedly.

"What's the matter?" he asked, puzzled.

"You sound so like a little boy all of a sudden. As though you thought I might not."

"Well," he said cautiously, "I didn't know."

"Well, now you do. The decision, unanimous, is yes. All right?"

"All right," he said humbly. "And thank you."

"Oh, my dear," she said, trying to sound light and bright and fashionably uncaring, but not really succeeding at all. "Thank *you*."

"I love you."

"I love you . . . where are you, incidentally? I haven't even asked. At home?"

"At the Court."

"At the Court!" she exclaimed with a sudden genuine dismay. "Haven't you heard that Earle Holgren has escaped?"

"So?"

"What do you mean, 'So?'" she demanded sharply. "He's killed Regard Stinnet—"

"We don't know that for sure, yet. There are plenty of fanatics running around loose on both sides of that issue."

"But—"

"Anyway, he's in the South somewhere, he isn't up here. And we have guards on duty. The Court's safe. Everything's back to normal."

"I know you have guards," she said impatiently, "but he's psychotic, and if he's set out on some jag to murder everybody connected with his trial that he can lay his hands on—"

"Cathy, Cathy!" he said. "Stop being so melodramatic! They're after him, they'll get him. He wouldn't do anything so obvious as try to kill *me* in any case. After all, why should he? I only spoke for the Court. And I saved his life, didn't I? I could have voted for the death penalty."

"But he doesn't *reason* like that. He's *crazy!*"

"Well, I assure you he isn't here," he said firmly. "The place is practically deserted, the guards are on the job—"

"I'm worried," she said bleakly. "And I think you should be too. I think you should have your own special guards—"

"Oh, Cathy! That would be ridiculous."

"You men are so—so—*stupid* sometimes," she said. "So phony-brave-*macho*. I'm scared, can't I get that through to you?"

"Well, look," he said patiently. "Will you feel any better if I come over soon? I'll be through in a little while. Why don't I hide out with you for the night? Surely he won't know how to find me there!"

"Now you're making fun of me," she said soberly, "and I find I resent it. I am *worried about this.*"

"Well, don't be," he said comfortably. "Everything is quite all right. Believe me."

"I hope so," she said bleakly. "Oh, my dear, *I hope so.*"

"It is," he said firmly. "It is. I'll see you soon. Don't worry, now. I'll be along within the hour."

"Yes," she said, still troubled and uncertain.

And that, he supposed as he returned to his papers, was just another example of the leftovers that would probably haunt him for a long time from the damnable case.

It had been hard enough to come to terms with his own actions in the matter. He had finally done so; had reached serenity; and had no desire to be troubled further now by what he regarded as exaggerated, if loving, fears.

For the first few hours after his confrontation with Debbie following the decision, the epithet *Clever coward!* had hung in the air, a malignant presence. He was honest enough to acknowledge that there was some truth in it—not a great deal, but enough at first to make him uneasy and far from being at peace with himself. The memory of Ray Ullstein's advice had proved invaluable then.

Ray had told him in a pre-decision telephone conversation that on the Court there was nothing to be gained by looking back. He had made no comment on the merits or demerits of Tay's decision, only expressed regret that they would not be together. And he had admonished, in his usual gentle, non-judgmental way, that Tay himself should neither regret nor brood upon his decision.

Some brooding, as Cathy had perceived in their first conversation after the decision, had perhaps been inevitable. Criticism of his stand, balanced so ironically between Justice NOW! and his fellow liberals, had been made even sharper and more stinging by the letters, phone calls and telegrams he had received from many old associates and many unknown countrymen. Approval had come from those he least respected: denunciation from those whose opinion he most valued and whose admiration he had always had. For a while, this had not been easy.

He had taken the middle ground, for reasons humanly understandable—and to him legally valid—and neither side ever valued the middle ground. You had to go to extremes to please one or the other. And his nature had never been extreme. To that he had been true.

It was this perhaps more than anything that had at last brought him peace of mind. In a sense it could be said that he *had* sidestepped the issues of the death penalty and television, but there would be other cases and other opportunities for them arising in this hectic age, of that he was very sure. And then, when the issues were clear-cut and free from personal emotion, he could take the stand so automatically expected of him in all cases but not so simple in this.

In the Holgren case he had made a ruling consistent, as he saw it, with the commands of the law and the necessities of a stable society. He had managed to conquer his personal hatred for the defendant and render justice that he was convinced would someday, after present passions passed, be seen to be fair and evenhanded. He had been fair to Janie, constructive to his country and just to Earle Holgren.

He had been consistent with himself.

He went into his bathroom, sloshed hot and cold water alternately on his face, dried it, suddenly felt completely at peace. Cathy was waiting. The future was waiting. He was ready to welcome it. He felt amazingly happy.

On a sudden impulse he picked up the phone and called his parents in California to tell them of his divorce and of Cathy. Then he called his brother Carl and his sister Anne and told them, too. Then he called Erma Tillson and told *her*. Everything seemed to have come full circle. The pain of Janie would never end but so much other unhappiness had rolled away. He felt suddenly very close to his family, very humbly grateful to Cathy.

In mind's eye he could see the beautiful valley of his youth stretched out before him in the gentle lovely light of California evening. The fertile earth conferred its old familiar solace. To it an infinite blessing had been added.

He forced himself to remain at his desk another fifteen minutes. Then it became too much. He said, "Oh, hell!" in a laughing voice, slapped his books shut, turned off his desk light, went into the outer office, snapped off the lamps and overheads, stepped into the corridor, back to it.

He locked his door and started to turn.

Just behind him, someone moved.

5

Here he had been wondering how to find his old pal Tay, Earle told himself with disbelieving glee as the elevator rose slowly upward, and suddenly Tay had been delivered into his hands. Suddenly the major problems were solved. He was confident now that what he had to do could be completed without much further trouble. The final details were a little hazy at the moment but he knew they would come to him. It was like a miracle. It was obviously meant to be. Earle Holgren rides again! he told himself, laughing aloud in the little cubicle. What made anybody in the world think that it was possible to stand against *him?*

He had arrived in the District on a late flight yesterday afternoon, having slipped easily across the state line into Georgia not too long after his date with Boomer, and then driven like hell for Atlanta. Security seemed to be lax along the way. The hue and cry for Regard's assassin was apparently still centered in the Columbia area, and the DO NOT DISTURB sign he had left on the motel door was apparently still successfully delaying the discovery of Debbie. He had only been stopped once and then rather lackadaisically, he thought; it had occurred because at one point he had been forced to leave back roads for half an hour and use a main highway. The officers at the roadblock had glanced quickly at the driver's license he had thoughtfully lifted from the back pocket of the motel manager and waved him on his way.

The fellow, who did resemble the clean-shaven Earle in a quick-glance sort of way, had responded to his call to come check the air con-

ditioner, right after he and Debbie arrived. It was working fine, actually,
but when he turned his back on Earle to check it, with Debbie's voluble
assistance, his half-out billfold was removed from his pocket and skillfully reinserted ten seconds later minus license. This was enough to get
Earle through the roadblock now, and after that it was clear sailing. No
particular interest was shown at the Atlanta airport. Armored in self-
righteous confidence he walked through security without a hitch and
was on his way.

In Washington he had grabbed a quick hamburger at the airport and
then taken a taxi into town where he found a cheap boardinghouse on
Ninth Street N.W. and holed up for the night. He had spent today
haunting the Court and trying without success to find out where Tay
Barbour lived. He had taken a couple of public tours of the building.
(It was an odd feeling to stand in the chamber and think, This is the
place where they did it to me. If he had needed any strengthening of his
resolve, which he did not, that would have done it.) He had picked up
the handy booklet, "The Supreme Court of the United States," at the
bookstand on the ground floor, finding in it which floor—the first—
housed Tay's chambers. He had then eaten lunch in the cafeteria along
with other tourists and some younger, more-at-home characters who he
assumed must be law clerks.

He had tried unsuccessfully to pump a couple of these as to Tay's
whereabouts; had shied away when they suddenly looked a little suspicious and had gone over to the Capitol for a while, where he roamed
about and saw a few things, playing Mr. Average Tourist. Finally he
had plopped himself down under one of the giant oaks on the Capitol
Plaza lawn and gone peacefully to sleep for a couple of hours.

When he awoke he sat for a while thinking before going back once
more to the Court. A young black couple lay entwined nearby, oblivious to the world. A transistor radio blared at their side:

"The hunt for Earle Holgren, the escaped killer who is suspected of
gunning down Attorney General Regard Stinnet of South Carolina,
leader of Justice NOW!, spread throughout the South today as the pro-
law-and-order group turned to its new chairman, Attorney General Ted
Phillips of California, for guidance in a stepped-up drive to enforce the
nation's anti-crime laws. Stinnet was largely responsible for Holgren's
conviction on earlier murder charges. His assassination is believed likely
to draw even more Americans into the ranks of the vigilante-type organization. Meanwhile Holgren's lawyer and presumed girl friend, Debbie
Donnelson, who is believed to have assisted his escape, continues miss-

ing and is believed to be with the convicted killer somewhere in the Carolinas . . ."

Well, he thought with a wry grimace, she's somewhere in the Carolinas, all right, and you'll find her soon enough. But you won't find your "escaped killer," you bastards, because your "escaped killer" is just too damned smart for you. He's a long way from where you think he is and he's got a job to do. You think Yahoo's death was a sensation! You wait and see what your "escaped killer's" going to do next, you damned goofballs!

For just a moment, a split second that passed so swiftly he was able to persuade himself that it had never happened, there clamped upon his being an unexpected and inexplicable thought that sickened him so that he almost literally swayed with its impact:

Suppose it all meant nothing, when all was said and done? Suppose his Purpose, his Manifesto, his lifelong pretense that he represented some kind of valid social justice and reasoned challenge to the social system were only that—pretenses? Suppose it was all just empty blood lust, prompted always by pointless rebellion, spurred on now by nothing more than blind revenge? Suppose he *was* psychotic, insane, forever and eternally twisted, deranged and damned, just as Yahoo and Debbie and the rest had said. *Suppose there really was nothing to Earle Holgren at all?*

The abyss opened for an instant at his feet, was as instantaneously forced shut.

A shudder shook his body for one awful, searing second.

Then it was gone.

His world was back in place.

A smile, arrogant, contemptuous and as always superior, crossed his lips.

The only damned problem at that point was, how was he to achieve his final objective? For the moment he felt himself stymied. It wasn't a feeling he liked and after a while—it was by now almost 6 P.M.—he got up, hailed a cab and went downtown to the Capitol Hilton at K and Sixteenth streets N.W. He had a couple of drinks in the bar, ate a leisurely meal in the Twigs restaurant—the clothes Debbie had bought for him were quite respectable and anyway it was summer, he looked no more casual than any other sports-shirted tourist—and then decided, restlessly, to go back up to the Court. No particular reason. It just kept drawing him, somehow. And suddenly, as he stood on the street looking for another cab, the idea hit him.

Somewhere out of the two tours he had taken—he hadn't dared take any more because a couple of the guards (they would recall him the next day, but it would be pointless, he would be gone by then) were beginning to look at him a little funny—some words came back about the Supreme Court Library. Brief tribute was paid to its beauty and excellence, his group was told regretfully that they couldn't see it because it was only open to "Justices, their staffs, specially qualified lawyers and occasional researchers from Congressional committees or staffs." The guide had been one such researcher herself, she said, checking on some legal point for her Senator, and that was what had started her interest in the law. Now she did guide work just as a part-time thing while she studied law at Howard University Law School and hoped to be a clerk to Justice Demsted someday. Everybody had smiled encouragingly but probably only Earle remembered.

He spun around abruptly, walked along K Street until he came to a stationery store, went in and bought himself a couple of yellow legal pads and a couple of ball-point pens. Then he found a cab and went back up to the Court. At least he could give it a test and find out how easy it would be to get in. If he succeeded he could scout around a little and get the lay of the land, maybe even pinpoint exactly where Tay's chambers were. He knew they were on the first floor, all of the Justices were. If he got in he might even do the same thing several nights running, that way everybody would get used to him. Hell, he might even come back a lot of times, if that's what it took to find Tay. He had plenty of time and plenty of money, both the defense fund money he had removed from Debbie and what he was sure Harry Aboud would get him from the trust if he asked him for it (Harry would be startled to hear from him, but not surprised: he ran a lot of errands like that, for the right people). He could spend the whole summer waiting for Tay, if he had to.

But the miracle happened; and he didn't have to.

He hadn't gone right into the building when he got back to the Hill. Possibly it was because for the first time he felt a little afraid that he might be challenged and denied entry: not because of who he was— nobody up here, he was confident, would have the slightest inkling—but just because the guide might have been wrong about the relative ease of access. That soon passed. He had learned long ago that if you approached people with an easy air, a show of certainty and a reasonable amount of charm, you could crack most places. So he couldn't say exactly why he lingered for a while outside in the hot, oppressive night air, but linger he did. And there, amazingly, came Tay, for some reason not going into the garage but instead parking his car alongside and coming up the steps like any tourist.

It did not occur to Earle that this might be because Tay simply wanted to see the building against the night sky, that he might consider it beautiful and moving and still be in considerable awe of it. Earle wasn't constructed to be touched or moved by beauty and he wasn't in awe of anything. If he had any thought about the building at all, it was to calculate idly how many pounds of explosives it would take to blow it up; but blowing it up wasn't his thing, tonight. His thing was good old half-assed wishy-washy Tay.

And here he was.

Instinctively Earle started to shrink back a little toward one of the trees along the sidewalk. And then he thought scornfully, Hell! Why hide? I don't have my beard any more, this is the last place he'd be expecting me. Why worry?

And straightening up, he had walked quietly along the street as Tay went up the steps. He had even whistled a bit in a thoughtful, unconcerned way, not looking at him.

Tay had not even noticed him.

So, presently, he had followed, walking meanwhile along to the Library of Congress, going in casually for a few moments to look at the exhibit of photographs from the annual White House Correspondents dinner for the President, acting like a tourist, killing time. After what he considered a decent interval, about twenty minutes, he had walked back, made sure that Tay's car was still there, and gone on in. The stupid dope on the door had let him by without a quibble, further confirming Tay's presence by his blatant lying about it, and had sent him along up to the library, virtually on his own. There was only one thing missing now, he thought as the elevator came to a halt and the doors opened.

He didn't have a weapon.

He hadn't dared bring the gun this first day, not knowing what the security would be.

But one miracle had happened and maybe another would. He smiled at the third-floor guard, asked, "Library?" received a nod of the head, saw the entrance and stepped through. For just a moment he was really impressed.

Stacks and stacks and stacks of books; an enormous high ceiling; dark wood paneling everywhere; soft lights glowing over long desks piled with tumbled volumes; a librarian or two moving quietly through the silence, perhaps ten people at work, scattered through stately rooms opening one upon another; painted medallions of famous lawgivers whom he didn't know, decorating the paneled ceiling above; a hush of study, concentration, devotion—majesty.

For just one split second Earle Holgren was in awe and across his mind shot again the frightful conundrum that he had to banish again and forever, since to try to solve it would be to destroy himself: *Who am I, what have I done and what am I doing here?*

He shook his head to clear it of such nonsense, smiled at one of the librarians, an older lady with an earnest face and gray hair; went to an isolated table and sat down, opened a book at random and pretended to read.

"Is there something particular you want, sir?" the librarian whispered in his ear, making him jump. He laughed deprecatingly, shook his head.

"No ma'am, thanks. I know where to find what I want. I'll get to it in a few minutes."

"Good," she said. "Just make yourself at home."

"Thanks," he said with a sudden sunny smile that quite touched her, he looked so young—well, not really, but at least a lot younger than she was—so serious and so handsome. "I will."

For perhaps ten minutes, surreptitiously but with a fierce intensity that fortunately for him remained unsensed by anyone around, he studied the library and its occupants. Weapon—weapon—*weapon*. There must be one, but what? Where?

His fearsome concentration was broken for a moment when he heard a laugh, quickly stifled, and looked up at the librarian's desk to see her chatting discreetly but with obvious enjoyment with a friend. In her hand she held the weapon.

A couple of minutes later when the friend left he closed his book and his notepads, sauntered up casually, engaged her in conversation, diverted her attention, bade her a pleasant good-bye and walked out with it.

The elevator reached the first floor. He got out, glanced quickly to right and left. A gleaming wooden barrier marked "Private" barred the way to the Justices' corridor. No one was in sight. He stepped over swiftly, shifted the barrier, which was not anchored, enough to get by, and moved swiftly on tiptoe, almost running, down the empty marble hallway. Just as he turned the corner he ran into a guard, walking toward him with a cup of coffee in his hand.

"Hey!" the guard said, startled. "Can I help you, mister?"

"I'm a friend of Justice Barbour," he said quickly, pleasantly, firmly. "He's expecting me."

"Oh," the guard said, accepting as people always did when Earle Holgren commanded them for his special purpose. "On down the hall a bit."

"Thank you," he said, smiled again pleasantly and moved on. He heard the guard's footsteps die away, glanced back quickly, saw the corridor empty, kept going.

Justice McIntosh . . . Justice Demsted . . . The Chief Justice . . . Justice Wallenberg . . . Justice Hemmelsford . . . Justice—

He had found it.

He stopped and listened intently. Outside, no sound broke the silence of the hallway.

Inside, he heard someone moving, coming toward him.

He wrapped the weapon's handle swiftly in his handkerchief, flattened himself against the wall to the right of the door.

It opened. Tay backed out. Earle raised the weapon. Tay turned.

"*No!*" he cried. There was no doubt of recognition here.

Earle raised the letter opener high, plunged it into his chest, withdrew it, stabbed again.

Tay started to fall forward upon him, blood beginning to spurt, arms flailing wildly. Earle leaped back, out of the way. Tay slumped to the floor.

Earle threw the letter opener on his body.

He ran quickly back along the corridor, slowed abruptly at the corner, saw no one, ran on to the barrier, swung swiftly through, replaced it; turned right into the Great Hall, slowed instantly to a walk, began to amble casually toward the door. The man on duty had changed. The one he had encountered in the hallway was at the desk.

"Did you find him?" the guard asked.

"Yep," he said. "He's still busy but he said he'd be along in a few minutes. Told me to wait for him outside."

"Better wait in here," the guard said. "It's kind of a dangerous neighborhood around here at night."

"No, thanks," he said pleasantly. "I'll stay under the lights. I won't go far. I'll be safe."

"Well," the guard said doubtfully. "O.K. But be careful."

"I will," he said. "Thanks a lot, and good night."

"Good night," the guard said. "Take care of yourself."

"Right," he said as he went out through the great bronze doors. "I'll do that."

In the house off Stanton Square Cathy busied herself with the kids for a while. They watched television and then at ten o'clock she sent them to bed.

At 10:05 the news program was interrupted by a flash.

"The bodies of two more of the principals in the Earle Holgren murder case have just been discovered in South Carolina," the bleached blonde, exuding personality, informed the world with the exact proper degree of hushed concern. "Holgren's lawyer, Debbie Donnelson, has been discovered strangled in a run-down motel outside Columbia. The body of Boomer Johnson, the black youth who was the only witness to place Holgren definitely at the scene of the Pomeroy Station bombing six weeks ago, has been discovered near his home in that small rural community. A nationwide alert has now been issued for Holgren and law officers everywhere are being mobilized to try to find him."

Cathy's first impulse was to call Tay and tell him. Then she thought, No, he's still working, he'll be here soon, I won't disturb him.

Then she thought, But perhaps I should. After all, he'll want to know.

Then she thought, Oh, that's silly, I just want to talk to him because he's such a wonderful guy and we're going to have such a really great life together.

Then she thought, I wonder when he *is* coming.

Then she thought, *Tay*—I wish you were here, Tay.

Then she thought, Where are you, Tay? Tay, it's getting late, *where are you?*

Then she told herself sternly once again, But this is silly. He said he's perfectly all right and he *is* perfectly all right. *This is really silly!*

She did have a strong character, and for a few more minutes she was almost able to convince herself of this.

It was not until a couple of minutes past eleven that she suddenly began to be really afraid.

At 11:06 she called the Court.

His chambers did not answer.

At 11:07 she called the guardroom.

Earle walked casually out the door and down the steps. At their foot he turned and looked back. Stately, white and serene, the great building defied the night. EQUAL JUSTICE UNDER LAW, it assured the world. Nothing, he told himself with a happy exultation, could be more fitting at this particular moment.

EQUAL JUSTICE UNDER LAW! That's what it was, all right; that's what it was. All scores were settled, justice had been done. The crazy law had been set right. The world that had tried to bend Earle Holgren to its stupid will had been shown that his was a spirit that did not fit such narrow categories. His was a spirit that was free. He was a being who could not be chained. He had shown them, once and for all.

He felt utterly divorced from reality, floating out there in some great high from which he would never come down.

Yet there was nothing to distinguish him, really, as he decided he had better cover his tracks and on sudden impulse turned right and started off through the dimly lighted tree-shrouded streets behind the Court.

Anyone who had been watching then—and as he moved deeper into the shadows, only one person was—would have had the impression of an individual stocky, open-faced, pleasant, amiable. No one to notice, particularly—not one to stand out in anybody's mind as worthy of any particular attention.

Not the sort you would turn to look at twice.

Or even once, for that matter.

The kind of face that gets lost in a crowd.

An ordinary guy.

So passed Earle Holgren—or Billy Ray Holgren, or Billy Ray, or Holgren Williams, or William Holgren, or Henry McAfee, or McAfee Johnson, or Everett Thompson or Everett Ray.

Normally, no one would have noticed: except that this time, in this place, someone did.

He was about to meet, although he did not know it, a classic case.

6

Bubba Whitby, unlike Boomer Johnson, was not a good boy. Bubba, as his mother Julia was always telling her employers, the Barbours, was a bad, *bad* boy. Yet there was, possibly, something to be said for Bubba—much, some would assert, because Bubba in many ways *was* a classic case.

It was rather too bad, actually, that *he* had not been the Pomeroy Station bomber. All those who found it a little difficult to sympathize with Earle—though they felt they must—would have been able with a clear conscience to sympathize with Bubba.

He fitted so snugly into so many patterns.

Bubba had just turned eighteen, as Julia had told Mr. Barbour; and Bubba's immediate family, aside from earnest, God-fearing, hardworking Julia and her other three kids, had contained some fairly worthless stuff.

Two weeks after their marriage, with Bubba already *in utero*, Julia had found Bubba's father with another woman; and since she was a small woman herself, rather frail, which was why she was allowed to take her own time about doing the housework, she did not respond as one of her girl friends might have, with shrieks and wails and teeth and nails and hair-pullings and face gougings, to hold her man. Not that she didn't do a lot of wailing of course, but that was all she did, and it didn't do her much good.

After that, Bubba's dad was right back where he'd always been, cattin' around; and Julia, unable to do much else, put her head down,

hired herself out for housework and plowed ahead, only taking time out
to have Bubba, his two younger brothers and their kid sister. When
Bubba was six years old and his sister three, after Julia and Bubba's
dad had been "married," if you could call his occasional visits that, for
five hectic years, Bubba's dad left to go off on some mysterious life of
his own that nobody knew much about but that everybody suspected
might have something to do with numbers and, later on, more fashionably and profitably, dope. From then right on up to now, Julia was on
her own in raising the kids.

Bubba, in the minds of many, might have been said to have two
strikes against him.

Julia herself, though, was a pretty powerful strike in the other direction, because Julia was, as Janie Barbour used to say back before that
terrible accident, "a very *good* lady." She was decent, she was kind, she
was hardworking, she was devoted and loyal and God-fearing and
church-going and a lot of other good things that weren't as fashionable
as dope, maybe, but still were pretty nice. She was also absolutely
devoted to her children and absolutely determined that they should be
reared to be "a credit to me and to your race." She often told them this,
and she lavished a lot of love and care and attention upon them. So
much so that some might have said that Bubba *had a mother problem
and was being smothered.*

As with Earle Holgren's younger sister, however, this did not seem to
bother Bubba's siblings. Bubba, like Earle, was the only one who went
bad. And Julia, like the elder Holgrens though with infinitely less to
give in the way of material comforts, was equally baffled and dismayed.

"We're poor but we're decent," she often told the kids; and she and
three of them were. But from about the time Bubba was eight it began
to be alarmingly apparent to her that Bubba wasn't. And it just defeated
her. Thereupon, some might have said, Bubba *began to lack parental
support and guidance.*

Still, though, Julia couldn't honestly see that this was her fault, because the Lord knew she did her very best to change his ways and make
him behave. When he was found with little girls she spanked him. When
he and little boys began to steal things and break windows, she spanked
him even more.

Bubba, before long, became what some might call *intimidated and re-
pressed.*

He could not—and did he ever let people know about it!—*express
himself.*

At least, he couldn't express himself—with his mother's knowledge, anyway—in the ways he wanted to express himself. And he refused to express himself the way she wanted him to, which was just to be a nice, decent, well-behaved kid.

There were a lot of kids in their neighborhood in suburban Maryland, and later on in Northeast near Stanton Square where they had come to live five or six years ago, who had much the same background and upbringing as Bubba. And somehow most of them turned out all right even with rough economic times and the never-ending struggle to find decent jobs. There were an awful lot of nice, decent, well-behaved kids around—some bad apples, too, of course, but many more who were just plain nice kids. Bubba was not among them.

In the eyes of some he could have been regarded as *decidedly thwarted*.

He took it out, as he grew rapidly older and bigger—much too big for his age, always, which was another problem, making him feel self-conscious and physically laughable—by becoming increasingly foul-mouthed, brutish and insubordinate to his mother and increasingly bullying to his brothers and sister.

He began to show signs of an inevitable reaction—to what, except Julia's desperate and often tearful attempts to raise him right, it was hard to explain, although there were some, including the social worker at the school he attended—sporadically—who tried very earnestly to do so.

It was not long before she began to refer to him as *a classic case*.

Overhearing this one day when she was talking to a teacher he had just straight-armed out of his way in the hall, he took it home and repeated it often and proudly—"I's a classic case." The social worker begged his teacher to have *understanding and patience and try to forgive*. The teacher, a male who was not quite as big as Bubba but capable of holding a long grudge, flunked him later. Bubba waylaid him after school in the parking lot and beat the holy shit out of him, giving him a broken jaw, a couple of broken ribs and a broken arm.

That was the first time Bubba went to juvenile home.

Now outside forces began to take a hand in Bubba's life. *Society,* the social worker said earnestly was becoming *harsh and repressive* to Bubba.

Julia, however, just thought her son was getting what was coming to him. It was about then that she began to confide in Mr. Barbour, since Mrs. Barbour didn't seem all that interested. She got sympathy from him, and, in these recent years, offers of small but respectable jobs suited to Bubba's years and inexperience—which Bubba always turned down. She was very hopeful (she told herself tonight as she wondered forlornly, for the thousandth time, where Bubba was) now that Mr. Barbour was on the Court, that he really might be able to offer something Bubba would accept, before it was too late.

By the time he was fifteen, there had been three more juvenile detentions for Bubba, one for trashing a store and two for stealing cars.

He was now defiantly showing signs of *rebellion and protest*—in fact, Julia thought, he wasn't showing much else, most of the time. But after all, what did society expect? He was *obviously misunderstood*. Not only that, he was *socially handicapped*. And to top it all, he was *definitely disadvantaged*. How could you beat that for a classic case?

He was also insufferable and insupportable to his mother and to all her decent friends, who were many. An armed truce came to exist between them, and she began to feel that the less Bubba was around, the better for them all. This broke her heart for a while, but once again she put her head down and plowed ahead. Bubba increasingly went his own way, a truant, a renegade, refusing to accept any of the modest but decent jobs that also came his way from others, and increasingly, from some source she did not know and did not dare surmise, affluent.

Now, though she did not know it, Bubba was using and peddling dope. He had already impregnated two giggly little junior high school girls who were taken with his enormous size and not bad looks; was participating regularly in petty thefts and robberies—and some not so petty; and had already killed another youth, entirely unbeknownst to the police and fortunately also not known to his mother, who would have perished of fright and mortification. And underneath it all were a growing disillusion and resentment against the things—himself, mostly, as he recognized dimly but felt hopeless to change—that were defeating him. A restless boredom began to prompt him to seek release in ever greater violence and ever more dangerous thrills.

And all the time, Bubba's two younger brothers and little sister, coming from exactly the same background, just as socially handicapped, just as disadvantaged, just as subject to the appeals of a mother who only sought to raise them decently—in their cases, with success—were coming right along, getting steadily more mature and reliable, growing up into good, decent, responsible citizens. So were many dozens of other kids, all around. Life was often hard for all of them, but a great many were managing to come through it quite all right.

Somewhere in Bubba there was something sadly and inherently awry that the social worker simply could not—in fact, deliberately *would* not —recognize.

This was not Julia's fault and probably, although he wasn't much good, it wasn't his evanescent father's fault either.

It was just in him.

It was there.

And it made of Bubba Whitby a dangerous youth, just as it was surely and inevitably and before very much longer going to make him a very dangerous man.

He was very rapidly on his way to becoming, in fact, everything that the great majority of his countrymen despised and feared and wanted to get rid of. He was everything that many perfectly sincere and well-meaning people wanted to help and educate and succor and save.

But unfortunately they would die—and some of them probably would, sooner or later, at his hands—rather than accept the thought that saving Bubba was something that it was impossible for them to do.

He was Death, as Earle Holgren was Death; and in this moment of their meeting he was, perhaps, if it were possible to draw comparisons between two such, the more fearsome—because unlike Earle, who even in this insane, utterly disconnected hour when he was floating out there cut off from all human goodness and decency, could persuade himself, if rather desperately now, that he had a purpose, and that it had been achieved, Bubba had none except possibly a great resentment, a great boredom and a great desire to just *do somethin'*, and the worse the better, to entertain himself on this hot . . . muggy . . . oppressive . . . dreadful night . . .

At first Earle thought he heard a funny skittering sound, as though someone were skipping toward him under the dimly lighted trees ahead.

Then it stopped.

He stopped.

Then he shrugged, though the hairs rose on the back of his neck, and started to walk on.

As abruptly as Earle had stepped before Boomer, the tall, hulking figure emerged silently from the trees and stood before him on the old uneven brick sidewalk. He could not see its face, for a streetlamp was behind it, but the menace in its stance was unmistakable.

"Hey, man," it said in a softly crooning tone that he knew instantly spelled deadly danger, "where you goin', man?"

"Just walking along, man," he said, heart suddenly beating fast but speaking casually. "Just taking a walk."

"Funny place for a white dude to be walkin'," the figure said, in the same soft way. "This here's a funny place. What you got in mind, man?"

"Nothing much, man," Earle said, thinking: keep him talking and maybe something will divert him. "It's a nice night, just thought I'd take a walk."

"I still think it's funny, man," the figure said. "You ain't no honkie fuzz come to git me, are you? Not any of them *under*cover folks they set on people like me?"

"I'm not any fuzz, man," Earle said carefully, shifting his weight ever so slowly onto the balls of his feet, positioning himself to strike with his fists since he realized with a devastating clarity that he had no weapon: the gun was in his room, the letter opener with Tay. "I hate 'em as much as you do."

"That's good, man," the figure said and suddenly shot out a long arm and gave Earle a quick little shove in the chest that knocked him off balance for a moment so that he had to scramble awkwardly and obviously to regain it. "Don't get ready to try nothin', man. It won't work."

"I'm not getting ready to try anything," Earle said, beginning to breathe a little hard, but reassuring. "Do you know where this street comes out?"

"It comes out at the end," the figure said contemptuously. "Where'd you think it comes out? And what you want to know for, anyway?"

"I'm on my way to Union Station," Earle said, casting desperately about for something—anything—to prolong the conversation until he could figure out how to destroy his tormentor. "Want to find the Metro. You know where the Metro is?"

"I know where the Metro is," the figure said, "and I know where Union Station is. And this is a funny way to get to 'em. What you doin' back here in these parts, I said!"

And suddenly he shot out the long arm again and grabbed Earle by his arm, twisting it suddenly so that Earle almost yelled with pain when he found himself pinned with his back to his captor.

"There's a car coming," he said with desperate relief. "You better let me go, man, or somebody's goin' to think something funny's going on."

"You think anybody's goin' to stop in *this* ay-reah?" the figure demanded, still contemptuously but releasing him and simultaneously spinning him around so that he faced him again. "Not if they know what's good for 'em, man. And everybody does—except maybe you, man," the figure added, its voice dropping again to the soft, crooning note. "Except you."

"Maybe it's the fuzz," Earle said desperately as the car drew slowly nearer.

"And maybe it ain't," the figure said. "If it is, we're just standin' here talkin', right? Just two old buddies. Just some inner—innerrayshal—conversation. And if it ain't, well, then, they ain't goin' to stop, anyway."

"We'll see," Earle said, half-turning to look at the battered old Cadillac.

"Hey, Bubba, man!" a voice cried. "What you got there, man? Somethin' you need some help with?"

"Hey, Elvis, baby!" the figure called happily. "How you doin', man? I got me a live one, I think, but I don't need no help. I can handle this. You jes' drive on by, now, and everything's goin' be O.K."

"O.K., man," the voice from the car said with a chuckle. "Give it to him good, man. See you roun'."

"Hey!" Earle shouted, suddenly finding his voice. "Help!"

The car stopped abruptly and a sarcastic voice came back.

"Don't do you no good to shout, man. Nobody goin' hear."

And slowly it resumed speed and dwindled away down the street under the tunnel of beautiful old trees.

"Help!" Earle called again, his voice suddenly cracking. "Help, somebody!"

"Ain't nobody goin' help, man," the figure assured him gently. "Bet you they's a hundred people behind those doors up and down this street, and *not one* of 'em is goin' stir out to lift a finger. They's scared to death, man, just like you are. They's scared of the night and they's scared of Bubba Whitby. Now, God damn!" the figure added with a laugh that made Earle begin to sweat. "There I gone and done it! I give you my name. Now I guess I got to go ahead and kill you, man."

"Why?" Earle demanded, voice in spite of him rising a notch. "*Why?*"

"Just 'cause you know who I am," the figure said. "And just 'cause I'm kind of bored and maybe a little killin' 'd pep me up. I got me a date later with some little gal and maybe a little killin' would get me hot for it. Too bad you won't be around then, man. You could come watch. She's a real ackerbat. So," he added with satisfaction, "am I."

"Listen," Earle said, trying to get things back on a rational basis, trying to reason, trying to be sane, though he could tell the bastard was a maniac and a real killer: he wasn't just threatening for the hell of it, Earle knew that. "Listen. What's the point in killing anybody, man? You don't solve things that way. You've got to talk things out. If I've offended you in some way, tell me what it is and we'll talk. What's wrong with that?"

"Nothin' wrong with that," the figure said, " 'cept that's not what I'm goin' do. It's just not what I'm goin' do."

"Why not?" Earle demanded desperately. "Why *not?*"

" 'Cause I'm Bubba," the figure said, "and I does what I pleases. People been tryin' hassle me all my life, man, but it don' do 'em no good. I's a free speerit, man. I's a classic case. Ain't *nobody* goin' tell me what to do."

"But that isn't civilized!" Earle protested. "That isn't right, man! We've got laws in this country! You can't just go around killing people!"

"*I* can," the figure said softly, and suddenly one long arm had Earle by the throat and he was aware that the other was raised with something gleaming at the end of it where the light fell flickering through the trees.

"*No!*" Earle cried. "*Not a knife!*"

"Oh, sure, man," the figure said, the arm pausing at the top of its plunge while the figure chuckled a little. "Oh, sure. Quick, clean, silent. And you can carve 'em up a bit, too, if you want to. I just might do that, before I let you die, man. I just might."

"*No!*" Earle cried again, struggling futilely in the iron grip. "*You're not going to kill me!*"

"Why, sure I am, man," the figure said amicably as the arm with tantalizing slowness began its sure descent. "Sure I am."

"*But I haven't got a weapon!*" Earle screamed as the arm began to pick up speed. "*I can't defend myself.*"

"That's too bad, man," the figure said as the knife struck home for the first time and Earle, feeling an awful pain in his chest, began to slump toward the sidewalk. "You should have thought of that before you came out here tonight."

Two more times the arm rose and fell while the world began to dissolve in a bloody haze around the bomber of Pomeroy Station, the deliberate destroyer of so many lives.

The last thing he felt was a terrible raking pain across his eyes.

And then he felt nothing more.

For a couple of minutes Bubba stood quivering with a fierce excitement, hovering over his victim who still gasped and groaned, though with steadily diminishing intensity. Then he straightened and looked sharply up and down the silent street.

Nothing stirred.

Nothing moved.

No one came.

Calmly then, with a deliberation that expressed all the sad, futile frustrations of his already sad and futile life, he drew back a huge hobnailed foot and aimed a savage kick at the face of Earle Holgren, slowly bleeding to death on the lovely, worn old bricks.

Then he turned and skipped away into the darkness as emptily, senselessly and pointlessly as he had come.

The great white building stood serene and untroubled in the hot, steamy night, once more looking as majestic and pure as it had before the throngs of Justice NOW! had seen fit to desecrate its lampposts and paint graffiti on its outside walls.

All that was gone, now.

The edifice seemed the same as ever.

Softly lighted, stately and beautiful, it stood again as it had for five decades, the high and impressive citadel of the law.

In the streets around, hardly anyone still lingered as Washington's suffocating velvet summer night closed down completely at last upon the city. An occasional tourist couple still wandered arm in arm, careful to walk close to the streetlamps whose pools of light shone down comfortingly through the thickly bending trees. An occasional slow-moving taxi passed, its occupants bent upon the same sightseeing mission. A few late students and researchers hurried nervously to their cars from the Court library or the neighboring Library of Congress, feeling fortunate if they had been able to find parking spaces in a lighted area, walking with an extra quickness if they had not. An occasional late-working law clerk, loaded down with books and papers, emerged from the building to make the same quick, uneasy progress to car, taxi or bus.

It was not a very good area to be in at night and was deserted accordingly.

Hardly any people, hardly any traffic . . . not much doing at the Court, this night.

Very soon, now, there would be activity, police cars, sirens, flashing lights, an ambulance, the convergence of frantically scrambling media and, unnoticed in the hubbub, a white-faced young woman with horror in her eyes.

But for the moment, all remained calm and serene.

Above the great bronze doors through which so many thousands of litigants, so many fateful cases and great causes had passed down the years, the calm affirmation sought, as always, to hold back the night.

EQUAL JUSTICE UNDER LAW.

She sat beside the bed, never taking her eyes off the still white face. Doctors and nurses came and went, the hours passed without break or relief. Fear and terror dragged upon her heart.

She had tried to cry but could not.

She had tried to penetrate the impenetrable mask but could not.

She had tried to keep hope alive but could not.

It was not until the first faint light touched the stately avenues, the beautiful buildings and monuments, the slow, winding river, the lush green hills of Maryland and Virginia and the tops of the trees through which Earle Holgren stared up unseeing at the empty sky that there was, at last, the tiniest stirring in the bed.

Slowly the eyes opened, slowly they focused. Slowly the ghost of a smile, the faintest of recognitions, crossed the face.

She and the nurse cried out, doctors and other nurses came running.

"Hi," he whispered very faintly.

"Hi," she said and at last began to cry.

The senior doctor passed a hand before the eyes, which flickered and followed; listened carefully to heart and chest, took pulse, studied temperature; finally nodded and gave her hand a hard encouraging squeeze.

"He'll make it," he said and she cried the more. "He's on his way back."

Justice of a sort—though not in all respects of a kind the Court or John Marshall might have intended—had been rendered.

And, human nature being what it is—and professed intentions having given way in some degree, as they so often do, to the human inadequacies of all concerned—a decision.

November 1980–January 1982.